WALTER SCOTT (1771–1832) was born in Edinburgh of a Border family. After attending the High School and the University of Edinburgh he followed his father into the law, becoming an advocate (barrister) in 1792. In 1799 he was appointed Sheriff-Depute for the county of Selkirk, and in 1806 a Clerk of the Court of Session— appointments which he retained until the end of his life. His first major publication was a collection of ballads entitled *The Minstrelsy of the Scottish Border* (1802–3). He became famous as a poet with *The Lay of the Last Minstrel* (1805), *Marmion* (1808), and *The Lady of the Lake* (1810). In 1814 he published his first novel, *Waverley*, set during the Jacobite rising of 1745. Its success encouraged him to produce more historical novels, set in different countries and periods, of which those set in Scotland, like *The Antiquary*, have usually been regarded as his best. Scott's work was widely acclaimed and influential in Europe and America. He spent the income from his writings on establishing a house and estate at Abbotsford, near Melrose. He was awarded a baronetcy by the Prince Regent in 1818. Partnership in the printing firm of James Ballantyne & Co. involved him in a financial crash in 1826; his last years were darkened by illness and the need to continue his output of writing to pay off his debts. He died at Abbotsford in 1832; his biography was written by his son-in-law, John Gibson Lockhart.

NICOLA J. WATSON is Lecturer in English at the Open University.

OXFORD WORLD'S CLASSICS

SIR WALTER SCOTT

The Antiquary

Edited with an Introduction and Notes by
NICOLA J. WATSON

OXFORD
UNIVERSITY PRESS

OXFORD
UNIVERSITY PRESS

Great Clarendon Street, Oxford OX2 6DP

Oxford University Press is a department of the University of Oxford.
It furthers the University's objective of excellence in research, scholarship,
and education by publishing worldwide in

Oxford New York

Auckland Bangkok Buenos Aires Cape Town Chennai
Dar es Salaam Delhi Hong Kong Istanbul Karachi Kolkata
Kuala Lumpur Madrid Melbourne Mexico City Mumbai Nairobi
São Paulo Shanghai Singapore Taipei Tokyo Toronto

and an associated company in Berlin

Oxford is a registered trade mark of Oxford University Press
in the UK and in certain other countries

Published in the United States
by Oxford University Press Inc., New York

Editorial matter © Nicola J. Watson 2002

British Library Cataloguing in Publication Data

Data available

Library of Congress Cataloging in Publication Data

Scott, Walter, Sir, 1771–1832.
The antiquary/Sir Walter Scott ; edited with an introduction and notes by Nicola J. Watson.
p. cm.—(Oxford world's classics).
Includes bibliographical references.
ISBN 0–19–283187–9 (acid-free paper)
1. Fathers and daughters—Fiction. 2. Antiquarians—Fiction. 3. Scotland—Fiction.
4. Beggars—Fiction. I. Watson, Nicola J., 1958– . II. Title. III. Oxford world's classics.
(Oxford University Press)
PR5317.A68 2002 823'.7—dc21 2001036905

ISBN 0–19–283187–9

1 3 5 7 9 10 8 6 4 2

Typeset in Ehrhardt
by RefineCatch Limited, Bungay, Suffolk
Printed in Great Britain by
Cox & Wyman Ltd.
Reading, Berkshire

CONTENTS

INTRODUCTION

In July 1815, about a month after the second fall of Napoleon and his exile to St Helena, the 44-year-old Walter Scott left Scotland on his way to Brussels to visit the field of Waterloo. There he picked up his share of relics and souvenirs from the battle, including a French cuirass which, if you care to, you can still go and see hanging (among many other historical artefacts of all kinds) at Scott's house in the Borders, Abbotsford. (Abbotsford is in itself an excellent introduction to *The Antiquary*: at once a home and a museum, it is as multiple and ambivalent as Scott's fiction, a modern domestic residence designed in the style of a medieval castle, sited in Scotland but looking south across the Borders into England.) Scott spent much of the rest of his visit to the Continent hobnobbing with high society in Brussels and Paris, meeting, amongst other military celebrities, the victor of Waterloo, the Duke of Wellington. He was one of the first wave of British tourists and souvenir-hunters, which included other literary celebrities such as the poets Robert Southey and Lord Byron, also newly released from the confinement to the British Isles necessitated by the long-running wars with revolutionary France. Like Southey and Byron, Scott wrote about his experiences, although unlike them he couched his most-considered reactions in prose, using the persona of a prosy letter-writing provincial bachelor in his travel book, *Paul's Letters to His Kinsfolk* (1816). Back at quiet provincial Abbotsford, in late September 1815, he turned his attention to a new novel, his third, for which he had already signed a contract in January 1815, and which should have been delivered in June. It too would take as its central personage a provincial middle-aged bachelor, often regarded as in some sense a self-portrait, and it would be built emotionally around the difference that Scott remarked upon on his return in a letter to his friend Morritt: 'The contrast between this quiet birds' nest of a place with the late scenes of confusion and military splendour which I have witnessed is something of a stunning nature.'[1] Scott's letters reveal that by December 1815 he had the germ of an idea for *The Antiquary*; composition

---

[1] H. J. C. Grierson (ed.), *The Letters of Sir Walter Scott*, 12 vols. (1932–7), iv. 99–100.

proceeded rapidly, and the latest novel by the anonymous and already celebrated 'Author of Waverley' was published in three smart volumes on 4 May 1816. It was to become a best-seller, selling 6,000 copies within a week of publication. Scott was to say towards the end of his life that it was his favourite of the entire series of Waverley novels.

The Story

Despite this initial success and authorial endorsement, *The Anti-quary* has been perhaps the most persistently underestimated work of (since the end of the nineteenth century) our most persistently underestimated major writer. Many of the complaints made against it have resulted simply from baffled readers approaching the book expecting much simpler fare than it offers. *The Antiquary*'s critics have in general been disappointed that it is not at heart a costume-drama thriller in the mode of Scott's first historical novel, *Waverley* (1814), the action-packed tale of a naive Englishman who finds him-self caught up in the 1745 Jacobite rebellion and is man-hunted across Scotland under suspicion of high treason. Although *The Anti-quary*, too, reveals Scott as the founder of a line in the novel which leads in one direction to *The Thirty-Nine Steps* and in another to *War and Peace*, this particular specimen of historical fiction is Scott for sophisticates: instead of thriving on the personal danger of a hero caught up to his astonishment and terror in great decisive public crises, *The Antiquary* takes a mature, even middle-aged, pleasure in the desultory and the loitering as a way of managing anxiety and melancholy, and it finds a consoling delight in the varieties and vagaries of language as a palliative for loss and failure. It is a generous-spirited, virtuoso exercise in comic bathos, woven of obsessive talk and aborted action, in which more seems to be at stake than is ever quite at risk. Although *The Antiquary* is no less invested than *Waverley* in the re-establishment of dying houses, the restora-tion of dynasties, and, metaphorically speaking, the repair of the British nation in the face of past and present war, it pursues its interest in the suppression of rebellions of all kinds with a self-mocking diffidence which is in itself part of its moral. It carefully weans its readers from their sensation-hungry expectations of high adventure and Gothic frisson in order to celebrate instead the victory of the very mildly interesting—of the ordinary, quotidian, and provincial, of the modestly and good-temperedly modern, and of the luxuries of silliness and garrulity—over the perpetually threatened eruption of violence, disorder, war, and death. To achieve this, *The Antiquary* devises notably elaborate and subtle ways of making us read it, proceeding by juxtaposing emblematic tableaux and episodes designed to repeat each other with significant variations, while its formal, surface plot provides a narrative resolution to these reiterated architectures of emotion.

At first glance, indeed, the story of *The Antiquary* seems slight to the point of flimsiness, and in terms of its purchase upon the reader's imagination it is even slighter than the following brief description will suggest. A young Englishman travels to north-east Scotland in the wartime year of 1794 on mysterious business and under an improbable name, meets the local bores and worthies, rescues the local baronet and his daughter from a watery grave, fights and wins a duel when his identity is questioned, and promptly disappears lengthily until the end of the novel, when his identity is finally revealed, his legitimacy is established, and he is able to marry the woman he loves and restore both her tottering family fortunes and his own. During his absence, the centre of the novel dramatizes the slow and uncertain detection and authentication of various buried pasts and buried treasures, presided over by the antiquary of the title, Jonathan Oldbuck, squire of Monkbarns, and involving his neighbour Sir Arthur Wardour, who is nearly bankrupted by a swindling but ultimately discomfited German, Dousterswivel, who claims to be able to refine lead and copper from ore found on his land. During the sometimes whimsical pursuit of all this, Scott nonetheless quietly achieves a sweeping panorama of turn-of-the-century Scottish society, largely through a virtuosic ventriloquy of social languages: from the fisherman's and beggar's Scots vernacular, through the jargons of antiquarianism, of the law, of the Church, and of heraldry, all diversified by proverbs, biblical scraps and rhythms, snatches of Latin and French, and innumerable tags and rags of quoted and misquoted poetry. The whole ends with a famous set-piece, with the countryside all in arms—under the leadership of the lost heir, on the alarm of a supposed French invasion. As in detective fiction, the forensic investigation and reinterpretation of the past provides the ground for understanding the present and building the future; *The Antiquary* deals in how, to what ends, and in what forms the miscellaneous tragedy of the past can be alchemized into modern comedy.

Critical Verdicts

The Antiquary has justly been celebrated ever since publication for its lively comic characterization of Jonathan Oldbuck and his anti-quarian follies, and for its rich documentary-style portrayal of Scot-tish life in the manor, the burgh town, and the fisherman's village, rendered in vigorous and colloquial style. Scott's contemporaries would also value the novel very highly for 'traits of feeling that melt, and strokes of humour that enliven the heart'[2]—sentiment sharp-ened by comedy, a sort of healthy moral work-out for the affections. The Victorians would especially enjoy, as the illustrations to the long series of nineteenth-century editions indicate, the novel's piquant juxtapositions of sentimental beauty, exemplified by the heroine Isabella Wardour, with the intransigently earthy, embodied by the beggar Edie Ochiltree. This taste meant that certain scenes—Edie talking to Isabella over the window-sill of Knockwinnock, for example—became standard scenarios to act out in home *tableaux vivants*; other celebrated painterly set-pieces included the stranding of Isabella and her father Sir Arthur Wardour by the rising tide and their rescue, and the funeral of the young fisherman Steenie Mucklebackit (the storm scene was famous enough as a spectacular to be included in the commemorative pageant mounted by the Theatre Royal, Covent Garden, on Scott's death in 1832). So diminished has Scott's reputation become since the 1890s saw the Waverley novels all but vanish into the hinterland of children's classics, however, that we now need to remind ourselves of how deeply embedded in the culture *The Antiquary* once was. It was still possible for Virginia Woolf to allude to it as part of Mr Ramsay's consoling reading in *To the Lighthouse* (1927) and to expect her readers to pick up the suggestion that her novel, like Scott's, concerned itself at that point with fatherhood and bereavement. Since then, however, its echoes have moved down-market into genre fiction. Michael Innes (a.k.a. the Oxford don J. I. M. Stewart) used

---

[2] *Quarterly Review*, 15 (Apr.–July 1816), 126.

The Antiquary as the basis for a patriotic wartime thriller, *The Secret Vanguard* (in 1941, when Innes apparently still expected his more cultivated readers to recognize structures, characters, scenes, and themes drawn from Scott's novel), and, most recently, its ghost hovers behind Patrick O'Brian's series of naval thrillers set during the Napoleonic Wars, in the shape of Captain Aubrey's disastrous involvement in a fraudulent mining scheme.

Even during the heyday of Scott's popularity, though, *The Antiquary* enjoyed a curious reception history for a much-loved Waverley novel. Short on action, conflict, heroism and romance, long on loquacious fustiness and anticlimax, it was destined never to be staged successfully as drama (despite three attempts), never to be burlesqued, and never to be adapted in any of the many modes and forms into which Scott's other novels spread themselves, whether as opera, children's fiction, schoolroom drama, or television costume spectacular. Like the book's would-be adapters, critics have regularly been baffled by the way that *The Antiquary*, paradoxically, has at once too little and too much plot. As commentators have been pointing out since 1816, the novel's foreground is occupied by figures who apparently have little directly invested in the outcome of the story, though they may assist ultimately in unravelling it; to quote Francis Jeffrey (the editor of the important literary journal the *Quarterly Review*):

though the antiquary [Oldbuck] gives his name to the work, he can hardly be called its hero; and, indeed, though the peculiarity of his character induces the author to produce him very frequently and forwardly in the scene, he has not any great share in the plot, and is evidently recommended to the high situation which he occupies by his humour rather than his use.[3]

The same has frequently been felt to be true of the portrait of the fishing family the Mucklebackits, or even of the picturesque vagrant Edie Ochiltree. The *Monthly*'s reviewer commented that the author's 'art' 'consists far less in the involution of plot, variety of incident, or command over the stronger feelings of our nature, than in that minute, happy, and frequently very humorous delineation of manners'.[4] The value of the piece was supposed to be found in its picture-gallery quality, in 'all the chequered scenes of life which he

[3] *Quarterly Review*, 129.
[4] *Monthly Review*, 82, (Jan.–Apr. 1817), 39.

presents to our view'.[5] As Scott himself said (though it is often unwise to take Scott's art at his own estimation): 'It is not so interesting as its predecessors—the period did not admit of so much romantic situation.'[6] On the other hand, buried deep in the novel's infrastructure there is a positive superfluity of sensational, if conventional, plot ('not very novel, nor yet very probable' as Jeffrey put it) in the shape of the Glenallan mystery, a Gothic romance of crippling incestuous guilt redeemed along with the lost heir.[7] The genre of this plot, horrible, unnatural, hackneyed, and commercial, associated at the time especially with women writers and readers and with Byron, has been a source of anxiety for reviewers from publication to the present; at the very least, it has seemed to be out of drawing with the rest. The chief link between this traumatic past and the urbane present, the juvenile lead Lovel, has seemed weak, if only because he is so conspicuously absent for so much of the time. Although all the strands of the novel weave together at the climax, the tonal and generic disjunctions between the conversational comedy of the Oldbuck circle, the documentary realism of the Mucklebackits, the melodramatic Gothic of the Glenallan mystery, the slapstick of the Dousterswivel plot, and the mechanical *coup de théâtre* of the denouement have persistently troubled critics. All in all, the novel has seemed wilfully and unnecessarily miscellaneous. The verdict, in short, has until recently been that the novel has many incidental 'beauties' (as the Victorians would perhaps have put it), but does not really hold together (although, in an era when postmodern historical romance is fast becoming the acknowledged mainstream of both middlebrow and highbrow fiction, it has now become possible to regard this tendency to dislimn as excitingly experimental).[8] *The Antiquary*'s insistence on making historical events spectacularly peripheral and even vanishing them into farcical non-events, and its rather recent setting in the 1790s, furthermore, have made it seem puzzlingly anomalous within the canon of the Author of Waverley constructed by the Magnum

[5] *British Critic*, 5 (Jan.–June 1816), 633.

[6] *Letters*, iv. 233.

[7] *Quarterly Review*, 128.

[8] For an approach that valorizes the disjunctions between Gothic and realism in *The Antiquary* and other Waverley novels, see Fiona Robertson, *Legitimate Histories: Scott, Gothic, and the Authorities of Fiction* (1994); on Scott, romance and the postmodern, see Diane Elam, *Romancing the Post-Modern* (1992), esp. 51–79.

Opus (Scott's final collected edition of his historical novels, published 1829–33).

The Figure of the Antiquary

While it is true that it is not in any simple sense a historical novel, *The Antiquary*, in its self-conscious and highly ironized exploration of the problems of retrieving and interpreting the historical, may be in fact less the odd one out among Scott's novels than the key to the entire project of the Waverley *opus*. To recognize this entails taking Scott's choice of title seriously. The title points to Jonathan Oldbuck (rather than Lovel) as the 'hero' of the novel and, insistently, to his amateur hobby of antiquarianism as the governing aesthetic or methodology of the whole book. Although Scott endeavoured to bring off his customary authorial disappearing trick by identifying his acquaintance George Constable rather than himself as the original for Oldbuck in the introduction he wrote for the Magnum Opus, it was recognized very early that Oldbuck was to some important degree a self-portrait: as his son-in-law Lockhart wrote shortly after his death,

the truth is, that although Scott's Introduction of 1830 represents himself as pleased with fancying that, in his principal personage, he had embalmed a worthy friend of his boyish days, his own antiquarian propensities ... had by degrees so developed themselves, that he could hardly, even when the Antiquary was published, have scrupled about recognising a quaint caricature of the founder of the Abbotsford Museum, in the inimitable portraiture of the Laird of Monkbarns.[9]

Lockhart's suggestion of Scott's complicity with this 'caricature' (and of its deliberate acknowledgement in the near-synonym of 'Monkbarns' and 'Abbotsford') is reinforced by the way Scott himself occasionally took on the alias of Oldbuck in later letters, and used it as part of the frame for later Waverley novels. It is also illuminated by an anecdote retailed by Scott's friend James Hogg in 1834, which could be said to construct Scott in Oldbuck mode and, moreover, to forerun the ironic structure of *The Antiquary* itself. Hogg, Scott, and party visited Rankleburn in the summer of 1801 to

[9] J. G. Lockhart, *Memoirs of the Life of Sir Walter Scott, Bart.* (1837–8), 7 vols., 4, 12.

search for family relics of the Scotts of Buccleuch, and in particular
for a font-stone that supposedly lay hidden in the ruins of an old
church:

As there appeared, however, to have been a sort of recess in the eastern
gable, we fell a turning over some loose stones, to see if the baptismal font
was not there, when we came to one-half of a small pot encrusted thick
with rust. Mr Scott's eyes brightened and he swore it was part of an
ancient consecrated helmet. Laidlaw, however, fell a picking and scratch-
ing with great patience until at last he came to a layer of pitch inside, and
then, with a malicious sneer, he said, 'The truth is, Mr Scott, it's nouther
mair nor less than an auld tar-pot, that some of the farmers hae been
buisting their sheep out o' i' the kirk lang syne.' Sir Walter's shaggy
eyebrows dipped deep over his eyes, and, suppressing a smile, he turned
and strode way as fast as he could, saying, that 'we had just rode all the
way to see that there was nothing to *be* seen.'[10]

Scott's most recent biographer John Sutherland points out the startling similarities between author and character: like Scott, Oldbuck is
a younger brother, apprenticed to an attorney, who falls in love in
youth with a noble young lady. Jilted for a better-connected and
richer lover, both retreat for consolation into antiquarian pursuits on
a modest competence provided on the death of father and older
brother. In short, Oldbuck represents both what Scott might have
become, and perhaps what Scott feels an author, even 'The Author
of Waverley', might be—outside history, society, and the repro-
ductive family.[11] The quasi-autobiographical creation of Oldbuck
and his positioning within the novel's schema suggests that part of
the business of *The Antiquary* is to explore the paradoxes of history
and fiction for Scott as inventor of a new genre.

Waterloo and the Romance of Restoration

The Antiquary is also central to Scott's canon, paradoxically, by virtue of its insistence on recent history; for in some rather general
sense all the early Waverley novels deal covertly with what is fore-
grounded in *The Antiquary*—the implications of the French Revolution, the Napoleonic Empire, and the Bourbon restoration for ways

[10] James Hogg, *Familiar Anecdotes of Sir Walter Scott* (1834), ed. Douglas S. Mack
(1972), 139.
[11] John Sutherland, *The Life of Sir Walter Scott* (1995), 190–1.

of imagining the nation. The third in the first series of Waverley novels, coming after *Waverley* and *Guy Mannering*, Scott advertised *The Antiquary* as 'complet[ing] a series of fictitious narratives, intended to illustrate the manners of Scotland at three different periods' (p. 3), in practice, a survey of the history of Scotland from the 1745 rebellion to the wars against revolutionary France. *The Antiquary*, indeed, can be seen as Scott's full-scale meditation upon Waterloo as a defining event in world history. For contemporaries, the fall of Napoleon marked not only the end of war but the end of the many social experiments instituted by the French Revolution. Like the the fall of the Berlin Wall (which, abruptly marking the end of the Cold War, closed an epoch of cultural no less than of political history), Bonaparte's defeat instantly constituted all that went before as 'history', as having taken place under an altogether vanished dispensation. In taking as its setting the summer of 1794 (though the denouement also owes something to the invasion scare of 1804), *The Antiquary* effectively takes stock of the revolutionary and Napoleonic past, seen through the lens of hindsight. It is not difficult to pick out the ways in which the novel carefully marks its wartime setting: the disguised hero Lovel is a military man, as is the belligerent Captain Hector M'Intyre; the pompous baronet Wardour feels the whiff of insurrection at home and proposes to take up the beggar Edie Ochiltree as its source; the tittle-tattle of the countryside imagines that Lovel is a French spy, or associated with the republican sympathizers the Friends of the People; the mystery surrounding Lovel's birth is partly generated by the killing of the woman who knows the family secret by the revolutionaries and partly solved by the return from France as a royalist émigré of the tutor who solemnized the marriage between his parents; there are references to the 1794 royalist uprising in La Vendée; the naval fleet stands just off-shore commanded by Lieutenant Taffril and disgorging secret chests of silver; the German charlatan and swindler Dousterswivel is generated straight out of contemporary hysteria about the imagined Napoleonic equivalent of the Fifth Column, the Illuminati, and he is duly threatened with the sanctions of both the Aliens Act and the Traitorous Correspondences Act of 1793; and the denouement, with the whole country rising in patriotic haste from baronet to beggar to fight the French on the lighting of the warning beacon fires, has often been celebrated. Concentrating on this aspect of the book, it is possible to construe *The Antiquary* as an exercise in patriotic nostalgia, a sort of late Georgian *Dad's Army* which looks back to the wartime past (in which all classes united against an invasion that never came) as an escape from the complexities of post-war change. As Sutherland notes, the novel's virtuous beggar, the loyal king's-bedesman Edie Ochiltree, is transparently a wish-fulfilling fiction produced in the face of the mass vagrancy occasioned by the demobilization of 1815, when starving, disaffected, unemployed, and begging soldiers and sailors were flooding the countryside.[12] Similarly the novel's investment in the unmasking of fraud—most importantly, the Countess of Glenallan's crippling fiction that her son's marriage is incestuous, doubled in Dousterswivel's swindling of Wardour, and finally repeated in farcical mode, in the imaginary invasion—can be read as a way of airbrushing the Revolution and the Napoleonic Empire out of history: it was all a sham, or at worst an error, now exploded forever.

Yet *The Antiquary* does not feel precisely like the crowing of a Tory triumphalist, hymning a total victory on the gentry's own terms; instead, it gives off a whiff of good-tempered, even rueful disillusionment and *ennui*. The novel is suffused with the general mood of what Scott himself registered as the 'vacancy' that afflicted him and his contemporaries upon the final disappearance of Napoleon as centre of attention and a source of anxiety.[13] The immediate euphoria of 1814 when Napoleon seemed defeated and safely exiled to Elba had first been soured by Napoleon's comeback, and then compromised by what was seen by admirers and haters of the Emperor alike as his ignoble surrender after Waterloo. As Scott was to write, Napoleon's return had seemed like

an unexpected convulsion, the recollection of whose unexpected fury will long make us feel like men who tread on the surface of a volcano. The victory of Waterloo, and the second capture of Paris, agitating, affecting, and interesting, as far as it is possible for human events to be so, had not power again to lull us into the pleasing delusion, that war was vanished from the earth, and that contending nations might in future hang the trumpet in the hall, and vie only in the arts of commerce and of peace. The eyes which wept for joy at the first restoration of the Bourbons,

---

[12] Sutherland, *The Life of Sir Walter Scott*, 193.
[13] *Letters*, iii. 450.

cannot look upon their second re-establishment without painful and anxious apprehensions, concerning the stability of their throne.[14]

The pan-European patching-up of dodgy dynastic fictions that was to follow, as obscure branches of exiled royal families were 'restored' to power in states now unrecognizable from their pre-Imperial forms, surely motivates the destabilizing heterogeneity of *The Antiquary*. Its aesthetic investment in irony, disappointment, and anti-climax dramatizes the post-Napoleonic insubstantiality of the romance of restoration.

Making History

The Antiquary, then, partly because of its own position in history as a novel about 1794 composed in 1815–16, is preoccupied on every level by the relation between past and present. Throughout its pages the past takes many forms and meanings, some of them conspicuously incompatible. The antiquarianism of Oldbuck, for example, is invested in a miscellaneous jumble of decontextualized objects and inscriptions which are variously obsolete, misplaced, inauthentic, or unreadable. The dilettantish quality of this antiquarianism is incarnated in his study: 'The floor, as well as the table and chairs, was overflowed by the same *mare magnum* of miscellaneous trumpery, where it would have been as impossible to find any individual article wanted, as to put it to any use when discovered' (p. 33). Littered with 'old armour, swords, dirks, helmets, and Highland targets' (p. 32), the study both domesticates and denies war; appropriately enough for the retreat of a confirmed bachelor, the business of reproduction—weddings and babies represented respectively by the tapestry depicting Sir Gawaine's wedding and the 'jolter-headed' Dutch cherubs—are safely reduced to caricature by the old-fashioned conventions through which they are represented. Like Oldbuck himself, his collectibles have fallen away from narrative, history, agency, and reproduction—and this constitutes their chief charm, for they speak of a cultured, peacetime, bachelor modernity in which there is leisure to indulge self-aggrandizing fantasies and follies of all sorts. Books about supernatural occurrences and ballads

---

[14] 'History of Europe, 1814', *The Edinburgh Annual Register for 1814, Edinburgh Annual Register*, (1816), 7, pt 1, 366–7.

about war alike turn into artefacts, valuable by virtue of their scarcity and aesthetic quaintness rather than for what they say.

Such antiquarianism makes history into property, and it does so typically through its investment in the idea of writing. The long and seemingly pointless bibliophile conversation in which Oldbuck displays his book collection makes this point; so too does his pride in his Whiggish heritage as the descendant of a printer, someone who turns knowledge into intellectual and financial capital. The other antiquaries of Oldbuck's circle are equally concerned to appropriate history as property, whether in the shape of Sir Arthur Wardour's pride in his family history as recorded in the Ragman Roll, or Oldbuck's nephew Hector M'Intyre's Highland touchiness when the authenticity of Ossian is queried, or the Revd Blattergowl's greedy interest in the past intricacies of church rents. This scholarly and antiquarian form of history—invested in the artefact and the written—is insistently counterposed to oral, living history and memory—vested in the body. The two types of historian confront each other early over the vexed matter of an earthwork, the Kaim of Kinprunes, claimed by Jonathan Oldbuck to be the site of an important Roman battle, and by the beggar Edie Ochiltree, 'the news-carrier, the minstrel, and sometimes the historian of the district' (p. 47), to have been dug by his friends for a local wedding. A good deal is at stake over the correct interpretation of the inscription A.D.D.L. which appears on a stone found there; Oldbuck has exchanged good grazing-land for this supposed site of special historical interest, but more metaphorically this scene sets up the whole question of whether this novel will concern itself with epic, war, and invasion, or whether it will settle for romance and weddings.

Siting History

The episode at the Kaim of Kinprunes sets written and oral history at loggerheads in a conflict of authentication. This drama of historical authentication—and its relation to real estate—is played out most elaborately upon the novel's most charged and palimpsestic setting, the romantic ruins of St Ruth's Priory. A remarkable number of the novel's incidents take place in or near these ruins: the picnic and the reading of the story of Martin Waldeck, the duel between the mysterious stranger Lovel and Hector M'Intyre, Lovel's flight into

OTTAKAR'S

a love for books

The Edinburgh Bookshop
57 George Street
Edinburgh, EH2 2JQ
0131 225 4495
george.street@ottakars.co.uk

SALE
27 3 179576   02 Feb 2006 13:37

CASHIER: ALISON
9780099472285 Out   8.99
9781841493695 Coyote Runtime   6.99

TOTAL   ITEMS   2   13.98

Cash   13.98
CHANGE   0.00

Head Office: St John's House,
72 St John's Road, London, SW11 1PT

Vat No: 561997200
Company Reg No: 2133199
Refunds or exchanges will be given
within 28 days of purchase on production
of a valid receipt providing goods are
in saleable condition.

hiding within the ruin's secret caves and passages, the duping first of
Sir Arthur Wardour by Dousterswivel and then of Dousterswivel by
Ochiltree and Steenie Mucklebackit, and, finally, the funeral of the
Countess of Glenallan, which inaugurates the last major section of
the novel. This site, 'ruin within ruin, structure upon structure,
inscription under inscription' as Judith Wilt has put it,[15] works as the
unconscious of the book, mined below with caves, passages, and
graves which variously emblematize obliteration, isolation, alien-
ation, the illicit and illegitimate, lost histories, violence and death. It
is a place compounded, like the whole fabric of *The Antiquary*, of
improbable stories, black secrets and comic lies, of burial and
exhumation, of treasure of dubious provenance and doubtful value.
It functions as the physical connection between the story of Martin
Waldeck's ill-gotten and fatal supernatural wealth and the 'discovery' of Dousterswivel's fraudulent hoard (complete with its
apparently supernatural spirits); both are associated with alchemy,
both come to a bad end. It doubles the stories of Waldeck and that of
Wardour's ancestor Malcolm the Misbegot a.k.a. Misticot—both
obtain their wealth by dubious means—and of Misticot and Lovel,
both associated with forbidden love, treasure, and illegitimacy.
Dreamlike, St Ruth's is a place of repetition and inversion. The
multiple exhumation from Misticot's grave of treasures by turn
fraudulent (Dousterswivel's bait for Wardour), real (the chest of
silver with the erased provenances—the concealed chest-lid and the
melted-off Glenallan arms), and non-existent (the imaginary second
chest of gold), is repeated and inverted in the burial of the Countess
of Glenallan, whose interment, paradoxically, will lead to the
exhumation of her fraud, resurrecting from the various living deaths
that have entombed them first her senile servant Elspeth Mucklebackit, then her guilt-broken son the Earl of Glenallan, and finally
her grandson Lovel himself, nameless and outlawed. The sequence
of readings and misreadings, recognitions and misrecognitions iden-
tifies the problem of the novel as being the discovery of the true,
buried treasure and its provision with a legitimate provenance—in
short, its authentication. That treasure, virtuous and magic rather
than fatal and fraudulent, will eventually turn out to be the heir

---

[15] Judith Wilt, *Secret Leaves: The Novels of Sir Walter Scott* (1985), 158.

Lovel himself, emblematically buried alive in the ruins at this pivotal moment of the novel.

Identity, Legitimacy, and Inheritance

The formal plot of *The Antiquary* accordingly repeats this metaphoric investment in dynastic history, detailing the detection of a Gothic narrative of buried crimes, broken families, and failed inheritance. It is centrally concerned with re-establishing the proper transmission of identity and inheritance from fathers to sons, with making the illegitimate legitimate, and thereby with restoring proper relations between past and present. The fabric of *The Antiquary* is shot through with childless fathers and fatherless sons and the possibilities of restoration. Lovel alone can lay claim to one supposed father (Edward Neville), one genetic father (the Earl of Glenallan), and two adoptive fathers (Jonathan Oldbuck and Edie Ochiltree). At the most literal level of the main plot, the novel restores the lost heir of Glenallan to his genetic father. Lovel's successive metamorphoses of identity from a renounced and reduced identity expressed in his alias, an imperfect and truncated anagram of Neville (the name derived from his supposed father, and also from his mother Eveline Neville) through to reinstatement as Lord Geraldin literalize the redemption of his father, 'so broken down with disease and mental misery, so gaunt and ghastly, that he appeared but a wreck of manhood' (p. 276), locked within the mausoleum of Glenallan House, hung with mourning and hatchments, filled with out-of-date furnishings and emblems of suffering and torture.

Lovel's alias also points to another of his functions—love-begot, he is there to love and to be loved, no less by Isabella Wardour than by Jonathan Oldbuck, another of the novel's childless fathers. If Glenallan is entombed in perpetual guilt and mourning (in an archaically cluttered house which looks like a tragic variant on the Antiquary's own), Oldbuck is equally crippled by the failure of his long-past courtship of Eveline Neville—deformed into comic misogyny and cranky scholarship. Lovel, whom the Antiquary calls his 'phoenix', is in some metaphoric sense Oldbuck's love-child, the son he never had by his dead love, the past miraculously brought back to life. Indeed, structurally Lovel usurps the place of the Antiquary's nephew and actual heir, the fatherless Hector M'Intyre. Whereas

Lovel in some sense restores the lost love and the lost past by being married with the Antiquary's ring, Hector is the cause of the loss of Oldbuck's walking-stick, associated with the Antiquary's doomed love for Eveline through having been cut 'in the classic woods of Hawthornden, when I did not expect always to have been a bachelor' (p. 296–7). The duel between the two young bloods is thus at least in part 'about' the threatened supplanting of Hector as the Antiquary's blood heir, and Lovel's title to do so. Oldbuck hints as much when he invites Lovel to live in his family:

'Why, I thought I had hit on the very arrangement that would suit us both, and who knows what might happen in the long run, and whether we might ever part?—Why, I am master of my acres, man—there is the advantage of being descended from a man of more sense than pride—they cannot oblige me to transmit my goods, chattels, and heritages, any way but as I please. No strings of substitute heirs of entail, as empty and unsubstantial as the morsels of paper strung to the train of a boy's kite, to cumber my flights of inclination, and my humours of predilection.' (p. 155)

If Lovel is Glenallan's genetic heir in the full strength of entail, he is therefore also elective heir to the Antiquary—a love-child in this sense, too. Oldbuck's claim on him as a sort of son is strengthened by his eventual role as investigator and authenticator of his legitimacy and as the man who introduces Lovel to his real father in the denouement.

Yet another childless father-figure, Edie Ochiltree, is crucial to securing Lovel's identity. Ochiltree is associated with the notion of love, continuity, and community. Whereas other characters are persistently connected with the idea of broken transmission and failed lines of communication, Ochiltree embodies connection. The lost and diverted letters, the delayed and frustrated journeys, the rash of misreadings that are characteristic of this novel—all are redeemed by Ochiltree. He is a knower of love-secrets, a plotter of plots, a reader of riddles; he incarnates provincial geography, connecting house to house across the social spectrum. He presides over the delivery of rings and letters, treasure and truths. This surely is the point of the little post-Wordsworthian scene in which Ochiltree finds the lost son of the postmaster and delivers him and his important letter to Lovel. Considered as an allegorical picture, here the childless beggar acquires a quasi-son—and we later discover that this letter brings the news of the loss of a quasi-father and Lovel's first inheritance. Ochiltree is involved in delivery in another sense too: his knowledge of both sea and land allows him to rescue the Wardours on the beach, and Lovel in the aftermath of the duel into the secret caves and passages beneath St Ruth's Priory. It is he who delivers Lovel's treasure into Misticot's grave and then delivers Lovel's letter in time to save the Wardours from being turned out of Knockwinnock.

The centrality of the restoration of sons to fathers is realized in the counterposed episodes of the death and funeral of Steenie Mucklebackit. Justly celebrated for their power, these scenes have not always been understood as integral to the logic of *The Antiquary*. Yet it is surely possible to see Steenie Mucklebackit's accident not as arbitrary but as motivated by the patterning of the text—Steenie is lost to the sea, so that Lovel can return from it. This son drowns in place of others: in place of Eveline Neville, rescued from the sea to die giving birth; in place of Isabella and her father, so nearly lost on Knockwinnock sands; in place, above all, of the other lost son, Lovel, who is at one point thought to have been lost at sea in the imagined wreck of Taffril's brig. In this scheme of fictional debits and credits, Mucklebackit is bereaved of his first-born so that others, Glenallan and Oldbuck, shall have their first-born restored to them; Jenny Rintherout loses her disapproved love so that Isabella Wardour can marry hers. The almost folkloric, primal opposition between the sea and the land founds the underlying metaphoric logic of the novel. The sea devours values associated with the land, notably property and inheritance, as is neatly played out in the storm scene, when Sir Arthur Wardour and his daughter Isabella are nearly drowned by an unusually high spring tide. Offended by a supposed slur on the ancestry of which he is so vain, Wardour flounces from the Monkbarns dinner-table to take the road home, and, seeing his recent dinner-companion Lovel in the distance, and prompted by his daughter (who has her own reasons for avoiding Lovel), he resolves to avoid further intimacy by taking the route by the sands. Their subsequent danger is thus directly traceable to Wardour's over-tender pride in his ancestry which itself (as we learn later) has prompted his daughter to sever relations with Lovel on the discovery that he is (apparently) illegitimate. Wardour's folly will nearly cost him dear. Caught between cliff and sea, he will be reduced, as Ochiltree so memorably says, to the landlessness of the itinerant beggar: 'Our riches will soon be equal . . . they are sae already; for I hae nae land, and you would give your fair bounds and barony for a square yard of rock that would be dry for twal hours' (p. 75). Their predicament foreshadows the catastrophe of the house of Wardour; their escape up the cliffs, assisted in turn by Ochiltree, Lovel, and the Antiquary himself, plays out in little the saving of that house in which all three will be involved towards the end of the novel.[16] In the chapters set in the fishing village this drama of loss and restoration is played out again on the beach, the indeterminate, literally (or littorally) liminal place between the sea and the land. For all its acclaimed documentary realism, the Mucklebackits' cottage on the beach serves just as much as a romance space associated with death, burial, and resurrection, a space within which fathers lose and regain sons. It is here, after all, that Oldbuck abandons the position of sceptical onlooker for participation, taking on the paternal position in carrying Steenie's head to the grave. It is here that the funeral wake over the dead body of Steenie gives the living dead, his grandmother Elspeth Mucklebackit, the power to tell Glenallan that his son may still be living.

Re-establishing inheritance from father to son, as here, depends both literally and metaphorically upon the deaths of mothers and proxy mothers—in particular, the deaths of the Countess of Glenallan and her onetime servant Elspeth Mucklebackit. In this sense, *The Antiquary* is structurally misogynistic, a misogyny recapitulated in comic mode by the Antiquary's would-be despotic management of his grotesque sister Grizzel and the rest of his all-female household, all the way down to Juno, the badly behaved spaniel belonging to his nephew, jokily named after the goddess who was Hector's enemy in the Trojan wars, and, even, far out on that dangerous beach, by the unruly female seal which vanquishes Hector (in an episode which, miraculously, becomes funnier every time the Antiquary tediously reminds him about it). If we understand that women in this novel are always threatening to misappropriate things that don't belong to them, we can see emerging, like invisible ink, a metaphoric linkage between the misappropriation of toast by the disobedient spaniel, the interception of Taffril's love-letter by the harpy-like matrons of the post office, and the more serious crimes of the Countess of

---

[16] For an extended reading of this scene along these lines see Joan S. Elbers, 'Isolation and Community in *The Antiquary*', *Nineteenth-Century Fiction*, 27 (1972–3), 405–23.

Glenallan. This stealing of property and the fabrication of fictions typically break up heterosexual romance. In comic mode, this is played out in the scene in the post office in which the older women withhold the love-letter from its addressee and expend considerable energy on misreading it into a web of wild rumours.[17] At the tragic end of the scale, this pattern is repeated in the Countess of Glenallan's invention of a fiction of incest in order to prevent her son marrying and so demoting her to the status of dowager. The overcoming of the secrets and lies associated with these older women is the drama of *The Antiquary*: the oral, bodily history of Elspeth and her mistress is translated into masculine structures of written authentication—depositions and statements collected up by Oldbuck in his capacity as magistrate—which resuture the past to the present and enable heterosexual romance. The antiquarian's investment in the redundancy of the past is hereby reinvested with paternal energy and agency: the comic expression of this is the moment when Oldbuck calls for his sword to repel the supposed French invasion; the women of the house come running with a choice of weapons unceremoniously plucked from his study—'a Roman falchion of brass', 'an Andrea Ferrara without a handle', 'a two-handed sword of the twelfth century' (p. 422). He chooses instead 'the sword which my father wore in the year forty-five' (p. 422). What is at stake seems, to judge by the outcome, nothing less than national security: the women of the post office are formally reprimanded for having endangered the national interest; the restored son and lover turns out also to be the military hero who will lead the town of Fairport against the supposed invaders.

What, then, is this heritage into which the book finally allows the triumphant Lovel to enter? His marriage to Isabella Wardour exchanges the pedigree that he starts off with—a fatherless illegitimacy with more than a suggestion of something worse superadded—for two inheritances: one Catholic, Jacobite, Scottish, and aristocratic from the Glenallans and the Wardours, and one Whig, middle-class, and meritocratic from Oldbuck, whose ancestor Aldobrand bestows upon Lovel in his important dream the motto 'Kunst Macht Gunst' which spurs him to continue to pursue Isabella and which is engraved on the wedding ring. One speaks

---

[17] For an extended reading of this episode see Nicola J. Watson, *Revolution and the Form of the British Novel, 1790–1825* (1994), 142–8.

hereditary right and continuity located in the body and the land, one speaks individual ability and an ideology of progress located with the idea of writing and documentation. These two inheritances are rescheduled by Lovel's own inheritance from his adoptive father Edward Neville—his professional Protestant Englishness—to construct a model of a new and fertile British identity, a new Protestant legitimacy which subsumes and harnesses the variously archaic and subversive energies of the past.

Language and Genre

The construction of this broad-based national legitimacy is played out in the verbal texture of the novel no less elaborately than in its plot. Perhaps more than any other of the Waverley novels, *The Antiquary* is concerned with the invention of competing idiolects: the mishmash of language drawn from natural philosophy that Dousterswivel mis-speaks in his German dialect; the prosy borings of Blattergowl and Wardour on the subjects of church tithe laws and heraldry; the earthy language of Ochiltree, moving to proverbial and biblical rhythms; the carefully differentiated vernacular of the locals; and the highly individuated language of the Antiquary himself, peppered with rags and tags of Latin, legal imagery, and poetry of all kinds. Both the original and subsequent editions of *The Antiquary* came equipped by Scott with a glossary which was gradually expanded over the rest of the nineteenth century, which indicates that the difficulty of these idiolects is quite deliberate on Scott's part: his readers, so far from being assumed to be fluent already in lowland Scots and archaic jargons, are invited to become delighted connoisseurs of recherché obscurity, aesthetically enjoying the multiply opaque surfaces of the novel's language before using the glossary to decode (as its characters do its plot) its partially buried senses. The potential for incomprehensibility in the various discourses is integral not merely to Scott's new brand of realism but to the overall preoccupation of the novel. Like its story, *The Antiquary*'s richly variegated verbal texture effectively argues by the end that beggar and baron, if divided by dialect, are united by a similar stake in the land. (Less conspicuously, the glossary points to another part of Scott's project, the integration of Scots and Scotland into mainstream British commercial culture.) And as with language, so, as I have already suggested, with literary form. For *The Antiquary* is woven not just from competing dialects but from competing genres: and not only the clash between the Gothic associated with the past and the comedy of manners associated with the present, but a deeper fundamental clash between ancient epic and modern farce. If Gothic incest, Catholic aristocracy, and Jacobitism in the person of the Earl of Glenallan is hauled into the light of modern day and comically talked to death at the progressive Antiquary's dinner-table, epic, associated most persistently with the warlike figure of the modern-day Hector and with the Antiquary's ambitions to shine in print as author of the notes to 'The Caledoniad; or, Invasion Repelled' is transmuted as ruthlessly into the farcical. Hector's shaming encounter with the seal is a miniaturization of this dwarfing of epic conflict within modernity, and prefigures the wonderfully twisty joke of the invasion scare, a joke which insists that invasion has in practice already been repelled (in the shape of the foreign Dousterswivel's burning machinery, which looks like a warning beacon) and that it is (therefore) simply imaginary. Epic violence is cleared away into bathetic farce, and leaves us with romance as a structure for the nation.

We are left, in fact, with just a very little more over and above romance. If the Antiquary's projected epic poem 'The Caledoniad; or, Invasion Repelled' is never completed by Lovel (there is no need for Lovel to write the poem, since he *is* the poem realized in flesh and blood, epic turned into a romance of national solidarity), the notes themselves do get written, and according to the resounding onto-logical joke of the novel's final sentence, they are not just extant but are 'at the service of any one who chooses to make them public, without risk or expense to THE ANTIQUARY' (p. 430). This parting shot may well make us pause when faced with Scott's famously baffling apparatus of introduction and notes, present in the first edition, and extended for the Magnum Opus, written in his best Oldbuck manner. The reader would be wise to beware of taking these notes at their face value as securely grounding Scott's fictions in 'history', in the context of a novel in which history is, at best, multiple and conflicted and, at worst, definitely fraudulent. It is not merely coincidental laziness that this is the novel in which Scott first starts simply to make up the quotations that he uses as the epigraphs to chapters—a symptomatic joke on any literal-minded editor who tries to out-edit Scott in the literary game of source-authentication. Associated with the Antiquary, ambiguously redundant and authenticating, the paratext's often playful and mocking interest in historical sources and originals extends sidelong the concerns of the host text with history as property. Yet if history is the respectable element in Scott's new genre, fiction is what alchemizes it thoroughly into wealth. No wonder then, that having put out what William Hazlitt admiringly described as 'a new edition of human nature',[18] the 'Author of Waverley' laboured to transform the fairy gold that came from it back into real history in the shape of the solid and heritable land of the Abbotsford estate.

[18] William Hazlitt, 'Sir Walter Scott', *The Spirit of the Age* (1825) in *The Complete Works of William Hazlitt*, ed. P. P. Howe, 21 vols. (1932), 11, 64.

NOTE ON THE TEXT

The Antiquary was published in May 1816, going into a second edition in July, which was subsequently reprinted in 1818 and 1821. It appeared also in the twelve-volume *Novels and Tales of the Author of Waverley* (1819), reprinted, sometimes in different formats, in 1821, 1822, 1823, and 1825. There were also a number of pirated editions which appeared in America and Europe. In 1829, Scott began publishing the extensively revised, collected edition of the Waverley novels known as the Magnum Opus, which, appearing in instalments, was completed in 1833, just after Scott's death.

The text that follows reprints the Magnum Opus edition of 1829, the final form in which Scott himself wished the novel to appear. Given that one current editorial fashion in Scott studies is for publishing Scott in something supposedly approximating to the earliest state of his writing, however, some readers may require a justification for this decision. My principal reason is a strong scepticism about the possibility and even the desirability of tracing Scott's novels back to some imagined uncontaminated original inspiration. It is an impulse rebuked by the care with which Scott edited, revised, and elaborated his own work. Secondly, the Magnum Opus quite extensively supplements the earlier editions of *The Antiquary*, providing an extended Advertisement (including a section on the originals for Oldbuck and Ochiltree), and adding twenty-three new notes, including the long 'Gyneocracy' and 'Alarm of Invasion'. Scott also modified the text here and there, but not in any very substantive fashion beyond the usual matters of presentation, punctuation, and the modernization of spelling: however, he did occasionally strengthen up the dosage of the vernacular. I can see no rationale for discarding this material as embarrassingly secondary and inauthentic, particularly given *The Antiquary*'s playful (if ever-ambiguous) satire on antiquarian pedantry and the fetishizing of authentic documents. Given this novel's thematic drive, Scott's pragmatic working practices, and the particular fictional aesthetic within which he worked—which is in any case more invested in structure and sentiment than it is in verbal minutiae—it would probably be just as misguided to regard the Magnum Opus version of *The Antiquary* as 'definitive' as it would be to treat any other variant, previously published or otherwise, as such: but subjecting its familiar text to a makeover threatens to erase the Scott who has been beloved by generations of writers and readers. It seems more important that present-day readers should be able to acquaint themselves with the Scott who to a remarkable extent invented nineteenth-century culture than that they should be offered his works in a version which he neither saw nor authorized.

A Note on the Notes

Originally, all the notes for the first edition were printed at the foot of the page; the longer notes composed later for the Magnum Opus were printed at the end of the relevant chapter. All of Scott's notes are here reprinted together at the end of the text, and are indicated in the text by a superscript numeral. My own explanatory notes are signalled in the text with an asterisk, and printed after Scott's notes.

SELECT BIBLIOGRAPHY

Walter Scott: Works, Personal Writings, and Biography

If you have become interested in Walter Scott as a novelist, you should read further within the series of the other Waverley novels set in Scotland; the most celebrated of these are probably *Waverley* (1814), *Old Mortality* (1816), *The Heart of Midlothian* (1818), and *The Bride of Lammermoor* (1819). Of nineteenth-century editions, the best are the Magnum Opus (Edinburgh 1829–33) (upon which all subsequent editions are based), the Centenary Edition (London, 1871), the Dryburgh Edition (London, 1892–4), and the Border Edition (London, 1892–4). The current definitive critical edition is the Edinburgh edition (1993–   ). Scott's poetry is to be found in *The Poetical Works of Sir Walter Scott, Bart.*, ed. J. G. Lockhart, 12 vols. (Edinburgh, 1833–4), and his prose in *The Prose Works of Sir Walter Scott, Bart.*, 28 vols. (Edinburgh, 1834–6).

The Journal of Sir Walter Scott, ed. W. E. K. Anderson, 1972.
The Letters of Sir Walter Scott, ed. H. J. C. Grierson, 12 vols. (1932–7).
Scott on Himself: A Selection of the Autobiographical Writings of Sir Walter Scott, ed. David Hewitt (1981).
Lockhart, John Gibson, *Memoirs of the Life of Sir Walter Scott, Bart.*, 7 vols. (1837–8), and the expanded second edition of 1839.
Johnson, Edgar, *Sir Walter Scott: The Great Unknown*, 2 vols. (1970).
Sutherland, John, *The Life of Sir Walter Scott* (1995).

Early Criticism

Carlyle, Thomas, 'Sir Walter Scott' (1838), in *The Works of Thomas Carlyle*, ed. H. D. Traill, 30 vols. (1896–9), xxix. 22–87.
Hayden, John O., *Scott: The Critical Heritage* (1970).
Hazlitt, William, 'Sir Walter Scott', in *The Spirit of the Age* (1825).
Secombe, Thomas, et al., *Scott Centenary Articles* (1932), ch. 3.
Stephen, Leslie, 'Hours in a Library No. III—Some Words about Sir Walter Scott', *Cornhill Magazine*, 24 (Sept. 1871), 278–93.

Recent Criticism

This section includes general studies of Scott as a novelist, together with books that put him into literary and historical context. Sections of particular interest to students of *The Antiquary* are indicated where relevant.

Brown, David, *Walter Scott and the Historical Imagination* (1979), ch. 3.

Butler, Marilyn, *Romantics, Rebels and Reactionaries: English Literature and its Background 1760–1830* (1981).

—— 'Antiquarianism (Popular)', in Ian MacCalman (ed.), *An Oxford Companion to the Romantic Age* (1999), 328–38.

Cockshut, A. O. J., *The Achievement of Sir Walter Scott* (1969), ch. 3.

Cottom, Daniel, *The Civilized Imagination: A Study of Ann Radcliffe, Jane Austen, and Sir Walter Scott* (1985).

Daiches, David, 'Scott's Achievement as a Novelist', reprinted in *Scott's Mind and Art*, ed. A. Norman Jeffares (1969), 21–52.

Elam, Diane, *Romancing the Post-Modern* (1992).

Elbers, Joan S., 'Isolation and Community in *The Antiquary*', *Nineteenth Century Fiction*, 27 (1973), 405–23.

Farrell, John P., *Revolution as Tragedy: The Dilemma of the Moderate from Scott to Arnold* (1980).

Fleishman, Avrom, *The English Historical Novel* (1971).

Gamerschlag, Kurt, 'The Non-Explosive Mixture: Historical Analysis and Social Ideals in Scott's *The Antiquary*', in *Studies in Scottish Fiction: Nineteenth Century*, ed. Horst W. Drescher and Joachim Schwend (1985), 65–81.

Garside, Peter, 'Scott, the Eighteenth Century and the New Man of Sentiment', *Anglia* 103 (1985), 71–89.

Gordon, Robert C., *Under Which King? A Study of the Scottish Waverley Novels* (1969), ch. 3.

Hart, Francis R., *Scott's Novels: The Plotting of Historic Survival* (1966), section 4, 1.

Hayden, John O. (ed.), *Scott: The Critical Heritage* (1970) (contemporary reviews).

Kerr, James, *Fiction against History: Scott as Storyteller* (1989).

Kidd, Colin, *Subverting Scotland's Past: Scottish Whig Historians and the Creation of Anglo-British Identity, 1689–1830* (1993), 255–67.

Lascelles, Mary, *The Story-Teller Retrieves the Past* (1980).

Lee, Yoon Sun, 'A Divided Inheritance: Scott's Antiquarian Novel and the British Nation', *ELH* 64 (1997), 571–601.

Levine, George, *The Realistic Imagination* (1981).

Lukács, Georg, *The Historical Novel* (1937), trans. Hannah and Stanley Mitchell (1962).

McMaster, Graham, *Scott and Society* (1981).

Mayhead, Robin, 'The Problem of Coherence in *The Antiquary*', in *Scott Bicentenary Essays*, ed. Alan Bell (1973), 134–46.

Millgate, Jane, *Walter Scott and the Making of the Novelist* (1984), ch. 5.

Reed, James, *Sir Walter Scott: Landscape and Locality* (1980), ch. 5.

Robertson, Fiona, *Legitimate Histories: Scott, Gothic and the Authorities of Fiction* (1994), ch. 5.

Shaw, Harry, *The Forms of Historical Fiction: Sir Walter Scott and His Successors* (1983) 70–81.

Watson, Nicola J., *Revolution and the Form of the British Novel 1790–1825* (1994), 142–8.

Welsh, Alexander, *The Hero of the Waverley Novels* (1963).

Wilson, A. N., *The Laird of Abbotsford: A View of Sir Walter Scott* (1980).

Wilt, Judith, *Secret Leaves: The Novels of Sir Walter Scott* (1985), ch. 5.

—— 'Steamboat Surfacing: Scott and the English Novelists', *Nineteenth Century Fiction*, 35 (1981), 459–86.

Further Reading in Oxford World's Classics

Scott, Sir Walter, *The Bride of Lammermoore*, ed. Fiona Robertson.

—— *The Heart of Midlothian*, ed. Claire Lamont.

—— *Ivanhoe*, ed. Ian Duncan.

—— *Old Mortality*, ed. Peter Davidson and Jane Stevenson.

—— *Redgauntlet*, ed. Kathryn Sutherland.

—— *Rob Roy*, ed. Ian Duncan.

—— *Waverley*, ed. Claire Lamont.

A CHRONOLOGY OF SIR WALTER SCOTT

	Life	Cultural and Historical Background
1760		Macpherson, *Fragments of Ancient Poetry Collected in the Highlands of Scotland*.
1765		Percy, *Reliques of Ancient English Poetry*.
1770		Hogg born; Wordsworth born.
1771	Born in Edinburgh, the ninth child of Walter Scott, a lawyer, and Anne Rutherford.	
1771–3	Contracts poliomyelitis, which leaves him permanently lame.	
1772–8	Resides mostly with his grandparents in Sandyknowe.	
1774		Southey born.
1775		Austen born.
1778		Death of Charles Stewart, claimant to the British throne, and leader of the 1745 Jacobite rising in Scotland.
1779–83	Attends the High School, Edinburgh.	
1783–6	Attends classes at Edinburgh University (Latin, Greek, Logic, Metaphysics, and Moral Philosophy).	
1786	Illness brings a temporary end to his studies; he is apprenticed to his father.	Burns, *Poems, Chiefly in the Scottish Dialect*.
1788		The Revolution Society celebrates the centenary of the Glorious Revolution which established a constitutional Hanoverian monarchy. French States General summoned. Byron born.
1789		Storming of the Bastille in Paris and the Declaration of the Rights of Man inaugurate Revolution in France.
1789–92	Studies for the bar at Edinburgh University, taking classes in History, Moral Philosophy, Scots Law, and Civil Law and ultimately qualifies.	

| 1790 | | Burke, *Reflections on the Revolution in France*. |

1791 — Louis XVI's flight and capture at Varennes; Boswell, *Life of Johnson*; Ritson, *Ancient Popular Poetry*.

1792 — London Corresponding Society is formed; Friends of the People, a reform-minded society, formed in Scotland; in France, the French royal family is imprisoned; September massacres in Paris; Paine, *Rights of Man* (rapidly banned and Paine sentenced to death *in absentia* for high treason and sedition).

1793 — Trial and execution of Louis XVI of France; France declares war on England; the Terror begins under Robespierre's direction; executions of Marie Antoinette and the Girondins; royalist rising in La Vendée ruthlessly crushed; Scottish treason trials of Muir and Palmer, sentenced to transportation for sedition; British Convention, assembled in Edinburgh on the French model, is forcibly broken up and its leaders arrested; the Aliens Act brought in, designed to control the influx of refugees and with them, suspected French spies.

1794 — Treason Trials (Horne Tooke, Holcroft, and Thelwall and others); Jacobins Danton and Robespierre executed; Radcliffe, *The Mysteries of Udolpho*.

c.1794–6 — In love with Wilhelmina Belsches, who marries William Forbes in 1796.

1795 — Seditious Meetings Act and Treasonable Practices Act, restricting freedoms of speech, of assembly, and of the press.

1796 — Publishes translations of Bürger's ballad-poems *The Chase* and *William and Helen*. — Attempted French invasion of Ireland; Lewis, *The Monk*.

1797 — Joins the Royal Edinburgh Light Dragoons, a volunteer cavalry regiment, and meets and marries Charlotte Carpenter (a.k.a. Charpentier) within three months. They settle in Edinburgh. — Attempted French invasion of Wales; naval mutinies; Bank of England suspends payment.

1798	Birth and death of first son.	Rebellion in Ireland coincident with French landing in Ireland; Nelson's victory at the battle of the Nile; Wordsworth and Coleridge, *Lyrical Ballads*.
1799	Publishes his translation of Goethe's tragedy *Goetz of Berlichingen*; death of his father; birth of his daughter, Charlotte; appointed Sheriff-Depute of Selkirkshire.	Suppression of Corresponding Societies and other radical groups by the Combination Acts; in France, the directorate falls and Napoleon becomes First Consul; Godwin, *St. Leon*.
1800	*An Apology for Tales of Terror*, an anthology.	Wordsworth, *Preface to Lyrical Ballads*.
1801	Contributions to Matthew Lewis's gothic *Tales of Wonder*; birth of son, Walter.	
1802	*Minstrelsy of the Scottish Border* (vols. i & ii), an edition of traditional border ballads.	Peace of Amiens concluded with France; *Edinburgh Review* founded.
1803	*Minstrelsy of the Scottish Border* (2nd edn. of first 2 vols. & vol. iii). Birth of daughter, Anne; begins a career as reviewer for the *Edinburgh Review*.	War breaks out again with France.
1804	Leases Ashetiel near Selkirk as country retreat; publishes edition of the medieval romance, *Sir Tristrem*.	Napoleon made Emperor and prepares to invade England.
1805	*The Lay of the Last Minstrel*, the first of a series of verse romances which were a commercial and literary success, and transformed Scott into a national celebrity. Enters into partnership with the printers James Ballantyne & Co., which will endure until the financial crash of 1826; birth of son, Charles; by his own account, starts and lays aside his first novel, *Waverley* (though current scholarship suggests 1808 as a more likely date).	Nelson's victory at Trafalgar.
1806	Appointed Principal Clerk of Session; lionized by London society during his visit to secure the appointment.	

1808	*Marmion*. Appointed secretary to the Parliamentary Commission to Inquire into the Administration of Justice in Scotland; publishes his edition of the works of John Dryden; completes Joseph Strutt's historical romance *Queenhoo Hall*.	Jameison, *Dictionary of the Scottish Tongue*.
1809	*A Collection of Scarce and Valuable Tracts*, an edition (13 vols., 1809–12).	
1810	*The Lady of the Lake*, Scott's most commercially successful poem.	
1811	*The Vision of Don Roderick*.	George III's illness means that his son takes over as Prince Regent; Austen, *Sense and Sensibility*.
1812	Moves from Ashestiel to Abbotsford, and begins planning alterations to the farmhouse there.	Napoleon's retreat from Moscow and defeat at Leipzig.
1813	*Rokeby* and *The Bridal of Triermain*. Financial crisis at Ballantyne's, eventually resolved in 1817; is offered and declines the Poet Laureateship.	Southey appointed Poet Laureate.
1814	*Waverley* (the first of the Waverley novels, and a bestseller). Edition of the works of Jonathan Swift.	Fall of Paris, abdication and exile of Napoleon, and restoration of the Bourbons. Austen, *Mansfield Park*; Byron, *Ode to Napoleon Buonaparte*.
1815	*The Lord of the Isles* (poem), *The Field of Waterloo* (poem), and *Guy Mannering*, Scott's second novel. Visits the Continent to view the field of Waterloo, and is lionized in Brussels and Paris.	Napoleon returns from Elba (March), is defeated at Waterloo (June), surrenders (July), and goes into exile on St Helena; restoration of Louis XVIII.
1816	*Paul's Letters to His Kinsfolk*, *The Antiquary*, *Tales of My Landlord 1st series* (*The Black Dwarf* and *The Tale of Old Mortality*).	Depression, discontent, and riots; Austen, *Emma*; Byron, *Childe Harold* (*Canto III*); Southey, *Poet's Pilgrimage to Waterloo*.

1817	*Harold the Dauntless* (Scott's last long poem), *Rob Roy*. Begins elaborate building-works at Abbotsford, which last for the next two years.	Habeas Corpus suspended.
1818	*Tales of My Landlord 2nd series* (*The Heart of Midlothian*). Accepts baronetcy (gazetted 1820).	Austen, *Persuasion*; Mary Shelley, *Frankenstein;* Hogg, *The Brownie of Bodsbeck*.
1819	Seriously ill, but completes and publishes *Tales of My Landlord 2nd series* (*The Bride of Lammermoor* and *A Legend of Montrose*), and *Ivanhoe*. Death of Scott's mother.	Some years of civil unrest culminate in the 'Peterloo' massacre and the Six Acts restricting the right to hold meetings and the freedom of the press.
1820	*The Monastery* and *The Abbot*. Daughter Sophia marries Scott's future biographer, John Gibson Lockhart; elected president of the Royal Society of Edinburgh.	Death of George III, accession of George IV.
1821	*Kenilworth* and *The Pirate*. Begins contributing prefatory lives of novelists to *Ballantyne's Novelist's Library*.	Death of Napoleon; Galt, *Annals of the Parish*.
1822	*The Fortunes of Nigel* and *Peveril of the Peak*. Demolition of the original farmhouse at Abbotsford and the beginning of the second phase of building works which last for the next three years.	
1823	*Quentin Durward* and *St Ronan's Well*.	
1824	*Redgauntlet*.	Repeal of Combination Acts.
1825	*Tales of the Crusaders* (*The Betrothed* and *The Talisman*). Son Walter marries.	Hazlitt, *The Spirit of the Age*; T. C. Croker, *Fairy Legends and Traditions of the South of Ireland* (concluded 1828).
1826	*Woodstock*. Financial insolvency precipitated by the bankruptcy of Scott's publishers, Hurst, Robinson & Co., Constable, and Ballantyne's; Scott undertakes to pay off resultant debts, amounting in total to some £126,000, all repaid by 1833. Death of wife.	

1827	Acknowledges authorship of the Waverley novels, an open secret; *The Life of Napoleon Buonaparte*; *Chronicles of the Canongate* ('The Highland Widow', 'The Two Drovers', 'The Surgeon's Daughter'); *Tales of a Grandfather* (a popular history of Scotland).	
1827–8	*Chronicles of the Canongate*, 2nd series (*The Fair Maid of Perth*) and *Tales of a Grandfather*, 2nd series.	
1828	*Anne of Geierstein* and *Tales of a Grandfather*, 3rd series. First volume of Magnum Opus appears.	
1829	*Letters on Demonology and Witchcraft*; *Tales of a Grandfather*, 4th series. Seriously ill; retires as Clerk to the Court of Session.	Catholic Emancipation Act.
1830	*Tales of My Landlord*, 4th series (*Count Robert of Paris* and *Castle Dangerous*). Travels to the Mediterranean in hopes of restoring his health.	Death of George IV, accession of William IV; Tennyson, *Poems, Chiefly Lyrical*.
1832	Returns to Abbotsford and dies on 21st September.	First Reform Act.

THE ANTIQUARY

I knew Anselmo. He was shrewd and prudent,
Wisdom and cunning had their shares of him;
But he was shrewish as a wayward child,
And pleased again by toys which childhood please;
As—book of fables graced with print of wood,
Or else the jingling of a rusty medal,
Or the rare melody of some old ditty,
That first was sung to please King Pepin's cradle.*

ADVERTISEMENT

THE present Work completes a series of fictitious narratives, intended to illustrate the manners of Scotland at three different periods. WAVERLEY embraced the age of our fathers, GUY MANNERING that of our own youth, and the ANTIQUARY refers to the last ten years of the eighteenth century.* I have, in the two last narratives especially, sought my principal personages in the class of society who are the last to feel the influence of that general polish which assimilates to each other the manners of different nations. Among the same class I have placed some of the scenes, in which I have endeavoured to illustrate the operation of the higher and more violent passions; both because the lower orders are less restrained by the habit of suppressing their feelings, and because I agree with my friend Wordsworth, that they seldom fail to express them in the strongest and most powerful language.* This is, I think, peculiarly the case with the peasantry of my own country, a class with whom I have long been familiar. The antique force and simplicity of their language, often tinctured with the Oriental eloquence of Scripture, in the mouths of those of an elevated understanding, give pathos to their grief, and dignity to their resentment.

I have been more solicitous to describe manners minutely, than to arrange in any case an artificial and combined narrative, and have but to regret that I felt myself unable to unite these two requisites of a good Novel.

The knavery of the Adept in the following sheets may appear forced and improbable; but we have had very late instances of the force of superstitious credulity* to a much greater extent, and the reader may be assured, that this part of the narrative is founded on a fact of actual occurrence.

I have now only to express my gratitude to the public, for the distinguished reception which they have given to works, that have little more than some truth of colouring to recommend them, and to take my respectful leave, as one who is not likely again to solicit their favour.*

To the above advertisement, which was prefixed to the first

edition of the Antiquary, it is necessary in the present edition to add a few words, transferred from the Introduction to the Chronicles of the Canongate,* respecting the character of Jonathan Oldbuck.

'I may here state generally, that although I have deemed historical personages free subjects of delineation, I have never on any occasion violated the respect due to private life. It was indeed impossible that traits proper to persons, both living and dead, with whom I have had intercourse in society, should not have risen to my pen in such works as Waverley, and those which followed it. But I have always studied to generalize the portraits, so that they should still seem, on the whole, the productions of fancy, though possessing some resemblance to real individuals. Yet I must own my attempts have not in this last particular been uniformly successful. There are men whose characters are so peculiarly marked, that the delineation of some leading and principal feature, inevitably places the whole person before you in his individuality. Thus, the character of Jonathan Oldbuck, in the Antiquary, was partly founded on that of an old friend of my youth, to whom I am indebted for introducing me to Shakspeare, and other invaluable favours; but I thought I had so completely disguised the likeness, that it could not be recognised by any one now alive. I was mistaken, however, and indeed had endangered what I desired should be considered as a secret; for I afterwards learned that a highly respectable gentleman, one of the few surviving friends of my father, and an acute critic, had said, upon the appearance of the work, that he was now convinced who was the author of it, as he recognised, in the Antiquary, traces of the character of a very intimate friend of my father's family.'

I have only farther to request the reader not to suppose that my late respected friend resembled Mr Oldbuck, either in his pedigree, or the history imputed to the ideal personage. There is not a single incident in the Novel which is borrowed from his real circumstances, excepting the fact that he resided in an old house near a flourishing seaport, and that the author chanced to witness a scene betwixt him and the female proprietor of a stage-coach, very similar to that which commences the history of the Antiquary. An excellent temper, with a slight degree of subacid humour; learning, wit, and drollery, the more poignant that they were a little marked by the peculiarities of an old bachelor; a soundness of thought, rendered more forcible by an occasional quaintness of expression, were, the author conceives, the only qualities in which the creature of his imagination resembled his benevolent and excellent old friend.

The prominent part performed by the Beggar in the following narrative, induces the author to prefix a few remarks on that character, as it formerly existed in Scotland, though it is now scarcely to be traced.

Many of the old Scottish mendicants were by no means to be confounded with the utterly degraded class of beings who now practise that wandering trade. Such of them as were in the habit of travelling through a particular district, were usually well received both in the farmer's ha', and in the kitchens of the country gentlemen. Martin,* author of the *Reliquiæ Divi Sancti Andreæ*, written in 1683, gives the following account of one class of this order of men in the seventeenth century, in terms which would induce an antiquary like Mr Oldbuck to regret its extinction. He conceives them to be descended from the ancient bards, and proceeds:—'They are called by others, and by themselves, Jockies, who go about begging; and use still to recite the Sloggorne (gathering-words or war-cries) of most of the true ancient surnames of Scotland, from old experience and observation. Some of them I have discoursed, and found to have reason and discretion. One of them told me there were not now above twelve of them in the whole isle; but he remembered when they abounded, so as at one time he was one of five that usually met at St Andrews.'

The race of Jockies (of the above description) has, I suppose, been long extinct in Scotland; but the old remembered beggar, even in my own time, like the Baccoch, or travelling cripple of Ireland, was expected to merit his quarters by something beyond an exposition of his distresses. He was often a talkative, facetious fellow, prompt at repartee, and not withheld from exercising his powers that way by any respect of persons, his patched cloak giving him the privilege of the ancient jester. To be a *gude crack*, that is, to possess talents for conversation, was essential to the trade of a 'puir body' of the more esteemed class; and Burns, who delighted in the amusement their discourse afforded, seems to have looked forward with gloomy firmness to the possibility of himself becoming one day or other a member of their itinerant society. In his poetical works, it is alluded to so often, as perhaps to indicate that he considered the consummation as not utterly impossible. Thus, in the fine dedication of his works to Gavin Hamilton, he says,—

> 'And when I downa yoke a naig,
> Then, Lord be thankit, I can beg.'

Again, in his Epistle to Davie, a brother Poet, he states, that in their closing career—

> 'The last o't, the warst o't,
> Is only just to beg.'

And after having remarked, that

> 'To lie in kilns and barns at e'en,
> When banes are crazed and blude is thin,
> Is doubtless great distress;'

the bard reckons up, with true poetical spirit, the free enjoyment of the beauties of nature, which might counterbalance the hardship and uncertainty of the life even of a mendicant. In one of his prose letters, to which I have lost the reference, he details this idea yet more seriously, and dwells upon it, as not ill adapted to his habits and powers.*

As the life of a Scottish mendicant of the eighteenth century, seems to have been contemplated without much horror by Robert Burns, the author can hardly have erred in giving to Edie Ochiltree something of poetical character and personal dignity, above the more abject of his miserable calling. The class had, in fact, some privileges. A lodging, such as it was, was readily granted to them in some of the out-houses, and the usual *awmous* (alms) of a handful of meal (called a *gowpen*) was scarce denied by the poorest cottager. The mendicant disposed these, according to their different quality, in various bags around his person, and thus carried about with him the principal part of his sustenance, which he literally received for the asking. At the houses of the gentry, his cheer was mended by scraps of broken meat, and perhaps a Scottish 'twalpenny,' or English penny, which was expended in snuff or whisky. In fact, these indolent peripatetics suffered much less real hardship and want of food, than the poor peasants from whom they received alms.

If, in addition to his personal qualifications, the mendicant chanced to be a King's Bedesman, or Blue-Gown, he belonged, in virtue thereof, to the aristocracy of his order, and was esteemed a person of great importance.

These Bedesmen are an order of paupers to whom the Kings of Scotland were in the custom of distributing a certain alms, in conformity with the ordinances of the Catholic Church, and who were expected in return to pray for the royal welfare and that of the state. This order is still kept up. Their number is equal to the number of years which his Majesty has lived; and one Blue-Gown additional is put on the roll for every returning royal birth-day. On the same auspicious era, each Bedesman receives a new cloak, or gown of coarse cloth, the colour light blue, with a pewter badge, which confers on them the general privilege of asking alms through all Scotland, all laws against sorning, masterful beggary, and every other species of mendicity, being suspended in favour of this privileged class. With his cloak, each receives a leathern purse, containing as many shillings Scots (videlicet, pennies sterling) as the sovereign is years old; the zeal of their intercession for the king's long life receiving, it is to be supposed, a great stimulus from their own present and increasing interest in the object of their prayers. On the same occasion one of the Royal Chaplains preaches a sermon to the Bedesmen, who (as one of the reverend gentlemen expressed himself) are the most impatient and inattentive audience in the world. Something of this may arise from a feeling on the part of the Bedesmen, that they are paid for their own devotions, not for listening to those of others. Or, more probably, it arises from impatience, natural, though indecorous in men bearing so venerable a character, to arrive at the conclusion of the ceremonial of the royal birth-day, which, so far as they are concerned, ends in a lusty breakfast of bread and ale; the whole moral and religious exhibition terminating in the advice of Johnson's 'Hermit hoar' to his proselyte,

'Come, my lad, and drink some beer.'*

Of the charity bestowed on these aged Bedesmen in money and clothing, there are many records in the Treasurer's accompts. The following extract, kindly supplied by Mr MacDonald of the Register House, may interest those whose taste is akin to that of Jonathan Oldbuck of Monkbarns.

BLEW GOWNIS

In the Account of Sir Robert Melvill of Murdocarny, Treasurer-Depute of King James VI., there are the following payments:

'Junij 1590.

'Item, to Mr Peter Young, Elimosinar, twentie four gownis of blew clayth, to be gevin to xxiiij auld men, according to the yeiris of his hienes age, extending to viij^{xx} viij elnis clayth; price of the elne xxviij š. . . . . Inde, ij £ j ħ. xij š.

'Item, for sextene elnis bukrum to the saidis gownis, price of the elne x š. . . . . Inde, viij ħ.

'Item, twentie four pursis, and in ilk purse twentie four schilling, ...Inde, xxviij ħ. xvj š.

'Item, the price of ilk purse iiij đ. . . . . .Inde, viij š.

'Item, for making of the saidis gownis, ...viij ħ.'

In the Account of John, Earl of Mar, Great Treasurer of Scotland, and of Sir Gideon Murray of Elibank, Treasurer-Depute, the Blue Gowns also appear—thus:

'Junij 1617.

'Item, to James Murray, merchant, for fyftene scoir sex elnis and ane half elne of blew claith to be gownis to fyftie ane aigeit men according to the yeiris of his Majesteis age, at xl š. the elne,Inde, vj £ xiij ħ.

'Item, to workmen for careing the blewis to James Aikman, tailyeour, his hous,. . . . . xiij š. iiij đ.

'Item, for sex elnis and ane half of harden to the saidis gownis, at vj š. viij đ. the elne,. . . . . Inde, xliij š. iiij đ.

'Item, to the said workmen for careing of the gownis fra the said James Aikman's hous to the palace of Halyrudehous,. . . . . . xviij š.

'Item, for making the saidis fyftie ane gownis, at xij š. the peice,. . . . . Inde, xxx ħi. xij š.

'Item, for fyftie ane pursis to the said puire men,. . . . . .ħj š.

'Item, to Sir Peter Young, ħj š. to be put in everie ane of the saidis ħj pursis to the said poore men,. . . . . j £ xxx ħj j š.

'Item, to the said Sir Peter, to buy breid and drink to the said puir men,. . . . . vj ħi. xiij š iiij đ.

'Item, to the said Sir Peter, to be delt amang uther puire folk,j £ ħj.

'Item, upoun the last day of Junij to Doctor Young, Deane of

Winchester, Elimozinar Deput to his Majestie, twentie fyve pund sterling, to be gevin to the puir be the way in his Majesteis progress,. . . . . .Inde, iij *&* li.'

I have only to add, that although the institution of King's Bedesmen still subsists, they are now seldom to be seen on the streets of Edinburgh, of which their peculiar dress made them rather a characteristic feature.

Having thus given an account of the genus and species to which Edie Ochiltree appertains, the author may add, that the individual he had in his eye was Andrew Gemmells, an old mendicant of the character described, who was many years since well known, and must still be remembered, in the vales of Gala, Tweed, Ettrick, Yarrow, and the adjoining country.

The author has in his youth repeatedly seen and conversed with Andrew, but cannot recollect whether he held the rank of Blue-Gown. He was a remarkably fine old figure, very tall, and maintaining a soldierlike, or military manner and address. His features were intelligent, with a powerful expression of sarcasm. His motions were always so graceful, that he might almost have been suspected of having studied them; for he might, on any occasion, have served as a model for an artist, so remarkably striking were his ordinary attitudes. Andrew Gemmells had little of the cant of his calling; his wants were food and shelter, or a trifle of money, which he always claimed, and seemed to receive, as his due. He sung a good song, told a good story, and could crack a severe jest with all the acumen of Shakspeare's jesters, though without using, like them, the cloak of insanity. It was some fear of Andrew's satire, as much as a feeling of kindness or charity, which secured him the general good reception which he enjoyed everywhere. In fact, a jest of Andrew Gemmells, especially at the expense of a person of consequence, flew round the circle which he frequented, as surely as the bon-mot of a man of established character for wit glides through the fashionable world. Many of his good things are held in remembrance, but are generally too local and personal to be introduced here.

Andrew had a character peculiar to himself among his tribe, for aught I ever heard. He was ready and willing to play at cards or dice with any one who desired such amusement. This was more in the character of the Irish itinerant gambler, called in that country a *carrow*, than of the Scottish beggar. But the late Reverend Doctor Robert Douglas, minister of Galashiels, assured the author, that the last time he saw Andrew Gemmells, he was engaged in a game at brag with a gentleman of fortune, distinction, and birth. To preserve the due gradations of rank, the party was made at an open window of the chateau, the laird sitting on his chair in the inside, the beggar on a stool in the yard; and they played on the window-sill. The stake was a considerable parcel of silver. The author expressing some surprise, Dr Douglas observed, that the laird was no doubt a humourist or original; but that many decent persons in those times would, like him, have thought there was nothing extraordinary in passing an hour, either in card-playing or conversation, with Andrew Gemmells.

This singular mendicant had generally, or was supposed to have, as much money about his person, as would have been thought the value of his life among modern foot-pads. On one occasion, a country gentleman, generally esteemed a very narrow man, happening to meet Andrew, expressed great regret that he had no silver in his pocket, or he would have given him sixpence:—'I can give you change for a note, laird,' replied Andrew.

Like most who have arisen to the head of their profession, the modern degradation which mendicity has undergone was often the subject of Andrew's lamentations. As a trade, he said, it was forty pounds a-year worse since he had first practised it. On another occasion he observed, begging was in modern times scarcely the profession of a gentleman, and that if he had twenty sons, he would not easily be induced to breed one of them up in his own line. When or where this *laudator temporis acti** closed his wanderings, the author never heard with certainty; but most probably, as Burns says,

> '——he died a cadger-powny's death
> At some dike side.'*

The author may add another picture of the same kind as Edie Ochiltree and Andrew Gemmells; considering these illustrations as a sort of gallery, open to the reception of any thing which may elucidate former manners, or amuse the reader.

The author's contemporaries at the university of Edinburgh will probably remember the thin wasted form of a venerable old Bedesman, who stood by the Potter-row port, now demolished, and, without speaking a syllable, gently inclined his head, and offered his hat, but with the least possible degree of urgency, towards each individual who passed. This man gained, by silence and the extenu- ated and wasted appearance of a palmer from a remote country, the same tribute which was yielded to Andrew Gemmells's sarcastic humour and stately deportment. He was understood to be able to maintain a son a student in the theological classes of the University, at the gate of which the father was a mendicant. The young man was modest and inclined to learning, so that a student of the same age, and whose parents were rather of the lower order, moved by seeing him excluded from the society of other scholars when the secret of his birth was suspected, endeavoured to console him by offering him some occasional civilities. The old mendicant was grateful for this attention to his son, and one day, as the friendly student passed, he stooped forward more than usual, as if to intercept his passage. The scholar drew out a halfpenny, which he concluded was the beggar's object, when he was surprised to receive his thanks for the kindness he had shown to Jemmie, and at the same time a cordial invitation to dine with them next Saturday, 'on a shoulder of mutton and pota- toes,' adding, 'ye'll put on your clean sark, as I have company.' The student was strongly tempted to accept this hospitable proposal, as many in his place would probably have done; but, as the motive might have been capable of misrepresentation, he thought it most prudent, considering the character and circumstances of the old man, to decline the invitation.

Such are a few traits of Scottish mendicity, designed to throw light on a Novel in which a character of that description plays a promin- ent part. We conclude, that we have vindicated Edie Ochiltree's right to the importance assigned him; and have shown, that we have known one beggar take a hand at cards with a person of distinction, and another give dinner parties.

I know not if it be worth while to observe, that the Antiquary was not so well received on its first appearance as either of its predeces- sors, though in course of time it rose to equal, and with some readers, superior popularity.

THE ANTIQUARY

CHAPTER I

'Go call a coach, and let a coach be call'd,
And let the man who calleth be the caller;
And in his calling let him nothing call,
But Coach! Coach! Coach! O for a coach, ye gods!'

*Chrononhotonthologos.**

IT was early on a fine summer's day, near the end of the eighteenth
century, when a young man, of genteel appearance, journeying
towards the north-east of Scotland, provided himself with a ticket in
one of those public carriages which travel between Edinburgh and
the Queensferry, at which place, as the name implies, and as is well
known to all my northern readers, there is a passage-boat for crossing the Frith of Forth. The coach was calculated to carry six regular
passengers, besides such interlopers as the coachman could pick up
by the way, and intrude upon those who were legally in possession.
The tickets, which conferred right to a seat in this vehicle of little
ease,* were dispensed by a sharp-looking old dame, with a pair of
spectacles on a very thin nose, who inhabited a 'laigh shop,' *anglicè*, a
cellar, opening to the High-street by a strait and steep stair, at the
bottom of which she sold tape, thread, needles, skeans of worsted,
coarse linen cloth, and such feminine gear, to those who had the
courage and skill to descend to the profundity of her dwelling, without falling headlong themselves, or throwing down any of the
numerous articles which, piled on each side of the descent, indicated
the profession of the trader below.

The written hand-bill, which, pasted on a projecting board,
announced that the Queensferry Diligence, or Hawes Fly,* departed
precisely at twelve o'clock on Tuesday, the fifteenth July, 17—, in
order to secure for travellers the opportunity of passing the Frith
with the flood-tide, lied on the present occasion like a bulletin;* for
although that hour was pealed from Saint Giles's steeple, and
repeated by the Tron,* no coach appeared upon the appointed stand.
It is true, only two tickets had been taken out, and possibly the lady

of the subterranean mansion might have an understanding with her Automedon,* that, in such cases, a little space was to be allowed for the chance of filling up the vacant places—or the said Automedon might have been attending a funeral, and be delayed by the necessity of stripping his vehicle of its lugubrious trappings—or he might have staid to take a half-mutchkin extraordinary with his crony the hostler—or—in short, he did not make his appearance.

The young gentleman, who began to grow somewhat impatient, was now joined by a companion in this petty misery of human life—the person who had taken out the other place. He who is bent upon a journey is usually easily to be distinguished from his fellow-citizens. The boots, the greatcoat, the umbrella, the little bundle in his hand, the hat pulled over his resolved brows, the determined importance of his pace, his brief answers to the salutations of lounging acquaintances, are all marks by which the experienced traveller in mail-coach or diligence can distinguish, at a distance, the companion of his future journey, as he pushes onward to the place of rendezvous. It is then that, with worldly wisdom, the first comer hastens to secure the best birth in the coach for himself, and to make the most convenient arrangement for his baggage before the arrival of his competitors. Our youth, who was gifted with little prudence of any sort, and who was, moreover, by the absence of the coach, deprived of the power of availing himself of his priority of choice, amused himself, instead, by speculating upon the occupation and character of the personage who was now come to the coach-office.

He was a good-looking man of the age of sixty, perhaps older, but his hale complexion and firm step announced that years had not impaired his strength or health. His countenance was of the true Scottish cast, strongly marked, and rather harsh in features, with a shrewd and penetrating eye, and a countenance in which habitual gravity was enlivened by a cast of ironical humour. His dress was uniform, and of a colour becoming his age and gravity; a wig, well dressed and powdered, surmounted by a slouched hat, had something of a professional air. He might be a clergyman, yet his appearance was more that of a man of the world than usually belongs to the kirk of Scotland, and his first ejaculation put the matter beyond question.

He arrived with a hurried pace, and, casting an alarmed glance towards the dial-plate of the church, then looking at the place where the coach should have been, exclaimed, 'Deil's in it—I am too late after all!'

The young man relieved his anxiety, by telling him the coach had not yet appeared. The old gentleman, apparently conscious of his own want of punctuality, did not at first feel courageous enough to censure that of the coachman. He took a parcel, containing apparently a large folio, from a little boy who followed him, and, patting him on the head, bid him go back and tell Mr B——, that if he had known he was to have had so much time, he would have put another word or two to their bargain,—then told the boy to mind his business, and he would be as thriving a lad as ever dusted a duodecimo. The boy lingered, perhaps in hopes of a penny to buy marbles; but none was forthcoming. Our senior leaned his little bundle upon one of the posts at the head of the staircase, and, facing the traveller who had first arrived, waited in silence for about five minutes the arrival of the expected diligence.

At length, after one or two impatient glances at the progress of the minute-hand of the clock, having compared it with his own watch, a huge and antique gold repeater, and having twitched about his features to give due emphasis to one or two peevish pshaws, he hailed the old lady of the cavern.

'Good woman,—what the d—l is her name?—Mrs Macleuchar!'

Mrs Macleuchar, aware that she had a defensive part to sustain in the encounter which was to follow, was in no hurry to hasten the discussion by returning a ready answer.

'Mrs Macleuchar—Good woman,' (with an elevated voice)—then apart, 'Old doited hag, she's as deaf as a post—I say, Mrs Macleuchar!'

'I am just serving a customer.—Indeed, hinny, it will not be a bodle cheaper than I tell ye.'

'Woman,' reiterated the traveller, 'do you think we can stand here all day till you have cheated that poor servant wench out of her half-year's fee and bountith?'

'Cheated!' retorted Mrs Macleuchar, eager to take up the quarrel upon a defensible ground; 'I scorn your words, sir; you are an uncivil person, and I desire you will not stand there to slander me at my ain stairhead.'

'The woman,' said the senior, looking with an arch glance at his destined travelling companion, 'does not understand the words of action.*—Woman,' again turning to the vault, 'I arraign not thy character, but I desire to know what is become of thy coach?'

'What's your wull?' answered Mrs Macleuchar, relapsing into deafness.

'We have taken places, ma'am,' said the younger stranger, 'in your diligence for Queensferry.'—'Which should have been half-way on the road before now,' continued the elder and more impatient traveller, rising in wrath as he spoke; 'and now in all likelihood we shall miss the tide, and I have business of importance on the other side—and your cursed coach'—

'The coach?—gude guide us, gentlemen, is it no on the stand yet?' answered the old lady, her shrill tone of expostulation sinking into a kind of apologetic whine. 'Is it the coach ye hae been waiting for?'

'What else could have kept us broiling in the sun by the side of the gutter here, you—you faithless woman? Eh?'

Mrs Macleuchar now ascended her trap stair, (for such it might be called, though constructed of stone,) until her nose came upon a level with the pavement; then, after wiping her spectacles to look for that which she well knew was not to be found, she exclaimed, with well-feigned astonishment, 'Gude guide us—saw ever ony body the like o' that!'

'Yes, you abominable woman,' vociferated the traveller, 'many have seen the like of it, and all will see the like of it, that have any thing to do with your trolloping sex;' then, pacing with great indignation before the door of the shop, still as he passed and repassed, like a vessel who gives her broadside as she comes abreast of a hostile fortress, he shot down complaints, threats, and reproaches, on the embarrassed Mrs Macleuchar. He would take a post-chaise—he would call a hackney-coach—he would take four horses—he must—he would be on the north side today—and all the expense of his journey, besides damages, direct and consequential, arising from delay, should be accumulated on the devoted head of Mrs Macleuchar.

There was something so comic in his pettish resentment, that the younger traveller, who was in no such pressing hurry to depart, could not help being amused with it, especially as it was obvious, that every now and then the old gentleman, though very angry, could not help laughing at his own vehemence. But when Mrs Macleuchar began also to join in the laughter, he quickly put a stop to her ill-timed merriment.

'Woman,' said he, 'is that advertisement thine?' showing a bit of crumpled printed paper: 'Does it not set forth, that, God willing, as you hypocritically express it, the Hawes Fly, or Queensferry Diligence, would set forth today at twelve o'clock; and is it not, thou falsest of creatures, now a quarter past twelve, and no such fly or diligence to be seen?—Dost thou know the consequence of seducing the lieges by false reports?—Dost thou know it might be brought under the statute of leasing-making?* Answer; and for once in thy long, useless, and evil life, let it be in the words of truth and sincerity—hast thou such a coach?—Is it *in rerum natura?*—or is this base annunciation a mere swindle on the incautious, to beguile them of their time, their patience, and three shillings of sterling money of this realm?—Hast thou, I say, such a coach? ay or no?'

'O dear, yes, sir; the neighbours ken the diligence weel, green picked out wi' red—three yellow wheels and a black ane.'

'Woman, thy special description will not serve—it may be only a lie with a circumstance.'*

'O, man, man!' said the overwhelmed Mrs Macleuchar, totally exhausted by having been so long the butt of his rhetoric, 'take back your three shillings, and mak me quit o' ye.'

'Not so fast, not so fast, woman—will three shillings transport me to Queensferry, agreeably to thy treacherous program?—or will it requite the damage I may sustain by leaving my business undone, or repay the expenses which I must disburse if I am obliged to tarry a day at the South Ferry for lack of tide?—Will it hire, I say, a pinnace, for which alone the regular price is five shillings?'

Here his argument was cut short by a lumbering noise, which proved to be the advance of the expected vehicle, pressing forward with all the dispatch to which the broken-winded jades that drew it could possibly be urged. With ineffable pleasure, Mrs Macleuchar saw her tormentor deposited in the leathern convenience; but still, as it was driving off, his head thrust out of the window reminded her, in words drowned amid the rumbling of the wheels, that, if the diligence did not attain the Ferry in time to save the flood-tide, she, Mrs Macleuchar, should be held responsible for all the consequences that might ensue.

The coach had continued in motion for a mile or two before the stranger had completely repossessed himself of his equanimity, as was manifested by the doleful ejaculations, which he made from time to time, on the too great probability, or even certainty, of their missing the flood-tide. By degrees, however, his wrath subsided; he wiped his brows, relaxed his frown, and, undoing the parcel in his hand, produced his folio, on which he gazed from time to time with the knowing look of an amateur, admiring its height and condition, and ascertaining, by a minute and individual inspection of each leaf, that the volume was uninjured and entire from title-page to colophon. His fellow-traveller took the liberty of inquiring the subject of his studies. He lifted up his eyes with something of a sarcastic glance, as if he supposed the young querist would not relish, or perhaps understand, his answer, and pronounced the book to be Sandy Gordon's Itinerarium Septentrionale,* a book illustrative of the Roman remains in Scotland. The querist, unappalled by this learned title, proceeded to put several questions, which indicated, that he had made good use of a good education, and, although not possessed of minute information on the subject of antiquities, had yet acquaintance enough with the classics to render him an interested and intelligent auditor when they were enlarged upon. The elder traveller, observing with pleasure the capacity of his temporary companion to understand and answer him, plunged, nothing loath, into a sea of discussion concerning urns, vases, votive altars, Roman camps, and the rules of castrametation.*

The pleasure of this discourse had such a dulcifying tendency, that, although two causes of delay occurred, each of much more serious duration than that which had drawn down his wrath upon the unlucky Mrs Macleuchar, our ANTIQUARY only bestowed on the delay the honour of a few episodical poohs and pshaws, which rather seemed to regard the interruption of his disquisition than the retardation of his journey.

The first of these stops was occasioned by the breaking of a spring, which half an hour's labour hardly repaired. To the second, the Antiquary was himself accessory, if not the principal cause of it; for, observing that one of the horses had cast a fore-foot shoe, he apprized the coachman of this important deficiency. 'It's Jamie Martingale that furnishes the naigs on contract, and uphauds them,' answered John, 'and I am not entitled to make any stop, or to suffer prejudice by the like of these accidents.'

'And when you go to—I mean to the place you deserve to go to, you scoundrel,—who do you think will uphold *you* on contract? If you don't stop directly and carry the poor brute to the next smithy, I'll have you punished, if there's a justice of peace in Mid-Lothian;' and, opening the coach door, out he jumped, while the coachman obeyed his orders, muttering, that 'if the gentlemen lost the tide now, they could not say but it was their ain fault, since he was willing to get on.'

I like so little to analyze the complication of the causes which influence actions, that I will not venture to ascertain whether our Antiquary's humanity to the poor horse was not in some degree aided by his desire of showing his companion a Pict's camp, or Round-about,* a subject which he had been elaborately discussing, and of which a specimen, 'very curious and perfect indeed,' happened to exist about a hundred yards distant from the place where this interruption took place. But were I compelled to decompose the motives of my worthy friend, (for such was the gentleman in the sober suit, with powdered wig and slouched hat,) I should say, that, although he certainly would not in any case have suffered the coachman to proceed while the horse was unfit for service, and likely to suffer by being urged forward, yet the man of whipcord escaped some severe abuse and reproach by the agreeable mode which the traveller found out to pass the interval of delay.

So much time was consumed by these interruptions of their journey, that when they descended the hill above the Hawes, (for so the inn on the southern side of the Queensferry is denominated,) the experienced eye of the Antiquary at once discerned, from the extent of wet sand, and the number of black stones and rocks, covered with seaweed, which were visible along the skirts of the shore, that the hour of tide was past. The young traveller expected a burst of indignation; but whether, as Croaker says in 'The Good-natured Man,'* our hero had exhausted himself in fretting away his misfortunes beforehand, so that he did not feel them when they actually arrived, or whether he found the company in which he was placed too congenial to lead him to repine at any thing which delayed his journey, it is certain that he submitted to his lot with much resignation.

'The d—l's in the diligence and the old hag it belongs to!— Diligence, quoth I? Thou shouldst have called it the Sloth—Fly!— quoth she? why, it moves like a fly through a glue-pot, as the

Irishman says. But, however, time and tide tarry for no man; and so, my young friend, we'll have a snack here at the Hawes, which is a very decent sort of a place, and I'll be very happy to finish the account I was giving you of the difference between the mode of entrenching *castra stativa* and *castra æstiva*,* things confounded by too many of our historians. Lack-a-day, if they had ta'en the pains to satisfy their own eyes, instead of following each other's blind guidance!—Well! we shall be pretty comfortable at the Hawes; and besides, after all, we must have dined somewhere, and it will be pleasanter sailing with the tide of ebb and the evening breeze.'

In this Christian temper of making the best of all occurrences, our travellers alighted at the Hawes.

CHAPTER II

Sir, they do scandal me upon the road here!
A poor quotidian rack of mutton roasted
Dry to be grated! and that driven down
With beer and butter-milk, mingled together.
It is against my freehold, my inheritance.
WINE is the word that glads the heart of man,
And mine's the house of wine. *Sack*, says my bush,*
Be merry and drink Sherry, that's my posie.

BEN JONSON'S *New Inn**

As the senior traveller descended the crazy steps of the diligence at the inn, he was greeted by the fat, gouty, pursy landlord, with that mixture of familiarity and respect which the Scotch innkeepers of the old school used to assume towards their more valued customers.

'Have a care o' us, Monkbarns, (distinguishing him by his territorial epithet, always most agreeable to the ear of a Scottish proprietor,) is this you? I little thought to have seen your honour here till the summer session* was ower.'

'Ye donnard auld deevil,' answered his guest, his Scottish accent predominating when in anger, though otherwise not particularly remarkable,—'ye donnard auld crippled idiot, what have I to do with the session, or the geese that flock to it, or the hawks that pick their pinions for them?'

'Troth, and that's true,' said mine host, who, in fact, only spoke upon a very general recollection of the stranger's original education, yet would have been sorry not to have been supposed accurate as to the station and profession of him, or any other occasional guest—-'That's very true—but I thought ye had some law affair of your ain to look after—I have ane mysell—a ganging plea* that my father left me, and his father afore left to him. It's about our back-yard—ye'll maybe hae heard of it in the Parliament-house,* Hutchinson against Mackitchinson—it's a weel-kenn'd plea—it's been four times in afore the fifteen, and deil ony thing the wisest o' them could make o't, but just to send it out again to the outer-house*—O it's a beautiful thing to see how lang and how carefully justice is considered in this country!'

'Hold your tongue, you fool,' said the traveller, but in great good-humour, 'and tell us what you can give this young gentleman and me for dinner.'

'Ou, there's fish, nae doubt,—that's sea-trout and caller had-docks,' said Mackitchinson, twisting his napkin; 'and ye'll be for a mutton-chop, and there's cranberry tarts, very weel preserved, and—and there's just ony thing else ye like.'

'Which is to say, there is nothing else whatever? Well, well, the fish and the chop, and the tarts, will do very well. But don't imitate the cautious delay that you praise in the courts of justice. Let there be no remits from the inner to the outer-house, hear ye me?'

'Na, na,' said Mackitchinson, whose long and heedful perusal of volumes of printed session papers* had made him acquainted with some law phrases—'the denner shall be served *quamprimum*, and that *peremptorie*.'* And with the flattering laugh of a promising host, he left them in his sanded parlour,* hung with prints of the Four Seasons.

As, notwithstanding his pledge to the contrary, the glorious delays of the law were not without their parallel in the kitchen of the inn, our younger traveller had an opportunity to step out and make some inquiry of the people of the house concerning the rank and station of his companion. The information which he received was of a general and less authentic nature, but quite sufficient to make him acquainted with the name, history, and circumstances of the gentle-man, whom we shall endeavour, in a few words, to introduce more accurately to our readers.

Jonathan Oldenbuck, or Oldinbuck, by popular contraction Old-buck, of Monkbarns, was the second son of a gentleman possessed of a small property in the neighbourhood of a thriving seaport town on the north-eastern coast of Scotland, which, for various reasons, we shall denominate Fairport. They had been established for several generations, as landholders in the county, and in most shires of England would have been accounted a family of some standing. But the shire of —— was filled with gentlemen of more ancient descent and larger fortune. In the last generation also, the neighbouring gen-try had been almost uniformly Jacobites, while the proprietors of Monkbarns, like the burghers of the town near which they were settled, were steady assertors of the Protestant succession.* The latter had, however, a pedigree of their own, on which they prided

themselves as much as those who despised them valued their respective Saxon, Norman, or Celtic genealogies. The first Oldenbuck, who
had settled in their family mansion shortly after the Reformation,*
was, they asserted, descended from one of the original printers of
Germany, and had left his country in consequence of the persecutions directed against the professors of the Reformed religion. He
had found a refuge in the town near which his posterity dwelt, the
more readily that he was a sufferer in the Protestant cause, and
certainly not the less so, that he brought with him money enough to
purchase the small estate of Monkbarns, then sold by a dissipated
laird, to whose father it had been gifted, with other church lands, on
the dissolution of the great and wealthy monastery* to which it had
belonged. The Oldenbucks were therefore loyal subjects on all occasions of insurrection; and, as they kept up a good intelligence with
the borough, it chanced that the Laird of Monkbarns, who flourished in 1745, was provost of the town during that ill-fated year, and
had exerted himself with much spirit in favour of King George, and
even been put to expenses on that score, which, according to the
liberal conduct of the existing government towards their friends, had
never been repaid him. By dint of solicitation, however, and borough
interest, he contrived to gain a place in the customs, and, being a
frugal, careful man, had found himself enabled to add considerably
to his paternal fortune. He had only two sons, of whom, as we have
hinted, the present laird was the younger, and two daughters, one of
whom still flourished in single blessedness,* and the other, who was
greatly more juvenile, made a love-match with a captain in the *Forty-
twa*,* who had no other fortune but his commission and a Highland
pedigree. Poverty disturbed a union which love would otherwise
have made happy, and Captain M'Intyre, in justice to his wife and
two children, a boy and girl, had found himself obliged to seek his
fortune in the East Indies. Being ordered upon an expedition against
Hyder Ally,* the detachment to which he belonged was cut off, and no
news ever reached his unfortunate wife whether he fell in battle, or
was murdered in prison, or survived, in what the habits of the Indian
tyrant rendered a hopeless captivity. She sunk under the accumulated load of grief and uncertainty, and left a son and daughter to the
charge of her brother, the existing laird of Monkbarns.

The history of that proprietor himself is soon told. Being, as we
have said, a second son, his father destined him to a share in a

substantial mercantile concern, carried on by some of his maternal relations. From this Jonathan's mind revolted in the most irreconcilable manner. He was then put apprentice to the profession of a writer, or attorney, in which he profited so far, that he made himself master of the whole forms of feudal investitures,* and showed such pleasure in reconciling their incongruities, and tracing their origin, that his master had great hope he would one day be an able conveyancer. But he halted upon the threshold, and, though he acquired some knowledge of the origin and system of the law of his country, he could never be persuaded to apply it to lucrative and practical purposes. It was not from any inconsiderate neglect of the advantages attending the possession of money that he thus deceived the hopes of his master. 'Were he thoughtless or light-headed, or *rei suæ prodigus*,'* said his instructor, 'I would know what to make of him. But he never pays away a shilling without looking anxiously after the change, makes his sixpence go farther than another lad's half-crown, and will ponder over an old black-letter* copy of the acts of parliament for days, rather than go to the golf or the change-house; and yet he will not bestow one of these days on a little business of routine, that would put twenty shillings in his pocket—a strange mixture of frugality and industry, and negligent indolence—I don't know what to make of him.'

But in process of time his pupil gained the means of making what he pleased of himself; for his father having died, was not long survived by his eldest son, an arrant fisher and fowler, who departed this life, in consequence of a cold caught in his vocation, while shooting ducks in the swamp called Kittlefitting-moss, notwithstanding his having drunk a bottle of brandy that very night to keep the cold out of his stomach. Jonathan, therefore, succeeded to the estate, and with it to the means of subsisting without the hated drudgery of the law. His wishes were very moderate; and as the rent of his small property rose with the improvement of the country, it soon greatly exceeded his wants and expenditure; and though too indolent to make money, he was by no means insensible to the pleasure of beholding it accumulate. The burghers of the town near which he lived regarded him with a sort of envy, as one who affected to divide himself from their rank in society, and whose studies and pleasures seemed to them alike incomprehensible. Still, however, a sort of hereditary respect for the Laird of Monkbarns, augmented by the knowledge of his being a ready-money man,* kept up his consequence with this class of his neighbours. The country gentlemen were generally above him in fortune, and beneath him in intellect, and, excepting one with whom he lived in habits of intimacy, had little intercourse with Mr Oldbuck of Monkbarns. He had, however, the usual resources, the company of the clergyman, and of the doctor, when he chose to request it, and also his own pursuits and pleasures, being in correspondence with most of the virtuosi of his time, who, like himself, measured decayed entrenchments, made plans of ruined castles, read illegible inscriptions, and wrote essays on medals in the proportion of twelve pages to each letter of the legend. Some habits of hasty irritation he had contracted, partly, it was said in the borough of Fairport, from an early disappointment in love, in virtue of which he had commenced misogynist, as he called it, but yet more by the obsequious attention paid to him by his maiden sister and his orphan niece, whom he had trained to consider him as the greatest man upon earth, and whom he used to boast of as the only women he had ever seen who were well broke in and bitted to obedience; though, it must be owned, Miss Grizzy Oldbuck was sometimes apt to *jibb* when he pulled the reins too tight. The rest of his character must be gathered from the story, and we dismiss with pleasure the tiresome task of recapitulation.

During the time of dinner, Mr Oldbuck, actuated by the same curiosity which his fellow-traveller had entertained on his account, made some advances, which his age and station entitled him to do in a more direct manner, towards ascertaining the name, destination, and quality of his young companion.

His name, the young gentleman said, was Lovel.

'What! the cat, the rat, and Lovel our dog?* Was he descended from King Richard's favourite?'

'He had no pretensions,' he said, 'to call himself a whelp of that litter; his father was a north-of-England gentleman. He was at present travelling to Fairport, (the town near to which Monkbarns was situated,) and, if he found the place agreeable, might perhaps remain there for some weeks.'

'Was Mr Lovel's excursion solely for pleasure?'

'Not entirely.'

'Perhaps on business with some of the commercial people of Fairport?'

'It was partly on business, but had no reference to commerce.'

Here he paused; and Mr Oldbuck having pushed his inquiries as far as good manners permitted, was obliged to change the conversation. The Antiquary, though by no means an enemy to good cheer, was a determined foe to all unnecessary expense on a journey; and upon his companion giving a hint concerning a bottle of port wine, he drew a direful picture of the mixture, which, he said, was usually sold under that denomination, and affirming that a little punch* was more genuine and better suited for the season, he laid his hand upon the bell to order the materials. But Mackitchinson had, in his own mind, settled their beverage otherwise, and appeared bearing in his hand an immense double quart bottle, or magnum, as it is called in Scotland, covered with saw-dust and cobwebs, the warrants of its antiquity.

'Punch!' said he, catching that generous sound as he entered the parlour, 'the deil a drap punch ye'se get here the day, Monkbarns, and that ye may lay your account wi'.'*

'What do you mean, you impudent rascal?'

'Ay, ay, it's nae matter for that—but do you mind the trick ye served me the last time ye were here?'

'I trick you!'

'Ay, just yoursell, Monkbarns. The Laird o' Tamlowrie, and Sir Gilbert Grizzlecleugh, and Auld Rossballoh, and the Bailie, were just setting in to make an afternoon o't, and you, wi' some o' your auld-warld stories, that the mind o' man canna resist, whirl'd them to the back o' beyont to look at the auld Roman camp—Ah, sir!' turning to Lovel, 'he wad wile the bird aff the tree wi' the tales he tells about folk lang syne—and did not I lose the drinking o' sax pints o' gude claret, for the deil ane wad hae stirred till he had seen that out at the least?'

'D'ye hear the impudent scoundrel!' said Monkbarns, but laughing at the same time; for the worthy landlord, as he used to boast, knew the measure of a guest's foot as well as e'er a souter on this side Solway;* 'well, well, you may send us in a bottle of port.'

'Port! na, na! ye maun leave port and punch to the like o' us, it's claret that's fit for you lairds; and, I dare say, nane of the folk ye speak so much o' ever drank either of the twa.'

'Do you hear how absolute the knave is?* Well, my young friend, we must for once prefer the *Falernian* to the *vile Sabinum*.'*

The ready landlord had the cork instantly extracted, decanted the wine into a vessel of suitable capaciousness, and, declaring it *parfumed* the very room, left his guests to make the most of it.

Mackitchinson's wine was really good, and had its effect upon the spirits of the elder guest, who told some good stories, cut some sly jokes, and at length entered into a learned discussion concerning the ancient dramatists; a ground on which he found his new acquaintance so strong, that at length he began to suspect he had made them his professional study. 'A traveller partly for business and partly for pleasure?—Why, the stage partakes of both; it is a labour to the performers, and affords, or is meant to afford, pleasure to the spectators. He seems, in manner and rank, above the class of young men who take that turn; but I remember hearing them say, that the little theatre at Fairport was to open with the performance of a young gentleman, being his first appearance on any stage.—If this should be thee, Lovel?—Lovel? yes, Lovel or Belville* are just the names which youngsters are apt to assume on such occasions—on my life, I am sorry for the lad.'

Mr Oldbuck was habitually parsimonious, but in no respects mean; his first thought was to save his fellow-traveller any part of the expense of the entertainment, which he supposed must be in his situation more or less inconvenient. He therefore took an opportunity of settling privately with Mr Mackitchinson. The young traveller remonstrated against his liberality, and only acquiesced in deference to his years and respectability.

The mutual satisfaction which they found in each other's society induced Mr Oldbuck to propose, and Lovel willingly to accept, a scheme for travelling together to the end of their journey. Mr Oldbuck intimated a wish to pay two-thirds of the hire of a post-chaise, saying, that a proportional quantity of room was necessary to his accommodation; but this Mr Lovel resolutely declined. Their expense then was mutual, unless when Lovel occasionally slipt a shilling into the hand of a growling positilion; for Oldbuck, tenacious of ancient customs, never extended his guerdon beyond eighteen-pence a-stage.* In this manner they travelled, until they arrived at Fairport about two o'clock on the following day.

Lovel probably expected that his travelling companion would have invited him to dinner on his arrival; but his consciousness of a want of ready preparation for unexpected guests, and perhaps some other reasons, prevented Oldbuck from paying him that attention. He only begged to see him as early as he could make it convenient to call in a forenoon, recommended him to a widow who had apartments to let, and to a person who kept a decent ordinary; cautioning both of them apart, that he only knew Mr Lovel as a pleasant companion in a post-chaise, and did not mean to guarantee any bills which he might contract while residing at Fairport. The young gentleman's figure and manners, not to mention a well-furnished trunk, which soon arrived by sea, to his address at Fairport, probably went as far in his favour as the limited recommendation of his fellow-traveller.

CHAPTER III

He had a routh o' auld nick-nackets,
Rusty airn caps, and jinglin-jackets,
Would held the Loudons three in tickets
    A towmond gude;
And parritch-pats, and auld saut-backets,
    Afore the flude.

BURNS.*

AFTER he had settled himself in his new apartments at Fairport, Mr Lovel bethought him of paying the requested visit to his fellow-traveller. He did not make it earlier, because, with all the old gentleman's good-humour and information, there had sometimes glanced forth in his language and manner towards him an air of superiority, which his companion considered as being fully beyond what the difference of age warranted. He therefore waited the arrival of his baggage from Edinburgh, that he might arrange his dress according to the fashion of the day, and make his exterior corresponding to the rank in society which he supposed or felt himself entitled to hold.

It was the fifth day after his arrival, that, having made the necessary inquiries concerning the road, he went forth to pay his respects at Monkbarns. A footpath leading over a heathy hill, and through two or three meadows, conducted him to this mansion, which stood on the opposite side of the hill aforesaid, and commanded a fine prospect of the bay and shipping. Secluded from the town by the rising ground, which also screened it from the north-west wind, the house had a solitary and sheltered appearance. The exterior had little to recommend it. It was an irregular old-fashioned building, some part of which had belonged to a grange, or solitary farm-house, inhabited by the bailiff, or steward, of the monastery, when the place was in possession of the monks. It was here that the community stored up the grain, which they received as ground-rent* from their vassals; for, with the prudence belonging to their order, all their conventional revenues were made payable in kind, and hence, as the present proprietor loved to tell, came the name of Monkbarns. To the remains of the bailiff's house, the succeeding lay inhabitants had made various additions in proportion to the accommodation

required by their families; and, as this was done with an equal contempt of convenience within and architectural regularity without,
the whole bore the appearance of a hamlet which had suddenly
stood still when in the act of leading down one of Amphion's,
or Orpheus's, country dances.* It was surrounded by tall clipped
hedges of yew and holly, some of which still exhibited the skill of the
topiarian artist,[1] and presented curious arm-chairs, towers, and the
figures of Saint George and the dragon. The taste of Mr Oldbuck
did not disturb these monuments of an art now unknown, and he
was the less tempted so to do, as it must necessarily have broken
the heart of the old gardener. One tall embowering holly was, however, sacred from the shears; and, on a garden seat beneath its shade,
Lovel beheld his old friend with spectacles on nose, and pouch on
side,* busily employed in perusing the London Chronicle,* soothed
by the summer breeze through the rustling leaves, and the distant
dash of the waves as they rippled upon the sand.

Mr Oldbuck immediately rose, and advanced to greet his travelling acquaintance with a hearty shake of the hand. 'By my faith,'
said he, 'I began to think you had changed your mind, and found the
stupid people of Fairport so tiresome, that you judged them
unworthy of your talents, and had taken French leave,* as my old
friend and brother antiquary, Mac-Cribb did, when he went off with
one of my Syrian medals.'*

'I hope, my good sir, I should have fallen under no such
imputation.'

'Quite as bad, let me tell you, if you had stolen yourself away
without giving me the pleasure of seeing you again. I had rather you
had taken my copper Otho* himself.—But come, let me show you the
way into my *sanctum sanctorum*,* my cell I may call it, for, except two
idle hussies of womankind, (by this contemptuous phrase, borrowed
from his brother antiquary, the cynic Anthony a Wood,* Mr Oldbuck
was used to denote the fair sex in general, and his sister and niece in
particular,) that, on some idle pretext of relationship, have established themselves in my premises, I live here as much a Cœnobite* as
my predecessor, John o' the Girnell, whose grave I will show you by
and by.'

Thus speaking, the old gentleman led the way through a low door;
but, before entrance, suddenly stopped short to point out some
vestiges of what he called an inscription, and shaking his head as he

pronounced it totally illegible, 'Ah! if you but knew, Mr Lovel, the time and trouble that these mouldering traces of letters have cost me! No mother ever travailed so for a child—and all to no purpose—although I am almost positive that these two last marks imply the figures, or letters, LV, and may give us a good guess at the real date of the building, since we know, *aliunde*, that it was founded by Abbot Waldimir about the middle of the fourteenth century—and, I profess, I think that centre ornament might be made out by better eyes than mine.'

'I think,' answered Lovel, willing to humour the old man, 'it has something the appearance of a mitre.'

'I protest you are right! you are right! it never struck me before—see what it is to have younger eyes—a mitre, a mitre, it corresponds in every respect.'

The resemblance was not much nearer than that of Polonius's cloud to a whale, or an owzel;* it was sufficient, however, to set the Antiquary's brains to work. 'A mitre, my dear sir,' continued he, as he led the way through a labyrinth of inconvenient and dark passages, and accompanied his disquisition with certain necessary cautions to his guest—'A mitre, my dear sir, will suit our abbot as well as a bishop—he was a mitred abbot, and at the very top of the roll—take care of these three steps—I know Mac-Cribb denies this, but it is as certain as that he took away my Antigonus,* no leave asked—you'll see the name of the Abbot of Trotcosey, *Abbas Trottocosiensis*, at the head of the rolls of parliament in the fourteenth and fifteenth centuries—there is very little light here, and these cursed womankind always leave their tubs in the passage—now take care of the corner—ascend twelve steps, and ye are safe!'

Mr Oldbuck had, by this time, attained the top of the winding stair which led to his own apartment, and opening a door, and pushing aside a piece of tapestry with which it was covered, his first exclamation was, 'What are you about here, you sluts?' A dirty barefooted chambermaid threw down her duster, detected in the heinous fact of arranging the *sanctum sanctorum*, and fled out of an opposite door from the face of her incensed master. A genteel-looking young woman, who was superintending the operation, stood her ground, but with some timidity.

'Indeed, uncle, your room was not fit to be seen, and I just came to see that Jenny laid every thing down where she took it up.'

'And how dare you, or Jenny either, presume to meddle with my private matters? (Mr Oldbuck hated *putting to rights* as much as Dr Orkborne,* or any other professed student.) Go sew your sampler, you monkey, and do not let me find you here again, as you value your ears.—I assure you, Mr Lovel, that the last inroad of these pretended friends to cleanliness was almost as fatal to my collection as Hudibras's visit to that of Sidrophel;* and I have ever since missed

> "My copperplate, with almanacks
> Engraved upon't, and other knacks;
> My moon-dial, with Napier's bones,*
> And several constellation stones;*
> My flea, my morepeon, and punaise,*
> I purchased for my proper ease."

And so forth, as old Butler has it.'

The young lady, after curtseying to Lovel, had taken the opportunity to make her escape during this enumeration of losses. 'You'll be poisoned here with the volumes of dust they have raised,' continued the Antiquary; 'but I assure you the dust was very ancient, peaceful, quiet dust,* about an hour ago, and would have remained so for a hundred years, had not these gipsies disturbed it, as they do every thing else in the world.'

It was, indeed, some time before Lovel could, through the thick atmosphere, perceive in what sort of den his friend had constructed his retreat. It was a lofty room of middling size, obscurely lighted by high narrow latticed windows. One end was entirely occupied by book-shelves, greatly too limited in space for the number of volumes placed upon them, which were, therefore, drawn up in ranks of two or three files deep, while numberless others littered the floor and the tables, amid a chaos of maps, engravings, scraps of parchment, bundles of papers, pieces of old armour, swords, dirks, helmets, and Highland targets. Behind Mr Oldbuck's seat, (which was an ancient leathern-covered easy-chair, worn smooth by constant use,) was a huge oaken cabinet, decorated at each corner with Dutch cherubs, having their little duck-wings displayed, and great jolter-headed visages placed between them. The top of this cabinet was covered with busts, and Roman lamps and pateræ, intermingled with one or two bronze figures. The walls of the apartment were partly clothed with grim old tapestry, representing the memorable story of Sir

Gawaine's wedding, in which full justice was done to the ugliness of the Lothely Lady;* although, to judge from his own looks, the gentle knight had less reason to be disgusted with the match on account of disparity of outward favour, than the romancer has given us to understand. The rest of the room was panelled, or wainscotted, with black oak, against which hung two or three portraits in armour, being characters in Scottish history, favourites of Mr Oldbuck, and as many in tie-wigs and laced coats, staring representatives of his own ancestors. A large old-fashioned oak table was covered with a profusion of papers, parchments, books, and nondescript trinkets and gewgaws, which seemed to have little to recommend them, besides rust and the antiquity which it indicates. In the midst of this wreck of ancient books and utensils, with a gravity equal to Marius among the ruins of Carthage,* sat a large black cat, which, to a super-stitious eye, might have presented the *genius loci*, the tutelar demon* of the apartment. The floor, as well as the table and chairs, was overflowed by the same *mare magnum** of miscellaneous trumpery, where it would have been as impossible to find any individual article wanted, as to put it to any use when discovered.

Amid this medley, it was no easy matter to find one's way to a chair, without stumbling over a prostrate folio, or the still more awkward mischance of overturning some piece of Roman or ancient British pottery. And, when the chair was attained, it had to be dis-encumbered, with a careful hand, of engravings which might have received damage, and of antique spurs and buckles, which would certainly have occasioned it to any sudden occupant. Of this the Antiquary made Lovel particularly aware, adding, that his friend, the Rev. Doctor Heavysterne from the Low Countries, had sustained much injury by sitting down suddenly and incautiously on three ancient calthrops, or *craw-taes*, which had been lately dug up in the bog near Bannockburn, and which, dispersed by Robert Bruce to lacerate the feet of the English chargers,* came thus in process of time to endamage the sitting part of a learned professor of Utrecht.

Having at length fairly settled himself, and being nothing loath to make inquiry concerning the strange objects around him, which his host was equally ready, as far as possible, to explain, Lovel was intro-duced to a large club, or bludgeon, with an iron spike at the end of it, which, it seems, had been lately found in a field on the Monkbarns property, adjacent to an old burying ground. It had mightily the air

of such a stick as the Highland reapers use to walk with on their
annual peregrinations from their mountains; but Mr Oldbuck was
strongly tempted to believe, that, as its shape was singular, it might
have been one of the clubs with which the monks armed their peasants in lieu of more martial weapons, whence, he observed, the
villains were called *Colve-carles*, or *Kolb-kerls*, that is, *Clavigeri*,* or
club-bearers. For the truth of this custom, he quoted the chronicle
of Antwerp and that of St Martin;* against which authorities Lovel
had nothing to oppose, having never heard of them till that moment.

Mr Oldbuck next exhibited thumb-screws, which had given the
Covenanters* of former days the cramp in their joints, and a collar*
with the name of a fellow convicted of theft, whose services, as the
inscription bore, had been adjudged to a neighbouring baron, in lieu
of the modern Scottish punishment,* which, as Oldbuck said, sends
such culprits to enrich England by their labour, and themselves by
their dexterity. Many and various were the other curiosities which he
showed; but it was chiefly upon his books that he prided himself,
repeating, with a complacent air, as he led the way to the crowded
and dusty shelves, the verses of old Chaucer—

> 'For he would rather have, at his bed-head,
> A twenty books, clothed in black or red,
> Of Aristotle, or his philosophy,
> Than robes rich, rebeck, or saltery.'*

This pithy motto he delivered, shaking his head, and giving each
guttural the true Anglo-Saxon enunciation, which is now forgotten
in the southern parts of this realm.

The collection was, indeed, a curious one, and might well be
envied by an amateur. Yet it was not collected at the enormous prices
of modern times, which are sufficient to have appalled the most
determined, as well as earliest bibliomaniac upon record, whom we
take to have been none else than the renowned Don Quixote de la
Mancha, as, among other slight indications of an infirm understanding, he is stated, by his veracious historian, Cid Hamet Benengeli, to
have exchanged fields and farms for folios and quartos of chivalry. In
this species of exploit, the good knight-errant has been imitated by
lords, knights, and squires of our own day, though we have not yet
heard of any that has mistaken an inn for a castle, or laid his lance in
rest against a windmill.* Mr Oldbuck did not follow these collectors

in such excess of expenditure; but, taking a pleasure in the personal labour of forming his library, saved his purse at the expense of his time and toil. He was no encourager of that ingenious race of peripatetic middle-men, who, trafficking between the obscure keeper of a stall and the eager amateur, make their profit at once of the ignorance of the former, and the dear-bought skill and taste of the latter. When such were mentioned in his hearing, he seldom failed to point out how necessary it was to arrest the object of your curiosity in its first transit, and to tell his favourite story of Snuffy Davie and Caxton's Game at Chess.*—'Davy Wilson,' he said, 'commonly called Snuffy Davy, from his inveterate addiction to black rappee, was the very prince of scouts for searching blind alleys, cellars, and stalls, for rare volumes. He had the scent of a slow-hound, sir, and the snap of a bull-dog. He would detect you an old black-letter ballad among the leaves of a law-paper, and find an *editio princeps** under the mask of a school Corderius.* Snuffy Davie bought the "Game of Chess, 1474," the first book ever printed in England, from a stall in Holland, for about two groschen, or two-pence of our money. He sold it to Osborne for twenty pounds, and as many books as came to twenty pounds more. Osborne resold this inimitable windfall to Dr Askew for sixty guineas. At Dr Askew's sale,' continued the old gentleman, kindling as he spoke, 'this inestimable treasure blazed forth in its full value, and was purchased by Royalty* itself, for one hundred and seventy pounds! Could a copy now occur, Lord only knows,' he ejaculated, with a deep sigh and lifted-up hands, 'Lord only knows what would be its ransom; and yet it was originally secured, by skill and research, for the easy equivalent of twopence sterling.[2]* Happy, thrice happy, Snuffy Davie! and blessed were the times when thy industry could be so rewarded!

'Even I, sir,' he went on, 'though far inferior in industry, and discernment, and presence of mind, to that great man, can show you a few, a very few things, which I have collected, not by force of money, as any wealthy man might,—although, as my friend Lucian* says, he might chance to throw away his coin only to illustrate his ignorance,—but gained in a manner that shows I know something of the matter. See this bundle of ballads, not one of them later than 1700, and some of them an hundred years older. I wheedled an old woman out of these, who loved them better than her psalm-book. Tobacco, sir, snuff, and the Complete Syren,* were the equivalent!

For that mutilated copy of the Complaynt of Scotland,* I sat out the drinking of two dozen bottles of strong ale with the late learned proprietor, who, in gratitude, bequeathed it to me by his last will. These little Elzevirs* are the memoranda and trophies of many a walk by night and morning through the Cowgate, the Canongate, the Bow, Saint Mary's Wynd,*—wherever, in fine, there were to be found brokers and trokers, those miscellaneous dealers in things rare and curious. How often have I stood haggling on a halfpenny, lest, by a too ready acquiescence in the dealer's first price, he should be led to suspect the value I set upon the article!—how have I trembled, lest some passing stranger should chop in between me and the prize, and regarded each poor student of divinity that stopped to turn over the books at the stall, as a rival amateur, or prowling bookseller in disguise!—And then, Mr Lovel, the sly satisfaction with which one pays the consideration, and pockets the article, affecting a cold indifference, while the hand is trembling with pleasure!—Then to dazzle the eyes of our wealthier and emulous rivals by showing them such a treasure as this—(displaying a little black smoked book about the size of a primer)—to enjoy their surprise and envy, shrouding meanwhile under a veil of mysterious consciousness our own superior knowledge and dexterity—these, my young friend, these are the white moments of life, that repay the toil, and pains, and sedulous attention, which our profession, above all others, so peculiarly demands!'

Lovel was not a little amused at hearing the old gentleman run on in this manner, and, however incapable of entering into the full merits of what he beheld, he admired, as much as could have been expected, the various treasures which Oldbuck exhibited. Here were editions esteemed as being the first, and there stood those scarcely less regarded as being the last and best; here was a book valued because it had the author's final improvements, and there another which (strange to tell!) was in request because it had them not. One was precious because it was a folio, another because it was a duodecimo; some because they were tall, some because they were short; the merit of this lay in the title-page, of that in the arrangement of the letters in the word Finis. There was, it seemed, no peculiar distinction, however trifling or minute, which might not give value to a volume, providing the indispensable quality of scarcity, or rare occurrence, was attached to it.

Not the least fascinating was the original broadside—the Dying Speech, Bloody Murder, or Wonderful Wonder of Wonders,* in its primary tattered guise, as it was hawked through the streets, and sold for the cheap and easy price of one penny, though now worth the weight of that penny in gold. On these the Antiquary dilated with transport, and read, with a rapturous voice, the elaborate titles, which bore the same proportion to the contents that the painted signs without a showman's booth do to the animals within. Mr Oldbuck, for example, piqued himself especially in possessing an *unique* broadside, entitled and called 'Strange and Wonderful News from Chipping-Norton, in the County of Oxon, of certain dreadful Apparitions which were seen in the Air on the 26th of July, 1610, at Half an Hour after Nine o'Clock at Noon, and continued till Eleven, in which Time was seen Appearances of several flaming Swords, strange Motions of the superior Orbs; with the unusual Sparkling of the Stars, with their dreadful Continuations: With the Account of the Opening of the Heavens, and strange Appearances therein disclosing themselves, with several other prodigious Circumstances not heard of in any Age, to the great Amazement of the Beholders, as it was communicated in a Letter to one Mr Colley, living in West Smithfield, and attested by Thomas Brown, Elizabeth Greenaway, and Anne Gutheridge, who were Spectators of the dreadful Apparitions: And if any one would be further satisfied of the Truth of this Relation, let them repair to Mr Nightingale's, at the Bear Inn, in West Smithfield, and they may be satisfied.'[3]

'You laugh at this,' said the proprietor of the collection, 'and I forgive you. I do acknowledge that the charms on which we doat are not so obvious to the eyes of youth as those of a fair lady; but you will grow wiser, and see more justly, when you come to wear spectacles.—Yet stay, I have one piece of antiquity which you, perhaps, will prize more highly.'

So saying, Mr Oldbuck unlocked a drawer, and took out a bundle of keys, then pulled aside a piece of the tapestry which concealed the door of a small closet, into which he descended by four stone steps, and, after some tinkling among bottles and cans, produced two long-stalked wine-glasses with bell mouths, such as are seen in Teniers'* pieces, and a small bottle of what he called rich racy canary, with a little bit of diet-cake, on a small silver server of exquisite old workmanship. 'I will say nothing of the server,' he remarked, 'though it is said to have been wrought by the old mad Florentine, Benvenuto Cellini.* But, Mr Lovel, our ancestors drunk sack*—you, who admire the drama, know where that's to be found.—Here's success to your exertions at Fairport, sir!'

'And to you, sir, and an ample increase to your treasure, with no more trouble on your part than is just necessary to make the acquisitions valuable.'

After a libation so suitable to the amusement in which they had been engaged, Lovel rose to take his leave, and Mr Oldbuck prepared to give him his company a part of the way, and show him something worthy of his curiosity on his return to Fairport.

CHAPTER IV

The pawky auld carle cam ower the lea,
Wi' mony good-e'ens and good-morrows to me,
Saying, Kind sir, for your courtesy,
Will ye lodge a silly poor man?

*The Gaberlunzie Man.**

OUR two friends moved through a little orchard, where the aged
apple-trees, well loaded with fruit, showed, as is usual in the neighbourhood of monastic buildings, that the days of the monks had not
always been spent in indolence, but often dedicated to horticulture
and gardening. Mr Oldbuck failed not to make Lovel remark, that
the planters of those days were possessed of the modern secret of
preventing the roots of the fruit-trees from penetrating the till, and
compelling them to spread in a lateral direction, by placing paving-
stones beneath the trees when first planted, so as to interpose
between their fibres and the subsoil. 'This old fellow,' he said, 'which
was blown down last summer, and still, though half reclined on the
ground, is covered with fruit, has been, as you may see, accom-
modated with such a barrier between his roots and the unkindly till.
That other tree has a story: the fruit is called the Abbot's Apple; the
lady of a neighbouring baron was so fond of it, that she would often
pay a visit to Monkbarns, to have the pleasure of gathering it from
the tree. The husband, a jealous man, belike, suspected that a taste so
nearly resembling that of Mother Eve prognosticated a similar fall.
As the honour of a noble family is concerned, I will say no more on
the subject, only that the lands of Lochard and Cringlecut still pay a
fine of six bolls of barley annually, to atone the guilt of their auda-
cious owner, who intruded himself and his worldly suspicions upon
the seclusion of the Abbot and his penitent. Admire the little belfry
rising above the ivy-mantled porch—there was here a *hospitium, hospitale*, or *hospitamentum*, (for it is written all these various ways in the
old writings and evidents,)* in which the monks received pilgrims—I
know our minister has said, in the Statistical Account,* that the *hospitium* was situated either on the lands of Haltweary, or upon those of
Half-starvet; but he is incorrect, Mr Lovel—that is the gate called

still the Palmer's Port, and my gardener found many hewn stones, when he was trenching the ground for winter celery, several of which I have sent as specimens to my learned friends, and to the various antiquarian societies of which I am an unworthy member. But I will say no more at present; I reserve something for another visit, and we have an object of real curiosity before us.'

While he was thus speaking, he led the way briskly through one or two rich pasture meadows to an open heath or common, and so to the top of a gentle eminence. 'Here,' he said, 'Mr Lovel, is a truly remarkable spot.'

'It commands a fine view,' said his companion, looking around him.

'True: but it is not for the prospect I brought you hither; do you see nothing else remarkable?—nothing on the surface of the ground?'

'Why, yes; I do see something like a ditch, indistinctly marked.'

'Indistinctly!—pardon me, sir, but the indistinctness must be in your powers of vision—nothing can be more plainly traced—a proper *agger* or *vallum*, with its corresponding ditch or *fossa*. Indistinctly! why, Heaven help you, the lassie, my niece, as light-headed a goose as womankind affords, saw the traces of the ditch at once. Indistinct! why, the great station at Ardoch, or that at Burnswark* in Annandale, may be clearer, doubtless, because they are stative forts, whereas this was only an occasional encampment. Indistinct! why, you must suppose that fools, boors, and idiots, have ploughed up the land, and, like beasts and ignorant savages, have thereby obliterated two sides of the square, and greatly injured the third; but you see, yourself, the fourth side is quite entire!'

Lovel endeavoured to apologize, and to explain away his ill-timed phrase, and pleaded his inexperience. But he was not at once quite successful. His first expression had come too frankly and naturally not to alarm the Antiquary, and he could not easily get over the shock it had given him.

'My dear sir,' continued the senior, 'your eyes are not inexperienced: you know a ditch from level ground, I presume, when you see them? Indistinct! why, the very common people, the very least boy that can herd a cow, calls it the Kaim of Kinprunes; and if that does not imply an ancient camp, I am ignorant what does.'

Lovel having again acquiesced, and at length lulled to sleep the irritated and suspicious vanity of the Antiquary, he proceeded in his task of cicerone. 'You must know,' he said, 'our Scottish antiquaries have been greatly divided about the local situation of the final conflict between Agricola and the Caledonians—some contend for Ardoch in Strathallan, some for Innerpeffrey, some for the Raedykes in the Mearns, and some are for carrying the scene of action as far north as Blair in Athole. Now, after all this discussion,' continued the old gentleman, with one of his slyest and most complacent looks, 'what would you think, Mr Lovel,—I say, what would you think,—if the memorable scene of conflict should happen to be on the very spot called the Kaim of Kinprunes, the property of the obscure and humble individual who now speaks to you?'—Then, having paused a little, to suffer his guest to digest a communication so important, he resumed his disquisition in a higher tone. 'Yes, my good friend, I am indeed greatly deceived if this place does not correspond with all the marks of that celebrated place of action. It was near to the Grampian mountains—lo! yonder they are, mixing and contending with the sky on the skirts of the horizon!—it was *in conspectu classis*,*—in sight of the Roman fleet; and would any admiral, Roman or British, wish a fairer bay to ride in than that on your right hand? It is astonishing how blind we professed antiquaries sometimes are; Sir Robert Sibbald,* Saunders Gordon,* General Roy,* Dr Stukely,* why, it escaped all of them.—I was unwilling to say a word about it till I had secured the ground, for it belonged to auld Johnnie Howie, a bonnet-laird[4] hard by, and many a communing we had before he and I could agree. At length—I am almost ashamed to say it—but I even brought my mind to give acre for acre of my good corn-land for this barren spot. But then it was a national concern; and when the scene of so celebrated an event became my own, I was overpaid.—Whose patriotism would not grow warmer, as old Johnson says, on the plains of Marathon?* I began to trench the ground, to see what might be discovered; and the third day, sir, we found a stone, which I have transported to Monkbarns, in order to have the sculpture taken off with plaster of Paris;* it bears a sacrificing vessel, and the letters A. D. L. L. which may stand, without much violence, for *Agricola Dicavit Libens Lubens.*'*

'Certainly, sir; for the Dutch antiquaries claim Caligula as the founder of a light-house, on the sole authority of the letters C. C. P. F., which they interpret *Caius Caligula Pharum Fecit*.'*

'True, and it has ever been recorded as a sound exposition. I see we shall make something of you even before you wear spectacles, notwithstanding you thought the traces of this beautiful camp indistinct when you first observed them.'

'In time, sir, and by good instruction'—

'—You will become more apt—I doubt it not. You shall peruse, upon your next visit to Monkbarns, my trivial Essay upon Castrametation, with some particular Remarks upon the Vestiges of Ancient Fortifications lately discovered by the Author at the Kaim of Kinprunes. I think I have pointed out the infallible touchstone of supposed antiquity. I premise a few general rules on that point, on the nature, namely, of the evidence to be received in such cases. Meanwhile be pleased to observe, for example, that I could press into my service Claudian's famous line,

"Ille Caledoniis posuit qui castra pruinis."*

For *pruinis*, though interpreted to mean *hoar frosts*, to which I own we are somewhat subject in this north-eastern sea-coast, may also signify a locality, namely, *Prunes*; the *Castra Pruinis posita* would therefore be the Kaim of Kinprunes. But I waive this, for I am sensible it might be laid hold of by cavillers as carrying down my Castra to the time of Theodosius, sent by Valentinian into Britain as late as the year 367,* or thereabout. No, my good friend, I appeal to people's eye-sight—is not here the Decuman gate? and there, but for the ravage of the horrid plough, as a learned friend calls it, would be the Prætorian gate.—On the left hand you may see some slight vestiges of the *porta sinistra*, and on the right, one side of the *porta dextra* wellnigh entire—Here, then, let us take our stand, on this tumulus, exhibiting the foundation of ruined buildings,—the central point—the *prætorium*,* doubtless, of the camp. From this place, now scarce to be distinguished, but by its slight elevation and its greener turf, from the rest of the fortification, we may suppose Agricola to have looked forth on the immense army of Caledonians, occupying the declivities of yon opposite hill, the infantry rising rank over rank as the form of ground displayed their array to its utmost advantage, the cavalry and *covinarii*, by which I understand the charioteers—another guise of folks from your Bond-street four-in-hand men,* I trow—scouring the more level space below—

—————See, then, Lovel—See——
See that huge battle moving from the mountains,
Their gilt coats shine like dragon scales;—their march
Like a rough tumbling storm—See them, and view them,
And then see Rome no more!——*

Yes, my dear friend, from this stance it is probable,—nay, it is nearly certain, that Julius Agricola beheld what our Beaumont has so admirably described!—From this very Prætorium'—

A voice from behind interrupted his ecstatic description—- 'Prætorian here, Prætorian there, I mind the bigging o't.'

Both at once turned round, Lovel with surprise, and Oldbuck with mingled surprise and indignation, at so uncivil an interruption. An auditor had stolen upon them, unseen and unheard, amid the energy of the Antiquary's enthusiastic declamation, and the attentive civility of Lovel. He had the exterior appearance of a mendicant. A slouched hat of huge dimensions; a long white beard, which mingled with his grizzled hair, an aged, but strongly marked and expressive countenance, hardened, by climate and exposure, to a right brick-dust complexion; a long blue gown, with a pewter badge on the right arm; two or three wallets, or bags, slung across his shoulder, for holding the different kinds of meal, when he received his charity in kind from those who were but a degree richer than himself,—all these marked at once a beggar by profession, and one of that privileged class which are called in Scotland the King's Bedes-men, or, vulgarly, Blue-gowns.

'What is that you say, Edie?' said Oldbuck, hoping, perhaps, that his ears had betrayed their duty; 'What were you speaking about?'

'About this bit bourock, your honour,' answered the undaunted Edie; 'I mind the bigging o't.'

'The devil you do! Why, you old fool, it was here before you were born, and will be after you are hanged, man!'

'Hanged or drowned, here or awa, dead or alive, I mind the bigging o't.'

'You—you—you,' said the Antiquary, stammering between confusion and anger, 'you strolling old vagabond, what the devil do you know about it?'

'Ou, I ken this about it, Monkbarns, and what profit have I for telling ye a lie—I just ken this about it, that about twenty years syne, I, and a wheen hallenshakers like mysell, and the mason-lads that built the lang dyke that gaes down the loaning, and twa or three herds maybe, just set to wark, and built this bit thing here that ye ca' the—the—Prætorian, and a' just for a bield at auld Aiken Drum's* bridal, and a bit blithe gae-down wi' had in't, some sair rainy weather. Mair by token, Monkbarns, if ye howk up the bourock, as ye seem to have begun, ye'll find, if ye hae not fund it already, a stane that ane o' the mason-callants cut a ladle on to have a bourd at the bridegroom, and he put four letters on't, that's A.D.L.L.—Aiken Drum's Lang Ladle—for Aiken was ane o' the kale-suppers o' Fife.'

This, thought Lovel to himself, is a famous counterpart to the story of *Keip on this syde.**—He then ventured to steal a glance at our Antiquary, but quickly withdrew it in sheer compassion. For, gentle reader, if thou hast ever beheld the visage of a damsel of sixteen, whose romance of true love has been blown up by an untimely discovery, or of a child of ten years, whose castle of cards has been blown down by a malicious companion, I can safely aver to you, that Jonathan Oldbuck of Monkbarns looked neither more wise nor less disconcerted.

'There is some mistake about this,' he said, abruptly turning away from the mendicant.

'Deil a bit on my side o' the wa',' answered the sturdy beggar; 'I never deal in mistakes, they aye bring mischances.—Now, Monkbarns, that young gentleman, that's wi' your honour, thinks little of a carle like me; and yet, I'll wager I'll tell him whar he was yestreen at the gloamin, only he maybe wadna like to hae't spoken o' in company.'

Lovel's soul rushed to his cheeks, with the vivid blush of two-and-twenty.

'Never mind the old rogue,' said Mr Oldbuck; 'don't suppose I think the worse of you for your profession; they are only prejudiced fools and coxcombs that do so. You remember what old Tully* says in his oration, *pro Archia poeta*, concerning one of your confraternity—- *Quis nostrum tam animo agresti ac duro fuit—ut—ut—** I forget the Latin—the meaning is, which of us was so rude and barbarous as to remain unmoved at the death of the great Roscius,* whose advanced age was so far from preparing us for his death, that we rather hoped one so graceful, so excellent in his art, ought to be exempted from the common lot of mortality? So the Prince of Orators spoke of the stage and its professors.'

The words of the old man fell upon Lovel's ears, but without conveying any precise idea to his mind, which was then occupied in thinking by what means the old beggar, who still continued to regard him with a countenance provokingly sly and intelligent, had contrived to thrust himself into any knowledge of his affairs. He put his hand in his pocket as the readiest mode of intimating his desire of secrecy, and securing the concurrence of the person whom he addressed; and while he bestowed him an alms, the amount of which rather bore proportion to his fears than to his charity, looked at him with a marked expression, which the mendicant, a physiognomist by profession, seemed perfectly to understand.—'Never mind me, sir, I am no tale-pyet; but there are mair een in the warld than mine,' answered he, as he pocketed Lovel's bounty, but in a tone to be heard by him alone, and with an expression which amply filled up what was left unspoken. Then turning to Oldbuck—'I am awa to the manse, your honour. Has your honour ony word there, or to Sir Arthur, for I'll come in by Knockwinnock Castle again e'en?'

Oldbuck started as from a dream; and, in a hurried tone, where vexation strove with a wish to conceal it, paying, at the same time, a tribute to Edie's smooth, greasy, unlined hat, he said, 'Go down, go down to Monkbarns—let them give you some dinner—or stay; if you do go to the manse, or to Knockwinnock, ye need say nothing about that foolish story of yours.'

'Who, I?' said the mendicant—'Lord bless your honour, naebody sall ken a word about it frae me, mair than if the bit bourock had been there since Noah's flood. But, Lord, they tell me your honour has gien Johnnie Howie acre for acre of the laigh crofts for this heathery knowe! Now, if he has really imposed the bourock on ye for an ancient wark, it's my real opinion the bargain will never haud gude, if you would just bring down your heart to try it at the law, and say that he beguiled ye.'

'Provoking scoundrel,' muttered the indignant Antiquary between his teeth,—'I'll have the hangman's lash and his back acquainted for this!'—And then in a louder tone,—'Never mind, Edie—it is all a mistake.'

'Troth, I am thinking sae,' continued his tormentor, who seemed to have pleasure in rubbing the galled wound, 'troth, I aye thought sae; and it's no sae lang since I said to Luckie Gemmels, "Never think you, Luckie," said I, "that his honour, Monkbarns, would hae done sic a daft-like thing, as to gie grund weel worth fifty shillings an acre, for a mailing that would be dear o' a pund Scots. Na, na," quo' I, "depend upon't the laird's been imposed upon wi' that wily do-little deevil, Johnnie Howie." "But Lord haud a care o' us, sirs, how can that be," quo' she again, "when the laird's sae book-learned, there's no the like o' him in the country side, and Johnnie Howie has hardly sense eneugh to ca' the cows out o' his kale-yard?" "Aweel, aweel," quo' I, "but ye'll hear he's circumvented him with some of his auld-warld stories,"—for ye ken, laird, yon other time about the bodle that ye thought was an auld coin'—

'Go to the devil!' said Oldbuck; and then in a more mild tone, as one that was conscious his reputation lay at the mercy of his antagonist, he added—'Away with you down to Monkbarns, and when I come back, I'll send ye a bottle of ale to the kitchen.'

'Heaven reward your honour!' This was uttered with the true mendicant whine, as, setting his pike-staff before him, he began to move in the direction of Monkbarns—'But did your honour,' turning round, 'ever get back the siller ye gae to the travelling packman for the bodle?'

'Curse thee, go about thy business!'

'Aweel, aweel, sir, God bless your honour!—I hope ye'll ding Johnnie Howie yet, and that I'll live to see it.' And so saying, the old beggar moved off, relieving Mr Oldbuck of recollections which were any thing rather than agreeable.

'Who is this familiar old gentleman?' said Lovel, when the mendicant was out of hearing.

'O, one of the plagues of the country—I have been always against poor's-rates and a work-house*—I think I'll vote for them now, to have that scoundrel shut up. O, your old-remembered guest of a beggar becomes as well acquainted with you as he is with his dish—as intimate as one of the beasts familiar to man which signify love,* and with which his own trade is especially conversant. Who is he?—why, he has gone the vole—has been soldier, ballad-singer, travelling tinker, and is now a beggar. He is spoiled by our foolish gentry, who laugh at his jokes, and rehearse Edie Ochiltree's good things as regularly as Joe Miller's.'*

'Why, he uses freedom apparently, which is the soul of wit,' answered Lovel.

'O ay, freedom enough,' said the Antiquary; 'he generally invents some damned improbable lie or another to provoke you, like that nonsense he talked just now—not that I'll publish my tract till I have examined the thing to the bottom.'

'In England,' said Lovel, 'such a mendicant would get a speedy check.'

'Yes, your churchwardens and dog-whips would make slender allowance for his vein of humour! But here, curse him, he is a sort of privileged nuisance—one of the last specimens of the old-fashioned Scottish mendicant, who kept his rounds within a particular space, and was the news-carrier, the minstrel, and sometimes the historian of the district. That rascal, now, knows more old ballads and traditions than any other man in this and the four next parishes. And after all,' continued he, softening as he went on describing Edie's good gifts, 'the dog has some good-humour. He has borne his hard fate with unbroken spirits, and it's cruel to deny him the comfort of a laugh at his betters. The pleasure of having quizzed me, as you gay folk would call it, will be meat and drink to him for a day or two. But I must go back and look after him, or he will spread his d—d nonsensical story over half the country.'

So saying, our heroes parted, Mr Oldbuck to return to his *hospitium* at Monkbarns, and Lovel to pursue his way to Fairport, where he arrived without farther adventure.

CHAPTER V

Launcelot Gobbo. Mark me now: Now will I raise the waters.

*Merchant of Venice.**

THE theatre at Fairport had opened, but no Mr Lovel appeared
on the boards, nor was there any thing in the habits or deportment of
the young gentleman so named, which authorized Mr Oldbuck's
conjecture that his fellow-traveller was a candidate for the public
favour. Regular were the Antiquary's inquiries at an old-fashioned
barber who dressed the only three wigs in the parish, which, in
defiance of taxes and times,* were still subjected to the operation of
powdering and frizzling, and who for that purpose divided his time
among the three employers whom fashion had yet left him—regular,
I say, were Mr Oldbuck's inquiries at this personage concerning the
news of the little theatre at Fairport, expecting every day to hear of
Mr Lovel's appearance; on which occasion the old gentleman had
determined to put himself to charges in honour of his young friend,
and not only to go to the play himself, but to carry his womankind
along with him. But old Jacob Caxon conveyed no information
which warranted his taking so decisive a step as that of securing a
box.

He brought information, on the contrary, that there was a young
man residing at Fairport, of whom the *town* (by which he meant all
the gossips, who, having no business of their own, fill up their leisure
moments by attending to that of other people) could make nothing.
He sought no society, but rather avoided that, which the apparent
gentleness of his manners, and some degree of curiosity, induced
many to offer him. Nothing could be more regular, or less resembling an adventurer, than his mode of living, which was simple, but
so completely well arranged, that all who had any transactions with
him were loud in their approbation.

These are not the virtues of a stage-struck hero, thought Oldbuck
to himself; and, however habitually pertinacious in his opinions, he
must have been compelled to abandon that which he had formed
in the present instance, but for a part of Caxon's communication.
'The young gentleman,' he said, 'was sometimes heard speaking to

himself, and rampauging about in his room, just as if he was ane o' the player folk.'

Nothing, however, excepting this single circumstance, occurred to confirm Mr Oldbuck's supposition, and it remained a high and doubtful question, what a well-informed young man, without friends, connexions, or employment of any kind, could have to do as a resident at Fairport. Neither port wine nor whist had apparently any charms for him. He declined dining with the mess of the volunteer cohort, which had been lately embodied,* and shunned joining the convivialities of either of the two parties which then divided Fairport, as they did more important places. He was too little of an aristocrat to join the club of Royal True Blues,* and too little of a democrat to fraternize with an affiliated society of the *soi-disant* Friends of the People,* which the borough had also the happiness of possessing. A coffee-room was his detestation; and, I grieve to say it, he had as few sympathies with the tea-table. In short, since the name was fashionable in novel-writing, and that is a great while agone, there was never a Master Lovel of whom so little positive was known, and who was so universally described by negatives.

One negative, however, was important—nobody knew any harm of Lovel. Indeed, had such existed, it would have been speedily made public; for the natural desire of speaking evil of our neighbour could in his case have been checked by no feelings of sympathy for a being so unsocial. On one account alone he fell somewhat under suspicion. As he made free use of his pencil in his solitary walks, and had drawn several views of the harbour, in which the signal-tower, and even the four-gun battery, were introduced, some zealous friends of the public sent abroad a whisper, that this mysterious stranger must certainly be a French spy. The Sheriff paid his respects to Mr Lovel accordingly, but in the interview which followed, it would seem that he had entirely removed that magistrate's suspicions, since he not only suffered him to remain undisturbed in his retirement, but, it was credibly reported, sent him two invitations to dinner-parties, both which were civilly declined. But what the nature of the explanation was, the magistrate kept a profound secret, not only from the public at large, but from his substitute,* his clerk, his wife, and his two daughters, who formed his privy council on all questions of official duty.

All these particulars being faithfully reported by Mr Caxon to his patron at Monkbarns, tended much to raise Lovel in the opinion of his former fellow-traveller. 'A decent sensible lad,' said he to himself, 'who scorns to enter into the fooleries and nonsense of these idiot people at Fairport.—I must do something for him—I must give him a dinner—and I will write Sir Arthur to come to Monkbarns to meet him—I must consult my womankind.'

Accordingly, such consultation having been previously held, a special messenger, being no other than Caxon himself, was ordered to prepare for a walk to Knockwinnock Castle with a letter, 'For the honoured Sir Arthur Wardour, of Knockwinnock, Bart.' The contents ran thus:

'DEAR SIR ARTHUR,

'On Tuesday the 17th curt. *stilo novo*,* I hold a cænobitical symposion at Monkbarns, and pray you to assist thereat, at four o'clock* precisely. If my fair enemy, Miss Isabel, can and will honour us by accompanying you, my womankind will be but too proud to have the aid of such an auxiliary in the cause of resistance to awful rule and right supremacy.* If not, I will send the womankind to the manse for the day. I have a young acquaintance to make known to you, who is touched with some strain of a better spirit than belongs to these giddy-paced times*—reveres his elders, and has a pretty notion of the classics—and, as such a youth must have a natural contempt for the people about Fairport, I wish to show him some rational as well as worshipful society. I am, dear Sir Arthur, &c. &c. &c.'

'Fly with this letter, Caxon,' said the senior, holding out his missive, *signatum atque sigillatum*,* 'fly to Knockwinnock, and bring me back an answer. Go as fast as if the town-council were met, and waiting for the provost, and the provost was waiting for his new-powdered wig.'

'Ah! sir,' answered the messenger, with a deep sigh, 'thae days hae lang gane by. Deil a wig has a provost of Fairport worn sin' auld Provost Jervie's time—and he had a quean of a servant-lass that dressed it hersell, wi' the doup o' a candle and a drudging-box. But I hae seen the day, Monkbarns, when the town-council of Fairport wad hae as soon wanted their town-clerk, or their gill of brandy ower-head after the haddies, as they wad hae wanted ilk ane a weel-favoured, sonsy, decent periwig on his pow. Hegh, sirs! nae wonder the commons will be discontent and rise against the law, when they see magistrates and bailies, and deacons, and the provost himsell, wi' heads as bald and as bare as ane o' my blocks!'

'And as well furnished within, Caxon. But away with you—you have an excellent view of public affairs, and, I dare say, have touched the cause of our popular discontent as closely as the provost could have done himself. But away with you, Caxon.'

And off went Caxon upon his walk of three miles—

> 'He hobbled—but his heart was good;
> Could he go faster than he could?'—*

While he is engaged in his journey and return, it may not be impertinent to inform the reader to whose mansion he was bearing his embassy.

We have said that Mr Oldbuck kept little company with the surrounding gentlemen, excepting with one person only. This was Sir Arthur Wardour, a baronet of ancient descent, and of a large but embarrassed fortune. His father, Sir Anthony, had been a Jacobite, and had displayed all the enthusiasm of that party, while it could be served with words only. No man squeezed the orange* with more significant gesture; no one could more dexterously intimate a dangerous health* without coming under the penal statutes; and, above all, none drank success to the cause more deeply and devoutly. But, on the approach of the Highland army in 1745, it would appear that the worthy baronet's zeal became a little more moderate just when its warmth was of most consequence. He talked much, indeed, of taking the field for the rights of Scotland and Charles Stewart;* but his demi-pique saddle would suit only one of his horses, and that horse could by no means be brought to stand fire. Perhaps the worshipful owner sympathized in the scruples of this sagacious quadruped, and began to think, that what was so much dreaded by the horse could not be very wholesome for the rider. At any rate, while Sir Anthony Wardour talked, and drank, and hesitated, the sturdy provost of Fairport (who, as we before noticed, was the father of our Antiquary) sallied from his ancient burgh, heading a body of whigburghers, and seized at once, in the name of George II., upon the Castle of Knockwinnock, and on the four carriage-horses, and person of the proprietor. Sir Anthony was shortly after sent off to the Tower of London by a secretary of state's warrant, and with him went his son, Arthur, then a youth. But as nothing appeared like an overt act of treason, both father and son were soon set at liberty, and returned to their own mansion of Knockwinnock, to drink healths five fathoms deep, and talk of their sufferings in the royal cause. This became so much a matter of habit with Sir Arthur, that, even after his father's death, the non-juring chaplain* used to pray regularly for the restoration of the rightful sovereign, for the downfall of the usurper, and for deliverance from their cruel and bloodthirsty enemies; although all idea of serious opposition to the house of Hanover had long mouldered away, and this treasonable liturgy was kept up rather as a matter of form than as conveying any distinct meaning. So much was this the case, that, about the year 1770, upon a disputed election occurring in the county, the worthy knight fairly gulped down the oaths of abjuration and allegiance,* in order to serve a candidate in whom he was interested;—thus renouncing the heir for whose restoration he weekly petitioned Heaven, and acknowledging the usurper, whose dethronement he had never ceased to pray for. And to add to this melancholy instance of human inconsistency, Sir Arthur continued to pray for the house of Stewart even after the family had been extinct,* and when, in truth, though in his theoretical loyalty he was pleased to regard them as alive, yet, in all actual service and practical exertion, he was a most zealous and devoted subject of George III.

In other respects, Sir Arthur Wardour lived like most country gentlemen in Scotland—hunted and fished—gave and received dinners—attended races and county meetings—was a deputy-lieutenant and trustee upon turnpike acts.* But, in his more advanced years, as he became too lazy or unwieldy for field-sports, he supplied them by now and then reading Scottish history; and, having gradually acquired a taste for antiquities, though neither very deep nor very correct, he became a crony of his neighbour, Mr Oldbuck of Monkbarns, and a joint labourer with him in his antiquarian pursuits.

There were, however, points of difference between these two humourists, which sometimes occasioned discord. The faith of Sir Arthur, as an antiquary, was boundless, and Mr Oldbuck (notwithstanding the affair of the Prætorium at the Kaim of Kinprunes) was much more scrupulous in receiving legends as current and authentic coin. Sir Arthur would have deemed himself guilty of the crime of leze-majesty had he doubted the existence of any single individual of that formidable bead-roll of one hundred and four kings of Scotland, received by Boethius, and rendered classical by Buchanan,* in virtue of whom James VI. claimed to rule his ancient kingdom, and whose portraits still frown grimly upon the walls of the gallery of Holyrood.* Now Oldbuck, a shrewd and suspicious man, and no respecter of divine hereditary right,* was apt to cavil at this sacred list, and to affirm, that the procession of the posterity of Fergus* through the pages of Scottish history, was as vain and unsubstantial as the gleamy pageant of the descendants of Banquo through the cavern of Hecate.*

Another tender topic, was the good fame of Queen Mary,* of which the knight was a most chivalrous assertor, while the esquire impugned it, in spite both of her beauty and misfortunes. When, unhappily, their conversation turned on yet later times, motives of discord occurred in almost every page of history. Oldbuck was upon principle a stanch Presbyterian, a ruling elder of the kirk,* and a friend to revolution principles and Protestant succession,* while Sir Arthur was the very reverse of all this. They agreed, it is true, in dutiful love and allegiance to the sovereign who now fills[5] the throne, but this was their only point of union. It therefore often happened, that bickerings hot broke out between them, in which Oldbuck was not always able to suppress his caustic humour, while it would sometimes occur to the Baronet, that the descendant of a German printer, whose sires had 'sought the base fellowship of paltry burghers,'* forgot himself, and took an unlicensed freedom of debate, considering the rank and ancient descent of his antagonist. This, with the old feud of the coach-horses, and the seizure of his manor-place and tower of strength by Mr Oldbuck's father, would at times rush upon his mind, and inflame at once his cheeks and his arguments. And, lastly, as Mr Oldbuck thought his worthy friend and compeer was, in some respects, little better than a fool, he was apt to come more near communicating to him that unfavourable opinion, than the rules of modern politeness warrant. In such cases, they often parted in deep dudgeon, and with something like a resolution to forbear each other's company in future:

'But with the morning calm reflection came;'

and as each was sensible that the society of the other had become, through habit, essential to his comfort, the breach was speedily made up between them. On such occasions, Oldbuck, considering that the

Baronet's pettishness resembled that of a child, usually showed his superior sense by compassionately making the first advances to reconciliation. But it once or twice happened, that the aristocratic pride of the far-descended knight took a flight too offensive to the feelings of the representative of the typographer. In these cases, the breach between these two originals might have been immortal, but for the kind exertions and interposition of the Baronet's daughter, Miss Isabella Wardour, who, with a son, now absent upon foreign and military service, formed his whole surviving family. She was well aware how necessary Mr Oldbuck was to her father's amusement and comfort, and seldom failed to interpose with effect, when the office of a mediator between them was rendered necessary, by the satirical shrewdness of the one, or the assumed superiority of the other. Under Isabella's mild influence, the wrongs of Queen Mary were forgotten by her father, and Mr Oldbuck forgave the blasphemy which reviled the memory of King William.* However, as she used in general to take her father's part playfully in these disputes, Oldbuck was wont to call Isabella his fair enemy, though in fact he made more account of her than any other of her sex, of whom, as we have seen, he was no admirer.

There existed another connexion betwixt these worthies, which had alternately a repelling and attractive influence upon their intimacy. Sir Arthur always wished to borrow; Mr Oldbuck was not always willing to lend. Mr Oldbuck, per contra,* always wished to be repaid with regularity; Sir Arthur was not always, nor indeed often, prepared to gratify this reasonable desire; and, in accomplishing an arrangement between tendencies so opposite, little *miffs* would occasionally take place. Still there was a spirit of mutual accommodation upon the whole, and they dragged on like dogs in couples, with some difficulty and occasional snarling, but without absolutely coming to a stand-still or throttling each other.

Some little disagreement, such as we have mentioned, arising out of business, or politics, had divided the houses of Knockwinnock and Monkbarns, when the emissary of the latter arrived to discharge his errand. In his ancient Gothic parlour, whose windows on one side looked out upon the restless ocean, and, on the other, upon the long straight avenue, was the Baronet seated, now turning over the leaves of a folio, now casting a weary glance where the sun quivered on the dark-green foliage and smooth trunks of the large and branching limes, with which the avenue was planted. At length, sight of joy! a moving object is seen, and it gives rise to the usual inquiries, Who is it? and what can be his errand? The old whitish grey coat, the hobbling gait, the hat, half-slouched, half-cocked, announced the forlorn maker of periwigs, and left for investigation only the second query. This was soon solved by a servant entering the parlour,—'A letter from Monkbarns, Sir Arthur.'

Sir Arthur took the epistle with a due assumption of consequential dignity.

'Take the old man into the kitchen, and let him get some refreshment,' said the young lady, whose compassionate eye had remarked his thin grey hair and wearied gait.

'Mr Oldbuck, my love, invites us to dinner on Tuesday the 17th,' said the Baronet, pausing; 'he really seems to forget that he has not of late conducted himself so civilly towards me as might have been expected.'

'Dear sir, you have so many advantages over poor Mr Oldbuck, that no wonder it should put him a little out of humour; but I know he has much respect for your person and your conversation; nothing would give him more pain than to be wanting in any real attention.'

'True, true, Isabella; and one must allow for the original descent: something of the German boorishness still flows in the blood; something of the whiggish and perverse opposition to established rank and privilege. You may observe that he never has any advantage of me in dispute, unless when he avails himself of a sort of pettifogging intimacy with dates, names, and trifling matters of fact, a tiresome and frivolous accuracy of memory which is entirely owing to his mechanical descent.'

'He must find it convenient in historical investigation, I should think, sir?' said the young lady.

'It leads to an uncivil and positive mode of disputing; and nothing seems more unreasonable than to hear him impugn even Bellenden's rare translation of Hector Boece,* which I have the satisfaction to possess, and which is a black-letter folio of great value, upon the authority of some old scrap of parchment which he has saved from its deserved destiny of being cut up into tailors' measures. And, besides, that habit of minute and troublesome accuracy leads to a mercantile manner of doing business, which ought to be beneath a landed proprietor, whose family has stood two or three

generations—I question if there's a dealer's clerk in Fairport that
can sum an account of interest* better than Monkbarns.'

'But you'll accept his invitation, sir?'

'Why, ye—yes; we have no other engagement on hand, I think.
Who can the young man be he talks of? he seldom picks up new
acquaintance; and he has no relation that I ever heard of.'

'Probably some relation of his brother-in-law, Captain M'Intyre.'

'Very possibly; yes, we will accept; the M'Intyres are of a very
ancient Highland family. You may answer his card in the affirmative,
Isabella; I believe I have no leisure to be *Dear Sirring* myself.'

So this important matter being adjusted, Miss Wardour intimated
'her own and Sir Arthur's compliments, and that they would have
the honour of waiting upon Mr Oldbuck. Miss Wardour takes this
opportunity to renew her hostility with Mr Oldbuck, on account of
his late long absence from Knockwinnock, where his visits give so
much pleasure.' With this *placebo* she concluded her note, with
which old Caxon, now refreshed in limbs and wind, set out on his
return to the Antiquary's mansion.

CHAPTER VI

Moth. By Woden, God of Saxons,
From whence comes Wensday; that is Wodnesday,
Truth is a thing that I will ever keep
Unto thylke day in which I creep into
My sepulcre————

CARTWRIGHT'S *Ordinary*.*

OUR young friend, Lovel, who had received a corresponding invitation, punctual to the hour of appointment, arrived at Monkbarns about five minutes before four o'clock on the 17th of July. The day had been remarkably sultry, and large drops of rain had occasionally fallen, though the threatened showers had as yet passed away.

Mr Oldbuck received him at the Palmer's-port in his complete brown suit, grey silk stockings, and wig powdered with all the skill of the veteran Caxon, who, having smelt out the dinner, had taken care not to finish his job till the hour of eating approached.

'You are welcome to my symposion, Mr Lovel; and now let me introduce you to my Clogdogdo's, as Tom Otter calls them; my unlucky and good-for-nothing womankind—*malæ bestiæ*,* Mr Lovel.'

'I shall be disappointed, sir, if I do not find the ladies very undeserving of your satire.'

'Tilley-valley, Mr Lovel,—which, by the way, one commentator derives from *tittivillitium*, and another from *talley-ho*—but tilley-valley, I say, a truce with your politeness. You will find them but samples of womankind—But here they be, Mr Lovel. I present to you, in due order, my most discreet sister Griselda, who disdains the simplicity, as well as patience, annexed to the poor old name of Grizzel;* and my most exquisite niece Maria, whose mother was called Mary, and sometimes Molly.'

The elderly lady rustled in silks and satins, and bore upon her head a structure resembling the fashion in the ladies' memorandum-book* for the year 1770—a superb piece of architecture—not much less than a modern Gothic castle, of which the curls might represent the turrets, the black pins the *chevaux de frize*, and the lappets the banners.

The face, which, like that of the ancient statues of Vesta,* was thus crowned with towers, was large and long, and peaked at nose and chin, and bore, in other respects, such a ludicrous resemblance to the physiognomy of Mr Jonathan Oldbuck, that Lovel, had they not appeared at once, like Sebastian and Viola in the last scene of the 'Twelfth Night,'* might have supposed that the figure before him was his old friend masquerading in female attire. An antique flowered silk gown graced the extraordinary person to whom belonged this unparalleled *tête*, which her brother was wont to say was fitter for a turban for Mahound or Termagant,* than a head-gear for a reasonable creature, or Christian gentlewoman. Two long and bony arms were terminated at the elbows by triple blond ruffles, and, being folded saltire-ways in front of her person, and decorated with long gloves of a bright vermilion colour, presented no bad resemblance to a pair of gigantic lobsters. High-heeled shoes, and a short silk cloak, thrown in easy negligence over her shoulders, completed the exterior of Miss Griselda Oldbuck.

Her niece, the same whom Lovel had seen transiently during his first visit, was a pretty young woman, genteelly dressed according to the fashion of the day, with an air of *espièglerie* which became her very well, and which was perhaps derived from the caustic humour peculiar to her uncle's family, though softened by transmission.

Mr Lovel paid his respects to both ladies, and was answered by the elder with the prolonged curtsey of 1760, drawn from the righteous period,

> When folks conceived a grace
> Of half an hour's space,
>   And rejoiced in a Friday's capon,*

and by the younger with a modern reverence, which, like the festive benediction of a modern divine, was of much shorter duration.

While this salutation was exchanging, Sir Arthur, with his fair daughter hanging upon his arm, having dismissed his chariot, appeared at the garden door, and in all due form paid his respects to the ladies.

'Sir Arthur,' said the Antiquary, 'and you, my fair foe, let me make known to you my young friend Mr Lovel, a gentleman who, during the scarlet-fever which is epidemic at present in this our island, has the virtue and decency to appear in a coat of a civil complexion.* You see, however, that the fashionable colour has mustered in his cheeks which appears not in his garments. Sir Arthur, let me present to you a young gentleman, whom your farther knowledge will find grave, wise, courtly, and scholar-like, well seen, deeply read, and thoroughly grounded, in all the hidden mysteries of the green-room and stage, from the days of Davie Lindsay* down to those of Dibdin*—he blushes again, which is a sign of grace.'

'My brother,' said Miss Griselda, addressing Lovel, 'has a humorous way of expressing himself, sir; nobody thinks any thing of what Monkbarns says—so I beg you will not be so confused for the matter of his nonsense; but you must have had a warm walk beneath this broiling sun—would you take ony thing?—a glass of balm wine?'

Ere Lovel could answer, the Antiquary interposed. 'Aroint thee, witch!* wouldst thou poison my guests with thy infernal decoctions? Dost thou not remember how it fared with the clergyman whom you seduced to partake of that deceitful beverage?'

'O fy, fy, brother—Sir Arthur, did you ever hear the like!—he must have every thing his ain way, or he will invent such stories—But there goes Jenny to ring the old bell to tell us that the dinner is ready.'

Rigid in his economy, Mr Oldbuck kept no male-servant. This he disguised under the pretext that the masculine sex was too noble to be employed in those acts of personal servitude, which, in all early periods of society, were uniformly imposed on the female. 'Why,' would he say, 'did the boy, Tam Rintherout, whom, at my wise sister's instigation, I, with equal wisdom, took upon trial—why did he pilfer apples, take birds' nests, break glasses, and ultimately steal my spectacles, except that he felt that noble emulation which swells in the bosom of the masculine sex, which has conducted him to Flanders* with a musket on his shoulder, and doubtless will promote him to a glorious halbert, or even to the gallows? And why does this girl, his full sister, Jenny Rintherout, move in the same vocation with safe and noiseless step—shod, or unshod—soft as the pace of a cat, and docile as a spaniel—Why? but because she is in her vocation. Let them minister to us, Sir Arthur,—let them minister, I say,—it's the only thing they are fit for. All ancient legislators, from Lycurgus* to Mahommed,* corruptly called Mahomet, agree in putting them in their proper and subordinate rank, and it is only the crazy heads of our old chivalrous ancestors that erected their Dulcineas* into despotic princesses.'

Miss Wardour protested loudly against this ungallant doctrine; but the bell now rung for dinner.

'Let me do all the offices of fair courtesy to so fair an antagonist,' said the old gentleman, offering his arm. 'I remember, Miss Wardour, Mahommed (vulgarly Mahomet) had some hesitation about the mode of summoning his Moslemah to prayer. He rejected bells as used by Christians, trumpets as the summons of the Guebres,* and finally adopted the human voice. I have had equal doubt concerning my dinner-call. Gongs, now in present use, seemed a newfangled and heathenish invention, and the voice of the female womankind I rejected as equally shrill and dissonant; wherefore, contrary to the said Mahommed, or Mahomet, I have resumed the bell. It has a local propriety, since it was the conventual signal for spreading the repast in their refectory, and it has the advantage over the tongue of my sister's prime minister, Jenny, that, though not quite so loud and shrill, it ceases ringing the instant you drop the bell-rope; whereas we know, by sad experience, that any attempt to silence Jenny, only wakes the sympathetic chime of Miss Oldbuck and Mary M'Intyre to join in chorus.'

With this discourse he led the way to his dining parlour, which Lovel had not yet seen; it was wainscotted, and contained some curious paintings. The dining-table was attended by Jenny; but an old superintendent, a sort of female butler, stood by the side-board, and underwent the burden of bearing several reproofs from Mr Oldbuck, and innuendos, not so much marked, but not less cutting, from his sister.

The dinner was such as suited a professed antiquary, comprehending many savoury specimens of Scottish viands, now disused at the tables of those who affect elegance. There was the relishing Solan goose,* whose smell is so powerful that he is never cooked within doors. Blood-raw he proved to be on this occasion, so that Oldbuck half-threatened to throw the greasy sea-fowl at the head of the negligent housekeeper, who acted as priestess in presenting this odoriferous offering. But, by good-hap, she had been most fortunate in the hotch-potch, which was unanimously pronounced to be inimitable. 'I knew we should succeed here,' said Oldbuck exultingly, 'for Davie Dibble, the gardener, (an old bachelor like myself,) takes care the rascally women do not dishonour our vegetables. And here is fish and sauce, and crappit-heads—I acknowledge our womankind excel in that dish—it procures them the pleasure of scolding, for half an hour at least, twice a-week, with auld Maggy Mucklebackit, our fish-wife. The chicken-pie, Mr Lovel, is made after a recipe bequeathed to me by my departed grandmother of happy memory—And if you will venture on a glass of wine, you will find it worthy of one who professes the maxim of King Alphonso of Castile—Old wood to burn—old books to read—old wine to drink*—and old friends, Sir Arthur—ay, Mr Lovel, and young friends too, to converse with.'

'And what news do you bring us from Edinburgh, Monkbarns?' said Sir Arthur; 'how wags the world* in Auld Reekie?'*

'Mad, Sir Arthur, mad—irretrievably frantic—far beyond dipping in the sea, shaving the crown, or drinking hellebore.* The worst sort of frenzy, a military frenzy, hath possessed man, woman, and child.'

'And high time, I think,' said Miss Wardour, 'when we are threatened with invasion from abroad, and insurrection at home.'

'O, I did not doubt you would join the scarlet host against me—women, like turkeys, are always subdued by a red rag—But what says Sir Arthur, whose dreams are of standing armies and German oppression?'*

'Why, I say, Mr Oldbuck,' replied the knight, 'that, so far as I am capable of judging, we ought to resist *cum toto corpore regni*,*—as the phrase is, unless I have altogether forgotten my Latin—an enemy who comes to propose to us a Whiggish sort of government, a republican system, and who is aided and abetted by a sort of fanatics of the worst kind in our own bowels. I have taken some measures, I assure you, such as become my rank in the community; for I have directed the constables to take up that old scoundrelly beggar, Edie Ochiltree, for spreading disaffection against church and state through the whole parish. He said plainly to old Caxon, that Willie Howie's Kilmarnock cowl* covered more sense than all the three wigs in the parish—I think it is easy to make out that innuendo—But the rogue shall be taught better manners.'

'O no, my dear sir,' exclaimed Miss Wardour, 'not old Edie, that we have known so long—I assure you no constable shall have my good graces that executes such a warrant.'

'Ay, there it goes,' said the Antiquary; 'you, to be a stanch Tory,

Sir Arthur, have nourished a fine sprig of Whiggery in your bosom—Why, Miss Wardour is alone sufficient to control a whole quarter-session—a quarter-session? ay, a general assembly or convocation* to boot—a Boadicea, she—an Amazon, a Zenobia.'*

'And yet, with all my courage, Mr Oldbuck, I am glad to hear our people are getting under arms.'

'Under arms, Lord love thee! didst thou ever read the history of Sister Margaret,* which flowed from a head, that, though now old and somedele grey, has more sense and political intelligence than you find now-a-days in a whole synod? Dost thou remember the Nurse's dream in that exquisite work, which she recounts in such agony to Hubble Bubble?—When she would have taken up a piece of broad cloth in her vision, lo! it exploded like a great iron cannon; when she put out her hand to save a pirn, it perked up in her face in the form of a pistol. My own vision in Edinburgh has been something similar. I called to consult my lawyer; he was clothed in a dragoon's dress, belted and casqued, and about to mount a charger, which his writing-clerk (habited as a sharp-shooter) walked to and fro before his door—I went to scold my agent for having sent me to advise with a madman; he had stuck into his head the plume, which in more sober days he wielded between his fingers, and figured as an artillery-officer. My mercer had his spontoon in his hand, as if he measured his cloth by that implement, instead of a legitimate yard. The banker's clerk, who was directed to sum my cashaccount, blundered it three times, being disordered by the recollection of his military *tellings-off* at the morning drill. I was ill, and sent for a surgeon—

> He came—but valour so had fired his eye,
> And such a falchion glitter'd on his thigh,
> That, by the gods, with such a load of steel,
> I thought he came to murder,—not to heal!*

I had recourse to a physician, but he also was practising a more wholesale mode of slaughter than that which his profession had been supposed at all times to open to him. And now, since I have returned here, even our wise neighbours of Fairport have caught the same valiant humour. I hate a gun like a hurt wild-duck—I detest a drum like a quaker;*—and they thunder and rattle out yonder upon the town's common, so that every volley and roll goes to my very heart.'

'Dear brother, dinna speak that gate o' the gentlemen

volunteers—I am sure they have a most becoming uniform—Weel I
wot they have been wet to the very skin twice last week—I met them
marching in terribly doukit, an mony a sair hoast was amang them—
And the trouble they take, I am sure it claims our gratitude.'

'And I am sure,' said Miss M'Intyre, 'that my uncle sent twenty
guineas to help out their equipments.'

'It was to buy liquorice and sugar-candy,' said the cynic, 'to
encourage the trade of the place, and to refresh the throats of the
officers who had bawled themselves hoarse in the service of their
country.'

'Take care, Monkbarns! we shall set you down among the black-
nebs by and by.'

'No, Sir Arthur, a tame grumbler I. I only claim the privilege of
croaking in my own corner here, without uniting my throat to the
grand chorus of the marsh*—*Ni quito Rey, ni pongo Rey*—I neither
make king nor mar king, as Sancho says,* but pray heartily for our
own sovereign, pay scot and lot,* and grumble at the exciseman—But
here comes the ewe-milk cheese in good time; it is a better digestive
than politics.'

When dinner was over, and the decanters placed on the table, Mr
Oldbuck proposed the King's health in a bumper, which was readily
acceded to both by Lovel and the Baronet, the Jacobitism of the
latter being now a sort of speculative opinion merely,—the shadow
of a shade.

After the ladies had left the apartment, the landlord and Sir
Arthur entered into several exquisite discussions, in which the
younger guest, either on account of the abstruse erudition which
they involved, or for some other reason, took but a slender share, till
at length he was suddenly started out of a profound reverie by an
unexpected appeal to his judgment.

'I will stand by what Mr Lovel says; he was born in the north of
England, and may know the very spot.'

Sir Arthur thought it unlikely that so young a gentleman should
have paid much attention to matters of that sort.

'I am avised of the contrary,' said Oldbuck.—'How say you, Mr
Lovel?—speak up, for your own credit, man.'

Lovel was obliged to confess himself in the ridiculous situation of
one, alike ignorant of the subject of conversation and controversy
which had engaged the company for an hour.

'Lord help the lad, his head has been wool-gathering!—I thought how it would be when the womankind were admitted—no getting a word of sense out of a young fellow for six hours after. Why, man, there was once a people called the Piks'—

'More properly *Picts*,' interrupted the Baronet.

'I say the *Pikar, Pihar, Piochtar, Piaghter,* or *Peughtar*,' vociferated Oldbuck; 'they spoke a Gothic dialect'—

'Genuine Celtic,' again asseverated the knight.

'Gothic! Gothic, I'll go to death upon it!' counter-asseverated the squire.

'Why, gentlemen,' said Lovel, 'I conceive that is a dispute which may be easily settled by philologists, if there are any remains of the language.'

'There is but one word,' said the Baronet, 'but, in spite of Mr Oldbuck's pertinacity, it is decisive of the question.'

'Yes, in my favour,' said Oldbuck: 'Mr Lovel, you shall be judge— I have the learned Pinkerton* on my side.'

'I, on mine, the indefatigable and erudite Chalmers.'*

'Gordon* comes into my opinion.'

'Sir Robert Sibbald* holds mine.'

'Innes* is with me!' vociferated Oldbuck.

'Ritson* has no doubt!' shouted the Baronet.

'Truly, gentlemen,' said Lovel, 'before you muster your forces and overwhelm me with authorities, I should like to know the word in dispute.'

'*Benval*,' said both the disputants at once.

'Which signifies *caput valli*,' said Sir Arthur.

'The head of the wall,' echoed Oldbuck.

There was a deep pause.—'It is rather a narrow foundation to build a hypothesis upon,' observed the arbiter.

'Not a whit, not a whit,' said Oldbuck; 'men fight best in a narrow ring—an inch is as good as a mile for a home-thrust.'

'It is decidedly Celtic,' said the Baronet; 'every hill in the Highlands begins with *Ben*.'

'But what say you to *Val*, Sir Arthur—is it not decidedly the Saxon *wall*?'

'It is the Roman *vallum*,' said Sir Arthur; 'the Picts borrowed that part of the word.'

'No such thing; if they borrowed any thing, it must have been your

Ben, which they might have from the neighbouring Britons of Strath Cluyd.'

'The Piks, or Picts,' said Lovel, 'must have been singularly poor in dialect, since, in the only remaining word of their vocabulary, and that consisting only of two syllables, they have been confessedly obliged to borrow one of them from another language; and, methinks, gentlemen, with submission, the controversy is not unlike that which the two knights fought, concerning the shield that had one side white and the other black. Each of you claim one-half of the word, and seem to resign the other. But what strikes me most, is the poverty of the language which has left such slight vestiges behind it.'

'You are in an error,' said Sir Arthur; 'it was a copious language, and they were a great and powerful people—built two steeples; one at Brechin, one at Abernethy. The Pictish maidens of the blood-royal were kept in Edinburgh Castle, thence called *Castrum Puellarum.*'*

'A childish legend,' said Oldbuck, 'invented to give consequence to trumpery womankind. It was called the Maiden Castle, *quasi lucus a non lucendo*,* because it resisted every attack, and women never do.'

'There is a list of the Pictish kings,' persisted Sir Arthur, 'well . authenticated, from Crentheminachcryme (the date of whose reign is somewhat uncertain) down to Drusterstone, whose death concluded their dynasty. Half of them have the Celtic patronymic *Mac* prefixed—*Mac, id est filius**—what do you say to that, Mr Oldbuck? There is Drust Macmorachin, Trynel Maclachlin, (first of that ancient clan, as it may be judged,) and Gormach Macdonald, Alpin Macmetegus, Drust Mactallargam, (here he was interrupted by a fit of coughing,) ugh, ugh, ugh—Golarge Macchan—ugh, ugh—Macchanan—ugh Macchananail—Kenneth—ugh,—ugh—Macferedith, Eachan Macfungus—and twenty more, decidedly Celtic names, which I could repeat, if this damned cough would let me.'

'Take a glass of wine, Sir Arthur, and drink down that bead-roll of unbaptized jargon, that would choke the devil—why, that last fellow has the only intelligible name you have repeated—they are all of the tribe of Macfungus—mushroom monarchs every one of them; sprung up from the fumes of conceit, folly, and falsehood, fermenting in the brains of some mad Highland seannachie.'

'I am surprised to hear you, Mr Oldbuck; you know, or ought to know, that the list of these potentates was copied, by Henry Maule* of Melgum, from the Chronicles of Loch-Leven and Saint Andrews,* and put forth by him in his short but satisfactory history of the Picts, printed by Robert Freebairn of Edinburgh, and sold by him at his shop in the Parliament-close, in the year of God seventeen hundred and five, or six, I am not precisely certain which—but I have a copy at home that stands next to my twelvemo copy of the Scots Acts, and ranges on the shelf with them very well—What say you to that, Mr Oldbuck?'

'Say? Why, I laugh at Harry Maule and his history,' answered Oldbuck, 'and thereby comply with his request, of giving it entertainment according to its merits.'

'Do not laugh at a better man than yourself,' said Sir Arthur, somewhat scornfully.

'I do not conceive I do, Sir Arthur, in laughing either at him or his history.'

'Henry Maule of Melgum was a gentleman, Mr Oldbuck.'

'I presume he had no advantage of me in *that* particular,' replied the Antiquary, somewhat tartly.

'Permit me, Mr Oldbuck—he was a gentleman of high family, and ancient descent, and therefore'——

'The descendant of a Westphalian printer should speak of him with deference?—Such may be your opinion, Sir Arthur—it is not mine. I conceive that my descent from that painful and industrious typographer, Wolfbrand Oldenbuck, who, in the month of December, 1493, under the patronage, as the colophon tells us, of Sebaldus Scheyter and Sebastian Kammermaister, accomplished the printing of the great Chronicle of Nuremberg*—I conceive, I say, that my descent from that great restorer of learning is more creditable to me as a man of letters, than if I had numbered in my generalogy all the brawling, bullet-headed, iron-fisted, old Gothic barons since the days of Crentheminachcryme—not one of whom, I suppose, could write his own name.'

'If you mean the observation as a sneer at my ancestry,' said the knight, with an assumption of dignified superiority and composure, 'I have the pleasure to inform you, that the name of my ancestor, Gamelyn de Guardover, Miles,* is written fairly with his own hand in the earliest copy of the Ragman-roll.'*

'Which only serves to show that he was one of the earliest who set the mean example of submitting to Edward I. What have you to say for the stainless loyalty of your family, Sir Arthur, after such a backsliding as that?'

'It's enough, sir,' said Sir Arthur, starting up fiercely, and pushing back his chair, 'I shall hereafter take care how I honour with my company, one who shows himself so ungrateful for my condescension.'

'In that you will do as you find most agreeable, Sir Arthur; I hope, that, as I was not aware of the extent of the obligation which you have done me, by visiting my poor house, I may be excused for not having carried my gratitude to the extent of servility.'

'Mighty well—mighty well, Mr Oldbuck—I wish you a good evening—Mr a—a—a—Shovel—I wish you a very good evening.'

Out of the parlour door flounced the incensed Sir Arthur, as if the spirit of the whole Round Table* inflamed his single bosom, and traversed with long strides the labyrinth of passages which conducted to the drawing-room.

'Did you ever hear such an old tup-headed ass?' said Oldbuck, briefly apostrophizing Lovel; 'but I must not let him go in this mad-like way neither.'

So saying, he pushed off after the retreating Baronet, whom he traced by the clang of several doors which he opened in search of the apartment for tea, and slammed with force behind him at every disappointment. 'You'll do yourself a mischief,' roared the Antiquary; '*Qui ambulat in tenebris, nescit quo vadit*—You'll tumble down the back-stair.'

Sir Arthur had now got involved in darkness, of which the sedative effect is well known to nurses and governesses who have to deal with pettish children. It retarded the pace of the irritated Baronet, if it did not abate his resentment, and Mr Oldbuck, better acquainted with the *locale*, got up with him as he had got his grasp upon the handle of the drawing-room door.

'Stay a minute, Sir Arthur,' said Oldbuck, opposing his abrupt entrance; 'don't be quite so hasty, my good old friend—I was a little too rude with you about Sir Gamelyn—why, he is an old acquaintance of mine, man, and a favourite—he kept company with Bruce and Wallace*—and, I'll be sworn on a black-letter Bible, only subscribed the Ragman-roll with the legitimate and justifiable intention of circumventing the false Southern—'twas right Scottish craft, my good knight—hundreds did it—come, come, forget and forgive—confess we have given the young fellow here a right to think us two testy old fools.'

'Speak for yourself, Mr Jonathan Oldbuck,' said Sir Arthur, with much majesty.

'A-well, a-well—a wilful man must have his way.'

With that the door opened, and into the drawing-room marched the tall gaunt form of Sir Arthur, followed by Lovel and Mr Oldbuck, the countenances of all three a little discomposed.

'I have been waiting for you, sir,' said Miss Wardour, 'to propose we should walk forward to meet the carriage, as the evening is so fine.'

Sir Arthur readily assented to this proposal, which suited the angry mood in which he found himself; and having, agreeably to the established custom in cases of pet, refused the refreshment of tea and coffee, he tucked his daughter under his arm; and, after taking a ceremonious leave of the ladies, and a very dry one of Oldbuck—off he marched.

'I think Sir Arthur has got the black dog* on his back again,' said Miss Oldbuck.

'Black dog!—black devil!—he's more absurd than womankind—What say you, Lovel?—Why, the lad's gone too.'

'He took his leave, uncle, while Miss Wardour was putting on her things; but I don't think you observed him.'

'The devil's in the people! This is all one gets by fussing and bustling, and putting one's self out of one's way in order to give dinners, besides all the charges they are put to.—O Seged, Emperor of Ethiopia!' said he, taking up a cup of tea in the one hand, and a volume of the Rambler* in the other,—for it was his regular custom to read while he was eating or drinking in presence of his sister, being a practice which served at once to evince his contempt for the society of womankind, and his resolution to lose no moment of instruction,—-'O Seged, Emperor of Ethiopia! well hast thou spoken—No man should presume to say, This shall be a day of happiness.'

Oldbuck proceeded in his studies for the best part of an hour, uninterrupted by the ladies, who each, in profound silence, pursued some female employment. At length, a light and modest tap was heard at the parlour door. 'Is that you, Caxon?—come in, come in, man.'

The old man opened the door, and, thrusting in his meagre face, thatched with thin grey locks, and one sleeve of his white coat, said in a subdued and mysterious tone of voice, 'I was wanting to speak to you, sir.'

'Come in then, you old fool, and say what you have got to say.'

'I'll maybe frighten the ladies,' said the ex-friseur.

'Frighten!' answered the Antiquary, 'What do you mean?—never mind the ladies. Have you seen another ghaist at the Humlock-know?'

'Na, sir; it's no a ghaist this turn,' replied Caxon—'but I'm no easy in my mind.'

'Did you ever hear of any body that was?' answered Oldbuck; 'what reason has an old battered powder-puff like you to be easy in your mind, more than all the rest of the world besides?'

'It's no for mysell, sir; but it threatens an awfu' night; and Sir Arthur, and Miss Wardour, poor thing'—

'Why, man, they must have met the carriage at the head of the loaning, or thereabouts; they must be home long ago.'

'Na, sir; they didna gang the road by the turnpike to meet the carriage, they gaed by the sands.'

The word operated like electricity on Oldbuck. 'The sands!' he exclaimed; 'impossible!'

'Ou, sir, that's what I said to the gardener; but he says he saw them turn down by the Musselcraig—in troth, says I to him, an that be the case, Davie, I am misdoubting'—

'An almanack! an almanack!' said Oldbuck, starting up in great alarm—'not that bauble!' flinging away a little pocket almanack which his niece offered him—'Great God! my poor dear Miss Isabella!—Fetch me instantly the Fairport Almanack.'—It was brought, consulted, and added greatly to his agitation. 'I'll go myself—call the gardener and ploughman—bid them bring ropes and ladders—bid them raise more help as they come along—keep the top of the cliffs, and halloo down to them—I'll go myself.'

'What is the matter?' inquired Miss Oldbuck and Miss M'Intyre.

'The tide!—the tide!' answered the alarmed Antiquary.

'Had not Jenny better—but no, I'll run myself,' said the younger lady, partaking in all her uncle's terrors—'I'll run myself to Saunders Mucklebackit, and make him get out his boat.'

'Thank you, my dear, that's the wisest word that has been spoken yet—run! run! To go by the sands!' seizing his hat and cane; 'was there ever such madness heard of!'

CHAPTER VII

───────────Pleased awhile to view
The watery waste, the prospect wild and new;
The now receding waters gave them space,
On either side, the growing shores to trace;
And then, returning, they contract the scene,
Till small and smaller grows the walk between.

                              CRABBE.*

THE information of Davie Dibble, which had spread such general alarm at Monkbarns, proved to be strictly correct. Sir Arthur and his daughter had set out, according to their first proposal, to return to Knockwinnock by the turnpike road; but, when they reached the head of the loaning, as it was called, or great lane, which on one side made a sort of avenue to the house of Monkbarns, they discerned a little way before them, Lovel, who seemed to linger on the way as if to give him an opportunity to join them. Miss Wardour immediately proposed to her father that they should take another direction; and, as the weather was fine, walk home by the sands, which, stretching below a picturesque ridge of rocks, afforded at almost all times a pleasanter passage between Knockwinnock and Monkbarns than the high-road.

Sir Arthur acquiesced willingly. 'It would be unpleasant,' he said, 'to be joined by that young fellow, whom Mr Oldbuck had taken the freedom to introduce them to.' And his old-fashioned politeness had none of the ease of the present day, which permits you, if you have a mind, to *cut* the person you have associated with for a week, the instant you feel or suppose yourself in a situation which makes it disagreeable to own him. Sir Arthur only stipulated, that a little ragged boy, for the guerdon of one penny sterling, should run to meet his coachman, and turn his equipage back to Knockwinnock.

When this was arranged, and the emissary dispatched, the knight and his daughter left the high-road, and, following a wandering path among sandy hillocks, partly grown over with furze and the long grass called bent, soon attained the side of the ocean. The tide was by no means so far out as they had computed; but this gave them no alarm; there were seldom ten days in the year when it approached so near the cliffs as not to leave a dry passage. But, nevertheless, at periods of spring-tide, or even when the ordinary flood was accelerated by high winds, this road was altogether covered by the sea; and tradition had recorded several fatal accidents which had happened on such occasions. Still, such dangers were considered as remote and improbable; and rather served, with other legends, to amuse the hamlet fireside, than to prevent any one from going between Knockwinnock and Monkbarns by the sands.

As Sir Arthur and Miss Wardour paced along, enjoying the pleasant footing afforded by the cool moist hard sand, Miss Wardour could not help observing, that the last tide had risen considerably above the usual water-mark. Sir Arthur made the same observation, but without its occurring to either of them to be alarmed at the circumstance. The sun was now resting his huge disk upon the edge of the level ocean, and gilded the accumulation of towering clouds through which he had travelled the livelong day, and which now assembled on all sides, like misfortunes and disasters around a sinking empire, and falling monarch. Still, however, his dying splendour gave a sombre magnificence to the massive congregation of vapours, forming out of their unsubstantial gloom, the show of pyramids and towers, some touched with gold, some with purple, some with a hue of deep and dark red. The distant sea, stretched beneath this varied and gorgeous canopy, lay almost portentously still, reflecting back the dazzling and level beams of the descending luminary, and the splendid colouring of the clouds amidst which he was setting. Nearer to the beach, the tide rippled onward in waves of sparkling silver, that imperceptibly, yet rapidly, gained upon the sand.

With a mind employed in admiration of the romantic scene, or perhaps on some more agitating topic, Miss Wardour advanced in silence by her father's side, whose recently offended dignity did not stoop to open any conversation. Following the windings of the beach, they passed one projecting point or headland of rock after another, and now found themselves under a huge and continued extent of the precipices by which that iron-bound coast is in most places defended. Long projecting reefs of rock, extending under water, and only evincing their existence by here and there a peak entirely bare, or by the breakers which foamed over those that were partially covered, rendered Knockwinnock bay dreaded by pilots and ship-masters. The crags which rose between the beach and the mainland, to the height of two or three hundred feet, afforded in their crevices shelter for unnumbered sea-fowl, in situations seemingly secured by their dizzy height from the rapacity of man. Many of these wild tribes, with the instinct which sends them to seek the land before a storm arises, were now winging towards their nests with the shrill and dissonant clang which announces disquietude and fear. The disk of the sun became almost totally obscured ere he had altogether sunk below the horizon, and an early and lurid shade of darkness blotted the serene twilight of a summer evening. The wind began next to arise; but its wild and moaning sound was heard for some time, and its effects became visible on the bosom of the sea, before the gale was felt on shore. The mass of waters, now dark and threatening, began to lift itself in larger ridges, and sink in deeper furrows, forming waves that rose high in foam upon the breakers, or burst upon the beach with a sound resembling distant thunder.

Appalled by this sudden change of weather, Miss Wardour drew close to her father, and held his arm fast. 'I wish,' at length she said, but almost in a whisper, as if ashamed to express her increasing apprehensions, 'I wish we had kept the road we intended, or waited at Monkbarns for the carriage.'

Sir Arthur looked round, but did not see, or would not acknowledge, any signs of an immediate storm. They would reach Knockwinnock, he said, long before the tempest began. But the speed with which he walked, and with which Isabella could hardly keep pace, indicated a feeling that some exertion was necessary to accomplish his consolatory prediction.

They were now near the centre of a deep but narrow bay, or recess, formed by two projecting capes of high and inaccessible rock, which shot out into the sea like the horns of a crescent; and neither durst communicate the apprehension which each began to entertain, that, from the unusually rapid advance of the tide, they might be deprived of the power of proceeding by doubling the promontory which lay before them, or of retreating by the road which brought them thither.

As they thus pressed forward, longing doubtless to exchange the easy curving line, which the sinuosities of the bay compelled them to adopt, for a straighter and more expeditious path, though less comformable to the line of beauty,* Sir Arthur observed a human figure on the beach advancing to meet them. 'Thank God,' he exclaimed, 'we shall get round Halket-head! that person must have passed it;' thus giving vent to the feeling of hope, though he had suppressed that of apprehension.

'Thank God indeed!' echoed his daughter, half audibly, half internally, as expressing the gratitude which she strongly felt.

The figure which advanced to meet them made many signs, which the haze of the atmosphere, now disturbed by wind and by a drizzling rain, prevented them from seeing or comprehending distinctly. Some time before they met, Sir Arthur could recognise the old blue-gowned beggar, Edie Ochiltree. It is said that even the brute creation lay aside their animosities and antipathies when pressed by an instant and common danger. The beach under Halket-head, rapidly diminishing in extent by the encroachments of a spring-tide and a north-west wind, was in like manner a neutral field, where even a justice of peace and a strolling mendicant might meet upon terms of mutual forbearance.

'Turn back! turn back!' exclaimed the vagrant; 'why did ye not turn when I waved to you?'

'We thought,' replied Sir Arthur, in great agitation, 'we thought we could get round Halket-head.'

'Halket-head! The tide will be running on Halket-head, by this time, like the Fall of Fyers!* It was a' I could do to get round it twenty minutes since—it was coming in three feet abreast. We will maybe get back by Bally-burgh Ness Point yet. The Lord help us, it's our only chance. We can but try.'

'My God, my child!'—'My father, my dear father!' exclaimed the parent and daughter, as, fear lending them strength and speed, they turned to retrace their steps, and endeavoured to double the point, the projection of which formed the southern extremity of the bay.

'I heard ye were here, frae the bit callant ye sent to meet your carriage,' said the beggar, as he trudged stoutly on a step or two behind Miss Wardour, 'and I couldna bide to think o' the dainty young leddy's peril, that has aye been kind to ilka forlorn heart that cam near her. Sae I lookit at the lift and the rin o' the tide, till I settled it that if I could get down time eneugh to gie you warning, we wad do weel yet. But I doubt, I doubt, I have been beguiled! for what mortal ee ever saw sic a race as the tide is rinning e'en now? See, yonder's the Ratton's Skerry—he aye held his neb abune the water in my day—but he's aneath it now.'

Sir Arthur cast a look in the direction in which the old man pointed. A huge rock, which in general, even in spring-tides, displayed a hulk like the keel of a large vessel, was now quite under water, and its place only indicated by the boiling and breaking of the eddying waves which encountered its submarine resistance.

'Mak haste, mak haste, my bonny leddy,' continued the old man, 'mak haste, and we may do yet! Take haud o' my arm—an auld and frail arm it's now, but it's been in as sair stress as this is yet. Take haud o' my arm, my winsome leddy! D'ye see yon wee black speck amang the wallowing waves yonder? This morning it was as high as the mast o' a brig—it's sma' eneugh now—but, while I see as muckle black about it as the crown o' my hat, I winna believe but we'll get round the Bally-burgh Ness, for a' that's come and gane yet.'

Isabella, in silence, accepted from the old man the assistance which Sir Arthur was less able to afford her. The waves had now encroached so much upon the beach, that the firm and smooth footing which they had hitherto had on the sand must be exchanged for a rougher path close to the foot of the precipice, and in some places even raised upon its lower ledges. It would have been utterly impossible for Sir Arthur Wardour, or his daughter, to have found their way along these shelves without the guidance and encouragement of the beggar, who had been there before in high tides, though never, he acknowledged, 'in sae awsome a night as this.'

It was indeed a dreadful evening. The howling of the storm mingled with the shrieks of the seafowl, and sounded like the dirge of the three devoted beings, who, pent between two of the most magnificent, yet most dreadful objects of nature—a raging tide and an insurmountable precipice—toiled along their painful and dangerous path, often lashed by the spray of some giant billow, which threw itself higher on the beach than those that had preceded it. Each minute did their enemy gain ground perceptibly upon them! Still, however, loath to relinquish the last hopes of life, they bent their eyes on the black rock pointed out by Ochiltree. It was yet distinctly visible among the breakers, and continued to be so, until they came to a turn in their precarious path, where an intervening projection of rock hid it from their sight. Deprived of the view of the beacon on which they had relied, they now experienced the double agony of terror and suspense. They struggled forward, however; but, when they arrived at the point from which they ought to have seen the crag, it was no longer visible. The signal of safety was lost among a thousand white breakers, which, dashing upon the point of the promontory, rose in prodigious sheets of snowy foam, as high as the mast of a first-rate man-of-war,* against the dark brow of the precipice.

The countenance of the old man fell. Isabella gave a faint shriek, and, 'God have mercy upon us!' which her guide solemnly uttered, was piteously echoed by Sir Arthur—'My child! my child!—to die such a death!'

'My father! my dear father!' his daughter exclaimed, clinging to him,—'and you too, who have lost your own life in endeavouring to save ours!'

'That's not worth the counting,' said the old man. 'I hae lived to be weary o' life; and here or yonder—at the back o' a dyke, in a wreath o' snaw, or in the wame o' a wave, what signifies how the auld gaberlunzie dies?'

'Good man,' said Sir Arthur, 'can you think of nothing?—of no help?—I'll make you rich—I'll give you a farm—I'll'—

'Our riches will be soon equal,' said the beggar, looking out upon the strife of the waters—'they are sae already; for I hae nae land, and you would give your fair bounds and barony for a square yard of rock that would be dry for twal hours.'

While they exchanged these words, they paused upon the highest ledge of rock to which they could attain; for it seemed that any further attempt to move forward could only serve to anticipate their fate. Here, then, they were to await the sure though slow progress of the raging element, something in the situation of the martyrs of the early church, who, exposed by heathen tyrants to be slain by wild beasts, were compelled for a time to witness the impatience and rage by which the animals were agitated, while awaiting the signal for undoing their grates, and letting them loose upon the victims.

Yet even this fearful pause gave Isabella time to collect the powers of a mind naturally strong and courageous, and which rallied itself at this terrible juncture. 'Must we yield life,' she said, 'without a struggle? Is there no path, however dreadful, by which we could climb the crag, or at least attain some height above the tide, where we could remain till morning, or till help comes? They must be aware of our situation, and will raise the country to relieve us.'

Sir Arthur, who heard, but scarcely comprehended, his daughter's

question, turned, nevertheless, instinctively and eagerly to the old
man, as if their lives were in his gift. Ochiltree paused. 'I was a bauld
craigsman,' he said, 'ance in my life, and mony a kittywake's and
lungie's nest hae I harried up amang thae very black rocks; but it's
lang, lang syne, and nae mortal could speel them without a rope—
and if I had ane, my ee-sight, and my footstep, and my hand-grip,
hae a' failed mony a day sinsyne—and then how could I save *you?*—
But there was a path here ance, though maybe, if we could see it, ye
would rather bide where we are—His name be praised!' he ejaculated suddenly, 'there's ane coming down the crag e'en now!'—
Then, exalting his voice, he hilloa'd out to the daring adventurer
such instructions as his former practice, and the remembrance of
local circumstances, suddenly forced upon his mind:—'Ye're right—
ye're right!—that gate, that gate!—fasten the rope weel round
Crummie's-horn, that's the muckle black stane—cast twa plies
round it—that's it!—now, weize yoursell a wee easel-ward—a wee
mair yet to that ither stane—we ca'd it the Cat's-lug—there used to
be the root o' an aik-tree there—that will do!—canny now, lad—
canny now—tak tent and tak time—Lord bless ye, tak time.—Vera
weel!—Now ye maun get to Bessy's Apron, that's the muckle braid
flat blue stane—and then, I think, wi' your help and the tow thegither, I'll win at ye, and then we'll be able to get up the young leddy
and Sir Arthur.'

The adventurer, following the directions of old Edie, flung him
down the end of the rope, which he secured around Miss Wardour,
wrapping her previously in his own blue gown, to preserve her as
much as possible from injury. Then, availing himself of the rope,
which was made fast at the other end, he began to ascend the face of
the crag—a most precarious and dizzy undertaking, which, however,
after one or two perilous escapes, placed him safe on the broad flat
stone beside our friend Lovel. Their joint strength was able to raise
Isabella to the place of safety which they had attained. Lovel then
descended in order to assist Sir Arthur, around whom he adjusted
the rope; and again mounting to their place of refuge, with the
assistance of old Ochiltree, and such aid as Sir Arthur himself could
afford, he raised himself beyond the reach of the billows.

The sense of reprieve from approaching and apparently inevitable
death, had its usual effect. The father and daughter threw themselves into each other's arms, kissed and wept for joy, although their

escape was connected with the prospect of passing a tempestuous night upon a precipitous ledge of rock, which scarce afforded footing for the four shivering beings, who now, like the sea-fowl around them, clung there in hopes of some shelter from the devouring element which raged beneath. The spray of the billows, which attained in fearful succession the foot of the precipice, overflowing the beach on which they so lately stood, flew as high as their place of temporary refuge; and the stunning sound with which they dashed against the rocks beneath, seemed as if they still demanded the fugitives in accents of thunder as their destined prey. It was a summer night doubtless; yet the probability was slender, that a frame so delicate as that of Miss Wardour should survive till morning the drenching of the spray; and the dashing of the rain, which now burst in full violence, accompanied with deep and heavy gusts of wind, added to the constrained and perilous circumstances of their situation.

'The lassie—the puir sweet lassie,' said the old man; 'mony such a night have I weathered at hame and abroad, but, God guide us, how can she ever win through it!'

His apprehension was communicated in smothered accents to Lovel; for, with the sort of free-masonry by which bold and ready spirits correspond in moments of danger, and become almost instinctively known to each other, they had established a mutual confidence.—'I'll climb up the cliff again,' said Lovel, 'there's daylight enough left to see my footing; I'll climb up, and call for more assistance.'

'Do so, do so, for heaven's sake!' said Sir Arthur eagerly.

'Are ye mad?' said the mendicant; 'Francie o' Fowlsheugh, and he was the best craigsman that ever speel'd heugh, (mair by token, he brake his neck upon the Dunbuy of Slaines,)* wadna hae ventured upon the Halket-head craigs after sun-down—It's God's grace, and a great wonder besides, that ye are not in the middle o' that roaring sea wi' what ye hae done already—I didna think there was the man left alive would hae come down the craigs as ye did. I question an I could hae done it mysell, at this hour and in this weather, in the youngest and yaldest of my strength—But to venture up again—it's a mere and a clear tempting o' Providence.'

'I have no fear,' answered Lovel; 'I marked all the stations perfectly as I came down, and there is still light enough left to see them quite well—I am sure I can do it with perfect safety. Stay here, my good friend, by Sir Arthur and the young lady.'

'Deil be in my feet then,' answered the bedesman sturdily; 'if ye gang, I'll gang too; for between the twa o'us, we'll hae mair than wark eneugh to get to the tap o' the heugh.'

'No, no—stay you here and attend to Miss Wardour—you see Sir Arthur is quite exhausted.'

'Stay yoursell then, and I'll gae,' said the old man; 'let death spare the green corn and take the ripe.'

'Stay both of you, I charge you,' said Isabella, faintly, 'I am well, and can spend the night very well here—I feel quite refreshed.' So saying, her voice failed her—she sunk down, and would have fallen from the crag, had she not been supported by Lovel and Ochiltree, who placed her in a posture half sitting, half reclining, beside her father, who, exhausted by fatigue of body and mind so extreme and unusual, had already sat down on a stone in a sort of stupor.

'It is impossible to leave them,' said Lovel—'What is to be done?—Hark! hark!—Did I not hear a halloo?'

'The skriegh of a Tammie Norie,' answered Ochiltree, 'I ken the skirl weel.'

'No, by Heaven,' replied Lovel, 'it was a human voice.'

A distant hail was repeated, the sound plainly distinguishable among the various elemental noises, and the clang of the sea-mews by which they were surrounded. The mendicant and Lovel exerted their voices in a loud halloo, the former waving Miss Wardour's handkerchief on the end of his staff to make them conspicuous from above. Though the shouts were repeated, it was some time before they were in exact response to their own, leaving the unfortunate sufferers uncertain whether, in the darkening twilight and increasing storm, they had made the persons who apparently were traversing the verge of the precipice to bring them assistance, sensible of the place in which they had found refuge. At length their halloo was regularly and distinctly answered, and their courage confirmed, by the assurance that they were within hearing, if not within reach, of friendly assistance.

CHAPTER VIII

There is a cliff, whose high and bending head
Looks fearfully on the confined deep;
Bring me but to the very brim of it,
And I'll repair the misery thou dost bear.

*King Lear.**

THE shout of human voices from above was soon augmented, and the gleam of torches mingled with those lights of evening which still remained amidst the darkness of the storm. Some attempt was made to hold communication between the assistants above, and the sufferers beneath, who were still clinging to their precarious place of safety; but the howling of the tempest limited their intercourse to cries, as inarticulate as those of the winged denizens of the crag, which shrieked in chorus, alarmed by the reiterated sound of human voices, where they had seldom been heard.

On the verge of the precipice an anxious group had now assembled. Oldbuck was the foremost and most earnest, pressing forward with unwonted desperation to the very brink of the crag, and extending his head (his hat and wig secured by a handkerchief under his chin) over the dizzy height, with an air of determination which made his more timorous assistants tremble.

'Haud a care, haud a care, Monkbarns,' cried Caxon, clinging to the skirts of his patron, and withholding him from danger as far as his strength permitted—'God's sake, haud a care!—Sir Arthur's drowned already, and an ye fa' over the cleugh too, there will be but ae wig left in the parish, and that's the minister's.'

'Mind the peak there,' cried Mucklebackit, an old fisherman and smuggler—'mind the peak—Steenie, Steenie Wilks, bring up the tackle—I'se warrant we'll sune heave them on board, Monkbarns, wad ye but stand out o' the gate.'

'I see them,' said Oldbuck, 'I see them low down on that flat stone—Hilli-hilloa, hilli-ho-a!'

'I see them mysell weel eneugh,' said Mucklebackit; 'they are sitting down yonder like hoodie-craws in a mist; but d'ye think ye'll help them wi' skirling that gate like an auld skart before a flaw o' weather?—Steenie, lad, bring up the mast—Odd, I'se hae them up as we used to bouse up the kegs o' gin and brandy lang syne*—Get up the pick-axe, make a step for the mast—make the chair fast with the rattlin—haul taught and belay!'

The fishers had brought with them the mast of a boat, and as half of the country fellows about had now appeared, either out of zeal or curiosity, it was soon sunk in the ground, and sufficiently secured. A yard, across the upright mast, and a rope stretched along it, and reeved through a block at each end, formed an extempore crane, which afforded the means of lowering an arm-chair, well secured and fastened, down to the flat shelf on which the sufferers had roosted. Their joy at hearing the preparations going on for their deliverance was considerably qualified when they beheld the precarious vehicle, by means of which they were to be conveyed to upper air. It swung about a yard free of the spot which they occupied, obeying each impulse of the tempest, the empty air all around it, and depending upon the security of a rope, which, in the increasing darkness, had dwindled to an almost imperceptible thread. Besides the hazard of committing a human being to the vacant atmosphere in such a slight means of conveyance, there was the fearful danger of the chair and its occupant being dashed, either by the wind or the vibrations of the cord, against the rugged face of the precipice. But to diminish the risk as much as possible, the experienced seamen had let down with the chair another line, which, being attached to it, and held by the persons beneath, might serve by way of *gy*, as Mucklebackit expressed it, to render its descent in some measure steady and regular. Still, to commit one's self in such a vehicle, through a howling tempest of wind and rain, with a beetling precipice above, and a raging abyss below, required that courage which despair alone can inspire. Yet wild as the sounds and sights of danger were, both above, beneath, and around, and doubtful and dangerous as the mode of escaping appeared to be, Lovel and the old mendicant agreed, after a moment's consultation, and after the former, by a sudden strong pull, had, at his own imminent risk, ascertained the security of the rope, that it would be best to secure Miss Wardour in the chair, and trust to the tenderness and care of those above for her being safely craned up to the top of the crag.

'Let my father go first,' exclaimed Isabella; 'for God's sake, my friends, place him first in safety.'

'It cannot be, Miss Wardour,' said Lovel; 'your life must be first secured—the rope which bears your weight may'—

'I will not listen to a reason so selfish!'

'But ye maun listen to it, my bonny lassie,' said Ochiltree, 'for a' our lives depend on it—besides, when ye get on the tap o' the heugh yonder, ye can gie them a round guess o' what's ganging on in this Patmos* o' ours—and Sir Arthur's far by that, as I am thinking.'

Struck with the truth of this reasoning, she exclaimed, 'True, most true; I am ready and willing to undertake the first risk—What shall I say to our friends above?'

'Just to look that their tackle does not graze on the face o' the craig, and to let the chair down, and draw it up hooly and fairly—we will halloo when we are ready.'

With the sedulous attention of a parent to a child, Lovel bound Miss Wardour with his handkerchief, neckcloth, and the mendicant's leathern belt, to the back and arms of the chair, ascertaining accurately the security of each knot, while Ochiltree kept Sir Arthur quiet. 'What are ye doing wi' my bairn?—What are ye doing?—She shall not be separated from me—Isabel, stay with me, I command you.'

'Lordsake, Sir Arthur, haud your tongue, and be thankful to God that there's wiser folk than you to manage this job,' cried the beggar, worn out by the unreasonable exclamations of the poor Baronet.

'Farewell, my father,' murmured Isabella—'farewell, my—my friends;' and, shutting her eyes, as Edie's experience recommended, she gave the signal to Lovel, and he to those who were above. She rose, while the chair in which she sate was kept steady by the line which Lovel managed beneath. With a beating heart he watched the flutter of her white dress, until the vehicle was on a level with the brink of the precipice.

'Canny now, lads, canny now!' exclaimed old Mucklebackit, who acted as commodore; 'swerve the yard a bit—Now—there! there she sits safe on dry land!'

A loud shout announced the successful experiment to her fellow-sufferers beneath, who replied with a ready and cheerful halloo. Monkbarns, in his ecstasy of joy, stripped his great-coat to wrap up the young lady, and would have pulled off his coat and waistcoat for the same purpose, had he not been withheld by the cautious Caxon. 'Haud a care o' us, your honour will be killed wi' the hoast—ye'll no

get out o' your night-cowl this fortnight—and that will suit us unco
ill.—Na, na,—there's the chariot down by, let twa o' the folk carry
the young leddy there.'

'You're right,' said the Antiquary, re-adjusting the sleeves and
collar of his coat, 'you're right, Caxon; this is a naughty night to
swim in.*—Miss Wardour, let me convey you to the chariot.'

'Not for worlds, till I see my father safe.'

In a few distinct words, evincing how much her resolution had
surmounted even the mortal fear of so agitating a hazard, she
explained the nature of the situation beneath, and the wishes of
Lovel and Ochiltree.

'Right, right, that's right too—I should like to see the son of Sir
Gamelyn de Guardover on dry land myself—I have a notion he
would sign the abjuration oath, and the Ragman-roll to boot, and
acknowledge Queen Mary to be nothing better than she should be, to
get alongside my bottle of old port that he ran away from, and left
scarce begun. But he's safe now, and here a' comes—(for the chair
was again lowered, and Sir Arthur made fast in it, without much
consciousness on his own part)—here a' comes—bowse away, my
boys—canny wi' him—a pedigree of a hundred links is hanging on a
tenpenny tow—the whole barony of Knockwinnock depends on
three plies of hemp—*respice finem, respice funem*—look to your end—
look to a rope's end.—Welcome, welcome, my good old friend, to
firm land, though I cannot say to warm land or to dry land—a cord
for ever against fifty fathom of water, though not in the sense of the
base proverb*—a fico for the phrase—better *sus. per funem*, than *sus.
per coll.*'*

While Oldbuck ran on in this way, Sir Arthur was safely wrapped
in the close embraces of his daughter, who, assuming that authority
which the circumstances demanded, ordered some of the assistants
to convey him to the chariot, promising to follow in a few minutes.
She lingered on the cliff, holding an old countryman's arm, to
witness probably the safety of those whose dangers she had shared.

'What have we here?' said Oldbuck, as the vehicle once more
ascended. 'What patched and weather-beaten matter is this?' Then,
as the torches illumined the rough face and grey hairs of old
Ochiltree,—'What! is it thou?—come, old Mocker,* I must needs be
friends with thee—but who the devil makes up your party besides?'

'Ane that's weel worth ony twa o' us, Monkbarns—it's the young stranger lad they ca' Lovel—and he's behaved this blessed night, as if he had three lives to rely on, and was willing to waste them a' rather than endanger ither folk's—Ca' hooly, sirs, as ye wad win an auld man's blessing!—mind there's naebody below now to haud the gy—Hae a care o' the Cat's-lug-corner—bide weel aff Crummie's-horn!'

'Have a care indeed,' echoed Oldbuck; 'What! is it my *rara avis**— my black swan—my phœnix of companions in a post-chaise?—take care of him, Mucklebackit.'

'As muckle care as if he were a greybeard o' brandy; and I canna take mair if his hair were like John Harlowe's.—Yo ho, my hearts, bowse away with him!'

Lovel did, in fact, run a much greater risk than any of his precursors. His weight was not sufficient to render his ascent steady amid such a storm of wind, and he swung like an agitated pendulum at the mortal risk of being dashed against the rocks. But he was young, bold, and active, and, with the assistance of the beggar's stout piked staff, which he had retained by advice of the proprietor, contrived to bear himself from the face of the precipice, and the yet more hazardous projecting cliffs which varied its surface. Tossed in empty space, like an idle and unsubstantial feather, with a motion that agitated the brain at once with fear and with dizziness, he retained his alertness of exertion and presence of mind; and it was not until he was safely grounded upon the summit of the cliff, that he felt temporary and giddy sickness. As he recovered from a sort of half swoon, he cast his eyes eagerly around. The object which they would most willingly have sought, was already in the act of vanishing. Her white garment was just discernible as she followed on the path which her father had taken. She had lingered till she saw the last of their company rescued from danger, and until she had been assured by the hoarse voice of Mucklebackit, that 'the callant had come off wi' unbrizzed banes, and that he was but in a kind of dwam.' But Lovel was not aware that she had expressed in his fate even this degree of interest, which, though nothing more than was due to a stranger who had assisted her in such an hour of peril, he would have gladly purchased by braving even more imminent danger than he had that evening been exposed to. The beggar she had already commanded to come to Knockwinnock that night. He made an excuse,—'Then tomorrow let me see you.'

The old man promised to obey. Oldbuck thrust something into his hand—Ochiltree looked at it by the torch-light, and returned it.—'Na, na! I never tak gowd—besides, Monkbarns, ye wad maybe be rueing it the morn.' Then turning to the group of fishermen and peasants,—'Now, sirs, wha will gie me a supper and some clean pease-strae?'

'I,' 'and I,' 'and I,' answered many a ready voice.

'Aweel, since sae it is, and I can only sleep in ae barn at ance, I'll gae down wi' Saunders Mucklebackit—he has aye a soup o' something comfortable about his bigging—and, bairns, I'll maybe live to put ilka ane o' ye in mind some ither night that ye hae promised me quarters and my awmous;' and away he went with the fisherman.

Oldbuck laid the hand of strong possession on Lovel—'Deil a stride ye's go to Fairport this night, young man—you must go home with me to Monkbarns.—Why, man, you have been a hero—a perfect Sir William Wallace by all accounts.—Come, my good lad, take hold of my arm—I am not a prime support in such a wind—but Caxon shall help us out—Here, you old idiot, come on the other side of me.—And how the deil got you down to that infernal Bessy's-apron, as they call it?—Bess, said they—why, curse her, she has spread out that vile pennon or banner of womankind, like all the rest of her sex, to allure her votaries to death and head-long ruin.'

'I have been pretty well accustomed to climbing, and I have long observed fowlers practise that pass down the cliff.'

'But how, in the name of all that is wonderful, came you to discover the danger of the pettish Baronet and his far more deserving daughter?'

'I saw them from the verge of the precipice.'

'From the verge!—umph—And what possessed you, *dumosa pendere procul de rupe?**—though *dumosa* is not the appropriate epithet—What the deil, man, tempted ye to the verge of the craig?'

'Why—I like to see the gathering and growling of a coming storm—or, in your own classical language, Mr Oldbuck, *suave mari magno**—and so forth—but here we reach the turn to Fairport. I must wish you good night.'

'Not a step, not a pace, not an inch, not a shathmont, as I may say; the meaning of which word has puzzled many that think themselves antiquaries. I am clear we should read *salmon-length* for *shathmont's-length*. You are aware that the space allotted for the passage of a salmon through a dam, dike, or wier, by statute, is the length within which a full-grown pig can turn himself round—now I have a scheme to prove, that, as terrestrial objects were thus appealed to for ascertaining submarine measurement, so it must be supposed that the productions of the water were established as gages of the extent of land.—Shathmont—salmont—you see the close alliance of the sounds; dropping out two *h*'s and a *t*, and assuming an *l*, makes the whole difference—I wish to Heaven no antiquarian derivation had demanded heavier concessions.'

'But, my dear sir, I really must go home—I am wet to the skin.'

'Shalt have my night-gown, man, and slippers, and catch the antiquarian fever as men do the plague, by wearing infected garments—nay, I know what you would be at—you are afraid to put the old bachelor to charges. But is there not the remains of that glorious chicken-pie—which, *meo arbitrio,** is better cold than hot—and that bottle of my oldest port, out of which the silly brain-sick Baronet (whom I cannot pardon, since he has escaped breaking his neck) had just taken one glass, when his infirm noddle went a wool-gathering after Gamelyn de Guardover?'

So saying, he dragged Lovel forward, till the Palmer's-port of Monkbarns received them. Never, perhaps, had it admitted two pedestrians more needing rest; for Monkbarns's fatigue had been in a degree very contrary to his usual habits, and his more young and robust companion had that evening undergone agitation of mind which had harassed and wearied him even more than his extraordinary exertions of body.

CHAPTER IX

> 'Be brave,' she cried, 'you yet may be our guest,
> Our haunted room was ever held the best.
> If, then, your valour can the sight sustain
> Of rustling curtains and the clinking chain;
> If your courageous tongue have powers to talk,
> When round your bed the horrid ghost shall walk;
> If you dare ask it why it leaves its tomb,
> I'll see your sheets well air'd, and show the room.'
>
> *True Story.**

THEY reached the room in which they had dined, and were clamorously welcomed by Miss Oldbuck.

'Where's the younger womankind?' said the Antiquary.

'Indeed, brother, amang a' the steery, Maria wadna be guided by me—she set away to the Halket-craig-head—I wonder ye didna see her.'

'Eh!—what—what's that you say, sister?—did the girl go out in a night like this to the Halket-head?—Good God! the misery of the night is not ended yet!'

'But ye winna wait, Monkbarns—ye are so imperative and impatient'—

'Tittle-tattle, woman,' said the impatient and agitated Antiquary, 'where is my dear Mary?'

'Just where ye suld be yoursell, Monkbarns—up-stairs, and in her warm bed.'

'I could have sworn it,' said Oldbuck, laughing, but obviously much relieved, 'I could have sworn it—the lazy monkey did not care if we were all drowned together—why did you say she went out?'

'But ye wadna wait to hear out my tale, Monkbarns—she gaed out, and she came in again with the gardener sae sune as she saw that nane o' ye were clodded ower the craig, and that Miss Wardour was safe in the chariot—she was hame a quarter of an hour syne, for it's now ganging ten—sair droukit was she, puir thing, sae I e'en put a glass o' sherry in her water-gruel.'

'Right, Grizel, right—let womankind alone for coddling each other. But hear ye, my venerable sister—Start not at the word venerable; it implies many praise-worthy qualities besides age; though that too is honourable, albeit it is the last quality for which womankind would wish to be honoured—but perpend my words; let Lovel and me have forthwith the relics of the chicken-pie, and the reversion of the port.'

'The chicken-pie—the port—ou dear! brother—there was but a wheen banes, and scarce a drap o' the wine.'

The Antiquary's countenance became clouded, though he was too well bred to give way, in the presence of a stranger, to his displeased surprise at the disappearance of the viands on which he had reckoned with absolute certainty. But his sister understood these looks of ire. 'Ou dear! Monkbarns, what's the use of making a wark?'

'I make no wark, as ye call it, woman.'

'But what's the use o' looking sae glum and glunch about a pickle banes?—an ye will hae the truth, ye maun ken the minister came in, worthy man—sair distressed he was, nae doubt, about your precaurious situation, as he ca'd it, (for ye ken how weel he's gifted wi' words,) and here he wad bide till he could hear wi' certainty how the matter was likely to gang wi' ye a'—He said fine things on the duty of resignation to Providence's will, worthy man! that did he.'

Oldbuck replied, catching the same tone, 'Worthy man!—he cared not how soon Monkbarns had devolved on an heir female, I've a notion—and while he was occupied in this Christian office of consolation against impending evil, I reckon that the chicken-pie and my good port disappeared?'

'Dear brother, how can you speak of sic frivolities, when you have had sic an escape from the craig?'

'Better than my supper has had from the minister's *craig*, Grizzie—it's all discussed, I suppose?'

'Hout, Monkbarns, ye speak as if there was nae mair meat in the house—wad ye not have had me offer the honest man some slight refreshment after his walk frae the manse?'

Oldbuck half-whistled, half-hummed, the end of the old Scottish ditty,

> 'O, first they eated the white puddings,
> And then they eated the black, O,
> And thought the gudeman unto himself,
> The deil clink down wi' that, O!'*

His sister hastened to silence his murmurs, by proposing some of
the relics of the dinner. He spoke of another bottle of wine, but
recommended in preference a glass of brandy which was really excellent. As no entreaties could prevail on Lovel to indue the velvet
night-cap and branched morning-gown of his host, Oldbuck, who
pretended to a little knowledge of the medical art, insisted on his
going to bed as soon as possible, and proposed to dispatch a messenger (the indefatigable Caxon) to Fairport early in the morning, to
procure him a change of clothes.

This was the first intimation Miss Oldbuck had received that the
young stranger was to be their guest for the night; and such was the
surprise with which she was struck by a proposal so uncommon,
that, had the superincumbent weight of her head-dress, such as we
before described, been less preponderant, her grey locks must have
started up on end, and hurled it from its position.

'Lord haud a care o' us!' exclaimed the astounded maiden.

'What's the matter now, Grizel?'

'Wad ye but just speak a moment, Monkbarns?'

'Speak!—What should I speak about?—I want to get to my bed—
and this poor young fellow—let a bed be made ready for him
instantly.'

'A bed?—The Lord preserve us,' again ejaculated Grizel.

'Why, what's the matter now? are there not beds and rooms
enough in the house? Was it not an ancient *hospitium*, in which I am
warranted to say, beds were nightly made down for a score of
pilgrims?'

'O dear, Monkbarns! wha kens what they might do lang syne?—
but in our time—beds—ay, troth, there's beds enow sic as they are—
and rooms enow too—but ye ken yoursell the beds haena been
sleepit in, Lord kens the time, nor the rooms aired.—If I had kenn'd,
Mary and me might hae gane down to the manse—Miss Beckie is
aye fond to see us (and sae is the minister, brother)—But now, gude
save us!'—

'Is there not the Green Room, Grizel?'

'Troth is there, and it is in decent order too, though naebody has
sleepit there since Dr Heavysterne, and'—

'And what?'

'And what! I'm sure ye ken yoursell what a night he had—ye
wadna expose the young gentleman to the like o' that, wad ye?'

Lovel interfered upon hearing this altercation, and protested he would far rather walk home than put them to the least inconvenience—that the exercise would be of service to him—that he knew the road perfectly, by night or day, to Fairport—that the storm was abating, and so forth; adding all that civility could suggest as an excuse for escaping from a hospitality which seemed more inconvenient to his host than he could possibly have anticipated. But the howling of the wind, and pattering of the rain against the windows, with his knowledge of the preceding fatigues of the evening, must have prohibited Oldbuck, even had he entertained less regard for his young friend than he really felt, from permitting him to depart. Besides, he was piqued in honour to show that he himself was not governed by womankind—'Sit ye down, sit ye down, sit ye down, man,' he reiterated; 'an ye part so, I would I might never draw a cork again, and here comes out one from a prime bottle of—strong ale—right *anno domini**—none of your Wassia Quassia* decoctions, but brewed of Monkbarns barley—John of the Girnel never drew a better flagon to entertain a wandering minstrel, or palmer, with the freshest news from Palestine.—And to remove from your mind the slightest wish to depart, know, that if you do so, your character as a gallant knight is gone for ever—Why, 'tis an adventure, man, to sleep in the Green Room at Monkbarns—Sister, pray see it got ready—And, although the bold adventurer, Heavysterne, dree'd pain and dolour in that charmed apartment, it is no reason why a gallant knight like you, nearly twice as tall, and not half so heavy, should not encounter and break the spell.'

'What! a haunted apartment, I suppose?'

'To be sure, to be sure—every mansion in this country of the slightest antiquity has its ghosts and its haunted chamber, and you must not suppose us worse off than our neighbours. They are going, indeed, somewhat out of fashion. I have seen the day when, if you had doubted the reality of the ghost in an old manor-house, you ran the risk of being made a ghost* yourself, as Hamlet says—Yes, if you had challenged the existence of Redcowl in the castle of Glenstirym, old Sir Peter Pepperbrand would have had ye out to his courtyard, made you betake yourself to your weapon, and if your trick of fence were not the better, would have sticked you like a paddock, on his own baronial middenstead. I once narrowly escaped such an affray—but I humbled myself and apologized to Redcowl; for, even in my younger days, I was no friend to the *monomachia*, or duel, and would rather walk with Sir Priest than with Sir Knight,* I care not who knows so much of my valour—thank God I am old now, and can indulge my irritabilities without the necessity of supporting them by cold steel.'

Here Miss Oldbuck re-entered, with a singularly sage expression of countenance. 'Mr Lovel's bed's ready, brother—clean sheets—weel aired—a spunk of fire in the chimney—I am sure, Mr Lovel, (addressing him,) it's no for the trouble—and I hope you will have a good night's rest—But'—

'You are resolved,' said the Antiquary, 'to do what you can to prevent it.'

'Me?—I am sure I have said naething, Monkbarns.'

'My dear madam,' said Lovel, 'allow me to ask you the meaning of your obliging anxiety on my account.'

'Ou, Monkbarns does not like to hear of it—but he kens himself that the room has an ill name. It's weel minded that it was there auld Rab Tull the town-clerk was sleeping when he had that marvellous communication about the grand law-plea between us and the feuars at the Mussel-craig. It had cost a hantle siller, Mr Lovel; for law-pleas were no carried on without siller lang syne mair than they are now—and the Monkbarns of that day—our gudesire, Mr Lovel, as I said before—was like to be waured afore the Session for want of a paper—Monkbarns there kens weel what paper it was, but I'se warrant he'll no help me out wi' my tale—but it was a paper of great significance to the plea, and we were to be waured for want o't. Aweel, the cause was to come on before the fifteen—in presence, as they ca't—and auld Rab Tull, the town-clerk, he cam ower to make a last search for the paper that was wanting, before our gudesire gaed into Edinburgh to look after his plea—so there was little time to come and gang on—He was but a doited snuffy body, Rab, as I've heard—but then he was the town-clerk of Fairport, and the Monkbarns heritors aye employed him on account of their connexion wi' the burgh, ye ken.'

'Sister Grizel, this is abominable,' interrupted Oldbuck; 'I vow to Heaven ye might have raised the ghosts of every abbot of Trotcosey, since the days of Waldimir, in the time you have been detailing the introduction to this single spectre—Learn to be succinct in your narrative—Imitate the concise style of old Aubrey, an experienced ghost-seer, who entered his memoranda on these subjects in a terse business-like manner; *exempli gratia**—"At Cirencester, 5th March, 1670, was an apparition—Being demanded whether good spirit or bad, made no answer, but instantly disappeared with a curious perfume, and a melodious twang."—*Vide* his Miscellanies, p. eighteen, as well as I can remember, and near the middle of the page.'*

'O, Monkbarns, man! do ye think every body is as book-learned as yoursell?—But ye like to gar folk look like fools—ye can do that to Sir Arthur, and the minister his very sell.'

'Nature has been beforehand with me, Grizel, in both these instances, and in another which shall be nameless;—but take a glass of ale, Grizel, and proceed with your story, for it waxes late.'

'Jenny's just warming your bed, Monkbarns, and ye maun e'en wait till she's done.—Weel, I was at the search that our gudesire, Monkbarns that then was, made wi' auld Rab Tull's assistance;—but ne'er-be-licket could they find that was to their purpose. And sae after they had touzled out mony a leather poke-full o' papers, the town-clerk had his drap punch at o'en to wash the dust out of his throat—we never were glass-breakers in this house, Mr Lovel, but the body had got sic a trick of sippling and tippling wi' the bailies and deacons when they met (which was amaist ilka night) concerning the common gude o' the burgh, that he couldna weel sleep without it—But his punch he gat, and to bed he gaed—and in the middle of the night he gat a fearfu' wakening!—he was never just himself after it, and he was strucken wi' the dead palsy* that very day four years—He thought, Mr Lovel, that he heard the curtains o' his bed fissil, and out he lookit, fancying, puir man, it might hae been the cat—But he saw—God hae a care o' us, it gars my flesh aye creep, though I hae tauld the story twenty times—he saw a weel-fa'ard auld gentleman standing by his bedside, in the moonlight, in a queer-fashioned dress, wi' mony a button and band-string about it, and that part o' his garments, which it does not become a leddy to particulareeze, was baith side and wide, and as mony plies o't as of ony Hamburgh skipper's—He had a beard too, and whiskers turned upwards on his upper-lip, as lang as baudron's—and mony mair particulars there were that Rab Tull tauld o', but they are forgotten now—it's an auld story.—Aweel, Rab was a just-living man for a country writer—and he was less fear'd than maybe might just hae been expected—and he asked in the name o' goodness what the apparition wanted—And the spirit answered in an unknown tongue.—Then Rab said he tried him wi' Erse, for he cam in his youth frae the braes of Glenlivat—but it wadna do—Aweel, in this strait, he bethought him of the twa or three words o' Latin, that he used in making out the town's deeds, and he had nae sooner tried the spirit wi' that, than out cam sic a blatter o' Latin about his lugs, that poor Rab Tull, wha was nae great scholar, was clean owerwhelmed. Od, but he was a bauld body, and he minded the Latin name for the deed that he was wanting. It was something about a cart I fancy, for the ghaist cried aye, *Carter, carter'*—

'*Carta*, you transformer of languages,' cried Oldbuck; 'if my ancestor had learned no other language in the other world, at least he would not forget the Latinity for which he was so famous while in this.'

'Weel, weel, *carta* be it then, but they ca'd it *carter* that tell'd me the story—It cried aye *carta*, if sae be that it was *carta*, and made a sign to Rab to follow it. Rab Tull keepit a highland heart, and bang'd out o' bed, and till some of his readiest claes—and he did follow the thing up stairs and down stairs to the place we ca' the high dow-cot, (a sort of a little tower in the corner of the auld house, where there was a rickle o' useless boxes and trunks,) and there the ghaist gae Rab a kick wi' the tae foot, and a kick wi' the tother, to that very auld east-country tabernacle of a cabinet that my brother has standing beside his library table, and then disappeared like a fuff o' tobacco, leaving Rab in a very pitiful condition.'

'*Tenues secessit in auras*,' quoth Oldbuck. 'Marry, sir, *mansit odor**— But, sure enough, the deed was there found in a drawer of this forgotten repository, which contained many other curious old papers, now properly labelled and arranged, and which seem to have belonged to my ancestor, the first possessor of Monkbarns. The deed, thus strangely recovered, was the original Charter of Erection of the Abbey, Abbey Lands, and so forth, of Trotcosey, comprehending Monkbarns and others, into a Lordship of Regality* in favour of the first Earl of Glengibber, a favourite of James the Sixth. It is subscribed by the King at Westminster, the seventeenth day of January, A. D. one thousand six hundred and twelve–thirteen.* It's not worth while to repeat the witnesses' names.'

'I would rather,' said Lovel, with awakened curiosity, 'I would rather hear your opinion of the way in which the deed was discovered.'

'Why, if I wanted a patron for my legend, I could find no less a one than Saint Augustine,* who tells the story of a deceased person appearing to his son, when sued for a debt which had been paid, and directing him where to find the discharge.[6] But I rather opine with Lord Bacon,* who says that imagination is much akin to miracle-working faith. There was always some idle story of the room being haunted by the spirit of Aldobrand Oldenbuck, my great-great-great-grandfather—it's a shame to the English language that we have not a less clumsy way of expressing a relationship, of which we have occasion to think and speak so frequently—he was a foreigner, and wore his national dress, of which tradition had preserved an accurate description; and indeed there is a print of him, supposed to be by Reginald Elstracke,* pulling the press with his own hand, as it works off the sheets of his scarce edition of the Augsburg Confession.* He was a chemist, as well as a good mechanic, and either of these qualities in this country was at that time sufficient to constitute a white witch at least. This superstitious old writer had heard all this, and probably believed it, and in his sleep the image and idea of my ancestor recalled that of his cabinet, which, with the grateful attention to antiquities and the memory of our ancestors not unusually met with, had been pushed into the pigeon-house to be out of the way—Add a *quantum sufficit** of exaggeration, and you have a key to the whole mystery.'

'Oh, brother, brother! But Dr Heavysterne, brother—whose sleep was so sore broken, that he declared he wadna pass another night in the Green Room to get all Monkbarns, so that Mary and I were forced to yield our'—

'Why, Grizel, the doctor is a good, honest, pudding-headed German, of much merit in his own way, but fond of the mystical, like many of his countrymen. You and he had a traffic the whole evening, in which you received tales of Mesmer, Shropfer, Cagliostro,* and other modern pretenders to the mystery of raising spirits, discovering hidden treasure, and so forth, in exchange for your legends of the green bedchamber—and considering that the *Illustrissimus* ate a pound and a half of Scotch collops* to supper, smoked six pipes, and drank ale and brandy in proportion, I am not surprised at his having a fit of the night-mare—But every thing is now ready. Permit me to light you to your apartment, Mr Lovel—I am sure you have need of rest—and I trust my ancestor is too sensible of the duties of hospitality to interfere with the repose which you have so well merited by your manly and gallant behaviour.'

So saying, the Antiquary took up a bedroom candlestick of massive silver and antique form, which, he observed, was wrought out of the silver found in the mines of the Harz mountains, and had been the property of the very personage who had supplied them with a subject for conversation. And having so said, he led the way through many a dusky and winding passage, now ascending and anon descending again, until he came to the apartment destined for his young guest.

CHAPTER X

When midnight o'er the moonless skies
Her pall of transient death has spread,
When mortals sleep, when spectres rise,
And none are wakeful but the dead;
No bloodless shape my way pursues,
No sheeted ghost my couch annoys,
Visions more sad my fancy views,—
Visions of long-departed joys.

W. R. SPENSER.*

WHEN they reached the Green Room, as it was called, Oldbuck placed the candle on the toilet-table, before a huge mirror with a black japanned frame, surrounded by dressing-boxes of the same, and looked around him with something of a disturbed expression of countenance. 'I am seldom in this apartment,' he said, 'and never without yielding to a melancholy feeling—not, of course, on account of the childish nonsense that Grizel was telling you, but owing to circumstances of an early and unhappy attachment. It is at such moments as these, Mr Lovel, that we feel the changes of time. The same objects are before us—those inanimate things which we have gazed on in wayward infancy and impetuous youth, in anxious and scheming manhood—they are permanent and the same; but when we look upon them in cold unfeeling old age, can we, changed in our temper, our pursuits, our feelings,—changed in our form, our limbs, and our strength,—can we be ourselves called the same? or do we not rather look back with a sort of wonder upon our former selves, as beings separate and distinct from what we now are? The philosopher, who appealed from Philip inflamed with wine to Philip in his hours of sobriety,* did not choose a judge so different, as if he had appealed from Philip in his youth to Philip in his old age. I cannot but be touched with the feeling so beautifully expressed in a poem which I have heard repeated;⁷*

My eyes are dim with childish tears,
My heart is idly stirr'd,
For the same sound is in my ears
Which in those days I heard.

> Thus fares it still in our decay;
>   And yet the wiser mind
> Mourns less for what time takes away,
>   Than what he leaves behind.*

Well, time cures every wound, and though the scar may remain and occasionally ache, yet the earliest agony of its recent infliction is felt no more.'—So saying, he shook Lovel cordially by the hand, wished him good night, and took his leave.

Step after step Lovel could trace his host's retreat along the various passages, and each door which he closed behind him fell with a sound more distant and dead. The guest, thus separated from the living world, took up the candle and surveyed the apartment. The fire blazed cheerfully. Mrs Grizel's attention had left some fresh wood, should he choose to continue it, and the apartment had a comfortable, though not a lively appearance. It was hung with tapestry, which the looms of Arras had produced in the sixteenth century, and which the learned typographer, so often mentioned, had brought with him as a sample of the arts of the Continent. The subject was a hunting-piece; and as the leafy boughs of the forest-trees, branching over the tapestry, formed the predominant colour, the apartment had thence acquired its name of the Green Chamber. Grim figures, in the old Flemish dress, with slashed doublets, covered with ribbands, short cloaks, and trunk-hose, were engaged in holding grey-hounds or stag-hounds in the leash, or cheering them upon the objects of their game. Others, with boar-spears, swords, and old-fashioned guns, were attacking stags or boars whom they had brought to bay. The branches of the woven forest were crowded with fowls of various kinds, each depicted with its proper plumage. It seemed as if the prolific and rich invention of old Chaucer had animated the Flemish artist with its profusion, and Oldbuck had accordingly caused the following verses, from that ancient and excellent poet, to be embroidered in Gothic letters, on a sort of border which he had added to the tapestry:—

> Lo! here be oakis grete, streight as a lime,
>   Under the which the grass, so fresh of line,
> Be'th newly sprung—at eight foot or nine.
>   Everich tree well from his fellow grew,
> With branches broad laden with leaves new,

That sprongen out against the sonne sheene,
Some golden red, and some a glad bright green.*

And in another canton was the following similar legend:

And many an hart, and many an hind,
Was both before me and behind.
Of fawns, sownders, bucks, and does
Was full the wood, and many roes,
And many squirrells that ysate
High on the trees and nuts ate.*

The bed was of a dark and faded green, wrought to correspond with the tapestry, but by a more modern and less skilful hand. The large and heavy stuff-bottomed chairs, with black ebony backs, were embroidered after the same pattern, and a lofty mirror, over the antique chimney-piece, corresponded in its mounting with that on the old-fashioned toilet.

'I have heard,' muttered Lovel, as he took a cursory view of the room and its furniture, 'that ghosts often chose the best room in the mansion to which they attached themselves; and I cannot disapprove of the taste of the disembodied printer of the Augsburg Confession.' But he found it so difficult to fix his mind upon the stories which had been told him of an apartment, with which they seemed so singularly to correspond, that he almost regretted the absence of those agitated feelings, half fear half curiosity, which sympathize with the old legends of awe and wonder, from which the anxious reality of his own hopeless passion at present detached him. For he now only felt emotions like those expressed in the lines,—

Ah! cruel maid, how hast thou changed
The temper of my mind!
My heart, by thee from all estranged,
Becomes like thee unkind.*

He endeavoured to conjure up something like the feelings which would, at another time, have been congenial to his situation, but his heart had no room for these vagaries of imagination. The recollection of Miss Wardour, determined not to acknowledge him when compelled to endure his society, and evincing her purpose to escape from it, would have alone occupied his imagination exclusively. But with this were united recollections more agitating if less painful— her hair-breadth escape—the fortunate assistance which he had been

able to render her—Yet, what was his requital?—She left the cliff
while his fate was yet doubtful, while it was uncertain whether her
preserver had not lost the life which he had exposed for her so
freely.—Surely gratitude, at least, called for some little interest in his
fate—But no—she could not be selfish or unjust—it was no part of
her nature. She only desired to shut the door against hope, and, even
in compassion to him, to extinguish a passion which she could never
return.

But this lover-like mode of reasoning was not likely to reconcile
him to his fate, since the more amiable his imagination presented
Miss Wardour, the more inconsolable he felt he should be rendered
by the extinction of his hopes. He was, indeed, conscious of possessing the power of removing her prejudices on some points; but, even
in extremity, he determined to keep the original determination
which he had formed, of ascertaining that she desired an explanation
ere he intruded one upon her. And turn the matter as he would, he
could not regard his suit as desperate. There was something of
embarrassment as well as of grave surprise in her look when Oldbuck
presented him, and, perhaps, upon second thoughts, the one was
assumed to cover the other. He would not relinquish a pursuit which
had already cost him such pains. Plans, suiting the romantic temper
of the brain that entertained them, chased each other through his
head, thick and irregular as the motes of the sun-beam, and long
after he had laid himself to rest, continued to prevent the repose
which he greatly needed. Then, wearied by the uncertainty and
difficulties with which each scheme appeared to be attended, he bent
up his mind to the strong effort of shaking off his love, 'like dewdrops from the lion's mane,'* and resuming those studies and that
career of life which his unrequited affection had so long and so
fruitlessly interrupted. In this last resolution, he endeavoured to
fortify himself by every argument which pride, as well as reason,
could suggest. 'She shall not suppose,' he said, 'that, presuming on
an accidental service to her or to her father, I am desirous to intrude
myself upon that notice, to which, personally, she considered me as
having no title. I will see her no more. I will return to the land which,
if it affords none fairer, has at least many as fair, and less haughty
than Miss Wardour. Tomorrow I will bid adieu to these northern
shores, and to her who is as cold and relentless as her climate.' When
he had for some time brooded over this sturdy resolution, exhausted

nature at length gave way, and, despite of wrath, doubt, and anxiety, he sunk into slumber.

It is seldom that sleep, after such violent agitation, is either sound or refreshing. Lovel's was disturbed by a thousand baseless and confused visions.* He was a bird—he was a fish—or he flew like the one, and swam like the other,—qualities which would have been very essential to his safety a few hours before. Then Miss Wardour was a syren,* or a bird of Paradise; her father a triton,* or a sea-gull; and Oldbuck alternately a porpoise and a cormorant. These agreeable imaginations were varied by all the usual vagaries of a feverish dream; the air refused to bear the visionary, the water seemed to burn him—the rocks felt like down-pillows as he was dashed against them—whatever he undertook failed in some strange and unexpected manner—and whatever attracted his attention, underwent, as he attempted to investigate it, some wild and wonderful metamorphosis, while his mind continued all the while in some degree conscious of the delusion, from which it in vain struggled to free itself by awaking—feverish symptoms all, with which those who are haunted by the night-hag, whom the learned call Ephialtes,* are but too well acquainted. At length these crude phantasmata arranged themselves into something more regular, if indeed the imagination of Lovel, after he awoke, (for it was by no means the faculty in which his mind was least rich,) did not gradually, insensibly, and unintentionally, arrange in better order the scene, of which his sleep presented, it may be, a less distinct outline. Or it is possible that his feverish agitation may have assisted him in forming the vision.

Leaving this discussion to the learned, we will say, that, after a succession of wild images, such as we have above described, our hero, for such we must acknowledge him, so far regained a consciousness of locality as to remember where he was, and the whole furniture of the Green Chamber was depicted to his slumbering eye. And here, once more, let me protest, that if there should be so much old-fashioned faith left among this shrewd and sceptical generation, as to suppose that what follows was an impression conveyed rather by the eye than by the imagination, I do not impugn their doctrine. He was then, or imagined himself, broad awake in the Green Chamber, gazing upon the flickering and occasional flame which the unconsumed remnants of the fagots sent forth, as, one by one, they fell down upon the red embers, into which the principal part of the boughs to which they belonged had crumbled away. Insensibly the legend of Aldobrand Oldenbuck, and his mysterious visits to the inmates of the chamber, awoke in his mind, and with it, as we often feel in dreams, an anxious and fearful expectation, which seldom fails instantly to summon up before our mind's eye the object of our fear. Brighter sparkles of light flashed from the chimney with such intense brilliancy, as to enlighten all the room. The tapestry waved wildly on the wall, till its dusky forms seemed to become animated. The hunters blew their horns—the stag seemed to fly, the boar to resist, and the hounds to assail the one and pursue the other; the cry of deer, mangled by throttling dogs—the shouts of men, and the clatter of horses' hoofs, seemed at once to surround him—while every group pursued, with all the fury of the chase, the employment in which the artist had represented them as engaged. Lovel looked on this strange scene devoid of wonder, (which seldom intrudes itself upon the sleeping fancy,) but with an anxious sensation of awful fear. At length an individual figure among the tissued hunts-men, as he gazed upon them more fixedly, seemed to leave the arras and to approach the bed of the slumberer. As he drew near, his figure appeared to alter. His bugle-horn became a brazen clasped volume; his hunting-cap changed to such a furred head-gear as graces the burgo-masters of Rembrandt;* his Flemish garb remained, but his features, no longer agitated with the fury of the chase, were changed to such a state of awful and stern composure, as might best pourtray the first proprietor of Monkbarns, such as he had been described to Lovel by his descendants in the course of the preceding evening. As this metamorphosis took place, the hubbub among the other person-ages in the arras disappeared from the imagination of the dreamer, which was now exclusively bent on the single figure before him. Lovel strove to interrogate this awful person in the form of exorcism proper for the occasion; but his tongue, as is usual in frightful dreams, refused its office, and clung, palsied, to the roof of his mouth. Aldobrand held up his finger, as if to impose silence upon the guest who had intruded on his apartment, and began deliberately to unclasp the venerable volume which occupied his left hand. When it was unfolded, he turned over the leaves hastily for a short space, and then raising his figure to its full dimensions, and holding the book aloft in his left hand, pointed to a passage in the page which he thus displayed. Although the language was unknown to our dreamer, his eye and attention were both strongly caught by the line which the figure seemed thus to press upon his notice, the words of which appeared to blaze with a supernatural light, and remained riveted upon his memory. As the vision shut his volume, a strain of delightful music seemed to fill the apartment—Lovel started, and became completely awake. The music, however, was still in his ears, nor ceased till he could distinctly follow the measure of an old Scottish tune.

He sate up in bed, and endeavoured to clear his brain of the phantoms which had disturbed it during this weary night. The beams of the morning sun streamed through the half-closed shutters, and admitted a distinct light into the apartment. He looked round upon the hangings, but the mixed groups of silken and worsted huntsmen were as stationary as tenter-hooks could make them, and only trembled slightly as the early breeze, which found its way through an open crevice of the latticed window, glided along their surface. Lovel leapt out of bed, and, wrapping himself in a morning-gown, that had been considerately laid by his bedside, stepped towards the window, which commanded a view of the sea, the roar of whose billows announced it still disquieted by the storm of the preceding evening, although the morning was fair and serene. The window of a turret, which projected at an angle with the wall, and thus came to be very near Lovel's apartment, was half open, and from that quarter he heard again the same music which had probably broken short his dream. With its visionary character it had lost much of its charms—it was now nothing more than an air on the harpsichord, tolerably well performed—such is the caprice of imagination as affecting the fine arts. A female voice sung, with some taste and great simplicity, something between a song and a hymn, in words to the following effect:—

> 'Why sit'st thou by that ruin'd hall,
>   Thou aged carle so stern and grey?
> Dost thou its former pride recall,
>   Or ponder how it pass'd away?'—
>
> 'Know'st thou not me!' the Deep Voice cried;
>   'So long enjoy'd, so oft misused—
> Alternate, in thy fickle pride,
>   Desired, neglected, and accused?

'Before my breath, like blazing flax,
    Man and his marvels pass away;
And changing empires wane and wax,
    Are founded, flourish, and decay.

'Redeem mine hours—the space is brief—
    While in my glass the sand-grains shiver,
And measureless thy joy or grief,
    When TIME and thou shall part for ever!'*

While the verses were yet singing, Lovel had returned to his bed; the train of ideas which they awakened was romantic and pleasing, such as his soul delighted in, and, willingly adjourning, till more broad day, the doubtful task of determining on his future line of conduct, he abandoned himself to the pleasing languor inspired by the music, and fell into a sound and refreshing sleep, from which he was only awakened at a late hour by old Caxon, who came creeping into the room to render the offices of a valet-de-chambre.

'I have brushed your coat, sir,' said the old man, when he perceived Lovel was awake; 'the callant brought it frae Fairport this morning, for that ye had on yesterday is scantly feasibly dry, though it's been a' night at the kitchen fire—and I hae cleaned your shoon—I doubt ye'll no be wanting me to tie your hair, for (with a gentle sigh) a' the young gentlemen wear crops now—but I hae the curling-tangs here to gie it a bit turn ower the brow, if ye like, before ye gae down to the leddies.'

Lovel, who was by this time once more on his legs, declined the old man's professional offices, but accompanied the refusal with such a douceur as completely sweetened Caxon's mortification.

'It's a pity he disna get his hair tied and pouthered,' said the ancient frizeur, when he had got once more into the kitchen, in which, on one pretence or other, he spent three parts of his idle time—that is to say, of his *whole* time—'it's a great pity, for he's a comely young gentleman.'

'Hout awa, ye auld gowk,' said Jenny Rintherout, 'would ye creesh his bonny brown hair wi' your nasty ulyie, and then moust it like the auld minister's wig?—Ye'll be for your breakfast, I'se warrant?—hae, there's a soup parritch for ye—it will set ye better to be slaistering at them and the lapper-milk than middling wi' Mr Lovel's head—ye wad spoil the maist natural and beautifaest head o' hair in a' Fairport, baith burgh and county.'

The poor barber sighed over the disrespect into which his art had so universally fallen, but Jenny was a person too important to offend by contradiction; so sitting quietly down in the kitchen, he digested at once his humiliation, and the contents of a bicker which held a Scotch pint* of substantial oatmeal porridge.

CHAPTER XI

Sometimes he thinks that Heaven this pageant sent,
And order'd all the pageants as they went;
Sometimes that only 'twas wild Fancy's play,—
The loose and scatter'd relics of the day.*

WE must now request our readers to adjourn to the breakfast-parlour
of Mr Oldbuck, who, despising the modern slops of tea and coffee,
was substantially regaling himself, *more majorum*,* with cold roast-
beef, and a glass of a sort of beverage called *mum*, a species of fat ale,*
brewed from wheat and bitter herbs, of which the present generation
only know the name by its occurrence in revenue acts of parliament,
coupled with cider, perry, and other excisable commodities. Lovel,
who was seduced to taste it, with difficulty refrained from pro-
nouncing it detestable, but *did* refrain, as he saw he should otherwise
give great offence to his host, who had the liquor annually prepared
with peculiar care, according to the approved recipe bequeathed to
him by the so-often mentioned Aldobrand Oldenbuck. The hospitality of the ladies offered Lovel a breakfast more suited to modern
taste, and while he was engaged in partaking of it, he was assailed by
indirect inquiries concerning the manner in which he had passed the
night.

'We canna compliment Mr Lovel on his looks this morning,
brother—but he winna condescend on any ground of disturbance he
has had in the night time—I am certain he looks very pale, and when
he came here, he was as fresh as a rose.'

'Why, sister, consider this rose of yours has been knocked about by
sea and wind all yesterday evening, as if he had been a bunch of kelp
or tangle, and how the devil would you have him retain his colour?'

'I certainly do still feel somewhat fatigued,' said Lovel, 'notwithstanding the excellent accommodations with which your hospitality
so amply supplied me.'

'Ah, sir!' said Miss Oldbuck, looking at him with a knowing smile,
or what was meant to be one, 'ye'll not allow of ony inconvenience,
out of civility to us.'

'Really, madam,' replied Lovel, 'I had no disturbance; for I cannot
term such the music with which some kind fairy favoured me.'

'I doubted Mary wad waken you wi' her skreighing; she didna ken I had left open a chink of your window, for, forbye the ghaist, the Green Room disna vent weel in a high wind—But, I am judging, ye heard mair than Mary's lilts yestreen—weel, men are hardy creatures, they can gae through wi' a' thing. I am sure had I been to undergo ony thing of that nature,—that's to say that's beyond nature—I would hae skreigh'd out at once, and raised the house, be the consequence what liket—and, I dare say, the minister wad hae done as mickle, and sae I hae tauld him,—I ken naebody but my brother, Monkbarns himsell, wad gae through the like o't, if, indeed, it binna you, Mr Lovel.'

'A man of Mr Oldbuck's learning, madam,' answered the questioned party, 'would not be exposed to the inconvenience sustained by the Highland gentleman you mentioned last night.'

'Ay! ay! ye understand now where the difficulty lies—language? he has ways o' his ain wad banish a' thae sort o' worricows as far as the hindermost parts of Gideon, (meaning possibly Midian,)* as Mr Blattergowl says—only ane wadna be uncivil to ane's forbear though he be a ghaist—I am sure I will try that receipt of yours, brother, that ye showed me in a book, if ony body is to sleep in that room again, though, I think, in Christian charity, ye should rather fit up the matted-room—it's a wee damp and dark, to be sure, but then we hae sae seldom occasion for a spare bed.'

'No, no, sister; dampness and darkness are worse than spectres—ours are spirits of light—and I would rather have you try the spell.'

'I will do that blythely, Monkbarns, an I had the ingredients, as my cookery book ca's them—There was *vervain* and *dill*—I mind that—Davie Dibble will ken about them, though, maybe, he'll gie them Latin names—and peppercorn, we hae walth o' them, for'—

'Hypericon,* thou foolish woman!' thundered Oldbuck; 'd'ye suppose you're making a haggis—or do you think that a spirit, though he be formed of air, can be expelled by a receipt against wind?—This wise Grizel of mine, Mr Lovel, recollects (with what accuracy you may judge) a charm which I once mentioned to her, and which, happening to hit her superstitious noddle, she remembers better than any thing tending to a useful purpose I may chance to have said for this ten years—But many an old woman besides herself'—

'Auld woman! Monkbarns,' said Miss Oldbuck, roused something above her usual submissive tone, 'ye really are less than civil to me.'

'Not less than just, Grizel; however, I include in the same class many a sounding name, from Jamblichus* down to Aubrey, who have wasted their time in devising imaginary remedies for non-existing diseases—But I hope, my young friend, that, charmed or uncharmed—secured by the potency of Hypericon,

> With vervain and with dill,
> That hinder witches of their will,*

or left disarmed and defenceless to the inroads of the invisible world, you will give another night to the terrors of the haunted apartment, and another day to your faithful and feal friends.'

'I heartily wish I could, but'—

'Nay, but me no *buts*—I have set my heart upon it.'

'I am greatly obliged, my dear sir, but'—

'Look ye there, now—*but* again!—I hate *but*; I know no form of expression in which he can appear, that is amiable, excepting as a *butt* of sack—*but* is to me a more detestable combination of letters than *no* itself. *No* is a surly, honest fellow, speaks his mind rough and round at once. *But* is a sneaking, evasive, half-bred, exceptious sort of a conjunction, which comes to pull away the cup just when it is at your lips—

> ——————it does allay
> The good precedent—fie upon *but yet!*
> *But yet* is as a jailor to bring forth
> Some monstrous malefactor.'*

'Well, then,' answered Lovel, whose motions were really undetermined at the moment, 'you shall not connect the recollection of my name with so churlish a particle—I must soon think of leaving Fairport, I am afraid—and I will, since you are good enough to wish it, take this opportunity of spending another day here.'

'And you shall be rewarded, my boy—First you shall see John o' the Girnel's grave, and then we'll walk gently along the sands, the state of the tide being first ascertained, (for we will have no more Peter Wilkins adventures, no more Glum and Gawrie* work,) as far as Knockwinnock Castle, and inquire after the old knight and my fair foe—which will but be barely civil, and then'—

'I beg pardon, my dear sir; but, perhaps, you had better adjourn your visit till tomorrow—I am a stranger, you know.'

'And are, therefore, the more bound to show civility, I should suppose—But I beg your pardon for mentioning a word that perhaps belongs only to a collector of antiquities—I am one of the old school,

> When courtiers gallop'd o'er four counties
> The ball's fair partner to behold,
> And humbly hope she caught no cold.'*

'Why, if—if—if you thought it would be expected—but I believe I had better stay.'

'Nay, nay, my good friend, I am not so old-fashioned as to press you to what is disagreeable, neither—it is sufficient that I see there is some *remora*, some cause of delay, some mid impediment,* which I have no title to inquire into.—Or you are still somewhat tired perhaps—I warrant I find means to entertain your intellects without fatiguing your limbs—I am no friend to violent exertion myself—a walk in the garden once a-day is exercise enough for any thinking being—none but a fool or a fox-hunter would require more.—Well, what shall we set about?—my Essay on Castrametation—but I have that in *petto* for our afternoon cordial—or I will show you the controversy upon Ossian's Poems between Mac-Cribb and me—I hold with the acute Orcadian*—he with the defenders of the authenticity—the controversy began in smooth, oily, lady-like terms, but is now waxing more sour and eager as we get on—it already partakes somewhat of old Scaliger's* style.—I fear the rogue will get some scent of that story of Ochiltree's—but at worst, I have a hard repartee for him on the affair of the abstracted Antigonus—I will show you his last epistle, and the scroll of my answer—egad, it is a trimmer!'

So saying, the Antiquary opened a drawer, and began rummaging among a quantity of miscellaneous papers, ancient and modern. But it was the misfortune of this learned gentleman, as it may be that of many learned and unlearned, that he frequently experienced, on such occasions, what Harlequin calls *l'embarras des richesses*—in other words, the abundance of his collection often prevented him from finding the article he sought for. 'Curse the papers!—I believe,' said Oldbuck, as he shuffled them to and fro,—'I believe they make themselves wings like grashoppers, and fly away bodily—but here, in the meanwhile, look at that little treasure.' So saying, he put into his hand a case made of oak, fenced at the corner with silver roses and

studs—'Pr'ythee, undo this button,'* said he, as he observed Lovel
fumbling at the clasp;—he did so, the lid opened, and discovered a
thin quarto curiously bound in black shagreen—'There, Mr Lovel—
there is the work I mentioned to you last night—the rare quarto of
the Augsburg Confession, the foundation at once and the bulwark of
the Reformation, drawn up by the learned and venerable Melancthon,* defended by the Elector of Saxony,* and the other valiant hearts
who stood up for their faith, even against the front of a powerful and
victorious emperor,* and imprinted by the scarcely less venerable and
praiseworthy Aldobrand Oldenbuck, my happy progenitor, during
the yet more tyrannical attempts of Philip II.* to suppress at once
civil and religious liberty. Yes, sir—for printing this work, that eminent man was expelled from his ungrateful country, and driven to
establish his household gods even here at Monkbarns, among the
ruins of papal superstition and domination. Look upon his venerable
effigies, Mr Lovel, and respect the honourable occupation in which
it presents him, as labouring personally at the press for the diffusion
of Christian and political knowledge—And see here his favourite
motto, expressive of his independence and self-reliance, which
scorned to owe any thing to patronage, that was not earned by
desert—expressive also of that firmness of mind and tenacity of
purpose, recommended by Horace.* He was, indeed, a man who
would have stood firm, had his whole printing-house, presses, fonts,
forms, great and small pica, been shivered to pieces around him—
Read, I say, his motto,—for each printer had his motto, or device,
when that illustrious art was first practised. My ancestor's was
expressed as you see in the Teutonic phrase, KUNST MACHT
GUNST—that is, skill, or prudence, in availing ourselves of our natural talents and advantages, will compel favour and patronage, even
where it is withheld from prejudice, or ignorance.'

'And that,' said Lovel, after a moment's thoughtful silence, 'that
then is the meaning of these German words?'

'Unquestionably—you perceive the appropriate application to a
consciousness of inward worth, and of eminence in an useful and
honourable art.—Each printer in those days, as I have already
informed you, had his device, his impresa, as I may call it, in the
same manner as the doughty chivalry of the age, who frequented tilt
and tournament. My ancestor boasted as much in his, as if he had
displayed it over a conquered field of battle, though it betokened the

diffusion of knowledge, not the effusion of blood. And yet there is a family tradition which affirms him to have chosen it from a more romantic circumstance.'

'And what is that said to have been, my good sir?' enquired his young friend.

'Why, it rather encroaches on my respected predecessor's fame for prudence and wisdom—*Sed semel insanivimus omnes**—every body has played the fool in their turn. It is said, my ancestor, during his apprenticeship with the descendant of old Fust,* whom popular tradition hath sent to the devil, under the name of Faustus, was attracted by a paltry slip of womankind, his master's daughter, called Bertha—They broke rings, or went through some idiotical ceremony, as is usual on such idle occasions as the plighting of a true-love troth, and Aldobrand set out on his journey through Germany, as became an honest *hand-werker*; for such was the custom of mechanics at that time, to make a tour through the empire, and work at their trade for a time in each of the most eminent towns, before they finally settled themselves for life. It was a wise custom; for, as such travellers were received like brethren in each town by those of their own handicraft, they were sure, in every case, to have the means either of gaining or communicating knowledge. When my ancestor returned to Nuremburg, he is said to have found his old master newly dead, and two or three gallant young suitors, some of them half-starved sprigs of nobility forsooth, in pursuit of the *Yung-fraw* Bertha, whose father was understood to have bequeathed her a dowry which might weigh against sixteen armorial quarters.* But Bertha, not a bad sample of womankind, had made a vow she would only marry that man who could work her father's press. The skill, at that time, was as rare as wonderful; besides that the expedient rid her at once of most of her *gentle* suitors, who would have as soon wielded a conjuring wand as a composing stick—some of the more ordinary typographers made the attempt; but none were sufficiently possessed of the mystery—But I tire you.'

'By no means; pray, proceed, Mr Oldbuck; I listen with uncommon interest.'

'Ah! it is all folly—however—Aldobrand arrived in the ordinary dress, as we would say, of a journeyman printer—the same with which he had traversed Germany, and conversed with Luther, Melancthon, Erasmus,* and other learned men, who disdained not his knowledge, and the power he possessed of diffusing it, though hid under a garb so homely. But what appeared respectable in the eyes of wisdom, religion, learning, and philosophy, seemed mean, as might readily be supposed, and disgusting, in those of silly and affected womankind, and Bertha refused to acknowledge her former lover, in the torn doublet, skin cap, clouted shoes, and leathern apron, of a travelling handicraftsman or mechanic. He claimed his privilege, however, of being admitted to a trial; and when the rest of the suitors had either declined the contest, or made such work as the devil could not read if his pardon depended on it, all eyes were bent on the stranger. Aldobrand stepped gracefully forward, arranged the types without omission of a single letter, hyphen, or comma, imposed them without deranging a single space, and pulled off the first proof as clear and free from errors, as if it had been a triple revise!* All applauded the worthy successor of the immortal Faustus—the blushing maiden acknowledged her error in trusting to the eye more than the intellect, and the elected bridegroom thenceforward chose for his impress or device the appropriate words, "*Skill wins favour.*"—But what is the matter with you?—you are in a brown study?—Come, I told you this was but trumpery conversation for thinking people—and now I have my hand on the Ossianic controversy.'

'I beg your pardon,' said Lovel; 'I am going to appear very silly and changeable in your eyes, Mr Oldbuck, but you seemed to think Sir Arthur might in civility expect a call from me?'

'Psha, psha, I can make your apology; and if you must leave us so soon as you say, what signifies how you stand in his honour's good graces?—And I warn you that the Essay on Castrametation is something prolix, and will occupy the time we can spare after dinner, so you may lose the Ossianic Controversy if we do not dedicate this morning to it—we will go out to my ever-green bower, my sacred holly-tree yonder, and have it *fronde super viridi.**

> "Sing hey-ho! hey-ho! for the green holly,
> Most friendship is feigning, most loving mere folly."*

But, egad,' continued the old gentleman, 'when I look closer at you, I begin to think you may be of a different opinion. Amen, with all my heart—I quarrel with no man's hobby, if he does not run it a tilt* against mine, and if he does—let him beware his eyes—What say you?—in the language of the world and worldlings base,* if you can condescend to so mean a sphere, shall we stay or go?'

'In the language of selfishness then, which is of course the language of the world—let us go by all means.'

'Amen, amen, quo' the Earl Marshall,'* answered Oldbuck, as he exchanged his slippers for a pair of stout walking shoes, with *cutikins*, as he called them, of black cloth. He only interrupted the walk by a slight deviation to the tomb of John o' the Girnel, remembered as the last bailiff of the abbey, who had resided at Monkbarns. Beneath an old oak-tree upon a hillock, sloping pleasantly to the south, and catching a distant view of the sea over two or three rich enclosures, and the Musselcrag, lay a moss-grown stone, and, in memory of the departed worthy, it bore an inscription, of which, as Mr Oldbuck affirmed, (though many doubted,) the defaced characters could be distinctly traced to the following effect:—

Heir lyeth John o' ye Girnell,
Erth has ye nit and heuen ye kirnell.
In hys tyme ilk wyfe's hennis clokit,
Ilka gud mannis herth wi' bairnis was stokit,
He deled a boll o' bear in firlottis fyve,
Four for ye halie kirke and ane for pure mennis wyvis.*

'You see how modest the author of this sepulchral commendation was—he tells us, that honest John could make five firlots, or quarters, as you would say, out of the boll, instead of four,—that he gave the fifth to the wives of the parish, and accounted for the other four to the abbot and chapter,—that in his time the wives' hens always laid eggs, and devil thank them, if they got one-fifth of the abbey rents; and that honest men's hearths were never unblest with offspring,—an addition to the miracle, which they, as well as I, must have considered as perfectly unaccountable. But come on—leave we Jock o' the Girnel, and let us jog on to the yellow sands, where the sea, like a repulsed enemy, is now retreating from the ground on which he gave us battle last night.'

Thus saying, he led the way to the sands. Upon the links or downs close to them, were seen four or five huts inhabited by fishers, whose boats, drawn high upon the beach, lent the odoriferous vapours of pitch melting under a burning sun, to contend with those of the offals of fish and other nuisances, usually collected round Scottish cottages. Undisturbed by these complicated steams of abomination, a middle-aged woman, with a face which had defied a thousand storms, sat mending a net at the door of one of the cottages. A handkerchief close bound about her head, and a coat, which had formerly been that of a man, gave her a masculine air, which was increased by her strength, uncommon stature, and harsh voice. 'What are ye for the day, your honour?' she said, or rather screamed, to Oldbuck; 'caller haddocks and whitings—a bannock-fluke and a cock-padle.'

'How much for the bannock-fluke and cock-padle?' demanded the Antiquary.

'Four white shillings and saxpence,' answered the Naiad.*

'Four devils and six of their imps!' retorted the Antiquary; 'do ye think I am mad, Maggie?'

'And div ye think,' rejoined the virago, setting her arms a-kimbo, 'that my man and my sons are to gae to the sea in weather like yestreen and the day—sic a sea as it's yet outby—and get naething for their fish, and be misca'd into the bargain, Monkbarns? It's no fish ye're buying—it's men's lives.'

'Well, Maggie, I'll bid you fair—I'll bid you a shilling for the fluke and the cock-padle, or sixpence separately—and if all your fish are as well paid, I think your man, as you call him, and your sons, will make a good voyage.'

'Deil gin their boat were knockit against the Bell-Rock* rather! it wad be better, and the bonnier voyage o' the twa. A shilling for thae twa bonny fish! Od, that's ane indeed!'

'Well, well, you old beldam, carry your fish up to Monkbarns, and see what my sister will give you for them.'

'Na, na, Monkbarns, deil a fit—I'll rather deal wi' yoursell; for, though you're near eneugh, yet Miss Grizel has an unco close grip— I'll gie ye them (in a softened tone) for three-and-saxpence.'

'Eighteen-pence, or nothing!'

'Eighteen-pence!!!' (in a loud tone of astonishment, which declined into a sort of rueful whine, when the dealer turned as if to walk away)—'Ye'll no be for the fish then?'—(then louder, as she saw him moving off)—'I'll gie them—and—and—and a half-a-dozen o' partans to make the sauce, for three shillings and a dram.'

'Half-a-crown then, Maggie, and a dram.'

'Aweel, your honour maun hae't your ain gate, nae doubt; but a dram's worth siller now—the distilleries is no working.'*

'And I hope they'll never work again in my time,' said Oldbuck.

'Ay, ay—it's easy for your honour, and the like o' you gentle-folks, to say sae, that hae stouth and routh, and fire and fending, and meat and claith, and sit dry and canny by the fireside—but an ye wanted fire, and meat, and dry claise, and were deeing o' cauld, and had a sair heart, whilk is warst ava', wi' just tippence in your pouch, wadna ye be glad to buy a dram wi't, to be eilding and claise, and a supper and heart's ease into the bargain, till the morn's morning?'

'It's even too true an apology, Maggie. Is your goodman off to sea this morning, after his exertions last night?'

'In troth is he, Monkbarns; he was awa this morning by four o'clock, when the sea was working like barm wi' yestreen's wind, and our bit coble dancing in't like a cork.'

'Well, he's an industrious fellow. Carry the fish up to Monkbarns.'

'That I will—or I'll send little Jenny, she'll rin faster; but I'll ca' on Miss Grizy for the dram mysell, and say ye sent me.'

A nondescript animal, which might have passed for a mermaid, as it was paddling in a pool among the rocks, was summoned ashore by the shrill screams of its dam; and having been made decent, as her mother called it, which was performed by adding a short red cloak to a petticoat, which was at first her sole covering, and which reached scantly below her knee, the child was dismissed with the fish in a basket, and a request on the part of Monkbarns, that they might be prepared for dinner. 'It would have been long,' said Oldbuck, with much self-complacency, 'ere my womankind could have made such a reasonable bargain with that old skinflint, though they sometimes wrangle with her for an hour together under my study window, like three sea-gulls screaming and sputtering in a gale of wind. But, come, wend we on our way to Knockwinnock.'

CHAPTER XII

Beggar?—the only freeman of your commonwealth;
Free above Scot-free, that observe no laws,
Obey no governor, use no religion
But what they draw from their own ancient custom,
Or constitute themselves, yet they are no rebels.

BROME.*

WITH our readers' permission, we will outstep the slow, though sturdy pace of the Antiquary, whose halts, as he turned round to his companion at every moment to point out something remarkable in the landscape, or to enforce some favourite topic more emphatically than the exercise of walking permitted, delayed their progress considerably.

Notwithstanding the fatigues and dangers of the preceding evening, Miss Wardour was able to rise at her usual hour, and to apply herself to her usual occupations, after she had first satisfied her anxiety concerning her father's state of health. Sir Arthur was no farther indisposed than by the effects of great agitation and unusual fatigue, but these were sufficient to induce him to keep his bedchamber.

To look back on the events of the preceding day, was, to Isabella, a very unpleasing retrospect. She owed her life, and that of her father, to the very person by whom, of all others, she wished least to be obliged, because she could hardly even express common gratitude towards him without encouraging hopes which might be injurious to them both. 'Why should it be my fate to receive such benefits, and conferred at so much personal risk, from one whose romantic passion I have so unceasingly laboured to discourage? Why should chance have given him this advantage over me? and why, oh why, should a half-subdued feeling in my own bosom, in spite of my sober reason, almost rejoice that he has attained it!'

While Miss Wardour thus taxed herself with wayward caprice, she beheld advancing down the avenue, not her younger and more dreaded preserver, but the old beggar who had made such a capital figure in the melo-drama of the preceding evening.

She rang the bell for her maid-servant. 'Bring the old man up stairs.'

The servant returned in a minute or two—'He will come up at no rate, madam—he says his clouted shoes never were on a carpet in his life, and that, please God, they never shall.—Must I take him into the servants' hall?'

'No; stay, I want to speak with him—Where is he?' for she had lost sight of him as he approached the house.

'Sitting in the sun on the stone-bench in the court, beside the window of the flagged parlour.'

'Bid him stay there—I'll come down to the parlour, and speak with him at the window.'

She came down accordingly, and found the mendicant half-seated, half-reclining, upon the bench beside the window. Edie Ochiltree, old man and beggar as he was, had apparently some internal consciousness of the favourable impressions connected with his tall form, commanding features, and long white beard and hair. It used to be remarked of him, that he was seldom seen but in a posture which showed these personal attributes to advantage. At present, as he lay half-reclined, with his wrinkled yet ruddy cheek, and keen grey eye, turned up towards the sky, his staff and bag laid beside him, and a cast of homely wisdom and sarcastic irony in the expression of his countenance, while he gazed for a moment around the court-yard, and then resumed his former look upward, he might have been taken by an artist as the model of an old philosopher of the Cynic school,* musing upon the frivolity of mortal pursuits, and the precarious tenure of human possessions, and looking up to the source from which aught permanently good can alone be derived. The young lady, as she presented her tall and elegant figure at the open window, but divided from the court-yard by a grating, with which, according to the fashion of ancient times, the lower windows of the castle were secured, gave an interest of a different kind, and might be supposed, by a romantic imagination, an imprisoned damsel communicating a tale of her durance to a palmer, in order that he might call upon the gallantry of every knight whom he should meet in his wanderings, to rescue her from her oppressive thraldom.

After Miss Wardour had offered, in the terms she thought would be most acceptable, those thanks which the beggar declined, as far beyond his merit, she began to express herself in a manner which she supposed would speak more feelingly to his apprehension. 'She did not know,' she said, 'what her father intended particularly to do for their preserver, but certainly it would be something that would make him easy for life; if he chose to reside at the castle, she would give orders'—

The old man smiled, and shook his head. 'I wad be baith a grievance and a disgrace to your fine servants, my leddy, and I have never been a disgrace to ony body yet, that I ken of.'

'Sir Arthur would give strict orders'—

'Ye're very kind—I doubtna, I doubtna; but there are some things a master can command, and some he canna—I daresay he wad gar them keep hands aff me—(and troth, I think they wad hardly venture on that ony gate)—and he wad gar them gie me my soup parritch and bit meat.—But trow ye that Sir Arthur's command could forbid the gibe o' the tongue or the blink o' the ee, or gar them gie me my food wi' the look o' kindness that gars it digest sae weel, or that he could make them forbear a' the slights and taunts that hurt ane's spirit mair nor downright misca'ing?—Besides, I am the idlest auld carle that ever lived; I downa be bound down to hours o' eating and sleeping; and, to speak the honest truth, I wad be a very bad example in ony weel-regulated family.'

'Well then, Edie, what do you think of a neat cottage and a garden, and a daily dole, and nothing to do but to dig a little in your garden when you pleased yourself?'

'And how often wad that be, trow ye, my leddy? maybe no ance atween Candlemas and Yule—and if a' thing were done to my hand, as if I was Sir Arthur himsell, I could never bide the staying still in ae place, and just seeing the same joists and couples aboon my head night after night.—And then I have a queer humour o' my ain, that sets a strolling beggar weel eneugh, whase word naebody minds—but ye ken Sir Arthur has odd sort o' ways—and I wad be jesting or scorning at them—and ye wad be angry, and then I wad be just fit to hang mysell.'

'O, you are a licensed man,' said Isabella; 'we shall give you all reasonable scope: So you had better be ruled, and remember your age.'

'But I am no that sair failed yet,' replied the mendicant. 'Od, ance I gat a wee soupled yestreen, I was as yauld as an eel.—And then what wad a' the country about do for want o' auld Edie Ochiltree, that brings news and country cracks frae ae farm-steading to anither, and gingerbread to the lasses, and helps the lads to mend their fiddles, and the gudewives to clout their pans, and plaits rush-swords and grenadier caps for the weans, and busks the laird's flees, and has skill o' cow-ills and horse-ills, and kens mair auld sangs and tales than a' the barony besides, and gars ilka body laugh wherever he comes?—troth, my leddy, I canna lay down my vocation; it would be a public loss.'

'Well, Edie, if your idea of your importance is so strong as not to be shaken by the prospect of independence'—

'Na, na, Miss—it's because I am mair independent as I am,' answered the old man; 'I beg nae mair at ony single house than a meal o' meat, or maybe but a mouthfou o't—if it's refused at ae place, I get it at anither—sae I canna be said to depend on ony body in particular, but just on the country at large.'

'Well, then, only promise me that you will let me know should you ever wish to settle as you turn old, and more incapable of making your usual rounds; and, in the meantime, take this.'

'Na, na, my leddy; I downa take muckle siller at anes, it's against our rule—and—though it's maybe no civil to be repeating the like o' that—they say that siller's like to be scarce wi' Sir Arthur himsell, and that he's run himsell out o' thought wi' his houkings and minings for lead and copper yonder.'

Isabella had some anxious anticipations to the same effect, but was shocked to hear that her father's embarrassments were such public talk; as if scandal ever failed to stoop upon so acceptable a quarry, as the failings of the good man, the decline of the powerful, or the decay of the prosperous.—Miss Wardour sighed deeply—'Well, Edie, we have enough to pay our debts, let folks say what they will, and requiting you is one of the foremost—let me press this sum upon you.'

'That I might be robbed and murdered some night between town and town? or, what's as bad, that I might live in constant apprehension o't?—I am no—(lowering his voice to a whisper, and looking keenly around him)—I am no that clean unprovided for neither; and though I should die at the back of a dike, they'll find as muckle quilted in this auld blue gown as will bury me like a Christian, and gie the lads and lasses a blythe lykewake too; sae there's the gaber-lunzie's burial provided for, and I need nae mair.—Were the like o' me ever to change a note, wha the deil d'ye think wad be sic fules as to gie me charity after that?—it wad flee through the country like wild-fire, that auld Edie suld hae done siccan a like thing, and then, I'se warrant, I might grane my heart out or ony body wad gie me either a bane or a bodle.'

'Is there nothing, then, that I can do for you?'

'Ou ay—I'll aye come for my awmous as usual,—and whiles I wad be fain o' a pickle sneeshin, and ye maun speak to the constable and ground-officer just to owerlook me, and maybe ye'll gie a gude word for me to Sandie Netherstanes, the miller, that he may chain up his muckle dog—I wadna hae him to hurt the puir beast, for it just does its office in barking at a gaberlunzie like me.—And there's ae thing maybe mair, but ye'll think it's very bauld o' the like o' me to speak o't.'

'What is it, Edie?—if it respects you it shall be done, if it is in my power.'

'It respects yoursell, and it is in your power, and I maun come out wi't.—Ye are a bonny young leddy, and a gude ane, and maybe a weel-tochered ane—but dinna ye sneer awa the lad Lovel, as ye did a while sinsyne on the walk beneath the Brierybank, when I saw ye baith, and heard ye too, though ye saw nae me. Be canny wi' the lad, for he loes ye weel, and it's to him, and no to ony thing I could have done for you, that Sir Arthur and you wan ower yestreen.'

He uttered these words in a low but distinct tone of voice; and, without waiting for an answer, walked towards a low door which led to the apartments of the servants, and so entered the house.

Miss Wardour remained for a moment or two in the situation in which she had heard the old man's last extraordinary speech, leaning, namely, against the bars of the window, nor could she determine upon saying even a single word, relative to a subject so delicate, until the beggar was out of sight. It was, indeed, difficult to determine what to do. That her having had an interview and private conversation with this young and unknown stranger, should be a secret possessed by a person of the last class in which a young lady would seek a confident, and at the mercy of one who was by profession gossip-general to the whole neighbourhood, gave her acute agony. She had no reason, indeed, to suppose that the old man would wilfully do any thing to hurt her feelings, much less to injure her; but the mere freedom of speaking to her upon such a subject, showed, as might have been expected, a total absence of delicacy; and what he might take it into his head to do or say next, *that* she was pretty sure so professed an admirer of liberty would not hesitate to do or say without scruple. This idea so much hurt and vexed her, that she half-wished the officious assistance of Lovel and Ochiltree had been absent upon the preceding evening.

While she was in this agitation of spirits, she suddenly observed Oldbuck and Lovel entering the court. She drew instantly so far back from the window, that she could, without being seen, observe how the Antiquary paused in front of the building, and, pointing to the various scutcheons of its former owners, seemed in the act of bestowing upon Lovel much curious and erudite information, which, from the absent look of his auditor, Isabella might shrewdly guess was entirely thrown away. The necessity that she should take some resolution became instant and pressing—she rang, therefore, for a servant, and ordered him to show the visitors to the drawing-room, while she, by another staircase, gained her own apartment, to consider, ere she made her appearance, what line of conduct were fittest for her to pursue. The guests, agreeably to her instructions, were introduced into the room where company was usually received.

CHAPTER XIII

Miss Isabella Wardour's complexion was considerably heightened, when, after the delay necessary to arrange her ideas, she presented herself in the drawing-room.

'I am glad you are come, my fair foe,' said the Antiquary, greeting her with much kindness, 'for I have had a most refractory, or at least negligent, auditor, in my young friend here, while I endeavoured to make him acquainted with the history of Knockwinnock Castle. I think the danger of last night has mazed the poor lad. But you, Miss Isabel, why, you look as if flying through the night air had been your natural and most congenial occupation. Your colour is even better than when you honoured my *hospitium* yesterday—And Sir Arthur—how fares my good old friend?'

'Indifferently well, Mr Oldbuck; but, I am afraid, not quite able to receive your congratulations, or to pay—to pay—Mr Lovel his thanks for his unparalleled exertions.'

'I dare say not—A good down pillow for his good white head were more meet than a couch so churlish* as Bessy's Apron, plague on her!'

'I had no thought of intruding,' said Lovel, looking upon the ground, and speaking with hesitation and suppressed emotion; 'I did not—did not mean to intrude upon Sir Arthur or Miss Wardour the presence of one who—who must necessarily be unwelcome—as associated, I mean, with painful reflections.'

'Do not think my father so unjust and ungrateful,' said Miss Wardour. 'I dare say,' she continued, participating in Lovel's embarrassment—'I dare say—I am certain—that my father would be happy to show his gratitude—in any way—that is, which Mr Lovel could consider it as proper to point out.'

'Why, the deuce,' interrupted Oldbuck, 'what sort of a qualification is that?—On my word, it reminds me of our minister, who, choosing, like a formal old fop as he is, to drink to my sister's inclinations, thought it necessary to add the saving clause, Provided, madam, they be virtuous. Come, let us have no more of this nonsense—I dare say Sir Arthur will bid us welcome on some future day.—And what news from the kingdom of subterranean darkness and airy hope?—what says the swart spirit of the mine?*—Has Sir Arthur had any good intelligence of his adventure lately in Glen-Withershins?'

Miss Wardour shook her head—'But indifferent, I fear, Mr Oldbuck; but there lie some specimens which have lately been sent down.'

'Ah! my poor dear hundred pounds, which Sir Arthur persuaded me to give for a share in that hopeful scheme, would have bought a porter's load of mineralogy—But let me see them.'

And so saying, he sat down at the table in the recess, on which the mineral productions were lying, and proceeded to examine them, grumbling and pshawing at each, which he took up and laid aside.

In the meantime, Lovel, forced as it were by this secession of Oldbuck, into a sort of tête-à-tête with Miss Wardour, took an opportunity of addressing her in a low and interrupted tone of voice. 'I trust Miss Wardour will impute, to circumstances almost irresistible, this intrusion of a person who has reason to think himself—so unacceptable a visitor.'

'Mr Lovel,' answered Miss Wardour, observing the same tone of caution, 'I trust you will not—I am sure you are incapable of abusing the advantages given to you by the services you have rendered us, which, as they affect my father, can never be sufficiently acknowledged or repaid—Could Mr Lovel see me without his own peace being affected—could he see me as a friend—as a sister—no man will be—and, from all I have ever heard of Mr Lovel, ought to be, more welcome; but'—

Oldbuck's anathema against the preposition *but* was internally echoed by Lovel—'Forgive me, if I interrupt you, Miss Wardour—you need not fear my intruding upon a subject where I have been already severely repressed—but do not add to the severity of repelling my sentiments the rigour of obliging me to disavow them.'

'I am much embarrassed, Mr Lovel,' replied the young lady, 'by your—I would not willingly use a strong word—your romantic and hopeless pertinacity—it is for yourself I plead, that you would consider the calls which your country has upon your talents, that you will not waste, in an idle and fanciful indulgence of an ill-placed predilection, time, which, well redeemed by active exertion, should lay the foundation of future distinction—let me entreat that you would form a manly resolution'—

'It is enough, Miss Wardour; I see plainly that'—

'Mr Lovel, you are hurt—and, believe me, I sympathize in the pain which I inflict—but can I, in justice to myself, in fairness to you, do otherwise?—Without my father's consent, I never will entertain the addresses of any one, and how totally impossible it is that he should countenance the partiality with which you honour me, you are yourself fully aware—and, indeed'—

'No, Miss Wardour,' answered Lovel, in a tone of passionate entreaty; 'do not go farther—is it not enough to crush every hope in our present relative situation?—do not carry your resolutions farther—why urge what would be your conduct if Sir Arthur's objections could be removed?'

'It is indeed vain, Mr Lovel,' said Miss Wardour, 'because their removal is impossible; and I only wish, as your friend, and as one who is obliged to you for her own and her father's life, to entreat you to suppress this unfortunate attachment—to leave a country which affords no scope for your talents, and to resume the honourable line of the profession which you seem to have abandoned.'

'Well, Miss Wardour, your wishes shall be obeyed—have patience with me one little month, and if, in the course of that space, I cannot show you such reasons for continuing my residence at Fairport, as even you shall approve of, I will bid adieu to its vicinity, and, with the same breath, to all my hopes of happiness.'

'Not so, Mr Lovel; many years of deserved happiness, founded on a more rational basis than your present wishes, are, I trust, before you—But it is full time to finish this conversation.—I cannot force you to adopt my advice—I cannot shut the door of my father's house against the preserver of his life and mine—but the sooner Mr Lovel can teach his mind to submit to the inevitable disappointment of wishes which have been so rashly formed, the more highly he will rise in my esteem—and, in the meanwhile, for his sake as well as mine, he must excuse my putting an interdict upon conversation on a subject so painful.'

A servant at this moment announced, that Sir Arthur desired to speak with Mr Oldbuck in his dressing-room.

'Let me show you the way,' said Miss Wardour, who apparently dreaded a continuation of her tête-à-tête with Lovel, and she conducted the Antiquary accordingly to her father's apartment.

Sir Arthur, his legs swathed in flannel, was stretched on the couch. 'Welcome, Mr Oldbuck,' he said; 'I trust you have come better off than I have done from the inclemency of yesterday evening?'

'Truly, Sir Arthur, I was not so much exposed to it—I kept *terra firma**—you fairly committed yourself to the cold night-air in the most literal of all senses. But such adventures become a gallant knight better than a humble esquire—to rise on the wings of the night-wind—to dive into the bowels of the earth.—What news from our subterranean Good Hope? the *terra incognita** of Glen-Withershins?'

'Nothing good as yet,' said the Baronet, turning himself hastily, as if stung by a pang of the gout; 'but Dousterswivel does not despair.'

'Does he not?' quoth Oldbuck; 'I do though, under his favour— Why, old Dr H——n^{8}* told me, when I was in Edinburgh, that we should never find copper enough, judging from the specimens I showed him, to make a pair of sixpenny knee-buckles—and I cannot see that those samples on the table below differ much in quality.'

'The learned doctor is not infallible, I presume?'

'No; but he is one of our first chemists; and this tramping philosopher of yours—this Dousterswivel, is, I have a notion, one of those learned adventurers, described by Kircher,* *Artem habent sine arte, partem sine parte, quorum medium est mentiri, vita eorum mendicatum ire*;* that is to say, Miss Wardour'—

'It is unnecessary to translate,' said Miss Wardour; 'I comprehend your general meaning—but I hope Mr Dousterswivel will turn out a more trustworthy character.'

'I doubt it not a little,' said the Antiquary, 'and we are a foul way out if we cannot discover this infernal vein that he has prophesied about these two years.'

'*You* have no great interest in the matter, Mr Oldbuck,' said the Baronet.

'Too much, too much, Sir Arthur—and yet, for the sake of my fair foe here, I would consent to lose it all so you had no more on the venture.'

There was a painful silence of a few moments, for Sir Arthur was too proud to acknowledge the downfall of his golden dreams, though he could no longer disguise to himself that such was likely to be the termination of the adventure. 'I understand,' he at length said, 'that the young gentleman, to whose gallantry and presence of mind we were so much indebted last night, has favoured me with a visit—I am distressed that I am unable to see him, or indeed any one, but an old friend like you, Mr Oldbuck.'

A declination of the Antiquary's stiff backbone acknowledged the preference.

'You made acquaintance with this young gentleman in Edinburgh, I suppose?'

Oldbuck told the circumstances of their becoming known to each other.

'Why, then, my daughter is an older acquaintance of Mr Lovel than you are,' said the Baronet.

'Indeed! I was not aware of that,' answered Oldbuck, somewhat surprised.

'I met Mr Lovel,' said Isabella, slightly colouring, 'when I resided this last spring with my aunt, Mrs Wilmot.'

'In Yorkshire?—and what character did he bear then, or how was he engaged?' said Oldbuck,—'and why did not you recognise him when I introduced you?'

Isabella answered the least difficult question, and passed over the other. 'He had a commission in the army, and had, I believe, served with reputation; he was much respected, as an amiable and promising young man.'

'And pray, such being the case,' replied the Antiquary, not disposed to take one reply in answer to two distinct questions, 'why did you not speak to the lad at once when you met him at my house?—I thought you had less of the paltry pride of womankind about you, Miss Wardour.'

'There was a reason for it,' said Sir Arthur, with dignity; 'you know the opinions—prejudices, perhaps, you will call them—of our house concerning purity of birth; this young gentleman is, it seems, the illegitimate son of a man of fortune; my daughter did not choose to renew their acquaintance till she should know whether I approved of her holding any intercourse with him.'

'If it had been with his mother instead of himself,' answered Old-buck, with his usual dry causticity of humour, 'I could see an excellent reason for it. Ah, poor lad! that was the cause then that he seemed so absent and confused while I explained to him the reason of the bend of bastardy* upon the shield yonder under the corner turret!'

'True,' said the Baronet with complacency, 'it is the shield of Malcolm the Usurper, as he is called. The tower which he built is termed, after him, Malcolm's Tower, but more frequently Misticot's Tower, which I conceive to be a corruption for *Misbegot*. He is denominated, in the Latin pedigree of our family, *Milcolumbus Nothus*;* and his temporary seizure of our property, and most unjust attempt to establish his own illegitimate line in the estate of Knock-winnock, gave rise to such family feuds and misfortunes, as strongly to found us in that horror and antipathy to defiled blood and illegitimacy, which has been handed down to me from my respected ancestry.'

'I know the story,' said Oldbuck, 'and I was telling it to Lovel this moment, with some of the wise maxims and consequences which it has engrafted on your family politics. Poor fellow! he must have been much hurt; I took the wavering of his attention for negligence, and was something piqued at it, and it proves to be only an excess of feeling. I hope, Sir Arthur, you will not think the less of your life, because it has been preserved by such assistance?'

'Nor the less of my assistant either,' said the Baronet; 'my doors and table shall be equally open to him as if he had descended of the most unblemished lineage.'

'Come, I am glad of that—he'll know where he can get a dinner, then, if he wants one. But what views can he have in this neighbourhood?—I must catechise him; and if I find he wants it—or, indeed, whether he does or not—he shall have my best advice.' As the Antiquary made this liberal promise, he took his leave of Miss Wardour and her father, eager to commence operations upon Mr Lovel. He informed him abruptly that Miss Wardour sent her compliments, and remained in attendance on her father, and then taking him by the arm, he led him out of the castle.

Knockwinnock still preserved much of the external attributes of a baronial castle. It had its drawbridge, though now never drawn up, and its dry moat, the sides of which had been planted with shrubs, chiefly of the evergreen tribes. Above these rose the old building, partly from a foundation of red rock scarped down to the sea-beach, and partly from the steep green verge of the moat. The trees of the avenue have been already mentioned, and many others rose around of large size, as if to confute the prejudice, that timber cannot be raised near to the ocean. Our walkers paused, and looked back upon the castle, as they attained the height of a small knoll, over which lay their homeward road, for it is to be supposed they did not tempt the risk of the tide by returning along the sands. The building flung its broad shadow upon the tufted foliage of the shrubs beneath it, while the front windows sparkled in the sun. They were viewed by the gazers with very different feelings. Lovel, with the fond eagerness of that passion which derives its food and nourishment from trifles, as the cameleon is said to live on the air, or upon the invisible insects which it contains, endeavoured to conjecture which of the numerous windows belonged to the apartment now graced by Miss Wardour's presence. The speculations of the Antiquary were of a more melancholy cast, and were partly indicated by the ejaculation of *cito peritura!** as he turned away from the prospect. Lovel, roused from his reverie, looked at him as if to inquire the meaning of an exclamation so ominous. The old man shook his head. 'Yes, my young friend,' said he, 'I doubt greatly—and it wrings my heart to say it—this ancient family is going fast to the ground!'

'Indeed!' answered Lovel—'You surprise me greatly!'

'We harden ourselves in vain,' continued the Antiquary, pursuing his own train of thought and feeling—'We harden ourselves in vain to treat with the indifference they deserve the changes of this trumpery whirligig world—We strive ineffectually to be the self-sufficing invulnerable being, the *teres atque rotundus** of the poet—the stoical exemption which philosophy affects to give us over the pains and vexations of human life, is as imaginary as the state of mystical quietism and perfection aimed at by some crazy enthusiasts.'

'And Heaven forbid that it should be otherwise!' said Lovel warmly—'Heaven forbid that any process of philosophy were cap-able so to sear and indurate our feelings, that nothing should agitate

them but what arose instantly and immediately out of our own selfish interests! I would as soon wish my hand to be as callous as horn,
that it might escape an occasional cut or scratch, as I would be
ambitious of the stoicism which should render my heart like a piece
of the nether mill-stone.'

The Antiquary regarded his youthful companion with a look half
of pity, half of sympathy, and shrugged up his shoulders as he
replied, 'Wait, young man,—wait till your bark has been battered by
the storm of sixty years of mortal vicissitude—you will learn by that
time to reef your sails, that she may obey the helm—or, in the
language of this world, you will find distresses enough, endured and
to endure, to keep your feelings and sympathies in full exercise,
without concerning yourself more in the fate of others than you
cannot possibly avoid.'

'Well, Mr Oldbuck, it may be so; but as yet I resemble you more in
your practice than in your theory, for I cannot help being deeply
interested in the fate of the family we have just left.'

'And well you may,' replied Oldbuck; 'Sir Arthur's embarrassments have of late become so many and so pressing, that I am
surprised you have not heard of them—And then his absurd and
expensive operations carried on by this High-German landlouper,
Dousterswivel'—

'I think I have seen that person, when, by some rare chance, I
happened to be in the coffee-room at Fairport—a tall, beetle-
browed, awkward-built man, who entered upon scientific subjects, as
it appeared to my ignorance at least, with more assurance than knowledge, was very arbitrary in laying down and asserting his opinions,
and mixed the terms of science with a strange jargon of mysticism; a
simple youth whispered me that he was an *Illuminé*,* and carried on
an intercourse with the invisible world.'

'O the same—the same—he has enough of practical knowledge to
speak scholarly and wisely to those of whose intelligence he stands in
awe; and, to say the truth, this faculty, joined to his matchless impudence, imposed upon me for some time when I first knew him. But I
have since understood, that when he is among fools and womankind,
he exhibits himself as a perfect charlatan—talks of the *magisterium*—
of sympathies and antipathies—of the cabala—of the divining rod—
and all the trumpery with which the Rosycrucians cheated a darker
age, and which, to our eternal disgrace, has in some degree revived

in our own.* My friend Heavysterne knew this fellow abroad, and unintentionally (for he, you must know, is, God bless the mark, a sort of believer) let me into a good deal of his real character. Ah! were I caliph for a day, as honest Abon Hassan* wished to be, I would scourge me these jugglers out of the commonwealth with rods of scorpions*—They debauch the spirit of the ignorant and credulous with mystical trash as effectually as if they had besotted their brains with gin, and then pick their pockets with the same facility. And now has this strolling blackguard and mountebank put the finishing blow to the ruin of an ancient and honourable family!'

'But how could he impose upon Sir Arthur to any ruinous extent?'

'Why, I don't know—Sir Arthur is a good honourable gentleman—but, as you may see from his loose ideas concerning the Pikish language, he is by no means very strong in the understanding. His estate is strictly entailed,* and he has been always an embarrassed man. This rapparee promised him mountains of wealth, and an English company was found to advance large sums of money—I fear on Sir Arthur's guarantee. Some gentlemen—I was ass enough to be one—took small shares in the concern, and Sir Arthur himself made great outlay; we were trained on by specious appearances, and more specious lies, and now, like John Bunyan,* we awake, and behold it is a dream.'

'I am surprised that you, Mr Oldbuck, should have encouraged Sir Arthur by your example.'

'Why,' said Oldbuck, dropping his large grizzled eye-brow, 'I am something surprised and ashamed at it myself; it was not the lucre of gain—nobody cares less for money (to be a prudent man) than I do—but I thought I might risk this small sum. It will be expected (though I am sure I cannot see why) that I should give something to any one who will be kind enough to rid me of that slip of woman-kind, my niece, Mary M'Intyre; and perhaps it may be thought I should do something to get that jackanapes, her brother, on in the army. In either case, to treble my venture, would have helped me out. And, besides, I had some idea that the Phœnicians had in former times wrought copper in that very spot. That cunning scoundrel, Dousterswivel, found out my blunt side, and brought strange tales (d—n him) of appearances of old shafts, and vestiges of mining operations, conducted in a manner quite different from those of modern times; and I—in short, I was a fool, and there is an end.

My loss is not much worth speaking about; but Sir Arthur's engagements are, I understand, very deep, and my heart aches for him, and the poor young lady who must share his distress.'

Here the conversation paused, until renewed in the next chapter.

CHAPTER XIV

If I may trust the flattering eye of sleep,
My dreams presage some joyful news at hand:
My bosom's lord sits lightly on his throne,
And all this day, an unaccustom'd spirit
Lifts me above the ground with cheerful thoughts.

*Romeo and Juliet.**

THE account of Sir Arthur's unhappy adventure had led Oldbuck somewhat aside from his purpose of catechising Lovel concerning the cause of his residence at Fairport. He was now, however, resolved to open the subject. 'Miss Wardour was formerly known to you, she tells me, Mr Lovel?'

'He had had the pleasure,' Lovel answered, 'to see her at Mrs Wilmot's, in Yorkshire.'

'Indeed! you never mentioned that to me before, and you did not accost her as an old acquaintance.'

'I—I did not know,' said Lovel, a good deal embarrassed, 'it was the same lady, till we met; and then it was my duty to wait till she should recognise me.'

'I am aware of your delicacy; the knight's a punctilious old fool, but I promise you his daughter is above all nonsensical ceremony and prejudice. And now, since you have found a new set of friends here, may I ask if you intend to leave Fairport as soon as you proposed?'

'What if I should answer your question by another,' replied Lovel, 'and ask you what is your opinion of dreams?'

'Of dreams, you foolish lad!—why, what should I think of them but as the deceptions of imagination when reason drops the reins?—I know no difference betwixt them and the hallucinations of madness—the unguided horses run away with the carriage in both cases, only in the one the coachman is drunk, and in the other he slumbers. What says our Marcus Tullius—*Si insanorum visis fides non est habenda, cur credatur somnientium visis, quæ multo etiam perturbatiora sunt, non intelligo.'**

'Yes, sir, but Cicero also tells us, that as he who passes the whole day in darting the javelin must sometimes hit the mark, so, amid the cloud of nightly dreams, some may occur consonant to future events.'*

'Ay—that is to say, *you* have hit the mark in your own sage opinion? Lord! Lord! how this world is given to folly! Well, I will allow for once the Oneirocritical science—I will give faith to the exposition of dreams, and say a Daniel* hath arisen to interpret them, if you can prove to me that that dream of yours has pointed to a prudent line of conduct.'

'Tell me then,' answered Lovel, 'why, when I was hesitating whether to abandon an enterprise, which I have perhaps rashly undertaken, I should last night dream I saw your ancestor pointing to a motto which encouraged me to perseverance? Why should I have thought of those words which I cannot remember to have heard before, which are in a language unknown to me, and which yet conveyed, when translated, a lesson which I could so plainly apply to my own circumstances?'

The Antiquary burst into a fit of laughing. 'Excuse me, my young friend, but it is thus we silly mortals deceive ourselves, and look out of doors for motives which originate in our own wilful will. I think I can help out the cause of your vision. You were so abstracted in your contemplations yesterday after dinner, as to pay little attention to the discourse between Sir Arthur and me, until we fell upon the controversy concerning the Piks, which terminated so abruptly; but I remember producing to Sir Arthur a book printed by my ancestor, and making him observe the motto; your mind was bent elsewhere, but your ear had mechanically received and retained the sounds, and your busy fancy, stirred by Grizel's legend, I presume, had introduced this scrap of German into your dream. As for the waking wisdom which seized on so frivolous a circumstance as an apology for perserving in some course which it could find no better reason to justify, it is exactly one of those juggling tricks which the sagest of us play off now and then, to gratify our inclination at the expense of our understanding.'

'I own it,' said Lovel, blushing deeply—'I believe you are right, Mr Oldbuck, and I ought to sink in your esteem for attaching a moment's consequence to such a frivolity; but I was tossed by contradictory wishes and resolutions, and you know how slight a line will tow a boat when afloat on the billows, though a cable would hardly move her when pulled up on the beach.'

'Right, right,' exclaimed the Antiquary; 'fall in my opinion?—not a whit—I love thee the better, man—why, we have story for story against each other, and I can think with less shame on having exposed myself about that cursed Prætorium—though I am still convinced Agricola's camp must have been somewhere in this neighbourhood. And now, Lovel, my good lad, be sincere with me—What make you from Wittenberg?—Why have you left your own country and professional pursuits, for an idle residence in such a place as Fairport?—A truant disposition,* I fear.'

'Even so,' replied Lovel, patiently submitting to an interrogatory which he could not well evade;—'yet I am so detached from all the world, have so few in whom I am interested, or who are interested in me, that my very state of destitution gives me independence. He, whose good or evil fortune affects himself alone, has the best right to pursue it according to his own fancy.'

'Pardon me, young man,' said Oldbuck, laying his hand kindly on his shoulder, and making a full halt—'*sufflamina*—a little patience if you please. I will suppose that you have no friends to share, or rejoice in your success in life, that you cannot look back to those to whom you owe gratitude, or forward to those to whom you ought to afford protection—but it is no less incumbent on you to move steadily in the path of duty—for your active exertions are due not only to society, but in humble gratitude to the Being who made you a member of it, with powers to serve yourself and others.'

'But I am unconscious of possessing such powers,' said Lovel, somewhat impatiently; 'I ask nothing of society but the permission of walking innoxiously through the path of life, without jostling others, or permitting myself to be jostled.—I owe no man any thing—I have the means of maintaining myself with complete independence, and so moderate are my wishes in this respect, that even these means, however limited, rather exceed than fall short of them.'

'Nay, then,' said Oldbuck, removing his hand, and turning again to the road, 'if you are so true a philosopher as to think you have money enough, there's no more to be said—I cannot pretend to be entitled to advise you—you have attained the *acmé*—the summit of perfection.—And how came Fairport to be the selected abode of so much self-denying philosophy? It is as if a worshipper of the true religion had set up his staff by choice among the multifarious idolaters of the land of Egypt. There is not a man in Fairport who is not a devoted worshipper of the Golden Calf—the Mammon of unrighteousness*—why, even I, man, am so infected by the bad neighbourhood, that I feel inclined occasionally to become an idolater myself.'

'My principal amusements being literary,' answered Lovel, 'and circumstances which I cannot mention having induced me, for a time at least, to relinquish the military service, I have pitched on Fairport as a place where I might follow my pursuits without any of those temptations to society, which a more elegant circle might have presented to me.'

'Aha!' replied Oldbuck, knowingly,—'I begin to understand your application of my ancestor's motto—you are a candidate for public favour, though not in the way I first suspected,—you are ambitious to shine as a literary character, and you hope to merit favour by labour and perseverance?'

Lovel, who was rather closely pressed by the inquisitiveness of the old gentleman, concluded it would be best to let him remain in the error which he had gratuitously adopted.

'I have been at times foolish enough,' he replied, 'to nourish some thoughts of the kind.'

'Ah, poor fellow! nothing can be more melancholy; unless, as young men sometimes do, you had fancied yourself in love with some trumpery specimen of womankind, which is, indeed, as Shakspeare truly says, pressing to death, whipping, and hanging* all at once.'

He then proceeded with inquiries, which he was sometimes kind enough to answer himself. For this good old gentleman had, from his antiquarian researches, acquired a delight in building theories out of premises which were often far from affording sufficient ground for them; and being, as the reader must have remarked, sufficiently opinionative, he did not readily brook being corrected, either in matter of fact or judgment, even by those who were principally interested in the subjects on which he speculated. He went on, therefore, chalking out Lovel's literary career for him.

'And with what do you propose to commence your debut as a man of letters?—but I guess—poetry—poetry—the soft seducer of youth. Yes! there is an acknowledging modesty of confusion in your eye and manner:—And where lies your vein? Are you inclined to soar to the higher regions of Parnassus, or to flutter around the base of the hill?'*

'I have hitherto attempted only a few lyrical pieces,' said Lovel.

'Just as I supposed—pruning your wing, and hopping from spray to spray. But I trust you intend a bolder flight—Observe, I would by no means recommend your persevering in this unprofitable pursuit—but you say you are quite independent of the public caprice?'

'Entirely so,' replied Lovel.

'And that you are determined not to adopt a more active course of life?'

'For the present, such is my resolution,' replied the young man.

'Why, then, it only remains for me to give you my best advice and assistance in the object of your pursuit. I have myself published two essays in the Antiquarian Repository*—and therefore am an author of experience. There was my Remarks on Hearne's edition of Robert of Gloucester,* signed *Scrutator*; and the other signed *Indagator*, upon a passage in Tacitus—I might add, what attracted considerable notice at the time, and that is my paper in the Gentleman's Magazine,* upon the inscription of Œlia Lelia, which I subscribed Œdipus*—So you see I am not an apprentice in the mysteries of author-craft, and must necessarily understand the taste and temper of the times.—And now once more, what do you intend to commence with?'

'I have no instant thoughts of publishing.'

'Ah! that will never do; you must have the fear of the public before your eyes in all your undertakings. Let us see now—A collection of fugitive pieces—but no—your fugitive poetry is apt to become stationary with the bookseller.—It should be something at once solid and attractive—none of your romances or anomalous novelties—I would have you take high ground at once—Let me see—What think you of a real epic?—the grand old-fashioned historical poem which moved through twelve or twenty-four books—we'll have it so—I'll supply you with a subject—The battle between the Caledonians and Romans—The Caledoniad; or, Invasion Repelled—Let that be the title—It will suit the present taste, and you may throw in a touch of the times.'

'But the invasion of Agricola was *not* repelled.'

'No; but you are a poet—free of the corporation,* and as little bound down to truth or probability as Virgil himself—You may defeat the Romans in spite of Tacitus.'

'And pitch Agricola's camp at the Kaim of—what do you call it,' answered Lovel, 'in defiance of Edie Ochiltree?'

'No more of that, an thou lovest me*—And yet, I dare say, ye may unwittingly speak most correct truth in both instances, in despite of the *toga* of the historian and the blue gown of the mendicant.'

'Gallantly counselled—Well, I will do my best—your kindness will assist me with local information.'

'Will I not, man?—why, I will write the critical and historical notes on each canto, and draw out the plan of the story myself. I pretend to some poetical genius, Mr Lovel, only I was never able to write verses.'

'It is a pity, sir, that you should have failed in a qualification somewhat essential to the art.'

'Essential?—not a whit—it is the mere mechanical department— A man may be a poet without measuring spondees and dactyls like the ancients, or clashing the ends of lines into rhyme like the moderns, as one may be an architect though unable to labour like a stonemason—Dost think Palladio or Vitruvius* ever carried a hod?'

'In that case, there should be two authors to each poem; one to think and plan, another to execute.'

'Why, it would not be amiss; at any rate, we'll make the experiment—not that I would wish to give my name to the public— assistance from a learned friend might be acknowledged in the preface after what flourish your nature will*—I am a total stranger to authorial vanity.'

Lovel was much entertained by a declaration not very consistent with the eagerness wherewith his friend seemed to catch at an opportunity of coming before the public, though in a manner which rather resembled stepping up behind a carriage than getting into one. The Antiquary was, indeed, uncommonly delighted; for, like many other men who spend their lives in obscure literary research, he had a secret ambition to appear in print, which was checked by cold fits of diffidence, fear of criticism, and habits of indolence and procrastination. But, thought he, I may, like a second Teucer,* discharge my shafts from behind the shield of my ally; and admit that he should not prove to be a first-rate poet, I am in no shape answerable for his deficiencies, and the good notes may very probably help

off an indifferent text.—But he is—he must be a good poet—he has
the real Parnassian abstraction—seldom answers a question till it is
twice repeated—drinks his tea scalding, and eats without knowing
what he is putting into his mouth. This is the real *æstus*, the *awen* of
the Welsh bards, the *divinus afflatus** that transports the poet beyond
the limits of sublunary things—His visions, too, are very sympto-
matical of poetic fury—I must recollect to send Caxon to see he puts
out his candle tonight—poets and visionaries are apt to be negligent
in that respect.—Then, turning to his companion, he expressed
himself aloud in continuation.

'Yes, my dear Lovel, you shall have full notes; and, indeed, I
think we may introduce the whole of the Essay on Castrametation
into the appendix—it will give great value to the work. Then we
will revive the good old forms so disgracefully neglected in modern
times.—You shall invoke the Muse—and certainly she ought to be
propitious to an author, who, in an apostatizing age, adheres with
the faith of Abdiel* to the ancient form of adoration—Then we
must have a vision—in which the genius of Caledonia shall appear
to Galgacus,* and show him a procession of the real Scottish
monarchs—and in the notes I will have a hit at Boethius—no; I
must not touch that topic, now that Sir Arthur is likely to have
vexation enough besides—but I'll annihilate Ossian, Macpherson,
and Mac-Cribb.'

'But we must consider the expense of publication,' said Lovel,
willing to try whether this hint would fall like cold water on the
blazing zeal of his self-elected coadjutor.

'Expense!' said Mr Oldbuck, pausing, and mechanically fumbling
in his pocket—'that is true—I would wish to do something—but
you would not like to publish by subscription?'*

'By no means,' answered Lovel.

'No, no!' gladly acquiesced the Antiquary. 'It is not respectable.—
I'll tell you what; I believe I know a bookseller who has a value for my
opinion, and will risk print and paper, and I will get as many copies
sold for you as I can.'

'O, I am no mercenary author,' answered Lovel, smiling; 'I only
wish to be out of risk of loss.'

'Hush! hush! we'll take care of that—throw it all on the pub-
lishers. I do long to see your labours commenced. You will choose
blank verse, doubtless?—it is more grand and magnificent for an

historical subject; and, what concerneth you, my friend, it is, I have an idea, more easily written.'

This conversation brought them to Monkbarns, where the Antiquary had to undergo a chiding from his sister, who, though no philosopher, was waiting to deliver a lecture to him in the portico. 'Guide us, Monkbarns, are things no dear eneugh already, but ye maun be raising the very fish on us, by giving that randy, Luckie Mucklebackit, just what she likes to ask?'

'Why, Grizel,' said the sage, somewhat abashed at this unexpected attack, 'I thought I made a very fair bargain.'

'A fair bargain! when ye gied the limmer a full half o' what she seekit!—An ye will be a wifecarle, and buy fish at your ain hands, ye suld never bid muckle mair than a quarter. And the impudent quean had the assurance to come up and seek a dram—But I trow, Jenny and I sorted her!'

'Truly,' said Oldbuck, (with a sly look to his companion,) 'I think our estate was gracious that kept us out of hearing of that controversy.—Well, well, Grizel, I was wrong for once in my life—*ultra crepidam**—I fairly admit. But hang expenses—care killed a cat*—we'll eat the fish, cost what it will.—And then, Lovel, you must know I pressed you to stay here today, the rather because our cheer will be better than usual, yesterday having been a gaudé-day*—I love the reversion of a feast better than the feast itself. I delight in the *analecta*, the *collectanea*,* as I may call them, of the preceding day's dinner, which appear on such occasions—And see, there is Jenny going to ring the dinner-bell.'

CHAPTER XV

'Be this letter delivered with haste—haste—post-haste! Ride,
villain, ride,—for thy life—for thy life—for thy life!'

*Ancient Indorsation of Letters of Importance.**

LEAVING Mr Oldbuck and his friend to enjoy their hard bargain of
fish, we beg leave to transport the reader to the back-parlour of the
postmaster's house at Fairport, where his wife, he himself being
absent, was employed in assorting for delivery the letters which had
come by the Edinburgh post. This is very often in country towns the
period of the day when gossips find it particularly agreeable to call
on the man or woman of letters, in order, from the outside of the
epistles, and, if they are not belied, occasionally from the inside also,
to amuse themselves with gleaning information, or forming conjectures about the correspondence and affairs of their neighbours.
Two females of this description were, at the time we mention,
assisting, or impeding, Mrs Mailsetter in her official duty.

'Eh, preserve us, sirs,' said the butcher's wife, 'there's ten,
eleven—twall letters to Tennant & Co.—thae folk do mair business
than a' the rest o' the burgh.'

'Ay; but see, lass,' answered the baker's lady, 'there's twa o' them
faulded unco square, and sealed at the tae side—I doubt there will be
protested bills* in them.'

'Is there ony letters come yet for Jenny Caxon?' inquired the
woman of joints and giblets—'the lieutenant's been awa three
weeks.'

'Just ane on Tuesday was a week,' answered the dame of letters.

'Was't a ship-letter?' asked the Fornarina.

'In troth was't.'

'It wad be frae the lieutenant then,' replied the mistress of the
rolls, somewhat disappointed—'I never thought he wad hae lookit
ower his shouther after her.'

'Odd, here's another,' quoth Mrs Mailsetter. 'A ship-letter—post-
mark, Sunderland.' All rushed to seize it.—'Na, na, leddies,' said
Mrs Mailsetter, interfering, 'I hae had eneugh o' that wark—Ken
ye that Mr Mailsetter got an unco rebuke frae the secretary at

Edinburgh, for a complaint that was made about the letter of Aily Bisset's that ye opened, Mrs Shortcake?'

'Me opened!' answered the spouse of the chief baker of Fairport; 'ye ken yoursell, madam, it just cam open o' free will in my hand—What could I help it?—folk suld seal wi' better wax.'

'Weel I wot that's true, too,' said Mrs Mailsetter, who kept a shop of small wares, 'and we have got some that I can honestly recommend, if ye ken ony body wanting it. But the short and the lang o't is, that we'll lose the place gin there's ony mair complaints o' the kind.'

'Hout, lass; the provost will take care o' that.'

'Na, na; I'll neither trust to provost nor bailie,' said the postmistress,—'but I wad aye be obliging and neighbourly, and I'm no again your looking at the outside of a letter neither—See, the seal has an anchor on't—he's done't wi' ane o' his buttons, I'm thinking.'

'Show me! show me!' quoth the wives of the chief butcher and chief baker; and threw themselves on the supposed love-letter, like the weird sisters in Macbeth upon the pilot's thumb,* with curiosity as eager and scarcely less malignant. Mrs Heukbane was a tall woman, she held the precious epistle up between her eyes and the window. Mrs Shortcake, a little squat personage, strained and stood on tiptoe to have her share of the investigation.

'Ay, it's frae him, sure eneugh,' said the butcher's lady,—'I can read Richard Taffril on the corner, and it's written, like John Thomson's wallet,* frae end to end.'

'Haud it lower down, madam,' exclaimed Mrs Shortcake, in a tone above the prudential whisper which their occupation required—-'haud it lower down—Div ye think naebody can read hand o' writ but yoursell?'

'Whisht, whisht, sirs, for God's sake!' said Mrs Mailsetter, 'there's somebody in the shop,'—then aloud—'Look to the customers, Baby!'—Baby answered from without in a shrill tone—'It's naebody but Jenny Caxon, ma'am, to see if there's ony letters to her.'

'Tell her,' said the faithful postmistress, winking to her compeers, 'to come back the morn at ten o'clock, and I'll let her ken—we havena had time to sort the mail letters yet—she's aye in sic a hurry, as if her letters were o' mair consequence than the best merchant's o' the town.'

Poor Jenny, a girl of uncommon beauty and modesty, could only draw her cloak about her to hide the sigh of disappointment, and return meekly home to endure for another night the sickness of the heart, occasioned by hope delayed.

'There's something about a needle and a pole,' said Mrs Shortcake, to whom her taller rival in gossiping had at length yielded a peep at the subject of their curiosity.

'Now, that's downright shamefu',' said Mrs Heukbane, 'to scorn the poor silly gait of a lassie after he's keepit company wi' her sae lang, and had his will o' her, as I make nae doubt he has.'

'It's but ower muckle to be doubted,' echoed Mrs Shortcake;—'to cast up to her that her father's a barber, and has a pole at his door,* and that she's but a manty-maker hersell! Hout! fy for shame!'

'Hout tout, leddies,' cried Mrs Mailsetter, 'ye're clean wrang— It's a line out o' ane o' his sailors' sangs that I have heard him sing, about being true like the needle to the pole.'

'Weel, weel, I wish it may be sae,' said the charitable Dame Heukbane,—'but it disna look weel for a lassie like her to keep up a correspondence wi ane o' the king's officers.'

'I'm no denying that,' said Mrs Mailsetter; 'but it's a great advantage to the revenue of the post-office thae love letters—See, here's five or six letters to Sir Arthur Wardour—maist o' them sealed wi' wafers, and no wi' wax*—there will be a downcome there, believe me.'

'Ay; they will be business letters, and no frae ony o' his grand friends, that seals wi' their coats of arms, as they ca' them,' said Mrs Heukbane; 'pride will hae a fa'—he hasna settled his account wi' my gudeman, the deacon, for this twalmonth—he's but slink, I doubt.'

'Nor wi' huz for sax months,' echoed Mrs Shortcake—'He's but a brunt crust.'

'There's a letter,' interrupted the trusty postmistress, 'from his son, the captain, I'm thinking—the seal has the same things wi' the Knockwinnock carriage. He'll be coming hame to see what he can save out o' the fire.'

The baronet thus dismissed, they took up the esquire—'Twa letters for Monkbarns—they're frae some o' his learned friends now— See sae close as they're written, down to the very seal—and a' to save sending a double letter*—that's just like Monkbarns himsell. When he gets a frank* he fills it up exact to the weight of an unce, that a carvy-seed would sink the scale—but he's ne'er a grain abune it. Weel I wot I wad be broken if I were to gie sic weight to the folk that come to buy our pepper and brimstone, and such like sweetmeats.'

'He's a shabby body the laird o' Monkbarns,' said Mrs Heukbane,—'he'll make as muckle about buying a forequarter o' lamb in August as about a back sey o' beef. Let's taste another drap o' the sinning—(perhaps she meant *cinnamon*)—waters, Mrs Mailsetter, my dear—Ah! lasses, an ye had kend his brother as I did— mony a time he wad slip in to see me wi' a brace o' wild-deukes in his pouch, when my first gudeman was awa at the Falkirk tryst*— weel, weel,—we'se no speak o' that e'enow.'

'I winna say ony ill o' this Monkbarns,' said Mrs Shortcake; 'his brother ne'er brought me ony wild-deukes, and this is a douce honest man—we serve the family wi' bread, and he settles wi' huz ilka week—only he was in an unco kippage when we sent him a book instead o' the *nick-sticks*,[9] * whilk, he said, were the true ancient way o' counting between tradesmen and customers; and sae they are, nae doubt.'

'But look here, lasses,' interrupted Mrs Mailsetter, 'here's a sight for sair e'en! What wad ye gie to ken what's in the inside o' this letter?—this is new corn—I haena seen the like o' this—For William Lovel, Esquire, at Mrs Hadoway's, High-street, Fairport, by Edinburgh, N. B.* This is just the second letter he has had since he was here.'

'Lord's sake, let's see, lass! Lord's sake, let's see!—that's him that the hale town kens naething about—and a weel-fa'ard lad he is—let's see, let's see!' Thus ejaculated the two worthy representatives of mother Eve.

'Na, na, sirs,' exclaimed Mrs Mailsetter; 'haud awa—bide aff, I tell you—this is nane o' your four-penny cuts that we might make up the value to the post-office amang ourselves if ony mischance befell it—the postage is five-and-twenty shillings—and here's an order frae the Secretary to forward it to the young gentleman by express, if he's no at hame. Na, na, sirs, bide aff; this maunna be roughly guided.'

'But just let's look at the outside o't, woman.'

Nothing could be gathered from the outside, except remarks on the various properties which philosophers ascribe to matter,— length, breadth, depth, and weight. The packet was composed of strong thick paper, imperviable by the curious eyes of the gossips, though they stared as if they would burst from their sockets. The seal was a deep and well-cut impression of arms, which defied all tampering.

'Odd, lass,' said Mrs Shortcake, weighing it in her hand, and wishing, doubtless, that the too, too solid wax would melt and dissolve itself,* 'I wad like to ken what's in the inside o' this, for that Lovel dings a' that ever set foot on the plainstanes o' Fairport—naebody kens what to make o' him.'

'Weel, weel, leddies,' said the postmistress, 'we'se sit down and crack about it—Baby, bring ben the tea-water—Muckle obliged to ye for your cookies, Mrs Shortcake—and we'll steek the shop, and cry ben Baby, and take a hand at the cartes till the gudeman comes hame—and then we'll try your braw veal sweet-bread that ye were so kind as send me, Mrs Heukbane.'

'But winna ye first send awa Mr Lovel's letter?' said Mrs Heukbane.

'Troth I kenna wha to send wi't till the gudeman comes hame, for auld Caxon tell'd me that Mr Lovel stays a' the day at Monkbarns—he's in a high fever wi' pu'ing the laird and Sir Arthur out o' the sea.'

'Silly auld doited carles,' said Mrs Shortcake; 'what gar'd them gang to the douking in a night like yestreen?'

'I was gi'en to understand it was auld Edie that saved them,' said Mrs Heukbane; 'Edie Ochiltree, the Blue-Gown, ye ken—and that he pu'd the hale three out of the auld fish-pound, for Monkbarns had threepit on them to gang in till't to see the wark o' the monks lang syne.'

'Hout, lass, nonsense,' answered the postmistress; 'I'll tell ye a' about it, as Caxon tell'd it to me. Ye see, Sir Arthur and Miss Wardour, and Mr Lovel, suld hae dined at Monkbarns'—

'But, Mrs Mailsetter,' again interrupted Mrs Heukbane, 'will ye no be for sending awa this letter by express? there's our powny and our callant hae gane express for the office or now, and the powny hasna gane abune thirty mile the day—Jock was sorting him up as I came ower by.'

'Why, Mrs Heukbane,' said the woman of letters, pursing up her mouth, 'ye ken my gudeman likes to ride the expresses himsell—we maun gie our ain fish-guts to our ain sea-maws—it's a red half-guinea to him every time he munts his mear—and I dare say he'll be in sune—or I dare to say, it's the same thing whether the gentleman gets the express this night or early next morning.'

'Only that Mr Lovel will be in town before the express gaes aff,' said Mrs Heukbane, 'and whare are ye then, lass?—but ye ken yere ain ways best.'

'Weel, weel, Mrs Heukbane;' answered Mrs Mailsetter, a little out of humour, and even out of countenance, 'I am sure I am never against being neighbour-like, and living, and letting live, as they say; and since I hae been sic a fule as to show you the post-office order— ou, nae doubt, it maun be obeyed—but I'll no need your callant, mony thanks to ye—I'll send little Davie on your powny, and that will be just five-and-threepence to ilka ane o' us, ye ken.'

'Davie! the Lord help ye, the bairn's no ten year auld; and, to be plain wi' ye, our powny reists a bit, and it's dooms sweer to the road,* and naebody can manage him but our Jock.'

'I'm sorry for that,' answered the postmistress gravely, 'it's like we maun wait then till the gudeman comes hame, after a'—for I wadna like to be responsible in trusting the letter to sic a callant as Jock— our Davie belangs in a manner to the office.'

'Aweel, aweel, Mrs Mailsetter, I see what ye wad be at—but an ye like to risk the bairn, I'll risk the beast.'

Orders were accordingly given. The unwilling pony was brought out of his bed of straw, and again equipped for service—Davie (a leathern post-bag strapped across his shoulders) was perched upon the saddle, with a tear in his eye, and a switch in his hand. Jock good-naturedly led the animal out of the town, and, by the crack of his whip, and the whoop and halloo of his too well-known voice, compelled it to take the road towards Monkbarns.

Meanwhile the gossips, like the sibyls after consulting their leaves,* arranged and combined the information of the evening, which flew next morning through a hundred channels, and in a hundred varieties, through the world of Fairport. Many, strange, and inconsistent, were the rumours to which their communications and conjectures gave rise. Some said Tennant & Co. were broken, and that all their bills had come back protested—others that they had got a great contract from government, and letters from the principal merchants at Glasgow, desiring to have shares upon a premium. One report stated, that Lieutenant Taffril had acknowledged a private marriage with Jenny Caxon—another, that he had sent her a letter, upbraiding her with the lowness of her birth and education, and bidding her an eternal adieu. It was generally rumoured that Sir Arthur Wardour's affairs had fallen into irretrievable confusion, and this report was only doubted by the wise, because it was traced to Mrs Mailsetter's shop, a source more famous for the circulation of news than for their accuracy. But all agreed that a packet from the Secretary of State's office had arrived, directed for Mr Lovel, and that it had been forwarded by an orderly dragoon, dispatched from the head-quarters at Edinburgh, who had galloped through Fairport without stopping, except just to inquire the way to Monkbarns. The reason of such an extraordinary mission to a very peaceful and retired individual, was variously explained. Some said Lovel was an emigrant noble, summoned to head an insurrection that had broken out in La Vendee*—others that he was a spy—others that he was a general officer, who was visiting the coast privately—others that he was a prince of the blood, who was travelling *incognito*.

Meanwhile the progress of the packet, which occasioned so much speculation, towards its destined owner at Monkbarns, had been perilous and interrupted. The bearer, Davie Mailsetter, as little resembling a bold dragoon as could well be imagined, was carried onwards towards Monkbarns by the pony, so long as the animal had in his recollection the crack of his usual instrument of chastisement, and the shout of the butcher's boy. But feeling how Davie, whose short legs were unequal to maintain his balance, swung to and fro upon his back, the pony began to disdain further compliance with the intimations he had received. First, then, he slackened his pace to a walk. This was no point of quarrel between him and his rider, who had been considerably discomposed by the rapidity of his former motion, and who now took the opportunity of his abated pace to gnaw a piece of gingerbread, which had been thrust into his hand by his mother, in order to reconcile this youthful emissary of the post-office to the discharge of his duty. By and by, the crafty pony availed himself of this surcease of discipline to twitch the rein out of Davie's hands, and apply himself to browse on the grass by the side of the lane. Sorely astounded by these symptoms of self-willed rebellion, and afraid alike to sit or to fall, poor Davie lifted up his voice and wept aloud. The pony, hearing this pudder over his head,* began apparently to think it would be best both for himself and Davie to return from whence they came, and accordingly commenced a retrograde movement towards Fairport. But, as all retreats are apt to end in utter rout, so the steed, alarmed by the boy's cries, and by the flapping of the reins, which dangled about his forefeet—finding also his nose turned homeward, began to set off at a rate which, if Davie kept the saddle, (a matter extremely dubious,) would soon have presented him at Heukbane's stable-door, when, at a turn of the road, an intervening auxiliary, in the shape of old Edie Ochiltree, caught hold of the rein, and stopped his farther proceeding. 'Wha's aught ye, callant? whaten a gate's that to ride?'

'I canna help it!' blubbered the express; 'they ca' me little Davie.'

'And where are ye gaun?'

'I'm gaun to Monkbarns wi' a letter.'

'Stirra, this is no the road to Monkbarns.'

But Davie could only answer the expostulation with sighs and tears.

Old Edie was easily moved to compassion where childhood was in the case.—I wasna gaun that gate, he thought, but it's the best o' my way o' life that I canna be weel out o' my road. They'll gie me quarters at Monkbarns readily eneugh, and I'll e'en hirple awa there wi' the wean, for it will knock its harns out, puir thing, if there's no somebody to guide the powny.—'Sae ye hae a letter, hinney? will ye let me see't?'

'I'm no gaun to let naebody see the letter,' sobbed the boy, 'till I gie't to Mr Lovel, for I am a faithfu' servant o' the office—if it werena for the powny.'

'Very right, my little man,' said Ochiltree, turning the reluctant pony's head towards Monkbarns, 'but we'll guide him atween us, if he's no a' the sweerer.'

Upon the very height of Kinprunes, to which Monkbarns had invited Lovel after their dinner, the Antiquary, again reconciled to the once-degraded spot, was expatiating upon the topics the scenery afforded for a description of Agricola's camp at the dawn of morning, when his eye was caught by the appearance of the mendicant and his protegé. 'What the devil!—here comes old Edie, bag and baggage, I think.'

The beggar explained his errand, and Davie, who insisted upon a literal execution of his commission by going on to Monkbarns, was with difficulty prevailed upon to surrender the packet to its proper owner, although he met him a mile nearer than the place he had been directed to. 'But my minnie said, I maun be sure to get twenty shillings and five shillings for the postage, and ten shillings and sixpence for the express—there's the paper.'

'Let me see—let me see,' said Oldbuck, putting on his spectacles, and examining the crumpled copy of regulations to which Davie appealed. 'Express, per man and horse, one day, not to exceed ten shillings and sixpence.—One day? why, it's not an hour—Man and horse? why, 'tis a monkey on a starved cat!'

'Father wad hae come himsell,' said Davie, 'on the muckle red mear, an ye wad hae bidden till the morn's night.'

'Four-and-twenty hours after the regular date of delivery!—You little cockatrice egg, do you understand the art of imposition so early?'

'Hout, Monkbarns, dinna set your wit against a bairn,' said the beggar; 'mind the butcher risked his beast, and the wife her wean, and I am sure ten and sixpence isna ower muckle. Ye didna gang sae near wi' Johnnie Howie, when'—

Lovel, who, sitting on the supposed *Prætorium*, had glanced over the contents of the packet, now put an end to the altercation by paying Davie's demand, and then turning to Mr Oldbuck, with a look of much agitation, he excused himself from returning with him to Monkbarns that evening. 'I must instantly go to Fairport, and perhaps leave it on a moment's notice; your kindness, Mr Oldbuck, I never can forget.'

'No bad news, I hope?' said the Antiquary.

'Of a very chequered complexion,' answered his friend—'Farewell—in good or bad fortune I will not forget your regard.'

'Nay, nay—stop a moment. If—if—(making an effort)—if there be any pecuniary inconvenience—I have fifty—or a hundred guineas at your service—till—till Whitsunday—or indeed as long as you please.'

'I am much obliged, Mr Oldbuck, but I am amply provided,' said his mysterious young friend. 'Excuse me—I really cannot sustain further conversation at present. I will write or see you, before I leave Fairport—that is, if I find myself obliged to go.' So saying, he shook the Antiquary's hand warmly, turned from him, and walked rapidly towards the town, 'staying no longer question.'*

'Very extraordinary indeed,' said Oldbuck; 'but there's something about this lad I can never fathom; and yet I cannot for my heart think ill of him neither. I must go home and take off the fire in the Green-Room, for none of my womankind will venture into it after twilight.'

'And how am I to win hame?' blubbered the disconsolate express.

'It's a fine night,' said the Blue-Gown, looking up to the skies; 'I had as gude gang back to the town, and take care o' the wean.'

'Do so, do so, Edie;' and, rummaging for some time in his huge waistcoat pocket till he found the object of his search, the Antiquary added, 'there's sixpence to ye to buy sneeshin.'

CHAPTER XVI

'I am bewitched with the rogue's company. If the rascal has not
given me medicines to make me love him, I'll be hang'd; it could
not be else. I have drunk medicines.'

*Second Part of Henry IV.**

REGULAR for a fortnight were the inquiries of the Antiquary at the
veteran Caxon, whether he had heard what Mr Lovel was about; and
as regular were Caxon's answers, 'that the town could learn naething
about him whatever, except that he had received anither muckle
letter or twa frae the south, and that he was never seen on the
plainstanes at a'.'

'How does he live, Caxon?'

'Ou, Mrs Hadoway just dresses him a beefsteak or a muttonchop,
or makes him some Friar's chicken,* or just what she likes hersell, and
he eats it in the little red parlour off his bedroom. She canna get him
to say that he likes ae thing better than anither; and she makes him
tea in a morning, and he settles honourably wi' her every week.'

'But does he never stir abroad?'

'He has clean gi'en up walking, and he sits a' day in his room
reading or writing; a hantle letters he has written, but he wadna put
them into our post-house, though Mrs Hadoway offered to carry
them hersell, but sent them a' under ae cover to the sheriff, and it's
Mrs Mailsetter's belief, that the sheriff sent his groom to put them
into the post-office at Tannonburgh; it's my puir thought, that he
jaloused their looking into his letters at Fairport; and weel had he
need, for my puir daughter Jenny'—

'Tut, don't plague me with your womankind, Caxon. About this
poor young lad—Does he write nothing but letters?'

'Ou, ay—hale sheets o' other things, Mrs Hadoway says. She
wishes muckle he could be gotten to take a walk; she thinks he's but
looking very puirly, and his appetite's clean gane; but he'll no hear o'
ganging ower the door-stane—him that used to walk sae muckle too.'

'That's wrong; I have a guess what he's busy about; but he must
not work too hard neither. I'll go and see him this very day—he's
deep, doubtless, in the Caledoniad.'

Having formed this manful resolution, Mr Oldbuck equipped himself for the expedition with his thick walking-shoes and gold-headed cane, muttering the while the words of Falstaff which we have chosen for the motto of this chapter; for the Antiquary was himself rather surprised at the degree of attachment which he could not but acknowledge he entertained for this stranger. The riddle was notwithstanding easily solved. Lovel had many attractive qualities, but he won our Antiquary's heart by being on most occasions an excellent listener.

A walk to Fairport had become somewhat of an adventure with Mr Oldbuck, and one which he did not often care to undertake. He hated greetings in the market-place; and there were generally loiterers in the streets to persecute him either about the news of the day, or about some petty pieces of business. So on this occasion, he had no sooner entered the streets of Fairport, than it was 'Good-morrow, Mr Oldbuck—a sight o' you's gude for sair een—what d'ye think of the news in the Sun* the day?—they say the great attempt* will be made in a fortnight.'

'I wish to the Lord it were made and over, that I might hear no more about it.'

'Monkbarns, your honour,' said the nursery and seeds-man, 'I hope the plants gied satisfaction? and if ye wanted ony flower-roots fresh frae Holland, or (this in a lower key) an anker or twa o' Cologne gin, ane o' our brigs cam in yestreen.'

'Thank ye, thank ye,—no occasion at present, Mr Crabtree,' said the Antiquary, pushing resolutely onward.

'Mr Oldbuck,' said the town-clerk, (a more important person, who came in front and ventured to stop the old gentleman,) 'the provost, understanding you were in town, begs on no account that you'll quit it without seeing him; he wants to speak to ye about bringing the water frae the Fairwell-spring through a part o' your lands.'

'What the deuce!—have they nobody's land but mine to cut and carve on?—I won't consent, tell them.'

'And the provost,' said the clerk, going on, without noticing the rebuff, 'and the council, wad be agreeable that you should hae the auld stanes at Donagild's chapel, that ye was wussing to hae.'

'Eh?—what?—Oho, that's another story—Well, well, I'll call upon the provost, and we'll talk about it.'

'But ye maun speak your mind on't forthwith, Monkbarns, if ye want the stanes; for Deacon Harlewalls thinks the carved through-stanes might be put with advantage on the front of the new council-house—that is, the twa cross-legged figures that the callants used to ca' Robin and Bobbin, ane on ilka door-cheek; and the other stane, that they ca'd Ailie Dailie, abune the door. It will be very tastefu', the deacon says, and just in the style of modern Gothic.'

'Lord deliver me from this Gothic generation!' exclaimed the Antiquary,—'A monument of a knight-templar on each side of a Grecian porch, and a Madonna on the top of it!—O *crimini!**—Well, tell the provost I wish to have the stones, and we'll not differ about the water-course.—It's lucky I happened to come this way, today.'

They parted mutually satisfied; but the wily clerk had most reason to exult in the dexterity he had displayed, since the whole proposal of an exchange between the monuments, (which the council had determined to remove as nuisance, because they encroached three feet upon the public road,) and the privilege of conveying the water to the burgh through the estate of Monkbarns, was an idea which had originated with himself upon the pressure of the moment.

Through these various entanglements, Monkbarns (to use the phrase by which he was distinguished in the country) made his way at length to Mrs Hadoway's. This good woman was the widow of a late clergyman at Fairport, who had been reduced, by her husband's untimely death, to that state of straitened and embarrassed circumstances in which the widows of the Scotch clergy are too often found. The tenement which she occupied, and the furniture of which she was possessed, gave her the means of letting a part of her house, and as Lovel had been a quiet, regular, and profitable lodger, and had qualified the necessary intercourse which they had together with a great deal of gentleness and courtesy, Mrs Hadoway, not, perhaps, much used to such kindly treatment, had become greatly attached to her lodger, and was profuse in every sort of personal attention which circumstances permitted her to render him. To cook a dish somewhat better than ordinary for 'the poor young gentleman's dinner;' to exert her interest with those who remembered her husband, or loved her for her own sake and his, in order to procure scarce vegetables, or something which her simplicity supposed might tempt her lodger's appetite, was a labour in which she delighted, although she anxiously concealed it from the person who was its object. She did not adopt this secrecy of benevolence to avoid the laugh of those who might suppose that an oval face and dark eyes, with a clear brown complexion, though belonging to a woman of five-and-forty, and enclosed within a widow's close-drawn pinners,* might possibly still aim at making conquests; for, to say truth, such a ridiculous suspicion having never entered into her own head, she could not anticipate its having birth in that of any one else. But she concealed her attentions solely out of delicacy to her guest, whose power of repaying them she doubted as much as she believed in his inclination to do so, and in his being likely to feel extreme pain at leaving any of her civilities unrequited. She now opened the door to Mr Oldbuck, and her surprise at seeing him brought tears into her eyes, which she could hardly restrain.

'I am glad to see you, sir—I am very glad to see you. My poor gentleman is, I am afraid, very unwell; and O, Mr Oldbuck, he'll see neither doctor, nor minister, nor writer! And think what it would be, if, as my poor Mr Hadoway used to say, a man was to die without advice of the three learned faculties!'

'Greatly better than with them,' grumbled the cynical Antiquary. 'I tell you, Mrs Hadoway, the clergy live by our sins, the medical faculty by our diseases, and the law gentry by our misfortunes.'

'O fie, Monkbarns, to hear the like o' that frae you!—But ye'll walk up and see the poor young lad?—Hegh, sirs, sae young and weel-favoured—and day by day he has eat less and less, and now he hardly touches ony thing, only just pits a bit on the plate to make fashion, and his poor cheek has turned every day thinner and paler, sae that he now really looks as auld as me, that might be his mother—no that I might be just that neither, but something very near it.'

'Why does he not take some exercise?' said Oldbuck.

'I think we have persuaded him to do that, for he has bought a horse from Gibbie Golightly, the galloping groom. A gude judge o' horse-flesh Gibbie tauld our lass that he was—for he offered him a beast he thought wad answer him weel eneugh, as he was a bookish man, but Mr Lovel wadna look at it, and bought ane might serve the Master o' Morphie*—they keep it at the Græme's Arms, ower the street—and he rode out yesterday morning and this morning before breakfast—But winna ye walk up to his room?'

'Presently, presently;—but has he no visitors?'

'O dear, Mr Oldbuck, not ane; if he wadna receive them when he was weel and sprightly, what chance is there of ony body in Fairport looking in upon him now?'

'Ay, ay, very true—I should have been surprised had it been otherwise—Come, show me up stairs, Mrs Hadoway, lest I make a blunder, and go where I should not.'

The good landlady showed Mr Oldbuck up her narrow staircase, warning him of every turn, and lamenting all the while that he was laid under the necessity of mounting up so high. At length, she gently tapped at the door of her guest's parlour. 'Come in,' said Lovel; and Mrs Hadoway ushered in the Laird of Monkbarns.

The little apartment was neat and clean, and decently furnished—ornamented too by such relics of her youthful arts of sempstress-ship as Mrs Hadoway had retained; but it was close, overheated, and, as it appeared to Oldbuck, an unwholesome situation for a young person in delicate health, an observation which ripened his resolution touching a project that had already occurred to him in Lovel's behalf. With a writing table before him, on which lay a quantity of books and papers, Lovel was seated on a couch, in his night gown and slippers. Oldbuck was shocked at the change which had taken place in his personal appearance. His cheek and brow had assumed a ghastly white, except where a round bright spot of hectic red formed a strong and painful contrast, totally different from the general cast of hale and hardy complexion which had formerly overspread and somewhat embrowned his countenance. Oldbuck observed, that the dress he wore belonged to a deep mourning suit, and a coat of the same colour hung on a chair near to him. As the Antiquary entered, Lovel arose and came forward to welcome him.

'This is very kind,' he said, shaking him by the hand, and thanking him warmly for his visit; 'this is very kind, and has anticipated a visit with which I intended to trouble you—you must know I have become a horseman lately.'

'I understand as much from Mrs Hadoway—I only hope, my good young friend, you have been fortunate in a quiet horse—I myself inadvertently bought one from the said Gibbie Golightly, which brute ran two miles on end with me after a pack of hounds, with which I had no more to do than the last year's snow, and after affording infinite amusement, I suppose, to the whole hunting field, he was so good as to deposit me in a dry ditch—I hope yours is a more peaceful beast?'

'I hope at least we shall make our excursions on a better plan of mutual understanding.'

'That is to say, you think yourself a good horseman?'

'I would not willingly,' answered Lovel, 'confess myself a very bad one.'

'No; all you young fellows think that would be equal to calling yourselves tailors at once—But, have you had experience? for, *crede experto*,* a horse in a passion is no joker.'

'Why, I should be sorry to boast myself as a great horseman, but when I acted as aid-de-camp to Sir —— —— in the cavalry-action at ——, last year, I saw many better cavaliers than myself dismounted.'

'Ah! you have looked in the face of the grisly God of arms then— you are acquainted with the frowns of Mars armipotent?* That experience fills up the measure of your qualifications for the epopea! The Britons, however, you will remember, fought in chariots— *covinarii* is the phrase of Tacitus—you recollect the fine description of their dashing among the Roman infantry—although the historian tells us how ill the rugged face of the ground was calculated for equestrian combat—and truly, upon the whole, what sort of chariots could be driven in Scotland anywhere but on turnpike roads, has been to me always matter of amazement. And well now—has the Muse visited you?—Have you got any thing to show me?'

'My time,' said Lovel, with a glance at his black dress, 'has been less pleasantly employed.'

'The death of a friend?' said the Antiquary.

'Yes, Mr Oldbuck; of almost the only friend I could ever boast of possessing.'

'Indeed? well, young man,' replied his visitor, in a tone of serious-ness very different from his affected gravity, 'be comforted—to have lost a friend by death while your mutual regard was warm and unchilled, while the tear can drop unembittered by any painful recol-lection of coldness or distrust or treachery, is perhaps an escape from a more heavy dispensation. Look round you—how few do you see grow old in the affections of those with whom their early friendships were formed! our sources of common pleasure gradually dry up as we journey on through the vale of Bacha,* and we hew out to ourselves other reservoirs, from which the first companions of our pilgrimage are excluded—jealousies, rivalries, envy, intervene to separate others from our side, until none remain but those who are connected with us, rather by habit than predilection, or who, allied more in blood than in disposition, only keep the old man company in his life, that they may not be forgotten at his death—

Hæc data pœna diu viventibus—*

Ah! Mr Lovel, if it be your lot to reach the chill, cloudy, and comfortless evening of life, you will remember the sorrows of your youth as the light shadowy clouds that intercepted for a moment the beams of the sun when it was rising.—But I cram these words into your ears against the stomach of your sense.'*

'I am sensible of your kindness,' answered the youth, 'but the wound that is of recent infliction must always smart severely, and I should be little comforted under my present calamity—forgive me for saying so—by the conviction that life had nothing in reserve for me but a train of successive sorrows. And permit me to add, you, Mr Oldbuck, have least reason of many men to take so gloomy a view of life—you have a competent and easy fortune—are generally respected—may, in your own phrase, *vacare musis*,* indulge yourself in the researches to which your taste addicts you—you may form your own society without doors, and within you have the affectionate and sedulous attention of the nearest relatives.'

'Why, yes; the womankind—for womankind—are, thanks to my training, very civil and tractable—do not disturb me in my morning studies—creep across the floor with the stealthy pace of a cat, when it suits me to take a nap in my easy-chair after dinner or tea. All this is very well—but I want something to exchange ideas with—something to talk to.'

'Then why do you not invite your nephew, Captain M'Intyre, who is mentioned by every one as a fine spirited young fellow, to become a member of your family?'

'Who?' exclaimed Monkbarns, 'my nephew Hector?—the Hotspur of the North?*—Why, Heaven love you, I would as soon invite a firebrand into my stackyard—he's an Almanzor,* a Chamont*—has a Highland pedigree as long as his claymore, and a claymore as long as the High-street of Fairport, which he unsheathed upon the surgeon the last time he was at Fairport—I expect him here one of these days, but I will keep him at staff's end, I promise you—He an inmate of my house! to make my very chairs and tables tremble at his brawls—No, no, I'll none of Hector M'Intyre. But hark ye, Lovel, you are a quiet, gentle-tempered lad; had not you better set up your staff* at Monkbarns for a month or two, since I conclude you do not immediately intend to leave this country?—I will have a door opened out to the garden—it will cost but a trifle—there is the space for an old one which was condemned long ago—by which said door you may pass and repass into the Green Chamber at pleasure, so you will not interfere with the old man, nor he with you. As for your fare, Mrs Hadoway tells me you are, as she terms it, very moderate of your mouth, so you will not quarrel with my humble table. Your washing'—

'Hold, my dear Mr Oldbuck,' interposed Lovel, unable to repress a smile; 'and before your hospitality settles all my accommodations, let me thank you most sincerely for so kind an offer—it is not at present in my power to accept of it; but very likely, before I bid adieu to Scotland, I shall find an opportunity to pay you a visit of some length.'

Mr Oldbuck's countenance fell. 'Why, I thought I had hit on the very arrangement that would suit us both, and who knows what might happen in the long run, and whether we might ever part?—Why, I am master of my acres, man—there is the advantage of being descended from a man of more sense than pride—they cannot oblige me to transmit my goods, chattels, and heritages, any way but as I please. No string of substitute heirs of entail,* as empty and unsubstantial as the morsels of paper strung to the train of a boy's kite, to cumber my flights of inclination, and my humours of predilection. Well,—I see you won't be tempted at present—But Caledonia goes on, I hope?'

'O, certainly!' said Lovel, 'I cannot think of relinquishing a plan so hopeful.'

'It is indeed,' said the Antiquary, looking gravely upward,—for, though shrewd and acute enough in estimating the variety of plans formed by others, he had a very natural, though rather disproportioned, good opinion of the importance of those which originated with himself—'It is indeed one of those undertakings which, if achieved with spirit equal to that which dictates its conception, may redeem from the charge of frivolity the literature of the present generation.'

Here he was interrupted by a knock at the room-door, which introduced a letter for Mr Lovel. The servant waited, Mrs Hadoway said, for an answer. 'You are concerned in this matter, Mr Oldbuck,' said Lovel, after glancing over the billet; and handed it to the Antiquary as he spoke.

It was a letter from Sir Arthur Wardour, couched in extremely civil language, regretting that a fit of the gout had prevented his hitherto showing Mr Lovel the attentions to which his conduct during a late perilous occasion had so well entitled him—apologizing for not paying his respects in person, but hoping Mr Lovel would dispense with that ceremony, and be a member of a small party which proposed to visit the ruins of St Ruth's priory on the following day, and afterwards to dine and spend the evening at Knockwinnock castle. Sir Arthur concluded with saying, that he had sent to request the Monkbarns family to join the party of pleasure which he thus proposed. The place of rendezvous was fixed at a turnpike-gate,* which was about an equal distance from all the points from which the company were to assemble.

'What shall we do?' said Lovel, looking at the Antiquary, but pretty certain of the part he would take.

'Go, man—we'll go, by all means. Let me see—it will cost a post-chaise though, which will hold you and me, and Mary M'Intyre, very well, and the other womankind may go to the manse, and you can come out in the chaise to Monkbarns, as I will take it for the day.'

'Why, I rather think I had better ride.'

'True, true, I forgot your Bucephalus.* You are a foolish lad, by the by, for purchasing the brute outright; you should stick to eighteen-pence a side,* if you will trust any creature's legs in preference to your own.'

'Why, as the horses have the advantage of moving considerably faster, and are, besides, two pair to one, I own I incline'—

'Enough said—enough said—do as you please. Well, then, I'll bring either Grizel or the minister, for I love to have my full penny-worth out of post-horses—and we meet at Tirlingen turnpike on Friday, at twelve o'clock precisely.'—And with this agreement the friends separated.

CHAPTER XVII

'Of seats they tell, where priests, 'mid tapers dim,
Breathed the warm prayer or tuned the midnight hymn;
To scenes like these the fainting soul retired,
Revenge and anger in these cells expired:
By Pity soothed, Remorse lost half her fears,
And soften'd Pride dropp'd penitential tears.'

*Crabbe's Borough.**

THE morning of Friday was as serene and beautiful as if no pleasure party had been intended; and that is a rare event, whether in novel-writing or real life. Lovel, who felt the genial influence of the weather, and rejoiced at the prospect of once more meeting with Miss Wardour, trotted forward to the place of rendezvous with better spirits than he had for some time enjoyed. His prospects seemed in many respects to open and brighten before him, and hope, although breaking like the morning sun through clouds and showers, appeared now about to illuminate the path before him. He was, as might have been expected from this state of spirits, first at the place of meeting, and, as might also have been anticipated, his looks were so intently directed towards the road from Knockwinnock Castle, that he was only apprized of the arrival of the Monkbarns division by the gee-hupping of the postilion, as the post-chaise lumbered up behind him. In this vehicle were pent up, first, the stately figure of Mr Oldbuck himself; secondly, the scarce less portly person of the Reverend Mr Blattergowl, minister of Trotcosey, the parish in which Monkbarns and Knockwinnock were both situated. The reverend gentleman was equipped in a buzz wig, upon the top of which was an equilateral cocked hat. This was the paragon of the three yet remaining wigs of the parish, which differed, as Monkbarns used to remark, like the three degrees of comparison—Sir Arthur's ramilies being the positive, his own bob-wig* the comparative, and the overwhelming grizzle of the worthy clergyman figuring as the superlative. The superintendent of these antique garnitures, deeming, or affecting to deem, that he could not well be absent on an occasion which assembled all three together, had seated himself on the board behind the carriage, 'just to be in the way in case they wanted a touch before the gentlemen sat down to dinner.' Between the two massive figures of Monkbarns and the clergyman was stuck, by way of bodkin,* the slim form of Mary M'Intyre, her aunt having preferred a visit to the manse, and a social chat with Miss Beckie Blattergowl, to investigating the ruins of the priory of Saint Ruth.

As greetings passed between the members of the Monkbarns party and Mr Lovel, the Baronet's carriage, an open barouche, swept onward to the place of appointment, making, with its smoking bays, smart drivers, arms, blazoned panels, and a brace of out-riders, a strong contrast with the battered vehicle and broken-winded hacks which had brought thither the Antiquary and his followers. The principal seat of the carriage was occupied by Sir Arthur and his daughter. At the first glance which passed betwixt Miss Wardour and Lovel, her colour rose considerably; but she had apparently made up her mind to receive him as a friend, and only as such, and there was equal composure and courtesy in the mode of her reply to his fluttered salutation. Sir Arthur halted the barouche to shake his preserver kindly by the hand, and intimate the pleasure he had on this opportunity of returning him his personal thanks; then mentioned to him, in a tone of slight introduction, 'Mr Dousterswivel, Mr Lovel.'

Lovel took the necessary notice of the German adept, who occupied the front seat of the carriage, which is usually conferred upon dependents or inferiors. The ready grin and supple inclination with which his salutation, though slight, was answered by the foreigner, increased the internal dislike which Lovel had already conceived towards him; and it was plain, from the lour of the Antiquary's shaggy eye-brow, that he too looked with displeasure on this addition to the company. Little more than distant greeting passed among the members of the party, until, having rolled on for about three miles beyond the place at which they met, the carriages at length stopped at the sign of the Four Horse-shoes, a small hedge inn,* where Caxon humbly opened the door, and let down the step of the hack-chaise, while the inmates of the barouche were, by their more courtly attendants, assisted to leave their equipage.

Here renewed greetings passed; the young ladies shook hands; and Oldbuck, completely in his element, placed himself as guide and Cicerone at the head of the party, who were now to advance on foot towards the object of their curiosity. He took care to detain Lovel close beside him as the best listener of the party, and occasionally glanced a word of explanation and instruction to Miss Wardour and Mary M'Intyre, who followed next in order. The Baronet and the clergyman he rather avoided, as he was aware both of them conceived they understood such matters as well, or better, than he did; and Dousterswivel, besides that he looked on him as a charlatan, was so nearly connected with his apprehended loss in the stock of the mining company, that he could not abide the sight of him. These two latter satellites, therefore, attended upon the orb of Sir Arthur, to whom, moreover, as the most important person of the society, they were naturally induced to attach themselves.

It frequently happens that the most beautiful points of Scottish scenery lie hidden in some sequestered dell, and that you may travel through the country in every direction without being aware of your vicinity to what is well worth seeing, unless intention or accident carry you to the very spot. This is particularly the case in the country around Fairport, which is, generally speaking, open, uninclosed, and bare. But here and there the progress of rills, or small rivers, has formed dells, glens, or, as they are provincially termed, *dens*, on whose high and rocky banks trees and shrubs of all kinds find a shelter, and grow with a luxuriant profusion, which is the more gratifying, as it forms an unexpected contrast with the general face of the country. This was eminently the case with the approach to the ruins of Saint Ruth, which was for some time merely a sheep-track, along the side of a steep and bare hill. By degrees, however, as this path descended, and winded round the hill-side, trees began to appear, at first singly, stunted, and blighted, with locks of wool upon their trunks, and their roots hollowed out into recesses, in which the sheep love to repose themselves,—a sight much more gratifying to the eye of an admirer of the picturesque than to that of a planter or forester. By and by the trees formed groups, fringed on the edges, and filled up in the middle, by thorns and hazel bushes; and at length these groups closed so much together, that, although a broad glade opened here and there under their boughs, or a small patch of bog or heath occurred which had refused nourishment to the seed which they sprinkled round, and consequently remained open and waste, the scene might on the whole be termed decidedly woodland. The sides of the valley began to approach each other more closely; the rush of a brook was heard below, and, between the intervals afforded by openings in the natural wood, its waters were seen hurling clear and rapid under their silvan canopy.

Oldbuck now took upon himself the full authority of Cicerone, and anxiously directed the company not to go a foot-breadth off the track which he pointed out to them, if they wished to enjoy in full perfection what they came to see. 'You are happy in me for a guide, Miss Wardour,' exclaimed the veteran, waving his hand and head in cadence as he repeated with emphasis,

> ' "I know each lane, and every alley green,
> Dingle, or bushy dell, of this wild wood,
> And every bosky bower from side to side."*

—Ah! deuce take it!—that spray of a bramble has demolished all Caxon's labours, and nearly canted my wig into the stream—so much for recitations, *hors de propos.*'*

'Never mind, my dear sir,' said Miss Wardour, 'you have your faithful attendant ready to repair such a disaster when it happens, and when you appear with it as restored to its original splendour, I will carry on the quotation:

> "So sinks the day-star in the ocean bed,
> And yet anon repairs his drooping head,
> And tricks his beams, and with new spangled ore
> Flames on the forehead" '—*

'O enough, enough!' answered Oldbuck; 'I ought to have known what it was to give you advantage over me—But here is what will stop your career of satire, for you are an admirer of nature I know.' In fact, when they had followed him through a breach in a low, ancient, and ruinous wall, they came suddenly upon a scene equally unexpected and interesting.

They stood pretty high upon the side of the glen, which had suddenly opened into a sort of amphitheatre to give room for a pure and profound lake of a few acres extent, and a space of level ground around it. The banks then arose every where steeply, and in some places were varied by rocks—in others covered with the copse which run up, feathering their sides lightly and irregularly, and breaking the uniformity of the green pasture-ground. Beneath, the lake discharged itself into the huddling and tumultuous brook, which had been their companion since they had entered the glen. At the point

at which it issued from 'its parent lake,'* stood the ruins which they
had come to visit. They were not of great extent; but the singular
beauty, as well as wild and sequestered character of the spot on
which they were situated, gave them an interest and importance
superior to that which attaches itself to architectural remains of
greater consequence, but placed near to ordinary houses, and possessing less romantic accompaniments. The eastern window of the
church remained entire, with all its ornaments and tracery work, and
the sides upheld by flying buttresses, whose airy support, detached
from the wall against which they were placed, and ornamented with
pinnacles and carved work, gave a variety and lightness to the building. The roof and western end of the church were completely ruinous, but the latter appeared to have made one side of a square, of
which the ruins of the conventual buildings formed other two, and
the gardens a fourth. The side of these buildings, which overhung
the brook, was partly founded on a steep and precipitous rock;
for the place had been occasionally turned to military purposes, and
had been taken with great slaughter, during Montrose's wars.* The
ground formerly occupied by the garden was still marked by a few
orchard trees. At a greater distance from the buildings were detached
oaks and elms and chestnuts, growing singly, which had attained
great size. The rest of the space between the ruins and the hill was a
close-cropt sward, which the daily pasture of the sheep kept in much
finer order than if it had been subjected to the scythe and broom.
The whole scene had a repose, which was still and affecting without
being monotonous. The dark, deep basin, in which the clear blue
lake reposed, reflecting the water lilies which grew on its surface,
and the trees which here and there threw their arms from the banks,
was finely contrasted with the haste and tumult of the brook which
broke away from the outlet, as if escaping from confinement, and
hurried down the glen, wheeling around the base of the rock on
which the ruins were situated, and brawling in foam and fury with
every shelve and stone which obstructed its passage. A similar contrast was seen between the level green meadow, in which the ruins
were situated, and the large timber-trees which were scattered over
it, compared with the precipitous banks which arose at a short distance around, partly fringed with light and feathery underwood,
partly rising in steeps clothed with purple heath, and partly more
abruptly elevated into fronts of grey rock, chequered with lichen,

and with those hardy plants which find root even in the most arid crevices of the crags.

'There was the retreat of learning in the days of darkness, Mr Lovel,' said Oldbuck, around whom the company had now grouped themselves while they admired the unexpected opening of a prospect so romantic; 'there reposed the sages who were aweary of the world, and devoted either to that which was to come, or to the service of the generations who should follow them in this. I will show you presently the library—see that stretch of wall with square-shafted windows—there it existed, stored, as an old manuscript in my possession assures me, with five thousand volumes—And here I might well take up the lamentation of the learned Leland,* who, regretting the downfall of the conventual libraries, exclaims, like Rachael weeping for her children,* that if the papal laws, decrees, decretals, clementines, and other such drugs of the devil, yea, if Heytesburg's sophisms, Porphyry's universals, Aristotle's logic, and Dunse's divinity,* with such other lousy legerdemains, (begging your pardon, Miss Wardour,) and fruits of the bottomless pit, had leapt out of our libraries, for the accommodation of grocers, candle-makers, soap-sellers, and other worldly occupiers,* we might have been therewith contented. But to put our ancient chronicles, our noble histories, our learned commentaries, and national muniments, to such offices of contempt and subjection, has greatly degraded our nation, and showed ourselves dishonoured in the eyes of posterity to the utmost stretch of time—O negligence, most unfriendly to our land!'

'And, O John Knox,'* said the baronet, 'through whose influence, and under whose auspices, the patriotic task was accomplished!'

The Antiquary, somewhat in the situation of a woodcock caught in his own springe,* turned short round and coughed, to excuse a slight blush as he mustered his answer—'As to the Apostle of Scottish Reformation'—

But Miss Wardour broke in to interrupt a conversation so dangerous. 'Pray, who was the author you quoted, Mr Oldbuck?'

'The learned Leland, Miss Wardour, who lost his senses on witnessing the destruction of the conventual libraries in England.'

'Now I think,' replied the young lady, 'his misfortune may have saved the rationality of some modern antiquaries, which would certainly have been drowned if so vast a lake of learning had not been diminished by draining.'

'Well, thank Heaven, there is no danger now—they have hardly left us a spoonful in which to perform the dire feat.'

So saying, Mr Oldbuck led the way down the bank, by a steep but secure path, which soon placed them on the verdant meadow where the ruins stood. 'There they lived,' continued the Antiquary, 'with nought to do but to spend their time in investigating points of remote antiquity, transcribing manuscripts, and composing new works for the information of posterity.'

'And,' added the baronet, 'in exercising the rites of devotion with a pomp and ceremonial worthy of the office of the priesthood.'

'And if Sir Arthur's excellence will permit,' said the German, with a low bow, 'the monksh might also make de vary curious experiment in deir laboraties, both in chemistry and *magia naturalis*.'*

'I think,' said the clergyman, 'they would have enough to do in collecting the teinds of the parsonage and vicarage of three good parishes.'

'And all,' added Miss Wardour, nodding to the Antiquary, 'without interruption from womankind.'

'True, my fair foe,' said Oldbuck; 'this was a paradise where no Eve was admitted, and we may wonder the rather by what chance the good fathers came to lose it.'

With such criticisms on the occupations of those by whom the ruins had been formerly possessed, they wandered for some time from one moss-grown shrine to another, under the guidance of Oldbuck, who explained, with much plausibility, the ground-plan of the edifice, and read and expounded to the company the various mouldering inscriptions which yet were to be traced upon the tombs of the dead, or under the vacant niches of the sainted images. 'What is the reason,' at length Miss Wardour asked the Antiquary, 'why tradition has preserved to us such meagre accounts of the inmates of these stately edifices, raised with such expense of labour and taste, and whose owners were in their times personages of such awful power and importance? The meanest tower of a freebooting baron, or squire, who lived by his lance and broadsword, is consecrated by its appropriate legend, and the shepherd will tell you with accuracy the names and feats of its inhabitants; but ask a countryman concerning these beautiful and extensive remains—these towers, these arches, and buttresses, and shafted windows, reared at such cost, three words fill up his answer—"they were made by the monks lang syne."'

The question was somewhat puzzling—Sir Arthur looked upward, as if hoping to be inspired with an answer—Oldbuck shoved back his wig—the clergyman was of opinion that his parishioners were too deeply impressed with the true presbyterian doctrine to preserve any records concerning the papistical cumberers of the land, offshoots as they were of the great overshadowing tree of iniquity, whose roots are in the bowels of the seven hills of abomination*—Lovel thought the question was best resolved by considering what are the events which leave the deepest impression on the minds of the common people—'These,' he contended, 'were not such as resemble the gradual progress of a fertilizing river, but the headlong and precipitous fury of some portentous flood. The eras, by which the vulgar compute time, have always reference to some period of fear and tribulation, and they date by a tempest, an earthquake, or burst of civil commotion. When such are the facts most alive in the memory of the common people, we cannot wonder,' he concluded, 'that the ferocious warrior is remembered, and the peaceful abbots are abandoned to forgetfulness and oblivion.'

'If you pleashe, gentlemans and ladies, and ashking pardon of Sir Arthur and Miss Wardour, and this worthy clergymansh, and my goot friend Mr Oldenbuck, who is my countrymansh, and of goot young Mr Lofel also, I think it is all owing to de hand of glory.'

'The hand of what?' exclaimed Oldbuck.

'De hand of glory, my goot Master Oldenbuck, which is a vary great and terrible secrets—which de monksh used to conceal their treasures when they were triven from their cloisters by what you call de Reform.'

'Ay, indeed! tell us about that,' said Oldbuck, 'for these are secrets worth knowing.'

'Why, my goot Master Oldenbuck, you will only laugh at me— But de hand of glory is vary well known in de countries where your worthy progenitors did live—and it is hand cut off from a dead man, as has been hanged for murther, and dried very nice in de shmoke of juniper wood, and if you put a little of what you call yew wid your juniper, it will not be any better—that is, it will not be no worse— then you do take something of de fatsh of de bear, and of de badger, and of de great eber, as you call de grand boar, and of de little sucking child as has not been christened, (for dat is very essentials,) and you do make a candle, and put it into de hand of glory at de proper hour and minute, with de proper ceremonish, and he who seeksh for treasuresh shall never find none at all.'

'I dare take my corporal oath of that conclusion,' said the Antiquary. 'And was it the custom, Mr Dousterswivel, in Westphalia, to make use of this elegant candelabrum?'

'Alwaysh, Mr Oldenbuck, when you did not want nobody to talk of nothing you wash doing about—And de monksh alwaysh did this when they did hide their church-plates, and their great chalices, and de rings, wid very preshious shtones and jewels.'

'But, notwithstanding, you knights of the Rosy Cross* have means, no doubt, of breaking the spell, and discovering what the poor monks have put themselves to so much trouble to conceal?'

'Ah! goot Mr Oldenbuck,' replied the adept, shaking his head mysteriously, 'you was very hard to believe; but if you had seen de great huge pieces of de plate so massive, Sir Arthur—so fine fashion, Miss Wardour—and de silver cross dat we did find (dat was Schrœpfer and my ownself) for de Herr Freygraff, as you call de Baron Von Blunderhaus, I do believe you would have believed then.'

'Seeing *is* believing indeed—But what was your art—what was your mystery, Mr Dousterswivel?'

'Aha, Mr Oldenbuck, dat is my little secret, mine goot sir—you sall forgife me that I not tell that—But I will tell you dere are various ways—yes, indeed, dere is de dream dat you dream tree times, dat is a vary goot way.'

'I am glad of that,' said Oldbuck; 'I have a friend (with a side-glance to Lovel) who is peculiarly favoured by the visits of Queen Mab.'*

'Den dere is de sympathies, and de antipathies, and de strange properties and virtues natural of divers herb, and of de little divining rod.'

'I would gladly rather see some of these wonders than hear of them,' said Miss Wardour.

'Ah, but, my much-honoured young lady, this is not de time or de way to do de great wonder of finding all de church's plate and treasure; but to oblige you, and Sir Arthur my patron, and de reverend clergymans, and goot Mr Oldenbuck, and young Mr Lofel, who is a very goot young gentleman also, I will show you dat it is possible, a vary possible, to discover de spring of water, and de little fountain hidden in de ground, without any mattock, or spade, or dig at all.'

'Umph!' quoth the Antiquary, 'I have heard of that conundrum. That will be no very productive art in our country—you should carry that property to Spain or Portugal, and turn it to good account.'

'Ah! my goot Master Oldenbuck, dere is de Inquisition, and de Auto-da-fe*—they would burn me, who am but a simple philosopher, for one great conjurer.'

'They would cast away their coals then,' said Oldbuck; 'but,' continued he, in a whisper to Lovel, 'were they to pillory him for one of the most impudent rascals that ever wagged a tongue, they would square the punishment more accurately with his deserts. But let us see—I think he is about to show us some of his legerdemain.'

In truth, the German was now got to a little copse-thicket at some distance from the ruins, where he affected busily to search for such a wand as should suit the purpose of his mystery; and after cutting, and examining, and rejecting several, he at length provided himself with a small twig of hazel terminating in a forked end, which he pronounced to possess the virtue proper for the experiment that he was about to exhibit. Holding the forked ends of the wand each between a finger and thumb, and thus keeping the rod upright, he proceeded to pace the ruined aisles and cloisters, followed by the rest of the company in admiring procession. 'I believe dere was no waters here,' said the adept, when he had made the round of several of the buildings, without perceiving any of those indications which he pretended to expect—'I believe those Scotch monksh did find de water too cool for de climate, and alwaysh drank de goot comfortable Rhine wine—but, aha!—see there.'—Accordingly, the assistants observed the rod to turn in his fingers, although he pretended to hold it very tight.—'Dere is water here about sure enough,'—and, turning this way and that way, as the agitation of the divining rod seemed to increase or diminish, he at length advanced into the midst of a vacant and roofless enclosure, which had been the kitchen of the priory, when the rod twisted itself so as to point almost straight downwards. 'Here is de place,' said the adept, 'and if you do not find de water here, I will give you all leave to call me an impudent knave.'

'I shall take that license,' whispered the Antiquary to Lovel, 'whether the water is discovered or no.'

A servant, who had come up with a basket of cold refreshments, was now dispatched to a neighbouring forester's hut for a mattock and pick-axe. The loose stones and rubbish being removed from the spot indicated by the German, they soon came to the sides of a regularly built well; and, when a few feet of rubbish were cleared out by the assistance of the forester and his sons, the water began to rise rapidly, to the delight of the philosopher, the astonishment of the ladies, Mr Blattergowl, and Sir Arthur, the surprise of Lovel, and the confusion of the incredulous Antiquary. He did not fail, however, to enter his protest in Lovel's ear against the miracle. 'This is a mere trick,' he said; 'the rascal had made himself sure of the existence of this old well, by some means or other, before he played off this mystical piece of jugglery. Mark what he talks of next. I am much mistaken if this is not intended as a prelude to some more serious fraud; see how the rascal assumes consequence, and plumes himself upon the credit of his success, and how poor Sir Arthur takes in the tide of nonsense which he is delivering to him as principles of occult science!'

'You do see, my goot patron, you do see, my goot ladies, you do see, worthy Dr Bladderhowl, and even Mr Lofel and Mr Oldenbuck may see, if they do will to see, how art has no enemy at all but ignorance. Look at this little slip of hazel nuts—it is fit for nothing at all but to whip de little child.'—('I would choose a cat and nine tails* for your occasions,' whispered Oldbuck apart,)—'and you put it in the hands of a philosopher—paf! it makes de grand discovery. But this is nothing, Sir Arthur,—nothing at all, worthy Dr Botherhowl—nothing at all, ladies—nothing at all, young Mr Lofel and goot Mr Oldenbuck, to what art can do. Ah! if dere was any man that had de spirit and de courage, I would show him better things than de well of water—I would show him'—

'And a little money would be necessary also, would it not?' said the Antiquary.

'Bah! one trifle, not worth talking about, might be necessaries,' answered the adept.

'I thought as much,' rejoined the Antiquary dryly; 'and I, in the meanwhile, without any divining rod, will show you an excellent venison pasty, and a bottle of London particular Madeira, and I think that will match all that Mr Dousterswivel's art is like to exhibit.'

The feast was spread *fronde super viridi*,* as Oldbuck expressed himself, under a huge old tree, called the Prior's Oak, and the company sitting down around it did ample honour to the contents of the basket.

CHAPTER XVIII

As when a Gryphon through the wilderness,
With winged course, o'er hill and moory dale,
Pursues the Arimaspian, who by stealth
Had from his wakeful custody purloin'd
The guarded gold: So eagerly the Fiend—

*Paradise Lost.**

WHEN their collation was ended, Sir Arthur resumed the account of the mysteries of the divining rod, as a subject on which he had formerly conversed with Dousterswivel. 'My friend Mr Oldbuck will now be prepared, Mr Dousterswivel, to listen with more respect to the stories you have told us of the late discoveries in Germany by the brethren of your association.'

'Ah, Sir Arthur, that was not a thing to speak to those gentlemans, because it is want of credulity—what you call faith—that spoils the great enterprise.'

'At least, however, let my daughter read the narrative she has taken down of the story of Martin Waldeck.'

'Ah, that was very true story—but Miss Wardour, she is so sly and so witty, that she has made it just like one romance—as well as Goethe or Wieland* could have done it, by mine honest wort.'

'To say the truth, Mr Dousterswivel,' answered Miss Wardour, 'the romantic predominated in the legend so much above the probable, that it was impossible for a lover of fairy-land like me to avoid lending a few touches to make it perfect in its kind—But here it is, and if you do not incline to leave this shade till the heat of the day has somewhat declined, and will have sympathy with my bad composition, perhaps Sir Arthur or Mr Oldbuck will read it to us.'

'Not I,' said Sir Arthur; 'I was never fond of reading aloud.'

'Nor I,' said Oldbuck, 'for I have forgot my spectacles—but here is Lovel, with sharp eyes, and a good voice; for Mr Blattergowl, I know, never reads any thing, lest he should be suspected of reading his sermons.'

The task was therefore imposed upon Lovel, who received, with some trepidation, as Miss Wardour delivered with a little embarrassment, a paper containing the lines traced by that fair hand, the possession of which he coveted as the highest blessing the earth could offer to him. But there was a necessity of suppressing his emotions; and, after glancing over the manuscript, as if to become acquainted with the character, he collected himself, and read the company the following tale.

The Fortunes of Martin Waldeck[10]

The solitudes of the Harz forest in Germany, but especially the mountains called Blockberg, or rather Brockenberg, are the chosen scene for tales of witches, demons, and apparitions. The occupation of the inhabitants, who are either miners or foresters, is of a kind that renders them peculiarly prone to superstition, and the natural phenomena which they witness in pursuit of their solitary or subterraneous profession, are often set down by them to the interference of goblins or the power of magic. Among the various legends current in that wild country, there is a favourite one, which supposes the Harz to be haunted by a sort of tutelar demon, in the shape of a wild man, of huge stature, his head wreathed with oak leaves, and his middle cinctured with the same, bearing in his hand a pine torn up by the roots. It is certain that many persons profess to have seen such a form traversing, with huge strides, in a line parallel to their own course, the opposite ridge of a mountain, when divided from it by a narrow glen; and indeed the fact of the apparition is so generally admitted, that modern scepticism has only found refuge by ascribing it to optical deception.[11]

In elder times, the intercourse of the demon with the inhabitants was more familiar, and, according to the traditions of the Harz, he was wont, with the caprice usually ascribed to these earth-born powers, to interfere with the affairs of mortals, sometimes for their weal, sometimes for their woe. But it was observed, that even his gifts often turned out, in the long run, fatal to those on whom they were bestowed, and it was no uncommon thing for the pastors, in their care of their flocks, to compose long sermons, the burden whereof was a warning against having any intercourse, direct or indirect, with the Harz demon. The fortunes of Martin Waldeck have been often quoted by the aged to their giddy children, when they were heard to scoff at a danger which appeared visionary.

A travelling capuchin had possessed himself of the pulpit of the thatched church at a little hamlet called *Morgenbrodt*, lying in the Harz district, from which he declaimed against the wickedness of the inhabitants, their communication with fiends, witches, and fairies, and, in particular, with the woodland goblin of the Harz. The doctrines of Luther had already begun to spread among the peasantry, for the incident is placed under the reign of Charles V., and they laughed to scorn the zeal with which the venerable man insisted upon his topic. At length, as his vehemence increased with opposition, so their opposition rose in proportion to his vehemence. The inhabitants did not like to hear an accustomed quiet demon, who had inhabited the Brockenberg for so many ages, summarily confounded with Baalpeor, Ashtaroth, and Beelzebub* himself, and condemned without reprieve to the bottomless Tophet.* The apprehensions that the spirit might avenge himself on them for listening to such an illiberal sentence, added to their national interest in his behalf. A travelling friar, they said, that is here today and away tomorrow, may say what he pleases: but it is we, the ancient and constant inhabitants of the country, that are left at the mercy of the insulted demon, and must, of course, pay for all. Under the irritation occasioned by these reflections, the peasants from injurious language betook themselves to stones, and having pebbled the priest pretty handsomely, they drove him out of the parish to preach against demons elsewhere.

Three young men, who had been present and assisting on this occasion, were upon their return to the hut where they carried on the laborious and mean occupation of preparing charcoal for the smelting furnaces. On the way, their conversation naturally turned upon the demon of the Harz and the doctrine of the capuchin. Max and George Waldeck, the two elder brothers, although they allowed the language of the capuchin to have been indiscreet and worthy of censure, as presuming to determine upon the precise character and abode of the spirit, yet contended it was dangerous, in the highest degree, to accept of his gifts, or hold any communication with him. He was powerful they allowed, but wayward and capricious, and those who had intercourse with him seldom came to a good end. Did he not give the brave knight, Ecbert of Rabenwald, that famous black steed, by means of which he vanquished all the champions at the great tournament at Bremen? and did not the same steed afterwards precipitate itself with its rider into an abyss so steep and fearful, that neither horse nor man were ever seen more? Had he not given to Dame Gertrude Trodden a curious spell for making butter come? and was she not burnt for a witch by the grand criminal judge of the Electorate,* because she availed herself of his gift? But these, and many other instances which they quoted, of mischance and ill-luck ultimately attending on the apparent benefits conferred by the Harz spirit, failed to make any impression upon Martin Waldeck, the youngest of the brothers.

Martin was youthful, rash, and impetuous; excelling in all the exercises which distinguish a mountaineer, and brave and undaunted from his familiar intercourse with the dangers that attend them. He laughed at the timidity of his brothers. 'Tell me not of such folly,' he said; 'the demon is a good demon—he lives among us as if he were a peasant like ourselves—haunts the lonely crags and recesses of the mountains like a huntsman or goatherd—and he who loves the Harz-forest and its wild scenes, cannot be indifferent to the fate of the hardy children of the soil. But, if the demon were as malicious as you would make him, how should he derive power over mortals, who barely avail themselves of his gifts, without binding themselves to submit to his pleasure? When you carry your charcoal to the furnace, is not the money as good that is paid you by blaspheming Blaize, the old reprobate overseer, as if you got it from the pastor himself? It is not the goblin's gifts which can endanger you then, but it is the use you shall make of them that you must account for. And were the demon to appear to me at this moment, and indicate to me a gold or silver mine, I would begin to dig away even before his back were turned, and I would consider myself as under protection of a much Greater than he, while I made a good use of the wealth he pointed out to me.'

To this the elder brother replied, that wealth ill won was seldom well spent; while Martin presumptuously declared, that the possession of all the treasures of the Harz would not make the slightest alteration on his habits, morals, or character.

His brother entreated Martin to talk less wildly upon this subject, and with some difficulty contrived to withdraw his attention, by calling it to the consideration of the approaching boar-chase. This talk brought them to their hut, a wretched wigwam, situated upon one side of a wild, narrow, and romantic dell, in the recesses of the

Brokenberg. They released their sister from attending upon the operation of charring the wood, which requires constant attention, and divided among themselves the duty of watching it by night, according to their custom, one always waking while his brothers slept.

Max Waldeck, the eldest, watched during the two first hours of the night, and was considerably alarmed, by observing, upon the opposite bank of the glen, or valley, a huge fire surrounded by some figures that appeared to wheel around it with antic gestures. Max at first bethought him of calling up his brothers; but recollecting the daring character of the youngest, and finding it impossible to wake the elder without also disturbing Martin—conceiving also what he saw to be an illusion of the demon, sent perhaps in consequence of the venturous expressions used by Martin on the preceding evening, he thought it best to betake himself to the safeguard of such prayers as he could murmur over, and to watch in great terror and annoyance this strange and alarming apparition. After blazing for some time, the fire faded gradually away into darkness, and the rest of Max's watch was only disturbed by the remembrance of its terrors.

George now occupied the place of Max, who had retired to rest. The phenomenon of a huge blazing fire, upon the opposite bank of the glen, again presented itself to the eye of the watchman. It was surrounded as before by figures, which, distinguished by their opaque forms, being between the spectator and the red glaring light, moved and fluctuated around it as if engaged in some mystical ceremony. George, though equally cautious, was of a bolder character than his elder brother. He resolved to examine more nearly the object of his wonder; and, accordingly, after crossing the rivulet which divided the glen, he climbed up the opposite bank, and approached within an arrow's flight of the fire, which blazed apparently with the same fury as when he first witnessed it.

The appearance of the assistants who surrounded it, resembled those phantoms which are seen in a troubled dream, and at once confirmed the idea he had entertained from the first, that they did not belong to the human world. Amongst these strange unearthly forms, George Waldeck distinguished that of a giant overgrown with hair, holding an uprooted fir in his hand, with which, from time to time, he seemed to stir the blazing fire, and having no other clothing than a wreath of oak leaves around his forehead and loins. George's heart sunk within him at recognising the well-known apparition of the Harz demon, as he had been often described to him by the ancient shepherds and huntsmen who had seen his form traversing the mountains. He turned, and was about to fly; but, upon second thoughts, blaming his own cowardice, he recited mentally the verse of the Psalmist, 'All good angels, praise the Lord!' which is in that country supposed powerful as an exorcism, and turned himself once more towards the place where he had seen the fire. But it was no longer visible.

The pale moon alone enlightened the side of the valley; and when George, with trembling steps, a moist brow, and hair bristling upright under his collier's cap, came to the spot on which the fire had been so lately visible, marked as it was by a scathed oak-tree, there appeared not on the heath the slightest vestiges of what he had seen. The moss and wild flowers were unscorched, and the branches of the oak-tree, which had so lately appeared enveloped in wreaths of flame and smoke, were moist with the dews of midnight.

George returned to his hut with trembling steps, and, arguing like his elder brother, resolved to say nothing of what he had seen, lest he should awake in Martin that daring curiosity which he almost deemed to be allied with impiety.

It was now Martin's turn to watch. The household cock had given his first summons, and the night was wellnigh spent. Upon examining the state of the furnace in which the wood was deposited in order to its being *coked* or *charred*, he was surprised to find that the fire had not been sufficiently maintained; for in his excursion and its consequences, George had forgot the principal object of his watch. Martin's first thought was to call up the slumberers; but, observing that both his brothers slept unwontedly deep and heavily, he respected their repose, and set himself to supply the furnace with fuel without requiring their aid. What he heaped upon it was apparently damp and unfit for the purpose, for the fire seemed rather to decay than revive. Martin next went to collect some boughs from a stack which had been carefully cut and dried for this purpose; but, when he returned, he found the fire totally extinguished. This was a serious evil, and threatened them with loss of their trade for more than one day. The vexed and mortified watchman set about to strike a light in order to re-kindle the fire, but the tinder was moist, and his labour proved in this respect also ineffectual. He was now about to call up his brothers, for circumstances seemed to be pressing, when flashes of light glimmered not only through the window, but through every crevice of the rudely-built hut, and summoned him to behold the same apparition which had before alarmed the successive watches of his brethren. His first idea was, that the Muhllerhaussers, their rivals in trade, and with whom they had had many quarrels, might have encroached upon their bounds for the purpose of pirating their wood, and he resolved to awake his brothers, and be revenged on them for their audacity. But a short reflection and observation on the gestures and manner of those who seemed to 'work in the fire,' induced him to dismiss this belief, and, although rather sceptical in such matters, to conclude that what he saw was a supernatural phenomenon. 'But be they men or fiends,' said the undaunted forester, 'that busy themselves yonder with such fantastical rites and gestures, I will go and demand a light to rekindle our furnace.' He relinquished, at the same time, the idea of awaking his brethren. There was a belief that such adventures as he was about to undertake were accessible only to one person at a time; he feared also that his brothers, in their scrupulous timidity, might interfere to prevent his pursuing the investigation he had resolved to commence; and, therefore, snatching his boar-spear from the wall, the undaunted Martin Waldeck set forth on the adventure alone.

With the same success as his brother George, but with courage far superior, Martin crossed the brook, ascended the hill, and approached so near the ghostly assembly, that he could recognise, in the presiding figure, the attributes of the Harz demon. A cold shuddering assailed him for the first time in his life; but the recollection that he had at a distance dared and even courted the intercourse which was now about to take place, confirmed his staggering courage, and pride supplying what he wanted in resolution, he advanced with tolerable firmness towards the fire, the figures which surrounded it appearing still more wild, fantastical, and supernatural, the more near he approached to the assembly. He was received with a loud shout of discordant and unnatural laughter, which, to his stunned ears, seemed more alarming than a combination of the most dismal and melancholy sounds that could be imagined. 'Who art thou?' said the giant, compressing his savage and exaggerated features into a sort of forced gravity, while they were occasionally agitated by the convulsion of the laughter which he seemed to suppress.

'Martin Waldeck, the forester,' answered the hardy youth;—'and who are you?'

'The King of the Waste and of the Mine,' answered the spectre;—'and why hast thou dared to encroach on my mysteries?'

'I came in search of light to rekindle my fire,' answered Martin hardily, and then resolutely asked in his turn, 'What mysteries are those that you celebrate here?'

'We celebrate,' answered the complaisant demon, 'the wedding of Hermes with the Black Dragon*—But take thy fire that thou camest to seek, and begone—No mortal may long look upon us and live.'

The peasant struck his spear point into a large piece of blazing wood, which he heaved up with some difficulty, and then turned round to regain his hut, the shouts of laughter being renewed behind him with treble violence, and ringing far down the narrow valley. When Martin returned to the hut, his first care, however much astonished with what he had seen, was to dispose the kindled coal among the fuel so as might best light the fire of his furnace; but after many efforts, and all exertions of bellows and fire-prong, the coal he had brought from the demon's fire became totally extinct, without kindling any of the others. He turned about and observed the fire still blazing on the hill, although those who had been busied around it had disappeared. As he conceived the spectre had been jesting with him, he gave way to the natural hardihood of his temper, and, determining to see the adventure to an end, resumed the road to the fire, from which, unopposed by the demon, he brought off in the same manner a blazing piece of charcoal, but still without being able to succeed in lighting his fire. Impunity having encreased his rashness, he resolved upon a third experiment, and was as successful as before in reaching the fire; but, when he had again appropriated a piece of burning coal, and had turned to depart, he heard the harsh and supernatural voice which had before accosted him, pronounce these words, 'Dare not to return hither a fourth time!'

The attempt to kindle the fire with this last coal having proved as ineffectual as on the former occasions, Martin relinquished the hopeless attempt, and flung himself on his bed of leaves, resolving to delay till the next morning the communication of his supernatural adventure to his brothers. He was awakened from a heavy sleep into which he had sunk, from fatigue of body and agitation of mind, by loud exclamations of surprise and joy. His brothers, astonished at finding the fire extinguished when they awoke, had proceeded to arrange the fuel in order to renew it, when they found in the ashes three huge metallic masses, which their skill (for most of the peasants in the Harz are practical mineralogists) immediately ascertained to be pure gold.

It was some damp upon their joyful congratulations when they learned from Martin the mode in which he had obtained this treasure, to which their own experience of the nocturnal vision induced them to give full credit. But they were unable to resist the temptation of sharing in their brother's wealth. Taking now upon him as head of the house, Martin Waldeck bought lands and forests, built a castle, obtained a patent of nobility, and, greatly to the indignation of the ancient aristocracy of the neighbourhood, was invested with all the privileges of a man of family. His courage in public war, as well as in private feuds, together with the number of retainers whom he kept in pay, sustained him for some time against the odium which was excited by his sudden elevation, and the arrogance of his pretensions.

And now it was seen in the instance of Martin Waldeck, as it has been in that of many others, how little mortals can foresee the effect of sudden prosperity on their own disposition. The evil propensities in his nature, which poverty had checked and repressed, ripened and bore their unhallowed fruit under the influence of temptation and the means of indulgence. As Deep calls unto Deep,* one bad passion awakened another;—the fiend of avarice invoked that of pride, and pride was to be supported by cruelty and oppression. Waldeck's character, always bold and daring, but rendered harsh and assuming by prosperity, soon made him odious, not to the nobles only, but likewise to the lower ranks, who saw, with double dislike, the oppressive rights of the feudal nobility of the empire so remorselessly exercised by one who had risen from the very dregs of the people. His adventure, although carefully concealed, began likewise to be whispered abroad, and the clergy already stigmatized as a wizard and accomplice of fiends, the wretch, who, having acquired so huge a treasure in so strange a manner, had not sought to sanctify it by dedicating a considerable portion to the use of the church. Surrounded by enemies, public and private, tormented by a thousand feuds, and threatened by the church with excommunication, Martin Waldeck, or, as we must now call him, the Baron Von Waldeck, often regretted bitterly the labours and sports of his unenvied poverty. But his courage failed him not under all these difficulties, and seemed rather to augment in proportion to the danger which darkened around him, until an accident precipitated his fall.

A proclamation by the reigning Duke of Brunswick had invited to a solemn tournament all German nobles of free and honourable descent, and Martin Waldeck, splendidly armed, accompanied by his two brothers, and a gallantly equipped retinue, had the arrogance to appear among the chilvalry of the province, and demand permission to enter the lists. This was considered as filling up the measure of his presumption. A thousand voices exclaimed, 'We will have no cinder-sifter mingle in our games of chivalry.' Irritated to frenzy, Martin drew his sword and hewed down the herald, who, in compliance with the general outcry, opposed his entry into the lists. An hundred swords were unsheathed to avenge what was in those days regarded as a crime only inferior to sacrilege, or regicide. Waldeck, after defending himself like a lion, was seized, tried on the spot by the judges of the lists, and condemned, as the appropriate punishment for breaking the peace of his sovereign, and violating the sacred person of a herald-at-arms, to have his right hand struck from his body, to be ignominiously deprived of the honour of nobility, of which he was unworthy, and to be expelled from the city. When he had been stripped of his arms, and sustained the mutilation imposed by this severe sentence, the unhappy victim of ambition was abandoned to the rabble, who followed him with threats and outcries levelled alternately against the necromancer and oppressor, which at length ended in violence. His brothers (for his retinue were fled and dispersed) at length succeeded in rescuing him from the hands of the populace, when, satiated with cruelty, they had left him half dead through loss of blood, and through the outrages he had sustained. They were not permitted, such was the ingenious cruelty of their enemies, to make use of any other means of removing him, excepting such a collier's cart as they had themselves formerly used, in which they deposited their brother on a truss of straw, scarcely expecting to reach any place of shelter ere death should release him from his misery.

When the Waldecks, journeying in this miserable manner, had approached the verge of their native country, in a hollow way, between two mountains, they perceived a figure advancing towards them, which at first sight seemed to be an aged man. But as he approached, his limbs and stature encreased, the cloak fell from his shoulders, his pilgrim's staff was changed into an uprooted pine-tree, and the gigantic figure of the Harz demon passed before them in his terrors. When he came opposite to the cart which contained the miserable Waldeck, his huge features dilated into a grin of unutterable contempt and malignity, as he asked the sufferer, 'How like you the fire MY coals have kindled?' The power of motion, which terror suspended in his two brothers, seemed to be restored to Martin by the energy of his courage. He raised himself on the cart, bent his brows, and, clenching his fist, shook it at the spectre with a ghastly look of hate and defiance. The goblin vanished with his usual tremendous and explosive laugh, and left Waldeck exhausted with this effort of expiring nature.

The terrified brethren turned their vehicle toward the towers of a convent, which arose in a wood of pine-trees beside the road. They were charitably received by a bare-footed and long-bearded capuchin, and Martin survived only to complete the first confession he had made since the day of his sudden prosperity, and to receive absolution from the very priest, whom, precisely on that day three years, he had assisted to pelt out of the hamlet of Morgenbrodt. The three years of precarious prosperity were supposed to have a mysterious correspondence with the number of his visits to the spectral fire upon the hill.

The body of Martin Waldeck was interred in the convent where he expired, in which his brothers, having assumed the habit of the order, lived and died in the performance of acts of charity and devotion. His lands, to which no one asserted any claim, lay waste until they were reassumed by the emperor as a lapsed fief,* and the ruins of the castle, which Waldeck had called by his own name, are still shunned by the miner and forester as haunted by evil spirits. Thus were the miseries attendant upon wealth, hastily attained and ill-employed, exemplified in the fortunes of Martin Waldeck.

CHAPTER XIX

Here has been such a stormy encounter
Betwixt my cousin Captain, and this soldier,
About I know not what!—nothing, indeed;
Competitions, degrees, and comparatives
Of soldiership!—

*A Fair Quarrel.**

THE attentive audience gave the fair transcriber of the foregoing legend the thanks which politeness required. Oldbuck alone curled up his nose, and observed, that Miss Wardour's skill was something like that of the alchemists, for she had contrived to extract a sound and valuable moral out of a very trumpery and ridiculous legend. 'It is the fashion, as I am given to understand, to admire those extravagant fictions—for me,

—————————I bear an English heart,
Unused at ghosts and rattling bones to start.'*

'Under your favour, my goot Mr Oldenbuck,' said the German, 'Miss Wardour has turned de story, as she does every thing as she touches, very pretty indeed; but all the history of de Harz goblin, and how he walks among de desolate mountains wid a great fir-tree for his walking-cane, and wid de great green bush around his head and his waist—that is as true as I am an honest man.'

'There is no disputing any proposition so well guarantee'd,' answered the Antiquary dryly. But at this moment the approach of a stranger cut short the conversation.

The new comer was a handsome young man, about five-and-twenty, in a military undress, and bearing, in his look and manner, a good deal of the martial profession, nay, perhaps a little more than is quite consistent with the ease of a man of perfect good-breeding, in whom no professional habit ought to predominate. He was at once greeted by the greater part of the company. 'My dear Hector!' said Miss M'Intyre, as she rose to take his hand—

'Hector, son of Priam,* whence comest thou?' said the Antiquary.

'From Fife, my liege,' answered the young soldier, and continued, when he had politely saluted the rest of the company, and particularly Sir Arthur and his daughter—'I learned from one of the servants, as I rode towards Monkbarns to pay my respects to you, that I should find the present company in this place, and I willingly embrace the opportunity to pay my respects to so many of my friends at once.'

'And to a new one also, my trusty Trojan,' said Oldbuck. 'Mr Lovel, this is my nephew, Captain M'Intyre—Hector, I recommend Mr Lovel to your acquaintance.'

The young soldier fixed his keen eye upon Lovel, and paid his compliment with more reserve than cordiality; and as our acquaintance thought his coldness almost supercilious, he was equally frigid and haughty in making the necessary return to it; and thus a prejudice seemed to arise between them at the very commencement of their acquaintance.

The observations which Lovel made during the remainder of this pleasure party did not tend to reconcile him with this addition to their society. Captain M'Intyre, with the gallantry to be expected from his age and profession, attached himself to the service of Miss Wardour, and offered her, on every possible opportunity, those marks of attention which Lovel would have given the world to have rendered, and was only deterred from offering by the fear of her displeasure. With forlorn dejection at one moment, and with irritated susceptibility at another, he saw this handsome young soldier assume and exercise all the privileges of a cavaliér servénte.* He handed Miss Wardour's gloves, he assisted her in putting on her shawl, he attached himself to her in the walks, had a hand ready to remove every impediment in her path, and an arm to support her where it was rugged or difficult; his conversation was addressed chiefly to her, and, where circumstances permitted, it was exclusively so. All this, Lovel well knew, might be only that sort of egotistical gallantry which induces some young men of the present day to give themselves the air of engrossing the attention of the prettiest woman in company, as if the others were unworthy of their notice. But he thought he observed in the conduct of Captain M'Intyre something of marked and peculiar tenderness, which was calculated to alarm the jealousy of a lover. Miss Wardour also received his attentions; and although his candour allowed they were of a kind which could not be repelled without some strain of affectation, yet it galled him to the heart to witness that she did so.

The heart-burning which these reflections occasioned proved very indifferent seasoning to the dry antiquarian discussions with which Oldbuck, who continued to demand his particular attention, was unremittingly persecuting him; and he underwent, with fits of impatience that amounted almost to loathing, a course of lectures upon monastic architecture, in all its styles, from the massive Saxon to the florid Gothic, and from that to the mixed and composite architecture of James the First's time, when, according to Oldbuck, all orders were confounded, and columns of various descriptions arose side by side, or were piled above each other, as if symmetry had been forgotten, and the elemental principles of art resolved into their primitive confusion. 'What can be more cutting to the heart than the sight of evils,' said Oldbuck, in rapturous enthusiasm, 'which we are compelled to behold, while we do not possess the power of remedying them?' Lovel answered by an involuntary groan. 'I see, my dear young friend, and most congenial spirit, that you feel these enormities almost as much as I do. Have you ever approached them, or met them, without longing to tear, to deface, what is so dishonourable?'

'Dishonourable!' echoed Lovel, 'in what respect dishonourable?'

'I mean disgraceful to the arts.'

'Where? how?'

'Upon the portico, for example, of the schools of Oxford,* where, at immense expense, the barbarous, fantastic, and ignorant architect has chosen to represent the whole five orders of architecture on the front of one building.'

By such attacks as these, Oldbuck, unconscious of the torture he was giving, compelled Lovel to give him a share of his attention,—as a skilful angler, by means of his line, maintains an influence over the most frantic movements of his agonized prey.

They were now on their return to the spot where they had left the carriages; and it is inconceivable how often, in the course of that short walk, Lovel, exhausted by the unceasing prosing of his worthy companion, mentally bestowed on the devil, or any one else that would have rid him of hearing more of them, all the orders and disorders of architecture which had been invented or combined from the building of Solomon's temple downwards. A slight incident occurred, however, which sprinkled a little patience on the heat of his distemperature.*

Miss Wardour, and her self-elected knight-companion, rather preceded the others in the narrow path, when the young lady apparently became desirous to unite herself with the rest of the party, and, to break off her tête-à-tête with the young officer, fairly made a pause until Mr Oldbuck came up. 'I wished to ask you a question, Mr Oldbuck, concerning the date of these interesting ruins.'

It would be doing injustice to Miss Wardour's *savoir faire*,* to suppose she was not aware that such a question would lead to an answer of no limited length. The Antiquary, starting like a war-horse at the trumpet sound,* plunged at once into the various arguments for and against the date of 1273, which had been assigned to the priory of St Ruth by a late publication on Scottish architectural antiquities. He raked up the names of all the priors who had ruled the institution, of the nobles who had bestowed lands upon it, and of the monarchs who had slept their last sleep among its roofless courts. As a train which takes fire* is sure to light another, if there be such in the vicinity, the Baronet, catching at the name of one of his ancestors which occurred in Oldbuck's disquisition, entered upon an account of his wars, his conquests, and his trophies; and worthy Dr Blattergowl was induced, from the mention of a grant of lands, *cum decimis inclusis tam vicariis quam garbalibus, et nunquam antea separatis*,* to enter into a long explanation concerning the interpretation given by the Teind Court* in the consideration of such a clause, which had occurred in a process for localling his last augmentation of stipend.* The orators, like three racers, each pressed forward to the goal, without much regarding how each crossed and jostled his competitors. Mr Oldbuck harangued, the Baronet declaimed, Mr Blattergowl prosed and laid down the law, while the Latin forms of feudal grants were mingled with the jargon of blazonry, and the yet more barbarous phraseology of the Teind Court of Scotland. 'He was,' exclaimed Oldbuck, speaking of the Prior Adhemar, 'indeed an exemplary prelate; and, from his strictness of morals, rigid execution of penance, joined to the charitable disposition of his mind, and the infirmities endured by his great age and ascetic habits'—

Here he chanced to cough, and Sir Arthur burst in, or rather continued—'was called popularly Hell-in-Harness; he carried a shield, gules with a sable fess,* which we have since disused, and was slain at the battle of Vernoil,* in France, after killing six of the English with his own'—

'Decreet of certification,' proceeded the clergyman, in that prolonged, steady, prosing tone, which, however overpowered at first by the vehemence of competition, promised, in the long run, to obtain the ascendency in this strife of narrators; 'Decreet of certification having gone out, and parties being held as confessed, the proof seemed to be held as concluded, when their lawyer moved to have it opened up, on the allegation that they had witnesses to bring forward, that they had been in the habit of carrying the ewes to lamb on the teind-free land; which was a mere evasion,* for'—

But here the Baronet and Mr Oldbuck having recovered their wind, and continued their respective harangues, the three *strands* of the conversation, to speak the language of a rope-work, were again twined together into one undistinguishable string of confusion.

Yet howsoever uninteresting this piebald jargon might seem, it was obviously Miss Wardour's purpose to give it her attention, in preference to yielding Captain M'Intyre an opportunity of renewing their private conversation. So that after waiting for a little time with displeasure ill concealed by his haughty features, he left her to enjoy her bad taste, and taking his sister by the arm, detained her a little behind the rest of the party.

'So I find, Mary, that your neighbourhood has neither become more lively nor less learned during my absence.'

'We lacked your patience and wisdom to instruct us, Hector.'

'Thank you, my dear sister. But you have got a wiser, if not so lively an addition to your society, than your unworthy brother—pray, who is this Mr Lovel, whom our old uncle has at once placed so high in his good graces?—he does not use to be so accessible to strangers.'

'Mr Lovel, Hector, is a very gentleman-like young man.'

'Ay, that is to say, he bows when he comes into a room, and wears a coat that is whole at the elbows.'

'No, brother; it says a great deal more. It says that his manners and discourse express the feelings and education of the higher class.'

'But I desire to know what is his birth and his rank in society; and what is his title to be in the circle in which I find him domesticated?'

'If you mean how he comes to visit at Monkbarns, you must ask my uncle, who will probably reply, that he invites to his own house such company as he pleases; and if you mean to ask Sir Arthur, you must know that Mr Lovel rendered Miss Wardour and him a service of the most important kind.'

'What! that romantic story is true then?—And pray, does the valorous knight aspire, as is befitting on such occasions, to the hand of the young lady whom he redeemed from peril?—It is quite in the rule of romance, I am aware; and I did think that she was uncommonly dry to me as we walked together, and seemed from time to time as if she watched whether she was not giving offence to her gallant cavalier.'

'Dear Hector,' said his sister, 'if you really continue to nourish any affection for Miss Wardour'—

'If, Mary?—what an *if* was there!'

'—I own I consider your perseverance as hopeless.'

'And why hopeless, my sage sister?' asked Captain M'Intyre; 'Miss Wardour, in the state of her father's affairs, cannot pretend to much fortune;—and, as to family, I trust that of M'Intyre is not inferior.'

'But, Hector,' continued his sister, 'Sir Arthur always considers us as members of the Monkbarns family.'

'Sir Arthur may consider what he pleases,' answered the Highlander, scornfully; 'but any one with common sense will consider that the wife takes rank from the husband, and that my father's pedigree of fifteen unblemished descents must have ennobled my mother, if her veins had been filled with printer's ink.'

'For God's sake, Hector,' replied his anxious sister, 'take care of yourself—a single expression of that kind, repeated to my uncle by an indiscreet or interested eves-dropper, would lose you his favour for ever, and destroy all chance of your succeeding to his estate.'

'Be it so,' answered the heedless young man; 'I am one of a profession which the world has never been able to do without, and will far less endure to want for half a century to come; and my good old uncle may tack his good estate and his plebeian name to your apron-string if he pleases, Mary, and you may wed this new favourite of his if you please, and you may both of you live quiet, peaceable, well-regulated lives if it pleases Heaven. My part is taken—I'll fawn on no man for an inheritance which should be mine by birth.'

Miss M'Intyre laid her hand on her brother's arm, and entreated him to suppress his vehemence. 'Who,' she said, 'injures or seeks to injure you, but your own hasty temper?—what dangers are you defying, but those you have yourself conjured up?—Our uncle has hitherto been all that is kind and paternal in his conduct to us, and why should you suppose he will in future be otherwise than what he has ever been, since we were left as orphans to his care?'

'He is an excellent old gentleman, I must own,' replied M'Intyre, 'and I am enraged at myself when I chance to offend him; but then his eternal harangues upon topics not worth the spark of a flint—his investigations about invalided pots and pans and tobacco-stoppers past service—all these things put me out of patience—I have something of Hotspur in me, sister, I must confess.'

'Too much, too much, my dear brother. Into how many risks, and, forgive me for saying, some of them little creditable, has this absolute and violent temper led you! Do not let such clouds darken the time you are now to pass in our neighbourhood, but let our old benefactor see his kinsman as he is,—generous, kind, and lively, without being rude, headstrong, and impetuous.'

'Well,' answered Captain M'Intyre, 'I am schooled—good manners be my speed!* I'll do the civil thing by your new friend—I'll have some talk with this Mr Lovel.'

With this determination, in which he was for the time perfectly sincere, he joined the party who were walking before them. The treble disquisition was by this time ended; and Sir Arthur was speaking on the subject of foreign news, and the political and military situation of the country, themes upon which every man thinks himself qualified to give an opinion. An action of the preceding year having come upon the *tapis*,* Lovel, accidentally mingling in the conversation, made some assertion concerning it, of the accuracy of which Captain M'Intyre seemed not to be convinced, although his doubts were politely expressed.

'You must confess yourself in the wrong here, Hector,' said his uncle, 'although I know no man less willing to give up an argument; but you were in England at the time, and Mr Lovel was probably concerned in the affair.'

'I am speaking to a military man, then,' said M'Intyre; 'may I enquire to what regiment Mr Lovel belongs?'—Mr Lovel gave him the number of the regiment.—'It happens strangely that we should never have met before, Mr Lovel. I know your regiment very well, and have served along with them at different times.'

A blush crossed Lovel's countenance. 'I have not lately been with my regiment,' he replied; 'I served the last campaign upon the staff of General Sir —— ——.'

'Indeed! that is more wonderful than the other circumstance; for, although I did not serve with General Sir —— ——, yet I had an opportunity of knowing the names of the officers who held situations in his family, and I cannot recollect that of Lovel.'

At this observation, Lovel again blushed so deeply, as to attract the attention of the whole company, while a scornful laugh seemed to indicate Captain M'Intyre's triumph. 'There is something strange in this,' said Oldbuck to himself, 'but I will not readily give up my phœnix of post-chaise companions—all his actions, language, and bearing, are those of a gentleman.'

Lovel, in the meanwhile, had taken out his pocket-book, and selecting a letter, from which he took off the envelope, he handed it to M'Intyre. 'You know the general's hand in all probability—I own I ought not to show these exaggerated expressions of his regard and esteem for me.' The letter contained a very handsome compliment from the officer in question for some military service lately performed. Captain M'Intyre, as he glanced his eye over it, could not deny that it was written in the general's hand, but dryly observed, as he returned it, that the address was wanting. 'The address, Captain M'Intyre,' answered Lovel in the same tone, 'shall be at your service whenever you choose to enquire after it.'

'I certainly shall not fail to do so,' rejoined the soldier.

'Come, come,' exclaimed Oldbuck, 'what is the meaning of all this?—Have we got Hiren here?*—We'll have no swaggering, youngsters. Are you come from the wars abroad, to stir up domestic strife in our peaceful land? Are you like bull-dog puppies, forsooth, that when the bull, poor fellow, is removed from the ring, fall to brawl among themselves, worry each other, and bite honest folk's shins that are standing by?'

Sir Arthur trusted, he said, that the young gentlemen would not so far forget themselves as to grow warm upon such a trifling subject as the back of a letter.

Both the disputants disclaimed any such intention, and, with high colour and flashing eyes, protested they were never so cool in their lives. But an obvious damp was cast over the party; they talked in future too much by the rule to be sociable, and Lovel, conceiving himself the object of cold and suspicious looks from the rest of the company, and sensible that his indirect replies had given them permission to entertain strange opinions respecting him, made a gallant determination to sacrifice the pleasure he had proposed in spending the day at Knockwinnock.

He affected, therefore, to complain of a violent headach, occasioned by the heat of the day, to which he had not been exposed since his illness, and made a formal apology to Sir Arthur, who, listening more to recent suspicion than to the gratitude due for former services, did not press him to keep his engagement more than good-breeding exactly demanded.

When Lovel took leave of the ladies, Miss Wardour's manner seemed more anxious than he had hitherto remarked it. She indicated by a glance of her eye towards Captain M'Intyre, perceptible only by Lovel, the subject of her alarm, and hoped, in a voice greatly under her usual tone, it was not a less pleasant engagement which deprived them of the pleasure of Mr Lovel's company. 'No engagement had intervened,' he assured her; 'it was only the return of a complaint by which he had been for some time occasionally attacked.'

'The best remedy in such a case is prudence, and I—every friend of Mr Lovel's, will expect him to employ it.'

Lovel bowed low and coloured deeply, and Miss Wardour, as if she felt that she had said too much, turned and got into the carriage. Lovel had next to part with Oldbuck, who, during this interval, had, with Caxon's assistance, been arranging his disordered periwig, and brushing his coat, which exhibited some marks of the rude path they had traversed. 'What, man!' said Oldbuck, 'you are not going to leave us on account of that foolish Hector's indiscreet curiosity and vehemence?—Why, he is a thoughtless boy—a spoiled child from the time he was in the nurse's arms—he threw his coral and bells* at my head for refusing him a bit of sugar—and you have too much sense to mind such a shrewish boy—*æquam servare mentem** is the motto of our friend Horace. I'll school Hector by and by, and put it all to rights.' But Lovel persisted in his design of returning to Fairport.

The Antiquary then assumed a graver tone. 'Take heed, young man, to your present feelings. Your life has been given you for useful and valuable purposes, and should be reserved to illustrate the literature of your country, when you are not called upon to expose it in her defence, or in the rescue of the innocent. Private war, a practice unknown to the civilized ancients, is, of all the absurdities introduced by the Gothic tribes, the most gross, impious, and cruel. Let me hear no more of these absurd quarrels, and I will show you the treatise upon the duello, which I composed when the town-clerk and provost Mucklewhame chose to assume the privileges of gentlemen, and challenged each other. I thought of printing my Essay, which is signed *Pacificator*; but there was no need, as the matter was taken up by the town-council of the borough.'

'But I assure you, my dear sir, there is nothing between Captain M'Intyre and me that can render such respectable interference necessary.'

'See it be so, for otherwise, I will stand second to both parties.'

So saying, the old gentleman got into the chaise, close to which Miss M'Intyre had detained her brother, upon the same principle that the owner of a quarrelsome dog keeps him by his side to prevent his fastening upon another. But Hector contrived to give her precaution the slip, for, as he was on horseback, he lingered behind the carriages until they had fairly turned the corner in the road to Knockwinnock, and then wheeling his horse's head round, gave him the spur in the opposite direction.

A very few minutes brought him up with Lovel, who, perhaps anticipating his intention, had not put his horse beyond a slow walk, when the clatter of hoofs behind him announced Captain M'Intyre. The young soldier, his natural heat of temper exasperated by the rapidity of motion, reined his horse up suddenly and violently by Lovel's side, and, touching his hat slightly, enquired, in a very haughty tone of voice, 'What am I to understand, sir, by your telling me that your address was at my service?'

'Simply, sir,' replied Lovel 'that my name is Lovel, and that my residence is, for the present, Fairport, as you will see by this card.'

'And this is all the information you are disposed to give me?'

'I see no right you have to require more.'

'I find you, sir, in company with my sister,' said the young soldier, 'and I have a right to know who is admitted into Miss M'Intyre's society.'

'I shall take the liberty of disputing that right,' replied Lovel, with a manner as haughty as that of the young soldier; 'you find me in society who are satisfied with the degree of information on my affairs which I have thought proper to communicate, and you, a mere stranger, have no right to enquire further.'

'Mr Lovel, if you served as you say you have'—

'If!' interrupted Lovel,—'*If* I have served as *I say* I have?'

'Yes, sir, such is my expression—*if* you have so served, you must know that you owe me satisfaction either in one way or other.'

'If that be your opinion, I shall be proud to give it to you, Captain M'Intyre, in the way in which the word is generally used among gentlemen.'

'Very well, sir,' rejoined Hector, and, turning his horse round, galloped off to overtake his party.

His absence had already alarmed them, and his sister, having stopped the carriage, had her neck stretched out of the window to see where he was.

'What is the matter with you now?' said the Antiquary, 'riding to and fro as your neck were upon the wager—why do you not keep up with the carriage?'

'I forgot my glove, sir,' said Hector.

'Forgot your glove!—I presume you meant to say you went to throw it down*—but I will take order with you, my young gentleman—you shall return with me this night to Monkbarns.' So saying, he bid the postilion go on.

CHAPTER XX

—————————If you fail Honour here,
Never presume to serve her any more;
Bid farewell to the integrity of armes,
And the honourable name of soldier
Fall from you, like a shivered wreath of laurel
By thunder struck from a desertlesse forehead.

*A Faire Quarrell.**

EARLY the next morning, a gentleman came to wait upon Mr Lovel, who was up and ready to receive him. He was a military gentleman, a friend of Captain M'Intyre's, at present in Fairport on the recruiting service. Lovel and he were slightly known to each other. 'I presume, sir,' said Mr Lesley, (such was the name of the visitor,) 'that you guess the occasion of my troubling you so early?'

'A message from Captain M'Intyre, I presume?'

'The same—he holds himself injured by the manner in which you declined yesterday to answer certain enquiries which he conceived himself entitled to make respecting a gentleman whom he found in intimate society with his family.'

'May I ask, if you, Mr Lesley, would have inclined to satisfy interrogatories so haughtily and unceremoniously put to you?'

'Perhaps not; and therefore, as I know the warmth of my friend M'Intyre on such occasions, I feel very desirous of acting as peacemaker. From Mr Lovel's very gentleman-like manners, every one must strongly wish to see him repel all that sort of dubious calumny which will attach itself to one whose situation is not fully explained. If he will permit me, in friendly conciliation, to inform Captain M'Intyre of his real name, for we are led to conclude that of Lovel is assumed'—

'I beg your pardon, sir, but I cannot admit that inference.'

'Or at least,' said Lesley, proceeding, 'that it is not the name by which Mr Lovel has been at all times distinguished—if Mr Lovel will have the goodness to explain this circumstance, which, in my opinion, he should do in justice to his own character, I will answer for the amicable arrangement of this unpleasant business.'

'Which is to say, Mr Lesley, that if I condescend to answer questions which no man has a right to ask, and which are now put to me under penalty of Captain M'Intyre's resentment, Captain M'Intyre will condescend to rest satisfied? Mr Lesley, I have just one word to say on this subject—I have no doubt my secret, if I had one, might be safely entrusted to your honour, but I do not feel called upon to satisfy the curiosity of any one. Captain M'Intyre met me in society which of itself was a warrant to all the world, and particularly ought to be such to him, that I was a gentleman. He has, in my opinion, no right to go any further, or to enquire the pedigree, rank, or circumstances of a stranger, who, without seeking any intimate connexion with him, or his, chances to dine with his uncle, or walk in company with his sister.'

'In that case, Captain M'Intyre requests you to be informed, that your farther visits at Monkbarns, and all connexion with Miss M'Intyre, must be dropt, as disagreeable to him.'

'I shall certainly,' said Lovel, 'visit Mr Oldbuck when it suits me, without paying the least respect to his nephew's threats or irritable feelings. I respect the young lady's name too much (though nothing can be slighter than our acquaintance) to introduce it into such a discussion.'

'Since that is your resolution, sir,' answered Lesley, 'Captain M'Intyre requests that Mr Lovel, unless he wishes to be announced as a very dubious character, will favour him with a meeting this evening, at seven, at the thorn-tree in the little valley, close by the ruins of St Ruth.'

'Most unquestionably, I will wait upon him. There is only one difficulty—I must find a friend to accompany me, and where to seek one on this short notice, as I have no acquaintances in Fairport—I will be on the spot, however, Captain M'Intyre may be assured of that.'

Lesley had taken his hat, and was as far as the door of the apartment, when, as if moved by the peculiarity of Lovel's situation, he returned, and thus addressed him: 'Mr Lovel, there is something so singular in all this, that I cannot help again resuming the argument. You must be yourself aware at this moment of the inconvenience of your preserving an incognito, for which, I am convinced, there can be no dishonourable reason. Still, this mystery renders it difficult for you to procure the assistance of a friend in a crisis so delicate—nay, let me add, that many persons will even consider it as a piece of

Quixotry in M'Intyre to give you a meeting, while your character and circumstances are involved in such obscurity.'

'I understand your innuendo, Mr Lesley,' rejoined Lovel, 'and though I might be offended at its severity, I am not so, because it is meant kindly. But, in my opinion, he is entitled to all the privileges of a gentleman, to whose charge, during the time he has been known in the society where he happens to move, nothing can be laid that is unhandsome or unbecoming. For a friend, I dare say I shall find some one or other who will do me that good turn; and if his experience be less than I could wish, I am certain not to suffer through that circumstance when you are in the field for my antagonist.'

'I trust you will not,' said Lesley; 'but as I must, for my own sake, be anxious to divide so heavy a responsibility with a capable assistant, allow me to say, that Lieutenant Taffril's gun-brig is come into the road-stead, and he himself is now at old Caxon's, where he lodges. I think you have the same degree of acquaintance with him as with me, and, as I am sure I should willingly have rendered you such a service were I not engaged on the other side, I am convinced he will do so at your first request.'

'At the thorn-tree, then, Mr Lesley, at seven this evening—the arms, I presume, are pistols?'

'Exactly; M'Intyre has chosen the hour at which he can best escape from Monkbarns—he was with me this morning by five in order to return and present himself before his uncle was up. Good morning to you, Mr Lovel.'—And Lesley left the apartment.

Lovel was as brave as most men; but none can internally regard such a crisis as now approached, without deep feelings of awe and uncertainty. In a few hours he might be in another world to answer for an action which his calmer thought told him was unjustifiable in a religious point of view, or he might be wandering about in the present like Cain, with the blood of his brother on his head.* And all this might be saved by speaking a single word. Yet pride whispered, that, to speak that word now, would be ascribed to a motive which would degrade him more low than even the most injurious reasons that could be assigned for his silence. Every one, Miss Wardour included, must then, he thought, account him a mean dishonoured poltroon, who gave to the fear of meeting Captain M'Intyre, the explanation he had refused to the calm and handsome expostulations of Mr Lesley. M'Intyre's insolent behaviour to himself personally, the air of pretension which he assumed towards Miss Wardour, and the extreme injustice, arrogance, and incivility, of his demands upon a perfect stranger, seemed to justify him in repelling his rude investigation. In short, he formed the resolution, which might have been expected from so young a man, to shut the eyes, namely, of his calmer reason, and follow the dictates of his offended pride. With this purpose he sought Lieutenant Taffril.

The lieutenant received him with the good-breeding of a gentleman, and the frankness of a sailor, and listened with no small surprise to the detail which preceded his request, that he might be favoured with his company at his meeting with Captain M'Intyre. When he had finished, Taffril rose up and walked through his apartment once or twice.

'This is a most singular circumstance,' he said, 'and really'—

'I am conscious, Mr Taffril, how little I am entitled to make my present request, but the urgency of circumstances hardly leaves me an alternative.'

'Permit me to ask you one question,' asked the sailor; 'is there any thing of which you are ashamed in the circumstances which you have declined to communicate?'

'Upon my honour, no; there is nothing but what, in a very short time, I trust I may publish to the whole world.'

'I hope the mystery arises from no false shame at the lowness of your friends perhaps, or connexions?'

'No, on my word,' replied Lovel.

'I have little sympathy for that folly,' said Taffril; 'indeed I cannot be supposed to have any; for, speaking of my relations, I may be said to have come myself from before the mast,* and I believe I shall very soon form a connexion, which the world will think low enough, with a very amiable girl, to whom I have been attached since we were next-door neighbours, at a time when I little thought of the good fortune which has brought me forward in the service.'

'I assure you, Mr Taffril,' replied Lovel, 'whatever were the rank of my parents, I should never think of concealing it from a spirit of petty pride. But I am so situated at present, that I cannot enter on the subject of my family with any propriety.'

'It is quite enough,' said the honest sailor, 'give me your hand; I'll see you as well through this business as I can, though it is but an unpleasant one after all—but what of that? our own honour has the next call on us after our country—you are a lad of spirit, and I own I think Mr Hector M'Intyre, with his long pedigree and his airs of family, very much of a jackanapes. His father was a soldier of fortune as I am a sailor—he himself, I suppose, is little better, unless just as his uncle pleases—and whether one pursues fortune by land, or sea, makes no great difference, I should fancy.'

'None in the universe, certainly,' answered Lovel.

'Well,' said his new ally, 'we will dine together and arrange matters for this rencounter. I hope you understand the use of the weapon?'

'Not particularly,' Lovel replied.

'I am sorry for that—M'Intyre is said to be a marksman.'

'I am sorry for it also,' said Lovel; 'both for his sake and my own— I must then, in self-defence, take my aim as well as I can.'

'Well,' added Taffril, 'I will have our surgeon's-mate on the field—a good clever young fellow at caulking a shot-hole.* I will let Lesley, who is an honest fellow for a landsman, know, that he attends for the benefit of either party.—Is there any thing I can do for you in case of an accident?'

'I have but little occasion to trouble you,' said Lovel; 'this small billet contains the key of my escritoir, and my very brief secret— there is one letter in the escritoir,' (digesting a temporary swelling of the heart as he spoke) 'which I beg the favour of you to deliver with your own hand.'

'I understand,' said the sailor; 'nay, my friend, never be ashamed for the matter—an affectionate heart may overflow for an instant at the eyes, if the ship were clearing for action—and, depend on it, whatever your injunctions are, Dan Taffril will regard them like the bequest of a dying brother. But this is all stuff—we must get our things in fighting order, and you will dine with me and my little surgeon's-mate at the Græmes'-arms, over the way, at four o'clock.'

'Agreed,' said Lovel.

'Agreed,' said Taffril; and the whole affair was arranged.

It was a beautiful summer evening, and the shadow of the solitary thorn-tree was lengthening upon the short green sward of the narrow valley, which was skirted by the woods that closed around the ruins of St Ruth.

Lovel and Lieutenant Taffril, with the surgeon, came upon the ground with a purpose of a nature very uncongenial to the soft, mild, and pacific character of the hour and scene. The sheep, which,

during the ardent heat of the day, had sheltered in the breaches and
hollows of the gravelly bank, or under the roots of the aged and
stunted trees, had now spread themselves upon the face of the hill to
enjoy their evening's pasture, and bleated to each other with that
melancholy sound, which at once gives life to a landscape and marks
its solitude. Taffril and Lovel came on in deep conference, having,
for fear of discovery, sent their horses back to the town by the Lieutenant's servant. The opposite party had not yet appeared on the
field. But, when they came upon the ground, there sat upon the
roots of the old thorn, a figure, as vigorous in his decay as the moss-
grown but strong and contorted boughs which served him for a
canopy. It was old Ochiltree. 'This is embarrassing enough,' said
Lovel; 'how shall we get rid of this old fellow?'

'Here, father Adam,'* cried Taffril, who knew the mendicant of
yore; 'here's half-a-crown for you—you must go to the Four Horse-
shoes yonder—the little inn, you know, and enquire for a servant
with blue and yellow livery. If he is not come, you'll wait for him, and
tell him we shall be with his master in about an hour's time. At any
rate wait there till we come back,—and—get off with you—come,
come, weigh anchor.'*

'I thank ye for your awmous,' said Ochiltree, pocketing the piece
of money; 'but I beg your pardon, Mr Taffril—I canna gang your
errand e'en now.'

'Why, not, man? what can hinder you?'

'I wad speak a word wi' young Mr Lovel.'

'With me?' answered Lovel; 'what would you say with me? come,
say on, and be brief.'

The mendicant led him a few paces aside. 'Are ye indebted ony
thing to the Laird o'Monkbarns?'

'Indebted!—no; not I—what of that?—what makes you think so?'

'Ye maun ken I was at the shirra's the day; for, God help me, I
gang about a' gates like the troubled spirit, and wha suld come
whirling there in a post-chaise, but Monkbarns in an unco
carfuffle—now it's no a little thing that will make his honour take a
chaise and post-horse twa days rinnin'.'

'Well, well; but what is all this to me?'

'Ou, ye'se hear, ye'se hear—Weel, Monkbarns is closeted wi' the
shirra whatever puir folk may be left thereout—ye needna doubt
that—the gentlemen are aye unco civil amang themsells.'

'For heaven's sake, my old friend'—

'Canna ye bid me gang to the deevil at ance, Mr Lovel? it wad be mair purpose fa'ard than to speak o' heaven in that impatient gate.'

'But I have private business with Lieutenant Taffril here.'

'Weel, weel, a' in gude time,' said the beggar—'I can use a little wee bit freedom wi' Mr Daniel Taffril—mony's the peery and the tap I worked for him lang syne, for I was a worker in wood as weel as a tinkler.'

'You are either mad, Adam, or have a mind to drive me mad.'

'Nane o' the twa,' said Edie, suddenly changing his manner from the protracted drawl of the mendicant to a brief and decided tone; 'the shirra sent for his clerk, and, as the lad is rather light o' the tongue, I fand it was for drawing a warrant to apprehend you—I thought it had been on a *fugie* warrant for debt;* for a' body kens the laird likes naebody to pit his hand in his pouch—But now I may haud my tongue, for I see the M'Intyre lad and Mr Lesley coming up, and I guess that Monkbarns's purpose was very kind, and that yours is muckle waur than it should be.'

The antagonists now approached, and saluted with the stern civility which befitted the occasion. 'What has this old fellow to do here?' said M'Intyre.

'I am an auld fallow,' said Edie, 'but I am also an auld soldier o' your father's, for I served wi' him in the 42d.'

'Serve where you please, you have no title to intrude on us,' said M'Intyre, 'or'—and he lifted his cane in terrorem,* though without the idea of touching the old man. But Ochiltree's courage was roused by the insult. 'Haud down your switch, Captain M'Intyre! I am an auld soldier, as I said before, and I'll take muckle frae your father's son; but no a touch o' the wand while my pike-staff will haud thegither.'

'Well, well, I was wrong—I was wrong,' said M'Intyre, 'here's a crown for you—go your ways—what's the matter now?'

The old man drew himself up to the full advantage of his uncommon height, and in despite of his dress, which indeed had more of the pilgrim than the ordinary beggar, looked, from height, manner, and emphasis of voice and gesture, rather like a grey palmer, or eremite preacher, the ghostly counsellor of the young men who were around him, than the object of their charity. His speech, indeed, was as homely as his habit, but as bold and unceremonious as his erect and dignified demeanour. 'What are ye come here for, young men?' he said, addressing himself to the surprised audience; 'are ye come amongst the most lovely works of God to break his laws? Have ye left the works of man, the houses and the cities that are but clay and dust, like those that built them; and are ye come here among the peaceful hills, and by the quiet waters, that will last whiles aught earthly shall endure, to destroy each other's lives, that will have but an unco short time, by the course of nature, to make up a lang account at the close o't? O sirs! hae ye brothers, sisters, fathers, that hae tended ye, and mothers that hae travailed for ye, friends that hae ca'd ye like a piece o' their ain heart? And is this the way ye tak to make them childless and brotherless and friendless? Ohon! it's an ill feight whar he that wins has the warst o't. Think on't, bairns,—I'm a puir man—but I'm an auld man too—and what my poverty takes awa frae the weight o' my counsel, grey hairs and a truthfu' heart should add it twenty times—Gang hame, gang hame, like gude lads—the French will be ower to harry us ane o' thae days, and ye'll hae feighting eneugh, and maybe auld Edie will hirple out himsell if he can get a feal-dike to lay his gun ower, and may live to tell you whilk o' ye does the best where there's a good cause afore ye.'

There was something in the undaunted and independent manner, hardy sentiment, and manly rude elocution of the old man, that had its effect upon the party, and particularly on the seconds, whose pride was uninterested in bringing the dispute to a bloody arbitrement, and who, on the contrary, eagerly watched for an opportunity to recommend reconciliation.

'Upon my word, Mr Lesley,' said Taffril, 'old Adam speaks like an oracle—Our friends here were very angry yesterday, and of course very foolish—Today they should be cool, or at least we must be so in their behalf—I think the word should be forget and forgive on both sides, that we should all shake hands, fire these foolish crackers in the air, and go home to sup in a body at the Græmes'-arms.'

'I would heartily recommend it,' said Lesley; 'for, amidst a great deal of heat and irritation on both sides, I confess myself unable to discover any rational ground of quarrel.'

'Gentlemen,' said M'Intyre very coldly, 'all this should have been thought of before. In my opinion, persons that have carried this matter so far as we have done, and who should part without carrying it any farther, might go to supper at the Græmes'-arms very joyously, but would rise the next morning with reputations as ragged as our friend here, who has obliged us with a rather unnecessary display of his oratory. I speak for myself, that I find myself bound to call upon you to proceed without more delay.'

'And I,' said Lovel, 'as I never desired any, have also to request these gentlemen to arrange preliminaries as fast as possible.'

'Bairns, bairns!' cried old Ochiltree; but, perceiving he was no longer attended to—'Madmen, I should say—but your blood be on your heads!'—And the old man drew off from the ground, which was now measured out by the seconds, and continued muttering and talking to himself in sullen indignation, mixed with anxiety, and with a strong feeling of painful curiosity. Without paying further attention to his presence or remonstrances, Mr Lesley and the Lieutenant made the necessary arrangements for the duel, and it was agreed that both parties should fire when Mr Lesley dropped his handkerchief.

The fatal sign was given, and both fired almost in the same moment. Captain M'Intyre's ball grazed the side of his opponent, but did not draw blood. That of Lovel was more true to the aim; M'Intyre reeled and fell. Raising himself on his arm, his first exclamation was, 'It is nothing—it is nothing—give us the other pistols.' But in an instant he said in a lower tone, 'I believe I have enough, and what's worse, I fear I deserve it. Mr Lovel, or whatever your name is, fly and save yourself—Bear all witness, I provoked this matter.' Then raising himself again on his arm, he added, 'Shake hands, Lovel—I believe you to be a gentleman—forgive my rudeness, and I forgive you my death—My poor sister!'

The surgeon came up to perform his part of the tragedy, and Lovel stood gazing on the evil of which he had been the active, though unwilling cause, with a dizzy and bewildered eye. He was roused from his trance by the grasp of the mendicant—'Why stand you gazing on your deed?—What's doomed is doomed—What's done is past recalling. But awa, awa, if ye wad save your young blood from a shamefu' death—I see the men out by younder that are come ower late to part ye—but out and alack! sune eneuch and ower sune to drag ye to prison.'

'He is right—he is right,' exclaimed Taffril, 'you must not attempt to get on the high-road—get into the wood till night. My brig will be under sail by that time, and at three in the morning, when the tide will serve, I shall have the boat waiting for you at the Mussel-crag. Away—away, for heaven's sake!'

'O yes, fly, fly!' repeated the wounded man, his words faltering with convulsive sobs.

'Come with me,' said the mendicant, almost dragging him off, 'the captain's plan is the best—I'll carry ye to a place where ye might be concealed in the meantime, were they to seek ye wi' sleuth-hounds.'

'Go, go,' again urged Lieutenant Taffril—'to stay here is mere madness.'

'It was worse madness to have come hither,' said Lovel, pressing his hand—'But farewell!' and he followed Ochiltree into the recesses of the wood.

CHAPTER XXI

——————The Lord Abbot had a soul
Subtile and quick and searching as the fire:
By magic stairs he went as deep as hell,
And if in devils' possession gold be kept,
He brought some sure from thence—'tis hid in caves,
Known, save to me, to none.—
*The Wonder of a Kingdome.**

LOVEL almost mechanically followed the beggar who led the way with a hasty and steady pace, through bush and bramble, avoiding the beaten path, and often turning to listen whether there were any sounds of pursuit behind them. They sometimes descended into the very bed of the torrent, sometimes kept a narrow and precarious path, that the sheep (which, with the sluttish negligence towards property of that sort universal in Scotland, were allowed to stray in the copse) had made along the very verge of its overhanging banks. From time to time Lovel had a glance of the path which he had traversed the day before in company with Sir Arthur, the Antiquary, and the young ladies. Dejected, embarrassed, and occupied by a thousand inquietudes, as he then was, what would he now have given to regain the sense of innocence which alone can counterbalance a thousand evils! 'Yet, then,' such was his hasty and involuntary reflections, 'even then, guiltless and valued by all around me, I thought myself unhappy. What am I now, with this young man's blood upon my hands?—the feeling of pride which urged me to the deed has now deserted me, as the actual fiend himself is said to do those whom he has tempted to guilt.' Even his affection for Miss Wardour sunk for the time before the first pangs of remorse, and he thought he could have encountered every agony of slighted love to have had the conscious freedom from blood-guiltiness which he possessed in the morning.

These painful reflections were not interrupted by any conversation on the part of his guide, who threaded the thicket before him, now holding back the sprays to make his path easy, now exhorting him to make haste, now muttering to himself, after the custom of solitary and neglected old age, words which might have escaped

Lovel's ear even had he listened to them, or which, apprehended and retained, were too isolated to convey any connected meaning,—a habit which may be often observed among people of the old man's age and calling.

At length, as Lovel, exhausted by his late indisposition, the harrowing feelings by which he was agitated, and the exertion necessary to keep up with his guide in a path so rugged, began to flag and fall behind, two or three very precarious steps placed him on the front of a precipice overhung with brushwood and copse. Here a cave, as narrow in its entrance as a fox-earth, was indicated by a small fissure in the rock, screened by the boughs of an aged oak, which, anchored by its thick and twisted roots in the upper part of the cleft, flung its branches almost straight outward from the cliff, concealing it effectually from all observation. It might indeed have escaped the attention even of those who had stood at its very opening, so uninviting was the portal at which the beggar entered. But within, the cavern was higher and more roomy, cut into two separate branches, which, intersecting each other at right angles, formed an emblem of the cross, and indicated the abode of an anchoret of former times. There are many caves of the same kind in different parts of Scotland. I need only instance those of Gorton, near Roslyn, in a scene well known to the admirers of romantic nature.

The light within the cave was a dusky twilight at the entrance, which failed altogether in the inner recesses. 'Few folks ken o' this place,' said the old man; 'to the best o' my knowledge, there's just twa living by mysell, and that's Jingling Jock and the Lang Linker. I have had mony a thought, that when I faund mysell auld and forfairn, and no able to enjoy God's blessed air ony langer, I wad drag mysell here wi' a pickle ait-meal—and see, there's a bit bonny drapping well that popples that self-same gate simmer and winter—and I wad e'en streek mysell out here, and abide my removal, like an auld dog that trails its useless ugsome carcass into some bush or bracken, no to gie living things a sconner wi' the sight o't when it's dead—Ay, and then, when the dogs barked at the lone farm-stead, the gudewife wad cry, "Whisht, stirra, that'll be auld Edie," and the bits o' weans wad up, puir things, and toddle to the door, to pu' in the auld Blue-Gown that mends a' their bonny-dies—but there wad be nae mair word o' Edie, I trow.'

He then led Lovel, who followed him unresistingly, into one of the interior branches of the cave. 'Here,' he said, 'is a bit turnpike-stair that gaes up to the auld kirk above. Some folks say this place was howkit out by the monks lang syne to hide their treasure in, and some said that they used to bring things into the abbey this gate by night, that they durstna sae weel hae brought in by the main port and in open day—And some said that ane o' them turned a saint, (or aiblins wad hae had folk think sae,) and settled him down in this Saint Ruth's cell, as the auld folks aye ca'd it, and garr'd big the stair, that he might gang up to the kirk when they were at the divine service. The Laird o' Monkbarns wad hae a hantle to say about it, as he has about maist things, if he kend only about the place. But whether it was made for man's devices or God's service, I have seen ower muckle sin done in it in my day, and far ower muckle have I been partaker of—ay, even here in this dark cove. Mony a gudewife's been wondering what for the red cock didna craw her up in the morning, when he's been roasting, puir fallow, in this dark hole—And, ohon! I wish that and the like o' that had been the warst o't! Whiles they wad hae heard the din we were making in the very bowels o' the earth, when Sanders Aikwood, that was forester in thae days, the father o' Ringan that now is, was gaun daundering about the wood at e'en to see after the laird's game—and whiles he wad hae seen a glance o' the light frae the door o' the cave, flaughtering against the hazels on the other bank—and then siccan stories as Sanders had about the worricows and gyre-carlins that haunted about the auld wa's at e'en, and the lights that he had seen, and the cries that he had heard, when there was nae mortal ee open but his ain; and eh! as he wad thrum them ower and ower to the like o' me ayont the ingle at e'en, and as I wad gie the auld silly carle grane for grane, and tale for tale, though I kend muckle better about it than ever he did. Ay, ay—they were daft days thae—but they were a' vanity and waur, and it's fitting that thae wha hae led a light and evil life, and abused charity when they were young, suld aiblins come to lack it when they are auld.'

While Ochiltree was thus recounting the exploits and tricks of his earlier life, with a tone in which glee and compunction alternately predominated, his unfortunate auditor had sat down upon the hermit's seat, hewn out of the solid rock, and abandoned himself to that lassitude, both of mind and body, which generally follows a course of events that have agitated both. The effect of his late indisposition, which had much weakened his system, contributed to this lethargic despondency. 'The puir bairn,' said auld Edie, 'an he sleeps in this damp hole, he'll maybe wauken nae mair, or catch some sair disease—it's no the same to him as to the like o' us, that can sleep ony gate an anes our wames are fu'. Sit up, Maister Lovel, lad—after a's come and gane, I dare say the captain-lad will do weel eneugh— and, after a', ye are no the first that has had this misfortune. I hae seen mony a man killed, and helped to kill them mysell, though there was nae quarrel between us—and if it isna wrang to kill folk we have nae quarrel wi', just because they wear another sort of a cockade, and speak a foreign language, I canna see but a man may have excuse for killing his ain mortal foe, that comes armed to the fair field to kill him. I dinna say it's right—God forbid—or that it isna sinfu' to take away what ye canna restore, and that's the breath of man, whilk is in his nostrils—but I say it is a sin to be forgiven if it's repented of. Sinfu' men are we a'; but if ye wad believe an auld grey sinner that has seen the evil o' his ways, there is as much promise atween the twa boards o' the Testament as wad save the warst o' us, could we but think sae.'

With such scraps of comfort and of divinity as he possessed, the mendicant thus continued to solicit and compel the attention of Lovel, until the twilight began to fade into night. 'Now,' said Ochiltree, 'I will carry ye to a mair convenient place, where I hae sat mony a time to hear the howlit crying out of the ivy tod, and to see the moonlight come through the auld windows o' the ruins. There can be naebody come here after this time o' night; and if they hae made ony search, thae blackguard shirra'-officers and constables, it will hae been ower lang syne. Odd, they are as great cowards as ither folk, wi' a' their warrants and king's keys[12]—I hae gien some o' them a gliff in my day, when they were coming rather ower near me—But, lauded be grace for it, they canna stir me now for ony waur than an auld man and a beggar, and my badge is a gude protection; and then Miss Isabella Wardour is a tower o' strength, ye ken—(Lovel sighed)—Aweel, dinna be cast down—bowls may a' row right yet— gie the lassie time to ken her mind—she's the wale o' the country for beauty, and a gude friend o' mine—I gang by the bridewell as safe as by the kirk on a Sabbath—deil ony o' them daur hurt a hair o' auld Edie's head now—I keep the crown o' the causey when I gae to the borough, and rub shouthers wi' a bailie wi' as little concern as an he were a brock.'

While the mendicant spoke thus, he was busied in removing a few loose stones in one angle of the cave which obscured the entrance of the staircase of which he had spoken, and led the way into it, followed by Lovel in passive silence.

'The air's free eneugh,' said the old man; 'the monks took care o' that, for they werena a lang-breathed generation, I reckon—they hae contrived queer tirlie-wirlie holes, that gang out to the open air, and keep the stair as caller as a kail-blade.'

Lovel accordingly found the staircase well aired, and, though narrow, it was neither ruinous nor long, but speedily admitted them into a narrow gallery contrived to run within the side wall of the chancel, from which it received air and light through apertures ingeniously hidden amid the florid ornaments of the Gothic architecture.

'This secret passage anes gaed round great part o' the biggin,' said the beggar, 'and through the wa' o' the place I've heard Monkbarns ca' the Refractory, [meaning probably *Refectory*,] and so awa to the Prior's ain house.—It's like he could use it to listen what the monks were saying at meal-time, and then he might come ben here and see that they were busy skreighing awa wi' the psalms doun below there—and then, when he saw a' was right and tight, he might step awa and fetch in a bonnie lass at the cove yonder, for they were queer hands the monks, unless mony lees is made on them. But our folk were at great pains lang syne to big up the passage in some parts, and pu' it down in others, for fear o' some uncanny body getting into it, and finding their way down to the cove—it wad hae been a fashious job that—by my certie, some o' our necks wad hae been ewking.'

They now came to a place where the gallery was enlarged into a small circle, sufficient to contain a stone seat. A niche, constructed exactly before it, projected forward into the chancel, and as its sides were latticed, as it were, with perforated stonework, it commanded a full view of the chancel in every direction, and was probably constructed, as Edie intimated, to be a convenient watch-tower, from which the superior priest, himself unseen, might watch the behaviour of his monks, and ascertain, by personal inspection, their punctual attendance upon those rites of devotion which his rank exempted him from sharing with them. As this niche made one of a regular series which stretched along the wall of the chancel, and in no respect differed from the rest when seen from below, the secret station, screened as it was by the stone figure of St Michael and the dragon* and the open tracery around the niche, was completely hid from observation. The private passage, confined to its pristine breadth, had originally continued beyond this seat; but the jealous precautions of the vagabonds who frequented the cave of St Ruth had caused them to build it carefully up with hewn stones from the ruin.

'We shall be better here,' said Edie, seating himself on the stone bench, and stretching the lappet of his blue gown upon the spot, when he motioned Lovel to sit down beside him—'We shall be better here than doun below—the air's free and mild, and the savour of the wallflowers, and siccan shrubs as grow on thae ruined wa's, is far mair refreshing than the damp smell doun below yonder. They smell sweetest by night-time thae flowers, and they're maist aye seen about ruined buildings—now, Maister Lovel, can ony o' your scholars gie a gude reason for that?'

Lovel replied in the negative.

'I am thinking,' resumed the beggar, 'that they'll be like mony folk's gude gifts, that often seem maist gracious in adversity—or maybe it's a parable, to teach us no to slight them that are in the darkness of sin and the decay of tribulation, since God sends odours to refresh the mirkest hour, and flowers and pleasant bushes to clothe the ruined buildings. And now I wad like a wise man to tell me whether Heaven is maist pleased wi' the sight we are looking upon— thae pleasant and quiet lang streaks o' moonlight that are lying sae still on the floor o' this auld kirk, and glancing through the great pillars and stanchions o' the carved windows, and just dancing like on the leaves o' the dark ivy as the breath o' wind shakes it—I wonder whether this is mair pleasing to Heaven than when it was lighted up wi' lamps, and candles nae doubt, and roughies,[13] and wi' the mirth and the frankincent* that they speak of in the Holy Scripture, and wi' organs assuredly, and men and women singers, and sackbuts, and dulcimers, and a' instruments o' music—I wonder if that was acceptable, or whether it is of these grand parafle o' cere-monies that holy writ says "it is an abomination to me"—I am think-ing, Maister Lovel, if twa puir contrite spirits like yours and mine fand grace to make our petition'—

Here Lovel laid his hand eagerly on the mendicant's arm, saying, 'Hush! I heard some one speak.'

'I am dull o' hearing,' answered Edie in a whisper, 'but we're surely safe here—where was the sound?'

Lovel pointed to the door of the chancel, which, highly orna-mented, occupied the west end of the building, surmounted by the carved window, which let in a flood of moonlight over it.

'They can be nane o' our folk,' said Edie in the same low and cautious tone; 'there's but twa o' them kens o' the place, and they're mony a mile off, if they are still bound on their weary pilgrimage. I'll never think it's the officers here at this time o' night. I am nae believer in auld wives' stories about ghaists, though this is gey like a place for them—But mortal, or of the other world, here they come!—twa men and a light.'

And in very truth, while the mendicant spoke, two human figures darkened with their shadows the entrance of the chancel which had before opened to the moonlight meadow beyond, and the small lan-tern which one of them displayed, glimmered pale in the clear and strong beams of the moon, as the evening star does among the lights of the departing day. The first and most obvious idea was, that, despite the asseverations of Edie Ochiltree, the persons who approached the ruins at an hour so uncommon must be the officers of justice in quest of Lovel. But no part of their conduct confirmed the suspicion. A touch and a whisper from the old man warned Lovel that his best course was to remain quiet, and watch their motions from their present place of concealment. Should any thing appear to render retreat necessary, they had behind them the private staircase and cavern, by means of which they could escape into the wood long before any danger of close pursuit. They kept them-selves, therefore, as still as possible, and observed, with eager and anxious curiosity, every accent and motion of these nocturnal wanderers.

After conversing together some time in whispers, the two figures advanced into the middle of the chancel, and a voice, which Lovel at once recognised, from its tone and dialect, to be that of Douster-swivel, pronounced in a louder but still a smothered tone, 'Indeed, mine goot sir, dere cannot be one finer hour nor season for dis great purpose. You shall see, mine goot sir, dat it is all one bibble-babble dat Mr Oldenbuck says, and dat he knows no more of what he speaks than one little shild. Mine soul! he expects to get as rich as one Jew for his poor dirty one hundred pounds, which I care no more about, by mine honest wort, than I care for an hundred stivers. But to you, my most munificent and reverend patron, I will show all de secrets dat art can show—ay, de secret of de great Pymander.'*

'That other ane,' whispered Edie, 'maun be, according to a' likelihood, Sir Arthur Wardour. I ken naebody but himsell wad come here at this time at e'en wi' that German blackguard—Ane wad think he's bewitched him—he gars him e'en trow that chalk is cheese—Let's see what they can be doing.'

This interruption, and the low tone in which Sir Arthur spoke, made Lovel lose all Sir Arthur's answer to the adept, excepting the three last emphatic words, 'Very great expense;'—to which Dousterswivel at once replied,—'Expenses—to be sure—dere must be de great expenses—you do not expect to reap before you do sow de seed—de expense is de seed—de riches and de mine of goot metal, and now de great big chests of plate, they are de crop—vary goot crop too, on mine wort. Now, Sir Arthur, you have sowed this night one little seed of ten guineas like one pinch of snuff, or so big—and if you do not reap de great harvest—dat is de great harvest for de little pinch of seed, for it must be proportions, you must know—then never call one honest man, Herman Dousterswivel. Now you see, mine patron—for I will not conceal mine secret from you at all—you see this little plate of silver—you know de moon measureth de whole zodiack in de space of twenty-eight day—every shild knows dat—well, I take a silver plate when she is in her fifteenth mansion, which mansion is in de head of *Libra*, and I engrave upon one side de worts, 𝕾𝖍𝖊𝖉𝖇𝖆𝖗𝖘𝖈𝖍𝖊𝖒𝖔𝖙𝖍 𝕾𝖈𝖍𝖆𝖗𝖙𝖆𝖈𝖍𝖆𝖓—dat is, de Emblems of de Intelligence of de moon—and I make his picture like a flying serpent with a turkey-cock's head—vary well—Then upon this side I make de table of de moon, which is a square of nine, multiplied into itself, with eighty-one numbers on every side, and diameter nine—dere it is done very proper—Now I will make dis avail me at de change of every quarter-moon dat I shall find by de same proportions of expenses I lay out in de suffumigations, as nine, to de product of nine multiplied into itself—But I shall find no more tonight as may be two or dree times nine, because dere is a thwarting power in de house of ascendency.'*

'But, Dousterswivel,' said the simple Baronet, 'does not this look like magic?—I am a true though unworthy son of the Episcopal church, and I will have nothing to do with the foul fiend.'

'Bah! bah!—not a bit magic in it at all—not a bit—It is all founded on de planetary influence, and de sympathy and force of numbers—I will show you much finer dan dis—I do not say dere is not de spirit in it, because of de suffumigation; but, if you are not afraid, he shall not be invisible.'

'I have no curiosity to see him at all,' said the Baronet, whose courage seemed, from a certain quaver in his accent, to have taken a fit of the ague.

'Dat is great pity,' said Dousterswivel; 'I should have liked to show you de spirit dat guard dis treasure like one fierce watch-dog—but I know how to manage him—you would not care to see him?'

'Not at all,' answered the Baronet, in a tone of feigned indifference; 'I think we have but little time.'

'You shall pardon me, my patron, it is not yet twelve, and twelve precise is just our planetary hours;* and I could show you de spirit vary well, in de meanwhile, just for pleasure. You see I would draw a pentagon within a circle, which is no trouble at all, and make my suffumigation within it, and dere we would be like in one strong castle, and you would hold de sword* while I did say de needful worts—Den you should see de solid wall open like de gate of ane city, and den—let me see—ay—you should see first one stag pursued by three black greyhounds, and they should pull him down as they do at de elector's great hunting-match—and den one ugly, little, nasty black negro should appear and take de stag from them—and paf—all should be gone—den you should hear horns winded dat all de ruins should ring—mine wort, they should play fine hunting piece, as goot as him you call'd Fischer with his oboi*—vary well—den comes one herald, as we call Ernhold, winding his horn—and den come de great Peolphan, called the Mighty Hunter of de North, mounted on hims black steed—but you would not care to see all this?'[14]

'Why, I am not afraid,' answered the poor Baronet,—'if—that is—does any thing—any great mischiefs, happen on such occasions?'

'Bah—mischiefs? no! sometimes if de circle be no quite just, or de beholder be de frightened coward, and not hold de sword firm and straight towards him, de Great Hunter will take his advantage, and drag him exorcist out of de circle and throttle him. Dat does happens.'

'Well then, Dousterswivel, with every confidence in my courage and your skill, we will dispense with this apparition, and go on to the business of the night.'

'With all mine heart—it is just one thing to me—and now it is de time—hold you de sword till I kindle de little what you call chip.'

Dousterswivel accordingly set fire to a little pile of chips, touched and prepared with some bituminous substance to make them burn fiercely; and when the flame was at the highest, and lightened, with its shortlived glare, all the ruins around, the German flung in a handful of perfumes, which produced a strong and pungent odour. The exorcist and his pupil both were so much affected as to cough and sneeze heartily; and, as the vapour floated around the pillars of the building, and penetrated every crevice, it produced the same effect on the beggar and Lovel.

'Was that an echo?' said the Baronet, astonished at the sternutation which resounded from above; 'or'—drawing close to the adept, 'can it be the spirit you talked of, ridiculing our attempt upon his hidden treasures?'

'N—n—no,' muttered the German, who began to partake of his pupil's terrors, 'I hope not.'

Here a violent explosion of sneezing, which the mendicant was unable to suppress, and which could not be considered by any means as the dying fall of an echo, accompanied by a grunting half-smothered cough, confounded the two treasure-seekers. 'Lord have mercy on us!' said the Baronet.

'*Alle guten Geistern, loben den Herrn!*'* ejaculated the terrified adept. 'I was begun to think,' he continued, after a moment's silence, 'that this would be de bestermost done in de day-light—we was bestermost to go away just now.'

'You juggling villain,' said the Baronet, in whom these expressions awakened a suspicion that overcame his terrors, connected as it was with the sense of desperation arising from the apprehension of impending ruin,—'you juggling mountebank, this is some legerdemain trick of yours to get off from the performance of your promise, as you have so often done before. But, before Heaven, I will this night know what I have trusted to when I suffered you to fool me on to my ruin!—Go on, then—come fairy, come fiend, you shall show me that treasure, or confess yourself a knave and an impostor, or, by the faith of a desperate and ruined man, I'll send you where you shall see spirits enough.'

The treasure-finder, trembling between his terror for the supernatural beings by whom he supposed himself to be surrounded, and for his life, which seemed to be at the mercy of a desperate man, could only bring out, 'Mine patron, this is not the allerbestmost usage. Consider, mine honoured sir, that de spirits'—

Here, Edie, who began to enter into the humour of the scene, uttered an extraordinary howl, being an exaltation and a prolongation of the most deplorable whine in which he was accustomed to solicit charity—Dousterswivel flung himself on his knees, 'Dear Sir Arthurs, let us go, or let me go!'

'No, you cheating scoundrel,' said the knight, unsheathing the sword which he had brought for the purposes of the exorcism, 'that shift shall not serve you—Monkbarns warned me long since of your juggling pranks—I will see this treasure before you leave this place, or I will have you confess yourself an impostor, or, by Heaven, I'll run this sword through you, though all the spirits of the dead should rise around us!'

'For de lofe of Heaven be patient, mine honoured patron, and you shall hafe all de treasure as I knows of—yes—you shall indeed—but do not speak about de spirits—it makes dem angry.'

Edie Ochiltree here prepared himself to throw in another groan, but was restrained by Lovel, who began to take a more serious interest, as he observed the earnest and almost desperate demeanour of Sir Arthur. Dousterswivel, having at once before his eyes the fear of the foul fiend, and the violence of Sir Arthur, played his part of a conjuror extremely ill, hesitating to assume the degree of confidence necessary to deceive the latter, lest it should give offence to the invisible cause of his alarm. However, after rolling his eyes, muttering and sputtering German exorcisms, with contortions of his face and person, rather flowing from the impulse of terror than of meditated fraud, he at length proceeded to a corner of the building where a flat stone lay upon the ground, bearing upon its surface the effigy of an armed warrior in a recumbent posture carved in bas-relief. He muttered to Sir Arthur, 'Mine patrons—it is here—Got save us all!'

Sir Arthur, who, after the first moment of his superstitious fear was over, seemed to have bent up all his faculties to the pitch of resolution necessary to carry on the adventure, lent the adept his assistance to turn over the stone, which, by means of a lever that the adept had provided, their joint force with difficulty effected. No supernatural light burst forth from below to indicate the subterranean treasury, nor was there any apparition of spirits, earthly or infernal. But when Dousterswivel had, with great trepidation, struck a few strokes with a mattock, and as hastily thrown out a shovelful or two of earth, (for they came provided with the tools necessary for digging,) something was heard to ring like the sound of a falling piece of metal, and Dousterswivel, hastily catching up the substance which produced it, and which his shovel had thrown out along with the earth, exclaimed, 'On mine dear wort, mine patrons, dis is all—it is indeed—I mean all we can do tonight,'—and he gazed round him with a cowering and fearful glance, as if to see from what corner the avenger of his imposture was to start forth.

'Let me see it,' said Sir Arthur; and then repeated still more sternly, 'I will be satisfied—I will judge by mine own eyes.' He accordingly held the object to the light of the lantern. It was a small case, or casket,—for Lovel could not at the distance exactly discern its shape, which, from the Baronet's exclamation as he opened it, he concluded was filled with coin. 'Ay,' said the Baronet, 'this is being indeed in good luck! and if it omens proportional success upon a larger venture, the venture shall be made. That six hundred of Goldieword's, added to the other incumbent claims, must have been ruin indeed. If you think we can parry it by repeating this experiment— suppose when the moon next changes,—I will hazard the necessary advance, come by it how I may.'

'O mine goot patrons, do not speak about all dat,' said Dousterswivel, 'as just now, but help me to put de shtone to de rights, and let us begone our own ways.' And accordingly, so soon as the stone was replaced, he hurried Sir Arthur, who was now resigned once more to his guidance, away from a spot, where the German's guilty conscience and superstitious fears represented goblins as lurking behind each pillar with the purpose of punishing his treachery.

'Saw ony body e'er the like o' that!' said Edie, when they had disappeared like shadows through the gate by which they had entered—'Saw ony creature living e'er the like o' that!—But what can we do for that puir doited deevil of a knight-baronet?—Odd, he showed muckle mair spunk, too, than I thought had been in him—I thought he wad hae sent cauld iron through the vagabond—Sir Arthur wasna half sae bauld at Bessie's-apron yon night—but then his blood was up even now, and that makes an unco difference. I hae seen mony a man wad hae felled another an anger him, that wadna muckle hae liked a clink against Crummie's-horn yon time. But what's to be done?'

'I suppose,' said Lovel, 'his faith in this fellow is entirely restored by this deception, which, unquestionably, he had arranged beforehand.'

'What! the siller?—Ay, ay—trust him for that—they that hide ken best where to find—he wants to wile him out o' his last guinea, and then escape to his ain country, the land-louper. I wad likeit weel just to hae come in at the clipping-time, and gien him a lounder wi' my pike-staff; he wad hae taen it for a bennison frae some o' the auld dead abbots—But it's best no to be rash—sticking disna gang by strength, but by the guiding o' the gully—I'se be upsides wi' him ae day.'

'What if you should inform Mr Oldbuck?' said Lovel.

'Ou, I dinna ken—Monkbarns and Sir Arthur are like, and yet they're no like neither—Monkbarns has whiles influence wi' him, and whiles Sir Arthur cares as little about him as about the like o' me. Monkbarns is no that ower wise himsell, in some things—he wad believe a bodle to be an auld Roman coin, as he ca's it, or a ditch to be a camp, upon ony leasing that idle folk made about it. I hae garr'd him trow mony a queer tale mysell, gude forgie me. But wi' a' that, he has unco little sympathy wi' ither folks; and he's snell and dure eneugh in casting up their nonsense to them, as if he had nane o' his ain. He'll listen the hale day, an ye'll tell him about tales o' Wallace, and Blind Harry,* and Davie Lindsay,* but ye maunna speak to him about ghaists or fairies, or spirits walking the earth, or the like o' that—he had amaist flung auld Caxon out o' the window, (and he might just as weel hae flung awa his best wig after him,) for threeping he had seen a ghaist at the humlock-knowe. Now, if he was taking it up in this way, he wad set up the tother's birse, and maybe do mair ill nor gude—he's done that twice or thrice about thae mine-warks—ye wad thought Sir Arthur had a pleasure in gaun on wi' them the deeper, the mair he was warn'd against it by Monkbarns.'

'What say you then,' said Lovel, 'to letting Miss Wardour know the circumstance?'

'Ou, puir thing, how could she stop her father doing his pleasure?—and, besides, what wad it help?—There's a sough in the country about that six hundred pounds, and there's a writer chield in Edinburgh has been driving the spur-rowels o' the law up to the head into Sir Arthur's sides to gar him pay it, and if he canna, he maun gang to jail or flee the country. He's like a desperate man, and just catches at this chance as a' he has left, to escape utter perdition; so what signifies plaguing the puir lassie about what canna be helped?—And besides, to say the truth, I wadna like to tell the secret o' this place. It's unco convenient, ye see yoursell, to hae a hiding-hole o'ane's ain, and though I be out o' the line o' needing ane e'en now, and trust in the power o' grace that I'll ne'er do ony thing to need ane again, yet naebody kens what temptation ane may be gien ower to—and, to be brief, I downa bide the thought of ony body kennin about the place—they say, keep a thing seven year, an' ye'll aye find a use for't—and maybe I may need the cove, either for mysell, or for some ither body.'

This argument, in which Edie Ochiltree, notwithstanding his scraps of morality and of divinity, seemed to take, perhaps from old habit, a personal interest, could not be handsomely controverted by Lovel, who was at that moment reaping the benefit of the secret of which the old man appeared to be so jealous.

This incident, however, was of great service to Lovel, as diverting his mind from the unhappy occurrence of the evening, and considerably rousing the energies which had been stupified by the first view of his calamity. He reflected, that it by no means necessarily followed that a dangerous wound must be a fatal one—that he had been hurried from the spot even before the surgeon had expressed any opinion of Captain M'Intyre's situation—and that he had duties on earth to perform, even should the very worst be true, which, if they could not restore his peace of mind or sense of innocence, would furnish a motive for enduring existence, and at the same time render it a course of active benevolence.

Such were Lovel's feelings when the hour arrived, when, according to Edie's calculation, who, by some train or process of his own in observing the heavenly bodies, stood independent of the assistance of a watch or timekeeper, it was fitting they should leave their hiding-place, and betake themselves to the sea-shore, in order to meet Lieutenant Taffril's boat according to appointment.

They retreated by the same passage which had admitted them to the prior's secret seat of observation, and when they issued from the grotto into the wood, the birds, which began to chirp, and even to sing, announced that the dawn was advanced. This was confirmed by the light and amber clouds that appeared over the sea as soon as their exit from the copse permitted them to view the horizon. Morning, said to be friendly to the muses, has probably obtained this character from its effect upon the fancy and feelings of mankind. Even to those who, like Lovel, have spent a sleepless and anxious night, the breeze of the dawn brings strength and quickening both of mind and body. It was therefore with renewed health and vigour that Lovel, guided by the trusty mendicant, brushed away the dew as he traversed the downs which divided the Den of St Ruth, as the woods surrounding the ruins were popularly called, from the sea-shore.

The first level beam of the sun, as his brilliant disk began to emerge from the ocean, shot full upon the little gun-brig which was lying-to in the offing—close to the shore the boat was already waiting, Taffril himself, with his naval cloak wrapped about him, seated in the stern. He jumped ashore when he saw the mendicant and Lovel approach, and, shaking the latter heartily by the hand, begged him not to be cast down. 'M'Intyre's wound,' he said, 'was doubtful, but far from desperate.' His attention had got Lovel's baggage privately sent on board the brig; 'and,' he said, 'he trusted that, if Lovel chose to stay with the vessel, the penalty of a short cruize would be the only disagreeable consequence of his rencontre. As for himself, his time and motions were a good deal at his own disposal,' he said, 'excepting the necessary obligation of remaining on his station.'

'We will talk of our farther motions,' said Lovel, 'as we go on board.'

Then turning to Edie, he endeavoured to put money into his hand. 'I think,' said Edie, as he tendered it back again, 'the hale folk here have either gane daft, or they hae made a vow to ruin my trade, as they say ower muckle water drowns the miller. I hae had mair gowd offered me within this twa or three weeks than I ever saw in my life afore. Keep the siller, lad, ye'll hae need o't, I'se warrant ye, and I hae nane—my claes is nae great things, and I get a blue gown every year, and as mony siller groats as the king, God bless him, is years auld—you and I serve the same master, ye ken, Captain Taffril—there's rigging provided for—and my meat and drink I get for the asking in my rounds, or, at an orra time, I can gang a day without it, for I make it a rule never to pay for nane—So that a' the siller I need is just to buy tobacco and sneeshin, and maybe a dram at a time in a cauld day, though I am nae dram-drinker to be a gaberlunzie—sae take back your gowd, and just gie me a lily-white shilling.'

Upon these whims, which he imagined intimately connected with the honour of his vagabond profession, Edie was flint and adamant, not to be moved by rhetoric or entreaty; and therefore Lovel was under the necessity of again pocketing his intended bounty, and taking a friendly leave of the mendicant by shaking him by the hand, and assuring him of his cordial gratitude for the very important services which he had rendered him, recommending, at the same time, secrecy as to what they had that night witnessed.—'Ye needna doubt that,' said Ochiltree; 'I never tell'd tales out o' yon cove in my life, though mony a queer thing I hae seen in't.'

The boat now put off. The old man remained looking after it as it made rapidly towards the brig under the impulse of six stout rowers, and Lovel beheld him again wave his blue bonnet as a token of farewell ere he turned from his fixed posture, and began to move slowly along the sands as if resuming his customary perambulations.

CHAPTER XXII

Wiser Raymond, as in his closet pent,
Laughs at such danger and adventurement,
When half his lands are spent in golden smoke,
And now his second hopeful glasse is broke;
But yet, if haply his third furnace hold,
Devoteth all his pots and pans to gold.*[15]

ABOUT a week after the adventures commemorated in our last chapter, Mr Oldbuck, descending to his breakfast-parlour, found that his womankind were not upon duty, his toast not made, and the silver jug, which wont to receive his libations of mum, not duly aired for its reception.

'This confounded hot-brained boy,' he said to himself, 'now that he begins to get out of danger, I can tolerate this life no longer—All goes to sixes and sevens—an universal saturnalia seems to be proclaimed in my peaceful and orderly family.—I ask for my sister—no answer—I call, I shout—I invoke my inmates by more names than the Romans gave to their deities—At length, Jenny, whose shrill voice I have heard this half hour lilting in the Tartarean regions of the kitchen, condescends to hear me and reply, but without coming up stairs, so the conversation must be continued at the top of my lungs.'—Here he again began to hollow aloud, 'Jenny, where's Miss Oldbuck?'

'Miss Grizzy's in the captain's room.'

'Umph, I thought so—and where's my niece?'

'Miss Mary's making the captain's tea.'

'Umph, I supposed as much again—and where's Caxon?'

'Awa to the town about the captain's fowling-gun and his setting-dog.'

'And who the devil's to dress my periwig, you silly jade?—when you knew that Miss Wardour and Sir Arthur were coming here early after breakfast, how could you let Caxon go on such a Tomfool's errand?'

'Me! what could I hinder him?—your honour wadna hae us contradict the captain e'en now, and him maybe deeing?'

'Dying!' said the alarmed Antiquary,—'eh!—what? has he been worse?'

'Na, he's no nae waur that I ken of.'[16]

'Then he must be better—and what good is a dog and a gun to do here, but the one to destroy all my furniture, steal from my larder, and perhaps worry the cat, and the other to shoot somebody through the head—he has had gunning and pistolling enough to serve him one while, I should think.'

Here Miss Oldbuck entered the parlour, at the door of which Oldbuck was carrying on this conversation, he bellowing downward to Jenny, and she again screaming upward in reply.

'Dear brother,' said the old lady, 'ye'll cry yoursell as hoarse as a corbie—is that the way to skreigh when there's a sick person in the house?'

'Upon my word, the sick person's like to have all the house to himself. I have gone without my breakfast, and am like to go without my wig; and I must not, I suppose, presume to say I feel either hunger or cold, for fear of disturbing the sick gentleman who lies six rooms off, and who feels himself well enough to send for his dog and gun, though he knows I detest such implements ever since our elder brother, poor Williewald, marched out of the world on a pair of damp feet caught in the Kittlefitting-moss—But that signifies nothing—I suppose I shall be expected by and by to lend a hand to carry Squire Hector out upon his litter, while he indulges his sportsman-like propensities by shooting my pigeons, or my turkeys—I think any of the *feræ naturæ** are safe from him for one while.'

Miss M'Intyre now entered, and began to her usual morning's task of arranging her uncle's breakfast, with the alertness of one who is too late in setting about a task, and is anxious to make up for lost time. But this did not avail her. 'Take care, you silly womankind—that mum's too near the fire—the bottle will burst—and I suppose you intend to reduce the toast to a cinder as a burnt-offering for Juno, or what do you call her—the female dog there, with some such Pantheon kind of a name,* that your wise brother has, in his first moments of mature reflection, ordered up as a fitting inmate of my house, (I thank him,) and meet company to aid the rest of the womankind of my household in their daily conversation and intercourse with him.'

'Dear uncle, don't be angry about the poor spaniel; she's been tied up at my brother's lodgings at Fairport, and she's broke her chain twice, and come running down here to him; and you would not have us beat the faithful beast away from the door—it moans as if it had some sense of poor Hector's misfortune, and will hardly stir from the door of his room.'

'Why,' said his uncle, 'they said Caxon had gone to Fairport after his dog and gun.'

'O dear sir, no,' answered Miss M'Intyre, 'it was to fetch some dressings that were wanted, and Hector only wished him to bring out his gun, as he was going to Fairport at any rate.'

'Well, then, it is not altogether so foolish a business, considering what a mess of womankind have been about it—Dressings, quotha?—and who is to dress my wig?—But I suppose Jenny will undertake'—continued the old bachelor, looking at himself in the glass,—'to make it somewhat decent. And now let us set to breakfast—with what appetite we may—Well may I say to Hector, as Sir Isaac Newton did to his dog Diamond, when the animal (I detest dogs) flung down the taper among calculations which had occupied the philosopher for twenty years, and consumed the whole mass of materials—Diamond, Diamond, thou little knowest the mischief thou hast done!'

'I assure you, sir,' replied his niece, 'my brother is quite sensible of the rashness of his own behaviour, and allows that Mr Lovel behaved very handsomely.'

'And much good that will do, when he has frightened the lad out of the country!—I tell thee, Mary, Hector's understanding, and far more that of feminity, is inadequate to comprehend the extent of the loss which he has occasioned to the present age and to posterity— *aureum quidem opus**—a poem on such a subject—with notes illustrative of all that is clear, and all that is dark, and all that is neither dark nor clear, but hovers in dusky twilight in the region of Caledonian antiquities. I would have made the Celtic panegyrists look about them—Fingal, as they conceitedly term Fin-Mac-Coul, should have disappeared before my search, rolling himself in his cloud like the spirit of Loda.* Such an opportunity can hardly again occur to an ancient and grey-haired man—and to see it lost by the madcap spleen of a hot-headed boy!—But I submit—Heaven's will be done.'

Thus continued the Antiquary to *maunder*, as his sister expressed it, during the whole time of breakfast, while, despite of sugar and honey, and all the comforts of a Scottish morning tea-table, his reflections rendered the meal bitter to all who heard them. But they knew the nature of the man. 'Monkbarns's bark,' said Miss Griselda Oldbuck, in confidential intercourse with Miss Rebecca Blattergowl, 'is muckle waur than his bite.'

In fact, Mr Oldbuck had suffered in mind extremely while his nephew was in actual danger, and now felt himself at liberty, upon his returning health, to indulge in complaints respecting the trouble he had been put to, and the interruption of his antiquarian labours. Listened to, therefore, in respectful silence, by his niece and sister, he unloaded his discontent in such grumblings as we have rehearsed, venting many a sarcasm against womankind, soldiers, dogs, and guns, all which implements of noise, discord, and tumult, as he called them, he professed to hold in utter abomination.

This expectoration of spleen was suddenly interrupted by the noise of a carriage without, when, shaking off all sullenness at the sound, Oldbuck ran nimbly up stairs and down stairs, for both operations were necessary, ere he could receive Miss Wardour and her father at the door of his mansion.

A cordial greeting passed on both sides. And Sir Arthur, referring to his previous enquiries by letter and message, requested to be particularly informed of Captain M'Intyre's health.

'Better than he deserves,' was the answer; 'better than he deserves, for disturbing us with his vixen brawls, and breaking God's peace and the king's.'

'The young gentleman,' Sir Arthur said, 'had been imprudent; but he understood they were indebted to him for the detection of a suspicious character in the young man Lovel.'

'No more suspicious than his own,' answered the Antiquary, eager in his favourite's defence; 'the young gentleman was a little foolish and headstrong, and refused to answer Hector's impertinent interrogatories—that is all. Lovel, Sir Arthur, knows how to choose his confidents better—ay, Miss Wardour, you may look at me—but it is very true—it was in my bosom that he deposited the secret cause of his residence at Fairport, and no stone should have been left unturned on my part to assist him in the pursuit to which he had dedicated himself.'

On hearing this magnanimous declaration on the part of the old Antiquary, Miss Wardour changed colour more than once, and could hardly trust her own ears. For of all confidents to be selected as the depositary of love affairs,—and such she naturally supposed must have been the subject of communication, next to Edie Ochiltree,— Oldbuck seemed the most uncouth and extraordinary; nor could she sufficiently admire or fret at the extraordinary combination of circumstances which thus threw a secret of such a delicate nature into the possession of persons so unfitted to be intrusted with it. She had next to fear the mode of Oldbuck's entering upon the affair with her father, for such she doubted not, was his intention. She well knew, that the honest gentleman, however vehement in his prejudices, had no great sympathy with those of others, and she had to fear a most unpleasant explosion upon an eclaircissement taking place between them. It was therefore with great anxiety that she heard her father request a private interview, and observed Oldbuck readily arise, and show the way to his library. She remained behind, attempting to converse with the ladies of Monkbarns, but with the distracted feelings of Macbeth, when compelled to disguise his evil conscience, by listening and replying to the observations of the attendant thanes upon the storm of the preceding night, while his whole soul is upon the stretch to listen for the alarm of murder, which he knows must be instantly raised by those who have entered the sleeping apartment of Duncan.* But the conversation of the two virtuosi turned on a subject very different from that which Miss Wardour apprehended.

'Mr Oldbuck,' said Sir Arthur, when they had, after a due exchange of ceremonies, fairly seated themselves in the *sanctum sanctorum* of the Antiquary,—'you, who know so much of my family matters, may probably be surprised at the question I am about to put to you.'

'Why, Sir Arthur, if it relates to money, I am very sorry, but'—

'It does relate to money matters, Mr Oldbuck.'

'Really then, Sir Arthur,' continued the Antiquary, 'in the present state of the money-market—and stocks being so low'—

'You mistake my meaning, Mr Oldbuck,' said the Baronet; 'I wished to ask your advice about laying out a large sum of money to advantage.'

'The devil!' exclaimed the Antiquary; and, sensible that his involuntary ejaculation of wonder was not over and above civil, he proceeded to qualify it by expressing his joy that Sir Arthur should have a sum of money to lay out when the commodity was so scarce. 'And as for the mode of employing it,' said he, pausing, 'the funds are low at present, as I said before, and there are good bargains of land to be had. But had you not better begin by clearing off encumbrances, Sir Arthur?—There is the sum in the personal bond*—and the three notes of hand,'*—continued he, taking out of the right-hand drawer of his cabinet a certain red memorandum-book, of which Sir Arthur, from the experience of former frequent appeals to it, abhorred the very sight—'with the interest thereon, amounting altogether to—let me see'—

'To about a thousand pounds,' said Sir Arthur, hastily; 'you told me the amount the other day.'

'But there's another term's interest due since that, Sir Arthur, and it amounts (errors excepted) to eleven hundred and thirteen pounds, seven shillings, five pennies, and three-fourths of a penny sterling—but look over the summation yourself.'

'I daresay you are quite right, my dear sir,' said the Baronet, putting away the book with his hand, as one rejects the old-fashioned civility that presses food upon you after you have eaten till you nauseate,—'perfectly right, I dare to say, and in the course of three days or less you shall have the full value—that is, if you choose to accept it in bullion.'

'Bullion! I suppose you mean lead. What the deuce! have we hit on the vein then at last?—But what could I do with a thousand pounds worth, and upwards, of lead?—the former abbots of Trotcosey might have roofed their church and monastery with it indeed—but for me'—

'By bullion,' said the Baronet, 'I mean the precious metals,—gold and silver.'

'Ay! indeed?—And from what Eldorado is this treasure to be imported?'

'Not far from hence,' said Sir Arthur, significantly; 'and now I think of it, you shall see the whole process on one small condition.'

'And what is that?' craved the Antiquary.

'Why, it will be necessary for you to give me your friendly assistance, by advancing one hundred pounds or thereabouts.'

Mr Oldbuck, who had already been grasping in idea the sum, principal and interest, of a debt which he had long regarded as wellnigh desperate, was so much astounded at the tables being so unexpectedly turned upon him, that he could only re-echo, in an accent of woe and surprise, the words, 'Advance one hundred pounds!'

'Yes, my good sir,' continued Sir Arthur; 'but upon the best possible security of being repaid in the course of two or three days.'

There was a pause—either Oldbuck's nether-jaw had not recovered its position, so as to enable him to utter a negative, or his curiosity kept him silent.

'I would not propose to you,' continued Sir Arthur, 'to oblige me thus far, if I did not possess actual proofs of the reality of those expectations which I now hold out to you. And, I assure you, Mr Oldbuck, that in entering fully upon this topic, it is my purpose to show my confidence in you, and my sense of your kindness on many former occasions.'

Mr Oldbuck professed his sense of obligation, but carefully avoided committing himself by any promise of farther assistance.

'Mr Dousterswivel,' said Sir Arthur, 'having discovered'—

Here Oldbuck broke in, his eyes sparkling with indignation. 'Sir Arthur, I have so often warned you of the knavery of that rascally quack, that I really wonder you should quote him to me.'

'But listen—listen,' interrupted Sir Arthur in his turn, 'it will do you no harm. In short, Dousterswivel persuaded me to witness an experiment which he had made in the ruins of St Ruth—and what do you think we found?'

'Another spring of water, I suppose, of which the rogue had beforehand taken care to ascertain the situation and source.'

'No, indeed—a casket of gold and silver coins—here they are.'

With that, Sir Arthur drew from his pocket a large ram's-horn, with a copper cover, containing a considerable quantity of coins, chiefly silver, but with a few gold pieces intermixed. The Antiquary's eyes glistened as he eagerly spread them out on the table.

'Upon my word—Scotch, English, and foreign coins, of the fifteenth and sixteenth centuries, and some of them *rari—et rariores—etiam rarissimi!** Here is the bonnet-piece of James V.—the unicorn of James II.—ay, and the gold testoon of Queen Mary, with her head and the Dauphin's.*—And these were really found in the ruins of St Ruth?'

'Most assuredly—my own eyes witnessed it.'

'Well,' replied Oldbuck, 'but you must tell me the when—the where—the how.'

'The when,' answered Sir Arthur, 'was at midnight the last full moon—the where, as I have told you, in the ruins of St Ruth's priory—the how, was by a nocturnal experiment of Dousterswivel, accompanied only by myself.'

'Indeed!' said Oldbuck, 'and what means of discovery did you employ?'

'Only a simple suffumigation,' said the Baronet, 'accompanied by availing ourselves of the suitable planetary hour.'

'Simple suffumigation? simple nonsensification—planetary hour? planetary fiddlestick—*Sapiens dominabitur astris.**—My dear Sir Arthur, that fellow has made a gull of you above ground and under ground, and he would have made a gull of you in the air too, if he had been by when you was craned up the devil's turnpike yonder at Halkethead—to be sure, the transformation would have been then peculiarly *apropos*.'

'Well, Mr Oldbuck, I am obliged to you for your indifferent opinion of my discernment; but I think you will give me credit for having seen what I *say* I saw.'

'Certainly, Sir Arthur,' said the Antiquary, 'to this extent at least, that I know Sir Arthur Wardour will not say he saw any thing but what he *thought* he saw.'

'Well then,' replied the Baronet, 'as there is a heaven above us, Mr Oldbuck, I saw, with my own eyes, these coins dug out of the chancel of St Ruth at midnight—And as to Dousterswivel, although the discovery be owing to his science, yet, to tell the truth, I do not think he would have had firmness of mind to have gone through with it if I had not been beside him.'

'Ay! indeed?' said Oldbuck, in the tone used when one wishes to hear the end of a story before making any comment.

'Yes, truly,' continued Sir Arthur, 'I assure you I was upon my guard—we did hear some very uncommon sounds, that is certain, proceeding from among the ruins.'

'Oh, you did?' said Oldbuck; 'an accomplice hid among them, I suppose?'

'Not a jot,' said the Baronet; 'the sounds, though of a hideous and preternatural character, rather resembled those of a man who sneezes violently than any other—one deep groan I certainly heard besides—and Dousterswivel assures me, that he beheld the spirit Peolphan, the Great Hunter of the North, (look for him in your

Nicolaus Remigius, or Petrus Thyracus,* Mr Oldbuck,) who mimicked the motion of snuff-taking and its effects.'

'These indications, however singular as proceeding from such a personage, seem to have been *apropos* to the matter,' said the Antiquary; 'for you see the case, which includes these coins, has all the appearance of being an old-fashioned Scottish snuff-mill. But you persevered, in spite of the terrors of this sneezing goblin?'

'Why, I think it probable that a man of inferior sense or consequence might have given way; but I was jealous of an imposture, conscious of the duty I owed to my family in maintaining my courage under every contingency, and therefore I compelled Dousterswivel, by actual and violent threats, to proceed with what he was about to do; and, sir, the proof of his skill and honesty is this parcel of gold and silver pieces, out of which I beg you to select such coins or medals as will best suit your collection.'

'Why, Sir Arthur, since you are so good, and on condition you will permit me to mark the value according to Pinkerton's catalogue* and appreciation, against your account in my red book, I will with pleasure select'—

'Nay,' said Sir Arthur Wardour, 'I do not mean you should consider them as any thing but a gift of friendship, and least of all would I stand by the valuation of your friend Pinkerton, who has impugned the ancient and trust-worthy authorities, upon which, as upon venerable and moss-grown pillars, the credit of Scottish antiquities reposed.'

'Ay, ay,' rejoined Oldbuck, 'you mean, I suppose, Mair* and Boece, the Jachin and Boaz,* not of history, but of falsification and forgery. And notwithstanding of all you have told me, I look on your friend Dousterswivel to be as apocryphal as any of them.'

'Why, then, Mr Oldbuck,' said Sir Arthur, 'not to awaken old disputes, I suppose you think, that because I believe in the ancient history of my country, I have neither eyes nor ears to ascertain what modern events pass before me?'

'Pardon me, Sir Arthur,' rejoined the Antiquary, 'but I consider all the affectation of terror which this worthy gentleman, your coadjutor, chose to play off, as being merely one part of his trick or mystery. And, with respect to the gold or silver coins, they are so mixed and mingled in country and date, that I cannot suppose they could be any genuine hoard, and rather suppose them to be, like the purses upon the table of Hudibras's lawyer—

> ————Money placed for show,
> Like nest-eggs, to make clients lay,
> And for his false opinions pay.*—

It is the trick of all professions, my dear Sir Arthur. Pray, may I ask you how much this discovery cost you?'

'About ten guineas.'

'And you have gained what is equivalent to twenty in actual bullion, and what may be perhaps worth as much more to such fools as ourselves, who are willing to pay for curiosity. This was allowing you a tempting profit on the first hazard, I must needs admit. And what is the next venture he proposes?'

'An hundred and fifty pounds; I have given him one-third part of the money, and I thought it likely you might assist me with the balance.'

'I should think that this cannot be meant as a parting blow—it is not of weight and importance sufficient; he will probably let us win this hand also, as sharpers manage a raw gamester.—Sir Arthur, I hope you believe I would serve you?'

'Certainly, Mr Oldbuck; I think my confidence in you on these occasions leaves no room to doubt that.'

'Well, then, allow me to speak to Dousterswivel. If the money can be advanced usefully and advantageously for you, why, for old neighbourhood's sake, you shall not want it; but if, as I think, I can recover the treasure for you without making such an advance, you will, I presume, have no objection?'

'Unquestionably, I can have none whatsoever.'

'Then where is Dousterswivel?' continued the Antiquary.

'To tell you the truth, he is in my carriage below; but knowing your prejudice against him'—

'I thank Heaven, I am not prejudiced against any man, Sir Arthur; it is systems, not individuals, that incur my reprobation.' He rang the bell. 'Jenny, Sir Arthur and I offer our compliments to Mr Dousterswivel, the gentleman in Sir Arthur's carriage, and beg to have the pleasure of speaking with him here.'

Jenny departed and delivered her message. It had been by no means a part of the project of Dousterswivel to let Mr Oldbuck into his supposed mystery. He had relied upon Sir Arthur's obtaining the necessary accommodation without any discussion as to the nature of the application, and only waited below for the purpose of possessing himself of the deposit as soon as possible, for he foresaw that his career was drawing to a close. But when summoned to the presence of Sir Arthur and Mr Oldbuck, he resolved gallantly to put confidence in his powers of impudence, of which, the reader may have observed, his natural share was very liberal.

CHAPTER XXIII

──────────And this Doctor,
Your sooty smoky-bearded compeer, he
Will close you so much gold in a bolt's head,
And, on a turn, convey in the stead another
With sublimed mercury, that shall burst i' the heat,
And all fly out *in fumo*—

*The Alchemist.**

'How do you do, goot Mr Oldenbuck? and I do hope your young gentleman, Captain M'Intyre, is getting better again?—Ach! it is a bat business when young gentlemens will put lead balls into each other's body.'

'Lead adventures of all kinds are very precarious, Mr Dousterswivel; but I am happy to learn,' continued the Antiquary, 'from my friend Sir Arthur, that you have taken up a better trade, and become a discoverer of gold.'

'Ach, Mr Oldenbuck, mine goot and honoured patron should not have told a word about dat little matter; for, though I have all reliance—yes, indeed, on goot Mr Oldenbuck's prudence and discretion, and his great friendship for Sir Arthur Wardour—yet, my heavens! it is an great ponderous secret.'

'More ponderous than any of the metal we shall make by it, I fear,' answered Oldbuck.

'Dat is just as you shall have de faith and de patience for de grand experiment—If you join wid Sir Arthur, as he is put one hundred and fifty—see, here is one fifty in your dirty Fairport banknote—you put one other hundred and fifty in de dirty notes, and you shall have de pure gold and silver, I cannot tell how much.'

'Nor any one for you, I believe,' said the Antiquary. 'But hark you, Mr Dousterswivel; suppose, without troubling this same sneezing spirit with any farther fumigations, we should go in a body, and having fair day-light and our good consciences to befriend us, using no other conjuring implements than good substantial pick-axes and shovels, fairly trench the area of the chancel in the ruins of St Ruth, from one end to the other, and so ascertain the existence of this supposed treasure, without putting ourselves to any farther expense: the ruins belong to Sir Arthur himself, so there can be no objection. Do you think we shall succeed in this way of managing the matter?'

'Bah!—you will not find one copper thimble—But Sir Arthur will do his pleasure—I have showed him how it is possible—very possible—to have de great sum of money for his occasions—I have showed him de real experiment—If he likes not to believe, goot Mr Oldenbuck, it is nothing to Herman Dousterswivel—he only loses de money and de gold and de silvers—dat is all.'

Sir Arthur Wardour cast an intimidated glance at Oldbuck, who, especially when present, held, notwithstanding their frequent difference of opinion, no ordinary influence over his sentiments. In truth, the Baronet felt what he would not willingly have acknowledged, that his genius stood rebuked* before that of the Antiquary. He respected him as a shrewd, penetrating, sarcastic character, feared his satire, and had some confidence in the general soundness of his opinions. He therefore looked at him as if desiring his leave before indulging his credulity. Dousterswivel saw he was in danger of losing his dupe, unless he could make some favourable impression on the adviser.

'I know, my goot Mr Oldenbuck, it is one vanity to speak to you about de spirit and de goblin. But look at this curious horn; I know you know de curiosity of all de countries, and how de great Oldenburgh horn, as they keep still in the Museum at Copenhagen, was given to de Duke of Oldenburgh by one female spirit of de wood.* Now I could not put one trick on you if I were willing, you who know all de curiosity so well, and dere it is de horn full of coins—if it had been a box or case, I would have said nothing.'

'Being a horn,' said Oldbuck, 'does indeed strengthen your argument. It was an implement of nature's fashioning, and therefore much used among rude nations, although it may be the metaphorical horn* is more frequent in proportion to the progress of civilisation. And this present horn,' he continued, rubbing it upon his sleeve, 'is a curious and venerable relic, and no doubt was intended to prove a *cornucopia*, or horn of plenty, to some one or other; but whether to the adept or his patron may be justly doubted.'

'Well, Mr Oldenbuck, I find you still hard of belief—but let me assure you, de monksh understood de *magisterium*.'

'Let us leave talking of the *magisterium*, Mr Dousterswivel, and think a little about the magistrate. Are you aware that this occupation of yours is against the law of Scotland, and that both Sir Arthur and myself are in the commission of the peace?'*

'Mine heaven! and what is dat to de purpose when I am doing you all de goot I can?'

'Why, you must know, that when the legislature abolished the cruel laws against witchcraft, they had no hope of destroying the superstitious feelings of humanity on which such chimeras had been founded, and to prevent those feelings from being tampered with by artful and designing persons, it is enacted by the *ninth* of George the Second, chap. 5, that whosoever shall pretend, by his alleged skill in any occult or crafty science, to discover such goods as are lost, stolen, or concealed, he shall suffer punishment by pillory and imprisonment, as a common cheat and impostor.'

'And is dat de laws?' asked Dousterswivel, with some agitation.

'Thyself shalt see the act,'* replied the Antiquary.

'Den, gentlemens, I shall take my leave of you, dat is all; I do not like to stand on your what you call pillory—it is very bad way to take de air, I think; and I do not like your prisons no more, where one cannot take de air at all.'

'If such be your taste, Mr Dousterswivel,' said the Antiquary, 'I advise you to stay where you are, for I cannot let you go, unless it be in the society of a constable; and, moreover, I expect you will attend us just now to the ruins of St Ruth, and point out the place where you propose to find this treasure.'

'Mine heaven, Mr Oldenbuck! what usage is this to your old friend, when I tell you so plain as I can speak, dat if you go now, you will get not so much treasure as one poor shabby sixpence?'

'I will try the experiment, however, and you shall be dealt with according to its success,—always with Sir Arthur's permission.'

Sir Arthur, during this investigation, had looked extremely embarrassed, and, to use a vulgar but expressive phrase, chop-fallen. Oldbuck's obstinate disbelief led him strongly to suspect the imposture of Dousterswivel, and the adept's mode of keeping his ground was less resolute than he had expected. Yet he did not entirely give him up.

'Mr Oldbuck,' said the Baronet, 'you do Mr Dousterswivel less than justice. He has undertaken to make this discovery by the use of his art, and by applying characters descriptive of the Intelligences presiding over the planetary hour in which the experiment is to be made; and you require him to proceed, under pain of punishment, without allowing him the use of any of the preliminaries which he considers as the means of procuring success.'

'I did not say that exactly—I only required him to be present when we make the search, and not to leave us during the interval.—I fear he may have some intelligence with the Intelligences you talk of, and that whatever may be now hidden at Saint Ruth may disappear before we get there.'

'Well, gentlemens,' said Dousterswivel sullenly, 'I will make no objections to go along with you; but I tell you beforehand, you shall not find so much of any thing as shall be worth your going twenty yard from your own gate.'

'We will put that to a fair trial,' said the Antiquary; and the Baronet's equipage being ordered, Miss Wardour received an intimation from her father, that she was to remain at Monkbarns until his return from an airing. The young lady was somewhat at a loss to reconcile this direction with the communication which she supposed must have passed between Sir Arthur and the Antiquary; but she was compelled, for the present, to remain in a most unpleasant state of suspense.

The journey of the treasure-seekers was melancholy enough. Dousterswivel maintained a sulky silence, brooding at once over disappointed expectation and the risk of punishment; Sir Arthur, whose golden dreams had been gradually fading away, surveyed, in gloomy prospect, the impending difficulties of his situation; and Oldbuck, who perceived that his having so far interfered in his neighbour's affairs gave the Baronet a right to expect some actual and efficient assistance, sadly pondered to what extent it would be necessary to draw open the strings of his purse. Thus each being wrapped in his own unpleasant ruminations, there was hardly a word said on either side, until they reached the Four Horse-shoes, by which sign the little inn was distinguished. They procured at this place the necessary assistance and implements for digging, and while they were busy about these preparations, were suddenly joined by the old beggar, Edie Ochiltree.

'The Lord bless your honour,' began the Blue-Gown, with the genuine mendicant whine, 'and long life to you—weel pleased am I to hear that young Captain M'Intyre is like to be on his legs again sune—Think on your poor bedesman the day.'

'Aha, old true-penny!'* replied the Antiquary. 'Why, thou hast never come to Monkbarns since thy perils by rock and flood—here's something for thee to buy snuff,'—and, fumbling for his purse, he pulled out at the same time the horn which enclosed the coins.

'Ay, and there's something to pit it in,' said the mendicant, eyeing the ram's horn—'that loom's an auld acquaintance o'mine. I could take my aith to that sneeshing-mull amang a thousand—I carried it for mony a year, till I niffered it for this tin ane wi' auld George Glen, the dammer and sinker, when he took a fancy till't doun at Glen-Withershins yonder.'

'Ay! indeed?' said Oldbuck,—'so you exchanged it with a miner? but I presume you never saw it so well filled before?'—and, opening it, he showed the coins.

'Troth, ye may swear that, Monkbarns—when it was mine it ne'er had abune the like o' saxpenny worth o' black rappee in't at ance; but I reckon ye'll be gaun to make an antic o't, as ye hae dune wi' mony an orra thing besides. Odd, I wish ony body wad make an antic o' me; but mony ane will find worth in rousted bits o' capper and horn and airn, that care unco little about an auld carle o' their ain country and kind.'

'You may now guess,' said Oldbuck, turning to Sir Arthur, 'to whose good offices you were indebted the other night. To trace this cornucopia of yours to a miner is bringing it pretty near a friend of ours—I hope we shall be as successful this morning without paying for it.'

'And whare is your honours gaun the day,' said the mendicant, 'wi' a' your picks and shules?—Odd, this will be some o' your tricks, Monkbarns; ye'll be for whirling some o' the auld monks down by yonder out o' their graves afore they hear the last call*—but, wi' your leave, I'se follow ye at ony rate, and see what ye make o't.'

The party soon arrived at the ruins of the priory, and, having gained the chancel, stood still to consider what course they were to pursue next. The Antiquary, meantime, addressed the adept.

'Pray, Mr Dousterswivel, what is your advice in this matter?— Shall we have most likelihood of success if we dig from east to west, or from west to east?—or will you assist us with your triangular vial of May-dew,* or with your divining-rod of witches-hazel?* Or will you have the goodness to supply us with a few thumping blustering terms of art, which, if they fail in our present service, may at least be useful to those who have not the happiness to be bachelors, to still their brawling children withal?'

'Mr Oldenbuck,' said Dousterswivel doggedly, 'I have told you already, you will make no good work at all, and I will find some way of mine own to thank you for your civilities to me—yes, indeed.'

'If your honours are thinking of tirling the floor,' said old Edie, 'and wad but take a puir body's advice, I would begin below that muckle stane that has the man there streekit out upon his back in the midst o't.'

'I have some reason for thinking favourably of that plan myself,' said the Baronet.

'And I have nothing to say against it,' said Oldbuck; 'it was not unusual to hide treasure in the tombs of the deceased—many instances might be quoted of that from Bartholinus* and others.'

The tomb-stone, the same beneath which the coins had been found by Sir Arthur and the German, was once more forced aside, and the earth gave easy way to the spade.

'It's travell'd earth that,' said Edie, 'it howks sae eithly—I ken it weel, for ance I wrought a simmer wi' auld Will Winnet, the bedral, and howkit mair graves than ane in my day; but I left him in winter, for it was unco cald wark; and then it cam a green Yule, and the folk died thick and fast—for ye ken a green Yule makes a fat kirkyard*—and I never dowed to bide a hard turn o' wark in my life—sae aff I gaed, and left Will to delve his last dwellings by himsell for Edie.'

The diggers were now so far advanced in their labours as to discover that the sides of the grave which they were clearing out had been originally secured by four walls of freestone, forming a parallelogram, for the reception, probably, of the coffin.

'It is worth while proceeding in our labours,' said the Antiquary to Sir Arthur, 'were it but for curiosity's sake. I wonder on whose sepulchre they have bestowed such uncommon pains.'

'The arms on the shield,' said Sir Arthur, and sighed as he spoke it, 'are the same with those on Misticot's tower, supposed to have been built by Malcolm the usurper. No man knew where he was buried, and there is an old prophecy in our family, that bodes us no good when his grave shall be discovered.'

'I wot,' said the beggar, 'I have often heard that when I was a bairn,

"If Malcolm the Misticot's grave were fun',
The lands of Knockwinnock are lost and won." '

Oldbuck, with his spectacles on his nose, had already knelt down on the monument, and was tracing, partly with his eye, partly with his finger, the mouldered devices upon the effigy of the deceased warrior. 'It is the Knockwinnock arms sure enough,' he exclaimed, 'quarterly with the coat of Wardour.'

'Richard, called the Red-handed Wardour, married Sybil Knockwinnock, the heiress of the Saxon family, and by that alliance,' said Sir Arthur, 'brought the castle and estate into the name of Wardour, in the year of God 1150.'

'Very true, Sir Arthur, and here is the baton-sinister, the mark of illegitimacy, extended diagonally through both coats upon the shield. Where can our eyes have been, that they did not see this curious monument before?'

'Na, whare was the through-stane that it didna come before our een till e'now?' said Ochiltree; 'for I hae kend this auld kirk, man and bairn, for saxty lang years, and I ne'er noticed it afore, and it's nae sic mote neither but what ane might see it in their parritch.'

All were now induced to tax their memory as to the former state of the ruins in that corner of the chancel, and all agreed in recollecting a considerable pile of rubbish which must have been removed and spread abroad in order to make the tomb visible. Sir Arthur might, indeed, have remembered seeing the monument on the former occasion, but his mind was too much agitated to attend to the circumstance as a novelty.

While the assistants were engaged in these recollections and discussions, the workmen proceeded with their labour. They had already dug to the depth of nearly five feet, and as the flinging out the soil became more and more difficult, they began at length to tire of the job.

'We're down to the till now,' said one of them, 'and the ne'er a coffin or ony thing else is here—some cunninger chiel's been afore us, I reckon;' and the labourer scrambled out of the grave.

'Hout, lad,' said Edie, getting down in his room, 'let me try my hand for an auld bedral—ye're gude seekers but ill finders.'

So soon as he got into the grave, he struck his pike-staff forcibly down—it encountered resistance in its descent, and the beggar exclaimed, like a Scotch schoolboy when he finds any thing, 'Nae halvers and quarters—hale o' mine ain and nane o' my neighbour's.'

Every body, from the dejected Baronet to the sullen adept, now caught the spirit of curiosity, crowded round the grave, and would have jumped into it could its space have contained them. The labourers, who had begun to flag in their monotonous and apparently hopeless task, now resumed their tools, and plied them with all the ardour of expectation. Their shovels soon grated upon a hard wooden surface, which, as the earth was cleared away, assumed the distinct form of a chest, but greatly smaller than that of a coffin. Now all hands were at work to heave it out of the grave, and all voices, as it was raised, proclaimed its weight and augured its value. They were not mistaken.

When the chest or box was placed on the surface, and the lid forced up by a pick-axe, there was displayed first a coarse canvass cover, then a quantity of oakum, and beneath that a number of ingots of silver. A general exclamation hailed a discovery so surprising and unexpected. The Baronet threw his hands and eyes up to heaven, with the silent rapture of one who is delivered from inexpressible distress of mind. Oldbuck, almost unable to credit his eyes, lifted one piece of silver after another. There was neither inscription nor stamp upon them, excepting one, which seemed to be Spanish. He could have no doubt of the purity and great value of the treasure before him. Still, however, removing piece by piece, he examined row by row, expecting to discover that the lower layers were of inferior value; but he could perceive no difference in this respect, and found himself compelled to admit, that Sir Arthur had possessed himself of bullion to the value perhaps of a thousand pounds sterling. Sir Arthur now promised the assistants a handsome recompense for their trouble, and began to busy himself about the mode of conveying this rich windfall to the Castle of Knockwinnock, when the adept, recovering from his surprise, which had equalled that exhibited by any other individual of the party, twitched his sleeve, and having offered his humble congratulations, turned next to Oldbuck with an air of triumph.

'I did tell you, my goot friend Mr Oldenbuck, dat I was to seek opportunity to thank you for your civility; now do you not think I have found out vary goot way to return thank?'

'Why, Mr Dousterswivel, do you pretend to have had any hand in our good success?—you forget you refused us all aid of your science, man. And you are here without your weapons that should have fought the battle, which you pretend to have gained in our behalf. You have used neither charm, lamen, sigil, talisman, spell, crystal, pentacle, magic mirror, nor geomantic figure. Where be your periapts, and your abracadabras, man? your May-fern, your vervain,

> "Your toad, your crow, your dragon, and your panther,
> Your sun, your moon, your firmament, your adrop,
> Your Lato, Azoch, Zernich, Chibrit, Heautarit,
> With all your broths, your menstrues, your materials,
> Would burst a man to name?"*—

Ah! rare Ben Jonson! long peace to thy ashes for a scourge of the quacks of thy day!—who expected to see them revive in our own?'

The answer of the adept to the Antiquary's tirade we must defer to our next chapter.

CHAPTER XXIV

Clause. You now shall know the king o' the beggars' treasure:—
Yes—ere tomorrow you shall find your harbour
Here,—fail me not, for if I live I'll fit you.

The Beggar's Bush.*

THE German, determined, it would seem, to assert the vantage-ground on which the discovery had placed him, replied with great pomp and stateliness to the attack of the Antiquary:

'Maister Oldenbuck, all dis may be very witty and comedy, but I have nothing to say—nothing at all—to people dat will not believe deir own eyesights. It is vary true dat I ave not any of de things of de art, and it makes de more wonder what I has done dis day.—But I would ask of you, mine honoured and goot and generous patron, to put your hand into your right-hand waistcoat pocket, and show me what you shall find dere.'

Sir Arthur obeyed his direction, and pulled out the small plate of silver which he had used under the adept's auspices upon the former occasion. 'It is very true,' said Sir Arthur, looking gravely at the Antiquary, 'this is the graduated and calculated sigil* by which Mr Dousterswivel and I regulated our first discovery.'

'Pshaw! pshaw! my dear friend,' said Oldbuck, 'you are too wise to believe in the influence of a trumpery crown-piece, beat out thin, and a parcel of scratches upon it. I tell thee, Sir Arthur, that if Dousterswivel had known where to get this treasure himself, you would not have been lord of the least share of it.'

'In troth, please your honour,' said Edie, who put in his word on all occasions, 'I think, since Mr Dunkerswivel has had sae muckle merit in discovering a' the gear, the least ye can do is to gie him that o't that's left behind for his labour, for doubtless he that kend where to find sae muckle will hae nae difficulty to find mair.'

Dousterswivel's brow grew very dark at this proposal of leaving him to his 'ain purchase,' as Ochiltree expressed it; but the beggar, drawing him aside, whispered a word or two in his ear, to which he seemed to give serious attention.

Meanwhile, Sir Arthur, his heart warm with his good fortune, said aloud, 'Never mind our friend Monkbarns, Mr Dousterswivel, but come to the Castle tomorrow, and I'll convince you that I am not ungrateful for the hints you have given me about this matter, and the fifty Fairport dirty notes, as you call them, are heartily at your service. Come, my lads, get the cover of this precious chest fastened up again.'

But the cover had in the confusion fallen aside among the rubbish, or the loose earth which had been removed from the grave—in short, it was not to be seen.

'Never mind, my good lads, tie the tarpaulin over it, and get it away to the carriage. Monkbarns, will you walk?—I must go back your way to take up Miss Wardour.'

'And, I hope, to take up your dinner also, Sir Arthur, and drink a glass of wine for joy of our happy adventure. Besides, you should write about the business to the Exchequer, in case of any interference on the part of the crown. As you are lord of the manor, it will be easy to get a deed of gift should they make any claim*—we must talk about it though.'

'And I particularly recommend silence to all who are present,' said Sir Arthur, looking round. All bowed and professed themselves dumb.

'Why, as to that,' said Monkbarns, 'recommending secrecy where a dozen of people are acquainted with the circumstance to be concealed, is only putting the truth in masquerade, for the story will be circulated under twenty different shapes. But never mind, we will state the true one to the Barons,* and that is all that is necessary.'

'I incline to send off an express tonight,' said the Baronet.

'I can recommend your honour to a sure hand,' said Ochiltree; 'little Davie Mailsetter and the butcher's reisting powny.'

'We will talk over the matter as we go to Monkbarns,' said Sir Arthur. 'My lads, (to the work-people,) come with me to the Four Horse-shoes, that I may take down all your names. Dousterswivel, I won't ask you to go down to Monkbarns, as the laird and you differ so widely in opinion; but do not fail to come to see me tomorrow.'

Dousterswivel growled out an answer, in which the words, 'duty,'—'mine honoured patron,'—and 'wait upon Sir Arthurs,'—were alone distinguishable; and after the Baronet and his friend had left the ruins, followed by the servants and workmen, who, in hope of reward and whisky, joyfully attended their leader, the adept remained in a brown study by the side of the open grave.

'Who was it as could have thought this?' he ejaculated unconsciously. 'Mine heiligkeit! I have heard of such things, and often spoken of such things—but, sapperment! I never thought to see them! And if I had gone but two or dree feet deeper down in the earth—mein himmel!* it had been all mine own—so much more as I have been muddling about to get from this fool's man.'

Here the German ceased his soliloquy, for, raising his eyes, he encountered those of Edie Ochiltree, who had not followed the rest of the company, but, resting as usual on his pike-staff, had planted himself on the other side of the grave. The features of the old man, naturally shrewd and expressive almost to an appearance of knavery, seemed in this instance so keenly knowing, that even the assurance of Dousterswivel, though a professed adventurer, sunk beneath their glances. But he saw the necessity of an eclaircissement, and, rallying his spirits, instantly began to sound the mendicant on the occurrences of the day. 'Goot Maister Edies Ochiltrees'—

'Edie Ochiltree, nae maister—your puir bedesman and the king's,' answered the Blue-Gown.

'Awell den, goot Edie, what do you think of all dis?'

'I was just thinking it was very kind (for I darena say very simple) o' your honour to gie thae twa rich gentles, wha hae lands and lairdships, and siller without end, this grand pose o' silver and treasure, (three times tried in the fire,* as the Scripture expresses it,) that might hae made yoursell and ony twa or three honest bodies beside, as happy and content as the day was lang.'

'Indeed, Edie, mine honest friends, dat is very true; only I did not know, dat is, I was not sure, where to find de gelt myself.'

'What! was it not by your honour's advice and counsel that Monkbarns and the Knight of Knockwinnock came here then?'

'Aha—yes—but it was by another circumstance; I did not know dat dey would have found de treasure, mein friend; though I did guess, by such a tintamarre, and cough, and sneeze, and groan, among de spirit one other night here, dat there might be treasure and bullion hereabout. Ach, mein himmel! the spirit will hone and groan over his gelt, as if he were a Dutch burgomaster counting his dollars after a great dinner at the Stadthaus.'*

'And do you really believe the like o' that, Mr Dusterdeevil?—a skeelfu' man like you—hout fie!'

'Mein friend,' answered the adept, forced by circumstances to speak something nearer the truth than he generally used to do, 'I believed it no more than you and no man at all, till I did hear them hone and moan and groan myself on de oder night, and till I did this day see de cause, which was an great chest all full of de pure silver from Mexico—and what would you ave me think den?'

'And what wad ye gie to ony ane,' said Edie, 'that wad help ye to sic another kistfu' o' silver?'

'Give?—mein himmel!—one great big quarter of it.'

'Now, if the secret were mine,' said the mendicant, 'I wad stand out for a half; for you see, though I am but a puir ragged body, and couldna carry silver or gowd to sell for fear o' being taen up, yet I could find mony folk would pass it awa for me at unco muckle easier profit than ye're thinking on.'

'Ach, himmel!—Mein goot friend, what was it I said?—I did mean to say you should have de tree quarter for your half, and de one quarter to be my fair half.'

'No, no, Mr Dusterdeevil, we will divide equally what we find, like brother and brother. Now look at this board that I just flung into the dark aisle out o' the way, while Monkbarns was glowering ower a' the silver yonder. He's a sharp chiel Monkbarns. I was glad to keep the like o' this out o' his sight. Ye'll maybe can read the character better than me—I am nae that book-learned, at least I'm no that muckle in practice.'

With this modest declaration of ignorance, Ochiltree brought forth from behind a pillar the cover of the box or chest of treasure, which, when forced from its hinges, had been carelessly flung aside during the ardour of curiosity to ascertain the contents which it concealed, and had been afterwards, as it seems, secreted by the mendicant. There was a word and a number upon the plank, and the beggar made them more distinct by spitting upon his ragged blue handkerchief, and rubbing off the clay by which the inscription was obscured. It was in the ordinary black letter.

'Can ye mak ought o't?' said Edie to the adept.

'S,' said the philosopher, like a child getting his lesson in the primer; 'S, T, A, R, C, H,—*Starch*—dat is what the women-washers put in to de neckerchers, and de shirt collar.'

'Starch!' echoed Ochiltree; 'na, na, Mr Dusterdeevil, ye are mair of a conjuror than a clerk—it's *search*, man, *search*—See, there's the *Ye* clear and distinct.'

'Aha!—I see it now—it is *search—number one*. Mein himmel, then there must be a *number two*, mein goot friend; for *search* is what you call to seek and dig, and this is but *number one!*—Mine wort, there is one great big prize in de wheel* for us, goot Maister Ochiltree.'

'Aweel, it maybe sae—but we canna howk for't enow—we hae nae shules, for they hae taen them a' awa—and it's like some o' them will be sent back to fling the earth into the hole, and mak a' things trig again. But an ye'll sit down wi' me a while in the wood, I'se satisfy your honour that ye hae just lighted on the only man in the country that could hae tauld about Malcolm Misticot and his hidden treasure—But first we'll rub out the letters on this board for fear it tell tales.'

And, by the assistance of his knife, the beggar erased and defaced the characters so as to make them quite unintelligible, and then daubed the board with clay so as to obliterate all traces of the erasure.

Dousterswivel stared at him in ambiguous silence. There was an intelligence and alacrity about all the old man's movements which indicated a person that could not be easily overreached, and yet (for even rogues acknowledge in some degree the spirit of precedence) our adept felt the disgrace of playing a secondary part, and dividing winnings with so mean an associate. His appetite for gain, however, was sufficiently sharp to overpower his offended pride, and though far more an impostor than a dupe, he was not without a certain degree of personal faith even in the gross superstitions by means of which he imposed upon others. Still, being accustomed to act as a leader on such occasions, he felt humiliated at feeling himself in the situation of a vulture marshalled to his prey by a carrion-crow. Let me, however, hear his story to an end, thought Dousterswivel, and it will be hard if I do not make mine account in it better, as Maister Edie Ochiltrees makes proposes.

The adept, thus transformed into a pupil from a teacher of the mystic art, followed Ochiltree in passive acquiescence to the Prior's Oak—a spot, as the reader may remember, at a short distance from the ruins, where the German sat down, and in silence waited the old man's communication.

'Maister Dustandsnivel,' said the narrator, 'it's an unco while since I heard this business treated anent—for the lairds of Knock-winnock, neither Sir Arthur, nor his father, nor his grandfather, and I mind a wee bit about them a', liked to hear it spoken about—nor they dinna like it yet—but nae matter, ye may be sure it was clattered about in the kitchen, like ony thing else in a great house, though it were forbidden in the ha'—and sae I hae heard the circumstance rehearsed by auld servants in the family; and in thir present days, when things o' that auld-warld sort arena keepit in mind round winter fire-sides as they used to be, I question if there's ony body in the country can tell the tale but mysell—aye out-taken the laird though, for there's a parchment book about it, as I have heard, in the charter-room at Knockwinnock Castle.'

'Well, all dat is vary well—but get you on with your stories, mine goot friend,' said Dousterswivel.

'Aweel, ye see,' continued the mendicant, 'this was a job in the auld times o' rugging and riving through the hale country, when it was ilka ane for himsell, and God for us a'; when nae man wanted property if he had strength to take it, or had it langer than he had power to keep it. It was just he ower her, and she ower him, which-ever could win upmost, a' through the east country here, and nae doubt through the rest o' Scotland in the self and same manner.

'Sae, in these days Sir Richard Wardour came into the land, and that was the first o' the name ever was in this country.—There's been mony of them sin' syne; and the maist, like him they ca'd Hell-in-Harness, and the rest o' them, are sleeping down in yon ruins. They were a proud dour set o' men, but unco brave, and aye stood up for the weel o' the country, God sain them a'—there's no muckle popery in that wish. They ca'd them the Norman Wardours, though they cam frae the south to this country—So this Sir Richard, that they ca'd Red-hand, drew up wi' the auld Knockwinnock o' that day, for then they were Knockwinnocks of that Ilk,* and wad fain marry his only daughter, that was to have the castle and the land. Laith, laith was the lass—(Sybil Knockwinnock they ca'd her that tauld me the tale)—laith, laith was she to gae into the match, for she had fa'en a wee ower thick wi' a cousin o' her ain that her father had some ill-will to; and sae it was, that after she had been married to Sir Richard jimp four months,—for marry him she maun it's like,—ye'll no hinder her gieing them a present o' a bonny knave bairn. Then there was siccan a ca'-thro', as the like was never seen; and she's be burnt, and he's be slain, was the best words o' their mouths. But it was a' sowdered up again some gait, and the bairn was sent awa, and bred up near the High lands, and grew up to be a fine wanle fallow, like mony ane that comes o' the wrang side o' the blanket;* and Sir Richard wi' the Red hand, he had a fair offspring o' his ain, and a' was lound and quiet till his head was laid in the ground. But then down came Malcolm Misticot—(Sir Arthur says it should be *Misbegot*, but they aye ca'd him Misticot that spoke o't lang syne)—down came this Malcolm, the love-begot, frae Glen-isla, wi' a string o' lang-legged Highlanders at his heels, that's aye ready for ony body's mischief, and he threeps the castle and lands are his ain as his mother's eldest son, and turns a' the Wardours out to the hill. There was a sort o' fighting and blude-spilling about it, for the gentles took different sides; but Malcolm had the uppermost for a lang time, and keepit the Castle of Knockwinnock, and strengthened it, and built that muckle tower, that they ca' Misticot's tower to this day.'

'Mine goot friend, old Mr Edie Ochiltree,' interrupted the German, 'this is all as one like de long histories of a baron of sixteen quarters in mine countries; but I would as rather hear of de silver and gold.'

'Why, ye see,' continued the mendicant, 'this Malcolm was weel helped by an uncle, a brother o' his father's, that was Prior o' St Ruth here, and muckle treasure they gathered between them, to secure the succession of their house in the lands of Knockwinnock—Folk said, that the monks in thae days had the art of multiplying metals—at ony rate they were very rich. At last it came to this, that the young Wardour, that was Red-hand's son, challenged Misticot to fight with him in the lists as they ca'd them—that's no lists or tailor's runds and selvedges o' claith, but a palin'-thing they set up for them to fight in like game-cocks. Aweel, Misticot was beaten, and at his brother's mercy—but he wadna touch his life, for the blood of Knockwinnock that was in baith their veins: so Malcolm was compelled to turn a monk, and he died soon after in the priory, of pure despite and vexation. Naebody ever kend whare his uncle the prior earded him, or what he did wi' his gowd and silver, for he stood on the right o' halie kirk, and wad gie nae account to ony body. But the prophecy gat abroad in the country, that whenever Misticot's grave was fund out, the estate of Knockwinnock should be lost and won.'

'Ach, mine goot old friend, Maister Edie, and dat is not so very unlikely, if Sir Arthurs will quarrel wit his goot friends to please Mr Oldenbuck—And so you do tink dat dis golds and silvers belonged to goot Mr Malcolm Mishdigoat?'

'Troth do I, Mr Dousterdeevil.'

'And you do believe dat dere is more of dat sorts behind?'

'By my certie do I—How can it be otherwise? —*Search—No. I.*— that is as muckle as to say, search and ye'll find number twa— besides, yon kist is only silver, and I aye heard that Misticot's pose had muckle yellow gowd in't.'

'Den, mine goot friends,' said the adept, jumping up hastily, 'why do we not set about our little job directly?'

'For twa gude reasons,' answered the beggar, who quietly kept his sitting posture; 'first, because, as I said before, we have naething to dig wi', for they hae taen awa the picks and shules; and, secondly, because there will be a wheen idle gowks coming to glower at the hole as lang as it is daylight, and maybe the laird may send somebody to fill it up—and ony way we wad be catched. But if you will meet me on this place at twal o'clock wi' a dark lantern,* I'll hae tools ready, and we'll gang quietly about our job our twa sells, and naebody the wiser for't.'

'Be—be—but, mine goot friend,' said Dousterswivel, from whose recollection his former nocturnal adventure was not to be altogether erased, even by the splendid hopes which Edie's narrative held forth, 'it is not so goot or so safe to be about goot Maister Mishdigoat's grave at dat time of night—you have forgot how I told you de spirits did hone and mone dere. I do assure you, dere is disturbance dere.'

'If ye're afraid of ghaists,' answered the mendicant coolly, 'I'll do the job mysell, and bring your share o' the siller to ony place ye like to appoint.'

'No—no—mine excellent old Mr Edie,—too much trouble for you—I will not have dat—I will come myself—and it will be better- most; for, mine old friend, it was I, Herman Dousterswivel, dis- covered Maister Mishdigoat's grave when I was looking for a place as to put away some little trumpery coins, just to play one little trick on my dear friend Sir Arthur, for a little sport and pleasures—yes, I did take some what you call rubbish, and did discover Maister Mish- digoat's own monumentsh—It is like dat he meant I should be his heirs—so it would not be civility in me not to come mineself for mine inheritance.'

'At twal o'clock, then,' said the mendicant, 'we meet under this tree—I'll watch for a while, and see that naebody meddles wi' the grave—it's only saying the lairds forbade it—then get my bit supper frae Ringan the poinder up by, and leave to sleep in his barn, and I'll slip out at night and ne'er be mist.'

'Do so, mine goot Maister Edie, and I will meet you here on this very place, though all de spirits should moan and sneeze deir very brains out.'

So saying, he shook hands with the old man, and, with this mutual pledge of fidelity to their appointment, they separated for the present.

CHAPTER XXV

———See thou shake the bags
Of hoarding abbots; angels imprisoned
Set thou at liberty—
Bell, book, and candle, shall not drive me back,
If gold and silver beckon to come on—

King John.*

THE night set in stormy, with wind and occasional showers of rain. 'Eh, sirs,' said the old mendicant, as he took his place on the sheltered side of the large oak-tree to wait for his associate—'Eh, sirs, but human nature's a wilful and wilyard thing!—Is it not an unco lucre o' gain wad bring this Dousterdivel out in a blast o' wind like this, at twal o'clock at night, to thir wild gousty wa's?—and amna I a bigger fule than himsell to bide here waiting for him?'

Having made these sage reflections, he wrapped himself close in his cloak, and fixed his eye on the moon as she waded amid the stormy and dusky clouds, which the wind from time to time drove across her surface. The melancholy and uncertain gleams that she shot from between the passing shadows fell full upon the rifted arches and shafted windows of the old building, which were thus for an instant made distinctly visible in their ruinous state, and anon became again a dark, undistinguished, and shadowy mass. The little lake had its share of these transient beams of light, and showed its waters broken, whitened, and agitated under the passing storm, which, when the clouds swept over the moon, were only distinguished by their sullen and murmuring plash against the beach. The wooded glen repeated, to every successive gust that hurried through its narrow trough, the deep and various groan with which the trees replied to the whirlwind, and the sound sunk again, as the blast passed away, into a faint and passing murmur, resembling the sighs of an exhausted criminal after the first pangs of his torture are over. In these sounds, superstition might have found ample gratification for that state of excited terror which she fears and yet loves. But such feelings made no part of Ochiltree's composition. His mind wandered back to the scenes of his youth.

'I have kept guard on the outposts baith in Germany and

America,' he said to himself, 'in mony a waur night than this, and when I kend there was maybe a dozen o' their riflemen in the thicket before me. But I was aye gleg at my duty—naebody ever catched Edie sleeping.'

As he muttered thus to himself, he instinctively shouldered his trusty pike-staff, assumed the port of a sentinel on duty, and, as a step advanced towards the tree, called, with a tone assorting better with his military reminiscences than his present state—'Stand—who goes there?'

'De devil, goot Edie,' answered Dousterswivel, 'why does you speak so loud as a baarenhauter, or what you call a factionary—I mean a sentinel?'

'Just because I thought I was a sentinel at that moment,' answered the mendicant. 'Here's an awsome night—hae ye brought the lantern and a pock for the siller?'

'Ay—ay—mine goot friend,' said the German, 'here it is—my pair of what you call saddlebag—one side will be for you, one side for me—I will put dem on my horse to save you de trouble, as you are old man.'

'Have you a horse here, then?' asked Edie Ochiltree.

'O yes, mine friend, tied yonder by de stile,' responded the adept.

'Weel, I hae just ae word to the bargain—there sall nane o' my gear gang on your beast's back.'

'What was it as you would be afraid of?' said the foreigner.

'Only of losing sight of horse, man, and money,' again replied the gaberlunzie.

'Does you know dat you make one gentlemans out to be one great rogue?'

'Mony gentlemen,' replied Ochiltree, 'can make that out for themselves—but what's the sense of quarrelling?—If ye want to gang on, gang on—If no, I'll gae back to the gude ait-straw in Ringan Aikwood's barn that I left wi' right ill-will e'now, and I'll pit back the pick and shule whar I got them.'

Dousterswivel deliberated a moment, whether, by suffering Edie to depart, he might not secure the whole of the expected wealth for his own exclusive use. But the want of digging implements, the uncertainty whether, if he had them, he could clear out the grave to a sufficient depth without assistance, and, above all, the reluctance which he felt, owing to the experience of the former night, to venture alone on the terrors of Misticot's grave, satisfied him the attempt would be hazardous. Endeavouring, therefore, to assume his usual cajoling tone, though internally incensed, he begged 'his goot friend Maister Edie Ochiltrees would lead the way, and assured him of his acquiescence in all such an excellent friend could propose.'

'Awell, aweel, then,' said Edie, 'tak gude care o' your feet amang the lang grass and the loose stanes—I wish we may get the light keepit in neist, wi' this fearsome wind—but there's a blink o' moonlight at times.'

Thus saying, old Edie, closely accompanied by the adept, led the way towards the ruins, but presently made a full halt in front of them.

'Ye're a learned man, Mr Dousterdeevil, and ken muckle o' the marvellous works o' nature—now, will ye tell me ae thing?—D'ye believe in ghaists and spirits that walk the earth?—d'ye believe in them, ay, or no?'

'Now, goot Mr Edie,' whispered Dousterwivel, in an expostulatory tone of voice, 'is this a times or a places for such a questions?'

'Indeed is it, baith the tane and the tother, Mr Dustanshovel; for I maun fairly tell ye, there's reports that auld Misticot walks. Now this wad be an uncanny night to meet him in, and wha kens if he wad be ower weel pleased wi' our purpose of visiting his pose?'

'*Alle guter Geister*'*—muttered the adept, the rest of the conjuration being lost in a tremulous warble of his voice,—'I do desires you not to speak so, Mr Edie, for, from all I heard dat one other night, I do much believes'—

'Now I,' said Ochiltree, entering the chancel, and flinging abroad his arm with an air of defiance, 'I wadna gie the crack o' my thumb for him were he to appear at this moment—he's but a disembodied spirit as we are embodied anes.'

'For the lofe of heavens,' said Dousterswivel, 'say nothing at all neither about somebodies or nobodies!'

'Aweel,' said the beggar, (expanding the shade of the lantern,) 'here's the stane, and, spirit or no spirit, I'se be a wee bit deeper in the grave'—and he jumped into the place from which the precious chest had that morning been removed. After striking a few strokes, he tired, or affected to tire, and said to his companion, 'I'm auld and failed now, and canna keep at it—Time about's fair play, neighbour—ye maun get in and tak the shule a bit, and shule out the loose earth, and then I'll tak turn about wi' you.'

Dousterswivel accordingly took the place which the beggar had evacuated, and toiled with all the zeal that awakened avarice, mingled with the anxious wish to finish the undertaking and leave the place as soon as possible, could inspire in a mind at once greedy, suspicious, and timorous.

Edie, standing much at his ease by the side of the hole, contented himself with exhorting his associate to labour hard. 'My certie! few ever wrought for siccan a day's wage; an it be but—say the tenth part o' the size o' the kist, No. I., it will double its value, being filled wi' gowd instead of silver.—Odd ye work as if ye had been bred to pick and shule—ye could win your round half-crown ilka day. Tak care o' your taes wi' that stane!' giving a kick to a large one which the adept had heaved out with difficulty, and which Edie pushed back again, to the great annoyance of his associate's shins.

Thus exhorted by the mendicant, Dousterswivel struggled and laboured among the stones and stiff clay, toiling like a horse, and internally blaspheming in German. When such an unhallowed syllable escaped his lips, Edie changed his battery upon him.

'O dinna swear, dinna swear!—wha kens wha's listening!—Eh! gude guide us, what's yon!—Hout, it's just a branch of ivy flightering awa frae the wa'; when the moon was in, it lookit unco like a dead man's arm wi' a taper in't; I thought it was Misticot himsell. But never mind, work you away—fling the earth weel up by out o' the gate—odd if ye're no as clean a worker at a grave as Will Winnet himsell! What gars ye stop now?—ye're just at the very bit for a chance.'

'Stop!' said the German, in a tone of anger and disappointment, 'why, I am down at de rocks dat de cursed ruins (God forgife me!) is founded upon.'

'Weel,' said the beggar, 'that's the likeliest bit of ony—it will be but a muckle through-stane laid doun to kiver the gowd; tak the pick till't, and pit mair strength, man—ae gude downright devvel will split it, I'se warrant ye—Ay, that will do—Odd, he comes on wi' Wallace's straiks!'

In fact, the adept, moved by Edie's exhortations, fetched two or three desperate blows, and succeeded in breaking, not indeed that against which he struck, which, as he had already conjectured, was the solid rock, but the implement which he wielded, jarring at the same time his arms up to the shoulder-blades.

'Hurra, boys!—there goes Ringan's pick-axe!' cried Edie; 'it's a shame o' the Fairport folk to sell siccan frail gear. Try the shule—at it again, Mr Dusterdeevil.'

The adept, without reply, scrambled out of the pit, which was now about six feet deep, and addressed his associate in a voice that trembled with anger. 'Does you know, Mr Edies Ochiltrees, who it is you put off your gibes and your jests upon?'

'Brawly, Mr Dusterdeevil—brawly do I ken ye, and has done mony a day; but there's nae jesting in the case, for I am wearying to see a' our treasures; we should hae had baith ends o' the pock-manky filled by this time—I hope it's bowk eneugh to haud a' the gear?'

'Look you, you base old person,' said the incensed philosopher, 'if you do put another jest upon me, I will cleave your skull-piece with this shovels!'

'And whare wad my hands and my pike-staff be a' the time?' replied Edie, in a tone that indicated no apprehension. 'Hout, tout, Maister Dusterdeevil, I haena lived sae lang in the warld neither, to be shuled out o't that gate. What ails ye to be cankered, man, wi' your friends? I'll wager I'll find out the treasure in a minute;' and he jumped into the pit and took up the spade.

'I do swear to you,' said the adept, whose suspicions were now fully awake, 'that if you have played me one big trick, I will give you one big beating, Mr Edies.'

'Hear till him now,' said Ochiltree; 'he kens how to gar folk find out the gear—Odd, I'm thinking he's been drilled that way himsell some day.'

At this insinuation, which alluded obviously to the former scene betwixt himself and Sir Arthur, the philosopher lost the slender remnant of patience he had left, and being of violent passions, heaved up the truncheon of the broken mattock to discharge it upon the old man's head. The blow would in all probability have been fatal, had not he at whom it was aimed exclaimed in a stern and firm voice, 'Shame to ye, man!—Do ye think Heaven or earth will suffer ye to murder an auld man that might be your father?—Look behind ye, man.'

Dousterswivel turned instinctively, and beheld, to his utter astonishment, a tall dark figure standing close behind him. The apparition gave him no time to proceed by exorcism or otherwise, but having instantly recourse to the *voie de fait*,* took measure of the adept's shoulders three or four times with blows so substantial, that he fell under the weight of them, and remained senseless for some minutes between fear and stupefaction. When he came to himself, he was alone in the ruined chancel, lying upon the soft and damp earth which had been thrown out of Misticot's grave. He raised himself with a confused sensation of anger, pain, and terror, and it was not until he had sat upright for some minutes that he could arrange his ideas sufficiently to recollect how he came there, or with what purpose. As his recollection returned, he could have little doubt that the bait held out to him by Ochiltree to bring him to that solitary spot, the sarcasms by which he had provoked him into a quarrel, and the ready assistance which he had at hand for terminating it in the manner in which it had ended, were all parts of a concerted plan to bring disgrace and damage on Herman Dousterswivel. He could hardly suppose that he was indebted for the fatigue, anxiety, and beating which he had undergone, purely to the malice of Edie Ochiltree singly, but concluded that the mendicant had acted a part assigned to him by some person of greater importance. His suspicions hesitated between Oldbuck and Sir Arthur Wardour. The former had been at no pains to conceal a marked dislike of him—but the latter he had deeply injured; and although he judged that Sir Arthur did not know the extent of his wrongs towards him, yet it was easy to suppose he had gathered enough of the truth to make him desirous of revenge. Ochiltree had alluded to at least one circumstance which the adept had every reason to suppose was private between Sir Arthur and himself, and therefore must have been learned from the former. The language of Oldbuck also intimated a conviction of his knavery, which Sir Arthur heard without making any animated defence. Lastly, the way in which Dousterswivel supposed the Baronet to have exercised his revenge, was not inconsistent with the practice of other countries with which the adept was better acquainted than with those of North Britain. With him, as with many bad men, to suspect an injury, and to nourish the purpose of revenge, was one and the same movement. And before Dousterswivel had fairly recovered his legs, he had mentally sworn the ruin of his benefactor, which, unfortunately, he possessed too much the power of accelerating.

But although a purpose of revenge floated through his brain, it was no time to indulge such speculations. The hour, the place, his own situation, and perhaps the presence or near neighbourhood of his assailants, made self-preservation the adept's first object. The lantern had been thrown down and extinguished in the scuffle. The wind, which formerly howled so loudly through the aisles of the ruin, had now greatly fallen, lulled by the rain, which was descending very fast. The moon, from the same cause, was totally obscured, and though Dousterswivel had some experience of the ruins, and knew that he must endeavour to regain the eastern door of the chancel, yet the confusion of his ideas was such, that he hesitated for some time ere he could ascertain in what direction he was to seek it. In this perplexity, the suggestions of superstition, taking the advantage of darkness and his evil conscience, began again to present themselves to his disturbed imagination. 'But bah!' quoth he valiantly to himself, 'it is all nonsense—all one part of de damn big trick and imposture. Devil! that one thick-skulled Scotch Baronet, as I have led by the nose for five year, should cheat Herman Dousterswivel!'

As he had come to this conclusion, an incident occurred which tended greatly to shake the grounds on which he had adopted it. Amid the melancholy *sough* of the dying wind, and the plash of the rain-drops on leaves and stones, arose, and apparently at no great distance from the listener, a strain of vocal music so sad and solemn, as if the departed spirits of the churchmen who had once inhabited these deserted ruins, were mourning the solitude and desolation to which their hallowed precincts had been abandoned. Dousterswivel, who had now got upon his feet, and was groping around the wall of the chancel, stood rooted to the ground on the occurrence of this new phenomenon. Each faculty of his soul seemed for the moment concentred in the sense of hearing, and all rushed back with the unanimous information, that the deep, wild, and prolonged chant which he now heard, was the appropriate music of one of the most solemn dirges of the church of Rome. Why performed in such a solitude, and by what class of choristers, were questions which the terrified imagination of the adept, stirred with all the German superstitions of nixies, oak-kings, wer-wolves, hobgoblings, black spirits and white, blue spirits and grey,* durst not even attempt to solve.

Another of his senses was soon engaged in the investigation. At the extremity of one of the transepts of the church, at the bottom of a few descending steps, was a small iron-grated door, opening, as far as he recollected, to a sort of low vault or sacristy. As he cast his eye in the direction of the sound, he observed a strong reflection of red light glimmering through these bars, and against the steps which descended to them. Dousterswivel stood a moment uncertain what to do; then, suddenly forming a desperate resolution, he moved down the aisle to the place from which the light proceeded.

Fortified with the sign of the cross, and as many exorcisms as his memory could recover, he advanced to the grate, from which, unseen, he could see what passed in the interior of the vault. As he approached with timid and uncertain steps, the chant, after one or two wild and prolonged cadences, died away into profound silence. The grate, when he reached it, presented a singular spectacle in the interior of the sacristy. An open grave, with four tall flambeaus, each about six feet high, placed at the four corners—a bier, having a corpse in its shroud, the arms folded upon the breast, rested upon tressels at one side of the grave, as if ready to be interred—A priest, dressed in his cope and stole, held open the service book—another churchman in his vestments bore a holy-water sprinkler—and two boys in white surplices held censers with incense—a man, of a figure once tall and commanding, but now bent with age or infirmity, stood alone and nearest to the coffin, attired in deep mourning—such were the most prominent figures of the group. At a little distance were two or three persons of both sexes, attired in long mourning hoods and cloaks; and five or six others in the same lugubrious dress, still farther removed from the body, around the walls of the vault, stood ranged in motionless order, each bearing in his hand a huge torch of black wax. The smoky light from so many flambeaus, by the red and indistinct atmosphere which it spread around, gave a hazy, dubious, and, as it were, phantom-like appearance to the outlines of this singular apparition. The voice of the priest—loud, clear, and sonorous, now recited, from the breviary which he held in his hand, those solemn words which the ritual of the Catholic church has consecrated to the rendering of dust to dust. Meanwhile, Dousterswivel, the place, the hour, and the surprise considered, still remained uncertain, whether what he saw was substantial, or an unearthly representation of the rites, to which, in former times, these walls were familiar, but which are now rarely practised in Protestant countries, and almost never in Scotland.* He was uncertain whether to abide the conclusion of the ceremony, or to endeavour to regain the chancel, when a change in his position made him visible through the grate to one of the attendant mourners. The person who first espied him, indicated his discovery to the individual who stood apart and nearest to the coffin by a sign, and upon his making a sign in reply, two of the group detached themselves, and, gliding along with noiseless steps, as if fearing to disturb the service, unlocked and opened the grate which separated them from the adept. Each took him by an arm, and exerting a degree of force, which he would have been incapable of resisting had his fear permitted him to attempt opposition, they placed him on the ground in the chancel, and sat down, one on each side of him, as if to detain him. Satisfied he was in the power of mortals like himself, the adept would have put some questions to them; but while one pointed to the vault, from which the sound of the priest's voice was distinctly heard, the other placed his finger upon his lips in token of silence, a hint which the German thought it most prudent to obey. And thus they detained him until a loud Alleluia, pealing through the deserted arches of St Ruth, closed the singular ceremony which it had been his fortune to witness.

When the hymn had died away with all its echoes, the voice of one of the sable personages under whose guard the adept had remained, said, in a familiar tone and dialect, 'Dear sirs, Mr Dousterswivel, is this you? could not ye have let us ken an ye had wussed till hae been present at the ceremony?—My lord couldna tak it weel your coming blinking and jinking in, in that fashion.'

'In de name of all dat is gootness, tell me what you are?' interrupted the German in his turn.

'What I am? why, wha should I be but Ringan Aikwood, the Knockwinnock poinder?—And what are ye doing here at this time o' night, unless ye were come to attend the leddy's burial?'

'I do declare to you, mine goot Poinder Aikwood,' said the German, raising himself up, 'that I have been this vary nights murdered, robbed, and put in fears of my life.'

'Robbed! wha wad do sic a deed here?—Murdered! odd, ye speak pretty blithe for a murdered man.—Put in fear! what put you in fear, Mr Dousterswivel?'

'I will tell you, Maister Poinder Aikwood Ringan, just dat old miscreant dog villain blue-gown, as you call Edie Ochiltrees.'

'I'll ne'er believe that,' answered Ringan; 'Edie was kend to me, and my father before me, for a true, loyal, and soothfast man; and, mair by token, he's sleeping up yonder in our barn, and has been since ten at e'en—Sae touch ye wha liket, Mr Dousterswivel, and whether ony body touched ye or no, I'm sure Edie's sackless.'

'Maister Ringan Aikwood Poinders, I do not know what you call sackless, but let alone all de oils and de soot dat you say he has, and I will tell you I was dis night robbed of fifty pounds by your oil and sooty friend, Edies Ochiltree; and he is no more in your barn even now dan I ever shall be in de kingdom of heafen.'

'Weel, sir, if ye will gae up wi' me, as the burial company has dispersed, we'se mak ye down a bed at the lodge, and we'se see if Edie's at the barn. There were twa wild-looking chaps left the auld kirk when we were coming up wi' the corpse, that's certain; and the priest, wha likes ill that ony heretics should look on at our church ceremonies, sent twa o' the riding saulies after them; sae we'll hear a' about it frae them.'

Thus speaking, the kindly apparition, with the assistance of the mute personage, who was his son, disencumbered himself of his cloak, and prepared to escort Dousterswivel to the place of that rest which the adept so much needed.

'I will apply to the magistrates tomorrow,' said the adept; 'oder, I will have de law put in force against all the peoples.'

While he thus muttered vengeance against the cause of his injury, he tottered from among the ruins, supporting himself on Ringan and his son, whose assistance his state of weakness rendered very necessary.

When they were clear of the priory, and had gained the little meadow in which it stands, Dousterswivel could perceive the torches which had caused him so much alarm issuing in irregular procession from the ruins, and glancing their light, like that of the *ignis fatuus*,* on the banks of the lake. After moving along the path for some short space with a fluctuating and irregular motion, the lights were at once extinguished.

'We aye put out the torches at the Halie-cross Well on sic occasions,' said the forester to his guest; and accordingly no farther visible sign of the procession offered itself to Dousterswivel, although his ear could catch the distant and decreasing echo of horses' hoofs in the direction towards which the mourners had bent their course.

CHAPTER XXVI

O weel may the boatie row,
  And better may she speed,
And weel may the boatie row
  That earns the bairnies' bread!
The boatie rows, the boatie rows,
  The boatie rows weel,
And lightsome be their life that bear
  The merlin and the creel!

*Old Ballad.**

WE must now introduce our reader to the interior of the fisher's cottage mentioned in chapter eleventh of this edifying history. I wish I could say that its inside was well arranged, decently furnished, or tolerably clean. On the contrary, I am compelled to admit, there was confusion,—there was dilapidation,—there was dirt good store. Yet, with all this, there was about the inmates, Luckie Mucklebackit and her family, an appearance of ease, plenty, and comfort, that seemed to warrant their old sluttish proverb, 'The clartier the cosier.' A huge fire, though the season was summer, occupied the hearth, and served at once for affording light, heat, and the means of preparing food. The fishing had been successful, and the family, with customary improvidence, had, since unlading the cargo, continued an unremitting operation of broiling and frying that part of the produce reserved for home consumption, and the bones and fragments lay on the wooden trenchers, mingled with morsels of broken bannocks and shattered mugs of half-drunk beer. The stout and athletic form of Maggie herself, bustling here and there among a pack of half-grown girls and younger children, of whom she chucked one now here and another now there, with an exclamation of 'Get out o' the gate, ye little sorrow!' was strongly contrasted with the passive and half stupified look and manner of her husband's mother, a woman advanced to the last stage of human life, who was seated in her wonted chair close by the fire, the warmth of which she coveted, yet hardly seemed to be sensible of, now muttering to herself, now smiling vacantly to the children as they pulled the strings of her *toy* or close cap, or twitched her blue checked apron. With her distaff in her

bosom, and her spindle in her hand, she plied lazily and mechanically the old-fashioned Scottish thrift, according to the old-fashioned
Scottish manner. The younger children, crawling among the feet of
the elder, watched the progress of grannie's spindle as it twisted, and
now and then ventured to interrupt its progress as it danced upon
the floor in those vagaries which the more regulated spinning-wheel*
has now so universally superseded, that even the fated Princess of
the fairy tale* might roam through all Scotland without the risk of
piercing her hand with a spindle, and dying of the wound. Late as
the hour was, (and it was long past midnight,) the whole family were
still on foot, and far from proposing to go to bed; the dame was still
busy broiling car-cakes on the girdle, and the elder girl, the half-
naked mermaid elsewhere commemorated, was preparing a pile of
Findhorn haddocks, (that is, haddocks smoked with green wood,) to
be eaten along with these relishing provisions.

While they were thus employed, a slight tap at the door, accompanied with the question, 'Are ye up yet, sirs?' announced a visitor.
The answer, 'Ay, ay,—come your ways ben, hinny,' occasioned the
lifting of the latch, and Jenny Rintherout, the female domestic of our
Antiquary, made her appearance.

'Ay, ay,' exclaimed the mistress of the family,—'Hegh, sirs! can
this be you, Jenny? a sight o' you's gude for sair een, lass.'

'O, woman, we've been sae taen up wi' Captain Hector's wound
up by, that I havena had my fit out ower the door this fortnight; but
he's better now, and auld Caxon sleeps in his room in case he wanted
ony thing. Sae, as soon as our auld folk gaed to bed, I e'en snooded
my head up a bit, and left the house-door on the latch, in case ony
body should be wanting in or out while I was awa, and just cam down
the gate to see an there was ony cracks amang ye.'

'Ay, ay,' answered Luckie Mucklebackit, 'I see ye hae gotten a'
your braws on—ye're looking about for Steenie now—but he's no at
hame the night—and ye'll no do for Steenie, lass—a feckless thing
like you's no fit to mainteen a man.'

'Steenie will no do for me,' retorted Jenny, with a toss of her head
that might have become a higher-born damsel,—'I maun hae a man
that can mainteen his wife.'

'Ou ay, hinny—thae's your landward and burrows-town notions.
My certie! fisher-wives ken better—they keep the man, and keep the
house, and keep the siller too, lass.'

'A wheen poor drudges ye are,' answered the nymph of the land to the nymph of the sea.—'As sune as the keel o' the coble touches the sand, deil a bit mair will the lazy fisher loons work, but the wives maun kilt their coats, and wade into the surf to tak the fish ashore. And then the man casts aff the wat and puts on the dry, and sits down wi' his pipe and his gill-stoup ahint the ingle, like ony auld houdie, and ne'er a turn will he do till the coble's afloat again!—And the wife, she maun get the scull on her back, and awa wi' the fish to the next burrows-town, and scauld and ban wi' ilka wife that will scauld and ban wi' her till it's sauld—and that's the gait fisher-wives live, puir slaving bodies.'

'Slaves? gae wa', lass!—Ca' the head o' the house slaves? little ye ken about it, lass—Show me a word my Saunders daur speak, or a turn he daur do about the house, without it be just to tak his meat, and his drink, and his diversion, like ony o' the weans. He has mair sense than to ca' ony thing about the bigging his ain, frae the rooftree down to a crackit trencher on the bink. He kens weel eneugh wha feeds him, and cleeds him, and keeps a' tight, thack and rape, when his coble is jowing awa in the Firth, puir fallow. Na, na, lass—them that sell the goods guide the purse—them that guide the purse rule the house—Show me ane o' your bits o' farmer-bodies that wad let their wife drive the stock to the market, and ca' in the debts. Na, na.'[17]

'Aweel, aweel, Maggie, ilka land has its ain lauch*—But where's Steenie the night, when a's come and gane? And where's the gudeman?'

'I hae puttin' the gudeman to his bed, for he was e'en sair forfairn; and Steenie's awa out about some barns-breaking wi' the auld gaber-lunzie, Edie Ochiltree—they'll be in sune, and ye can sit doun.'

'Troth, gudewife, (taking a seat,) I haena that muckle time to stop—but I maun tell ye about the news—Ye'll hae heard o' the muckle kist o' gowd that Sir Arthur has fund down by at St Ruth?—He'll be grander than ever now—he'll no can haud down his head to sneeze, for fear o' seeing his shoon.'

'Ou ay—a' the country's heard o' that; but auld Edie says they ca' it ten times mair than ever was o't, and he saw them howk it up. Odd, it would be lang or a puir body that needed it got sic a windfa'.'

'Na, that's sure eneugh.—And ye'll hae heard o' the Countess o' Glenallan being dead and lying in state, and how she's to be buried at

St Ruth's as this night fa's, wi' torch-light; and a' the papist servants, and Ringan Aikwood, that's a papist too, are to be there, and it will be the grandest show ever was seen.'

'Troth, hinny,' answered the Nereid, 'if they let naebody but papists come there, it'll no be muckle o' a show in this country; for the auld harlot,* as honest Mr Blattergowl ca's her, has few that drink o' her cup of enchantments in this corner of our chosen lands.—But what can ail them to bury the auld carlin (a rudas wife she was) in the night time?—I dare say our gudemither will ken.'

Here she exalted her voice, and exclaimed twice or thrice, 'Gudemither! gudemither!' but, lost in the apathy of age and deafness, the aged sibyl she addressed continued plying her spindle without understanding the appeal made to her.

'Speak to your grandmither, Jenny—odd, I wad rather hail the coble half a mile aff, and the norwast wind whistling again in my teeth.'

'Grannie,' said the little mermaid, in a voice to which the old woman was better accustomed, 'minnie wants to ken what for the Glenallan folk aye bury by candle-light in the ruins of St Ruth?'

The old woman paused in the act of twirling the spindle, turned round to the rest of the party, lifted her withered, trembling, and clay-coloured hand, raised up her ashen-hue'd and wrinkled face, which the quick motion of two light-blue eyes chiefly distinguished from the visage of a corpse, and, as if catching at any touch of association with the living world, answered, 'What gars the Glenallan family inter their dead by torch-light, said the lassie?—Is there a Glenallan dead e'en now?'

'We might be a' dead and buried too,' said Maggie, 'for ony thing ye wad ken about it;'—and then, raising her voice to the stretch of her mother-in-law's comprehension, she added, 'It's the auld Countess, gudemither.'

'And is she ca'd hame then at last?' said the old woman, in a voice that seemed to be agitated with much more feeling than belonged to her extreme old age, and the general indifference and apathy of her manner—'is she then called to her last account after her lang race o' pride and power?—O God forgie her!'

'But minnie was asking ye,' resumed the lesser querist, 'what for the Glenallan family aye bury their dead by torch-light?'

'They hae aye dune sae,' said the grandmother, 'since the time the

Great Earl fell in the sair battle o' the Harlaw,* when they say the coronach was cried in ae day from the mouth o' the Tay to the Buck of the Cabrach, that ye wad hae heard nae other sound but that of lamentation for the great folks that had fa'en fighting against Donald of the Isles.—But the Great Earl's mither was living—they were a doughty and a dour race the women o' the house o' Glenallan—and she wad hae nae coronach cried for her son, but had him laid in the silence o' midnight in his place o' rest, without either drinking the dirge, or crying the lament.—She said he had killed enow that day he died, for the widows and daughters o' the Highlanders he had slain to cry the coronach for them they had lost and for her son too; and sae she laid him in his grave wi' dry eyes, and without a groan or a wail—And it was thought a proud word o' the family, and they aye stickit by it—and the mair in the latter times, because in the night-time they had mair freedom to perform their popish ceremonies by darkness and in secrecy than in the daylight—at least that was the case in my time—they wad hae been disturbed in the day-time baith by the law and the commons of Fairport—they may be owerlooked now, as I have heard—the warld's changed—I whiles hardly ken whether I am standing or sitting, or dead or living.'

And looking round the fire, as if in the state of unconscious uncertainty of which she complained, old Elspeth relapsed into her habitual and mechanical occupation of twirling the spindle.

'Eh, sirs!' said Jenny Rintherout, under her breath to her gossip, 'it's awsome to hear your gudemither break out in that gait—it's like the dead speaking to the living.'

'Ye're no that far wrang, lass; she minds nae-thing o' what passes the day—but set her on auld tales, and she can speak like a prent buke. She kens mair about the Glenallan family than maist folk—the gudeman's father was their fisher mony a day. Ye maun ken the papists make a great point o' eating fish*—it's nae bad part o' their religion that, whatever the rest is—I could aye sell the best o' fish at the best o' prices for the Countess's ain table, grace be wi' her! especially on a Friday—But see as our gudemither's hands and lips are ganging—now it's working in her head like barm—she'll speak eneugh the night—whiles she'll no speak a word in a week, unless it be to the bits o' bairns.'

'Hegh, Mrs Mucklebackit, she's an awsome wife!' said Jenny in reply. 'D'ye think she's a'thegither right?—Folk says she downa gang to the kirk, or speak to the minister, and that she was ance a papist; but since her gudeman's been dead naebody kens what she is—D'ye think yoursell, that she's no uncanny?'

'Canny, ye silly tawpie! think ye ae auld wife's less canny than anither? unless it be Ailison Breck—I really couldna in conscience swear for her—I have kent the boxes she set fill'd wi' partans, when'—

'Whisht, whisht, Maggie,' whispered Jenny, 'your gudemither's gaun to speak again.'

'Wasna there some ane o' ye said,' asked the old sibyl, 'or did I dream, or was it revealed to me, that Joscelind, Lady Glenallan, is dead, an buried this night?'

'Yes, gudemither,' screamed the daughter-in-law, 'it's e'en sae.'

'And e'en sae let it be,' said old Elspeth; 'she's made mony a sair heart in her day—ay, e'en her ain son's—is he living yet?'

'Ay, he's living yet—but how lang he'll live—however, dinna ye mind his coming and asking after you in the spring, and leaving siller?'

'It may be sae, Maggie—I dinna mind it—but a handsome gentleman he was, and his father before him. Eh! if his father had lived, they might hae been happy folk!—But he was gane, and the lady carried it in-ower and out-ower wi' her son, and garr'd him trow the thing he never suld hae trowed, and do the thing he has repented a' his life, and will repent still, were his life as lang as this lang and wearisome ane o' mine.'

'O what was it, grannie?'—and 'What was it, gudemither?'—and 'What was it, Luckie Elspeth?' asked the children, the mother, and the visitor, in one breath.

'Never ask what it was,' answered the old sibyl, 'but pray to God that ye arena left to the pride and wilfu'ness o' your ain hearts. They may be as powerful in a cabin as in a castle—I can bear a sad witness to that.—O that weary and fearfu' night! will it never gang out o' my auld head?—Eh! to see her lying on the floor wi' her lang hair dreeping wi' the salt water!—Heaven will avenge on a' that had to do wi't.—Sirs! is my son out wi' the coble this windy e'en?'

'Na, na, mither—nae coble can keep the sea this wind—he's sleeping in his bed outower yonder ahint the hallan.'

'Is Steenie out at sea then?'

'Na, grannie—Steenie's awa out wi' auld Edie Ochiltree, the gaberlunzie—maybe they'll be gaun to see the burial.'

'That canna be,' said the mother of the family,—'We kent naething o't till Jock Rand cam in, and tauld us the Aikwoods had warning to attend; they keep thae things unco private, and they were to bring the corpse a' the way frae the castle, ten miles off, under cloud o' night. She has lain in state this ten days at Glenallan-house, in a grand chamber, a' hung wi' black, and lighted wi' wax cannle.'

'God assoilzie her!' ejaculated old Elspeth, her head apparently still occupied by the event of the Countess's death—'she was a hard-hearted woman, but she's gaen to account for it a', and His mercy is infinite—God grant she may find it sae!'—And she relapsed into silence, which she did not break again during the rest of the evening.

'I wonder what that auld daft beggar-carle and our son Steenie can be doing out in sic a night as this,' said Maggie Mucklebackit; and her expression of surprise was echoed by her visitor; 'Gang awa, ane o' ye, hinnies, up to the heugh head, and gie them a cry in case they're within hearing—the car-cakes will be burnt to a cinder.'

The little emissary departed, but in a few minutes came running back with the loud exclamation, 'Eh, minnie! eh, grannie! there's a white bogle chasing twa black anes down the heugh.'

A noise of footsteps followed this singular annunciation, and young Steenie Mucklebackit, closely followed by Edie Ochiltree, bounced into the hut. They were panting and out of breath. The first thing Steenie did was to look for the bar of the door, which his mother reminded him had been broken up for fire-wood in the hard winter three years ago; for what use, she said, had the like o' them for bars?

'There's naebody chasing us,' said the beggar, after he had taken his breath; 'we're e'en like the wicked, that flee when no one pursueth.'

'Troth, but we were chased,' said Steenie, 'by a spirit, or something little better.'

'It was a man in white on horseback,' said Edie, 'for the saft grund, that wadna bear the beast, flung him about, I wot that weel; but I didna think my auld legs could have brought me aff as fast; I ran amaist as fast as if I had been at Prestonpans.'*

'Hout, ye daft gowks,' said Luckie Mucklebackit, 'it will hae been some o' the riders at the Countess's burial.'

'What!' said Edie, 'is the auld Countess buried the night at St Ruth's?—Ou, that wad be the lights and the noise that scarr'd us awa: I wish I had kend—I wad hae stude them, and no left the man yonder—but they'll take care o' him. Ye strake ower hard, Steenie— I doubt ye foundered the chield.'

'Ne'er a bit,' said Steenie, laughing; 'he has braw broad shouthers, and I just took the measure o' them wi' the stang—Odd, if I hadna been something short wi' him, he wad hae knockit your auld harns out, lad.'

'Weel, an I win clear o' this scrape,' said Edie, 'I'se tempt Providence nae mair. But I canna think it an unlawfu' thing to pit a bit trick on sic a land-louping scoundrel, that just lives by tricking honester folk.'

'But what are we to do with this?' said Steenie, producing a pocket-book.

'Odd guide us, man,' said Edie, in great alarm, 'what gar'd ye touch the gear? a very leaf o' that pocket-book wad be eneugh to hang us baith.'

'I dinna ken,' said Steenie; 'the book had fa'en out o' his pocket, I fancy, for I fand it amang my feet when I was graping about to set him on his legs again, and I just pat it in my pouch to keep it safe; and then came the tramp of horse, and you cried "Rin, rin," and I had nae mair thought o' the book.'

'We maun get it back to the loon some gait or other; ye had better take it yoursell, I think, wi' peep o' light, up to Ringan Aikwood's. I wadna for a hundred pounds it was fund in our hands.'

Steenie undertook to do as he was directed.

'A bonny night ye hae made o't, Mr Steenie,' said Jenny Rinther-out, who, impatient of remaining so long unnoticed, now presented herself to the young fisherman—'A bonny night ye hae made o't, tramping about wi' gaberlunzies, and getting yoursell hunted wi' worricows, when ye suld be sleeping in your bed like your father, honest man.'

This attack called forth a suitable response of rustic raillery from the young fisherman. An attack was now commenced upon the car-cakes and smoked fish, and sustained with great perseverance by assistance of a bicker or two of twopenny ale and a bottle of gin. The mendicant then retired to the straw of an out-house adjoining,— the children had one by one crept into their nests,—the old grandmother was deposited in her flock-bed,—Steenie, notwithstanding his preceding fatigue, had the gallantry to accompany Miss Rintherout to her own mansion, and at what hour he returned the story saith not,—and the matron of the family, having laid the gathering-coal upon the fire, and put things in some sort of order, retired to rest the last of the family.

CHAPTER XXVII

——————Many great ones
Would part with half their states, to have the plan
And credit to beg in the first style—

Beggar's Bush.*

OLD EDIE was stirring with the lark, and his first enquiry was after
Steenie and the pocket-book. The young fisherman had been under
the necessity of attending his father before daybreak to avail themselves of the tide, but he had promised, that, immediately on his
return, the pocket-book, with all its contents, carefully wrapped up
in a piece of sail-cloth, should be delivered by him to Ringan
Aikwood, for Dousterswivel, the owner.

The matron had prepared the morning meal for the family, and,
shouldering her basket of fish, tramped sturdily away towards Fairport. The children were idling round the door, for the day was fair
and sun-shiney. The ancient grandame, again seated on her wicker-
chair by the fire, had resumed her eternal spindle, wholly unmoved
by the yelling and screaming of the children, and the scolding of the
mother, which had preceded the dispersion of the family. Edie had
arranged his various bags, and was bound for the renewal of his
wandering life, but first advanced with due courtesy to take his leave
of the ancient crone.

'Gude day to ye, cummer, and mony ane o' them. I will be back
about the fore-end o' har'st, and I trust to find ye baith haill and
fere.'

'Pray that ye may find me in my quiet grave,' said the old woman,
in a hollow and sepulchral voice, but without the agitation of a single
feature.

'Ye're auld, cummer, and sae am I mysell; but we maun abide HIS
will—we'll no be forgotten in His good time.'

'Nor our deeds neither,' said the crone; 'what's dune in the body
maun be answered in the spirit.'

'I wot that's true; and I may weel tak the tale hame to mysell, that
hae led a misruled and roving life. But ye were aye a canny wife.
We're a' frail—but ye canna hae sae muckle to bow ye down.'

'Less than I might have had—but mair, O far mair, than wad sink the stoutest brig e'er sailed out o' Fairport harbour!—Didna somebody say yestreen—at least sae it is borne in on my mind—but auld folk hae weak fancies—did not somebody say that Joscelind, Countess of Glenallan, was departed frae life?'

'They said the truth whaever said it,' answered old Edie; 'she was buried yestreen by torch-light at St Ruth's, and I, like a fule, gat a gliff wi' seeing the lights and the riders.'

'It was their fashion since the days of the Great Earl that was killed at Harlaw—They did it to show scorn that they should die and be buried like other mortals—The wives o' the house of Glenallan wailed nae wail for the husband, nor the sister for the brother.—But is she e'en ca'd to the lang account?'

'As sure,' answered Edie, 'as we maun a' abide it.'

'Then I'll unlade my mind, come o't what will.'

This she spoke with more alacrity than usually attended her expressions, and accompanied her words with an attitude of the hand, as if throwing something from her. She then raised up her form, once tall, and still retaining the appearance of having been so, though bent with age and rheumatism, and stood before the beggar like a mummy animated by some wandering spirit into a temporary resurrection. Her light-blue eyes wandered to and fro, as if she occasionally forgot and again remembered the purpose for which her long and withered hand was searching among the miscellaneous contents of an ample old-fashioned pocket. At length, she pulled out a small chip-box, and opening it, took out a handsome ring, in which was set a braid of hair, composed of two different colours, black and light brown, twined together, encircled with brilliants of considerable value.

'Gudeman,' she said to Ochiltree, 'as ye wad e'er deserve mercy, ye maun gang my errand to the house of Glenallan, and ask for the Earl.'

'The Earl of Glenallan, cummer! ou, he winna see ony o' the gentles o' the country, and what likelihood is there that he wad see the like o' an auld gaberlunzie?'

'Gang your ways and try—and tell him that Elspeth o' the Craigburnfoot—he'll mind me best by that name—maun see him or she be relieved frae her lang pilgrimage, and that she sends him that ring in token of the business she wad speak o'.'

Ochiltree looked on the ring with some admiration of its apparent value, and then carefully replacing it in the box, and wrapping it in an old ragged handkerchief, he deposited the token in his bosom.

'Weel, gudewife,' he said, 'I'se do your bidding, or it's no be my fault.—But surely there was never sic a braw propine as this sent to a yerl by an auld fish-wife, and through the hands of a gaberlunzie beggar.'

With this reflection, Edie took up his pike-staff, put on his broad-brimmed bonnet, and set forth upon his pilgrimage. The old woman remained for some time standing in a fixed posture, her eyes directed to the door through which her ambassador had departed. The appearance of excitation, which the conversation had occasioned, gradually left her features—she sunk down upon her accustomed seat, and resumed her mechanical labour of the distaff and spindle, with her wonted air of apathy.

Edie Ochiltree meanwhile advanced on his journey. The distance to Glenallan was ten miles, a march which the old soldier accomplished in about four hours. With the curiosity belonging to his idle trade and animated character, he tortured himself the whole way to consider what could be the meaning of this mysterious errand with which he was intrusted, or what connexion the proud, wealthy, and powerful Earl of Glenallan could have with the crimes or penitence of an old doting woman, whose rank in life did not greatly exceed that of her messenger. He endeavoured to call to memory all that he had ever known or heard of the Glenallan family, yet, having done so, remained altogether unable to form a conjecture on the subject. He knew that the whole extensive estate of this ancient and powerful family had descended to the Countess lately deceased, who inherited, in a most remarkable degree, the stern, fierce, and unbending character which had distinguished the house of Glenallan since they first figured in Scottish annals. Like the rest of her ancestors, she adhered zealously to the Roman Catholic faith, and was married to an English gentleman of the same communion, and of large fortune, who did not survive their union two years. The Countess was, therefore, left an early widow, with the uncontrolled management of the large estates of her two sons. The elder, Lord Geraldin, who was to succeed to the title and fortune of Glenallan, was totally dependent on his mother during her life. The second, when he came of age, assumed the name and arms of his father, and took possession of his estate, according to the provisions of the Countess's marriage-settlement. After this period, he chiefly resided in England, and paid very few and brief visits to his mother and brother; and these at length were altogether dispensed with, in consequence of his becoming a convert to the reformed religion.

But even before this mortal offence was given to its mistress, his residence at Glenallan offered few inducements to a gay young man like Edward Geraldin Neville, though its gloom and seclusion seemed to suit the retired and melancholy habits of his elder brother. Lord Geraldin, in the outset of life, had been a young man of accomplishment and hopes. Those who knew him upon his travels entertained the highest expectations of his future career. But such fair dawns are often strangely overcast. The young nobleman returned to Scotland, and after living about a year in his mother's society at Glenallan-house, he seemed to have adopted all the stern gloom and melancholy of her character. Excluded from politics by the incapacities attached to those of his religion,* and from all lighter avocations by choice, Lord Geraldin led a life of the strictest retirement. His ordinary society was composed of the clergymen of his communion, who occasionally visited his mansion; and very rarely, upon stated occasions of high festival, one or two families who still professed the Catholic religion were formally entertained at Glenallan-house. But this was all—their heretic neighbours knew nothing of the family whatever; and even the Catholics saw little more than the sumptuous entertainment and solemn parade which was exhibited on those formal occasions, from which all returned without knowing whether most to wonder at the stern and stately demeanour of the Countess, or the deep and gloomy dejection which never ceased for a moment to cloud the features of her son. The late event had put him in possession of his fortune and title, and the neighbourhood had already begun to conjecture whether gaiety would revive with independence, when those who had some occasional acquaintance with the interior of the family spread abroad a report, that the earl's constitution was undermined by religious austerities, and that, in all probability, he would soon follow his mother to the grave. This event was the more probable, as his brother had died of a lingering complaint, which, in the latter years of his life, had affected at once his frame and his spirits: so that heralds and genealogists were already looking back into their records to discover the heir of this ill-fated family, and lawyers were talking, with glee-some anticipation, of the probability of a 'great Glenallan cause.'

As Edie Ochiltree approached the front of Glenallan-house, an ancient building of great extent, the most modern part of which had been designed by the celebrated Inigo Jones,* he began to consider in what way he should be most likely to gain access for delivery of his message; and, after much consideration, resolved to send the token to the Earl by one of the domestics. With this purpose he stopped at a cottage, where he obtained the means of making up the ring in a sealed packet like a petition, addressed, *Forr his hounor the Yerl of Glenllan—These*. But being aware that missives delivered at the doors of great houses by such persons as himself, do not always make their way according to address, Edie determined, like an old soldier, to reconnoitre the ground before he made his final attack. As he approached the porter's-lodge, he discovered, by the number of poor ranked before it, some of them being indigent persons in the vicinity, and others itinerants of his own begging profession,—that there was about to be a general dole or distribution of charity.

'A good turn,' said Edie to himself, 'never goes unrewarded—I'll maybe get a good awmous that I wad hae missed, but for trotting on this auld wife's errand.'

Accordingly, he ranked up with the rest of this ragged regiment, assuming a station as near the front as possible,—a distinction due, as he conceived, to his blue gown and badge, no less than to his years and experience; but he soon found there was another principle of precedence in this assembly to which he had not adverted.

'Are ye a triple man, friend, that ye press forward sae bauldly?—I'm thinking no, for there's nae Catholics wear that badge.'

'Na, na, I am no a Roman,' said Edie.

'Then shank yoursell awa to the double folk, or single folk, that's the Episcopals or Presbyterians yonder—it's a shame to see a heretic hae sic a lang white beard, that would do credit to a hermit.'

Ochiltree, thus rejected from the society of the Catholic mendi-cants, or those who called themselves such, went to station himself with the paupers of the communion of the church of England, to whom the noble donor allotted a double portion of his charity. But never was a poor occasional conformist* more roughly rejected by a High-church congregation, even when that matter was furiously agitated in the days of good Queen Anne.

'See to him wi' his badge!' they said; 'he hears ane o' the king's Presbyterian chaplains sough out a sermon on the morning of every birth-day, and now he would pass himsell for ane o' the Episcopal church! Na, na! We'll take care o' that.'

Edie, thus rejected by Rome and prelacy, was fain to shelter himself from the laughter of his brethren among the thin group of Presbyterians, who had either disdained to disguise their religious opinions for the sake of an augmented dole, or perhaps knew they could not attempt the imposition without a certainty of detection.

The same degree of precedence was observed in the mode of distributing the charity, which consisted in bread, beef, and a piece of money, to each individual of all the three classes. The almoner, an ecclesiastic of grave appearance and demeanour, superintended in person the accommodation of the Catholic mendicants, asking a question or two of each as he delivered the charity, and recommending to their prayers the soul of Joscelind, late Countess of Glenallan, mother of their benefactor. The porter, distinguished by his long staff headed with silver, and by the black gown tufted with lace of the same colour, which he had assumed upon the general mourning in the family, overlooked the distribution of the dole among the prelatists. The less-favoured kirk-folk were committed to the charge of an aged domestic.

As this last discussed some disputed point with the porter, his name, as it chanced to be occasionally mentioned, and then his features, struck Ochiltree, and awakened recollections of former times. The rest of the assembly were now retiring, when the domestic, again approaching the place where Edie still lingered, said, in a strong Aberdeenshire accent, 'Fat is the auld feel-body deeing that he canna gang avay, now that he's gotten baith meat and siller?'

'Francie Macraw,' answered Edie Ochiltree, 'd'ye no mind Fontenoy,* and "Keep thegither, front and rear!"'

'Ohon, ohon!' cried Francie, with a true north-country yell of recognition, 'naebody could hae said that word but my auld front-rank man, Edie Ochiltree! But I'm sorry to see ye in sic a peer state, man.'

'No sae ill aff as ye may think, Francie. But I'm laith to leave this place without a crack wi' you, and I kenna when I may see you again, for your folk dinna mak Protestants welcome, and that's ae reason that I hae never been here before.'

'Fusht, fusht,' said Francie, 'let that flee stick i' the wa'—when the dirt's dry it will rub out—and come you awa wi' me, and I'll gie ye something better than that beef bane, man.'

Having then spoke a confidential word with the porter, (probably to request his connivance,) and having waited until the almoner had returned into the house with slow and solemn steps, Francie Macraw introduced his old comrade into the court of Glenallan-house, the gloomy gateway of which was surmounted by a huge scutcheon, in which the herald and undertaker had mingled, as usual, the emblems of human pride and of human nothingness; the Countess's hereditary coat-of-arms, with all its numerous quarterings, disposed in a lozenge, and surrounded by the separate shields of her paternal and maternal ancestry, intermingled with scythes, hour-glasses, skulls, and other symbols of that mortality which levels all distinctions. Conducting his friend as speedily as possible along the large paved court, Macraw led the way through a side-door to a small apartment near the servants'-hall, which, in virtue of his personal attendance upon the Earl of Glenallan, he was entitled to call his own. To produce cold meat of various kinds, strong beer, and even a glass of spirits, was no difficulty to a person of Francie's importance, who had not lost, in his sense of conscious dignity, the keen northern prudence which recommended a good understanding with the butler. Our mendicant envoy drank ale, and talked over old stories with his comrade, until, no other topic of conversation occurring, he resolved to take up the theme of his embassy, which had for some time escaped his memory.

'He had a petition to present to the Earl,' he said;—for he judged it prudent to say nothing of the ring, not knowing, as he afterwards observed, how far the manners of a single soldier[18] might have been corrupted by service in a great house.

'Hout, tout, man,' said Francie, 'the Earl will look at nae petitions—but I can gie't to the almoner.'

'But it relates to some secret, that maybe my lord wad like best to see't himsell.'

'I'm jeedging that's the very reason that the almoner will be for seeing it the first and foremost.'

'But I hae come a' this way on purpose to deliver it, Francie, and ye really maun help me at a pinch.'

'Ne'er speed then if I dinna,' answered the Aberdeenshire man; 'let them be as cankered as they like, they can but turn me awa, and I was just thinking to ask my discharge, and gang down to end my days at Inverurie.'

With this doughty resolution of serving his friend at all ventures, since none was to be encountered which could much inconvenience himself, Francie Macraw left the apartment. It was long before he returned, and when he did, his manner indicated wonder and agitation.

'I am nae seere gin ye be Edie Ochiltree o' Carrick's company* in the Forty-twa, or gin ye be the deil in his likeness!'

'And what makes ye speak in that gait?' demanded the astonished mendicant.

'Because my lord has been in sic a distress, and seerpreese, as I ne'er saw a man in my life. But he'll see you—I got that job cookit. He was like a man awa frae himsell for mony minutes, and I thought he wad hae swarv't a'thegither,—and fan he cam' to himsell, he asked fae brought the packet—and fat trow ye I said?'

'An auld soger,' says Edie; 'that does likeliest at a gentle's door—at a farmer's it's best to say ye're an auld tinkler, if ye need ony quarters, for maybe the gudewife will hae something to souther.'

'But I said ne'er ane o' the twa,' answered Francie; 'my lord cares as little about the tane as the tother—for he's best to them that can souther up our sins. Sae I e'en said the bit paper was brought by an auld man wi' a lang fite beard—he might be a capeechin freer for fat I kend, for he was dressed like an auld palmer.* Sae ye'll be sent for up fanever he can find mettle to face ye.'

I wish I was weel through this business, thought Edie to himself; mony folk surmise that the earl's no very right in the judgment, and wha can say how far he may be offended wi' me for taking upon me sae muckle?

But there was now no room for retreat—a bell sounded from a distant part of the mansion, and Macraw said, with a smothered accent, as if already in his master's presence, 'That's my lord's bell! —follow me, and step lightly and cannily, Edie.'

Edie followed his guide, who seemed to tread as if afraid of being overheard, through a long passage, and up a back stair, which admitted them into the family apartments. They were ample and extensive, furnished at such cost as showed the ancient importance and splendour of the family. But all the ornaments were in the taste of a former and distant period, and one would have almost supposed himself traversing the halls of a Scottish nobleman before the union of the crowns.* The late Countess, partly from a haughty contempt of the times in which she lived, partly from her sense of family pride, had not permitted the furniture to be altered or modernized during her residence at Glenallan-house. The most magnificent part of the decorations was a valuable collection of pictures by the best masters, whose massive frames were somewhat tarnished by time. In this particular also the gloomy taste of the family seemed to predominate. There were some fine family portraits by Vandyke* and other masters of eminence; but the collection was richest in the Saints and Martyrdoms of Domenichino,* Velasquez,* and Murillo,* and other subjects of the same kind, which had been selected in preference to landscapes or historical pieces. The manner in which these awful, and sometimes disgusting, subjects were represented, harmonized with the gloomy state of the apartments; a circumstance which was not altogether lost on the old man, as he traversed them under the guidance of his quondam fellow-soldier. He was about to express some sentiment of this kind, but Francie imposed silence on him by signs, and, opening a door at the end of the long picture-gallery, ushered him into a small antechamber hung with black. Here they found the almoner, with his ear turned to a door opposite that by which they entered, in the attitude of one who listens with attention, but is at the same time afraid of being detected in the act.

The old domestic and churchman started when they perceived each other. But the almoner first recovered his recollection, and, advancing towards Macraw, said under his breath, but with an authoritative tone, 'How dare you approach the Earl's apartment without knocking? and who is this stranger, or what has he to do here?—Retire to the gallery, and wait for me there.'

'It's impossible just now to attend your reverence,' answered Macraw, raising his voice so as to be heard in the next room, being conscious that the priest would not maintain the altercation within hearing of his patron,—'the Earl's bell has rung.'

He had scarce uttered the words, when it was rung again with greater violence than before; and the ecclesiastic, perceiving further expostulation impossible, lifted his finger at Macraw with a menacing attitude, as he left the apartment.

'I tell'd ye sae,' said the Aberdeen man in a whisper to Edie, and then proceeded to open the door near which they had observed the chaplain stationed.

CHAPTER XXVIII

——————————This ring,—
This little ring, with necromantic force,
Has raised the ghost of Pleasure to my fears,
Conjured the sense of honour and of love
Into such shapes, they fright me from myself.
                                        *The Fatal Marriage.**

THE ancient forms of mourning were observed in Glenallan-house, notwithstanding the obduracy with which the members of the family were popularly supposed to refuse to the dead the usual tribute of lamentation. It was remarked, that when she received the fatal letter announcing the death of her second, and, as was once believed, her favourite son, the hand of the Countess did not shake, nor her eyelid twinkle, any more than upon perusal of a letter of ordinary business. Heaven only knows whether the suppression of maternal sorrow, which her pride commanded, might not have some effect in hastening her own death. It was at least generally supposed, that the apoplectic stroke, which so soon afterwards terminated her existence, was, as it were, the vengeance of outraged Nature for the restraint to which her feelings had been subjected. But although Lady Glenallan forbore the usual external signs of grief, she had caused many of the apartments, amongst others her own and that of the Earl, to be hung with the exterior trappings of woe.

The Earl of Glenallan was therefore seated in an apartment hung with black cloth, which waved in dusky folds along its lofty walls. A screen, also covered with black baize, placed towards the high and narrow window, intercepted much of the broken light which found its way through the stained glass, that represented, with such skill as the fourteenth century possessed, the life and sorrows of the prophet Jeremiah. The table at which the Earl was seated was lighted with two lamps wrought in silver, shedding that unpleasant and doubtful light which arises from the mingling of artificial lustre with that of general daylight. The same table displayed a silver crucifix, and one or two clasped parchment books. A large picture, exquisitely painted by Spagnoletto,* represented the martyrdom of St Stephen,* and was the only ornament of the apartment.

The inhabitant and lord of this disconsolate chamber was a man not past the prime of life, yet so broken down with disease and mental misery, so gaunt and ghastly, that he appeared but a wreck of manhood; and when he hastily arose and advanced towards his visitor, the exertion seemed almost to overpower his emaciated frame. As they met in the midst of the apartment, the contrast they exhibited was very striking. The hale cheek, firm step, erect stature, and undaunted presence and bearing of the old mendicant, indicated patience and content in the extremity of age, and in the lowest condition to which humanity can sink; while the sunken eye, pallid cheek, and tottering form of the nobleman with whom he was confronted, showed how little wealth, power, and even the advantages of youth, have to do with that which gives repose to the mind, and firmness to the frame.

The Earl met the old man in the middle of the room, and having commanded his attendant to withdraw into the gallery, and suffer no one to enter the antechamber till he rung the bell, awaited, with hurried yet fearful impatience, until he heard first the door of his apartment, and then that of the antechamber, shut and fastened by the spring-bolt. When he was satisfied with this security against being overheard, Lord Glenallan came close up to the mendicant, whom he probably mistook for some person of a religious order in disguise, and said, in a hasty yet faltering tone, 'In the name of all our religion holds most holy, tell me, reverend father, what I am to expect from a communication, opened by a token connected with such horrible recollections?'

The old man, appalled by a manner so different from what he had expected from the proud and powerful nobleman, was at a loss how to answer, and in what manner to undeceive him—'Tell me,' continued the Earl, in a tone of increasing trepidation and agony—'tell me, do you come to say, that all that has been done to expiate guilt so horrible, has been too little and too trivial for the offence, and to point out new and more efficacious modes of severe penance?—I will not blench from it, father—let me suffer the pains of my crime here in the body, rather than hereafter in the spirit!'

Edie had now recollection enough to perceive, that if he did not interrupt the frankness of Lord Glenallan's admissions, he was likely to become the confident of more than might be safe for him to know. He therefore uttered with a hasty and trembling voice—'Your lordship's honour is mistaken—I am not of your persuasion, nor a clergyman, but, with all reverence, only puir Edie Ochiltree, the king's bedesman and your honour's.'

This explanation he accompanied by a profound bow after his manner, and then drawing himself up erect, rested his arm on his staff, threw back his long white hair, and fixed his eyes upon the Earl, as he waited for an answer.

'And you are not, then,' said Lord Glenallan, after a pause of surprise, 'you are not then a Catholic priest?'

'God forbid!' said Edie, forgetting in his confusion to whom he was speaking; 'I am only the king's bedesman and your honour's, as I said before.'

The Earl turned hastily away, and paced the room twice or thrice, as if to recover the effects of his mistake, and then, coming close up to the mendicant, he demanded, in a stern and commanding tone, what he meant by intruding himself on his privacy, and from whence he had got the ring which he had thought proper to send him. Edie, a man of much spirit, was less daunted at this mode of interrogation than he had been confused by the tone of confidence in which the Earl had opened their conversation. To the reiterated question from whom he had obtained the ring, he answered composedly, 'From one who was better known to the Earl than to him.'

'Better known to me, fellow?' said Lord Glenallan; 'what is your meaning? Explain yourself instantly, or you shall experience the consequence of breaking in upon the hours of family distress.'

'It was auld Elspeth Mucklebackit that sent me here,' said the beggar, 'in order to say'—

'You dote, old man!' said the Earl; 'I never heard the name—but this dreadful token reminds me'—

'I mind now, my lord,' said Ochiltree; 'she tauld me your lordship would be mair familiar wi' her, if I ca'd her Elspeth o' the Craigburnfoot—She had that name when she lived on your honour's land, that is, your honour's worshipful mother's that was then—Grace be wi' her!'

'Ay,' said the appalled nobleman, as his countenance sunk, and his cheek assumed a hue yet more cadaverous; 'that name is indeed written in the most tragic page of a deplorable history—But what can she desire of me? Is she dead or living?'

'Living, my lord; and entreats to see your lordship before she dies, for she has something to communicate that hangs upon her very soul, and she says she canna flit in peace until she sees you.'

'Not until she sees me!—what can that mean?—but she is doting with age and infirmity—I tell thee, friend, I called at her cottage myself, not a twelvemonth since, from a report that she was in distress, and she did not even know my face or voice.'

'If your honour wad permit me,' said Edie, to whom the length of the conference restored a part of his professional audacity and native talkativeness—'if your honour wad but permit me, I wad say, under correction of your lordship's better judgment, that auld Elspeth's like some of the ancient ruined strengths and castles that ane sees amang the hills. There are mony parts of her mind that appear, as I may say, laid waste and decayed, but then there's parts that look the steever, and the stronger, and the grander, because they are rising just like to fragments amang the ruins o' the rest—She's an awful woman.'

'She always was so,' said the Earl, almost unconsciously echoing the observation of the mendicant; 'she always was different from other women—likest perhaps to her who is now no more, in her temper and turn of mind.—She wishes to see me, then?'

'Before she dies,' said Edie, 'she earnestly entreats that pleasure.'

'It will be a pleasure to neither of us,' said the Earl sternly, 'yet she shall be gratified.—She lives, I think, on the sea shore to the southward of Fairport?'

'Just between Monkbarns and Knockwinnock Castle, but nearer to Monkbarns. Your lordship's honour will ken the laird and Sir Arthur, doubtless?'

A stare, as if he did not comprehend the question, was Lord Glenallan's answer. Edie saw his mind was elsewhere, and did not venture to repeat a query which was so little germain to the matter.

'Are you a Catholic, old man?' demanded the Earl.

'No, my lord,' said Ochiltree stoutly; for the remembrance of the unequal division of the dole rose in his mind at the moment; 'I thank Heaven I am a good Protestant.'

'He who can conscientiously call himself *good*, has indeed reason to thank Heaven, be his form of Christianity what it will.—But who is he that shall dare to do so!'

'Not I,' said Edie; 'I trust to beware of the sin of presumption.'

'What was your trade in your youth?' continued the Earl.

'A soldier, my lord; and mony a sair day's kemping I've seen. I was to have been made a sergeant, but'—

'A soldier! then you have slain and burnt, and sacked and spoiled?'

'I winna say,' replied Edie, 'that I have been better than my neighbours—it's a rough trade—war's sweet to them that never tried it.'

'And you are now old and miserable, asking from precarious charity, the food which in your youth you tore from the hand of the poor peasant?'

'I am a beggar, it is true, my lord; but I am nae just sae miserable neither—for my sins, I hae had grace to repent of them, if I might say sae, and to lay them where they may be better borne than by me—and for my food, naebody grudges an auld man a bit and a drink—Sae I live as I can, and am contented to die when I am ca'd upon.'

'And thus, then, with little to look back upon that is pleasant or praiseworthy in your past life, with less to look forward to on this side of eternity, you are contented to drag out the rest of your existence—Go, begone; and, in your age and poverty and weariness, never envy the lord of such a mansion as this, either in his sleeping or waking moments—Here is something for thee.'

The Earl put into the old man's hand five or six guineas. Edie would, perhaps, have stated his scruples, as upon other occasions, to the amount of the benefaction, but the tone of Lord Glenallan was too absolute to admit of either answer or dispute. The Earl then called his servant—'See this old man safe from the castle—let no one ask him any questions—and you, friend, begone, and forget the road that leads to my house.'

'That would be difficult for me,' said Edie, looking at the gold which he still held in his hand, 'that would be e'en difficult, since your honour has gien me such gude cause to remember it.'

Lord Glenallan stared, as hardly comprehending the old man's boldness in daring to bandy words with him, and, with his hand, made him another signal of departure, which the mendicant instantly obeyed.

CHAPTER XXIX

For he was one in all their idle sport,
And, like a monarch, ruled their little court;
The pliant bow he form'd, the flying ball,
The bat, the wicket, were his labours all.

Crabbe's Village.*

FRANCIS MACRAW, agreeably to the commands of his master, attended the mendicant, in order to see him fairly out of the estate, without permitting him to have conversation, or intercourse, with any of the Earl's dependants or domestics. But, judiciously considering that the restriction did not extend to himself, who was the person intrusted with the convoy, he used every measure in his power to extort from Edie the nature of his confidential and secret interview with Lord Glenallan. But Edie had been in his time accustomed to cross-examination, and easily evaded those of his quondam comrade. 'The secrets of grit folk,' said Ochiltree within himself, 'are just like the wild beasts that are shut up in cages. Keep them hard and fast snecked up, and it's a' very weel or better—but anes let them out, they will turn and rend you. I mind how ill Dugald Gunn cam aff for letting loose his tongue about the Major's leddy and Captain Bandilier.'

Francie was, therefore, foiled in his assaults upon the fidelity of the mendicant, and, like an indifferent chess-player, became, at every unsuccessful movement, more liable to the counter-checks of his opponent.

'Sae ye uphauld ye had nae particulars to say to my lord but about your ain matters?'

'Ay, and about the wee bits o' things I had brought frae abroad,' said Edie. 'I kend you papist folk are unco set on the relics that are fetched frae far—kirks and sae forth.'

'Troth, my lord maun be turned feel outright,' said the domestic, 'an he puts himsell into sic a curfuffle for ony thing ye could bring him, Edie.'

'I doubtna ye may say true in the main, neighbour,' replied the beggar; 'but maybe he's had some hard play in his younger days, Francie, and that whiles unsettles folk sair.'

'Troth, Edie, and ye may say that—and since it's like ye'll ne'er come back to the estate, or, if ye dee, that ye'll no find me there, I'se e'en tell you he had a heart in his young time sae wrecked and rent, that it's a wonder it hasna broken outright lang afore this day.'

'Ay, say ye sae?' said Ochiltree; 'that maun hae been about a woman, I reckon?'

'Troth, and ye hae guessed it,' said Francie—'jeest a cusin o' his nain—Miss Eveline Neville, as they suld hae ca'd her—there was a sough in the country about it, but it was hushed up, as the grandees were concerned—it's mair than twenty years syne—ay, it will be three-and-twenty.'

'Ay, I was in America then,'* said the mendicant, 'and no in the way to hear the country clashes.'

'There was little clash about it, man,' replied Macraw; 'he liked this young leddy, and suld hae married her, but his mother fand it out, and then the deil gaed o'er Jock Wabster.* At last, the peer lass clodded hersell o'er the scaur at the Craigburnfoot into the sea, and there was an end o't.'

'An end o't wi' the puir leddy,' said the mendicant, 'but, as I rackon, nae end o't wi' the yerl.'

'Nae end o't till his life makes an end,' answered the Aberdonian.

'But what for did the auld Countess forbid the marriage?' continued the persevering querist.

'Fat for!—she maybe didna weel ken for fat hersell, for she gar'd a' bow to her bidding, right or wrang—But it was kend the young leddy was inclined to some o' the heresies of the country*—mair by token, she was sib to him nearer than our Church's rule admits of*—Sae the leddy was driven to the desperate act, and the yerl has never since held his head up like a man.'

'Weel away!' replied Ochiltree; 'it's e'en queer I ne'er heard this tale afore.'

'It's e'en queer that ye hear it now, for deil ane o' the servants durst hae spoken o't had the auld Countess been living—Eh! man, Edie, but she was a trimmer—it wad hae taen a skeely man to hae squared wi' her!—But she's in her grave, and we may loose our tongues a bit fan we meet a friend.—But fare ye weel, Edie, I maun be back to the evening service.—An ye come to Inverurie maybe sax months awa, dinna forget to ask after Francie Macraw.'

What one kindly pressed, the other as firmly promised; and the friends having thus parted, with every testimony of mutual regard, the domestic of Lord Glenallan took his road back to the seat of his master, leaving Ochiltree to trace onward his habitual pilgrimage.

It was a fine summer evening, and the world, that is, the little circle which was all in all to the individual by whom it was trodden, lay before Edie Ochiltree, for the choosing of his night's quarters. When he had passed the less hospitable domains of Glenallan, he had in his option so many places of refuge for the evening, that he was nice and even fastidious in the choice. Ailie Sim's public was on the road-side about a mile before him; but there would be a parcel of young fellows there on the Saturday night, and that was a bar to civil conversation. Other 'gudemen and gudewives,' as the farmers and their dames are termed in Scotland, successively presented themselves to his imagination. But one was deaf, and could not hear him; another toothless, and could not make him hear; a third had a cross temper; and a fourth an ill-natured house-dog. At Monkbarns or Knockwinnock he was sure of a favourable and hospitable reception; but they lay too distant to be conveniently reached that night.

'I dinna ken how it is,' said the old man, 'but I am nicer about my quarters this night than ever I mind having been in my life. I think having seen a' the braws yonder, and finding out ane may be happier without them, has made me proud o' my ain lot—but I wuss it bode me gude, for pride goeth before destruction.* At ony rate, the warst barn e'er man lay in wad be a pleasanter abode than Glenallan-house, wi' a' the pictures and black velvet, and silver bonny-wawlies belanging to it—Sae I'll e'en settle at ance, and put in for Ailie Sim's.'

As the old man descended the hill above the little hamlet to which he was bending his course, the setting sun had relieved its inmates from their labour, and the young men, availing themselves of the fine evening, were engaged in the sport of long-bowls on a patch of common, while the women and elders looked on. The shout, the laugh, the exclamations of winners and losers, came in blended chorus up the path which Ochiltree was descending, and awakened in his recollection the days when he himself had been a keen competitor, and frequently victor, in games of strength and agility. These remembrances seldom fail to excite a sigh, even when the evening of life is cheered by brighter prospects than those of our poor mendicant.—At that time of day, was his natural reflection, I would have thought as little about ony auld palmering body that was coming down the edge of Kinblythemont, as ony o' thae stalwart young chiels does e'enow about auld Edie Ochiltree.

He was, however, presently cheered, by finding that more importance was attached to his arrival than his modesty had anticipated. A disputed cast had occurred between the bands of players, and as the gauger favoured the one party, and the schoolmaster the other, the matter might be said to be taken up by the higher powers. The miller and smith, also, had espoused different sides, and, considering the vivacity of two such disputants, there was reason to doubt whether the strife might be amicably terminated. But the first person who caught a sight of the mendicant exclaimed, 'Ah! here comes auld Edie, that kens the rules of a' country games better than ony man that ever drave a bowl, or threw an axle-tree, or putted a stane either—let's hae nae quarrelling, callants—we'll stand by auld Edie's judgment.'

Edie was accordingly welcomed, and installed as umpire, with a general shout of gratulation. With all the modesty of a bishop to whom the mitre is proffered, or of a new Speaker called to the chair,* the old man declined the high trust and responsibility with which it was proposed to invest him, and, in requital for his self-denial and humility, had the pleasure of receiving the reiterated assurances of young, old, and middle-aged, that he was simply the best qualified person for the office of arbiter 'in the haill country-side.' Thus encouraged, he proceeded gravely to the execution of his duty, and, strictly forbidding all aggravating expressions on either side, he heard the smith and gauger on one side, the miller and schoolmaster on the other, as junior and senior counsel. Edie's mind, however, was fully made up on the subject before the pleading began; like that of many a judge, who must, nevertheless, go through all the forms, and endure, in its full extent, the eloquence and argumentation of the bar. For when all had been said on both sides, and much of it said over oftener than once, our senior, being well and ripely advised, pronounced the moderate and healing judgment, that the disputed cast was a drawn one, and should therefore count to neither party. This judicious decision restored concord to the field of players; they began anew to arrange their match and their bets, with the clamorous mirth usual on such occasions of village sport, and the more eager were already stripping their jackets, and committing them, with their coloured handkerchiefs, to the care of wives, sisters, and mistresses. But their mirth was singularly interrupted.

On the outside of the group of players began to arise sounds of a description very different from those of sport—that sort of suppressed sigh and exclamation, with which the first news of calamity is received by the hearers, began to be heard indistinctly. A buzz went about among the women of 'Eh, sirs! sae young and sae suddenly summoned!'—It then extended itself among the men, and silenced the sounds of sportive mirth. All understood at once that some disaster had happened in the country, and each enquired the cause at his neighbour, who knew as little as the querist. At length the rumour reached, in a distinct shape, the ears of Edie Ochiltree, who was in the very centre of the assembly. The boat of Mucklebackit, the fisherman whom we have so often mentioned, had been swamped at sea, and four men had perished, it was affirmed, including Mucklebackit and his son. Rumour had in this, however, as in other cases, gone beyond the truth. The boat had indeed been overset; but Stephen, or, as he was called, Steenie Mucklebackit, was the only man who had been drowned. Although the place of his residence and his mode of life removed the young man from the society of the country folks, yet they failed not to pause in their rustic mirth to pay that tribute to sudden calamity, which it seldom fails to receive in cases of infrequent occurrence. To Ochiltree, in particular, the news came like a knell, the rather that he had so lately engaged this young man's assistance in an affair of sportive mischief; and though neither loss nor injury was designed to the German adept, yet the work was not precisely one in which the latter hours of life ought to be occupied.

Misfortunes never come alone. While Ochiltree, pensively leaning upon his staff, added his regrets to those of the hamlet which bewailed the young man's sudden death, and internally blamed himself for the transaction in which he had so lately engaged him, the old man's collar was seized by a peace-officer, who displayed his baton* in his right hand, and exclaimed, 'In the king's name.'

The gauger and schoolmaster united their rhetoric, to prove to the constable and his assistant that he had no right to arrest the king's bedesman as a vagrant; and the mute eloquence of the miller and smith, which was vested in their clenched fists, was prepared to give highland bail* for their arbiter; his blue gown, they said, was his warrant for travelling the country.

'But his blue gown,' answered the officer, 'is nae protection for assault, robbery, and murder; and my warrant is against him for these crimes.'

'Murder?' said Edie, 'murder? wha did I e'er murder?'

'Mr German Doustercivil, the agent at Glen-Withershins mining-works.'

'Murder Dustersnivel!—hout, he's living, and life-like, man.'

'Nae thanks to you if he be; he had a sair struggle for his life, if a' be true he tells, and ye maun answer for't at the bidding of the law.'

The defenders of the mendicant shrunk back at hearing the atrocity of the charges against him, but more than one kind hand thrust meat and bread and pence upon Edie, to maintain him in the prison, to which the officers were about to conduct him.

'Thanks to ye—God bless ye a', bairns—I've gotten out o' mony a snare when I was waur deserving o' deliverance—I shall escape like a bird from the fowler. Play out your play, and never mind me—I am mair grieved for the puir lad that's gane than for aught they can do to me.'

Accordingly, the unresisting prisoner was led off, while he mechanically accepted and stored in his wallets the alms which poured in on every hand, and ere he left the hamlet, was as deep-laden as a government victualler.* The labour of bearing this accumulating burden was, however, abridged, by the officer procuring a cart and horse to convey the old man to a magistrate, in order to his examination and committal.

The disaster of Steenie, and the arrest of Edie, put a stop to the sports of the village, the pensive inhabitants of which began to speculate upon the vicissitudes of human affairs, which had so suddenly consigned one of their comrades to the grave, and placed their master of the revels in some danger of being hanged. The character of Dousterswivel being pretty generally known, which was in his case equivalent to being pretty generally detested, there were many speculations upon the probability of the accusation being malicious. But all agreed, that, if Edie Ochiltree behoved in all events to suffer upon this occasion, it was a great pity he had not better merited his fate by killing Dousterswivel outright.

CHAPTER XXX

Who is he?—One that for the lack of land
Shall fight upon the water—he hath challenged
Formerly the grand whale; and by his titles
Of Leviathan, Behemoth, and so forth,
He tilted with a sword-fish—Marry, sir,
Th' aquatic had the best—the argument
Still galls our champion's breech.

*Old Play.**

'AND the poor young fellow, Steenie Mucklebackit, is to be buried this morning,' said our old friend the Antiquary, as he exchanged his quilted night-gown for an old-fashioned black coat in lieu of the snuff-coloured vestment which he ordinarily wore, 'and, I presume, it is expected that I should attend the funeral?'

'Ou ay,' answered the faithful Caxon, officiously brushing the white threads and specks from his patron's habit; 'the body, God help us, was sae broken against the rocks that they're fain to hurry the burial. The sea's a kittle cast,* as I tell my daughter, puir thing, when I want her to get up her spirits—the sea, says I, Jenny, is as uncertain a calling'—

'As the calling of an old periwig-maker, that's robbed of his business by crops and the powder-tax.* Caxon, thy topics of consolation are as ill chosen as they are foreign to the present purpose. *Quid mihi cum fæmina?** What have I to do with thy womankind, who have enough and to spare of mine own?—I pray of you again, am I expected by these poor people to attend the funeral of their son?'

'Ou doubtless, your honour is expected,' answered Caxon; 'weel I wot ye are expected. Ye ken in this country ilka gentleman is wussed to be sae civil as to see the corpse aff his grounds—Ye needna gang higher than the loan-head—it's no expected your honour suld leave the land—it's just a Kelso convoy, a step and a half ower the door-stane.'

'A Kelso convoy!' echoed the inquisitive Antiquary; 'and why a Kelso convoy more than any other?'

'Dear sir,' answered Caxon, 'how should I ken? it's just a by-word.'

'Caxon,' answered Oldbuck, 'thou art a mere periwig-maker—

Had I asked Ochiltree the question, he would have had a legend ready made to my hand.'

'My business,' replied Caxon, with more animation than he commonly displayed, 'is with the outside of your honour's head, as ye are accustomed to say.'

'True, Caxon, true; and it is no reproach to a thatcher that he is not an upholsterer.'

He then took out his memorandum-book and wrote down, 'Kelso convoy—said to be a step and a half ower the threshold. Authority—Caxon.—*Quaere*—Whence derived? *Mem*. To write to Dr Graysteel upon the subject.'

Having made this entry, he resumed—'And truly, as to this custom of the landlord attending the body of the peasant, I approve it, Caxon. It comes from ancient times, and was founded deep in the notions of mutual aid and dependence between the lord and cultivator of the soil. And herein I must say, the feudal system (as also in its courtesy towards womankind in which it exceeded)—herein I say, the feudal usages mitigated and softened the sternness of classical times. No man, Caxon, ever heard of a Spartan attending the funeral of a Helot*—yet I dare be sworn that John of the Girnell—ye have heard of him, Caxon?'

'Ay, ay, sir,' answered Caxon; 'naebody can hae been lang in your honour's company without hearing of that gentleman.'

'Well,' continued the Antiquary, 'I would bet a trifle there was not a *kolb kerl*,* or bondsman, or peasant, *ascriptus glebae*,* died upon the monks' territories down here, but John of the Girnell saw them fairly and decently interred.'

'Ay, but if it like your honour, they say he had mair to do wi' the births than the burials. Ha! ha! ha!' with a gleeful chuckle.

'Good, Caxon! very good! why, you shine this morning.'

'And besides,' added Caxon, slily, encouraged by his patron's approbation, 'they say too that the Catholic priests in thae times gat something for ganging about to burials.'*

'Right, Caxon, right as my glove—by the by, I fancy that phrase comes from the custom of pledging a glove as the signal of irrefragable faith—right, I say, as my glove, Caxon—but we of the Protestant ascendency have the more merit in doing that duty for nothing which cost money in the reign of that empress of superstition, whom Spenser, Caxon, terms, in his allegorical phrase,

　　　　　——The daughter of that woman blind,
　　Abessa, daughter of Corecca slow*——

But why talk I of these things to thee?—my poor Lovel has spoiled me, and taught me to speak aloud when it is much the same as speaking to myself—where's my nephew, Hector M'Intyre?'

'He's in the parlour, sir, wi' the leddies.'

'Very well,' said the Antiquary, 'I will betake me thither.'

'Now, Monkbarns,' said his sister, on his entering the parlour, 'ye maunna be angry.'

'My dear uncle!' began Miss M'Intyre.

'What's the meaning of all this?' said Oldbuck, in alarm of some impending bad news, and arguing upon the supplicating tone of the ladies, as a fortress apprehends an attack from the very first flourish of the trumpet which announces the summons;—'What's all this? What do you bespeak my patience for?'

'No particular matter, I should hope, sir,' said Hector, who, with his arm in a sling, was seated at the breakfast-table; 'however, what-ever it may amount to I am answerable for it, as I am for much more trouble that I have occasioned, and for which I have little more than thanks to offer.'

'No, no! heartily welcome, heartily welcome—only let it be a warning to you,' said the Antiquary, 'against your fits of anger, which is a short madness—*Ira furor brevis*—but what is this new disaster?'

'My dog, sir, has unfortunately thrown down'—

'If it please Heaven, not the lachrymatory from Clochnaben!' interjected Oldbuck.

'Indeed, uncle,' said the young lady, 'I am afraid—it was that which stood upon the sideboard—the poor thing only meant to eat the pat of fresh butter.'

'In which she has fully succeeded, I presume, for I see that on the table is salted. But that is nothing—my lachrymatory, the main pillar of my theory, on which I rested to show, in despite of the ignorant obstinacy of Mac-Cribb, that the Romans had passed the defiles of these mountains, and left behind them traces of their arts and arms, is gone—annihilated—reduced to such fragments as might be the shreds of a broken—flowerpot!

　　　　　——Hector, I love thee,
　　But never more be officer of mine.'*

'Why, really, sir, I am afraid I should make a bad figure in a regiment of your raising.'

'At least, Hector, I would have you dispatch your camp train,* and travel *expeditus* or *relictis impedimentis*.* You cannot conceive how I am annoyed by this beast—She commits burglary I believe, for I heard her charged with breaking into the kitchen after all the doors were locked, and eating up a shoulder of mutton.'—(Our readers, if they chance to remember Jenny Rintherout's precaution of leaving the door open when she went down to the fisher's cottage, will probably acquit poor Juno of that aggravation of guilt which the lawyers call a *claustrum fregit*,* and which makes the distinction between burglary and privately stealing.)

'I am truly sorry, sir,' said Hector, 'that Juno has committed so much disorder; but Jack Muirhead, the breaker, was never able to bring her under command. She has more travel than any bitch I ever knew, but'—

'Then, Hector, I wish the bitch would travel herself out of my grounds.'

'We will both of us retreat tomorrow, or today, but I would not willingly part from my mother's brother in unkindness about a paltry pipkin.'

'O brother, brother!' ejaculated Miss M'Intyre, in utter despair at this vituperative epithet.

'Why what would you have me call it?' continued Hector; 'it was just such a thing as they use in Egypt to cool wine, or sherbet, or water—I brought home a pair of them—I might have brought home twenty.'

'What!' said Oldbuck, 'shaped such as that your dog threw down?'

'Yes, sir, much such a sort of earthen jar as that which was on the sideboard. They are in my lodgings at Fairport; we brought a parcel of them to cool our wine on the passage—they answer wonderfully well—if I could think they would in any degree repay your loss, or rather that they could afford you pleasure, I am sure I should be much honoured by your accepting them.'

'Indeed, my dear boy, I should be highly gratified by possessing them. To trace the connexion of nations by their usages, and the similarity of the implements which they employ, has been long my favourite study. Every thing that can illustrate such connexions is most valuable to me.'

'Well, sir, I shall be much gratified by your acceptance of them, and a few trifles of the same kind.—And now, am I to hope you have forgiven me?'

'O, my dear boy, you are only thoughtless and foolish.'

'But Juno—she is only thoughtless too, I assure you—the breaker tells me she has no vice or stubbornness.'

'Well, I grant Juno also a free pardon—conditioned, that you will imitate her in avoiding vice and stubbornness, and that henceforward she banish herself forth of Monkbarns parlour.'

'Then, uncle,' said the soldier, 'I should have been very sorry and ashamed to propose to you any thing in the way of expiation of my own sins, or those of my follower, that I thought *worth* your acceptance; but now, as all is forgiven, will you permit the orphan-nephew, to whom you have been a father, to offer you a trifle, which I have been assured is really curious, and which only the cross accident of my wound has prevented my delivering to you before? I got it from a French Savant, to whom I rendered some service after the Alexandria affair.'

The captain put a small ring-case into the Antiquary's hands, which, when opened, was found to contain an antique ring of massive gold, with a cameo, most beautifully executed, bearing a head of Cleopatra. The Antiquary broke forth into unrepressed ecstasy, shook his nephew cordially by the hand, thanked him an hundred times, and showed the ring to his sister and niece, the latter of whom had the tact to give it sufficient admiration; but Miss Griselda (though she had the same affection for her nephew) had not address enough to follow the lead.

'It's a bonny thing,' she said, 'Monkbarns, and, I dare say, a valuable—but it's out o' my way—ye ken I am nae judge o' sic matters.'

'There spoke all Fairport in one voice!' exclaimed Oldbuck; 'it is the very spirit of the borough has infected us all; I think I have smelled the smoke these two days, that the wind has stuck, like a *remora*,* in the north-east—and its prejudices fly farther than its vapours. Believe me, my dear Hector, were I to walk up the High-street of Fairport, displaying this inestimable gem in the eyes of each one I met, no human creature, from the provost to the town-crier, would stop to ask me its history. But if I carried a bale of linen cloth under my arm, I could not penetrate to the Horsemarket ere I should be overwhelmed with queries about its precise texture and price. O, one might parody their brutal ignorance in the words of Gray:

> "Weave the warp and weave the woof,
>   The winding-sheet of wit and sense,
> Dull garment of defensive proof
>   'Gainst all that doth not gather pence." '*

The most remarkable proof of this peace-offering being quite acceptable, was that while the Antiquary was in full declamation, Juno, who held him in awe, according to the remarkable instinct by which dogs instantly discover those who like or dislike them, had peeped several times into the room, and encountering nothing very forbidding in his aspect, had at length presumed to introduce her full person, and finally, becoming bold by impunity, she actually ate up Mr Oldbuck's toast, as, looking first at one, then at another of his audience, he repeated with self-complacency,

> ' "Weave the warp and weave the woof," '—

'You remember the passage in the Fatal Sisters,* which, by the way, is not so fine as in the original—But, hey-day! my toast has vanished!—I see which way—Ah, thou type of womankind, no wonder they take offence at thy generic appellation!'—(So saying, he shook his fist at Juno, who scoured out of the parlour.)—'However, as Jupiter, according to Homer, could not rule Juno in heaven, and as Jack Muirhead, according to Hector M'Intyre, has been equally unsuccessful on earth, I suppose she must have her own way.' And this mild censure the brother and sister justly accounted a full pardon for Juno's offences, and sate down well pleased to the morning meal.

When breakfast was over, the Antiquary proposed to his nephew to go down with him to attend the funeral. The soldier pleaded the want of a mourning habit.

'O that does not signify—your presence is all that is requisite. I assure you, you will see something that will entertain—no, that's an improper phrase—but that will interest you, from the resemblances which I will point out betwixt popular customs on such occasions and those of the ancients.'

Heaven forgive me! thought M'Intyre; I shall certainly misbehave, and lose all the credit I have so lately and accidentally gained.

When they set out, schooled as he was by the warning and entreating looks of his sister, the soldier made his resolution strong to give no offence by evincing inattention or impatience. But our best resolutions are frail, when opposed to our predominant inclinations. Our Antiquary, to leave nothing unexplained, had commenced with the funeral rites of the ancient Scandinavians, when his nephew interrupted him in a discussion upon the 'age of hills,' to remark that a large sea-gull, which flitted around them, had come twice within shot. This error being acknowledged and pardoned, Oldbuck resumed his disquisition.

'These are circumstances you ought to attend to and be familiar with, my dear Hector; for, in the strange contingencies of the present war which agitates every corner of Europe, there is no knowing where you may be called upon to serve. If in Norway, for example, or Denmark, or any part of the ancient Scania, or Scandinavia, as we term it, what could be more convenient than to have at your fingers' ends the history and antiquities of that ancient country, the *officina gentium*,* the mother of modern Europe, the nursery of those heroes,

> Stern to inflict, and stubborn to endure,
> Who smiled in death?—*

How animating, for example, at the conclusion of a weary march, to find yourself in the vicinity of a Runic monument, and discover that you had pitched your tent beside the tomb of a hero!'

'I am afraid, sir, our mess would be better supplied if it chanced to be in the neighbourhood of a good poultry-yard.'

'Alas, that you should say so!—No wonder the days of Cressy and Agincourt* are no more, when respect for ancient valour has died away in the breasts of the British soldiery.'

'By no means, sir—by no manner of means. I dare say that Edward and Henry,* and the rest of these heroes, thought of their dinner, however, before they thought of examining an old tombstone. But I assure you, we are by no means insensible to the memory of our fathers' fame; I used often of an evening to get old Rory M'Alpin to sing us songs out of Ossian about the battles of Fingal and Lamon Mor, and Magnus and the spirit of Muirartach.'

'And did you believe,' asked the aroused Antiquary, 'did you absolutely believe that stuff of Macpherson's to be really ancient, you simple boy?'

'Believe it, sir?—how could I but believe it, when I have heard the songs sung from my infancy?'

'But not the same as Macpherson's English Ossian—you're not absurd enough to say that, I hope?' said the Antiquary, his brow darkening with wrath.

But Hector stoutly abode the storm; like many a sturdy Celt, he imagined the honour of his country and native language connected with the authenticity of these popular poems, and would have fought knee-deep, or forfeited life and land, rather than have given up a line of them. He therefore undauntedly maintained, that Rory M'Alpin could repeat the whole book from one end to another; and it was only upon cross-examination that he explained an assertion so general, by adding, 'At least, if he was allowed whisky enough, he could repeat as long as any body would hearken to him.'

'Ay, ay,' said the Antiquary; 'and that, I suppose, was not very long.'

'Why, we had our duty, sir, to attend to, and could not sit listening all night to a piper.'

'But do you recollect, now,' said Oldbuck, setting his teeth firmly together, and speaking without opening them, which was his custom when contradicted—'Do you recollect, now, any of these verses you thought so beautiful and interesting—being a capital judge, no doubt, of such things?'

'I don't pretend to much skill, uncle; but it's not very reasonable to be angry with me for admiring the antiquities of my own country more than those of the Harolds, Harfagers, and Hacos* you are so fond of.'

'Why, these, sir,—these mighty and unconquered Goths,—*were* your ancestors! The bare-breeched Celts whom they subdued, and suffered only to exist, like a fearful people, in the crevices of the rocks, were but their Mancipia and Serfs!'*

Hector's brow now grew red in his turn. 'Sir,' he said, 'I don't understand the meaning of Mancipia and Serfs, but I conceive such names are very improperly applied to Scotch Highlanders. No man but my mother's brother dared to have used such language in my presence; and I pray you will observe, that I consider it as neither hospitable, handsome, kind, nor generous usage towards your guest and your kinsman. My ancestors, Mr Oldbuck'—

'Were great and gallant chiefs, I dare say, Hector; and really I did not mean to give you such immense offence in treating a point of remote antiquity, a subject on which I always am myself cool, deliberate, and unimpassioned. But you are as hot and hasty, as if you were Hector and Achilles, and Agamemnon* to boot.'

'I am sorry I expressed myself so hastily, uncle, especially to you, who have been so generous and good—But my ancestors'—

'No more about it, lad; I meant them no affront—none.'

'I am glad of it, sir; for the house of M'Intyre'—

'Peace be with them all, every man of them,' said the Antiquary. 'But to return to our subject—Do you recollect, I say, any of those poems which afforded you such amusement?'

Very hard this, thought M'Intyre, that he will speak with such glee of every thing which is ancient, excepting my family.—Then, after some efforts at recollection, he added aloud, 'Yes, sir,—I think I do remember some lines; but you do not understand the Gaelic language.'

'And will readily excuse hearing it. But you can give me some idea of the sense in our own vernacular idiom?'

'I shall prove a wretched interpreter,' said M'Intyre, running over the original, well garnished with *aghes*, *aughs*, and *oughs*, and similar gutturals, and then coughing and hawking as if the translation stuck in his throat. At length, having premised that the poem was a dialogue between the poet Oisin, or Ossian, and Patrick, the tutelar Saint of Ireland,* and that it was difficult, if not impossible, to render the exquisite felicity of the first two or three lines, he said the sense was to this purpose:

'Patrick the psalm-singer,
Since you will not listen to one of my stories,
Though you never heard it before,
I am sorry to tell you
You are little better than an ass'—

'Good! good!' exclaimed the Antiquary; 'but go on. Why, this is, after all, the most admirable fooling*—I dare say the poet was very right. What says the Saint?'

'He replies in character,' said M'Intyre; 'but you should hear M'Alpin sing the original. The speeches of Ossian come in upon a strong deep bass—those of Patrick are upon a tenor key.'

'Like M'Alpin's drone and small pipes,* I suppose,' said Oldbuck. 'Well? Pray, go on.'

'Well then, Patrick replies to Ossian:

> "Upon my word, son of Fingal,
> While I am warbling the psalms,
> The clamour of your old women's tales
> Disturbs my devotional exercises."'

'Excellent!—why, this is better and better. I hope Saint Patrick sung better than Blattergowl's precentor, or it would be hang-choice between the poet and psalmist. But what I admire is the courtesy of these two eminent persons towards each other. It is a pity there should not be a word of this in Macpherson's translation.'

'If you are sure of that,' said M'Intyre, gravely, 'he must have taken very unwarrantable liberties with his original.'

'It will go near to be thought so shortly—but pray proceed.'

'Then,' said M'Intyre, 'this is the answer of Ossian:

> "Dare you compare your psalms,
> You son of a"'—

'Son of a what!' exclaimed Oldbuck.

'It means, I think,' said the young soldier, with some reluctance, 'son of a female dog:

> "Do you compare your psalms
> To the tales of the bare-arm'd Fenians?"'*

'Are you sure you are translating that last epithet correctly, Hector?'

'Quite sure, sir,' answered Hector, doggedly.

'Because I should have thought the nudity might have been quoted as existing in a different part of the body.'

Disdaining to reply to this insinuation, Hector proceeded in his recitation:

> 'I shall think it no great harm
> To wring your bald head from your shoulders—'

'But what is that yonder?' exclaimed Hector, interrupting himself.

'One of the herd of Proteus,'* said the Antiquary—'a *phoca*, or seal, lying asleep on the beach.'

Upon which M'Intyre, with the eagerness of a young sportsman, totally forgot both Ossian, Patrick, his uncle, and his wound, and exclaiming, 'I shall have her! I shall have her!' snatched the walking-stick out of the hand of the astonished Antiquary, at some risk of throwing him down, and set off at full speed to get between the animal and the sea, to which element, having caught the alarm, she was rapidly retreating.

Not Sancho, when his master interrupted his account of the combatants of Pentapolin with the naked arm, to advance in person to the charge of the flock of sheep,* stood more confounded than Oldbuck at this sudden escapade of his nephew.

'Is the devil in him,' was his first exclamation, 'to go to disturb the brute that was never thinking of him!'—Then elevating his voice, 'Hector—nephew—fool—let alone the *Phoca*—let alone the *Phoca*—they bite, I tell you, like furies.—He minds me no more than a post—there—there they are at it—Gad, the *Phoca* has the best of it! I am glad to see it,' said he, in the bitterness of his heart, though really alarmed for his nephew's safety; 'I am glad to see it, with all my heart and spirit.'

In truth, the seal, finding her retreat intercepted by the light-footed soldier, confronted him manfully, and having sustained a heavy blow without injury, she knitted her brows, as is the fashion of the animal when incensed, and making use at once of her fore paws and her unwieldy strength, wrenched the weapon out of the assailant's hand, overturned him on the sands, and scuttled away into the sea without doing him any farther injury. Captain M'Intyre, a good deal out of countenance at the issue of his exploit, just rose in time to receive the ironical congratulations of his uncle, upon a single combat, worthy to be commemorated by Ossian himself, 'since,' said the Antiquary, 'your magnanimous opponent hath fled, though not upon eagle's wings, from the foe that was low—Egad, she walloped away with all the grace of triumph, and has carried my stick off also, by way of *spolia opima*.'*

M'Intyre had little to answer for himself, except that a Highlander could never pass a deer, a seal, or a salmon, where there was a possibility of having a trial of skill with them, and that he had forgot one of his arms was in a sling. He also made his fall an apology for returning back to Monkbarns, and thus escaped the farther raillery of his uncle, as well as his lamentations for his walking-stick.

'I cut it,' he said, 'in the classic woods of Hawthornden, when I did not expect always to have been a bachelor—I would not have given it for an ocean of seals*—O Hector, Hector!—thy namesake was born to be the prop of Troy, and thou to be the plague of Monkbarns!'

CHAPTER XXXI

Tell me not of it, friend—when the young weep,
Their tears are luke-warm brine;—from our old eyes
Sorrow falls down like hail-drops of the North,
Chilling the furrows of our wither'd cheeks,
Cold as our hopes, and harden'd as our feeling—
Theirs, as they fall, sink sightless—ours recoil,
Heap the fair plain, and bleaken all before us.

*Old Play.**

THE Antiquary, being now alone, hastened his pace, which had been retarded by these various discussions, and the rencontre which had closed them, and soon arrived before the half-dozen cottages at Mussel-crag. They now had, in addition to their usual squalid and uncomfortable appearance, the melancholy attributes of the house of mourning. The boats were all drawn up on the beach; and, though the day was fine, and the season favourable, the chant, which is used by the fishers when at sea, was silent, as well as the prattle of the children, and the shrill song of the mother, as she sits mending her nets by the door. A few of the neighbours, some in their antique and well-saved suits of black, others in their ordinary clothes, but all bearing an expression of mournful sympathy with distress so sudden and unexpected, stood gathered around the door of Mucklebackit's cottage, waiting till 'the body was lifted.' As the Laird of Monkbarns approached, they made way for him to enter, doffing their hats and bonnets as he passed, with an air of melancholy courtesy, and he returned their salutes in the same manner.

In the inside of the cottage was a scene, which our Wilkie* alone could have painted, with that exquisite feeling of nature that characterises his enchanting productions.

The body was laid in its coffin within the wooden bedstead which the young fisher had occupied while alive. At a little distance stood the father, whose rugged weather-beaten countenance, shaded by his grizzled hair, had faced many a stormy night and night-like day. He was apparently revolving his loss in his mind with that strong feeling of painful grief, peculiar to harsh and rough characters, which almost breaks forth into hatred against the world, and all that remain in it, after the beloved object is withdrawn. The old man had made the most desperate efforts to save his son, and had only been withheld by main force from renewing them at a moment, when, without the possibility of assisting the sufferer, he must himself have perished. All this apparently was boiling in his recollection. His glance was directed sidelong towards the coffin, as to an object on which he could not steadfastly look, and yet from which he could not withdraw his eyes. His answers to the necessary questions which were occasionally put to him, were brief, harsh, and almost fierce. His family had not yet dared to address to him a word, either of sympathy or consolation. His masculine wife, virago as she was, and absolute mistress of the family, as she justly boasted herself, on all ordinary occasions, was, by this great loss, terrified into silence and submission, and compelled to hide from her husband's observation the bursts of her female sorrow. As he had rejected food ever since the disaster had happened, not daring herself to approach him, she had that morning, with affectionate artifice, employed the youngest and favourite child to present her husband with some nourishment. His first action was to push it from him with an angry violence, that frightened the child; his next, to snatch up the boy and devour him with kisses. 'Ye'll be a bra' fallow, an ye be spared, Patie,—but ye'll never—never can be—what he was to me!—He has sailed the coble wi' me since he was ten years auld, and there wasna the like o' him drew a net betwixt this and Buchan-ness—They say folks maun submit—I will try.'

And he had been silent from that moment until compelled to answer the necessary questions we have already noticed. Such was the disconsolate state of the father.

In another corner of the cottage, her face covered by her apron, which was flung over it, sat the mother, the nature of her grief sufficiently indicated, by the wringing of her hands, and the convulsive agitation of the bosom which the covering could not conceal. Two of her gossips, officiously whispering into her ear the commonplace topic of resignation under irremediable misfortune, seemed as if they were endeavouring to stun the grief which they could not console.

The sorrow of the children was mingled with wonder at the preparations they beheld around them, and at the unusual display of wheaten bread and wine, which the poorest peasant, or fisher, offers to the guests on these mournful occasions; and thus their grief for their brother's death was almost already lost in admiration of the splendour of his funeral.

But the figure of the old grandmother was the most remarkable of the sorrowing group. Seated on her accustomed chair, with her usual air of apathy, and want of interest in what surrounded her, she seemed every now and then mechanically to resume the motion of twirling her spindle—then to look towards her bosom for the distaff, although both had been laid aside—She would then cast her eyes about as if surprised at missing the usual implements of her industry, and appear struck by the black colour of the gown in which they had dressed her, and embarrassed by the number of persons by whom she was surrounded—then, finally, she would raise her head with a ghastly look, and fix her eyes upon the bed which contained the coffin of her grandson, as if she had at once, and for the first time, acquired sense to comprehend her inexpressible calamity. These alternate feelings of embarrassment, wonder, and grief, seemed to succeed each other more than once upon her torpid features. But she spoke not a word, neither had she shed a tear; nor did one of the family understand, either from look or expression, to what extent she comprehended the uncommon bustle around her. Thus she sat among the funeral assembly like a connecting link between the surviving mourners and the dead corpse which they bewailed—a being in whom the light of existence was already obscured by the encroaching shadows of death.

When Oldbuck entered this house of mourning, he was received by a general and silent inclination of the head, and according to the fashion of Scotland on such occasions, wine and spirits and bread were offered round to the guests. Elspeth, as these refreshments were presented, surprised and startled the whole company by motioning to the person who bore them to stop; then, taking a glass in her hand, she rose up, and, as the smile of dotage played upon her shrivelled features, she pronounced, with a hollow and tremulous voice, 'Wishing a' your healths, sirs, and often may we hae such merry meetings!'

All shrunk from the ominous pledge, and set down the untasted liquor with a degree of shuddering horror, which will not surprise those who know how many superstitions are still common on such occasions among the Scottish vulgar. But as the old woman tasted the liquor, she suddenly exclaimed with a sort of shriek, 'What's this?—this is wine—how should there be wine in my son's house?—Ay,' she continued with a suppressed groan, 'I mind the sorrowful cause now,' and, dropping the glass from her hand, she stood a moment gazing fixedly on the bed in which the coffin of her grandson was deposited, and then sinking gradually into her seat, she covered her eyes and forehead with her withered and pallid hand.

At this moment the clergyman entered the cottage. Mr Blattergowl, though a dreadful proser, particularly on the subject of augmentations, localities, teinds, and overtures in that session of the General Assembly, to which, unfortunately for his auditors, he chanced one year to act as moderator,* was nevertheless a good man, in the old Scottish presbyterian phrase, God-ward and man-ward. No divine was more attentive in visiting the sick and afflicted, in catechizing the youth, in instructing the ignorant, and in reproving the erring. And hence, notwithstanding impatience of his prolixity and prejudices, personal or professional, and notwithstanding, moreover, a certain habitual contempt for his understanding, especially on affairs of genius and taste, on which Blattergowl was apt to be diffuse, from his hope of one day fighting his way to a chair of rhetoric or belles lettres,*—notwithstanding, I say, all the prejudices excited against him by these circumstances, our friend the Antiquary looked with great regard and respect on the said Blattergowl, though I own he could seldom, even by his sense of decency and the remonstrances of his womankind, be *hounded out*, as he called it, to hear him preach. But he regularly took shame to himself for his absence when Blattergowl came to Monkbarns to dinner, to which he was always invited of a Sunday, a mode of testifying his respect which the proprietor probably thought fully as agreeable to the clergyman, and rather more congenial to his own habits.

To return from a digression which can only serve to introduce the honest clergyman more particularly to our readers, Mr Blattergowl had no sooner entered the hut, and received the mute and melancholy salutations of the company whom it contained, than he edged himself towards the unfortunate father, and seemed to endeavour to slide in a few words of condolence or of consolation. But the old man was incapable as yet of receiving either; he nodded, however, gruffly, and shook the clergyman's hand in acknowledgment of his good intentions, but was either unable or unwilling to make any verbal reply.

The minister next passed to the mother, moving along the floor as slowly, silently, and gradually, as if he had been afraid that the ground would, like unsafe ice, break beneath his feet, or that the first echo of a footstep was to dissolve some magic spell, and plunge the hut, with all its inmates, into a subterranean abyss. The tenor of what he had said to the poor woman could only be judged by her answers, as, half-stifled by sobs ill-repressed, and by the covering which she still kept over her countenance, she faintly answered at each pause in his speech—'Yes, sir, yes!—Ye're very gude—ye're very gude!—Nae doubt, nae doubt!—It's our duty to submit!—But, O dear, my poor Steenie, the pride o' my very heart, that was sae handsome and comely, and a help to his family, and a comfort to us a', and a pleasure to a' that lookit on him!—O my bairn, my bairn, my bairn! what for is thou lying there, and eh! what for am I left to greet for ye!'

There was no contending with this burst of sorrow and natural affection. Oldbuck had repeated recourse to his snuff-box to conceal the tears which, despite his shrewd and caustic temper, were apt to start on such occasions. The female assistants whimpered, the men held their bonnets to their faces, and spoke apart with each other. The clergyman, meantime, addressed his ghostly consolation to the aged grandmother. At first she listened, or seemed to listen, to what he said, with the apathy of her usual unconsciousness. But as, in pressing this theme, he approached so near to her ear, that the sense of his words became distinctly intelligible to her, though unheard by those who stood more distant, her countenance at once assumed that stern and expressive cast which characterised her intervals of intelligence. She drew up her head and body, shook her head in a manner that showed at least impatience, if not scorn of his counsel, and waved her hand slightly, but with a gesture so expressive, as to indicate to all who witnessed it a marked and disdainful rejection of the ghostly consolation proffered to her. The minister stepped back as if repulsed, and, by lifting gently and dropping his hand, seemed to show at once wonder, sorrow, and compassion for her dreadful state of mind. The rest of the company sympathized, and a stifled whisper went through them, indicating how much her desperate and determined manner impressed them with awe and even horror.

In the meantime the funeral company was completed, by the arrival of one or two persons who had been expected from Fairport.

The wine and spirits again circulated, and the dumb show of greeting was anew interchanged. The grandame a second time took a glass in her hand, drank its contents, and exclaimed, with a sort of laugh,—'Ha! ha! I hae tasted wine twice in ae day—Whan did I that before, think ye, cummers?—Never since'—And the transient glow vanishing from her countenance, she set the glass down and sunk upon the settle from whence she had risen to snatch at it.

As the general amazement subsided, Mr Oldbuck, whose heart bled to witness what he considered as the errings of the enfeebled intellect struggling with the torpid chill of age and of sorrow, observed to the clergyman that it was time to proceed with the ceremony. The father was incapable of giving directions, but the nearest relation of the family made a sign to the carpenter, who in such cases goes through the duty of the undertaker, to proceed in his office. The creak of the screw-nails presently announced that the lid of the last mansion of mortality was in the act of being secured above its tenant. The last act which separates us for ever, even from the mortal relics of the person we assemble to mourn, has usually its effect upon the most indifferent, selfish, and hard-hearted. With a spirit of contradiction, which we may be pardoned for esteeming narrow-minded, the fathers of the Scottish kirk rejected, even on this most solemn occasion, the form of an address to the Divinity, lest they should be thought to give countenance to the rituals of Rome or of England. With much better and more liberal judgment, it is the present practice of most of the Scottish clergymen to seize this opportunity of offering a prayer, and exhortation, suitable to make an impression upon the living, while they are yet in the very presence of the relics of him, whom they have but lately seen such as they themselves, and who now is such as they must in their time become. But this decent and praiseworthy practice was not adopted at the time of which I am treating, or, at least, Mr Blattergowl did not act upon it, and the ceremony proceeded without any devotional exercise.

The coffin, covered with a pall, and supported upon handspikes by the nearest relatives, now only waited the father to support the head, as is customary. Two or three of these privileged persons spoke to him, but he only answered by shaking his hand and his head in token of refusal. With better intention than judgment, the friends, who considered this as an act of duty on the part of the living, and of decency towards the deceased, would have proceeded to enforce their request, had not Oldbuck interfered between the distressed father and his well-meaning tormentors, and informed them, that he himself, as landlord and master to the deceased, 'would carry his head to the grave.' In spite of the sorrowful occasion, the hearts of the relatives swelled within them at so marked a distinction on the part of the laird; and old Alison Breck, who was present among other fish-women, swore almost aloud, 'His honour Monkbarns should never want sax warp of oysters in the season, (of which fish he was understood to be fond,) if she should gang to sea and dredge for them hersell, in the foulest wind that ever blew.' And such is the temper of the Scottish common people, that, by this instance of compliance with their customs, and respect for their persons, Mr Oldbuck gained more popularity than by all the sums which he had yearly distributed in the parish for purposes of private or general charity.

The sad procession now moved slowly forward, preceded by the beadles, or saulies, with their batons,—miserable-looking old men, tottering as if on the edge of that grave to which they were marshalling another, and clad, according to Scottish guise, with threadbare black coats, and hunting-caps, decorated with rusty crape. Monkbarns would probably have remonstrated against this superfluous expense, had he been consulted; but, in doing so, he would have given more offence than he gained popularity by condescending to perform the office of chief mourner. Of this he was quite aware, and wisely withheld rebuke, where rebuke and advice would have been equally unavailing. In truth, the Scottish peasantry are still infected with that rage for funeral ceremonial, which once distinguished the grandees of the kingdom so much, that a sumptuary law was made by the Parliament of Scotland for the purpose of restraining it; and I have known many in the lowest stations, who have denied themselves not merely the comforts, but almost the necessaries of life, in order to save such a sum of money as might enable their surviving friends to bury them like Christians, as they termed it; nor could their faithful executors be prevailed upon, though equally necessitous, to turn to the use and maintenance of the living, the money vainly wasted upon the interment of the dead.

The procession to the churchyard, at about half-a-mile's distance, was made with the mournful solemnity usual on these occasions,—

the body was consigned to its parent earth,—and when the labour of the gravediggers had filled up the trench, and covered it with fresh sod, Mr Oldbuck, taking his hat off, saluted the assistants, who had stood by in melancholy silence, and with that adieu dispersed the mourners.

The clergyman offered our Antiquary his company to walk homeward; but Mr Oldbuck had been so much struck with the deportment of the fisherman and his mother, that, moved by compassion, and perhaps also, in some degree, by that curiosity which induces us to seek out even what gives us pain to witness, he preferred a solitary walk by the coast, for the purpose of again visiting the cottage as he passed.

CHAPTER XXXII

What is this secret sin, this untold tale,
That art cannot extract, nor penance cleanse?
——————————Her muscles hold their place;
Nor discomposed, nor form'd to steadiness,
No sudden flushing, and no faltering lip.—

*Mysterious Mother.**

THE coffin had been borne from the place where it rested. The mourners, in regular gradation, according to their rank or their relationship to the deceased, had filed from the cottage, while the younger male children were led along to totter after the bier of their brother, and to view with wonder a ceremonial which they could hardly comprehend. The female gossips next rose to depart, and, with consideration for the situation of the parents, carried along with them the girls of the family, to give the unhappy pair time and opportunity to open their hearts to each other, and soften their grief by communicating it. But their kind intention was without effect. The last of them had darkened the entrance of the cottage, as she went out, and drawn the door softly behind her, when the father, first ascertaining by a hasty glance that no stranger remained, started up, clasped his hands wildly above his head, uttered a cry of the despair which he had hitherto repressed, and, in all the impotent impatience of grief, half rushed half staggered forward to the bed on which the coffin had been deposited, threw himself down upon it, and smothering, as it were, his head among the bed-clothes, gave vent to the full passion of his sorrow. It was in vain that the wretched mother, terrified by the vehemence of her husband's affliction—affliction still more fearful as agitating a man of hardened manners and a robust frame—suppressed her own sobs and tears, and, pulling him by the skirts of his coat, implored him to rise and remember, that, though one was removed, he had still a wife and children to comfort and support. The appeal came at too early a period of his anguish, and was totally unattended to; he continued to remain prostrate, indicating, by sobs so bitter and violent that they shook the bed and partition against which it rested, by clenched hands which grasped the bed-clothes, and by the vehement and convulsive motion of his legs, how deep and how terrible was the agony of a father's sorrow.

'O, what a day is this! what a day is this!' said the poor mother, her womanish affliction already exhausted by sobs and tears, and now almost lost in terror for the state in which she beheld her husband; 'O, what an hour is this! and naebody to help a poor lone woman—O, gudemither, could ye but speak a word to him!—wad ye but bid him be comforted!'

To her astonishment, and even to the increase of her fear, her husband's mother heard and answered the appeal. She rose and walked across the floor without support, and without much apparent feebleness, and standing by the bed on which her son had extended himself, she said, 'Rise up, my son, and sorrow not for him that is beyond sin and sorrow and temptation—Sorrow is for those that remain in this vale of sorrow and darkness*—I, wha dinna sorrow, and wha canna sorrow for ony ane, hae maist need that ye should a' sorrow for me.'

The voice of his mother, not heard for years as taking part in the active duties of life, or offering advice or consolation, produced its effect upon her son. He assumed a sitting posture on the side of the bed, and his appearance, attitude, and gestures, changed from those of angry despair to deep grief and dejection. The grandmother retired to her nook, the mother mechanically took in her hand her tattered Bible, and seemed to read, though her eyes were drowned with tears.

They were thus occupied, when a loud knock was heard at the door.

'Hegh, sirs!' said the poor mother, 'wha is it that can be coming in that gait e'enow?—They canna hae heard o' our misfortune, I'm sure.'

The knock being repeated, she rose and opened the door, saying querulously, 'Whatna gait's that to disturb a sorrowfu' house?'

A tall man in black stood before her, whom she instantly recognised to be Lord Glenallan.

'Is there not,' he said, 'an old woman lodging in this or one of the neighbouring cottages, called Elspeth, who was long resident at Craigburnfoot of Glenallan?'

'It's my gudemither, my lord,' said Margaret; 'but she canna see ony body e'enow—Ohon! we're dreeing a sair weird—we hae had a heavy dispensation!'

'God forbid,' said Lord Glenallan, 'that I should on light occasion disturb your sorrow—but my days are numbered—your mother-in-law is in the extremity of age, and, if I see her not today, we may never meet on this side of time.'

'And what,' answered the desolate mother, 'wad ye see at an auld woman, broken down wi' age and sorrow and heartbreak?—Gentle or semple shall not darken my doors the day my bairn's been carried out a corpse.'

While she spoke thus, indulging the natural irritability of disposition and profession, which began to mingle itself in some degree with her grief when its first uncontrolled bursts were gone by, she held the door about one-third part open, and placed herself in the gap, as if to render the visitor's entrance impossible. But the voice of her husband was heard from within—'Wha's that, Maggie? what for are ye steeking them out?—let them come in—it doesna signify an auld rope's end wha comes in or wha gaes out o' this house frae this time forward.'

The woman stood aside at her husband's command, and permitted Lord Glenallan to enter the hut. The dejection exhibited in his broken frame and emaciated countenance, formed a strong contrast with the effects of grief, as they were displayed in the rude and weatherbeaten visage of the fisherman, and the masculine features of his wife. He approached the old woman as she was seated on her usual settle, and asked her, in a tone as audible as his voice could make it, 'Are you Elspeth of the Craigburnfoot of Glenallan?'

'Wha is it that asks about the unhallowed residence of that evil woman?' was the answer returned to his query.

'The unhappy Earl of Glenallan.'

'Earl—Earl of Glenallan!'

'He who was called William Lord Geraldin,' said the Earl; 'and whom his mother's death has made Earl of Glenallan.'

'Open the bole,' said the old woman firmly and hastily to her daughter-in-law, 'open the bole wi' speed, that I may see if this be the right Lord Geraldin—the son of my mistress—him that I received in my arms within the hour after he was born—him that has reason to curse me that I didna smother him before the hour was past!'

The window, which had been shut, in order that a gloomy twilight might add to the solemnity of the funeral meeting, was opened as she commanded, and threw a sudden and strong light through the smoky and misty atmosphere of the stifling cabin. Falling in a stream upon the chimney, the rays illuminated, in the way that Rembrandt would have chosen, the features of the unfortunate nobleman, and those of the old sibyl, who now, standing upon her feet, and holding him by one hand, peered anxiously in his features with her light-blue eyes, and holding her long and withered fore-finger within a small distance of his face, moved it slowly as if to trace the outlines, and reconcile what she recollected with that she now beheld. As she finished her scrutiny, she said, with a deep sigh, 'It's a sair—sair change—and wha's fault is it?—but that's written down where it will be remembered—it's written on tablets of brass with a pen of steel, where all is recorded that is done in the flesh.—And what,' she said, after a pause, 'what is Lord Geraldin seeking from a puir auld creature like me, that's dead already, and only belangs sae far to the living that she isna yet laid in the moulds?'

'Nay,' answered Lord Glenallan, 'in the name of Heaven, why was it that you requested so urgently to see me? and why did you back your request by sending a token, which you knew well I dared not refuse?'

As he spoke thus, he took from his purse the ring which Edie Ochiltree had delivered to him at Glenallan-house. The sight of this token produced a strange and instantaneous effect upon the old woman. The palsy of fear was immediately added to that of age, and she began instantly to search her pockets with the tremulous and hasty agitation of one who becomes first apprehensive of having lost something of great importance—then, as if convinced of the reality of her fears, she turned to the Earl, and demanded, 'And how came ye by it, then?—how came ye by it?—I thought I had kept it sae securely—what will the Countess say?'

'You know,' said the Earl, 'at least you must have heard, that my mother is dead.'

'Dead! are ye no imposing upon me? has she left a' at last, lands and lordship and lineages?'

'All, all,' said the Earl, 'as mortals must leave all human vanities.'

'I mind now,' answered Elspeth, 'I heard of it before; but there has been sic distress in our house since, and my memory is sae muckle impaired—But ye are sure your mother, the Lady Countess, is gane hame?'

The Earl again assured her that her former mistress was no more.

'Then,' said Elspeth, 'it shall burden my mind nae langer!—When she lived, wha dared to speak what it would hae displeased her to hae had noised abroad?—But she's gane—and I will confess all.'

Then, turning to her son and daughter-in-law, she commanded them imperatively to quit the house, and leave Lord Geraldin (for so she still called him) alone with her. But Maggie Mucklebackit, her first burst of grief being over, was by no means disposed in her own house to pay passive obedience to the commands of her mother-in-law, an authority which is peculiarly obnoxious to persons in her rank of life, and which she was the more astonished at hearing revived, when it seemed to have been so long relinquished and forgotten.

'It was an unco thing,' she said, in a grumbling tone of voice,—for the rank of Lord Glenallan was somewhat imposing—'it was an unco thing to bid a mother leave her ain house wi' the tear in her ee, the moment her eldest son had been carried a corpse out at the door o't.'

The fisherman, in a stubborn and sullen tone, added to the same purpose, 'This is nae day for your auld-warld stories, mother—My lord, if he be a lord, may ca' some other day—or he may speak out what he has gotten to say if he likes it—There's nane here will think it worth their while to listen to him or you either. But neither for laird or loon, gentle or semple, will I leave my ain house to pleasure ony body on the very day my poor'—

Here his voice choked, and he could proceed no farther; but as he had risen when Lord Glenallan came in, and had since remained standing, he now threw himself doggedly upon a seat, and remained in the sullen posture of one who was determined to keep his word.

But the old woman, whom this crisis seemed to repossess in all those powers of mental superiority with which she had once been eminently gifted, arose, and, advancing towards him, said with a solemn voice, 'My son, as ye wad shun hearing of your mother's shame,—as ye wad not willingly be a witness of her guilt,—as ye wad deserve her blessing and avoid her curse, I charge ye, by the body that bore and that nursed ye, to leave me at freedom to speak with Lord Geraldin, what nae mortal ears but his ain maun listen to. Obey my words, that when ye lay the moulds on my head,—and O, that the day were come!—ye may remember this hour without the reproach of having disobeyed the last earthly command that ever your mother wared on you.'

The terms of this solemn charge revived in the fisherman's heart the habit of instinctive obedience, in which his mother had trained him up, and to which he had submitted implicitly while her powers of exacting it remained entire. The recollection mingled also with the prevailing passion of the moment; for, glancing his eye at the bed on which the dead body had been laid, he muttered to himself, '*He* never disobeyed *me*, in reason or out o' reason, and what for should I vex *her*?' Then, taking his reluctant spouse by the arm, he led her gently out of the cottage, and latched the door behind them as he left it.

As the unhappy parents withdrew, Lord Glenallan, to prevent the old woman from relapsing into her lethargy, again pressed her on the subject of the communication which she proposed to make to him.

'Ye will have it sune eneugh,' she replied; 'my mind's clear eneugh now, and there is not—I think there is not—a chance of my forgetting what I have to say. My dwelling at Craigburnfoot is before my een, as it were present in reality—the green bank, with its selvidge, just where the burn met wi' the sea—the twa little barks, wi' their sails furled, lying in the natural cove which it formed—the high cliff that joined it with the pleasure-grounds of the house of Glenallan, and hung right ower the stream—Ah! yes, I may forget that I had a husband and have lost him—that I hae but ane alive of our four fair sons—that misfortune upon misfortune has devoured our ill-gotten wealth—that they carried the corpse of my son's eldest-born frae the house this morning—But I never can forget the days I spent at bonny Craigburnfoot!'

'You were a favourite of my mother,' said Lord Glenallan, desirous to bring her back to the point, from which she was wandering.

'I was, I was,—ye needna mind me o' that. She brought me up abune my station, and wi' knowledge mair than my fellows—but, like the tempter of auld,* wi' the knowledge of gude she taught me the knowledge of evil.'

'For God's sake, Elspeth,' said the astonished Earl, 'proceed, if you can, to explain the dreadful hints you have thrown out!—I well know you are confident to one dreadful secret, which should split this roof even to hear it named—but speak on farther.'

'I will,' she said,—'I will—just bear wi' me for a little;'—and again she seemed lost in recollection, but it was no longer tinged with imbecility or apathy. She was now entering upon the topic which had long loaded her mind, and which doubtless often occupied her whole soul at times when she seemed dead to all around her. And I may add, as a remarkable fact, that such was the intense operation of mental energy upon her physical powers and nervous system, that, notwithstanding her infirmity of deafness, each word that Lord Glenallan spoke during this remarkable conference, although in the lowest tone of horror or agony, fell as full and distinct upon Elspeth's ear as it could have done at any period of her life. She spoke also herself clearly, distinctly, and slowly, as if anxious that the intelligence she communicated should be fully understood; concisely at the same time, and with none of the verbiage or circumlocutory additions natural to those of her sex and condition. In short, her language bespoke a better education, as well as an uncommonly firm and resolved mind, and a character of that sort from which great virtues or great crimes may be naturally expected. The tenor of her communication is disclosed in the following chapter.

CHAPTER XXXIII

Remorse—she ne'er forsakes us—
A bloodhound stanch—she tracks our rapid step
Through the wild labyrinth of youthful frenzy,
Unheard, perchance, until old age hath tamed us;
Then in our lair, when Time hath chill'd our joints,
And maim'd our hope of combat, or of flight,
We hear her deep-mouth'd bay, announcing all
Of wrath and woe and punishment that bides us.

Old Play.*

'I NEED not tell you,' said the old woman addressing the Earl of Glenallan, 'that I was the favourite and confidential attendant of Joscelind, Countess of Glenallan, whom God assoilzie!'—(here she crossed herself)—'and, I think farther, ye may not have forgotten, that I shared her regard for mony years. I returned it by the maist sincere attachment, but I fell into disgrace frae a trifling act of disobedience, reported to your mother by ane that thought, and she wasna wrang, that I was a spy upon her actions and yours.'

'I charge thee, woman,' said the Earl, in a voice trembling with passion, 'name not her name in my hearing!'

'I MUST,' returned the penitent firmly and calmly, 'or how can you understand me?'

The Earl leaned upon one of the wooden chairs of the hut, drew his hat over his face, clenched his hands together, set his teeth like one who summons up courage to undergo a painful operation, and made a signal to her to proceed.

'I say then,' she resumed, 'that my disgrace with my mistress was chiefly owing to Miss Eveline Neville, then bred up in Glenallan-house as the daughter of a cousin-german* and intimate friend of your father that was gane. There was muckle mystery in her history, but wha dared to enquire farther than the Countess liked to tell?— All in Glenallan-house loved Miss Neville—all but twa—your mother and mysell—we baith hated her.'

'God! for what reason, since a creature so mild, so gentle, so formed to inspire affection, never walked on this wretched world?'

'It may hae been sae,' rejoined Elspeth, 'but your mother hated a' that cam of your father's family—a' but himsell. Her reasons related to strife which fell between them soon after her marriage; the particulars are naething to this purpose. But, Oh, doubly did she hate Eveline Neville when she perceived that there was a growing kindness atween you and that unfortunate young leddy! Ye may mind that the Countess's dislike didna gang farther at first than just showing o' the cauld shouther—at least it wasna seen farther: but at the lang run it brak out into such downright violence that Miss Neville was even fain to seek refuge at Knockwinnock Castle with Sir Arthur's leddy, wha (God sain her) was then wi' the living.'

'You rend my heart by recalling these particulars—But go on, and may my present agony be accepted as additional penance for the involuntary crime!'

'She had been absent some months,' continued Elspeth, 'when I was ae night watching in my hut the return of my husband from fishing, and shedding in private those bitter tears that my proud spirit wrung frae me whenever I thought on my disgrace. The sneck was drawn, and the Countess, your mother, entered my dwelling. I thought I had seen a spectre, for, even in the height of my favour, this was an honour she had never done me, and she looked as pale and ghastly as if she had risen from the grave. She sate down and wrung the draps from her hair and cloak, for the night was drizzling, and her walk had been through the plantations, that were a' loaded with dew. I only mention these things that you may understand how weel that night lives in my memory,—and weel it may. I was surprised to see her, but I durstna speak first, mair than if I had seen a phantom—Na, I durst not, my lord, I that hae seen mony sights of terror, and never shook at them—Sae, after a silence, she said, "Elspeth Cheyne, (for she always gave me my maiden name,) are not ye the daughter of that Reginald Cheyne, who died to save his master, Lord Glenallan, on the field of Sheriffmuir?"* And I answered her as proudly as hersell nearly—"As sure as you are the daughter of that Earl of Glenallan whom my father saved that day by his own death."'

Here she made a deep pause.

'And what followed?—what followed?—For Heaven's sake, good woman—But why should I use that word?—Yet, good or bad, I command you to tell me.'

'And little I should value earthly command,' answered Elspeth, 'were there not a voice that has spoken to me sleeping and waking, that drives me forward to tell this sad tale.—Aweel, my lord—the Countess said to me, "My son loves Eveline Neville—they are agreed—they are plighted;—should they have a son, my right over Glenallan merges—I sink, from that moment, from a Countess into a miserable stipendiary dowager—I who brought lands and vassals, and high blood and ancient fame, to my husband, I must cease to be mistress when my son has an heir-male. But I care not for that—had he married any but one of the hated Nevilles, I had been patient— But for them—that they and their descendants should enjoy the right and honours of my ancestors, goes through my heart like a two-edged dirk. And this girl—I detest her!"—And I answered, for my heart kindled at her words, that her hate was equalled by mine.'

'Wretch!' exclaimed the Earl, in spite of his determination to preserve silence,—'Wretched woman! what cause of hate could have arisen from a being so innocent and gentle?'

'I hated what my mistress hated, as was the use with the liege vassals of the house of Glenallan; for though, my lord, I married under my degree, yet an ancestor of yours never went to the field of battle, but an ancestor of the frail, demented, auld, useless wretch wha now speaks with you, carried his shield before him.—But that was not a',' continued the beldam, her earthly and evil passions rekindling as she became heated in her narration; 'that was not a'—I hated Miss Eveline Neville for her ain sake—I brought her frae England, and, during our whole journey, she gecked and scorned at my northern speech and habit, as her southland leddies and kimmers had done at the boarding-school as they ca'd it,' (and, strange as it may seem, she spoke of an affront offered by a heedless school-girl without intention, with a degree of inveteracy, which, at such a distance of time, a mortal offence would neither have authorized or excited in any well-constituted mind)—'Yes, she scorned and jested at me—but let them that scorn the tartan fear the dirk!'

She paused, and then went on. 'But I deny not that I hated her mair than she deserved. My mistress, the Countess, persevered and said, "Elspeth Cheyne, this unruly boy will marry with the false English blood—were days as they have been, I could throw her into the Massymore[19] of Glenallan, and fetter him in the Keep of Strathbonnel—But these times are past, and the authority which the nobles of the land should exercise is delegated to quibbling lawyers and their baser dependents. Hear me, Elspeth Cheyne! If you are your father's daughter as I am mine, I will find means that they shall not marry—She walks often to that cliff that overhangs your dwelling to look for her lover's boat,—(ye may remember the pleasure ye then took on the sea, my lord)—let him find her forty fathom lower than he expects!"—Yes!—ye may stare and frown and clench your hand, but, as sure as I am to face the only Being I ever feared,—and O that I had feared him mair!—these were your mother's words—What avails it to me to lie to you?—But I wadna consent to stain my hand with blood.—Then she said, "By the religion of our holy Church they are ower *sibb* thegither. But I expect nothing but that both will become heretics as well as disobedient reprobates," that was her addition to that argument—And then, as the fiend is ever ower busy wi' brains like mine, that are subtle beyond their use and station, I was unhappily permitted to add—"But they might be brought to think themselves sae *sibb* as no Christian law will permit their wedlock."'

Here the Earl of Glenallan echoed her words with a shriek so piercing, as almost to rend the roof of the cottage—'Ah! then Eveline Neville was not the—the'—

'The daughter, ye would say, of your father?' continued Elspeth; 'No—be it a torment or be it a comfort to you—ken the truth, she was nae mair a daughter of your father's house than I am.'

'Woman, deceive me not—make me not curse the memory of the parent I have so lately laid in the grave, for sharing in a plot the most cruel, the most infernal'—

'Bethink ye, my Lord Geraldin, ere ye curse the memory of a parent that's gane, is there none of the blood of Glenallan living, whose faults have led to this dreadfu' catastrophe?'

'Mean you my brother?—he, too, is gone,' said the Earl.

'No,' replied the sibyl, 'I mean yoursell, Lord Geraldine. Had you not transgressed the obedience of a son by wedding Eveline Neville in secret while a guest at Knockwinnock, our plot might have separated you for a time, but would have left at least your sorrows without remorse to canker them—But your ain conduct had put poison in the weapon that we threw, and it pierced you with the mair force, because ye cam rushing to meet it. Had your marriage been a proclaimed and acknowledged action, our stratagem to throw an obstacle into your way that couldna be got ower, neither wad nor could hae been practised against ye.'

'Great Heaven!' said the unfortunate nobleman; 'it is as if a film fell from my obscured eyes!—Yes, I now well understand the doubtful hints of consolation thrown out by my wretched mother, tending indirectly to impeach the evidence of the horrors of which her arts had led me to believe myself guilty.'

'She could not speak mair plainly,' answered Elspeth, 'without confessing her ain fraud, and she would have submitted to be torn by wild horses, rather than unfold what she had done; and, if she had still lived, so would I for her sake. They were stout hearts the race of Glenallan, male and female, and sae were a' that in auld times cried their gathering-word of *Clochnaben*—they stood shouther to shouther—Nae man parted frae his chief for love of gold or of gain, or of right or of wrang.—The times are changed, I hear, now.'

The unfortunate nobleman was too much wrapped up in his own confused and distracting reflections to notice the rude expressions of savage fidelity, in which, even in the latest ebb of life, the unhappy author of his misfortunes seemed to find a stern and stubborn source of consolation.

'Great Heaven!' he exclaimed, 'I am then free from a guilt the most horrible with which man can be stained, and the sense of which, however involuntary, has wrecked my peace, destroyed my health, and bowed me down to an untimely grave. Accept,' he fervently uttered, lifting his eyes upwards, 'accept my humble thanks!—If I live miserable, at least I shall not die stained with that unnatural guilt!—And thou—proceed, if thou hast more to tell—proceed, while thou hast voice to speak it, and I have powers to listen.'

'Yes,' answered the beldam, 'the hour when you shall hear, and I shall speak, is indeed passing rapidly away—Death has crossed your brow with his finger, and I find his grasp turning every day caulder at my heart.—Interrupt me nae mair with exclamations and groans and accusations, but hear my tale to an end! And then—if ye be indeed sic a Lord of Glenallan as I hae heard of in *my* day—make your merrymen gather the thorn, and the brier, and the green hollin, till they heap them as high as the house-riggin', and burn! burn! burn! the auld witch Elspeth, and a' that can put ye in mind that sic a creature ever crawled upon the land!'

'Go on,' said the Earl, 'go on—I will not again interrupt you.'

He spoke in a half-suffocated yet determined voice, resolved that no irritability on his part should deprive him of this opportunity of acquiring proofs of the wonderful tale he then heard. But Elspeth had become exhausted by a continuous narration of such unusual length; the subsequent part of her story was more broken, and, though still distinctly intelligible in most parts, had no longer the lucid conciseness which the first part of her narrative had displayed to such an astonishing degree. Lord Glenallan found it necessary, when she had made some attempts to continue her narrative without success, to prompt her memory, by demanding, what proofs she could propose to bring of the truth of a narrative so different from that which she had originally told?

'The evidence,' she replied, 'of Eveline Neville's real birth was in the Countess's possession, with reasons for its being, for some time, kept private. They may yet be found, if she has not destroyed them, in the left-hand drawer of the ebony cabinet that stood in the dressing-room—these she meant to suppress for the time until you went abroad again, when she trusted, before your return, to send Miss Neville back to her ain country, or to get her settled in marriage.'

'But did you not show me letters of my father's, which seemed to me, unless my senses altogether failed me in that horrible moment, to avow his relationship to—to the unhappy'—

'We did; and, with my testimony, how could you doubt the fact, or her either?—But we suppressed the true explanation of these letters, and that was, that your father thought it right the young leddy should pass for his daughter for a while, on account o' some family reasons that were amang them.'

'But wherefore, when you learned our union, was this dreadful artifice persisted in?'

'It wasna,' she replied, 'till Lady Glenallan had communicated this fause tale that she suspected ye had actually made a marriage—nor even then did you avow it sae as to satisfy her, whether the ceremony had in verity passed atween ye or no—But ye remember, O ye canna but remember weel, what passed in that awfu' meeting!'

'Woman! you swore upon the gospels to the fact which you now disavow.'

'I did, and I wad hae taen a yet mair holy pledge on it, if there had been ane—I wad not hae spared the blood of my body, or the guilt of my soul, to serve the house of Glenallan.'

'Wretch! do you call that horried perjury, attended with consequences yet more dreadful—do you esteem that a service to the house of your benefactors?'

'I served her, wha was then the head of Glenallan, as she required me to serve her. The cause was between God and her conscience—the manner between God and mine—She is gane to her account, and I maun follow—Have I tauld you a'?'

'No,' answered Lord Glenallan; 'you have yet more to tell—you have to tell me of the death of the angel whom your perjury drove to despair, stained, as she thought herself, with a crime so horrible—Speak truth—was that dreadful—was that horrible incident'—he could scarcely articulate the words—'was it as reported? or was it an act of yet further, though not more atrocious cruelty, inflicted by others?'

'I understand you,' said Elspeth; 'but report spoke truth—our false witness was indeed the cause, but the deed was her ain distracted act—On that fearfu' disclosure, when ye rushed frae the Countess's presence, and saddled your horse, and left the castle like a fire-flaught, the Countess hadna yet discovered your private marriage; she hadna fund out that the union, which she had framed this awfu' tale to prevent, had e'en taen place. Ye fled from the house as if the fire o' Heaven was about to fa' upon it, and Miss Neville, atween reason and the want o't, was put under sure ward. But the ward sleep't, and the prisoner waked—the window was open—the way was before her—there was the cliff, and there was the sea!—O, when will I forget that!'

'And thus died,' said the Earl, 'even so as was reported?'

'No, my lord. I had gane out to the cove—the tide was in, and it flowed, as ye'll remember, to the foot of that cliff—it was a great convenience that for my husband's trade—Where am I wandering?—I saw a white object dart frae the tap o' the cliff like a sea-maw through the mist, and then a heavy flash and sparkle of the waters showed me it was a human creature that had fa'en into the waves. I was bold and strong, and familiar with the tide. I rushed in and grasped her gown, and drew her out and carried her on my shouthers—I could hae carried twa sic then—carried her to my hut, and laid her on my bed. Neighbours cam and brought help—but the words she uttered in her ravings, when she got back the use of speech, were such, that I was fain to send them awa, and get up word to Glenallan-house. The Countess sent down her Spanish servant Teresa—if ever there was a fiend on earth in human form, that woman was ane—She and I were to watch the unhappy leddy, and let no other person approach. God knows what Teresa's part was to hae been—she tauld it not to me—but Heaven took the conclusion in its ain hand. The poor leddy! she took the pangs of travail before her time, bore a male child, and died in the arms of me—of her mortal enemy! Ay, *ye* may weep—she was a sightly creature to see to—but think ye, if I didna mourn her then, that I can mourn her now?—Na, na!—I left Teresa wi' the dead corpse and new-born babe, till I gaed up to take the Countess's commands what was to be done. Late as it was, I ca'd her up, and she gar'd me ca' up your brother'—

'My brother?'

'Yes, Lord Geraldin, e'en your brother, that some said she aye wished to be her heir. At ony rate, he was the person maist concerned in the succession and heritance of the house of Glenallan.'

'And is it possible to believe, then, that my brother, out of avarice to grasp at my inheritance, would lend himself to such a base and dreadful stratagem?'

'Your mother believed it,' said the old beldam with a fiendish laugh—'it was nae plot of my making—but what they did or said I will not say, because I did not hear. Lang and sair they consulted in the black wainscot dressing-room; and when your brother passed through the room where I was waiting, it seemed to me (and I have often thought sae since syne) that the fire of hell was in his cheek and een. But he had left some of it with his mother at ony rate. She entered the room like a woman demented, and the first words she spoke were, "Elspeth Cheyne, did ye ever pull a new-budded flower?" I answered, as ye may believe, that I often had; "then," said she, "ye will ken the better how to blight the spurious and heretical blossom that has sprung forth this night to disgrace my father's noble house—See here;"—(and she gave me a golden bodkin)—-"Nothing but gold must shed the blood of Glenallan. This child is already as one of the dead, and since thou and Teresa alone ken that it lives, let it be dealt upon as ye will answer to me!" and she turned away in her fury, and left me with the bodkin in my hand. Here it is; that and the ring of Miss Neville are a' I hae preserved of my ill-gotten gear—for muckle was the gear I got. And weel hae I keepit the secret, but no for the gowd or gear either.'

Her long and bony hand held out to Lord Glenallan a gold bodkin, down which in fancy he saw the blood of his infant trickling.

'Wretch! had you the heart?'

'I kenna if I could hae had it or no. I returned to my cottage without feeling the ground that I trode on; but Teresa and the child were gane—a' that was alive was gane—naething left but the lifeless corpse.'

'And did you never learn my infant's fate?'

'I could but guess. I have tauld ye your mother's purpose, and I ken Teresa was a fiend. She was never mair seen in Scotland, and I have heard that she returned to her ain land. A dark curtain has fa'en ower the past, and the few that witnessed ony part of it could only surmise something of seduction and suicide. You yourself'—

'I know—I know it all,' answered the Earl.

'You indeed know all that I can say—And now, heir of Glenallan, can you forgive me?'

'Ask forgiveness of God, and not of man,' said the Earl, turning away.

'And how shall I ask of the pure and unstained what is denied to me by a sinner like mysell?—If I hae sinned, hae I not suffered?—Hae I had a day's peace or an hour's rest since these lang wet locks of hair first lay upon my pillow at Craigburnfoot?—Has not my house been burned, wi' my bairn in the cradle?—Have not my boats been wrecked, when a' others weathered the gale?—Have not a' that were near and dear to me dree'd penance for my sin?—Has not the fire had its share o' them—the winds had their part—the sea had her part?—And oh!' (she added, with a lengthened groan, looking first upwards towards heaven, and then bending her eyes on the floor)—'Oh! that the earth would take her part, that's been lang lang wearying to be joined to it!'

Lord Glenallan had reached the door of the cottage, but the generosity of his nature did not permit him to leave the unhappy woman in this state of desperate reprobation. 'May God forgive thee, wretched woman,' he said, 'as sincerely as I do!—turn for mercy to Him, who can alone grant mercy, and may your prayers be heard as if they were mine own!—I will send a religious man.'

'Na, na, nae priest! nae priest!' she ejaculated; and the door of the cottage opening as she spoke, prevented her from proceeding.

CHAPTER XXXIV

Still in his dead hand clench'd remain the strings
That thrill his father's heart—e'en as the limb,
Lopp'd off and laid in grave, retains, they tell us,
Strange commerce with the mutilated stump,
Whose nerves are twinging still in maim'd existence.

*Old Play.**

THE Antiquary, as we informed the reader in the end of the tenth chapter, had shaken off the company of worthy Mr Blattergowl, although he offered to entertain him with an abstract of the ablest speech he had ever known in the teind court, delivered by the procurator for the church* in the remarkable case of the parish of Gatherem. Resisting this temptation, our senior preferred a solitary path, which again conducted him to the cottage of Mucklebackit. When he came in front of the fisherman's hut, he observed a man working intently, as if to repair a shattered boat which lay upon the beach, and, going up to him, was surprised to find it was Mucklebackit himself. 'I am glad,' he said, in a tone of sympathy—'I am glad, Saunders, that you feel yourself able to make this exertion.'

'And what would ye have me to do,' answered the fisher gruffly, 'unless I wanted to see four children starve, because ane is drowned? It's weel wi' you gentles, that can sit in the house wi' handkerchers at your een when ye lose a friend; but the like o' us maun to our wark again, if our hearts were beating as hard as my hammer.'

Without taking more notice of Oldbuck he proceeded in his labour; and the Antiquary, to whom the display of human nature under the influence of agitating passions was never indifferent, stood beside him, in silent attention, as if watching the progress of the work. He observed more than once the man's hard features, as if by the force of association, prepare to accompany the sound of the saw and hammer with his usual symphony of a rude tune hummed or whistled, and as often a slight twitch of convulsive expression showed that, ere the sound was uttered, a cause for suppressing it rushed upon his mind. At length, when he had patched a considerable rent, and was beginning to mend another, his feelings appeared altogether to derange the power of attention necessary for his work.

The piece of wood which he was about to nail on was at first too long; then he sawed it off too short; then chose another equally ill adapted for the purpose. At length, throwing it down in anger, after wiping his dim eye with his quivering hand, he exclaimed, 'There is a curse either on me or on this auld black bitch of a boat, that I have hauled up high and dry, and patched and clouted sae mony years, that she might drown my poor Steenie at the end of them, an' be d—d to her!' and he flung his hammer against the boat, as if she had been the intentional cause of his misfortune. Then recollecting himself, he added, 'Yet what needs ane be angry at her, that has neither soul nor sense?—though I am no that muckle better mysell. She's but a rickle o' auld rotten deals nailed thegither, and warped wi' the wind and the sea—and I am a dour carle, battered by foul weather at sea and land till I am maist as senseless as hersell. She maun be mended though again' the morning tide—that's a thing o' necessity.'

Thus speaking, he went to gather together his instruments and attempt to resume his labour, but Oldbuck took him kindly by the arm. 'Come, come,' he said, 'Saunders, there is no work for you this day—I'll send down Shavings the carpenter to mend the boat, and he may put the day's work into my account—and you had better not come out tomorrow, but stay to comfort your family under this dispensation, and the gardener will bring you some vegetables and meal from Monkbarns.'

'I thank ye, Monkbarns,' answered the poor fisher; 'I am a plain-spoken man, and hae little to say for mysell; I might hae learned fairer fashions frae my mither lang syne, but I never saw muckle gude they did her; however, I thank ye. Ye were aye kind and neighbourly, whatever folk says o' your being near and close; and I hae often said in thae times when they were ganging to raise up the puir folk against the gentles—I hae often said, ne'er a man should steer a hair touching to Monkbarns while Steenie and I could wag a finger—and so said Steenie too. And, Monkbarns, when ye laid his head in the grave, (and mony thanks for the respect,) ye saw the mouls laid on an honest lad that likit you weel, though he made little phrase about it.'

Oldbuck, beaten from the pride of his affected cynicism, would not willingly have had any one by upon that occasion to quote to him his favourite maxims of the Stoic philosophy.* The large drops fell fast from his own eyes, as he begged the father, who was now melted at recollecting the bravery and generous sentiments of his son, to forbear useless sorrow, and led him by the arm towards his own home, where another scene awaited our Antiquary. As he entered, the first person whom he beheld was Lord Glenallan.

Mutual surprise was in their countenances as they saluted each other, with haughty reserve on the part of Mr Oldbuck, and embarrassment on that of the Earl.

'My Lord Glenallan, I think?' said Mr Oldbuck.

'Yes—much changed from what he was when he knew Mr Oldbuck.'

'I do not mean,' said the Antiquary, 'to intrude upon your lordship—I only came to see this distressed family.'

'And you have found one, sir, who has still greater claims on your compassion.'

'My compassion? Lord Glenallan cannot need *my* compassion—if Lord Glenallan could need it, I think he would hardly ask it.'

'Our former acquaintance,' said the Earl—

'Is of such ancient date, my lord—was of such short duration, and was connected with circumstances so exquisitely painful, that I think we may dispense with renewing it.'

So saying, the Antiquary turned away, and left the hut; but Lord Glenallan followed him into the open air, and, in spite of a hasty 'Good morning, my lord,' requested a few minutes' conversation, and the favour of his advice in an important matter.

'Your lordship will find many more capable to advise you, my lord, and by whom your intercourse will be deemed an honour. For me, I am a man retired from business and the world, and not very fond of raking up the past events of my useless life; and forgive me if I say, I have particular pain in reverting to that period of it when I acted like a fool, and your lordship like'—He stopped short.

'Like a villain, you would say,' said Lord Glenallan, 'for such I must have appeared to you.'

'My lord—my lord, I have no desire to hear your shrift,' said the Antiquary.

'But, sir, if I can show you that I am more sinned against than sinning*—that I have been a man miserable beyond the power of description, and who looks forward at this moment to an untimely grave as to a haven of rest, you will not refuse the confidence which, accepting your appearance at this critical moment as a hint from Heaven, I venture thus to press on you.'

'Assuredly, my lord, I shall shun no longer the continuation of this extraordinary interview.'

'I must then recall to you our occasional meetings upwards of twenty years since at Knockwinnock Castle, and I need not remind you of a lady who was then a member of that family.'

'The unfortunate Miss Eveline Neville, my lord—I remember it well.'

'Towards whom you entertained sentiments'—

'Very different from those with which I before and since have regarded her sex; her gentleness, her docility, her pleasure in the studies which I pointed out to her, attached my affections more than became my age, (though that was not then much advanced,) or the solidity of my character. But I need not remind your lordship of the various modes in which you indulged your gaiety at the expense of an awkward and retired student, embarrassed by the expression of feelings so new to him, and I have no doubt that the young lady joined you in the well-deserved ridicule—It is the way of womankind. I have spoken at once to the painful circumstances of my addresses and their rejection, that your lordship may be satisfied every thing is full in my memory, and may, so far as I am concerned, tell your story without scruple or needless delicacy.'

'I will,' said Lord Glenallan; 'but first let me say, you do injustice to the memory of the gentlest and kindest, as well as to the most unhappy of women, to suppose she could make a jest of the honest affection of a man like you. Frequently did she blame me, Mr Oldbuck, for indulging my levity at your expense—may I now presume you will excuse the gay freedoms which then offended you?—my state of mind has never since laid me under the necessity of apologizing for the inadvertencies of a light and happy temper.'

'My lord, you are fully pardoned,' said Mr Oldbuck. 'You should be aware, that, like all others, I was ignorant at the time that I placed myself in competition with your lordship, and understood that Miss Neville was in a state of dependence which might make her prefer a competent independence and the hand of an honest man—But I am wasting time—I would I could believe that the views entertained towards her by others were as fair and honest as mine!'

'Mr Oldbuck, you judge harshly.'

'Not without cause, my lord. When I only, of all the magistrates of this county, having neither, like some of them, the honour to be connected with your powerful family, nor, like others, the meanness to fear it—when I made some enquiry into the manner of Miss Neville's death—I shake you, my lord, but I must be plain—I do own I had every reason to believe that she had met most unfair dealing, and had either been imposed upon by a counterfeit marriage, or that very strong measures had been adopted to stifle and destroy the evidence of a real union. And I cannot doubt in my own mind, that this cruelty on your lordship's part, whether coming of your own free will, or proceeding from the influence of the late Countess, hurried the unfortunate young lady to the desperate act by which her life was terminated.'

'You are deceived, Mr Oldbuck, into conclusions which are not just, however naturally they flow from the circumstances. Believe me, I respected you even when I was most embarrassed by your active attempts to investigate our family misfortunes. You showed yourself more worthy of Miss Neville than I, by the spirit with which you persisted in vindicating her reputation even after her death. But the firm belief, that your well-meant efforts could only serve to bring to light a story too horrible to be detailed, induced me to join my unhappy mother in schemes to remove or destroy all evidence of the legal union which had taken place between Eveline and myself. And now let us sit down on this bank, for I feel unable to remain longer standing, and have the goodness to listen to the extraordinary discovery which I have this day made.'

They sate down accordingly; and Lord Glenallan briefly narrated his unhappy family history—his concealed marriage—the horrible invention by which his mother had designed to render impossible that union which had already taken place. He detailed the arts by which the Countess, having all the documents relative to Miss Neville's birth in her hands, had produced those only relating to a period during which, for family reasons, his father had consented to own that young lady as his natural daughter, and showed how impossible it was that he could either suspect or detect the fraud put upon him by his mother, and vouched by the oaths of her attendants, Teresa and Elspeth. 'I left my paternal mansion,' he concluded, 'as if the furies of hell had driven me forth, and travelled with frantic velocity I knew not whither. Nor have I the slightest recollection of what I did or whither I went, until I was discovered by my brother. I will not trouble you with an account of my sick-bed and recovery, or how, long afterwards, I ventured to enquire after the sharer of my misfortunes, and heard that her despair had found a dreadful remedy for all the ills of life. The first thing that roused me to thought was hearing of your enquiries into this cruel business; and you will hardly wonder, that, believing what I did believe, I should join in those expedients to stop your investigation, which my brother and mother had actively commenced. The information which I gave them concerning the circumstances and witnesses of our private marriage enabled them to baffle your zeal. The clergyman, therefore, and witnesses, as persons who had acted in the matter only to please the powerful heir of Glenallan, were accessible to his promises and threats, and were so provided for, that they had no objections to leave this country for another. For myself, Mr Oldbuck,' pursued this unhappy man, 'from that moment I considered myself as blotted out of the book of the living,* and as having nothing left to do with this world. My mother tried to reconcile me to life by every art—even by intimations which I can now interpret as calculated to produce a doubt of the horrible tale she herself had fabricated. But I construed all she said as the fictions of maternal affection.—I will forbear all reproach—she is no more—and, as her wretched associate said, she knew not how the dart was poisoned, or how deep it must sink, when she threw it from her hand. But, Mr Oldbuck, if ever, during these twenty years, there crawled upon earth a living being deserving of your pity, I have been that man. My food has not nourished me—my sleep has not refreshed me—my devotions have not comforted me—all that is cheering and necessary to man has been to me converted into poison. The rare and limited intercourse which I have held with others has been most odious to me. I felt as if I were bringing the contamination of unnatural and inexpressible guilt among the gay and the innocent. There have been moments when I had thoughts of another description—to plunge into the adventures of war, or to brave the dangers of the traveller in foreign and barbarous climates—to mingle in political intrigue, or to retire to the stern seclusion of the anchorites of our religion—All these are thoughts which have alternately passed through my mind, but each required an energy, which was mine no longer after the withering stroke I had received. I vegetated on as I could in the same spot,—fancy, feeling, judgment, and health, gradually decaying, like a tree whose bark has been destroyed,—when first the blossoms fade, then the boughs, until its state resembles the decayed and dying trunk that is now before you. Do you now pity and forgive me?'

'My lord,' answered the Antiquary, much affected, 'my pity—my forgiveness, you have not to ask, for your dismal story is of itself not only an ample excuse for whatever appeared mysterious in your conduct, but a narrative that might move your worst enemies (and I, my lord, was never of the number) to tears and to sympathy. But permit me to ask what you now mean to do, and why you have honoured me, whose opinion can be of little consequence, with your confidence on this occasion?'

'Mr Oldbuck,' answered the Earl, 'as I could never have foreseen the nature of that confession which I have heard this day, I need not say, that I had no formed plan of consulting you or any one upon affairs, the tendency of which I could not even have suspected. But I am without friends, unused to business, and, by long retirement, unacquainted alike with the laws of the land and the habits of the living generation; and when, most unexpectedly, I find myself immersed in the matters of which I know least, I catch, like a drowning man, at the first support that offers. You are that support, Mr Oldbuck. I have always heard you mentioned as a man of wisdom and intelligence—I have known you myself as a man of a resolute and independent spirit—and there is one circumstance,' said he, 'which ought to combine us in some degree—our having paid tribute to the same excellence of character in poor Eveline. You offered yourself to me in my need, and you were already acquainted with the beginning of my misfortunes. To you, therefore, I have recourse for advice, for sympathy, for support.'

'You shall seek none of them in vain, my lord,' said Oldbuck, 'so far as my slender ability extends; and I am honoured by the preference, whether it arises from choice or is prompted by chance. But this is a matter to be ripely considered. May I ask what are your principal views at present?'

'To ascertain the fate of my child,' said the Earl, 'be the consequences what they may, and to do justice to the honour of Eveline, which I have only permitted to be suspected to avoid discovery of the yet more horrible taint to which I was made to believe it liable.'

'And the memory of your mother?'

'Must bear its own burden,' answered the Earl, with a sigh; 'better that she were justly convicted of deceit, should that be found necessary, than that others should be unjustly accused of crimes so much more dreadful.'

'Then, my lord,' said Oldbuck, 'our first business must be to put the information of the old woman, Elspeth, into a regular and authenticated form.'

'That,' said Lord Glenallan, 'will be at present, I fear, impossible—She is exhausted herself, and surrounded by her distressed family. Tomorrow, perhaps, when she is alone—and yet I doubt, from her imperfect sense of right and wrong, whether she would speak out in any one's presence but my own—I too am sorely fatigued.'

'Then, my lord,' said the Antiquary, whom the interest of the moment elevated above points of expense and convenience, which had generally more than enough of weight with him, 'I would propose to your lordship, instead of returning, fatigued as you are, so far as to Glenallan-house, or taking the more uncomfortable alternative of going to a bad inn at Fairport, to alarm all the busy bodies of the town—I would propose, I say, that you should be my guest at Monkbarns for this night—By tomorrow these poor people will have renewed their out-of-doors vocation, for sorrow with them affords no respite from labour, and we will visit the old woman, Elspeth, alone, and take down her examination.'

After a formal apology for the encroachment, Lord Glenallan agreed to go with him, and underwent with patience in their return home the whole history of John of the Girnell, a legend which Mr Oldbuck was never known to spare any one who crossed his threshold.

The arrival of a stranger of such note, with two saddle horses and a servant in black, which servant had holsters on his saddle-bow, and a coronet upon the holsters, created a general commotion in the house of Monkbarns. Jenny Rintherout, scarce recovered from the hysterics which she had taken on hearing of poor Steenie's misfortune, chased about the turkeys and poultry, cackled and screamed louder than they did, and ended by killing one-half too many. Miss Griselda made many wise reflections on the hot-headed wilfulness of her brother, who had occasioned such a devastation, by suddenly bringing in upon them a papist nobleman. And she ventured to transmit to Mr Blattergowl some hint of the unusual slaughter which had taken place in the *basse-cour*, which brought the honest clergyman to enquire how his friend Monkbarns had got home, and whether he was not the worse of being at the funeral, at a period so near the ringing of the bell for dinner, that the Antiquary had no choice left but to invite him to stay and bless the meat. Miss M'Intyre had on her part some curiosity to see this mighty peer, of whom all had heard, as an Eastern caliph or sultan is heard of by his subjects, and felt some degree of timidity at the idea of encountering a person, of whose unsocial habits and stern manners so many stories were told, that her fear kept at least pace with her curiosity. The aged housekeeper was no less flustered and hurried in obeying the numerous and contradictory commands of her mistress, concerning preserves, pastry, and fruit, the mode of marshalling and dishing the dinner, the necessity of not permitting the melted butter to run to oil, and the danger of allowing Juno—who, though formally banished from the parlour, failed not to maraud about the out-settlements of the family—to enter the kitchen.

The only inmate of Monkbarns who remained entirely indifferent on this momentous occasion was Hector M'Intyre, who cared no more for an Earl than he did for a commoner, and who was only interested in the unexpected visit, as it might afford some protection against his uncle's displeasure, if he harboured any, for his not attending the funeral, and still more against his satire upon the subject of his gallant but unsuccessful single combat with the phoca, or seal.

To these, the inmates of his household, Oldbuck presented the Earl of Glenallan, who underwent, with meek and subdued civility, the prosing speeches of the honest divine, and the lengthened apologies of Miss Griselda Oldbuck, which her brother in vain endeavoured to abridge. Before the dinner hour, Lord Glenallan requested permission to retire a while to his chamber. Mr Oldbuck accompanied his guest to the Green Room, which had been hastily prepared for his reception. He looked around with an air of painful recollection.

'I think,' at length he observed, 'I think, Mr Oldbuck, that I have been in this apartment before.'

'Yes, my lord,' answered Oldbuck, 'upon occasion of an excursion hither from Knockwinnock—and since we are upon a subject so melancholy, you may perhaps remember whose taste supplied these lines from Chaucer, which now form the motto of the tapestry.'

'I guess,' said the Earl, 'though I cannot recollect—She excelled me, indeed, in literary taste and information, as in every thing else, and it is one of the mysterious dispensations of Providence, Mr Oldbuck, that a creature so excellent in mind and body should have been cut off in so miserable a manner, merely from her having formed a fatal attachment to such a wretch as I am.'

Mr Oldbuck did not attempt an answer to this burst of the grief which lay ever nearest to the heart of his guest, but, pressing Lord Glenallan's hand with one of his own, and drawing the other across his shaggy eyelashes, as if to brush away a mist that intercepted his sight, he left the Earl at liberty to arrange himself previous to dinner.

CHAPTER XXXV

————————Life, with you,
Glows in the brain and dances in the arteries;
'Tis like the wine some joyous guest hath quaff'd,
That glads the heart and elevates the fancy:—
Mine is the poor residuum of the cup,
Vapid, and dull, and tasteless, only soiling,
With its base dregs, the vessel that contains it.

*Old Play.**

'Now only think what a man my brother is, Mr Blattergowl, for a wise man and a learned man, to bring this Yerl into our house without speaking a single word to a body!—And there's the distress of thae Mucklebackits—we canna get a fin o' fish—and we hae nae time to send ower to Fairport for beef, and the mutton's but new killed—and that silly fliskmahoy, Jenny Rintherout, has taen the exies, and done naething but laugh and greet, the skirl at the tail o' the guffá, for twa days successively—and now we maun ask that strange man, that's as grand and as grave as the Yerl himsel, to stand at the sideboard! And I canna gang into the kitchen to direct ony thing, for he's hovering there making some pousowdie[20] for my lord, for he doesna eat like ither folk neither—And how to sort the strange servant man at dinner time—I am sure, Mr Blattergowl, a'thegither, it passes my judgment.'

'Truly, Miss Griselda,' replied the divine, 'Monkbarns was inconsiderate. He should have taen a day to see the invitation, as they do wi' the titular's condescendence in the process of valuation and sale.*—But the great man could not have come on a sudden to ony house in this parish where he could have been better served with *vivers*—that I must say—and also that the steam from the kitchen is very gratifying to my nostrils—and if ye have ony household affairs to attend to, Mrs Griselda, never make a stranger of me—I can amuse myself very weel with the larger copy of Erskine's Institutes.'*

And taking down from the window seat that amusing folio, (the Scottish Coke upon Littleton,*) he opened it, as if instinctively, at the tenth title of Book Second, 'of Teinds, or Tythes,' and was presently deeply wrapped up in an abstruse discussion concerning the temporality of benefices.

The entertainment, about which Miss Oldbuck expressed so much anxiety, was at length placed upon the table; and the Earl of Glenallan, for the first time since the date of his calamity, sat at a stranger's board surrounded by strangers. He seemed to himself like a man in a dream, or one whose brain was not fully recovered from the effects of an intoxicating potion. Relieved, as he had that morning been, from the image of guilt which had so long haunted his imagination, he felt his sorrows as a lighter and more tolerable load, but was still unable to take any share in the conversation that passed around him. It was, indeed, of a cast very different from that which he had been accustomed to. The bluntness of Oldbuck, the tiresome apologetic harangues of his sister, the pedantry of the divine, and the vivacity of the young soldier, which savoured much more of the camp than of the court, were all new to a nobleman who had lived in a retired and melancholy state for so many years, that the manners of the world seemed to him equally strange and unpleasing. Miss M'Intyre alone, from the natural politeness and unpretending simplicity of her manners, appeared to belong to that class of society to which he had been accustomed in his earlier and better days.

Nor did Lord Glenallan's deportment less surprise the company. Though a plain but excellent family-dinner was provided, (for, as Mr Blattergowl had justly said, it was impossible to surprise Miss Griselda when her larder was empty,) and though the Antiquary boasted his best port, and assimilated it to the Falernian of Horace, Lord Glenallan was proof to the allurements of both. His servant placed before him a small mess of vegetables, that very dish, the cooking of which had alarmed Miss Griselda, arranged with the most minute and scrupulous neatness. He eat sparingly of these provisions; and a glass of pure water, sparkling from the fountain head, completed his repast. Such, his servant said, had been his lordship's diet for very many years, unless upon the high festivals of the Church, or when company of the first rank were entertained at Glenallan-house, when he relaxed a little in the austerity of his diet, and permitted himself a glass or two of wine. But at Monkbarns, no anchoret could have made a more simple and scanty meal.

The Antiquary was a gentleman, as we have seen, in feeling, but blunt and careless in expression, from the habit of living with those before whom he had nothing to suppress. He attacked his noble guest without scruple on the severity of his regimen.

'A few half-cold greens and potatoes—a glass of ice-cold water to wash them down—antiquity gives no warrant for it, my lord. This house used to be accounted a *hospitium*, a place of retreat for Christians; but your lordship's diet is that of a heathen Pythagorean, or Indian Bramin*—nay, more severe than either, if you refuse these fine apples.'

'I am a Catholic, you are aware,' said Lord Glenallan, wishing to escape from the discussion, 'and you know that our church'—

'Lays down many rules of mortification,' proceeded the dauntless Antiquary; 'but I never heard that they were quite so rigorously practised—Bear witness my predecessor, John of the Girnell, or the jolly Abbot, who gave his name to this apple, my lord.'

And as he pared the fruit, in spite of his sister's 'O fie, Monkbarns,' and the prolonged cough of the minister, accompanied by a shake of his huge wig, the Antiquary proceeded to detail the intrigue which had given rise to the fame of the abbot's apple with more slyness and circumstantiality than was at all necessary. His jest (as may readily be conceived) missed fire, for this anecdote of conventual gallantry failed to produce the slightest smile on the visage of the Earl. Oldbuck then took up the subject of Ossian, Macpherson, and Mac-Cribb; but Lord Glenallan had never so much as heard of any of the three, so little conversant had he been with modern literature. The conversation was now in some danger of flagging, or of falling into the hands of Mr Blattergowl, who had just pronounced the formidable word, 'teind-free,' when the subject of the French Revolution was started; a political event on which Lord Glenallan looked with all the prejudiced horror of a bigoted Catholic and zealous aristocrat. Oldbuck was far from carrying his detestation of its principles to such a length.

'There were many men in the first Constituent Assembly,'* he said, 'who held sound Whiggish doctrines, and were for settling the Constitution with a proper provision for the liberties of the people. And if a set of furious madmen were now in possession of the government, it was,' he continued, 'what often happened in great revolutions, where extreme measures are adopted in the fury of the moment, and the state resembles an agitated pendulum which swings from side to side for some time ere it can acquire its due and perpendicular station. Or it might be likened to a storm or hurricane, which, passing over a region, does great damage in its passage, yet sweeps away stagnant and unwholesome vapours, and repays, in future health and fertility, its immediate desolation and ravage.'

The Earl shook his head; but having neither spirit nor inclination for debate, he suffered the argument to pass uncontested.

This discussion served to introduce the young soldier's experiences; and he spoke of the actions in which he had been engaged with modesty, and, at the same time, with an air of spirit and zeal which delighted the Earl, who had been bred up, like others of his house, in the opinion, that the trade of arms was the first duty of man, and believed that to employ them against the French was a sort of holy warfare.

'What would I give,' said he apart to Oldbuck, as they rose to join the ladies in the drawing-room, 'what would I give to have a son of such spirit as that young gentleman!—He wants something of address and manner, something of polish, which mixing in good society would soon give him—but with what zeal and animation he expresses himself—how fond of his profession—how loud in the praise of others—how modest when speaking of himself!'

'Hector is much obliged to you, my lord,' replied his uncle, gratified, yet not so much so as to suppress his consciousness of his own mental superiority over the young soldier; 'I believe in my heart nobody ever spoke half so much good of him before, except perhaps the sergeant of his company, when he was wheedling a Highland recruit to enlist with him. He is a good lad notwithstanding, although he be not quite the hero your lordship supposes him, and although my commendations rather attest the kindness, than the vivacity of his character. In fact, his high spirit is a sort of constitutional vehemence, which attends him in every thing he sets about, and is often very inconvenient to his friends. I saw him today engage in an animated contest with a *phoca*, or seal, (*sealgh*, our people more properly call them, retaining the Gothic guttural *gh*,) with as much vehemence as if he had fought against Dumourier*—Marry, my lord, the *phoca* had the better, as the said Dumourier had of some other folks. And he'll talk with equal if not superior rapture of the good behaviour of a pointer bitch, as of the plan of a campaign.'

'He shall have full permission to sport over my grounds,' said the Earl, 'if he is so fond of that exercise.'

'You will bind him to you, my lord,' said Monkbarns, 'body and soul; give him leave to crack off his birding-piece at a poor covey of partridges or moor-fowl, and he's yours for ever. I will enchant him by the intelligence. But O, my lord, that you could have seen my phœnix Lovel!—the very prince and chieftain of the youth of this age; and not destitute of spirit neither—I promise you he gave my termagant kinsman a *quid pro quo**—a Rowland for his Oliver,* as the vulgar say, alluding to the two celebrated Paladins of Charlemagne.'*

After coffee, Lord Glenallan requested a private interview with the Antiquary, and was ushered to his library.

'I must withdraw you from your own amiable family,' he said, 'to involve you in the perplexities of an unhappy man. You are acquainted with the world, from which I have long been banished; for Glenallan-house has been to me rather a prison than a dwelling, although a prison which I had neither fortitude nor spirit to break from.'

'Let me first ask your lordship,' said the Antiquary, 'what are your own wishes and designs in this matter?'

'I wish most especially,' answered Lord Glenallan, 'to declare my luckless marriage, and to vindicate the reputation of the unhappy Eveline; that is, if you see a possibility of doing so without making public the conduct of my mother.'

'*Suum cuique tribuito*,'* said the Antiquary, 'do right to every one. The memory of that unhappy young lady has too long suffered, and I think it might be cleared without further impeaching that of your mother, than by letting it be understood in general that she greatly disapproved and bitterly opposed the match. All—forgive me, my lord—all who ever heard of the late Countess of Glenallan, will learn that without much surprise.'

'But you forget one horrible circumstance, Mr Oldbuck,' said the Earl, in an agitated voice.

'I am not aware of it,' replied the Antiquary.

'The fate of the infant—its disappearance with the confidential attendant of my mother, and the dreadful surmises which may be drawn from my conversation with Elspeth.'

'If you would have my free opinion, my lord,' answered Mr Oldbuck, 'and will not catch too rapidly at it as matter of hope, I would say, that it is very possible the child yet lives. For thus much I ascertained, by my former enquiries concerning the event of that deplorable evening, that a child and woman were carried that night from the cottage at the Craigburnfoot in a carriage and four by your brother Edward Geraldin Neville, whose journey towards England with these companions I traced for several stages. I believed then it was a part of the family compact to carry a child whom you meant to stigmatize with illegitimacy, out of that country, where chance might have raised protectors and proofs of its rights. But I now think that your brother, having reason, like yourself, to believe the child stained with shame yet more indelible, had nevertheless withdrawn it, partly from regard to the honour of his house, partly from the risk to which it might have been exposed in the neighbourhood of the Lady Glenallan.'

As he spoke, the Earl of Glenallan grew extremely pale, and had nearly fallen from his chair. The alarmed Antiquary ran hither and thither looking for remedies; but his museum, though sufficiently well filled with a vast variety of useless matters, contained nothing that could be serviceable on the present or any other occasion. As he posted out of the room to borrow his sister's salts, he could not help giving a constitutional growl of chagrin and wonder at the various incidents which had converted his mansion, first into an hospital for a wounded duellist, and now into the sick chamber of a dying nobleman. 'And yet,' said he, 'I have always kept aloof from the soldiery and the peerage. My *cœnobitium* has only next to be made a lying-in hospital,* and then, I trow, the transformation will be complete.'

When he returned with the remedy, Lord Glenallan was much better. The new and unexpected light which Mr Oldbuck had thrown upon the melancholy history of his family had almost over-powered him. 'You think, then, Mr Oldbuck,—for you are capable of thinking, which I am not,—you think, then, that it is possible—that is, not impossible—my child may yet live?'

'I think,' said the Antiquary, 'it is impossible that it could come to any violent harm through your brother's means. He was known to be a gay and dissipated man, but not cruel nor dishonourable,—nor is it possible, that, if he had intended any foul play, he would have placed himself so forward in the charge of the infant, as I will prove to your lordship he did.'

So saying, Mr Oldbuck opened a drawer of the cabinet of his ancestor, Aldobrand, and produced a bundle of papers tied with a black ribband, and labelled, Examinations, &c. taken by Jonathan Oldbuck, J. P. upon the 18th of February, 17—; a little under was written, in a small hand, *Eheu Evelina!** The tears dropped fast from the Earl's eyes, as he endeavoured, in vain, to unfasten the knot which secured these documents.

'Your lordship,' said Mr Oldbuck, 'had better not read these at present. Agitated as you are, and having much business before you, you must not exhaust your strength. Your brother's succession is now, I presume, your own, and it will be easy for you to make enquiry among his servants and retainers, so as to hear where the child is, if, fortunately, it shall be still alive.'

'I dare hardly hope it,' said the Earl, with a deep sigh,—'why should my brother have been silent to me?'

'Nay, my lord! why should he have communicated to your lordship the existence of a being, whom you must have supposed the offspring of'—

'Most true—there is an obvious and a kind reason for his being silent. If any thing, indeed, could have added to the horror of the ghastly dream that has poisoned my whole existence, it must have been the knowledge that such a child of misery existed.'

'Then,' continued the Antiquary, 'although it would be rash to conclude, at the distance of more than twenty years, that your son must needs be still alive, because he was not destroyed in infancy, I own I think you should instantly set on foot enquiries.'

'It shall be done,' replied Lord Glenallan, catching eagerly at the hope held out to him, the first he had nourished for many years; 'I will write to a faithful steward of my father, who acted in the same capacity under my brother Neville—but, Mr Oldbuck, I am not my brother's heir.'

'Indeed!—I am sorry for that, my lord—it is a noble estate, and the ruins of the old castle of Neville's-Burgh alone, which are the most superb relics of Anglo-Norman architecture in that part of the country, are a possession much to be coveted. I thought your father had no other son or near relative.'

'He had not, Mr Oldbuck,' replied Lord Glenallan; 'but my brother adopted views in politics, and a form of religion, alien from those which had been always held by our house. Our tempers had long differed, nor did my unhappy mother always think him sufficiently observant to her. In short, there was a family quarrel, and my brother, whose property was at his own free disposal, availed himself of the power vested in him to choose a stranger for his heir. It is a matter which never struck me as being of the least consequence; for, if worldly possessions could alleviate misery, I have enough and to spare. But now I shall regret it, if it throws any difficulty in the way of our enquiries—and I bethink me that it may; for, in case of my having a lawful son of my body, and my brother dying without issue, my father's possessions stood entailed upon my son. It is not, therefore, likely that this heir, be who he may, will afford us assistance in making a discovery which may turn out so much to his own prejudice.'*

'And in all probability the steward your lordship mentions is also in his service,' said the Antiquary.

'It is most likely; and the man being a Protestant—how far it is safe to intrust him'—

'I should hope, my lord,' said Oldbuck, gravely, 'that a Protestant may be as trustworthy as a Catholic. I am doubly interested in the Protestant faith, my lord. My ancestor, Aldobrand Oldenbuck, printed the celebrated Confession of Augsburg, as I can show by the original edition now in this house.'

'I have not the least doubt of what you say, Mr Oldbuck,' replied the Earl, 'nor do I speak out of bigotry or intolerance; but probably the Protestant steward will favour the Protestant heir rather than the Catholic—if, indeed, my son has been bred in his father's faith—or, alas! if indeed he yet lives.'

'We must look close into this,' said Oldbuck, 'before committing ourselves. I have a literary friend at York, with whom I have long corresponded on the subject of the Saxon horn that is preserved in the Minster* there; we interchanged letters for six years, and have only as yet been able to settle the first line of the inscription. I will write forthwith to this gentleman, Dr Dryasdust,* and be particular in my enquiries concerning the character, &c. of your brother's heir, of the gentleman employed in his affairs, and what else may be likely to further your lordship's enquiries. In the meantime your lordship will collect the evidence of the marriage, which I hope can still be recovered?'

'Unquestionably,' replied the Earl; 'the witnesses who were formerly withdrawn from your research are still living. My tutor, who solemnized the marriage, was provided for by a living in France, and has lately returned to this country as an emigrant,* a victim of his zeal for loyalty, legitimacy, and religion.'

'That's one lucky consequence of the French Revolution, my lord—you must allow that, at least,' said Oldbuck; 'but no offence, I will act as warmly in your affairs as if I were of your own faith in politics and religion. And take my advice—If you want an affair of consequence properly managed, put it into the hands of an antiquary; for, as they are eternally exercising their genius and research upon trifles, it is impossible they can be baffled in affairs of importance—use makes perfect; and the corps that is most frequently drilled upon the parade, will be most prompt in its exercise upon the day of battle. And, talking upon that subject, I would willingly read to your lordship, in order to pass away the time betwixt and supper'—

'I beg I may not interfere with family arrangements,' said Lord Glenallan, 'but I never taste any thing after sunset.'

'Nor I either, my lord,' answered his host, 'notwithstanding it is said to have been the custom of the ancients—but then I dine differently from your lordship, and therefore am better enabled to dispense with those elaborate entertainments which my womankind (that is, my sister and niece, my lord) are apt to place on the table, for the display rather of their own housewifery than the accommodation of our wants. However, a broiled bone, or a smoked haddock, or an oyster, or a slice of bacon of our own curing, with a toast and a tankard—or something or other of that sort, to close the orifice of the stomach before going to bed, does not fall under my restriction, nor, I hope, under your lordship's.'

'My no-supper is literal, Mr Oldbuck; but I will attend you at your meal with pleasure.'

'Well, my lord,' replied the Antiquary, 'I will endeavour to entertain your ears at least, since I cannot banquet your palate. What I am about to read to your lordship relates to the upland glens.'

Lord Glenallan, though he would rather have recurred to the subject of his own uncertainties, was compelled to make a sign of rueful civility and acquiescence.

The Antiquary, therefore, took out his portfolio of loose sheets, and, after premising that the topographical details here laid down were designed to illustrate a slight essay upon castrametation, which had been read with indulgence at several societies of Antiquaries, he commenced as follows: 'The subject, my lord, is the hill-fort of Quickens-bog, with the site of which your lordship is doubtless familiar: It is upon your store-farm of Mantanner, in the barony of Clochnaben.'

'I think I have heard the names of these places,' said the Earl, in answer to the Antiquary's appeal.

'Heard the name? and the farm brings him six hundred a-year—O Lord!'

Such was the scarce subdued ejaculation of the Antiquary. But his hospitality got the better of his surprise, and he proceeded to read his essay with an audible voice, in great glee at having secured a patient, and, as he fondly hoped, an interested hearer.

'Quickens-bog may at first seem to derive its name from the plant *Quicken*, by which, *Scottice*, we understand couch-grass, dog-grass, or the *Triticum repens* of Linnæus;* and the common English monosyllable *Bog*, by which we mean, in popular language, a marsh or morass; in Latin, *Palus*. But it may confound the rash adopters of the more obvious etymological derivations, to learn, that the couch-grass or dog-grass, or, to speak scientifically, the *triticum repens* of Linnæus, does not grow within a quarter of a mile of this castrum or hill-fort, whose ramparts are uniformly clothed with short verdant turf; and that we must seek a bog or *palus* at a still greater distance, the nearest being that of Gird-the-mear, a full half-mile distant. The last syllable, *bog*, is obviously, therefore, a mere corruption of the Saxon *Burgh*, which we find in the various transmutations of *Burgh*, *Burrow*, *Brough*, *Bruff*, *Buff*, and *Boff*, which last approaches very near the sound in question—since, supposing the word to have been originally *borgh*, which is the genuine Saxon spelling, a slight change, such as modern organs too often make upon ancient sounds, will produce first *Bogh*, and then, *elisa H*,* or compromising and sinking the guttural, agreeable to the common vernacular practice, you have either *Boff* or *Bog* as it happens. The word *Quickens* requires in like manner to be altered,—decomposed, as it were,—and reduced to its original and genuine sound, ere we can discern its real meaning. By the ordinary exchange of the *Qu* into *Wh*, familiar to the rudest *tyro* who has opened a book of old Scottish poetry, we gain either Whilkens, or Whichens-borgh—put, we may suppose, by way of question, as if those who imposed the name, struck with the extreme antiquity of the place, had expressed in it an interrogation, "To whom did this fortress belong?"—Or, it might be *Whackens-burgh*, from the Saxon *Whacken*, to strike with the hand, as doubtless the skirmishes near a place of such apparent consequence must have legitimated such a derivation,' &c. &c. &c.

I will be more merciful to my readers than Oldbuck was to his guest; for, considering his opportunities of gaining patient attention from a person of such consequence as Lord Glenallan were not many, he used, or rather abused, the present to the uttermost.

CHAPTER XXXVI

Crabbed age and youth
   Cannot live together:—
Youth is full of pleasance,
   Age is full of care;
Youth like summer morn,
   Age like winter weather,
Youth like summer brave,
   Age like winter bare.

SHAKSPEARE.*

IN the morning of the following day, the Antiquary, who was something of a sluggard, was summoned from his bed a full hour earlier than his custom by Caxon.

'What's the matter now?' he exclaimed, yawning and stretching forth his hand to the huge gold repeater, which, bedded upon his India silk handkerchief, was laid safe by his pillow—'What's the matter now, Caxon?—it can't be eight o'clock yet.'

'Na, sir,—but my lord's man sought me out, for he fancies me your honour's valley-de-sham,—and sae I am, there's nae doubt o't, baith your honour's and the minister's—at least ye hae nae other that I ken o'—and I gie a help to Sir Arthur too, but that's mair in the way o' my profession.'

'Well, well—never mind that,' said the Antiquary, 'happy is he that is his own valley-de-sham, as you call it—but why disturb my morning's rest?'

'Ou, sir, the great man's been up since peep o' day, and he's steered the town to get awa an express to fetch his carriage, and it will be here briefly, and he wad like to see your honour afore he gaes awa.'

'Gadso!' ejaculated Oldbuck, 'these great men use one's house and time as if they were their own property. Well, it's once and away.—Has Jenny come to her senses yet, Caxon?'

'Troth, sir, but just middling,' replied the barber; 'she's been in a swither about the jocolate this morning, and was like to hae toomed it a' out into the slap-bason, and drank it hersell in her ecstasies— but she's won ower wi't, wi' the help o' Miss M'Intyre.'

'Then all my womankind are on foot and scrambling, and I must enjoy my quiet bed no longer, if I would have a well-regulated house—Lend me my gown.—And what are the news at Fairport?'

'Ou, sir, what can they be about but this grand news o' my lord,' answered the old man; 'that hasna been ower the door-stane, they threep to me, for this twenty years—this grand news of his coming to visit your honour!'

'Aha!' said Monkbarns, 'and what do they say of that, Caxon?'

''Deed, sir, they hae various opinions. Thae fallows that are the democraws, as they ca' them, that are again' the king and the law, and hair powder and dressing o' gentlemen's wigs—a wheen blackguards—they say he's come doun to speak wi' your honour about bringing doun his hill lads and Highland tenantry to break up the meetings of the Friends o' the People*—and when I said your honour never meddled wi' the like o' sic things where there was like to be straiks and bloodshed, they said, if ye didna, your nevoy did, and that he was weel kend to be a kingsman that wad fight knee-deep, and that ye were the head and he was the hand, and that the Yerl was to bring out the men and the siller.'

'Come,' said the Antiquary, laughing, 'I am glad the war is to cost me nothing but counsel.'

'Na, na,' said Caxon, 'naebody thinks your honour wad either fight yoursell, or gie ony feck o' siller to ony side o' the question.'

'Umph! well, that's the opinion of the democraws, as you call them—What say the rest of Fairport?'

'In troth,' said the candid reporter, 'I canna say it's muckle better—Captain Coquet, of the volunteers,—that's him that's to be the new collector,*—and some of the other gentlemen of the Blue and a' Blue Club,* are just saying it's no right to let papists, that hae sae mony French friends as the Yerl of Glenallan, gang through the country, and—but your honour will maybe be angry?'

'Not I, Caxon,' said Oldbuck—'fire away as if you were Captain Coquet's whole platoon,—I can stand it.'

'Weel, then, they say, sir, that as ye didna encourage the petition about the peace,* and wadna petition in favour of the new tax, and as ye were again' bringing in the yeomanry at the meal mob,* but just for settling the folk wi' the constables—they say ye're no a gude friend to government; and that thae sort o' meetings between sic a powerfu' man as the Yerl, and sic a wise man as you,—odd, they think they suld be lookit after, and some say ye should baith be shankit aff till Edinburgh Castle.'

'On my word,' said the Antiquary, 'I am infinitely obliged to my neighbours for their good opinion of me! And so, I, that have never interfered with their bickerings, but to recommend quiet and moderate measures, am given up on both sides as a man very likely to commit high treason, either against King or People?—Give me my coat, Caxon,—give me my coat—It's lucky I live not in their report.*—Have you heard any thing of Taffril and his vessel?'

Caxon's countenance fell.—'Na, sir, and the winds hae been high, and this is a fearfu' coast to cruise on in thae eastern gales,—the headlands rin sae far out, that a veshell's embayed afore I could sharp a razor; and then there's nae harbour or city of refuge on our coast, a' craigs and breakers. A veshell that rins ashore wi' us flees asunder like the powther when I shake the pluff—and it's as ill to gather ony o't again.—I aye tell my daughter thae things when she grows wearied for a letter frae Lieutenant Taffril—It's aye an apology for him— Ye suldna blame him, says I, hinnie, for ye little ken what may hae happened.'

'Ay, ay, Caxon, thou art as good a comforter as a valet-de-chambre.—Give me a white stock, man,—d'ye think I can go down with a handkerchief about my neck when I have company?'

'Dear sir, the Captain says a three-nookit hankercher is the maist fashionable overlay, and that stocks belang to your honour and me that are auld-warld folk.—I beg pardon for mentioning us twa thegither, but it was what he said.'

'The Captain's a puppy, and you are a goose, Caxon.'

'It's very like it may be sae,' replied the acquiescent barber,—'I am sure your honour kens best.'

Before breakfast, Lord Glenallan, who appeared in better spirits than he had evinced in the former evening, went particularly through the various circumstances of evidence which the exertions of Oldbuck had formerly collected; and pointing out the means which he possessed of completing the proof of his marriage, expressed his resolution instantly to go through the painful task of collecting and restoring the evidence concerning the birth of Eveline Neville, which Elspeth had stated to be in his mother's possession.

'And yet, Mr Oldbuck,' he said, 'I feel like a man who receives important tidings ere he is yet fully awake, and doubt whether they refer to actual life, or are not rather a continuation of his dream. This woman,—this Elspeth,—she is in the extremity of age, and approaching in many respects to dotage. Have I not,—it is a hideous question,—have I not been hasty in the admission of her present evidence, against that which she formerly gave me to a very—very different purpose?'

Mr Oldbuck paused a moment, and then answered with firmness—'No, my lord, I cannot think you have any reason to suspect the truth of what she has told you last, from no apparent impulse but the urgency of conscience. Her confession was voluntary, disinterested, distinct, consistent with itself, and with all the other known circumstances of the case. I would lose no time, however, in examining and arranging the other documents to which she has referred, and I also think her own statement should be taken down, if possible, in a formal manner. We thought of setting about this together. But it will be a relief to your lordship, and, moreover, have a more impartial appearance, were I to attempt the investigation alone, in the capacity of a magistrate. I will do this, at least I will attempt it, so soon as I shall see her in a favourable state of mind to undergo an examination.'

Lord Glenallan wrung the Antiquary's hand in token of grateful acquiescence. 'I cannot express to you,' he said, 'Mr Oldbuck, how much your countenance and co-operation in this dark and most melancholy business gives me relief and confidence. I cannot enough applaud myself for yielding to the sudden impulse which impelled me, as it were, to drag you into my confidence, and which arose from the experience I had formerly of your firmness, in discharge of your duty as a magistrate, and as a friend to the memory of the unfortunate. Whatever the issue of these matters may prove,—and I would fain hope there is a dawn breaking on the fortunes of my house, though I shall not live to enjoy its light,—but whatsoever be the issue, you have laid my family and me under the most lasting obligation.'

'My lord,' answered the Antiquary, 'I must necessarily have the greatest respect for your lordship's family, which I am well aware is one of the most ancient in Scotland, being certainly derived from Aymer de Geraldin, who sat in parliament at Perth, in the reign of Alexander II.,* and who, by the less vouched, yet plausible tradition of the country, is said to have been descended from the Marmor of

Clochnaben.—Yet, with all my veneration for your ancient descent, I must acknowledge that I find myself still more bound to give your lordship what assistance is in my limited power, from sincere sympathy with your sorrows, and detestation at the frauds which have so long been practised upon you.—But, my lord, the matin meal is, I see, now prepared—Permit me to show your lordship the way through the intricacies of my *cœnobitium*, which is rather a combination of cells, jostled oddly together, and piled one upon the top of the other, than a regular house.—I trust you will make yourself some amends for the spare diet of yesterday.'

But this was no part of Lord Glenallan's system: having saluted the company with the grave and melancholy politeness which distinguished his manners, his servant placed before him a slice of toasted bread, with a glass of fair water, being the fare on which he usually broke his fast. While the morning's meal of the young soldier and the old Antiquary was dispatched in a much more substantial manner, the noise of wheels was heard.

'Your lordship's carriage, I believe,' said Oldbuck, stepping to the window. 'On my word, a handsome *Quadriga*, for such, according to the best *scholium*, was the *vox signata** of the Romans for a chariot which, like that your lordship's, was drawn by four horses.'

'And I will venture to say,' cried Hector, eagerly gazing from the window, 'that four handsomer or better-matched bays never were put in harness—What fine fore-hands!—what capital chargers they would make!—Might I ask if they are of your lordship's own breeding?'

'I—I—rather believe so,' said Lord Glenallan; 'but I have been so negligent of my domestic matters, that I am ashamed to say I must apply to Calvert' (looking at the domestic).

'They are of your lordship's own breeding,' said Calvert, 'got by Mad Tom out of Jemima and Yarico, your lordship's brood mares.'

'Are there more of the set?' said Lord Glenallan.

'Two, my lord,—one rising four, the other five off this grass,* both very handsome.'

'Then let Dawkins bring them down to Monkbarns tomorrow,' said the Earl—'I hope Captain M'Intyre will accept them, if they are at all fit for service.'

Captain M'Intyre's eyes sparkled, and he was profuse in grateful acknowledgments; while Oldbuck, on the other hand, seizing the

Earl's sleeve, endeavoured to intercept a present which boded no good to his corn-chest and hay-loft.

'My lord—my lord—much obliged—much obliged—But Hector is a pedestrian, and never mounts on horseback in battle—he is a Highland soldier, moreover, and his dress ill adapted for cavalry service. Even Macpherson never mounted his ancestors on horseback, though he has the impudence to talk of their being car-borne—and that, my lord, is what is running in Hector's head—it is the vehicular, not the equestrian exercise, which he envies—

"Sunt quos curriculo pulverem Olympicum
Collegisse juvat."*

His noddle is running on a curricle, which he has neither money to buy, nor skill to drive if he had it; and I assure your lordship, that the possession of two such quadrupeds would prove a greater scrape than any of his duels, whether with human foe or with my friend the *phoca.*'

'You must command us all at present, Mr Oldbuck,' said the Earl politely, 'but I trust you will not ultimately prevent my gratifying my young friend in some way that may afford him pleasure?'

'Any thing useful, my lord,' said Oldbuck, 'but no *curriculum*—I protest he might as rationally propose to keep a *quadriga* at once—And now I think of it, what is that old post-chaise from Fairport come jingling here for?—I did not send for it.'

'*I* did, sir,' said Hector rather sulkily, for he was not much grati-fied by his uncle's interference to prevent the Earl's intended gener-osity, nor particularly inclined to relish either the disparagement which he cast upon his skill as a charioteer, or the mortifying allusion to his bad success in the adventures of the duel and the seal.

'You did, sir?' echoed the Antiquary, in answer to his concise information. 'And pray, what may be your business with a post-chaise?—Is this splendid equipage—this *biga*, as I may call it—to serve for an introduction to a *quadriga* or a *curriculum?*'

'Really, sir,' replied the young soldier, 'if it be necessary to give you such a specific explanation, I am going to Fairport on a little business.'

'Will you permit me to enquire into the nature of that business, Hector?' answered his uncle, who loved the exercise of a little brief authority over his relative—'I should suppose any regimental affairs might be transacted by your worthy deputy the sergeant,—an honest gentleman, who is so good as to make Monkbarns his home since his arrival among us—I should, I say, suppose that he may transact any business of yours, without your spending a day's pay on two dog-horses, and such a combination of rotten wood, cracked glass, and leather—such a skeleton of a post-chaise, as that before the door.'

'It is not regimental business, sir, that calls me; and, since you insist upon knowing, I must inform you, Caxon has brought word this morning that old Ochiltree, the beggar, is to be brought up for examination today, previous to his being committed for trial; and I am going to see that the poor old fellow gets fair play—that's all.'

'Ay?—I heard something of this, but could not think it serious. And pray, Captain Hector, who are so ready to be every man's second on all occasions of strife, civil or military, by land, by water, or on the sea-beach, what is your especial concern with old Edie Ochiltree?'

'He was a soldier in my father's company, sir,' replied Hector; 'and besides, when I was about to do a very foolish thing one day, he interfered to prevent me, and gave me almost as much good advice, sir, as you could have done yourself.'

'And with the same good effect, I dare be sworn for it—Eh, Hector?—Come, confess it was thrown away.'

'Indeed it was, sir; but I see no reason that my folly should make me less grateful for his intended kindness.'

'Bravo, Hector! that's the most sensible thing I ever heard you say—but always tell me your plans without reserve—why, I will go with you myself, man—I am sure the old fellow is not guilty, and I will assist him in such a scrape much more effectually than you can do. Besides, it will save thee half-a-guinea, my lad, a consideration which I heartily pray you to have more frequently before your eyes.'

Lord Glenallan's politeness had induced him to turn away and talk with the ladies, when the dispute between the uncle and nephew appeared to grow rather too animated to be fit for the ear of a stranger, but the Earl mingled again in the conversation when the placable tone of the Antiquary expressed amity. Having received a brief account of the mendicant, and of the accusation brought against him, which Oldbuck did not hesitate to ascribe to the malice of Dousterswivel, Lord Glenallan asked, whether the individual in question had not been a soldier formerly?—He was answered in the affirmative.

'Had he not,' continued his lordship, 'a coarse blue coat, or gown, with a badge?—Was he not a tall, striking-looking old man, with grey beard and hair, who kept his body remarkably erect, and talked with an air of ease and independence, which formed a strong contrast to his profession?'

'All this is an exact picture of the man,' returned Oldbuck.

'Why, then,' continued Lord Glenallan, 'although I fear I can be of no use to him in his present condition, yet I owe him a debt of gratitude for being the first person who brought me some tidings of the utmost importance. I would willingly offer him a place of comfortable retirement, when he is extricated from his present situation.'

'I fear, my lord,' said Oldbuck, 'he would have difficulty in reconciling his vagrant habits to the acceptance of your bounty, at least I know the experiment has been tried without effect. To beg from the public at large he considers as independence, in comparison to drawing his whole support from the bounty of an individual. He is so far a true philosopher, as to be a contemner of all ordinary rules of hours and times. When he is hungry he eats; when thirsty he drinks; when weary he sleeps; and with such indifference with respect to the means and appliances about which we make a fuss, that, I suppose, he was never ill dined or ill lodged in his life. Then he is, to a certain extent, the oracle of the district through which he travels—their genealogist, their newsman, their master of the revels, their doctor at a pinch, or their divine—I promise you he has too many duties, and is too zealous in performing them, to be easily bribed to abandon his calling. But I should be truly sorry if they sent the poor light-hearted old man to lie for weeks in a jail. I am convinced the confinement would break his heart.'

Thus finished the conference. Lord Glenallan, having taken leave of the ladies, renewed his offer to Captain M'Intyre of the freedom of his manors for sporting, which was joyously accepted.

'I can only add,' he said, 'that if your spirits are not liable to be damped by dull company, Glenallan-house is at all times open to you—On two days of the week, Friday and Saturday, I keep my apartment, which will be rather a relief to you, as you will be left to enjoy the society of my almoner, Mr Gladsmoor, who is a scholar and a man of the world.'

Hector, his heart exulting at the thoughts of ranging through the preserves of Glenallan-house, and over the well-protected moors of

Clochnaben, nay, joy of joys, the deer-forest of Strath-Bonnel, made many acknowledgments of the honour and gratitude he felt. Mr Oldbuck was sensible of the Earl's attention to his nephew; Miss M'Intyre was pleased because her brother was gratified; and Miss Griselda Oldbuck looked forward with glee to the potting of whole bags of moor-fowl and black game, of which Mr Blattergowl was a professed admirer. Thus,—which is always the case when a man of rank leaves a private family where he has studied to appear obliging,—all were ready to open in praise of the Earl as soon as he had taken his leave, and was wheeled off in his chariot by the four admired bays. But the panegyric was cut short, for Oldbuck and his nephew deposited themselves in the Fairport hack, which, with one horse trotting, and the other urged to a canter, creaked, jingled, and hobbled towards that celebrated seaport, in a manner that formed a strong contrast to the rapidity and smoothness with which Lord Glenallan's equipage had seemed to vanish from their eyes.

CHAPTER XXXVII

Yes! I love justice well—as well as you do—
But since the good dame's blind, she shall excuse me,
If, time and reason fitting, I prove dumb;—
The breath I utter now shall be no means
To take away from me my breath in future.

Old Play.*

By dint of charity from the town's people, in aid of the load of provisions he had brought with him into durance, Edie Ochiltree had passed a day or two's confinement without much impatience, regretting his want of freedom the less, as the weather proved broken and rainy.

'The prison,' he said, 'wasna sae dooms bad a place as it was ca'd. Ye had aye a good roof ower your head to fend aff the weather, and, if the windows werena glazed, it was the mair airy and pleasant for the summer season. And there were folk enow to crack wi', and he had bread eneugh to eat, and what need he fash himsell about the rest o't?'

The courage of our philosophical mendicant began, however, to abate, when the sunbeams shone fair on the rusty bars of his grated dungeon, and a miserable linnet, whose cage some poor debtor had obtained permission to attach to the window, began to greet them with his whistle.

'Ye're in better spirits than I am,' said Edie, addressing the bird, 'for I can neither whistle nor sing for thinking o' the bonnie burn-sides and green shaws that I should hae been dandering beside in weather like this.—But hae, there's some crumbs t'ye, an ye are sae merry; and troth ye hae some reason to sing an ye kent it, for your cage comes by nae faut o' your ain, and I may thank mysell that I am closed up in this weary place.'

Ochiltree's soliloquy was disturbed by a peace-officer, who came to summon him to attend the magistrate. So he set forth in awful procession between two poor creatures, neither of them so stout as he was himself, to be conducted into the presence of inquisitorial justice. The people, as the aged prisoner was led along by his decrepit guards, exclaimed to each other, 'Eh! see sic a grey-haired man as that is, to have committed a highway robbery, wi' ae fit in the grave!'—And the children congratulated the officers, objects of their alternate dread and sport, Puggie Orrock and Jock Ormston, on having a prisoner as old as themselves.

Thus marshalled forward, Edie was presented (by no means for the first time) before the worshipful Bailie Littlejohn,* who, contrary to what his name expressed, was a tall portly magistrate, on whom corporation crusts had not been conferred in vain. He was a zealous loyalist of that zealous time, somewhat rigorous and peremptory in the execution of his duty, and a good deal inflated with the sense of his own power and importance, otherwise an honest, well-meaning, and useful citizen.

'Bring him in, bring him in!' he exclaimed; 'upon my word these are awful and unnatural times—the very bedesmen and retainers of his majesty are the first to break his laws—Here has been an old Blue-Gown committing robbery! I suppose the next will reward the royal charity, which supplies him with his garb, pension, and begging license, by engaging in high-treason, or sedition at least—But bring him in.'

Edie made his obeisance, and then stood, as usual, firm and erect, with the side of his face turned a little upward, as if to catch every word which the magistrate might address to him. To the first general questions, which respected only his name and calling, the mendicant answered with readiness and accuracy; but when the magistrate, having caused his clerk to take down these particulars, began to enquire whereabout the mendicant was on the night when Douster-swivel met with his misfortune, Edie demurred to the motion. 'Can ye tell me now, Bailie, you that understands the law, what gude will it do me to answer ony o' your questions?'

'Good? no good certainly, my friend, except that giving a true account of yourself, if you are innocent, may entitle me to set you at liberty.'

'But it seems mair reasonable to me, now, that you, Bailie, or ony body that has ony thing to say against me, should prove my guilt, and no to be bidding me prove my innocence.'

'I don't sit here,' answered the magistrate, 'to dispute points of law with you. I ask you, if you choose to answer my question, whether you were at Ringan Aikwood the forester's, upon the day I have specified?'

'Really, sir, I dinna feel myself called on to remember,' replied the cautious bedesman.

'Or whether, in the course of that day or night,' continued the magistrate, 'you saw Steven, or Steenie, Mucklebackit?—you knew him, I suppose?'

'O brawlie did I ken Steenie, puir fallow,' replied the prisoner—-'but I canna condeshend on ony particular time I have seen him lately.'

'Were you at the ruins of St Ruth any time in the course of that evening?'

'Bailie Littlejohn,' said the mendicant, 'if it be your honour's pleasure, we'll cut a lang tale short, and I'll just tell ye, I am no minded to answer ony o' thae questions—I'm ower auld a traveller to let my tongue bring me into trouble.'

'Write down,' said the magistrate, 'that he declines to answer all interrogatories, in respect that by telling the truth he might be brought to trouble.'

'Na, na,' said Ochiltree, 'I'll no hae that set down as ony part o' my answer—but I just meant to say, that in a' my memory and practice, I never saw ony gude come o' answering idle questions.'

'Write down,' said the Bailie, 'that, being acquainted with judicial interrogatories by long practice, and having sustained injury by answering questions put to him on such occasions, the declarant refuses'—

'Na, na, Bailie,' reiterated Edie, 'ye are no to come in on me that gait neither.'

'Dictate the answer yourself then, friend,' said the magistrate, 'and the clerk will take it down from your own mouth.'

'Ay, ay,' said Edie, 'that's what I ca' fair play; I'se do that without loss o'time.—Sae, neighbour, ye may just write down, that Edie Ochiltree, the declarant, stands up for the liberty—na, I maunna say that neither—I am nae liberty-boy—I hae fought again' them in the riots in Dublin*—besides, I have ate the king's bread* mony a day.— Stay, let me see—Ay—write that Edie Ochiltree, the Blue-Gown, stands up for the prerogative—(see that ye spell that word right— it's a lang ane)—for the prerogative of the subjects of the land, and winna answer a single word that sall be asked at him this day, unless he sees a reason for't.—Put down that, young man.'

'Then, Edie,' said the magistrate, 'since you will give me no information on the subject, I must send you back to prison till you shall be delivered in due course of law.'

'A weel, sir, if it's Heaven's will and man's will, nae doubt I maun submit,' replied the mendicant. 'I hae nae great objection to the prison, only that a body canna win out o't; and if it wad please you as weel, Bailie, I wad gie you my word to appear afore the Lords at the Circuit,* or in ony other court ye like, on ony day ye are pleased to appoint.'

'I rather think, my good friend,' answered Bailie Littlejohn, 'your word might be a slender security where your neck may be in some danger. I am apt to think you would suffer the pledge to be forfeited.—If you could give me sufficient security, indeed'—

At this moment the Antiquary and Captain M'Intyre entered the apartment.—'Good morning to you, gentlemen,' said the magistrate; 'you find me toiling in my usual vocation—looking after the iniquities of the people—labouring for the *res-publica*,* Mr Oldbuck—serving the King our master, Captain M'Intyre,—for I suppose you know I have taken up the sword?'

'It is one of the emblems of justice, doubtless,' answered the Antiquary; 'but I should have thought the scales would have suited you better, Bailie, especially as you have them ready in the warehouse.'

'Very good, Monkbarns—excellent; but I do not take the sword up as justice, but as a soldier—indeed I should rather say the musket and bayonet—there they stand at the elbow of my gouty chair, for I am scarce fit for drill yet—A slight touch of our old acquaintance *padagra*—I can keep my feet, however, while our sergeant puts me through the manual.* I should like to know, Captain M'Intyre, if he follows the regulations correctly—he brings us but awkwardly to the *present*.'* And he hobbled towards his weapon to illustrate his doubts and display his proficiency.

'I rejoice we have such zealous defenders, Bailie,' replied Mr Oldbuck; 'and I dare say Hector will gratify you by communicating his opinion on your progress in this new calling. Why, you rival the Hecaté of the ancients,* my good sir—a merchant on the Mart, a magistrate in the Town-house, a soldier on the Links—*quid non pro patria?*★ But my business is with the justice; so let commerce and war go slumber.'

'Well, my good sir,' said the Bailie, 'and what commands have you for me?'

'Why, here's an old acquaintance of mine, called Edie Ochiltree, whom some of your myrmidons have mewed up in jail, on account of an alleged assault on that fellow Dousterswivel, of whose accusation I do not believe one word.'

The magistrate here assumed a very grave countenance. 'You ought to have been informed that he is accused of robbery, as well as assault; a very serious matter indeed—it is not often such criminals come under my cognizance.'

'And,' replied Oldbuck, 'you are tenacious of the opportunity of making the very most of such as occur. But is this poor old man's case really so very bad?'

'It is rather out of rule,' said the Bailie; 'but as you are in the commission,* Monkbarns, I have no hesitation to show you Douster-swivel's declaration, and the rest of the precognition.'* And he put the papers into the Antiquary's hands, who assumed his spectacles, and sat down in a corner to peruse them.

The officers in the meantime had directions to remove their prisoner into another apartment; but before they could do so, M'Intyre took an opportunity to greet old Edie, and to slip a guinea into his hand.

'Lord bless your honour,' said the old man; 'it's a young soldier's gift, and it should surely thrive wi' an auld ane. I'se no refuse it, though it's beyond my rules; for if they steek me up here, my friends are like eneugh to forget me—out o' sight out o' mind is a true proverb—And it wadna be creditable for me, that am the King's bedesman, and entitled to beg by word of mouth, to be fishing for bawbees out at the jail window wi' the fit o' a stocking and a string.' As he made this observation he was conducted out of the apartment.

Mr Dousterswivel's declaration contained an exaggerated account of the violence he had sustained, and also of his loss.

'But what I should have liked to have asked him,' said Monkbarns, 'would have been his purpose in frequenting the ruins of St Ruth, so lonely a place, at such an hour, and with such a companion as Edie Ochiltree. There is no road lies that way, and I do not conceive a mere passion for the picturesque would carry the German thither in such a night of storm and wind. Depend upon it, he has been about some roguery, and, in all probability, hath been caught in a trap of his own setting—*Nec lex justitior ulla*.'*

The magistrate allowed there was something mysterious in that circumstance, and apologized for not pressing Dousterswivel, as his declaration was voluntarily emitted. But for the support of the main charge, he showed the declaration of the Aikwoods concerning the state in which Dousterswivel was found, and establishing the important fact, that the mendicant had left the barn in which he was quartered, and did not return to it again. Two people belonging to the Fairport undertaker, who had that night been employed in attending the funeral of Lady Glenallan, had also given declarations, that, being sent to pursue two suspicious persons who left the ruins of St Ruth as the funeral approached, and who, it was supposed, might have been pillaging some of the ornaments prepared for the ceremony, they had lost and regained sight of them more than once, owing to the nature of the ground, which was unfavourable for riding, but had at length fairly lodged them both in Mucklebackit's cottage. And one of the men added, that 'he, the declarant, having dismounted from his horse, and gone close up to the window of the hut, he saw the old Blue-Gown and young Steenie Muckle-backit, with others, eating and drinking in the inside, and also observed the said Steenie Mucklebackit show a pocket-book to the others; and declarant has no doubt that Ochiltree and Steenie Mucklebackit were the persons whom he and his comrade had pursued, as above mentioned.' And being interrogated why he did not enter the said cottage, declares, 'he had no warrant so to do; and that as Mucklebackit and his family were understood to be rough-handed folk, he, the declarant, had no desire to meddle or make with their affairs. *Causa scientiæ patet.** All which he declares to be truth,' &c.

'What do you say to that body of evidence against your friend?' said the magistrate, when he had observed the Antiquary had turned the last leaf.

'Why, were it in the case of any other person, I own, I should say it looked, *prima facie*,* a little ugly; but I cannot allow any body to be in the wrong for beating Dousterswivel—Had I been an hour younger, or had but one single flash of your warlike genius, Bailie, I should have done it myself long ago—He is *nebulo nebulonum*,* an impudent, fraudulent, mendacious quack, that has cost me a hundred pounds by his roguery; and my neighbour Sir Arthur, God knows how much—And besides, Bailie, I do not hold him to be a sound friend to government.'

'Indeed?' said Bailie Littlejohn; 'if I thought that, it would alter the question considerably.'

'Right; for, in beating him,' observed Oldbuck, 'the bedesman must have shown his gratitude to the king by thumping his enemy; and in robbing him, he would only have plundered an Egyptian, whose wealth it is lawful to spoil.* Now, suppose this interview in the ruins of St Ruth had relation to politics,—and this story of hidden treasure, and so forth, was a bribe from the other side of the water* for some great man, or the funds destined to maintain a seditious club?'

'My dear sir,' said the magistrate, catching at the idea, 'you hit my very thoughts! How fortunate should I be if I could become the humble means of sifting such a matter to the bottom!—Don't you think we had better call out the volunteers, and put them on duty?'

'Not just yet, while *podagra* deprives them of an essential member of their body.—But will you let me examine Ochiltree?'

'Certainly; but you'll make nothing of him. He gave me distinctly to understand he knew the danger of a judicial declaration on the part of an accused person, which, to say the truth, has hanged many an honester man than he is.'

'Well, but, Bailie,' continued Oldbuck, 'you have no objection to let me try him?'

'None in the world, Monkbarns.—I hear the sergeant below,—I'll rehearse the manual in the meanwhile.—Baby, carry my gun and bayonet down to the room below—it makes less noise there when we ground arms.'—And so exit the martial magistrate, with his maid behind him bearing his weapons.

'A good squire that wench for a gouty champion,' observed Oldbuck.—'Hector, my lad, hook on, hook on—Go with him, boy—keep him employed, man, for half an hour or so—butter him with some warlike terms—praise his dress and address.'

Captain M'Intyre, who, like many of his profession, looked down with infinite scorn on those citizen soldiers, who had assumed arms without any professional title to bear them, rose with great reluctance, observing that he should not know what to say to Mr Littlejohn; and that to see an old gouty shopkeeper attempting the exercise and duties of a private soldier, was really too ridiculous.

'It may be so, Hector,' said the Antiquary, who seldom agreed with any person in the immediate proposition which was laid down,—'it may possibly be so in this and some other instances; but at present the country resembles the suitors in a small-debt court, where parties plead in person, for lack of cash to retain the professed heroes of the bar. I am sure in the one case we never regret the want of the acuteness and eloquence of the lawyers; and so, I hope, in the other, we may manage to make shift with our hearts and muskets, though we shall lack some of the discipline of you martinets.'

'I have no objection, I am sure, sir, that the whole world should fight if they please, if they will but allow me to be quiet,' said Hector, rising with dogged reluctance.

'Yes, you are a very quiet personage indeed,' said his uncle; 'whose ardour for quarrelling cannot pass so much as a poor *phoca* sleeping upon the beach!'

But Hector, who saw which way the conversation was tending, and hated all allusions to the foil he had sustained from the fish, made his escape before the Antiquary concluded the sentence.

CHAPTER XXVIII

Well, well, at worst, 'tis neither theft nor coinage,
Granting I knew all that you charge me with.
What, tho' the tomb hath borne a second birth,
And given the wealth to one that knew not on't,
Yet fair exchange was never robbery,
Far less pure bounty.—

*Old Play.**

THE Antiquary, in order to avail himself of the permission given him to question the accused party, chose rather to go to the apartment in which Ochiltree was detained, than to make the examination appear formal, by bringing him again into the magistrate's office. He found the old man seated by a window which looked out on the sea; and as he gazed on that prospect, large tears found their way, as if unconsciously, to his eye, and from thence trickled down his cheeks and white beard. His features were, nevertheless, calm and composed, and his whole posture and mien indicated patience and resignation. Oldbuck had approached him without being observed, and roused him out of his musing, by saying kindly, 'I am sorry, Edie, to see you so much cast down about this matter.'

The mendicant started, dried his eyes very hastily with the sleeve of his gown, and, endeavouring to recover his usual tone of indifference and jocularity, answered, but with a voice more tremulous than usual, 'I might weel hae judged, Monkbarns, it was you, or the like o' you, was coming in to disturb me—for it's ae great advantage o' prisons and courts o' justice, that ye may greet your een out an ye like, and nane o' the folk that's concerned about them will ever ask you what it's for.'

'Well, Edie,' replied Oldbuck, 'I hope your present cause of distress is not so bad but it may be removed.'

'And I had hoped, Monkbarns,' answered the mendicant in a tone of reproach, 'that ye had kend me better than to think that this bit trifling trouble o' my ain wad bring tears into my auld een, that hae seen far different kind o' distress—Na, na!—But here's been the puir lass, Caxon's daughter, seeking comfort, and has gotten unco little—there's been nae speerings o' Taffril's gunbrig since the last gale; and folk report on the key that a king's ship had struck on the Reef of Rattray, and a' hands lost—God forbid! for as sure as you live, Monkbarns, the puir lad Lovel, that ye liked sae weel, must have perished.'

'God forbid indeed!' echoed the Antiquary, turning pale; 'I would rather Monkbarns house were on fire. My poor dear friend and coadjutor!—I will down to the quay instantly.'

'I'm sure ye'll learn naething mair than I hae tauld ye, sir,' said Ochiltree, 'for the officer-folk here were very civil, (that is, for the like o' them,) and lookit up a' their letters and authorities, and could thraw nae light on't either ae way or another.'

'It can't be true—it shall not be true,' said the Antiquary, 'and I won't believe it if it were—Taffril's an excellent seaman—and Lovel (my poor Lovel!) has all the qualities of a safe and pleasant companion by land or by sea—one, Edie, whom, from the ingenuousness of his disposition, I would choose, did I ever go a sea voyage, (which I never do, unless across the ferry,*) *fragilem mecum solvere phaselum,** to be the companion of my risk, as one against whom the elements could nourish no vengeance. No, Edie, it is not, and cannot be true— it is a fiction of the idle jade Rumour, whom I wish hanged with her trumpet about her neck,* that serves only with its screech-owl tones to fright honest folks out of their senses.—Let me know how you got into this scrape of your own.'

'Are ye axing me as a magistrate, Monkbarns, or is it just for your ain satisfaction?'

'For my own satisfaction solely,' replied the Antiquary.

'Put up your pocket-book and your keelyvine pen then, for I downa speak out an ye hae writing materials in your hands—they're a scaur to unlearned folk like me—Odd, ane o' the clerks in the neist room will clink down, in black and white, as muckle as wad hang a man, before ane kens what he's saying.'

Monkbarns complied with the old man's humour, and put up his memorandum-book.

Edie then went with great frankness through the part of the story already known to the reader, informing the Antiquary of the scene which he had witnessed between Dousterswivel and his patron in the ruins of St Ruth, and frankly confessing that he could not resist the opportunity of decoying the adept once more to visit the tomb of Misticot, with the purpose of taking a comic revenge upon him for his quackery. He had easily persuaded Steenie, who was a bold thoughtless young fellow, to engage in the frolic along with him, and the jest had been inadvertently carried a great deal farther than was designed. Concerning the pocket-book, he explained that he had expressed his surprise and sorrow as soon as he found it had been inadvertently brought off; and that publicly, before all the inmates of the cottage, Steenie had undertaken to return it the next day, and had only been prevented by his untimely fate.

The Antiquary pondered a moment, and then said, 'Your account seems very probable, Edie, and I believe it from what I know of the parties—but I think it likely that you know a great deal more than you have thought it proper to tell me, about this matter of the treasure-trove—I suspect you have acted the part of the Lar Familiaris in Plautus*—a sort of Brownie,* Edie, to speak to your comprehension, who watched over hidden treasures.—I do bethink me you were the first person we met when Sir Arthur made his successful attack upon Misticot's grave, and also that when the labourers began to flag, you, Edie, were again the first to leap into the trench, and to make the discovery of the treasure. Now you must explain all this to me, unless you would have me use you as ill as Euclio does Staphyla in the *Aulularia*.'*

'Lordsake, sir,' replied the mendicant, 'what do I ken about your Howlowlaria?—it's mair like a dog's language than a man's.'

'You knew, however, of the box of treasure being there?' continued Oldbuck.

'Dear sir,' answered Edie, assuming a countenance of great simplicity, 'what likelihood is there o' that? d'ye think sae puir an auld creature as me wad hae kend o' sic a like thing without getting some gude out o't?—and ye wot weel I sought nane and gat nane, like Michael Scott's man.* What concern could I hae wi't?'

'That's just what I want you to explain to me,' said Oldbuck; 'for I am positive you knew it was there.'

'Your honour's a positive man, Monkbarns—and, for a positive man, I must needs allow ye're often in the right.'

'You allow, then, Edie, that my belief is well-founded?'

Edie nodded acquiescence.

'Then please to explain to me the whole affair from beginning to end,' said the Antiquary.

'If it were a secret o' mine, Monkbarns,' replied the beggar, 'ye suldna ask twice; for I hae aye said ahint your back, that, for a' the nonsense maggots that ye whiles take into your head, ye are the maist wise and discreet o' a' our country gentles. But I'se e'en be open-hearted wi' you, and tell you, that this is a friend's secret, and that they suld draw me wi' wild horses, or saw me asunder, as they did the children of Ammon,* sooner than I would speak a word mair about the matter, excepting this, that there was nae ill intended, but muckle gude, and that the purpose was to serve them that are worth twenty hundred o' me. But there's nae law, I trow, that makes it a sin to ken where ither folk's siller is, if we dinna pit hand till't oursell?'

Oldbuck walked once or twice up and down the room in profound thought, endeavouring to find some plausible reason for transactions of a nature so mysterious, but his ingenuity was totally at fault. He then placed himself before the prisoner.

'This story of yours, friend Edie, is an absolute enigma, and would require a second Œdipus* to solve it—who Œdipus was, I will tell you some other time, if you remind me—However, whether it be owing to the wisdom or to the maggots with which you compliment me, I am strongly disposed to believe that you have spoken the truth, the rather, that you have not made any of those obtestations of the superior powers, which I observe you and your comrades always make use of when you mean to deceive folks.' (Here Edie could not suppress a smile.) 'If, therefore, you will answer me one question, I will endeavour to procure your liberation.'

'If ye'll let me hear the question,' said Edie, with the caution of a canny Scotchman, 'I'll tell you whether I'll answer it or no.'

'It is simply,' said the Antiquary, 'Did Dousterswivel know any thing about the concealment of the chest of bullion?'

'He, the ill-fa'ard loon!' answered Edie, with much frankness of manner, 'there wad hae been little speerings o't had Dustansnivel kend it was there—it wad hae been butter in the black dog's hause.'*

'I thought as much,' said Oldbuck. 'Well, Edie, if I procure your freedom, you must keep your day, and appear to clear me of the bail-bond, for these are not times for prudent men to incur forfeitures, unless you can point out another *Aulam auri plenam quadrilibrem**—another *Search No. I.*'

'Ah!' said the beggar, shaking his head, 'I doubt the bird's flown that laid thae golden eggs—for I winna ca' her goose, though that's the gait it stands in the story-buick*—But I'll keep my day,

Monkbarns; ye'se no loss a penny by me—And troth I wad fain be out again, now the weather's fine—and then I hae the best chance o' hearing the first news o' my friends.'

'Well, Edie, as the bouncing and thumping beneath has somewhat ceased, I presume Bailie Littlejohn has dismissed his military preceptor, and has retired from the labours of Mars to those of Themis*—I will have some conversation with him—But I cannot and will not believe any of those wretched news you were telling me.'

'God send your honour may be right!' said the mendicant, as Oldbuck left the room.

The Antiquary found the magistrate, exhausted with the fatigues of the drill, reposing in his gouty chair, humming the air, 'How merrily we live that soldiers be!' and between each bar comforting himself with a spoonful of mock-turtle soup. He ordered a similar refreshment for Oldbuck, who declined it, observing, that, not being a military man, he did not feel inclined to break his habit of keeping regular hours for meals—'Soldiers like you, Bailie, must snatch their food as they find means and time. But I am sorry to hear ill news of young Taffril's brig.'

'Ah, poor fellow!' said the Bailie, 'he was a credit to the town—much distinguished on the first of June.'*

'But,' said Oldbuck, 'I am shocked to hear you talk of him in the preterite tense.'

'Troth, I fear there may be too much reason for it, Monkbarns; and yet let us hope the best. The accident is said to have happened in the Rattray reef of rocks, about twenty miles to the northward, near Dirtenalan Bay—I have sent to enquire about it—and your nephew run out himself as if he had been flying to get the Gazette* of a victory.'

Here Hector entered, exclaiming as he came in, 'I believe it's all a damned lie—I can't find the least authority for it, but general rumour.'

'And pray, Mr Hector,' said his uncle, 'if it had been true, whose fault would it have been that Lovel was on board?'

'Not mine, I am sure,' answered Hector; 'it would have been only my misfortune.'

'Indeed!' said his uncle; 'I should not have thought of that.'

'Why, sir, with all your inclination to find me in the wrong,' replied the young soldier, 'I suppose you will own my intention was not to blame in this case. I did my best to hit Lovel, and, if I had been successful, 'tis clear my scrape would have been his, and his scrape would have been mine.'

'And whom or what do you intend to hit now, that you are lugging with you that leathern magazine there, marked Gunpowder?'

'I must be prepared for Lord Glenallan's moors on the twelfth,* sir,' said M'Intyre.

'Ah, Hector! thy great *chasse*, as the French call it, would take place best—

"Omne cum Proteus pecus agitaret
Visere montes"—*

Could you meet but with a martial *phoca*, instead of an unwarlike heath-bird.'

'The devil take the seal, sir, or *phoca*, if you choose to call it so— it's rather hard one can never hear the end of a little piece of folly like that.'

'Well, well,' said Oldbuck, 'I am glad you have the grace to be ashamed of it.—As I detest the whole race of Nimrods,* I wish them all as well matched—Nay, never start off at a jest, man—I have done with the *phoca*—though, I dare say, the Bailie could tell us the value of seal-skins just now.'

'They are up,' said the magistrate, 'they are well up—the fishing has been unsuccessful lately.'

'We can bear witness to that,' said the tormenting Antiquary, who was delighted with the hank this incident had given him over the young sportsman: 'One word more, Hector, and

"We'll hang a seal-skin on thy recreant limbs."*

Aha my boy!—come, never mind it, I must go to business—Bailie, a word with you—you must take bail—moderate bail—you understand—for old Ochiltree's appearance.'

'You don't consider what you ask,' said the Bailie; 'the offence is assault and robbery.'

'Hush! not a word about it,' said the Antiquary, 'I gave you a hint before—I will possess you more fully hereafter—I promise you, there is a secret.'

'But, Mr Oldbuck, if the state is concerned, I, who do the whole drudgery business here, really have a title to be consulted, and until I am'—

'Hush! hush!' said the Antiquary, winking and putting his finger to his nose,—'you shall have the full credit, the entire management, whenever matters are ripe. But this is an obstinate old fellow, who will not hear of two people being as yet let into his mystery, and he has not fully acquainted me with the clew to Dousterswivel's devices.'

'Aha! so we must tip that fellow the alien act,* I suppose?'

'To say truth, I wish you would.'

'Say no more,' said the magistrate, 'it shall forthwith be done; he shall be removed *tanquam suspect**—I think that's one of your own phrases, Monkbarns?'

'It is classical, Bailie—you improve.'

'Why, public business has of late pressed upon me so much, that I have been obliged to take my foreman into partnership.—I have had two several correspondences with the Under Secretary of State; one on the proposed tax on Riga hemp-seed, and the other on putting down political societies. So you might as well communicate to me as much as you know of this old fellow's discovery of a plot against the state.'

'I will, instantly, when I am master of it,' replied Oldbuck—'I hate the trouble of managing such matters myself—Remember, however, I did not say decidedly a plot against the state; I only say, I hope to discover, by this man's means, a foul plot.'

'If it be a plot at all, there must be treason in it, or sedition at least,' said the Bailie—'Will you bail him for four hundred merks?'

'Four hundred merks for an old Blue-Gown!—Think on the act 1701 regulating bail-bonds!*—Strike off a cipher from the sum—I am content to bail him for forty merks.'

'Well, Mr Oldbuck, every body in Fairport is always willing to oblige you—and besides, I know that you are a prudent man, and one that would be as unwilling to lose forty, as four hundred merks. So I will accept your bail—*meo periculo**—what say you to that law phrase again?—I had it from a learned counsel.—I will vouch it, my lord, he said, *meo periculo*.'

'And I will vouch for Edie Ochiltree, *meo periculo*, in like manner,' said Oldbuck. 'So let your clerk draw out the bail-bond, and I will sign it.'

When this ceremony had been performed, the Antiquary communicated to Edie the joyful tidings that he was once more at liberty, and directed him to make the best of his way to Monkbarns-house, to which he himself returned with his nephew, after having perfected their good work.

CHAPTER XXXIX

Full of wise saws and modern instances.
*As You Like it.**

'I wish to Heaven, Hector,' said the Antiquary, next morning after breakfast, 'you would spare our nerves, and not be keeping snapping that arquebuss of yours.'

'Well, sir, I'm sure I'm sorry to disturb you,' said his nephew, still handling his fowling-piece; 'but it's a capital gun; it's a Joe Manton,* that cost forty guineas.'

'A fool and his money are soon parted, nephew—there is a Joe Miller for your Joe Manton,' answered the Antiquary; 'I am glad you have so many guineas to throw away.'

'Every one has their fancy, uncle,—you are fond of books.'

'Ay, Hector,' said the uncle, 'and if my collection were yours, you would make it fly to the gunsmith, the horse-market, the dog-breaker,—*Coemptos undique nobiles libros—mutare loricis Iberis.'*

'I could not use your books, my dear uncle,' said the young soldier, 'that's true; and you will do well to provide for their being in better hands—but don't let the faults of my head fall on my heart—I would not part with a Cordery* that belonged to an old friend, to get a set of horses like Lord Glenallan's.'

'I don't think you would, lad, I don't think you would,' said his softening relative—'I love to teaze you a little sometimes; it keeps up the spirit of discipline and habit of subordination—You will pass your time happily here having me to command you, instead of Captain, or Colonel, or "Knight in Arms," as Milton has it;* and instead of the French,' he continued, relapsing into his ironical humour, 'you have the *Gens humida ponti**—for, as Virgil says,

> "Sternunt se somno diversæ in littore phocæ,"*

which might be rendered,

> "Here phocæ slumber on the beach,
> Within our Highland Hector's reach."

Nay, if you grow angry I have done.—Besides, I see old Edie in the court-yard, with whom I have business. Good-by, Hector—Do you remember how she splashed into the sea like her master Proteus, *et se jactu dedit æquor in altum?**

M'Intyre,—waiting, however, till the door was shut,—then gave way to the natural impatience of his temper.

'My uncle is the best man in the world, and in his way the kindest; but rather than hear any more about that cursed *phoca*, as he is pleased to call it, I would exchange for the West Indies,* and never see his face again.'

Miss M'Intyre, gratefully attached to her uncle, and passionately fond of her brother, was, on such occasions, the usual envoy of reconciliation. She hastened to meet her uncle on his return, before he entered the parlour.

'Well, now, Miss Womankind, what is the meaning of that imploring countenance?—has Juno done any more mischief?'

'No, uncle; but Juno's master is in such fear of your joking him about the seal—I assure you, he feels it much more than you would wish—it's very silly of him, to be sure; but then you can turn every body so sharply into ridicule'——

'Well, my dear,' answered Oldbuck, propitiated by the compliment, 'I will rein in my satire, and, if possible, speak no more of the *phoca*—I will not even speak of sealing a letter, but say *umph*, and give a nod to you when I want the wax-light—I am not *monitoribus asper*,* but, Heaven knows, the most mild, quiet, and easy of human beings, whom sister, niece, and nephew guide just as best pleases them.'

With this little panegyric on his own docility, Mr Oldbuck entered the parlour, and proposed to his nephew a walk to the Mussel-crag. 'I have some questions to ask of a woman at Mucklebackit's cottage,' he observed, 'and I would willingly have a sensible witness with me—so, for fault of a better, Hector, I must be contented with you.'

'There is old Edie, sir, or Caxon—could not they do better than me?' answered M'Intyre, feeling somewhat alarmed at the prospect of a long tête-à-tête with his uncle.

'Upon my word, young man, you turn me over to pretty companions, and I am quite sensible of your politeness,' replied Mr Oldbuck. 'No, sir, I intend the old Blue-Gown shall go with me—not as a competent witness, for he is at present, as our friend Bailie Littlejohn says, (blessings on his learning!) *tanquam suspectus*, and you are *suspicione major*,* as our law has it.'

'I wish I were a major, sir,' said Hector, catching only the last, and, to a soldier's ear, the most impressive word in the sentence,—'but, without money or interest, there is little chance of getting the step.'

'Well, well, most doughty son of Priam,' said the Antiquary, 'be ruled by your friends, and there's no saying what may happen— Come away with me, and you shall see what may be useful to you should you ever sit upon a court-martial, sir.'

'I have been on many a regimental court-martial, sir,' answered Captain M'Intyre.—'But here's a new cane for you.'

'Much obliged, much obliged.'

'I bought it from our drum-major,' added M'Intyre, 'who came into our regiment from the Bengal army when it came down the Red Sea. It was cut on the banks of the Indus, I assure you.'

'Upon my word, 'tis a fine ratan, and well replaces that which the *ph*—Bah! what was I going to say?'

The party, consisting of the Antiquary, his nephew, and the old beggar, now took the sands towards Mussel-crag,—the former in the very highest mood of communicating information, and the others, under a sense of former obligation, and some hope for future favours, decently attentive to receive it. The uncle and nephew walked together, the mendicant about a step and a half behind, just near enough for his patron to speak to him by a slight inclination of his neck, and without the trouble of turning round. Petrie, in his Essay on Good-breeding,* dedicated to the magistrates of Edinburgh, recommends, upon his own experience, as tutor in a family of distinction, this attitude to all led captains,* tutors, dependants, and bottle-holders of every description. Thus escorted, the Antiquary moved along full of his learning, like a lordly man of war, and every now and then yawing to starboard and larboard to discharge a broadside upon his followers.

'And so it is your opinion,' said he to the mendicant, 'that this windfall—this *arca auri*,* as Plautus has it, will not greatly avail Sir Arthur in his necessities?'

'Unless he could find ten times as much,' said the beggar, 'and that I am sair doubtful of—I heard Puggie Orrock, and the tother thief of a sheriff-officer, or messenger, speaking about it—and things are ill aff when the like o' them can speak crously about ony gentleman's affairs. I doubt Sir Arthur will be in stane wa's for debt, unless there's swift help and certain.'

'You speak like a fool,' said the Antiquary.—'Nephew, it is a remarkable thing, that in this happy country no man can be legally imprisoned for debt.'

'Indeed, sir?' said M'Intyre; 'I never knew that before—that part of our law would suit some of our mess well.'

'And if they arena confined for debt,' said Ochiltree, 'what is't that tempts sae mony puir creatures to bide in the tolbooth o' Fairport yonder?—they a' say they were put there by their creditors—Odd! they maun like it better than I do if they're there o' free will.'

'A very natural observation, Edie, and many of your betters would make the same; but it is founded entirely upon ignorance of the feudal system.—Hector, be so good as to attend, unless you are looking out for another—Ahem! (Hector compelled himself to give attention at this hint.)—And you, Edie, it may be useful to you, *rerum cognoscere causas.** The nature and origin of warrant for caption is a thing *haud alienum a Scævolæ studiis.** You must know then once more, that nobody can be arrested in Scotland for debt.'

'I haena muckle concern wi' that, Monkbarns,' said the old man, 'for naebody wad trust a bodle to a gaberlunzie.'

'I pr'ythee peace, man—As a compulsitor, therefore, of payment,—that being a thing to which no debtor is naturally inclined, as I have too much reason to warrant from the experience I have had with my own,—we had first the letters of four forms,* a sort of gentle invitation, by which our sovereign lord the king, interesting himself, as a monarch should, in the regulation of his subjects' private affairs, at first by mild exhortation, and afterwards by letters of more strict enjoinment and more hard compulsion—What do you see extraordinary about that bird, Hector?—it's but a seamaw.'

'It's a pictarnie, sir,' said Edie.

'Well, what an if it were—what does that signify at present?—But I see you're impatient; so I will waive the letters of four forms, and come to the modern process of diligence.*—You suppose, now, a man's committed to prison because he cannot pay his debt? Quite otherwise; the truth is, the king is so good as to interfere at the request of the creditor, and to send the debtor his royal command to do him justice within a certain time—fifteen days, or six, as the case may be. Well, the man resists and disobeys—what follows? Why, that he be lawfully and rightfully declared a rebel to our gracious sovereign, whose command he has disobeyed, and that by three blasts of a horn at the market-place of Edinburgh, the metropolis of Scotland. And he is then legally imprisoned, not on account of any civil debt, but because of his ungrateful contempt of the royal mandate. What say you to that, Hector?—there's something you never knew before.'[21]

'No, uncle; but, I own, if I wanted money to pay my debts, I would rather thank the king to send me some, than to declare me a rebel for not doing what I could not do.'

'Your education has not led you to consider these things,' replied his uncle; 'you are incapable of estimating the elegance of the legal fiction, and the manner in which it reconciles that duress, which, for the protection of commerce, it has been found necessary to extend towards refractory debtors, with the most scrupulous attention to the liberty of the subject.'

'I don't know, sir,' answered the unenlightened Hector; 'but if a man must pay his debt or go to jail, it signifies but little whether he goes as a debtor or a rebel, I should think. But you say this command of the king's gives a license of so many days—now, egad, were I in the scrape, I would beat a march, and leave the king and the creditor to settle it among themselves before they came to extremities.'

'So wad I,' said Edie; 'I wad gie them leg-bail to a certainty.'

'True,' replied Monkbarns; 'but those whom the law suspects of being unwilling to abide her formal visit, she proceeds with by means of a shorter and more unceremonious call, as dealing with persons on whom patience and favour would be utterly thrown away.'

'Ay,' said Ochiltree, 'that will be what they ca' the fugie-warrants—I hae some skeel in them. There's Border-warrants* too in the south country, unco rash uncanny things—I was taen up on ane at Saint James's Fair, and keepit in the auld kirk at Kelso the haill day and night; and a cauld goustie place it was, I'se assure ye.—But whatna wife's this, wi' her creel on her back?—It's puir Maggie hersell, I'm thinking.'

It was so. The poor woman's sense of her loss, if not diminished, was become at least mitigated by the inevitable necessity of attending to the means of supporting her family; and her salutation to Oldbuck was made in an odd mixture, between the usual language of solicitation with which she plied her customers, and the tone of lamentation for her recent calamity.

'How's a' wi' ye the day, Monkbarns?—I havena had the grace yet to come down to thank your honour for the credit ye did puir Steenie, wi' laying his head in a rath grave, puir fallow.'—Here she whimpered and wiped her eyes with the corner of her blue apron.—— 'But the fishing comes on no that ill, though the gudeman hasna had the heart to gang to sea himsell—Atweel I wad fain tell him it wad do him gude to put hand to wark—but I'm maist fear'd to speak to him—and it's an unco thing to hear ane o' us speak that gate o' a man—however, I hae some dainty caller haddies, and they sall be but three shillings the dozen, for I hae nae pith to drive a bargain e'en-now, and maun just take what ony Christian body will gie, wi' few words and nae flyting.'

'What shall we do, Hector?' said Oldbuck, pausing: 'I got into disgrace with my womankind for making a bad bargain with her before. These maritime animals, Hector, are unlucky to our family.'

'Pooh, sir, what would you do?—give poor Maggie what she asks, or allow me to send a dish of fish up to Monkbarns.'

And he held out the money to her; but Maggie drew back her hand. 'Na, na, Captain; ye're ower young and ower free o' your siller—ye should never tak a fish-wife's first bode, and troth I think maybe a flyte wi' the auld housekeeper at Monkbarns, or Miss Grizel, would do me some gude—And I want to see what that hellicate quean Jenny Rintherout's doing—folk said she wasna weel— She'll be vexing hersell about Steenie, the silly tawpie, as if he wad ever hae lookit ower his shouther at the like o' her!—Weel, Monkbarns, they're braw caller haddies, and they'll bid me unco little indeed at the house if ye want crappit-heads the day.'

And so on she paced with her burden, grief, gratitude for the sympathy of her betters, and the habitual love of traffic and of gain, chasing each other through her thoughts.

'And now that we are before the door of their hut,' said Ochiltree, 'I wad fain ken, Monkbarns, what has gar'd ye plague yoursell wi' me a' this length? I tell ye sincerely I hae nae pleasure in ganging in there. I downa bide to think how the young hae fa'en on a' sides o' me, and left me an useless auld stump wi' hardly a green leaf on't.'

'This old woman,' said Oldbuck, 'sent you on a message to the Earl of Glenallan, did she not?'

'Ay!' said the surprised mendicant; 'how ken ye that sae weel?'

'Lord Glenallan told me himself,' answered the Antiquary; 'so there is no delation—no breach of trust on your part—and as he wishes me to take her evidence down on some important family matters, I chose to bring you with me, because in her situation, hovering between dotage and consciousness, it is possible that your voice and appearance may awaken trains of recollection which I should otherwise have no means of exciting. The human mind—what are you about, Hector?'

'I was only whistling for the dog, sir,' replied the Captain; 'she always roves too wide—I knew I should be troublesome to you.'

'Not at all, not at all,' said Oldbuck, resuming the subject of his disquisition—'The human mind is to be treated like a skein of ravelled silk, where you must cautiously secure one free end before you can make any progress in disentangling it.'

'I ken naething about that,' said the gaberlunzie; 'but an my auld acquaintance be hersell, or ony thing like hersell, she may come to wind us a pirn. It's fearsome baith to see and hear her when she wampishes about her arms, and gets to her English, and speaks as if she were a prent book,—let a-be an auld fisher's wife. But, indeed, she had a grand education, and was muckle taen out afore she married an unco bit beneath hersell. She's aulder than me by half a score years—but I mind well eneugh they made as muckle wark about her making a half-merk marriage* wi' Simon Mucklebackit, this Saunders's father, as if she had been ane o' the gentry. But she got into favour again, and then she lost it again, as I hae heard her son say, when he was a muckle chield; and then they got muckle siller, and left the Countess's land and settled here. But things never throve wi' them. Howsomever, she's a weel-educate woman, and an she win to her English, as I hae heard her do at an orra time, she may come to fickle us a'.'

CHAPTER XL

Life ebbs from such old age, unmark'd and silent,
As the slow neap-tide leaves yon stranded galley.—
Late she rock'd merrily at the least impulse
That wind or wave could give; but now her keel
Is settling on the sand, her mast has ta'en
An angle with the sky, from which it shifts not.
Each wave receding shakes her less and less,
Till, bedded on the strand, she shall remain
Useless as motionless.

*Old Play.**

As the Antiquary lifted the latch of the hut, he was surprised to hear the shrill tremulous voice of Elspeth chanting forth an old ballad in a wild and doleful recitative.

'The herring loves the merry moonlight,
    The mackerel loves the wind,
But the oyster loves the dredging sang,
    For they come of a gentle kind.'*

A diligent collector of these legendary scraps of ancient poetry, his foot refused to cross the threshold when his ear was thus arrested, and his hand instinctively took pencil and memorandum-book. From time to time the old woman spoke as if to the children—'O ay, hinnies, whisht, whisht! and I'll begin a bonnier ane than that—

"Now haud your tongue, baith wife and carle,
    And listen, great and sma',
And I will sing of Glenallan's Earl
    That fought on the red Harlaw.

"The cronach's cried on Bennachie,
    And doun the Don and a',
And hieland and lawland may mournfu' be
    For the sair field of Harlaw.—"*

I dinna mind the neist verse weel—my memory's failed, and there's unco thoughts come ower me—God keep us frae temptation!'

Here her voice sunk in indistinct muttering.

'It's a historical ballad,' said Oldbuck eagerly, 'a genuine and

undoubted fragment of minstrelsy!—Percy* would admire its
simplicity—Ritson* could not impugn its authenticity.'

'Ay, but it's a sad thing,' said Ochiltree, 'to see human nature sae
far owertaen as to be skirling at auld sangs on the back of a loss like
hers.'

'Hush, hush!' said the Antiquary,—'she has gotten the thread of
the story again.'—And as he spoke, she sung:

> 'They saddled a hundred milk-white steeds,
>   They hae bridled a hundred black,
> With a chafron of steel on each horse's head,
>   And a good knight upon his back.'—

'Chafron!' exclaimed the Antiquary,—'equivalent, perhaps, to
cheveron—the word's worth a dollar,'—and down it went in his red
book.

> 'They hadna ridden a mile, a mile,
>   A mile, but barely ten,
> When Donald came branking down the brae
>   Wi' twenty thousand men.
>
> 'Their tartans they were waving wide,
>   Their glaives were glancing clear,
> The pibrochs rung frae side to side,
>   Would deafen ye to hear.
>
> 'The great Earl in his stirrups stood
>   That Highland host to see:
> "Now here a knight that's stout and good
>   May prove a jeopardie:
>
> ' "What wouldst thou do, my squire so gay,
>   That rides beside my reyne,
> Were ye Glenallan's Earl the day,
>   And I were Roland Cheyne?
>
> ' "To turn the rein were sin and shame,
>   To fight were wondrous peril,
> What would ye do now, Roland Cheyne,
>   Were ye Glenallan's Earl?"'

Ye maun ken, hinnies, that this Roland Cheyne, for as poor and auld
as I sit in the chimney-neuk, was my forebear, and an awfu' man he
was that day in the fight, but specially after the Earl had fa'en; for he

blamed himsell for the counsel he gave, to fight before Mar came up wi' Mearns, and Aberdeen, and Angus.'

Her voice rose and became more animated as she recited the warlike counsel of her ancestor:

> ' "Were I Glenallan's Earl this tide,
>   And ye were Roland Cheyne,
> The spur should be in my horse's side,
>   And the bridle upon his mane.
>
> ' "If they hae twenty thousand blades,
>   And we twice ten times ten,
> Yet they hae but their tartan plaids,
>   And we are mail-clad men.
>
> ' "My horse shall ride through ranks sae rude,
>   As through the moorland fern,
> Then ne'er let the gentle Norman blude
>   Grow cauld for Highland kerne." '

'Do you hear that, nephew?' said Oldbuck; 'you observe your Gaelic ancestors were not held in high repute formerly by the Lowland warriors.'

'I hear,' said Hector, 'a silly old woman sing a silly old song. I am surprised, sir, that you, who will not listen to Ossian's songs of Selma,* can be pleased with such trash; I vow, I have not seen or heard a worse halfpenny ballad; I don't believe you could match it in any pedlar's pack in the country. I should be ashamed to think that the honour of the Highlands could be affected by such doggrel.'—And, tossing up his head, he snuffed the air indignantly.

Apparently the old woman heard the sound of their voices; for, ceasing her song, she called out, 'Come in, sirs, come in—good-will never halted at the door-stane.'

They entered, and found to their surprise Elspeth alone, sitting 'ghastly on the hearth,' like the personification of Old Age in the Hunter's song of the Owl,[22] 'wrinkled, tattered, vile, dim-eyed, discoloured, torpid.'*

'They're a' out,' she said, as they entered; 'but, an ye will sit a blink, somebody will be in. If ye hae business wi' my gude-daughter, or my son, they'll be in belyve,—I never speak on business mysell.—Bairns, gie them seats—the bairns are a gane out, I trow,'—looking around her,—'I was crooning to keep them quiet a wee while since;

but they hae cruppin out some gate—Sit down, sirs, they'll be in belyve;' and she dismissed her spindle from her hand to twirl upon the floor, and soon seemed exclusively occupied in regulating its motion, as unconscious of the presence of the strangers as she appeared indifferent to their rank or business there.

'I wish,' said Oldbuck, 'she would resume that canticle, or legendary fragment—I always suspected there was a skirmish of cavalry before the main battle of the Harlaw.'[23]

'If your honour pleases,' said Edie, 'had ye not better proceed to the business that brought us a' here? I'se engage to get ye the sang ony time.'

'I believe you are right, Edie—*Do manus**—I submit. But how shall we manage? She sits there, the very image of dotage—speak to her, Edie—try if you can make her recollect having sent you to Glenallan-house.'

Edie rose accordingly, and, crossing the floor, placed himself in the same position which he had occupied during his former conversation with her. 'I'm fain to see ye looking sae weel, cummer; the mair, that the black ox has tramped on ye since I was aneath your roof-tree.'

'Ay,' said Elspeth; but rather from a general idea of misfortune, than any exact recollection of what had happened,—'there has been distress amang us of late—I wonder how younger folk bide it—I bide it ill—I canna hear the wind whistle, and the sea roar, but I think I see the coble whombled keel up, and some o'them struggling in the waves!—Eh, sirs, sic weary dreams as folk hae between sleeping and waking, before they win to the lang sleep and the sound!—I could amaist think whiles, my son, or else Steenie, my oe, was dead, and that I had seen the burial. Isna that a queer dream for a daft auld carline? what for should ony o' them dee before me?—it's out o' the course o' nature, ye ken.'

'I think you'll make very little of this stupid old woman,' said Hector; who still nourished, perhaps, some feelings of the dislike excited by the disparaging mention of his countrymen in her lay—'I think you'll make but little of her, sir; and it's wasting our time to sit here and listen to her dotage.'

'Hector,' said the Antiquary indignantly, 'if you do not respect her misfortunes, respect at least her old age and grey hairs,—this is the last stage of existence, so finely treated by the Latin poet:

————————————————"Omni
Membrorum damno major dementia, quæ nec
Nomina servorum, nec vultus agnoscit amici,
Cum queis preterita cœnavit nocte, nec illos
Quos genuit, quos eduxit." '*

'That's Latin!' said Elspeth, rousing herself as if she attended to
the lines which the Antiquary recited with great pomp of diction,—–
'That's Latin!' and she cast a wild glance around her—'Has there a
priest fund me out at last?'

'You see, nephew, her comprehension is almost equal to your own
of that fine passage.'

'I hope you think, sir, that I knew it to be Latin as well as she did?'

'Why, as to that—But stay, she is about to speak.'

'I will have no priest—none,' said the beldam, with impotent
vehemence—'as I have lived I will die—none shall say that I
betrayed my mistress, though it were to save my soul!'

'That bespoke a foul conscience,' said the mendicant; 'I wuss she
wad mak a clean breast, an it were but for her ain sake,' and he again
assailed her.

'Weel, gudewife, I did your errand to the Yerl.'

'To what Earl? I ken nae Earl—I kend a Countess ance—I wish to
Heaven I had never kend her! for by that acquaintance, neighbour,
there cam,'—and she counted her withered fingers as she spoke—–
'first Pride, then Malice, then Revenge, then False Witness; and
Murder tirl'd at the door-pin, if he camna ben—And werena thae
pleasant guests, think ye, to take up their quarters in ae woman's
heart? I trow there was routh o' company.'

'But, cummer,' continued the beggar, 'it wasna the Countess of
Glenallan I meant, but her son, him that was Lord Geraldin.'

'I mind it now,' she said; 'I saw him no that lang syne, and we
had a heavy speech thegither.—Eh, sirs, the comely young lord is
turned as auld and frail as I am—it's muckle that sorrow and heartbreak, and crossing of true love, will do wi' young blood—But
suldna his mither hae lookit to that hersell?—We were but to do her
bidding, ye ken—I am sure there's naebody can blame me—he
wasna my son, and she was my mistress—Ye ken how the rhyme
says—I hae maist forgotten how to sing, or else the tune's left my
auld head:

"He turn'd him right and round again,
　　Said, Scorn na at my mither;
　Light loves I may get mony a ane,
　　But minnie ne'er anither."*

Then he was but of the half blude, ye ken, and hers was the right
Glenallan after a'. Na, na, I maun never maen doing and suffering
for the Countess Joscelin. Never will I maen for that.'

Then drawing her flax from the distaff, with the dogged air of one
who is resolved to confess nothing, she resumed her interrupted
occupation.

'I hae heard,' said the mendicant, taking his cue from what Oldbuck had told him of the family history,—'I hae heard, cummer,
that some ill tongue suld hae come between the Earl, that's Lord
Geraldin, and his young bride.'

'Ill tongue?' she said, in hasty alarm; 'and what had she to fear frae
an ill tongue?—she was gude and fair eneugh—at least a' body said
sae—But had she keepit her ain tongue aff ither folk, she might hae
been living like a leddy for a' that's come and gane yet.'

'But I hae heard say, gudewife,' continued Ochiltree, 'there was a
clatter in the country, that her husband and her were ower sibb when
they married.'

'Wha durst speak o' that?' said the old woman hastily; 'Wha durst
say they were married?—Wha kend o' that?—not the Countess—
not I—if they wedded in secret they were severed in secret—They
drank of the fountains of their ain deceit.'

'No, wretched beldam,' exclaimed Oldbuck, who could keep
silence no longer, 'they drank the poison that you and your wicked
mistress prepared for them.'

'Ha, ha!' she replied, 'I aye thought it would come to this—it's but
sitting silent when they examine me—there's nae torture in our
days—and if there is, let them rend me!—It's ill o' the vassal's
mouth that betrays the bread it eats.'

'Speak to her, Edie,' said the Antiquary, 'she knows your voice,
and answers to it most readily.'

'We shall mak naething mair out o' her,' said Ochiltree. 'When she
has clinkit hersell down that way, and faulded her arms, she winna
speak a word, they say, for weeks thegither. And besides, to my
thinking, her face is sair changed since we cam in. However, I'se try
her ance mair to satisfy your honour.—So ye canna keep in mind,

cummer, that your auld mistress, the Countess Joscelin, has been removed?'

'Removed!' she exclaimed; for that name never failed to produce its usual effect upon her; 'then we maun a' follow. A' maun ride when she is in the saddle—tell them to let Lord Geraldin ken we're on before them—bring my hood and scarf—ye wadna hae me gang in the carriage wi' my leddy, and my hair in this fashion?'

She raised her shrivelled arms, and seemed busied like a woman who puts on her cloak to go abroad, then dropped them slowly and stiffly; and the same idea of a journey still floating apparently through her head, she proceeded in a hurried and interrupted manner,—'Call Miss Neville—What do you mean by Lady Geraldin? I said Eveline Neville—not Lady Geraldin—there's no Lady Geraldin—tell her that, and bid her change her wet gown, and no' look sae pale.—Bairn! what should she do wi' a bairn?—maidens hae nane, I trow.—Teresa—Teresa—my lady calls us!—Bring a candle, the grand staircase is as mirk as a Yule midnight—We are coming, my lady!' With these words she sunk back on the settle, and from thence sidelong to the floor.[24]

Edie ran to support her, but hardly got her in his arms, before he said, 'It's a' ower, she has passed away even with that last word.'

'Impossible,' said Oldbuck, hastily advancing, as did his nephew. But nothing was more certain. She had expired with the last hurried word that left her lips; and all that remained before them, were the mortal relics of the creature who had so long struggled with an internal sense of concealed guilt, joined to all the distresses of age and poverty.

'God grant that she be gane to a better place!' said Edie, as he looked on the lifeless body; 'but, oh! there was something lying hard and heavy at her heart. I have seen mony a ane dee, baith in the field o' battle, and a fair-strae death* at hame; but I wad rather see them a' ower again, as sic a fearfu' flitting as hers!'

'We must call in the neighbours,' said Oldbuck, when he had somewhat recovered his horror and astonishment, 'and give warning of this additional calamity—I wish she could have been brought to a confession. And, though of far less consequence, I could have wished to transcribe that metrical fragment. But Heaven's will must be done!'

They left the hut accordingly, and gave the alarm in the hamlet, whose matrons instantly assembled to compose the limbs and arrange the body of her who might be considered as the mother of their settlement. Oldbuck promised his assistance for the funeral.

'Your honour,' said Ailison Breck, who was next in age to the deceased, 'suld send doun something to us for keeping up our hearts at the lyke-wake, for a' Saunders's gin, puir man, was drucken out at the burial o' Steenie, and we'll no get mony to sit dry-lipped aside the corpse. Elspeth was unco clever in her young days, as I can mind right weel, but there was aye a word o' her no being that chancy— Ane suldna speak ill o' the dead—mair by token, o' ane's cummer and neighbour—but there was queer things said about a leddy and a bairn or she left the Craigburnfoot. And sae, in gude troth, it will be a puir lyke-wake, unless your honour sends us something to keep us cracking.'

'You shall have some whisky,' answered Oldbuck, 'the rather that you have preserved the proper word for that ancient custom of watching the dead. — You observe, Hector, this is genuine Teutonic, from the Gothic *Leichnam*, a corpse. It is quite erroneously called *Late-wake*, though Brand* favours that modern corruption and derivation.'

'I believe,' said Hector to himself, 'my uncle would give away Monkbarns to any one who would come to ask it in genuine Teutonic! Not a drop of whisky would the old creatures have got, had their president asked it for the use of the *Late-wake*.'

While Oldbuck was giving some farther directions, and promising assistance, a servant of Sir Arthur's came riding very hard along the sands, and stopped his horse when he saw the Antiquary. 'There had something,' he said, 'very particular happened at the Castle,' (he could not, or would not, explain what,) 'and Miss Wardour had sent him off express to Monkbarns, to beg that Mr Oldbuck would come to them without a moment's delay.'

'I am afraid,' said the Antiquary, 'his course also is drawing to a close—What can I do?'

'Do, sir?' exclaimed Hector, with his characteristic impatience,— 'get on the horse, and turn his head homeward—you will be at Knockwinnock Castle in ten minutes.'

'He is quite a free goer,' said the servant, dismounting to adjust the girths and stirrups,—'he only pulls a little if he feels a dead weight on him.'

'I should soon be a dead weight *off* him, my friend,' said the Antiquary.—'What the devil, nephew, are you weary of me? or do you suppose me weary of my life, that I should get on the back of such a Bucephalus as that? No, no, my friend, if I am to be at Knockwinnock today, it must be by walking quietly forward on my own feet, which I will do with as little delay as possible. Captain M'Intyre may ride that animal himself, if he pleases.'

'I have little hope I could be of any use, uncle, but I cannot think of their distress without wishing to show sympathy at least—so I will ride on before, and announce to them that you are coming.—I'll trouble you for your spurs, my friend.'

'You will scarce need them, sir,' said the man, taking them off at the same time, and buckling them upon Captain M'Intyre's heels, 'he's very frank to the road.'

Oldbuck stood astonished at this last act of temerity. 'Are you mad, Hector?' he cried, 'or have you forgotten what is said by Quintus Curtius,* with whom, as a soldier, you must needs be familiar, *Nobilis equus umbra quidem virgæ regitur; ignavus ne calcari quidem excitari potest*;* which plainly shows that spurs are useless in every case, and, I may add, dangerous in most?'

But Hector, who cared little for the opinion of either Quintus Curtius, or of the Antiquary, upon such a topic, only answered with a heedless 'Never fear, never fear, sir.'

> 'With that he gave his able horse the head,
> And, bending forward, struck his armed heels
> Against the panting sides of his poor jade,
> Up to the rowel-head; and starting so,
> He seem'd in running to devour the way,
> Staying no longer question.'*

'There they go, well matched,' said Oldbuck, looking after them as they started,—'a mad horse and a wild boy, the two most unruly creatures in Christendom! and all to get half an hour sooner to a place where nobody wants him; for I doubt Sir Arthur's griefs are beyond the cure of our light horseman. It must be the villainy of Dousterswivel, for whom Sir Arthur has done so much; for I cannot help observing, that, with some natures, Tacitus's maxim holdeth good: *Beneficia eo usque læta sunt dum videntur exsolvi posse; ubi multum antevenere, pro gratia odium redditur*—from which a wise man

might take a caution, not to oblige any man beyond the degree in
which he may expect to be requited, lest he should make his debtor a
bankrupt in gratitude.'

Murmuring to himself such scraps of cynical philosophy, our
Antiquary paced the sands towards Knockwinnock; but it is necessary we should outstrip him, for the purpose of explaining the
reasons of his being so anxiously summoned thither.

CHAPTER XLI

So, while the Goose, of whom the fable told,
Incumbent, brooded o'er her eggs of gold,
With hand outstretch'd, impatient to destroy,
Stole on her secret nest the cruel Boy,
Whose gripe rapacious changed her splendid dream,
—For wings vain fluttering, and for dying scream.
                    *The Loves of the Sea-weeds.**

FROM the time that Sir Arthur Wardour had become possessor of the treasure found in Misticot's grave, he had been in a state of mind more resembling ecstasy than sober sense. Indeed, at one time his daughter had become seriously apprehensive for his intellect; for, as he had no doubt that he had the secret of possessing himself of wealth to an unbounded extent, his language and carriage were those of a man who had acquired the philosopher's stone. He talked of buying contiguous estates, that would have led him from one side of the island to the other, as if he were determined to brook no neighbour, save the sea. He corresponded with an architect of eminence, upon a plan of renovating the castle of his forefathers, on a style of extended magnificence that might have rivalled that of Windsor,* and laying out the grounds on a suitable scale. Troops of liveried menials were already, in fancy, marshalled in his halls, and—for what may not unbounded wealth authorize its possessor to aspire to?—the coronet of a marquis, perhaps of a duke, was glittering before his imagination. His daughter—to what matches might she not look forward? Even an alliance with the blood-royal was not beyond the sphere of his hopes. His son was already a general—and he himself whatever ambition could dream of in its wildest visions.

In this mood, if any one endeavoured to bring Sir Arthur down to the regions of common life, his replies were in the vein of Ancient Pistol:

'A fico for the world, and worldlings base!
I speak of Africa and golden joys!'*

The reader may conceive the amazement of Miss Wardour, when, instead of undergoing an investigation concerning the addresses of

Lovel, as she had expected from the long conference of her father with Mr Oldbuck, upon the morning of the fated day when the treasure was discovered, the conversation of Sir Arthur announced an imagination heated with the hopes of possessing the most unbounded wealth. But she was seriously alarmed when Dousterswivel was sent for to the Castle, and was closeted with her father— his mishap condoled with—his part taken, and his loss compensated. All the suspicions which she had long entertained respecting this man became strengthened, by observing his pains to keep up the golden dreams of her father, and to secure for himself, under various pretexts, as much as possible out of the windfall which had so strangely fallen to Sir Arthur's share.

Other evil symptoms began to appear, following close on each other. Letters arrived every post, which Sir Arthur, as soon as he had looked at the directions, flung into the fire without taking the trouble to open them. Miss Wardour could not help suspecting that these epistles, the contents of which seemed to be known to her father by a sort of intuition, came from pressing creditors. In the meanwhile, the temporary aid which he had received from the treasure, dwindled fast away. By far the greater part had been swallowed up by the necessity of paying the bill of six hundred pounds, which had threatened Sir Arthur with instant distress. Of the rest, some part was given to the adept, some wasted upon extravagances which seemed to the poor knight fully authorized by his full-blown hopes,—and some went to stop for a time the mouths of such claimants, who, being weary of fair promises, had become of opinion with Harpagon,* that it was necessary to touch something substantial. At length circumstances announced but too plainly, that it was all expended within two or three days after its discovery; and there appeared no prospect of a supply. Sir Arthur, naturally impatient, now taxed Dousterswivel anew with breach of those promises, through which he had hoped to convert all his lead into gold. But that worthy gentleman's turn was now served; and as he had grace enough to wish to avoid witnessing the fall of the house which he had undermined, he was at the trouble of bestowing a few learned terms of art upon Sir Arthur, that at least he might not be tormented before his time. He took leave of him, with assurances that he would return to Knockwinnock the next morning, with such information as would not fail to relieve Sir Arthur from all his distresses.

'For, since I have consulted in such matters, I ave never,' said Mr Herman Dousterswivel, 'approached so near de *arcanum*, what you call de great mystery,—de Panchresta—de Polychresta—I do know as much of it as Pelaso de Taranta, or Basilius*—and either I will bring you in two and tree days de No. III. of Mr Mishdigoat, or you shall call me one knave myself, and never look me in de face again no more at all.'

The adept departed with this assurance, in the firm resolution of making good the latter part of the proposition, and never again appearing before his injured patron. Sir Arthur remained in a doubtful and anxious state of mind. The positive assurances of the philosopher, with the hard words Panchresta, Basilius, and so forth, produced some effect on his mind. But he had been too often deluded by such jargon to be absolutely relieved of his doubt, and he retired for the evening into his library, in the fearful state of one who, hanging over a precipice, and without the means of retreat, perceives the stone on which he rests gradually parting from the rest of the crag, and about to give way with him.

The visions of hope decayed, and there increased in proportion that feverish agony of anticipation with which a man, educated in a sense of consequence, and possessed of opulence,—the supporter of an ancient name, and the father of two promising children,—foresaw the hour approaching which should deprive him of all the splendour which time had made familiarly necessary to him, and send him forth into the world to struggle with poverty, with rapacity, and with scorn. Under these dire forebodings, his temper, exhausted by the sickness of delayed hope, became peevish and fretful, and his words and actions sometimes expressed a reckless desperation, which alarmed Miss Wardour extremely. We have seen, on a former occasion, that Sir Arthur was a man of passions lively and quick, in proportion to the weakness of his character in other respects; he was unused to contradiction, and if he had been hitherto, in general, good-humoured and cheerful, it was probably because the course of his life had afforded no such frequent provocation as to render his irritability habitual.

On the third morning after Dousterswivel's departure, the servant, as usual, laid on the breakfast table the newspaper and letters of the day. Miss Wardour took up the former to avoid the continued ill-humour of her father, who had wrought himself into a violent passion, because the toast was over-browned.

'I perceive how it is,' was his concluding speech on this interesting subject,—'my servants, who have had their share of my fortune, begin to think there is little to be made of me in future. But while I *am* the scoundrels' master I will be so, and permit no neglect—no, nor endure a hair's-breadth diminution of the respect I am entitled to exact from them.'

'I am ready to leave your honour's service this instant,' said the domestic upon whom the fault had been charged, 'as soon as you order payment of my wages.'

Sir Arthur, as if stung by a serpent, thrust his hand into his pocket, and instantly drew out the money which it contained, but which was short of the man's claim. 'What money have you got, Miss Wardour?' he said, in a tone of affected calmness, but which concealed violent agitation.

Miss Wardour gave him her purse; he attempted to count the bank notes which it contained, but could not reckon them. After twice miscounting the sum, he threw the whole to his daughter, and saying in a stern voice, 'Pay the rascal, and let him leave the house instantly!' he strode out of the room.

The mistress and servant stood alike astonished at the agitation and vehemence of his manner.

'I am sure, ma'am, if I had thought I was particularly wrang, I wadna hae made ony answer when Sir Arthur challenged me—I hae been lang in his service, and he has been a kind master, and you a kind mistress, and I wad like ill ye should think I wad start for a hasty word—I am sure it was very wrang o' me to speak about wages to his honour, when maybe he has something to vex him. I had nae thoughts o' leaving the family in this way.'

'Go down stairs, Robert,' said his mistress—'something has happened to fret my father—go down stairs, and let Alick answer the bell.'

When the man left the room, Sir Arthur re-entered, as if he had been watching his departure. 'What's the meaning of this?' he said hastily, as he observed the notes lying still on the table—-'Is he not gone? Am I neither to be obeyed as a master or a father?'

'He is gone to give up his charge to the house-keeper, sir,—I thought there was not such instant haste.'

'There *is* haste, Miss Wardour,' answered her father, interrupting her;—'What I do henceforth in the house of my forefathers, must be done speedily, or never.'

He then sate down, and took up with a trembling hand the basin of tea prepared for him, protracting the swallowing of it, as if to delay the necessity of opening the post-letters which lay on the table, and which he eyed from time to time, as if they had been a nest of adders ready to start into life and spring upon him.

'You will be happy to hear,' said Miss Wardour, willing to withdraw her father's mind from the gloomy reflections in which he appeared to be plunged, 'you will be happy to hear, sir, that Lieutenant Taffril's gun-brig has got safe into Leith Roads—I observe there had been apprehensions for his safety—I am glad we did not hear them till they were contradicted.'

'And what is Taffril and his gun-brig to me?'

'Sir!' said Miss Wardour in astonishment; for Sir Arthur, in his ordinary state of mind, took a fidgety sort of interest in all the gossip of the day and country.

'I say,' he repeated, in a higher and still more impatient key, 'what do I care who is saved or lost?—It's nothing to me, I suppose?'

'I did not know you were busy, Sir Arthur; and thought, as Mr Taffril is a brave man, and from our own country, you would be happy to hear'—

'O, I am happy—as happy as possible—and, to make you happy too, you shall have some of my good news in return.' And he caught up a letter. 'It does not signify which I open first—they are all to the same tune.'

He broke the seal hastily, run the letter over, and then threw it to his daughter—'Ay; I could not have lighted more happily!—this places the cope-stone.'

Miss Wardour, in silent terror, took up the letter. 'Read it—read it aloud!' said her father; 'it cannot be read too often; it will serve to break you in for other good news of the same kind.'

She began to read with a faltering voice, 'Dear Sir.'

'He *dears* me too, you see—this impudent drudge of a writer's office,* who, a twelvemonth since, was not fit company for my second table*—I suppose I shall be "dear Knight" with him by and by.'

'Dear Sir,' resumed Miss Wardour; but, interrupting herself, 'I see the contents are unpleasant, sir—it will only vex you my reading them aloud.'

'If you will allow me to know my own pleasure, Miss Wardour, I entreat you to go on—I presume, if it were unnecessary, I should not ask you to take the trouble.'

'Having been of late taken into copartnery,' continued Miss Wardour, reading the letter, 'by Mr Gilbert Greenhorn, son of your late correspondent and man of business, Girnigo Greenhorn, Esq. writer to the signet,* whose business I conducted as parliament-house clerk for many years, which business will in future be carried on under the firm of Greenhorn and Grinderson, (which I memorandum for the sake of accuracy in addressing your future letters,) and having had of late favours of yours, directed to my aforesaid partner, Gilbert Greenhorn, in consequence of his absence at the Lamberton races, have the honour to reply to your said favours.'

'You see my friend is methodical, and commences by explaining the causes which have procured me so modest and elegant a correspondent—Go on—I can bear it.'

And he laughed that bitter laugh which is perhaps the most fearful expression of mental misery. Trembling to proceed, and yet afraid to disobey, Miss Wardour continued to read: 'I am, for myself and partner, sorry we cannot oblige you by looking out for the sums you mention, or applying for a suspension in the case of Goldiebirds' bond, which would be more inconsistent, as we have been employed to act as the said Goldiebirds' procurators and attorneys, in which capacity we have taken out a charge of horning* against you, as you must be aware by the schedule left by the messenger, for the sum of four thousand seven hundred and fifty-six pounds five shillings and sixpence one-fourth of a penny Sterling, which, with annual rent and expenses effeiring, we presume will be settled, during the currency of the charge, to prevent further trouble. Same time, I am under the necessity to observe our own account, amounting to seven hundred and sixty-nine pounds ten shillings and sixpence, is also due, and settlement would be agreeable; but as we hold your rights, title-deeds, and documents in hypothec,* shall have no objection to give reasonable time—say till the next money term.* I am, for myself and partner, concerned to add, that Messrs Goldiebirds' instructions to us are, to proceed *peremptorie* and *sine mora*,* of which I have the pleasure to advise you to prevent future mistakes, reserving to ourselves otherwise to *agé* as accords.* I am, for self and partner, dear sir, your obliged humble servant, Gabriel Grinderson, for Greenhorn and Grinderson.'

'Ungrateful villain!' said Miss Wardour.

'Why, no; it's in the usual rule, I suppose; the blow could not have been perfect if dealt by another hand—it's all just as it should be,' answered the poor Baronet, his affected composure sorely belied by his quivering lip and rolling eye—'But here's a postscript I did not notice—come, finish the epistle.'

'I have to add, (not for self but partner,) that Mr Greenhorn will accommodate you by taking your service of plate, or the bay horses, if sound in wind and limb, at a fair appreciation, in part payment of your accompt.'

'G—d confound him!' said Sir Arthur, losing all command of himself at this condescending proposal; 'his grandfather shod my father's horses, and this descendant of a scoundrelly blacksmith proposes to swindle me out of mine! But I will write him a proper answer.'

And he sate down and began to write with great vehemence, then stopped and read aloud: 'Mr Gilbert Greenhorn, in answer to two letters of a late date, I received a letter from a person calling himself Grinderson, and designing himself as your partner. When I address any one, I do not usually expect to be answered by deputy—I think I have been useful to your father, and friendly and civil to yourself, and therefore am now surprised—And yet,' said he, stopping short, 'why should I be surprised at that or any thing else—or why should I take up my time in writing to such a scoundrel?—I shan't be always kept in prison, I suppose, and to break that puppy's bones when I get out shall be my first employment.'

'In prison, sir?' said Miss Wardour faintly.

'Ay, in prison, to be sure. Do you make any question about that?—Why, Mr what's his name's fine letter for self and partner seems to be thrown away on you, or else you have got four thousand so many hundred pounds, with the due proportion of shillings, pence, and half-pence, to pay that aforesaid demand, as he calls it.'

'I, sir?—O if I had the means!—But where's my brother?—Why does he not come, and so long in Scotland? He might do something to assist us.'

'Who, Reginald?—I suppose he's gone with Mr Gilbert Greenhorn, or some such respectable person, to the Lamberton races—I have expected him this week past—but I cannot wonder that my children should neglect me as well as every other person. But I should beg your pardon, my love, who never either neglected or offended me in your life.'

And kissing her cheek as she threw her arms round his neck, he experienced that consolation which a parent feels, even in the most distressed state, in the assurance that he possesses the affection of a child.

Miss Wardour took the advantage of this revulsion of feeling, to endeavour to soothe her father's mind to composure. She reminded him that he had many friends.

'I *had* many once,' said Sir Arthur; 'but of some I have exhausted their kindness with my frantic projects—others are unable to assist me—others are unwilling—it is all over with me—I only hope Reginald will take example by my folly.'

'Should I not send to Monkbarns, sir?' said his daughter.

'To what purpose? He cannot lend me such a sum, and would not if he could, for he knows I am otherwise drowned in debt; and he would only give me scraps of misanthropy and quaint ends of Latin.'

'But he is shrewd and sensible, and was bred to business, and, I am sure, always loved this family.'

'Yes; I believe he did—it is a fine pass we are come to, when the affection of an Oldbuck is of consequence to a Wardour!—But when matters come to extremity, as I suppose they presently will—it may be as well to send for him.—And now go take your walk, my dear— my mind is more composed than when I had this cursed disclosure to make.—You know the worst, and may daily or hourly expect it. Go take your walk—I would willingly be alone for a little while.'

When Miss Wardour left the apartment, her first occupation was to avail herself of the half permission granted by her father, by dispatching to Monkbarns the messenger, who, as we have already seen, met the Antiquary and his nephew on the sea-beach.

Little recking, and indeed scarce knowing, where she was wandering, chance directed her into the walk beneath the Briery Bank, as it was called. A brook, which, in former days, had supplied the castle-moat with water, here descended through a narrow dell, up which Miss Wardour's taste had directed a natural path, which was rendered neat and easy of ascent, without the air of being formally made and preserved. It suited well the character of the little glen, which was overhung with thickets and underwood, chiefly of larch and hazel, intermixed with the usual varieties of the thorn and brier. In this walk had passed that scene of explanation between Miss Wardour and Lovel, which was overheard by old Edie Ochiltree. With a heart softened by the distress which approached her family, Miss Wardour now recalled every word and argument which Lovel had urged in support of his suit, and could not help confessing to herself, it was no small subject of pride to have inspired a young man of his talents with a passion so strong and disinterested. That he should have left the pursuit of a profession in which he was said to be rapidly rising, to bury himself in a disagreeable place like Fairport, and brood over an unrequited passion, might be ridiculed by others as romantic, but was naturally forgiven as an excess of affection by the person who was the object of his attachment. Had he possessed an independence, however moderate, or ascertained a clear and undisputed claim to the rank in society he was well qualified to adorn, she might now have had it in her power to offer her father, during his misfortunes, an asylum in an establishment of her own. These thoughts, so favourable to the absent lover, crowded in, one after the other, with such a minute recapitulation of his words, looks, and actions, as plainly intimated that his former repulse had been dictated rather by duty than inclination. Isabella was musing alternately upon this subject, and upon that of her father's misfortunes, when, as the path winded round a little hillock, covered with brushwood, the old Blue-Gown suddenly met her.

With an air as if he had something important and mysterious to communicate, he doffed his bonnet, and assumed the cautious step and voice of one who would not willingly be overheard. 'I hae been wishing muckle to meet wi' your leddyship—for ye ken I darena come to the house for Dousterswivel.'

'I heard indeed,' said Miss Wardour, dropping an alms into the bonnet, 'I heard that you had done a very foolish, if not a very bad thing, Edie, and I was sorry to hear it.'

'Hout, my bonny leddy—fulish?—A' the warld's fules—and how should auld Edie Ochiltree be aye wise?—and for the evil—let them wha deal wi' Dousterswivel tell whether he gat a grain mair than his deserts.'

'That may be true, Edie, and yet,' said Miss Wardour, 'you may have been very wrong.'

'Weel, weel, we'se no dispute that e'enow—it's about yoursell I'm gaun to speak—Div ye ken what's hanging ower the house of Knockwinnock?'

'Great distress, I fear, Edie,' answered Miss Wardour; 'but I am surprised it is already so public.'

'Public!—Sweepclean, the messenger, will be there the day wi' a' his tackle. I ken it frae ane o' his concurrents, as they ca' them, that's warned to meet him—and they'll be about their wark belyve—whare they clip there needs nae kame—they sheer close eneugh.'

'Are you sure this bad hour, Edie, is so very near?—come, I know, it will.'

'It's e'en as I tell you, leddy! but dinna be cast down—there's a heaven ower your head here, as weel as in that fearful night atween the Ballyburghness and the Halket-head. D'ye think He, wha rebuked the waters, canna protect you against the wrath of men, though they be armed with human authority?'

'It is, indeed, all we have to trust to.'

'Ye dinna ken—ye dinna ken—when the night's darkest, the dawn's nearest. If I had a gude horse, or could ride him when I had him, I reckon there wad be help yet.—I trusted to hae gotten a cast wi' the Royal Charlotte,* but she's coupit yonder, its like, at Kittlebrig. There was a young gentleman on the box, and he behuved to drive; and Tam Sang, that suld hae mair sense, he behuved to let him, and the daft callant couldna tak the turn at the corner o' the brig, and odd! he took the curb-stance, and he's whomled her as I wad whomle a toom bicker—it was a luck I hadna gotten on the tap o' her—Sae I came down atween hope and despair to see if ye wad send me on.'

'And, Edie—where would ye go?' said the young lady.

'To Tannonburgh, my leddy,' (which was the first stage from Fairport, but a good deal nearer to Knockwinnock,) 'and that without delay—it's a' on your ain business.'

'Our business, Edie? Alas! I give you all credit for your good meaning, but'—

'There's nae *buts* about it, my leddy, for gang I maun,' said the persevering Blue-Gown.

'But what is it that you would do at Tannonburgh?—or how can your going there benefit my father's affairs?'

'Indeed, my sweet leddy,' said the gaberlunzie, 'ye maun just trust that bit secret to auld Edie's grey pow, and ask nae questions about it—Certainly if I wad hae wared my life for you yon night, I can hae nae reason to play an ill pliskie t'ye in the day o' your distress.'

'Well, Edie, follow me then,' said Miss Wardour; 'and I will try to get you sent to Tannonburgh.'

'Mak haste then, my bonny leddy, mak haste, for the love o' goodness!'—and he continued to exhort her to expedition until they reached the castle.

CHAPTER XLII

Let those go see who will—I like it not—
For, say he was a slave to rank and pomp,
And all the nothings he is now divorced from
By the hard doom of stern necessity;
Yet is it sad to mark his alter'd brow,
Where Vanity adjusts her flimsy veil
O'er the deep wrinkles of repentant anguish.

*Old Play.**

WHEN Miss Wardour arrived in the court of the Castle, she was apprised by the first glance, that the visit of the officers of the law had already taken place. There was confusion, and gloom, and sorrow, and curiosity among the domestics, while the retainers of the law went from place to place, making an inventory of the goods and chattels falling under their warrant of distress, or poinding,* as it is called in the law of Scotland. Captain M'Intyre flew to her, as, struck dumb with the melancholy conviction of her father's ruin, she paused upon the threshold of the gateway.

'Dear Miss Wardour,' he said, 'do not make yourself uneasy; my uncle is coming immediately, and I am sure he will find some way to clear the house of these rascals.'

'Alas! Captain M'Intyre, I fear it will be too late.'

'No,' answered Edie, impatiently,—'could I but get to Tannonburgh. In the name of Heaven, Captain! contrive some way to get me on, and ye'll do this poor ruined family the best day's doing that has been done them since Redhand's days—for as sure as e'er an auld saw came true, Knockwinnock house and land will be lost and won this day.'

'Why, what good can you do, old man?' said Hector.

But Robert, the domestic with whom Sir Arthur had been so much displeased in the morning, as if he had been watching for an opportunity to display his zeal, stepped hastily forward and said to his mistress, 'If you please, ma'am, this auld man, Ochiltree, is very skeely and auld-farrant about mony things, as the diseases of cows, and horse, and sic like, and I am sure he disna want to be at Tannonburgh the day for naething, since he insists on't this gate; and, if your leddyship pleases, I'll drive him there in the taxed cart* in an hour's time.—I wad fain be of some use—I could bite my very tongue out when I think on this morning.'

'I am obliged to you, Robert,' said Miss Wardour; 'and if you really think it has the least chance of being useful'—

'In the name of God,' said the old man, 'yoke the cart, Robie, and if I am no o' some use, less or mair, I'll gie ye leave to fling me ower Kittlebrig as ye come back again. But O man, haste ye, for time's precious this day.'

Robert looked at his mistress as she retired into the house, and seeing he was not prohibited, flew to the stable-yard, which was adjacent to the court, in order to yoke the carriage; for, though an old beggar was the personage least likely to render effectual assistance in a case of pecuniary distress, yet there was among the common people of Edie's circle, a general idea of his prudence and sagacity, which authorized Robert's conclusion, that he would not so earnestly have urged the necessity of this expedition had he not been convinced of its utility. But so soon as the servant took hold of a horse to harness him for the tax-cart, an officer touched him on the shoulder—'My friend, you must let that beast alone, he's down in the schedule.'

'What,' said Robert, 'am I not to take my master's horse to go my young leddy's errand?'

'You must remove nothing here,' said the man of office, 'or you will be liable for all consequences.'

'What the devil, sir,' said Hector, who, having followed to examine Ochiltree more closely on the nature of his hopes and expectations, already began to bristle like one of the terriers of his own native mountains, and sought but a decent pretext for venting his displeasure, 'have you the impudence to prevent the young lady's servant from obeying her orders?'

There was something in the air and tone of the young soldier, which seemed to argue that his interference was not likely to be confined to mere expostulation; and which, if it promised finally the advantages of a process of battery and deforcement, would certainly commence with the unpleasant circumstances necessary for founding such a complaint. The legal officer, confronted with him of the military, grasped with one doubtful hand the greasy bludgeon which was to enforce his authority, and with the other produced his short official baton, tipped with silver, and having a movable ring upon it—'Captain M'Intyre,—Sir, I have no quarrel with you,—but if you interrupt me in my duty, I will break the wand of peace, and declare myself deforced.'*

'And who the devil cares,' said Hector, totally ignorant of the words of judicial action, 'whether you declare yourself divorced or married?—And as to breaking your wand, or breaking the peace, or whatever you call it, all I know is, that I will break your bones if you prevent the lad from harnessing the horses to obey his mistress's orders.'

'I take all who stand here to witness,' said the messenger, 'that I showed him my blazon and explained my character.—He that will to Cupar maun to Cupar,'*—and he slid his enigmatical ring from one end of the baton to the other, being the appropriate symbol of his having been forcibly interrupted in the discharge of his duty.

Honest Hector, better accustomed to the artillery of the field than to that of the law, saw this mystical ceremony with great indifference; and with like unconcern beheld the messenger sit down to write out an execution of deforcement. But at this moment, to prevent the well-meaning hot-headed Highlander from running the risk of a severe penalty, the Antiquary arrived puffing and blowing, with his handkerchief crammed under his hat, and his wig upon the end of his stick.

'What the deuce is the matter here?' he exclaimed, hastily adjusting his head-gear; 'I have been following you in fear of finding your idle loggerhead knocked against one rock or other, and here I find you parted with your Bucephalus, and quarrelling with Sweepclean. A messenger, Hector, is a worse foe than a *phoca*, whether it be the *phoca barbata*, or the *phoca vitulina** of your late conflict.'

'D—n the *phoca*, sir,' said Hector, 'whether it be the one or the other—I say d—n them both particularly!—I think you would not have me stand quietly by and see a scoundrel like this, because he calls himself a king's messenger, forsooth—(I hope the king has many better for his meanest errands)—insult a young lady of family and fashion like Miss Wardour?'

'Rightly argued, Hector,' said the Antiquary; 'but the king, like other people, has now and then shabby errands, and, in your ear, must have shabby fellows to do them. But even supposing you unacquainted with the statutes of William the Lion, in which, *capite quarto, versu quinto,** this crime of deforcement is termed *despectus*

*Domini Regis,** a contempt, to wit, of the king himself, in whose name all legal diligence issues, could you not have inferred, from the information I took so much pains to give you today, that those who interrupt officers who come to execute letters of caption, are *tanquam participes criminis rebellionis?** seeing that he who aids a rebel, is himself, *quodammodo*, an accessory to rebellion—But I'll bring you out of the scrape.'

He then spoke to the messenger, who, upon his arrival, had laid aside all thoughts of making a good by-job out of the deforcement, and accepted Mr Oldbuck's assurances that the horse and taxed-cart should be safely returned in the course of two or three hours.

'Very well, sir,' said the Antiquary, 'since you are disposed to be so civil, you shall have another job in your own best way—a little cast of state politics—a crime punishable *per Legem Juliam,** Mr Sweepclean—Hark thee hither.'

And, after a whisper of five minutes, he gave him a slip of paper, on receiving which, the messenger mounted his horse, and, with one of his assistants, rode away pretty sharply. The fellow who remained seemed to delay his operations purposely, proceeded in the rest of his duty very slowly, and with the caution and precision of one who feels himself overlooked by a skilful and severe inspector.

In the meantime, Oldbuck, taking his nephew by the arm, led him into the house, and they were ushered into the presence of Sir Arthur Wardour, who, in a flutter between wounded pride, agonized apprehension, and vain attempts to disguise both under a show of indifference, exhibited a spectacle of painful interest.

'Happy to see you, Mr Oldbuck—always happy to see my friends in fair weather or foul,' said the poor Baronet, struggling not for composure, but for gaiety, an affectation which was strongly contrasted by the nervous and protracted grasp of his hand, and the agitation of his whole demeanour; 'I am happy to see you—You are riding, I see—I hope in this confusion your horses are taken good care of—I always like to have my friends' horses looked after—Egad, they will have all my care now, for you see they are like to leave me none of my own—he! he! he! eh, Mr Oldbuck?'

This attempt at a jest was attended by a hysterical giggle, which poor Sir Arthur intended should sound as an indifferent laugh.

'You know I never ride, Sir Arthur,' said the Antiquary.

'I beg your pardon; but sure I saw your nephew arrive on

horseback a short time since. We must look after officers' horses, and
his was a handsome grey charger, as I have seen.'

Sir Arthur was about to ring the bell, when Mr Oldbuck said, 'My
nephew came on your own grey horse, Sir Arthur.'

'Mine!' said the poor Baronet, 'mine, was it? then the sun had
been in my eyes—Well, I'm not worthy having a horse any longer,
since I don't know my own when I see him.'

Good Heaven, thought Oldbuck, how is this man altered from the
formal stolidity of his usual manner!—he grows wanton under
adversity—*Sed pereunti mille figuræ*.*—He then proceeded aloud; 'Sir
Arthur, we must necessarily speak a little on business.'

'To be sure,' said Sir Arthur;—'but it was so good that I should
not know the horse I have ridden these five years—ha! ha! ha!'

'Sir Arthur,' said the Antiquary, 'don't let us waste time which is
precious; we shall have, I hope, many better seasons for jesting—-
*desipere in loco** is the maxim of Horace—I more than suspect this has
been brought on by the villainy of Dousterswivel.'

'Don't mention his name, sir!' said Sir Arthur; and his manner
entirely changed from a fluttered affectation of gaiety to all the agitation of fury—his eyes sparkled, his mouth foamed, his hands were
clenched; 'Don't mention his name, sir,' he vociferated, 'unless you
would see me go mad in your presence!—That I should have been
such a miserable dolt—such an infatuated idiot—such a beast,
endowed with thrice a beast's stupidity, to be led and driven and
spur-galled by such a rascal, and under such ridiculous pretences—
Mr Oldbuck, I could tear myself when I think of it.'

'I only meant to say,' answered the Antiquary, 'that this fellow is
like to meet his reward; and I cannot but think we shall frighten
something out of him that may be of service to you—He has certainly had some unlawful correspondence on the other side of the
water.'

'Has he?—has he?—has he, indeed?—then d—n the household-
goods, horses, and so forth—I will go to prison a happy man, Mr
Oldbuck—I hope in Heaven there's a reasonable chance of his being
hanged?'

'Why, pretty fair,' said Oldbuck, willing to encourage this diversion, in hopes it might mitigate the feelings which seemed like to
overset the poor man's understanding; 'honester men have stretched
a rope, or the law has been sadly cheated—But this unhappy

business of yours—can nothing be done?—Let me see the charge.'

He took the papers; and, as he read them, his countenance grew hopelessly dark and disconsolate. Miss Wardour had by this time entered the apartment, and fixing her eyes on Mr Oldbuck, as if she meant to read her fate in his looks, easily perceived, from the change in his eye and the dropping of his nether-jaw, how little was to be hoped.

'We are then irremediably ruined, Mr Oldbuck?' said the young lady.

'Irremediably?—I hope not—but the instant demand is very large, and others will, doubtless, pour in.'

'Ay, never doubt that, Monkbarns,' said Sir Arthur; 'where the slaughter is, the eagles will be gathered together.*—I am like a sheep which I have seen fall down a precipice, or drop down from sickness—if you had not seen a single raven or hooded crow for a fortnight before, he will not lie on the heather ten minutes before half-a-dozen will be picking out his eyes, (and he drew his hand over his own), and tearing at his heart-strings before the poor devil has time to die. But that d—d long-scented vulture that dogged me so long—you have got him fast, I hope?'

'Fast enough,' said the Antiquary; 'the gentleman wished to take the wings of the morning* and bolt in the what d'ye call it,—the coach and four there. But he would have found twigs limed for him at Edinburgh. As it is, he never got so far, for the coach being overturned—as how could it go safe with such a Jonah?*—he has had an infernal tumble, is carried into a cottage near Kittlebrig, and, to prevent all possibility of escape, I have sent your friend, Sweepclean, to bring him back to Fairport, *in nomine regis*,* or to act as his sick-nurse at Kittlebrig, as is most fitting.—And now, Sir Arthur, permit me to have some conversation with you on the present unpleasant state of your affairs, that we may see what can be done for their extrication;' and the Antiquary led the way into the library, followed by the unfortunate gentleman.

They had been shut up together for about two hours, when Miss Wardour interrupted them with her cloak on, as if prepared for a journey. Her countenance was very pale, yet expressive of the composure which characterised her disposition.

'The messenger is returned, Mr Oldbuck.'

'Returned?—What the devil! he has not let the fellow go?'

'No—I understand he has carried him to confinement; and now he is returned to attend my father, and says he can wait no longer.'

A loud wrangling was now heard on the staircase, in which the voice of Hector predominated. 'You an officer, sir, and these raga-muffins a party! a parcel of beggarly tailor fellows—tell yourselves off by nine, and we shall know your effective strength.'

The grumbling voice of the man of law was then heard indistinctly muttering a reply, to which Hector retorted—'Come, come, sir, this won't do; march your party, as you call them, out of this house directly, or I'll send you and them to the right about presently.'

'The devil take Hector,' said the Antiquary, hastening to the scene of action; 'his Highland blood is up again, and we shall have him fighting a duel with the bailiff—Come, Mr Sweepclean, you must give us a little time—I know you would not wish to hurry Sir Arthur.'

'By no means, sir,' said the messenger, putting his hat off, which he had thrown on to testify defiance of Captain M'Intyre's threats; 'but your nephew, sir, holds very uncivil language, and I have borne too much of it already; and I am not justified in leaving my prisoner any longer after the instructions I received, unless I am to get pay-ment of the sums contained in my diligence.'—And he held out the caption, pointing with the awful truncheon which he held in his right hand, to the formidable line of figures jotted upon the back thereof.

Hector, on the other hand, though silent from respect to his uncle, answered this gesture by shaking his clenched fist at the messenger with a frown of Highland wrath.

'Foolish boy, be quiet,' said Oldbuck, 'and come with me into the room—the man is doing his miserable duty, and you will only make matters worse by opposing him.—I fear, Sir Arthur, you must accompany this man to Fairport; there is no help for it in the first instance—I will accompany you to consult what farther can be done—My nephew will escort Miss Wardour to Monkbarns, which I hope she will make her residence until these unpleasant matters are settled.'

'I go with my father, Mr Oldbuck,' said Miss Wardour firmly—'I have prepared his clothes and my own—I suppose we shall have the use of the carriage?'

'Any thing in reason, madam,' said the messenger; 'I have ordered it out, and it's at the door—I will go on the box with the coachman—I have no desire to intrude—but two of the concurrents must attend on horseback.'

'I will attend too,' said Hector, and he ran down to secure a horse for himself.

'We must go then,' said the Antiquary.

'To jail,' said the Baronet, sighing involuntarily; 'And what of that?' he resumed, in a tone affectedly cheerful—'it is only a house we can't get out of, after all—Suppose a fit of the gout, and Knockwinnock would be the same—Ay, ay, Monkbarns, we'll call it a fit of the gout without the d—d pain.'

But his eyes swelled with tears as he spoke, and his faltering accent marked how much this assumed gaiety cost him. The Antiquary wrung his hand, and, like the Indian Banians,* who drive the real terms of an important bargain by signs, while they are apparently talking of indifferent matters, the hand of Sir Arthur, by its convulsive return of the grasp, expressed his sense of gratitude to his friend, and the real state of his internal agony. They stepped slowly down the magnificent staircase—every well-known object seeming to the unfortunate father and daughter to assume a more prominent and distinct appearance than usual, as if to press themselves on their notice for the last time.

At the first landing-place, Sir Arthur made an agonized pause; and as he observed the Antiquary look at him anxiously, he said with assumed dignity—'Yes, Mr Oldbuck, the descendant of an ancient line—the representative of Richard Redhand and Gamelyn de Guardover, may be pardoned a sigh when he leaves the castle of his fathers thus poorly escorted. When I was sent to the Tower with my late father, in the year 1745, it was upon a charge becoming our birth—upon an accusation of high treason, Mr Oldbuck—we were escorted from Highgate by a troop of life-guards, and committed upon a secretary of state's warrant; and now, here I am, in my old age, dragged from my household by a miserable creature like that, (pointing to the messenger,) and for a paltry concern of pounds, shillings, and pence.'

'At least,' said Oldbuck, 'you have now the company of a dutiful daughter, and a sincere friend, if you will permit me to say so, and that may be some consolation, even without the certainty that there can be no hanging, drawing, or quartering,* on the present occasion.—But I hear that choleric boy as loud as ever. I hope to God he has got into no new broil!—it was an accursed chance that brought him here at all.'

In fact, a sudden clamour, in which the loud voice and somewhat northern accent of Hector was again pre-eminently distinguished, broke off this conversation. The cause we must refer to the next chapter.

CHAPTER XLIII

Fortune, you say, flies from us—She but circles,
Like the fleet sea-bird round the fowler's skiff,—
Lost in the mist one moment, and the next
Brushing the white sail with her whiter wing,
As if to court the aim.—Experience watches,
And has her on the wheel.—

Old Play.*

THE shout of triumph in Hector's warlike tones was not easily distinguished from that of battle. But as he rushed up stairs with a packet in his hand, exclaiming, 'Long life to an old soldier! here comes Edie with a whole budget of good news!' it became obvious that his present cause of clamour was of an agreeable nature. He delivered the letter to Oldbuck, shook Sir Arthur heartily by the hand, and wished Miss Wardour joy, with all the frankness of Highland congratulation. The messenger, who had a kind of instinctive terror for Captain M'Intyre, drew towards his prisoner, keeping an eye of caution on the soldier's motions.

'Don't suppose I shall trouble myself about you, you dirty fellow,' said the soldier; 'there's a guinea for the fright I have given you; and here comes an old *forty-two* man, who is a fitter match for you than I am.'

The messenger (one of those dogs who are not too scornful to eat dirty puddings) caught in his hand the guinea which Hector chucked at his face; and abode warily and carefully the turn which matters were now to take. All voices meanwhile were loud in enquiries, which no one was in a hurry to answer.

'What is the matter, Captain M'Intyre?' said Sir Arthur.

'Ask old Edie,' said Hector; 'I only know all's safe and well.'

'What is all this, Edie?' said Miss Wardour to the mendicant.

'Your leddyship maun ask Monkbarns, for he has gotten the yepistolary correspondensh.'

'God save the king!' exclaimed the Antiquary, at the first glance of the contents of his packet, and, surprised at once out of decorum, philosophy, and phlegm, he skimmed his cocked-hat in the air, from which it descended not again, being caught in its fall by a branch of the chandelier. He next, looking joyously round, laid a grasp on his wig, which he perhaps would have sent after the beaver, had not Edie stopped his hand, exclaiming, 'Lordsake! he's gaun gyte—mind Caxon's no here to repair the damage.'

Every person now assailed the Antiquary, clamouring to know the cause of so sudden a transport, when, somewhat ashamed of his rapture, he fairly turned tail, like a fox at the cry of a pack of hounds, and ascending the stair by two steps at a time, gained the upper landing-place, where, turning round, he addressed the astonished audience as follows:—

'My good friends, *favete linguis**—To give you information, I must first, according to logicians, be possessed of it myself; and, therefore, with your leaves, I will retire into the library to examine these papers—Sir Arthur and Miss Wardour will have the goodness to step into the parlour—Mr Sweepclean, *secede paulisper*,* or, in your own language, grant us a supersedere of diligence* for five minutes— Hector, draw off your forces, and make your bear-garden* flourish elsewhere—And, finally, be all of good cheer till my return, which will be *instanter*.'

The contents of the packet were indeed so little expected, that the Antiquary might be pardoned, first his ecstasy, and next his desire of delaying to communicate the intelligence they conveyed, until it was arranged and digested in his own mind.

Within the envelope was a letter addressed to Jonathan Oldbuck, Esq. of Monkbarns, of the following purport:—

'Dear Sir,—To you, as my father's proved and valued friend, I venture to address myself, being detained here by military duty of a very pressing nature. You must, by this time, be acquainted with the entangled state of our affairs; and I know it will give you great pleasure to learn, that I am as fortunately as unexpectedly placed in a situation to give effectual assistance for extricating them. I understand Sir Arthur is threatened with severe measures by persons who acted formerly as his agents; and, by advice of a creditable man of business here, I have procured the enclosed writing, which I understand will stop their proceedings, until their claim shall be legally discussed, and brought down to its proper amount. I also enclose bills* to the amount of one thousand pounds to pay any other pressing demands, and request of your friendship to apply them according to your discretion. You will be surprised I give you this trouble, when it would seem more natural to address my father directly in his own affairs. But I have yet had no assurance that his eyes are opened to the character of a person against whom you have often, I know, warned him, and whose baneful influence has been the occasion of these distresses. And as I owe the means of relieving Sir Arthur to the generosity of a matchless friend, it is my duty to take the most certain measures for the supplies being devoted to the purpose for which they were destined, and I know your wisdom and kindness will see that it is done. My friend, as he claims an interest in your regard, will explain some views of his own in the enclosed letter. The state of the post-office at Fairport being rather notorious, I must send this letter to Tannonburgh; but the old man Ochiltree, whom particular circumstances have recommended as trustworthy, has information when the packet is likely to reach that place, and will take care to forward it. I expect to have soon an opportunity to apologize in person for the trouble I now give, and have the honour to be your very faithful servant—REGINALD GAMELYN WARDOUR. Edinburgh, 6th August, 179—.'

The Antiquary hastily broke the seal of the enclosure, the contents of which gave him equal surprise and pleasure. When he had in some measure composed himself after such unexpected tidings, he inspected the other papers carefully, which all related to business—put the bills into his pocket-book, and wrote a short acknowledgment to be dispatched by that day's post, for he was extremely methodical in money matters;—and, lastly, fraught with all the importance of disclosure, he descended to the parlour.

'Sweepclean,' said he, as he entered, to the officer who stood respectfully at the door, 'you must sweep yourself clean out of Knockwinnock Castle with all your followers, tag-rag and bob-tail. See'st thou this paper, man?'

'A sist on a bill o' suspension,'* said the messenger, with a disappointed look; 'I thought it would be a queer thing if ultimate diligence* was to be done against sic a gentleman as Sir Arthur—Weel, sir, I'se go my ways with my party—And who's to pay my charges?'

'They who employed thee,' replied Oldbuck, 'as thou full well dost know.—But here comes another express: this is a day of news, I think.'

This was Mr Mailsetter on his mare from Fairport, with a letter for Sir Arthur, another to the messenger, both of which, he said, he was directed to forward instantly. The messenger opened his, observing, that Greenhorn and Grinderson were good enough men for his expenses, and here was a letter from them desiring him to stop the diligence. Accordingly, he immediately left the apartment, and staying no longer than to gather his posse together, he did then, in the phrase of Hector, who watched his departure as a jealous mastiff eyes the retreat of a repulsed beggar, evacuate Flanders.*

Sir Arthur's letter was from Mr Greenhorn, and a curiosity in its way. We give it, with the worthy Baronet's comments.

'Sir—[Oh! I am *dear* sir no longer; folks are only dear to Messrs Greenhorn and Grinderson when they are in adversity]—Sir, I am much concerned to learn, on my return from the country, where I was called on particular business, [a bet on the sweepstakes, I suppose,] that my partner had the impropriety, in my absence, to undertake the concerns of Messrs Goldiebirds in preference to yours, and had written to you in an unbecoming manner. I beg to make my most humble apology, as well as Mr Grinderson's—[come, I see he can write for himself and partner too,]—and trust it is impossible you can think me forgetful of, or ungrateful for, the constant patronage which my family [*his* family! curse him for a puppy!] have uniformly experienced from that of Knockwinnock. I am sorry to find, from an interview I had this day with Mr Wardour, that he is much irritated, and, I must own, with apparent reason. But, in order to remedy as much as in me lies the mistake of which he complains, [pretty mistake, indeed! to clap his patron into jail,] I have sent this express to discharge all proceedings against your person or property; and at the same time to transmit my respectful apology. I have only to add, that Mr Grinderson is of opinion, that, if restored to your confidence, he could point out circumstances connected with Messrs Goldiebirds' present claim which would greatly reduce its amount [so, so, willing to play the rogue on either side]; and that there is not the slightest hurry in settling the balance of your accompt with us; and that I am, for Mr G. as well as myself, Dear Sir, [O, ay, he has written himself into an approach to familiarity,] your much obliged, and most humble servant, GILBERT GREENHORN.'

'Well said, Mr Gilbert Greenhorn,' said Monkbarns; 'I see now there is some use in having two attorneys in one firm. Their movements resemble those of the man and woman in a Dutch babyhouse.* When it is fair weather with the client, out comes the gentleman-partner to fawn like a spaniel; when it is foul, forth bolts the operative brother to pin like a bull–dog—Well, I thank God, that my man of business still wears an equilateral cocked hat, has a house in the Old Town, is as much afraid of a horse as I am myself, plays at golf of a Saturday, goes to the kirk of a Sunday, and, in respect he has no partner, hath only his own folly to apologize for.'

'There are some writers very honest fellows,' said Hector; 'I should like to hear any one say that my cousin, Donald M'Intyre, Strathtudlem's seventh son, (the other six are in the army,) is not as honest a fellow'—

'No doubt, no doubt, Hector, all the M'Intyres are so; they have it by patent, man—But, I was going to say, that in a profession where unbounded trust is necessarily reposed, there is nothing surprising that fools should neglect it in their idleness, and tricksters abuse it in their knavery—But it is the more to the honour of those, and I will vouch for many, who unite integrity with skill and attention, and walk honourably upright where there are so many pitfalls and stumbling blocks for those of a different character. To such men their fellow-citizens may safely intrust the care of protecting their patrimonial rights, and their country the more sacred charge of her laws and privileges.'

'They are best off, however, that hae least to do with them,' said Ochiltree, who had stretched his neck into the parlour door; for the general confusion of the family not having yet subsided, the domestics, like waves after the fall of a hurricane, had not yet exactly regained their due limits, but were roaming wildly through the house.

'Aha, old Truepenny,* art thou there?' said the Antiquary; 'Sir Arthur, let me bring in the messenger of good luck, though he is but a lame one. You talked of the raven that scented out the slaughter from afar; but here's a blue pigeon (somewhat of the oldest and toughest, I grant) who smelled the good news six or seven miles off, flew thither in the taxed-cart, and returned with the olive branch.'*

'Ye owe it a' to puir Robie that drave me—puir fallow,' said the beggar, 'he doubts he's in disgrace wi' my leddy and Sir Arthur.'

Robert's repentant and bashful face was seen over the mendicant's shoulder.

'In disgrace with me?' said Sir Arthur—'how so?'—for the irritation into which he had worked himself on occasion of the toast had been long forgotten—'O, I recollect—Robert, I was angry, and you were wrong—go about your work, and never answer a master that speaks to you in a passion.'

'Nor any one else,' said the Antiquary; 'for a soft answer turneth away wrath.'*

'And tell your mother, who is so ill with the rheumatism, to come down to the housekeeper tomorrow,' said Miss Wardour, 'and we will see what can be of service to her.'

'God bless your leddyship,' said poor Robert, 'and his honour Sir Arthur, and the young laird, and the house of Knockwinnock in a' its branches, far and near—it's been a kind and a gude house to the puir this mony hundred years.'

'There'—said the Antiquary to Sir Arthur—'we won't dispute—but there you see the gratitude of the poor people naturally turns to the civil virtues of your family. You don't hear them talk of Redhand, or Hell-in-Harness. For me, I must say, *Odi accipitrem qui semper vivit in armis**—so let us eat and drink in peace, and be joyful, Sir Knight.'

A table was quickly covered in the parlour, where the party sat joyously down to some refreshment. At the request of Oldbuck, Edie Ochiltree was permitted to sit by the sideboard in a great leathern chair, which was placed in some measure behind a screen.

'I accede to this the more readily,' said Sir Arthur, 'because I remember in my father's days that chair was occupied by Ailshie Gourlay, who, for aught I know, was the last privileged fool, or jester, maintained by any family of distinction in Scotland.'

'Aweel, Sir Arthur,' replied the beggar, who never hesitated an instant between his friend and his jest, 'mony a wise man sits in a fule's seat, and mony a fule in a wise man's, especially in families o' distinction.'

Miss Wardour, fearing the effect of this speech (however worthy of Ailshie Gourlay, or any other privileged jester) upon the nerves of her father, hastened to enquire whether ale or beef should not be distributed to the servants and people, whom the news had assembled around the Castle.

'Surely, my love,' said her father, 'when was it ever otherwise in our families when a siege had been raised?'

'Ay, a siege laid by Saunders Sweepclean the bailiff, and raised by Edie Ochiltree the gaberlunzie, *par nobile fratrum*,'* said Oldbuck, 'and well pitted against each other in respectability. But never mind, Sir Arthur—these are such sieges and such reliefs as our time of day admits of—and our escape is not less worth commemorating in a glass of this excellent wine—Upon my credit, it is Burgundy, I think.'

'Were there any thing better in the cellar,' said Miss Wardour, 'it would be all too little to regale you after your friendly exertions.'

'Say you so?' said the Antiquary—'why, then, a cup of thanks to you, my fair enemy, and soon may you be besieged as ladies love best to be, and sign terms of capitulation in the chapel of Saint Winnox.'*

Miss Wardour blushed, Hector coloured, and then grew pale.

Sir Arthur answered, 'My daughter is much obliged to you, Monkbarns; but unless you'll accept of her yourself, I really do not know where a poor knight's daughter is to seek for an alliance in these mercenary times.'

'Me, mean ye, Sir Arthur?—No, not I; I will claim the privilege of the duello, and, as being unable to encounter my fair enemy myself, I will appear by my champion—But of this matter hereafter.—What do you find in the papers there, Hector, that you hold your head down over them as if your nose were bleeding?'

'Nothing particular, sir; but only that, as my arm is now almost quite well, I think I shall relieve you of my company in a day or two, and go to Edinburgh. I see Major Neville is arrived there. I should like to see him.'

'Major whom?' said his uncle.

'Major Neville, sir,' answered the young soldier.

'And who the devil is Major Neville?' demanded the Antiquary.

'O, Mr Oldbuck,' said Sir Arthur, 'you must remember his name frequently in the newspapers—a very distinguished young officer indeed. But I am happy to say that Mr M'Intyre need not leave Monkbarns to see him, for my son writes that the Major is to come with him to Knockwinnock, and I need not say how happy I shall be to make the young gentlemen acquainted,—unless, indeed, they are known to each other already.'

'No, not personally,' answered Hector, 'but I have had occasion to hear a good deal of him, and we have several mutual friends—your son being one of them.—But I must go to Edinburgh; for I see my uncle is beginning to grow tired of me, and I am afraid'—

'That you will grow tired of him?' interrupted Oldbuck,—'I fear that's past praying for. But you have forgotten that the ecstatic twelfth of August approaches, and that you are engaged to meet one of Lord Glenallan's gamekeepers, God knows where, to persecute the peaceful feathered creation.'

'True, true, uncle—I had forgot that,' exclaimed the volatile Hector,—'but you said something just now that put every thing out of my head.'

'An it like your honours,' said old Edie, thrusting his white head from behind the screen, where he had been plentifully regaling himself with ale and cold meat—'an it like your honours, I can tell ye something that will keep the Captain wi' us amaist as weel as the pouting—Hear ye na the French are coming?'

'The French, you blockhead?' answered Oldbuck—'Bah!'

'I have not had time,' said Sir Arthur Wardour, 'to look over my lieutenancy correspondence for the week—indeed, I generally make a rule to read it only on Wednesdays, except in pressing cases,—for I do every thing by method—but from the glance I took of my letters, I observed some alarm was entertained.'

'Alarm?' said Edie,—'troth there's alarm, for the provost's gar'd the beacon light on the Halket-head be sorted up (that suld hae been sorted half a year syne) in an unco hurry, and the council hae named nae less a man than auld Caxon himsell to watch the light. Some say it was out o' compliment to Lieutenant Taffril,—for it's neist to certain that he'll marry Jenny Caxon—some say it's to please your honour and Monkbarns that wear wigs—and some say there's some auld story about a periwig that ane o' the bailies got and ne'er paid for—Ony way, there he is, sitting cockit up like a skart upon the tap o' the craig, to skirl when foul weather comes.'

'On mine honour, a pretty warder,' said Monkbarns; 'and what's my wig to do all the while?'

'I asked Caxon that very question,' answered Ochiltree, 'and he said he could look in ilka morning, and gie't a touch afore he gaed to his bed, for there's another man to watch in the day-time, and Caxon says he'll frizz your honour's wig as weel sleeping as wauking.'

This news gave a different turn to the conversation, which ran upon national defence, and the duty of fighting for the land we live in, until it was time to part. The Antiquary and his nephew resumed their walk homeward, after parting from Knockwinnock with the warmest expressions of mutual regard, and an agreement to meet again as soon as possible.

CHAPTER XLIV

Nay, if she love me not, I care not for her:
Shall I look pale because the maiden blooms?
Or sigh because she smiles, and smiles on others?
Not I, by Heaven!—I hold my peace too dear,
To let it, like the plume upon her cap,
Shake at each nod that her caprice shall dictate.

Old Play.*

'HECTOR,' said his uncle to Captain M'Intyre, in the course of their walk homeward, 'I am sometimes inclined to suspect that, in one respect, you are a fool.'

'If you only think me so in *one* respect, sir, I am sure you do me more grace than I expected or deserve.'

'I mean in one particular, *par excellence*,' answered the Antiquary. 'I have sometimes thought that you have cast your eyes upon Miss Wardour.'

'Well, sir,' said M'Intyre, with much composure.

'Well, sir!' echoed his uncle, 'deuce take the fellow, he answers me as if it were the most reasonable thing in the world, that he, a captain in the army, and nothing at all besides, should marry the daughter of a baronet.'

'I presume to think, sir,' said the young Highlander, 'there would be no degradation on Miss Wardour's part in point of family.'

'O, Heaven forbid we should come on that topic!—no, no, equal both—both on the table-land of gentility, and qualified to look down on every *roturier* in Scotland.'

'And in point of fortune we are pretty even, since neither of us have got any,' continued Hector. 'There may be an error, but I cannot plead guilty to presumption.'

'But here lies the error, then, if you call it so,' replied his uncle; 'she won't have you, Hector.'

'Indeed, sir?'

'It is very sure, Hector; and to make it double sure, I must inform you that she likes another man. She misunderstood some words I once said to her, and I have since been able to guess at the interpretation she put on them. At the time, I was unable to account for her hesitation and blushing; but, my poor Hector, I now understand them as a death-signal to your hopes and pretensions—So I advise you to beat your retreat, and draw off your forces as well as you can, for the fort is too well garrisoned for you to storm it.'

'I have no occasion to beat any retreat, uncle,' said Hector, holding himself very upright, and marching with a sort of dogged and offended solemnity; 'no man needs to retreat that has never advanced. There are women in Scotland besides Miss Wardour, of as good family'—

'And better taste,' said his uncle; 'doubtless there are, Hector; and though I cannot say but that she is one of the most accomplished as well as sensible girls I have seen, yet I doubt much of her merit would be cast away on you. A showy figure, now, with two cross feathers above her noddle—one green, one blue; who would wear a riding-habit of the regimental complexion, drive a gig one day, and the next review the regiment on the grey trotting pony which dragged that vehicle, *hoc erat in votis**—These are the qualities that would subdue you, especially if she had a taste for natural history, and loved a specimen of a *phoca*.'

'It's a little hard, sir,' said Hector, 'I must have that cursed seal thrown into my face on all occasions—but I care little about it—and I shall not break my heart for Miss Wardour. She is free to choose for herself, and I wish her all happiness.'

'Magnanimously resolved, thou prop of Troy! Why, Hector, I was afraid of a scene—Your sister told me you were desperately in love with Miss Wardour.'

'Sir,' answered the young man, 'you would not have me desperately in love with a woman that does not care about me?'

'Well, nephew,' said the Antiquary, more seriously, 'there is doubtless much sense in what you say; yet I would have given a great deal, some twenty or twenty-five years since, to have been able to think as you do.'

'Any body, I suppose, may think as they please on such subjects,' said Hector.

'Not according to the old school,' said Oldbuck; 'but, as I said before, the practice of the modern seems in this case the most prudential, though, I think, scarcely the most interesting. But tell me your ideas now on this prevailing subject of an invasion.—The cry is still, They come.'*

Hector, swallowing his mortification, which he was peculiarly anxious to conceal from his uncle's satirical observation, readily entered into a conversation which was to turn the Antiquary's thoughts from Miss Wardour and the seal. When they reached Monkbarns, the communicating to the ladies the events which had taken place at the Castle, with the counter-information of how long dinner had waited before the womankind had ventured to eat it in the Antiquary's absence, averted these delicate topics of discussion.

The next morning the Antiquary arose early, and, as Caxon had not yet made his appearance, he began mentally to feel the absence of the petty news and small talk, of which the ex-peruquier was a faithful reporter, and which habit had made as necessary to the Antiquary as his occasional pinch of snuff, although he held, or affected to hold, both to be of the same intrinsic value. The feeling of vacuity peculiar to such a deprivation, was alleviated by the appearance of old Ochiltree, sauntering beside the clipped yew and holly hedges, with the air of a person quite at home. Indeed, so familiar had he been of late, that even Juno did not bark at him, but contented herself with watching him with a close and vigilant eye. Our Antiquary stepped out in his night-gown, and instantly received and returned his greeting.

'They are coming now, in good earnest, Monkbarns—I just cam frae Fairport to bring ye the news, and then I'll step away back again—the Search has just come into the bay, and they say she's been chased by a French fleet.'

'The Search?' said Oldbuck, reflecting a moment. 'Oho!'

'Ay, ay, Captain Taffril's gun-brig, the Search.'

'What! any relation to *Search, No. II.?*' said Oldbuck, catching at the light which the name of the vessel seemed to throw on the mysterious chest of treasure.

The mendicant, like a man detected in a frolic, put his bonnet before his face, yet could not help laughing heartily.—'The deil's in you, Monkbarns, for garring odds and evens meet—Wha thought ye wad hae laid that and that thegither?—Odd, I am clean catch'd now.'

'I see it all,' said Oldbuck, 'as plain as the legend on a medal of high preservation—the box in which the bullion was found belonged to the gun-brig, and the treasure to my phœnix?'—(Edie nodded assent.)—'And was buried there that Sir Arthur might receive relief in his difficulties?'

'By me,' said Edie, 'and twa o' the brig's men —but they didna ken its contents; and thought it some bit smuggling concern o' the Captain's. I watched day and night till I saw it in the right hand; and then, when that German deevil was glowering at the lid o' the kist, (they liked mutton weel that licket where the yowe lay,) I think some Scottish deevil put it into my head to play him yon ither cantrip— Now, ye see, if I had said mair or less to Bailie Littlejohn, I behoved till hae come out wi' a' this story; and vexed would Mr Lovel hae been to have it brought to light—sae I thought I would stand to ony thing rather than that.'

'I must say he has chosen his confident well,' said Oldbuck, 'though somewhat strangely.'

'I'll say this for mysell, Monkbarns,' answered the mendicant, 'that I am the fittest man in the haill country to trust wi' siller, for I neither want it, nor wish for it, nor could use it if I had it. But the lad hadna muckle choice in the matter, for he thought he was leaving the country for ever (I trust he's mistaen in that though); and the night was set in when we learned, by a strange chance, Sir Arthur's sair distress, and Lovel was obliged to be on board as the day dawned. But five nights afterwards the brig stood into the bay, and I met the boat by appointment, and we buried the treasure where ye fand it.'

'This was a very romantic, foolish exploit,' said Oldbuck—'why not trust me, or any other friend?'

'The blood o' your sister's son,' replied Edie, 'was on his hands, and him maybe dead outright—what time had he to take counsel?— or how could he ask it of you, by ony body?'

'You are right.—But what if Dousterswivel had come before you?'

'There was little fear o' his coming there without Sir Arthur—he had gotten a sair gliff the night afore, and never intended to look near the place again, unless he had been brought there sting and ling*—He kend weel the first pose was o' his ain hiding, and how could he expect a second? He just havered on about it to make the mair o' Sir Arthur.'

'Then how,' said Oldbuck, 'should Sir Arthur have come there unless the German had brought him?'

'Umph!' answered Edie dryly, 'I had a story about Misticot wad hae brought him forty miles, or you either. Besides, it was to be thought he would be for visiting the place he fand the first siller in— he kend na the secret o' that job. In short, the siller being in this shape, Sir Arthur in utter difficulties, and Lovel determined he should never ken the hand that helped him,—for that was what he insisted maist upon,—we couldna think o' a better way to fling the gear in his gate, though we simmered it and wintered it* e'er sae lang. And if by ony queer mischance Doustercivil had got his claws on't, I was instantly to hae informed you or the Sheriff o' the haill story.'

'Well, notwithstanding all these wise precautions, I think your contrivance succeeded better than such a clumsy one deserved, Edie. But how the deuce came Lovel by such a mass of silver ingots?'

'That's just what I canna tell ye—But they were put on board wi' his things at Fairport, it's like, and we stowed them into ane o' the ammunition-boxes o' the brig, baith for concealment and convenience of carriage.'

'Lord!' said Oldbuck, his recollection recurring to the earlier part of his acquaintance with Lovel; 'and this young fellow, who was putting hundreds on so strange a hazard, I must be recommending a subscription to him, and paying his bill at the Ferry! I never will pay any person's bill again, that's certain.—And you kept up a constant correspondence with Lovel, I suppose?'

'I just gat ae bit scrape o' a pen frae him, to say there wad, as yesterday fell, be a packet at Tannonburgh, wi' letters o' great consequence to the Knockwinnock folk; for they jaloused the opening of our letters at Fairport—And that's as true, I hear Mrs Mailsetter is to lose her office for looking after other folk's business and neglecting her ain.'

'And what do you expect, now, Edie, for being the adviser, and messenger, and guard, and confidential person in all these matters?'

'Deil haet do I expect—excepting that a' the gentles will come to the gaberlunzie's burial; and maybe ye'll carry the head yoursell, as ye did puir Steenie Mucklebackit's.—What trouble was't to me? I was ganging about at ony rate—O but I was blythe when I got out of prison, though; for, I thought, what if that weary letter should come when I am closed up here like an oyster, and a' should gang wrang for want o't? and whiles I thought I maun make a clean breast and tell you a' about it; but then I couldna weel do that without contravening Mr Lovel's positive orders; and I reckon he had to see somebody at Edinburgh afore he could do what he wussed to do for Sir Arthur and his family.'

'Well, and to your public news, Edie—So they are still coming, are they?'

'Troth, they say sae, sir; and there's come down strict orders for the forces and volunteers to be alert; and there's a clever young officer to come here forthwith, to look at our means o' defence—I saw the Bailie's lass cleaning his belts and white breeks—I gae her a hand, for ye maun think she wasna ower clever at it, and sae I gat a' the news for my pains.'

'And what think you, as an old soldier?'

'Troth, I kenna—an they come sae mony as they speak o', they'll be odds against us—But there's mony yauld chields amang thae volunteers; and I maunna say muckle about them that's no weel and no very able, because I am something that gate myself—But we'se do our best.'

'What! so your martial spirit is rising again, Edie?

"Even in our ashes glow their wonted fires!"*

I would not have thought you, Edie, had so much to fight for?'

'*Me* no muckle to fight for, sir?—isna there the country to fight for, and the burnsides that I gang daundering beside, and the hearths o' the gudewives that gie me my bit bread, and the bits o' weans that come toddling to play wi' me when I come about a landward town?—Deil!' he continued, grasping his pikestaff with great emphasis, 'an I had as gude pith as I hae gude-will, and a gude cause, I should gie some o' them a day's kemping.'

'Bravo, bravo, Edie! The country's in little ultimate danger, when the beggar's as ready to fight for his dish as the laird for his land.'

Their further conversation reverted to the particulars of the night passed by the mendicant and Lovel in the ruins of St Ruth; by the details of which the Antiquary was highly amused.

'I would have given a guinea,' he said, 'to have seen the scoundrelly German under the agonies of those terrors, which it is part of his own quackery to inspire into others; and trembling alternately for the fury of his patron, and the apparition of some hobgoblin.'

'Troth,' said the beggar, 'there was time for him to be cowed; for ye wad hae thought the very spirit of Hell-in-Harness had taken possession o' the body o' Sir Arthur.—But what will come o' the land-louper?'

'I have had a letter this morning, from which I understand he has acquitted you of the charge he brought against you, and offers to make such discoveries as will render the settlement of Sir Arthur's affairs a more easy task than we apprehended—So writes the Sheriff; and adds, that he has given some private information of importance to government, in consideration of which, I understand he will be sent back to play the knave in his own country.'

'And a' the bonny engines, and wheels, and the coves, and sheughs, doun at Glenwithershins yonder, what's to come o' them?' said Edie.

'I hope the men, before they are dispersed, will make a bonfire of their gimcracks, as an army destroy their artillery when forced to raise a siege. And as for the holes, Edie, I abandon them as rat-traps, for the benefit of the next wise men who may choose to drop the substance to snatch at a shadow.'

'Hech, sirs! guide us a'! to burn the engines? that's a great waste— Had ye na better try to get back part o' your hundred pounds wi' the sale o' the materials?' he continued, with a tone of affected condolence.

'Not a farthing,' said the Antiquary peevishly; taking a turn from him, and making a step or two away. Then returning, half-smiling at his own pettishness, he said, 'Get thee into the house, Edie, and remember my counsel: never speak to me about a mine, or to my nephew Hector about a *phoca*, that is a sealgh, as you call it.'

'I maun be ganging my ways back to Fairport,' said the wanderer; 'I want to see what they're saying there about the invasion— but I'll mind what your honour says, no to speak to you about a sealgh, or to the Captain about the hundred pounds that you gied to Douster'—

'Confound thee!—I desired thee not to mention that to me.'

'Dear me!' said Edie, with affected surprise; 'weel, I thought there was naething but what your honour could hae studden in the way o' agreeable conversation, unless it was about the Prætorian yonder, or the bodle that the packman sauld to ye for an auld coin.'

'Pshaw, pshaw,' said the Antiquary, turning from him hastily, and retreating into the house.

The mendicant looked after him a moment, and with a chuckling laugh, such as that with which a magpie or parrot applauds a successful exploit of mischief, he resumed once more the road to

Fairport. His habits had given him a sort of restlessness, much increased by the pleasure he took in gathering news; and in a short time he had regained the town which he left in the morning, for no reason that he knew himself, unless just to 'hae a bit crack wi' Monkbarns.'

CHAPTER XLV

Red glared the beacon on Pownell,
On Skiddaw there were three;
The bugle-horn on moor and fell
Was heard continually.

JAMES HOGG.*

THE watch who kept his watch on the hill, and looked towards Birnam, probably conceived himself dreaming when he first beheld the fated grove put itself into motion for its march to Dunsinane.* Even so, old Caxon, as, perched in his hut, he qualified his thoughts upon the approaching marriage of his daughter, and the dignity of being father-in-law to Lieutenant Taffril, with an occasional peep towards the signal-post with which his own corresponded, was not a little surprised by observing a light in that direction. He rubbed his eyes, looked again, adjusting his observation by a cross-staff which had been placed so as to bear upon the point. And behold, the light increased, like a comet to the eye of the astronomer, 'with fear of change perplexing nations.'*

'The Lord preserve us!' said Caxon, 'what's to be done now?—But there will be wiser heads than mine to look to that, sae I'se e'en fire the beacon.'

And he lighted the beacon accordingly, which threw up to the sky a long wavering train of light, startling the sea-fowl from their nests, and reflected far beneath by the reddening billows of the sea. The brother warders of Caxon being equally diligent, caught and repeated his signal. The lights glanced on headlands and capes and inland hills, and the whole district was alarmed by the signal of invasion.[25]

Our Antiquary, his head wrapped warm in two double night-caps, was quietly enjoying his repose, when it was suddenly broken by the screams of his sister, his niece, and two maid-servants.

'What the devil is the matter?' said he, starting up in his bed,—'womankind in my room at this hour of night!—are ye all mad?'

'The beacon, uncle!' said Miss M'Intyre.

'The French coming to murder us!' screamed Miss Griselda.

'The beacon, the beacon!—the French, the French!—murder, murder! and waur than murder!'—cried the two handmaidens, like the chorus of an opera.

'The French?' said Oldbuck, starting up,—'get out of the room, womankind that you are, till I get my things on—And, hark ye, bring me my sword.'

'Whilk o' them, Monkbarns?' cried his sister, offering a Roman falchion of brass with the one hand, with the other an Andrea Ferrara* without a handle.

'The langest, the langest,' cried Jenny Rintherout, dragging in a two-handed sword of the twelfth century.

'Womankind,' said Oldbuck, in great agitation, 'be composed, and do not give way to vain terror—Are you sure they are come?'

'Sure!—sure!' exclaimed Jenny,—'ower sure!—a' the sea fencibles, and the land fencibles,* and the volunteers and yeomanry, are on fit, and driving to Fairport as hard as horse and man can gang—and auld Mucklebackit's gane wi'the lave—muckle good he'll do;—Hech, sirs!—*he'll* be missed the morn wha wad hae served king and country weel!'

'Give me,' said Oldbuck, 'the sword which my father wore in the year forty-five—it hath no belt or baldrick—but we'll make shift.'

So saying, he thrust the weapon through the cover of his breeches pocket. At this moment Hector entered, who had been to a neighbouring height to ascertain whether the alarm was actual.

'Where are your arms, nephew?' exclaimed Oldbuck—'where is your double-barrelled gun, that was never out of your hand when there was no occasion for such vanities?'

'Pooh! pooh! sir,' said Hector, 'who ever took a fowling-piece on action?—I have got my uniform on, you see—I hope I shall be of more use if they will give me a command, than I could be with ten double-barrels.—And you, sir, must get to Fairport, to give directions for the quartering and maintaining the men and horses, and preventing confusion.'

'You are right, Hector,—I believe I shall do as much with my head as my hand too—But here comes Sir Arthur Wardour, who, between ourselves, is not fit to accomplish much either one way or other.'

Sir Arthur was probably of a different opinion; for, dressed in his lieutenancy uniform, he was also on the road to Fairport, and called in his way to take Mr Oldbuck with him, having had his original opinion of his sagacity much confirmed by late events. And in spite of all the entreaties of the womankind that the Antiquary would stay to garrison Monkbarns, Mr Oldbuck, with his nephew, instantly accepted Sir Arthur's offer.

Those who have witnessed such a scene can alone conceive the state of bustle in Fairport. The windows were glancing with a hundred lights, which, appearing and disappearing rapidly, indicated the confusion within doors. The women of lower rank assembled and clamoured in the market-place. The yeomanry, pouring from their different glens, galloped through the streets, some individually, some in parties of five or six, as they had met on the road. The drums and fifes of the volunteers beating to arms, were blended with the voice of the officers, the sound of the bugles, and the tolling of the bells from the steeple. The ships in the harbour were lit up, and boats from the armed vessels added to the bustle, by landing men and guns, destined to assist in the defence of the place. This part of the preparations was superintended by Taffril with much activity. Two or three light vessels had already slipped their cables and stood out to sea, in order to discover the supposed enemy.

Such was the scene of general confusion, when Sir Arthur Wardour, Oldbuck, and Hector, made their way with difficulty into the principal square, where the town-house is situated. It was lighted up, and the magistracy, with many of the neighbouring gentlemen, were assembled. And here, as upon other occasions of the like kind in Scotland, it was remarkable how the good sense and firmness of the people supplied almost all the deficiencies of inexperience.

The magistrates were beset by the quarter-masters of the different corps for billets for men and horses. 'Let us,' said Bailie Littlejohn, 'take the horses into our warehouses, and the men into our parlours,—share our supper with the one, and our forage with the other. We have made ourselves wealthy under a free and paternal government, and now is the time to show we know its value.'

A loud and cheerful acquiescence was given by all present, and the substance of the wealthy, with the persons of those of all ranks, were unanimously devoted to the defence of the country.

Captain M'Intyre acted on this occasion as military adviser and aid-de-camp to the principal magistrate, and displayed a degree of presence of mind, and knowledge of his profession, totally unexpected by his uncle, who, recollecting his usual *insouciance* and impetuosity, gazed at him with astonishment from time to time, as he remarked the calm and steady manner in which he explained the various measures of precaution that his experience suggested, and gave directions for executing them. He found the different corps in good order, considering the irregular materials of which they were composed, in great force of numbers, and high confidence and spirits. And so much did military experience at that moment over-balance all other claims to consequence, that even old Edie, instead of being left, like Diogenes at Sinope,* to roll his tub when all around were preparing for defence, had the duty assigned him of superintending the serving out of the ammunition, which he executed with much discretion.

Two things were still anxiously expected—the presence of the Glenallan volunteers, who, in consideration of the importance of that family, had been formed into a separate corps, and the arrival of the officer before announced, to whom the measures of defence on that coast had been committed by the commander-in-chief, and whose commission would entitle him to take upon himself the full disposal of the military force.

At length the bugles of the Glenallan yeomanry were heard, and the Earl himself, to the surprise of all who knew his habits and state of health, appeared at their head in uniform. They formed a very handsome and well-mounted squadron, formed entirely out of the Earl's Lowland tenants, and were followed by a regiment of five hundred men, completely equipped in the Highland dress, whom he had brought down from the upland glens, with their pipes playing in the van. The clean and serviceable appearance of this band of feudal dependents called forth the admiration of Captain M'Intyre; but his uncle was still more struck by the manner in which, upon this crisis, the ancient military spirit of his house seemed to animate and invigorate the decayed frame of the Earl, their leader. He claimed, and obtained for himself and his followers, the post most likely to be that of danger, displayed great alacrity in making the necessary dis-positions, and showed equal acuteness in discussing their propriety. Morning broke in upon the military councils of Fairport, while all concerned were still eagerly engaged in taking precautions for their defence.

At length a cry among the people announced, 'There's the brave Major Neville come at last, with another officer;' and their post-chaise and four drove into the square, amidst the huzzas of the volunteers and inhabitants. The magistrates, with their assessors of the lieutenancy,* hastened to the door of their town-house to receive him; but what was the surprise of all present, but most especially that of the Antiquary, when they became aware, that the handsome uniform and military cap disclosed the person and features of the pacific Lovel! A warm embrace, and a hearty shake of the hand, were necessary to assure him that his eyes were doing him justice. Sir Arthur was no less surprised to recognise his son, Captain Wardour, in Lovel's, or rather Major Neville's company. The first words of the young officers were a positive assurance to all present, that the courage and zeal which they had displayed were entirely thrown away, unless in so far as they afforded an acceptable proof of their spirit and promptitude.

'The watchman at Halket-head,' said Major Neville, 'as we discovered by an investigation which we made in our route hither, was most naturally misled by a bonfire which some idle people had made on the hill above Glenwithershins, just in the line of the beacon with which his corresponded.'

Oldbuck gave a conscious look to Sir Arthur, who returned it with one equally sheepish, and a shrug of the shoulders.

'It must have been the machinery which we condemned to the flames in our wrath,' said the Antiquary, plucking up heart, though not a little ashamed of having been the cause of so much disturbance—'The devil take Dousterswivel with all my heart!—I think he has bequeathed us a legacy of blunders and mischief, as if he had lighted some train of fireworks at his departure—I wonder what cracker will go off next among our shins.—But yonder comes the prudent Caxon.—Hold up your head, you ass—your betters must bear the blame for you—And here, take this what-d'ye-call-it'—(giving him his sword)—'I wonder what I would have said yesterday to any man, that would have told me I was to stick such an appendage to my tail.'

Here he found his arm gently pressed by Lord Glenallan, who dragged him into a separate apartment. 'For God's sake, who is that young gentleman who is so strikingly like'—

'Like the unfortunate Eveline,' interrupted Oldbuck. 'I felt my heart warm to him from the first, and your lordship has suggested the very cause.'

'But who—who is he?' continued Lord Glenallan, holding the Antiquary with a convulsive grasp.

'Formerly I would have called him Lovel, but now he turns out to be Major Neville.'

'Whom my brother brought up as his natural son—whom he made his heir—Gracious Heaven! the child of my Eveline!'

'Hold, my lord—hold!' said Oldbuck, 'do not give too hasty way to such a presumption—what probability is there?'

'Probability? none! There is certainty! absolute certainty. The agent I mentioned to you wrote me the whole story—I received it yesterday, not sooner—Bring him, for God's sake, that a father's eyes may bless him before he departs.'

'I will; but, for your own sake and his, give him a few moments for preparation.'

And, determined to make still farther investigation before yielding his entire conviction to so strange a tale, he sought out Major Neville, and found him expediting the necessary measures for dispersing the force which had been assembled.

'Pray, Major Neville, leave this business for a moment to Captain Wardour and to Hector, with whom, I hope, you are thoroughly reconciled, (Neville laughed, and shook hands with Hector across the table,) and grant me a moment's audience.'

'You have a claim on me, Mr Oldbuck, were my business more urgent,' said Neville, 'for having passed myself upon you under a false name, and rewarding your hospitality by injuring your nephew.'

'You served him as he deserved,' said Oldbuck; 'though, by the way, he showed as much good sense as spirit today—Egad, if he would rub up his learning, and read Cæsar and Polybius, and the *Stratagemata Polyœni*,* I think he would rise in the army, and I will certainly lend him a lift.'

'He is heartily deserving of it,' said Neville; 'and I am glad you excuse me, which you may do the more frankly, when you know that I am so unfortunate as to have no better right to the name of Neville, by which I have been generally distinguished, than to that of Lovel, under which you knew me.'

'Indeed! then, I trust, we shall find out one for you to which you shall have a firm and legal title.'

'Sir !—I trust you do not think the misfortune of my birth a fit subject'—

'By no means, young man,' answered the Antiquary, interrupting him,—'I believe I know more of your birth than you do yourself—and, to convince you of it, you were educated and known as a natural son of Geraldin Neville of Neville's-burgh, in Yorkshire, and, I presume, as his destined heir?'

'Pardon me—no such views were held out to me; I was liberally educated, and pushed forward in the army by money and interest; but I believe my supposed father long entertained some ideas of marriage, though he never carried them into effect.'

'You say your *supposed* father?—What leads you to suppose Mr Geraldin Neville was not your real father?'

'I know, Mr Oldbuck, that you would not ask these questions on a point of such delicacy for the gratification of idle curiosity. I will, therefore, tell you candidly, that last year, while we occupied a small town in French Flanders, I found in a convent, near which I was quartered, a woman who spoke remarkably good English—She was a Spaniard—her name Teresa D'Acunha. In the process of our acquaintance, she discovered who I was, and made herself known to me as the person who had charge of my infancy. She dropped more than one hint of rank to which I was entitled, and of injustice done to me, promising a more full disclosure in case of the death of a lady in Scotland, during whose lifetime she was determined to keep the secret. She also intimated that Mr Geraldin Neville was not my father. We were attacked by the enemy, and driven from the town, which was pillaged with savage ferocity by the republicans. The religious orders were the particular objects of their hate and cruelty. The convent was burned, and several nuns perished, among others Teresa—and with her all chance of knowing the story of my birth—tragic by all accounts it must have been.'

'*Raro antecedentem scelestum*, or, as I may here say, *scelestam*,' said Oldbuck, '*deseruit pœna**—even Epicureans admitted that—and what did you do upon this?'

'I remonstrated with Mr Neville by letter, and to no purpose—I then obtained leave of absence, and threw myself at his feet, conjuring him to complete the disclosure which Teresa had begun. He refused, and, on my importunity, indignantly upbraided me with the favours he had already conferred; I thought he abused the power of a benefactor, as he was compelled to admit he had no title to that of a father, and we parted in mutual displeasure. I renounced the name of Neville, and assumed that under which you knew me.—It was at this time, when residing with a friend in the north of England who favoured my disguise, that I became acquainted with Miss Wardour, and was romantic enough to follow her to Scotland. My mind wavered on various plans of life, when I resolved to apply once more to Mr Neville for an explanation of the mystery of my birth. It was long ere I received an answer; you were present when it was put into my hands. He informed me of his bad state of health, and conjured me, for my own sake, to enquire no farther into the nature of his connexion with me, but to rest satisfied with his declaring it to be such and so intimate, that he designed to constitute me his heir. When I was preparing to leave Fairport to join him, a second express brought me word that he was no more. The possession of great wealth was unable to suppress the remorseful feelings with which I now regarded my conduct to my benefactor, and some hints in his letter appearing to intimate that there was on my birth a deeper stain than that of ordinary illegitimacy, I remembered certain prejudices of Sir Arthur.'

'And you brooded over these melancholy ideas until you were ill, instead of coming to me for advice, and telling me the whole story?' said Oldbuck.

'Exactly; then came my quarrel with Captain M'Intyre, and my compelled departure from Fairport and its vicinity.'

'From love and from poetry—Miss Wardour and the Caledoniad?'

'Most true.'

'And since that time you have been occupied, I suppose, with plans for Sir Arthur's relief?'

'Yes, sir; with the assistance of Captain Wardour at Edinburgh.'

'And Edie Ochiltree here—you see I know the whole story. But how came you by the treasure?'

'It was a quantity of plate which had belonged to my uncle, and was left in the custody of a person at Fairport. Some time before his death he had sent orders that it should be melted down. He perhaps did not wish me to see the Glenallan arms upon it.'

'Well, Major Neville, or—let me say—Lovel, being the name in which I rather delight, you must, I believe, exchange both of your *alias's* for the style and title of the Honourable William Geraldin, commonly called Lord Geraldin.'

The Antiquary then went through the strange and melancholy circumstances concerning his mother's death.

'I have no doubt,' he said, 'that your uncle wished the report to be believed, that the child of this unhappy marriage was no more—perhaps he might himself have an eye to the inheritance of his brother—he was then a gay wild young man—But of all intentions against your person, however much the evil conscience of Elspeth might lead her to suspect him from the agitation in which he appeared, Teresa's story and your own fully acquit him. And now, my dear sir, let me have the pleasure of introducing a son to a father.'

We will not attempt to describe such a meeting. The proofs on all sides were found to be complete, for Mr Neville had left a distinct account of the whole transaction with his confidential steward in a sealed packet, which was not to be opened until the death of the old Countess; his motive for preserving secrecy so long appearing to have been an apprehension of the effect which the discovery, fraught with so much disgrace, must necessarily produce upon her haughty and violent temper.

In the evening of that day, the yeomanry and volunteers of Glenallan drank prosperity to their young master. In a month afterwards, Lord Geraldin was married to Miss Wardour, the Antiquary making the lady a present of the wedding ring, a massy circle of antique chasing, bearing the motto of Aldobrand Oldenbuck, *Kunst macht gunst*.

Old Edie, the most important man that ever wore a blue-gown, bowls away easily from one friend's house to another, and boasts that he never travels unless on a sunny day. Latterly, indeed, he has given some symptoms of becoming stationary, being frequently found in the corner of a snug cottage between Monkbarns and Knockwinnock, to which Caxon retreated upon his daughter's marriage, in order to be in the neighbourhood of the three parochial wigs, which he continues to keep in repair, though only for amusement. Edie has been heard to say, 'This is a gey bein place, and it's a comfort to hae sic a corner to sit in in a bad day.' It is thought, as he grows stiffer in the joints, he will finally settle there.

The bounty of such wealthy patrons as Lord and Lady Geraldin flowed copiously upon Mrs Hadoway and upon the Mucklebackits. By the former it was well employed, by the latter wasted. They continue, however, to receive it, but under the administration of Edie

Ochiltree; and they do not accept it without grumbling at the channel through which it is conveyed.

Hector is rising rapidly in the army, and has been more than once mentioned in the Gazette, and rises proportionally high in his uncle's favour. And, what scarcely pleases the young soldier less, he has also shot two seals, and thus put an end to the Antiquary's perpetual harping upon the story of the *phoca*. People talk of a marriage between Miss M'Intyre and Captain Wardour; but this wants confirmation.

The Antiquary is a frequent visitor at Knockwinnock and Glenallan-house, ostensibly for the sake of completing two essays, one on the mail-shirt of the Great Earl, and the other on the left-hand gauntlet of Hell-in-Harness. He regularly enquires whether Lord Geraldin has commenced the Caledoniad, and shakes his head at the answers he receives. *En attendant*,* however, he has completed his notes, which, we believe, will be at the service of any one who chooses to make them public, without risk or expense to THE ANTIQUARY.

SCOTT'S NOTES

1. *Ars Topiaria*, the art of clipping yew hedges into fantastic figures. A Latin poem, entitled *Ars Topiaria*, contains a curious account of the process.
2. This bibliomaniacal anecdote is literally true; and David Wilson, the author need not tell his brethren of the Roxburghe and Bannatyne Clubs, was a real personage.
3. Of this thrice and four times rare broadside, the author possesses an exemplar.
4. A bonnet-laird signifies a petty proprietor, wearing the dress, along with the habits, of a yeoman.
5. The reader will understand that this refers to the reign of our late Gracious Sovereign, George the Third.
6. MR R——D'S DREAM. The legend of Mrs Grizel Oldbuck was partly taken from an extraordinary story which happened about seventy years since, in the South of Scotland, so peculiar in its circumstances, that it merits being mentioned in this place. Mr R——d of Bowland, a gentleman of landed property in the vale of Gala, was prosecuted for a very considerable sum, the accumulated arrears of teind (or tithe) for which he was said to be indebted to a noble family, the titulars (lay impropriators of the tithes). Mr R——d was strongly impressed with the belief that his father had, by a form of process peculiar to the law of Scotland, purchased these lands from the titular, and therefore that the present prosecution was groundless. But, after an industrious search among his father's papers, an investigation of the public records, and a careful inquiry among all persons who had transacted law business for his father, no evidence could be recovered to support his defence. The period was now near at hand when he conceived the loss of his lawsuit to be inevitable, and he had formed his determination to ride to Edinburgh next day, and make the best bargain he could in the way of compromise. He went to bed with this resolution, and, with all the circumstances of the case floating upon his mind, had a dream to the following purpose. His father, who had been many years dead, appeared to him, he thought, and asked him why he was disturbed in his mind. In dreams men are not surprised at such apparitions. Mr R——d thought that he informed his father of the cause of his distress, adding that the payment of a considerable sum of money was the more unpleasant to him, because he had a strong consciousness that it was not due, though he was unable to recover any evidence in support of his belief. 'You are right, my son,' replied the paternal shade; 'I did acquire right to these teinds, for payment of which you are now prosecuted. The papers relating to the transaction are in the hands of Mr——, a writer (or attorney), who is now retired from professional business, and resides at Inveresk, near Edinburgh. He was a person whom I employed on that occasion for a particular reason, but who never on any other occasion

transacted business on my account. It is very possible,' pursued the vision, 'that Mr——may have forgotten a matter which is now of a very old date; but you may call it to his recollection by this token, that when I came to pay his account, there was difficulty in getting change for a Portugal piece of gold, and that we were forced to drink out the balance at a tavern.'

Mr R——d awaked in the morning with all the words of the vision imprinted on his mind, and thought it worth while to ride across the country to Inveresk, instead of going straight to Edinburgh. When he came there he waited on the gentleman mentioned in the dream, a very old man; without saying any thing of the vision, he inquired whether he remembered having conducted such a matter for his deceased father. The old gentleman could not at first bring the circumstance to his recollection, but on mention of the Portugal piece of gold, the whole returned upon his memory; he made an immediate search for the papers, and recovered them,—so that Mr R——d carried to Edinburgh the documents necessary to gain the cause which he was on the verge of losing.

The author has often heard this story told by persons who had the best access to know the facts, who were not likely themselves to be deceived, and were certainly incapable of deception. He cannot therefore refuse to give it credit, however extraordinary the circumstances may appear. The circumstantial character of the information given in the dream, takes it out of the general class of impressions of the kind which are occasioned by the fortuitous coincidence of actual events with our sleeping thoughts. On the other hand, few will suppose that the laws of nature were suspended, and a special communication from the dead to the living permitted, for the purpose of saving Mr R——d a certain number of hundred pounds. The author's theory is, that the dream was only the recapitulation of information which Mr R——d had really received from his father while in life, but which at first he merely recalled as a general impression that the claim was settled. It is not uncommon for persons to recover, during sleep, the thread of ideas which they have lost during their waking hours.

It may be added, that this remarkable circumstance was attended with bad consequences to Mr R——d; whose health and spirits were afterwards impaired by the attention which he thought himself obliged to pay to the visions of the night.

7. Probably Wordsworth's Lyrical Ballads had not as yet been published.
8. Probably Dr Hutton, the celebrated geologist.
9. A sort of tally generally used by bakers of the olden time in settling with their customers. Each family had its own nick-stick, and for each loaf as delivered a notch was made on the stick. Accounts in Exchequer, kept by the same kind of check, may have occasioned the Antiquary's partiality. In Prior's time the English bakers had the same sort of reckoning.

> Have you not seen a baker's maid
> Between two equal panniers sway'd?
> Her tallies useless lie and idle,
> If placed exactly in the middle.

10. The outline of this story is taken from the German, though the author is at present unable to say in which of the various collections of the popular legends in that language, the original is to be found.

11. The shadow of the person who sees the phantom, being reflected upon a cloud of mist, like the image of the magic lantern upon a white sheet, is supposed to have formed the apparition.

12. The king's keys are, in law phrase, the crow-bars and hammers used to force doors and locks, in execution of the king's warrant.

13. Links, or torches.

14. A great deal of stuff to the same purpose with that placed in the mouth of the German adept, may be found in Reginald Scot's Discovery of Witch-craft. *Third Edition*, folio, London, 1665. The appendix is entitled, 'An Excellent Discourse of the Nature and Substance of Devils and Spirits, in two Books; the First by the aforesaid author, (Reginald Scot,) the Second now added in this Third Edition as succedaneous to the former, and conducing to the completing of the whole work.' This Second Book, though stated as succedaneous to the first, is, in fact, entirely at variance with it; for the work of Reginald Scot is a compilation of the absurd and superstitious ideas concerning witches so generally entertained at the time, and the pretended conclusion is a serious treatise on the various means of conjuring astral spirits.

15. The author cannot remember where these lines are to be found; perhaps in Bishop Hall's Satires.

16. It is, I believe, a piece of free-masonry, or a point of conscience, among the Scottish lower orders, never to admit that a patient is doing better. The closest approach to recovery which they can be brought to allow, is, that the party enquired after is 'Nae waur.'

17. In the fishing villages on the Friths of Forth and Tay, as well as elsewhere in Scotland, the government is gynecocracy, as described in the text. In the course of the late war, and during the alarm of invasion, a fleet of transports entered the Frith of Forth, under the convoy of some ships of war which would reply to no signals. A general alarm was excited, in consequence of which, all the fishers, who were enrolled as sea-fencibles, got on board the gun-boats, which they were to man as occasion should require, and sailed to oppose the supposed enemy. The foreigners proved to be Russians, with whom we were then at peace. The county gentlemen of Mid-Lothian, pleased with the zeal displayed by the sea-fencibles at a critical moment, passed a vote for presenting the community of fishers with a silver punch-bowl, to be used on occasions of festivity. But the fisher-women, on hearing what was intended, put in their claim to have some separate share in the intended honorary reward. The men, they said, were their husbands; it was they who would have been sufferers if their husbands had been killed, and it was by their permission and injunctions that they embarked on board the gun-boats for the public service. They therefore claimed to share the reward in some manner which should dis-tinguish the female patriotism which they had shown on the occasion. The gentlemen of the county willingly admitted the claim; and, without

diminishing the value of their compliment to the men, they made the females a present of a valuable brooch, to fasten the plaid of the queen of the fisher-women for the time.

It may be farther remarked, that these Nereids [sea-nymphs] are punctilious among themselves, and observe different ranks according to the commodities they deal in. One experienced dame was heard to characterise a younger damsel as 'a puir silly thing, who had no ambition, and would never,' she prophesied, 'rise above the *mussell-line* of business.'

18. A single soldier means, in Scotch, a private soldier.

19. *Massa-mora*, an ancient name for a dungeon, derived from the Moorish language, perhaps as far back as the time of the Crusades.

20. *Pousowdie*. Miscellaneous mess.

21. The doctrine of Monkbarns on the origin of imprisonment for civil debt in Scotland, may appear somewhat whimsical, but was referred to, and admitted to be correct, by the Bench of the Supreme Scottish Court, on 5th December, 1828, in the case of Thom *v.* Black. In fact, the Scottish law is in this particular more jealous of the personal liberty of the subject than any other code in Europe.

22. See Mrs Grant on the Highland Superstitions, vol. ii. p. 260, for this fine translation from the Gaelic.

23. BATTLE OF HARLAW. The great battle of Harlaw, here and formerly referred to, might be said to determine whether the Gaelic or the Saxon race should be predominant in Scotland. Donald, Lord of the Isles, who had at that period the power of an independent sovereign, laid claim to the Earldom of Ross during the Regency of Robert, Duke of Albany. To enforce his supposed right, he ravaged the north with a large army of Highlanders and Islesmen. He was encountered at Harlaw, in the Garioch, by Alexander, Earl of Mar, at the head of the northern nobility and gentry of Saxon and Norman descent. The battle was bloody and indecisive; but the invader was obliged to retire, in consequence of the loss he sustained, and afterwards was compelled to make submission to the Regent, and renounce his pretensions to Ross; so that all the advantages of the field were gained by the Saxons. The battle of Harlaw was fought 24th July, 1411.

24. ELSPETH'S DEATH. The concluding circumstance of Elspeth's death is taken from an incident said to have happened at the funeral of John, Duke of Roxburghe. All who were acquainted with that accomplished nobleman must remember, that he was not more remarkable for creating and possessing a most curious and splendid library, than for his acquaintance with the literary treasures it contained. In arranging his books, fetching and replacing the volumes which he wanted, and carrying on all the necessary intercourse which a man of letters holds with his library, it was the Duke's custom to employ, not a secretary or librarian, but a livery servant, called Archie, whom habit had made so perfectly acquainted with the library, that he knew every book, as a shepherd does the individuals of his flock, by what is called head-mark, and could bring his master whatever volume he wanted, and afford all the mechanical aid the Duke required in his

literary researches. To secure the attendance of Archie, there was a bell hung in his room, which was used on no occasion except to call him individually to the Duke's study.

His Grace died in Saint James's Square, London, in the year 1804; the body was to be conveyed to Scotland, to lie in state at his mansion of Fleurs, and to be removed from thence to the family burial-place at Bowden.

At this time, Archie, who had been long attacked by a liver-complaint, was in the very last stage of that disease. Yet he prepared himself to accompany the body of the master whom he had so long and so faithfully waited upon. The medical persons assured him he could not survive the journey. It signified nothing, he said, whether he died in England or Scotland; he was resolved to assist in rendering the last honours to the kind master from whom he had been inseparable for so many years, even if he should expire in the attempt. The poor invalid was permitted to attend the Duke's body to Scotland; but when they reached Fleurs he was totally exhausted, and obliged to keep his bed, in a sort of stupor which announced speedy dissolution. On the morning of the day fixed for removing the dead body of the Duke to the place of burial, the private bell by which he was wont to summon his attendant to his study, was rung violently. This might easily happen in the confusion of such a scene, although the people of the neighbourhood prefer believing that the bell sounded of its own accord. Ring, however, it did; and Archie, roused by the well-known summons, rose up in his bed, and faltered, in broken accents, 'Yes, my Lord Duke—yes—I will wait on your Grace instantly;' and with these words on his lips, he is said to have fallen back and expired.

25. ALARM OF INVASION. The story of the false alarm at Fairport, and the consequences, are taken from a real incident. Those who witnessed the state of Britain, and of Scotland in particular, from the period that succeeded the war which commenced in 1803 to the battle of Trafalgar, must recollect those times with feelings which we can hardly hope to make the rising generation comprehend. Almost every individual was enrolled either in a military or civil capacity, for the purpose of contributing to resist the long-suspended threats of invasion, which were echoed from every quarter. Beacons were erected along the coast, and all through the country, to give the signal for every one to repair to the post where his peculiar duty called him, and men of every description fit to serve held themselves in readiness on the shortest summons. During this agitating period, and on the evening of the 2d February, 1804, the person who kept watch on the commanding station of Home Castle, being deceived by some accidental fire in the county of Northumberland, which he took for the corresponding signal-light in that county with which his orders were to communicate, lighted up his own beacon. The signal was immediately repeated through all the valleys on the English Border. If the beacon at Saint Abbs-head had been fired, the alarm would have run northward, and roused all Scotland. But the watch at this important point judiciously considered, that if there had been an actual or threatened descent on our

eastern sea-coast, the alarm would have come along the coast, and not from the interior of the country.

Through the Border counties the alarm spread with rapidity, and on no occasion when that country was the scene of perpetual and unceasing war, was the summons to arms more readily obeyed. In Berwickshire, Roxburghshire, and Selkirkshire, the volunteers and militia got under arms with a degree of rapidity and alacrity which, considering the distance individuals lived from each other, had something in it very surprising—they poured to the alarm-posts on the sea-coast in a state so well armed and so completely appointed, with baggage, provisions, &c., as was accounted by the best military judges to render them fit for instant and effectual service.

There were some particulars in the general alarm which are curious and interesting. The men of Liddesdale, the most remote point to the westward which the alarm reached, were so much afraid of being late in the field, that they put in requisition all the horses they could find, and when they had thus made a forced march out of their own county, they turned their borrowed steeds loose to find their way back through the hills, and they all got back safe to their own stables. Another remarkable circumstances was, the general cry of the inhabitants of the smaller towns for arms, that they might go along with their companions. The Selkirkshire Yeomanry made a remarkable march, for although some of the individuals lived at twenty and thirty miles distance from the place where they mustered, they were nevertheless embodied and in order in so short a period, that they were at Dalkeith, which was their alarm-post, about one o'clock on the day succeeding the first signal, with men and horses in good order, though the roads were in a bad state, and many of the troopers must have ridden forty or fifty miles without drawing bridle. Two members of the corps chanced to be absent from their homes, and in Edinburgh on private business. The lately married wife of one of these gentlemen, and the widowed mother of the other, sent the arms, uniforms, and chargers of the two troopers, that they might join their companions at Dalkeith. The author was very much struck by the answer made to him by the last-mentioned lady, when he paid her some compliment on the readiness which she showed in equipping her son with the means of meeting danger, when she might have left him a fair excuse for remaining absent. 'Sir,' she replied, with the spirit of a Roman matron, 'none can know better than you that my son is the only prop by which, since his father's death, our family is supported. But I would rather see him dead on that hearth, than hear that he had been a horse's length behind his companions in the defence of his king and country.' The author mentions what was immediately under his own eye, and within his own knowledge; but the spirit was universal, wherever the alarm reached, both in Scotland and England.

The account of the ready patriotism displayed by the country on this occasion, warmed the hearts of Scottishmen in every corner of the world. It reached the ears of the well-known Dr Leyden, whose enthusiastic love of Scotland, and of his own district of Teviotdale, formed a distinguished part of his character. The account, which was read to him when on a sick-bed, stated (very truly) that the different corps, on arriving at their alarm-posts, announced themselves by their music playing the tunes peculiar to their own districts, many of which have been gathering-signals for centuries. It was particularly remembered, that the Liddesdale men, before mentioned, entered Kelso playing the lively tune—

> 'O wha dare meddle wi' me,
>   And wha dare meddle wi' me!
> My name it is little Jock Elliot,
>   And wha dare meddle wi' me!'

The patient was so delighted with this display of ancient Border spirit, that he sprung up in his bed, and began to sing the old song with such vehemence of action and voice, that his attendants, ignorant of the cause of excitation, concluded that the fever had taken possession of his brain; and it was only the entry of another Borderer, Sir John Malcolm, and the explanation which he was well qualified to give, that prevented them from resorting to means of medical coercion.

The circumstances of this false alarm, and its consequences, may be now held of too little importance even for a note upon a work of fiction; but, at the period when it happened, it was hailed by the country as a propitious omen, that the national force, to which much must naturally have been trusted, had the spirit to look in the face the danger which they had taken arms to repel; and every one was convinced, that on whichever side God might bestow the victory, the invaders would meet with the most determined opposition from the children of the soil.

EDITOR'S NOTES

The following notes are inevitably heavily indebted throughout to David Hewitt's definitive work in editing *The Antiquary* for the Edinburgh Edition (1993–). Standard modern scholarly editions have been used for references to plays and poems except where an early edition is indicated by a date in parenthesis. References to Shakespeare's plays are taken from the *Oxford Shakespeare*, ed. Wells and Taylor (1986). Names and terms used a number of times by Scott are only annotated on the first occasion that they appear.

1 *epigraph*: probably by Scott. King Pepin was the father of Charlemagne, reigning 751–68. The first edition prints it here; the Magnum Opus, perhaps accidentally, transposes it to the beginning of the second volume (vol. vi of the series).

3 *Waverley . . . eighteenth century*: *Waverley* (1814) is set in 1745–6, *Guy Mannering* (1815) in the 1780s, *The Antiquary* in 1794.

  principal personages . . . powerful language: Wordsworth's Preface to the Second Edition of *Lyrical Ballads* (1800): 'Low and rustic life was generally chosen because in that situation the essential passions of the heart find a better soil in which they can attain their maturity, are under less restraint, and speak a plainer and more emphatic language. . . . The language too of these men has been adopted . . . because, from their rank in society and the sameness and narrow circle of their intercourse . . . they convey their feelings and notions in simple and unelaborated expressions.'

  late instances of . . . superstitious credulity: the model for the 'adept' Dousterswivel according to Robert Chambers was a German Rodolphe Eric Raspe (1737–94) editor of *Baron Munchausen* (1785), archaeologist, librarian, and thief in Germany, and thereafter lecturer on geology and mineralogy in England, and fraudulent prospector in Scotland in 1789, conning one Sir John Sinclair (an enemy of Scott's and model for Sir Arthur Wardour).

  one who is not likely again to solicit their favour: Scott was, however, to publish *The Black Dwarf* and *The Tale of Old Mortality* in December 1816, but under yet another alias, that of Jedediah Cleishbotham.

4 *Chronicles of the Canongate*: Scott's compilation of three novellas, pub. 1827.

5 *Martin*: George Martine (1635–1712), *Reliquiae divi Andreae, or The state of the venerable and primitial see of St Andrews* (1797), 3.

6 *Burns . . . habits and powers*: Robert Burns (1759–96), *A Dedication to Gavin Hamilton Esq.* ll. 15–16; *Epistle to Davie* (1786), ll. 27–8, ll. 29–31, and see stanza 4 following. Prose letter untraced.

7 *Johnson's . . . some beer*: verse by Samuel Johnson (1709–84) recorded by James Boswell in his *Life of Johnson*, ed. G. B. Hill, rev. L. F. Powell, 4 vols. (1934–50), iii. 159.

10 *laudator temporis acti*: (Latin) he who praises the good old days.

as Burns says . . . dike side: Robert Burns, *Epistle to J. Lapraik, An Old Scottish Bard, April 1, 1785*, stanza 7.

13 *epigraph*: Henry Carey, *Chrononhotonthologos*, 5. 31–4.

little ease: a prison cell designed to make it impossible to stand upright, lie down, or sit comfortably.

Queensferry Diligence, or Hawes Fly: a public carriage which would have terminated at the Hawes Inn in Queensferry.

lied . . . like a bulletin: a military dispatch for domestic publication, and therefore economical with the truth.

Saint Giles's . . , the Tron: both churches situated on Edinburgh's High Street.

14 *Automedon*: the charioteer of Achilles in *The Iliad*.

16 *words of action*: words which would support an action for slander.

17 *seducing the lieges with false reports . . . statute of leasing-making*: a refer- ence to the Scottish laws of 1584, 1585, 1703 prohibiting slander calculated to 'seduce' the king's subjects from their proper loyalty; 'leasing-making' had been punished since the act of 1704 variously by a fine, corporal punishment, or jail.

in rerum natura: (Latin) within the natural order of things.

a lie with a circumstance: a lie with circumstantial evidence to back it up.

18 *Sandy Gordon's Itinerarium Septentrionale*: Alexander Gordon (1696?– 1754?), *Itinerarium Septentrionale: or, A Journey thro' most of the Counties of Scotland, and those in the North of England* (1726).

rules of castrametation: principles of camp fortification and layout.

19 *a Pict's camp, or Round-about*: a round camp or fort.

Croaker . . . 'The Good-natured Man': Oliver Goldsmith (1730?–74), *The Good-Natur'd Man*: 'There's the advantage of fretting away our mis- fortunes beforehand, we never feel them when they come', 5.211–13.

20 *castra stativa . . . castra æstiva*: (Latin) year-round camp and summer camp.

21 *bush*: ivy bush commonly hung up as a pub sign in reference to Bacchus, god of wine.

epigraph: Ben Jonson, *The New Inn*, 1.2.18–21, 23, 27–9.

the summer session: the summer sitting of the Court of Session, the supreme civil court of Scotland. The landlord has misremembered Monkbarns as a lawyer.

a ganging plea: a pending court-case.

the Parliament-house: location of the sittings of the highest Scottish civil and criminal courts.

21 *in afore the fifteen . . . the outer-house*: the fifteen judges of the Court of Session, organized into the Outer House and the Inner House. Cases started in the Outer House under a single judge, and might be sent in to the Inner House where all fifteen judges would give final decisions or rulings on ticklish legal points, whereupon the case would then be sent back down to the Outer House.

22 *printed session papers*: printed versions of papers concerned in cases before the Court of Session.

quamprimum . . . peremptorie: (Latin) first thing, as soon as possible, immediately.

sanded parlour: the small dining-room's stone floor would have been strewn with sand to absorb spills.

Jacobites . . . Protestant succession: the Jacobites supported the claims of the son and later the grandson of James II to the British throne. The Roman Catholic James II fled the country in the Glorious Revolution of 1688–9, and was replaced by a Protestant monarchy in the shape of James's daughter Mary and her husband William, then Mary's sister, Queen Anne, and finally by George I of Hanover in 1714. Throughout this period there were Jacobite risings, culminating in the last of 1745–6.

23 *Reformation*: the period of religious reform in the 16th century that led to the establishment of Protestantism in northern Europe, and a succession of religious wars and persecutions.

gifted . . . on the dissolution of the . . . monastery: on the Scottish Reformation (1560), supporters of the Protestant cause were often rewarded by gifts of church lands confiscated from Catholic monasteries.

single blessedness: *A Midsummer Night's Dream*, 1.1.78.

the Forty-twa: the Black Watch, the 42nd infantry regiment of loyal Highlanders.

East Indies . . . Hyder Ally: he seeks his fortune in India. Hyder Ali (1728–82), ruler of Mysore, waged two wars against the British, 1767–9 and 1778–81.

24 *the whole forms of feudal investitures*: the way in which title to land/real estate was conferred and registered.

rei suæ prodigus: (Latin) wasteful of his own wealth.

black-letter: a Gothic type used by printers in the fifteenth and sixteenth centuries.

25 *a ready-money man*: one who can pay in cash, without asking for credit.

the cat, the rat, and Lovel our dog: adapted from William Collingbourne (d. 1484), 'the Cat, the Rat and Lovell the dog | Rule all England under a hog', referring to Sir William Catesbie, Sir Richard Ratcliffe, and Lord Lovell (whose crest was a dog), favourites of Richard III, whose own emblem was a wild boar.

26 *punch*: being composed of spirits, water, lemon, sugar and spice, punch

was both a traditionally native drink and a good deal more economical than port or claret. It is probably hot punch that Monkbarns has in mind as more suitable for the season.

ye may lay your account wi': you can be sure.

this side Solway: the Solway firth divides England from Scotland, hence in Scotland.

how absolute the knave is: Hamlet, 5.1.133.

Falernian . . . vile Sabinum: Falernian is the more expensive wine.

27 *Lovel or Belville*: standard names for stage romantic leads: see John Caryll, *The English Princess* (1667); Aphra Behn's *The Rover* (1677); Thomas Shadwell, *The Sullen Lovers* (1668); Thomas d'Urfey, *Squire Oldsapp* (1679); Susanna Centlivre, *The Platonick Lady* (1707); James Townley, *High Life below Stairs* (1759); Charles Lamb, *John Woodvil* (1802), amongst many others.

eighteen-pence a-stage: Oldbuck is only prepared to pay 1s. 6d. per 'stage', at the end of which the horses would be changed at a posting inn.

29 *epigraph*: Robert Burns, 'On the late Captain Grose's Peregrinations thro' Scotland collecting the Antiquities of that Kingdom' (1789), 31–6.

ground-rent: the rent of land was customarily paid in kind as late as the end of the seventeenth century.

30 *Amphion's . . . country dances*: while fortifying Thebes, Amphion played the lyre with such skill that stones built themselves into a wall; Orpheus played the lyre so beautifully that not only wild beasts but trees and rocks came to listen to his song.

with spectacles on nose, and pouch on side: As You Like It, 2.7.159.

London Chronicle: a contemporary weekly newspaper.

taken French leave: to go away, or do anything, without permission.

Syrian medals: Roman coins from Syria.

copper Otho: rare and coveted coin thought in the eighteenth century to have originated from Antioch and Alexandria, but now regarded as a forgery.

sanctum sanctorum: (Latin) literally, holy of holies; here, his private study.

Anthony a Wood: (1632–95), Oxford antiquary and historian.

Cænobite: a monk, so called because they hold everything in common (*coeno*: Greek, common).

31 *Polonius's cloud to a whale, or an owzel*: 'owzel', a blackbird, following Pope's emendation of 'weasel'. *Hamlet*, 3.2.364–70.

Antigonus: the Romano–Syrian coin referred to above.

32 *Dr Orkborne*: Frances Burney's *Camilla* (1796), which contains a scene in which Dr Orkborne's study is, to his fury, tidied up.

32 *Hudibras's visit to that of Sidrophel*: in Samuel Butler's satiric poem *Hudibras* Hudibras visits Sidrophel, who is posing as an astrologer. There follows a patched-up quotation from 2.3.1091–2, 1095–6; and 3.1.437–8.

Napier's bones: calculator composed of ivory sticks invented by John Napier (1550–1617).

constellation stones: precious stones influenced by particular constellations.

My flea, my morepeon, and punaise: flea, crab-louse, and bed-bug.

very ancient, peaceful, quiet dust: *Much Ado About Nothing*, 3.3.38–9.

33 *Sir Gawaine's wedding . . . the Lothely Lady*: A reference to 'The Marriage of Sir Gawaine', included in Percy's *Reliques of Ancient English Poetry*, which tells the story of a knight who seeks the answer to the riddle of what women most desire from an ugly woman, who asks for a husband in return. Gawaine obliges and is rewarded by her transformation into a beautiful lady. A better-known variant on this story appears as 'The Wife of Bath's Tale' in Chaucer's *The Canterbury Tales (c.*1387).

Marius among the ruins of Carthage: the defeated Roman general Caius Marius (157–86 BC) fled to Africa, landing in Carthage in 88 BC. Ordered to leave by the Roman governor, he answered, 'Tell the praetor you have seen Caius Marius, a fugitive, sitting among the ruins of Carthage.' See Plutarch's *Life of Marius*.

the genius loci, the tutelar demon: (Latin) the guardian spirit of the place; the protecting spirit.

mare magnum: (Latin) great sea.

three ancient calthrops . . . English chargers: Robert the Bruce (1274–1329), prior to the battle of Bannockburn against the English under Edward II in 1314, booby-trapped the marshy ground over which the English cavalry had to pass with concealed pits and spikes.

34 *Colve-carles . . . Kolb-kerls . . . Clavigeri*: Middle English, German, Latin for 'club-bearers'.

the chronicle of Antwerp . . . that of St Martin: probably the Antwerp Chronicle for 1500–74 (pub. 1743), and the chronicle of St Martin of Tours (pub. 1738).

Covenanters: Presbyterian supporters of the National Covenant (1638) and the Solemn League and Covenant (1643) were persecuted under Charles II (1660–85) and James II (1685–8).

collar: a metal collar which marked a criminal as being under sentence of perpetual servitude.

modern Scottish punishment: banishment; often, in practice, emigration to England.

For he would rather have . . . saltery: adapted from Chaucer, *The Canterbury Tales*, 'General Prologue', 293–6.

Don Quixote . . . a windmill: Miguel de Cervantes Saavedra, author of

Don Quixote (1605; 1615), claimed that his source was a fictitious Arabian author, Cid Hamet Benengeli. Don Quixote exchanges land for books, takes an innkeeper's daughter for a lady, and duels with a windmill which he mistakes for a giant.

35 *Caxton's Game at Chess*: *The Game and Playe of the Chesse* (1474?), printed by William Caxton (1422–91).

editio princeps: (Latin) first (and most important) edition.

a school Corderius: a Latin grammar, so called after the popular textbook, *Colloquia Scholastica* (1564) by Mathurin Cordier (1478–1564).

Osborne . . . Askew . . . Royalty: Thomas Osborne (d. 1767), London bookseller and publisher; Dr Askew (1722–72), physician, classical scholar, book-collector; George III did own a copy of *The Game and Playe of the Chesse*. The anecdote is probably *not* true.

twopence sterling: Scott's note: both the Roxburghe Club and the Bannatyne Club were for antiquaries.

Lucian: Greek belles-lettrist and wit (b. *c.* AD 120), author of 'To an Un-educated Book-Collector'.

the Complete Syren: *The Syren, containing a collection of four hundred and thirty-two of the most celebrated English songs* (1739).

36 *the Complaynt of Scotland*: by Robert Wedderburn (d. 1557) pub. *c.*1548.

Elzevirs: books published by the seventeenth-century Dutch family printers.

the Cowgate . . . St Mary's Wynd: Edinburgh streets.

37 *Dying Speech, Bloody Murder, or Wonderful Wonder of Wonders*: a com-posite of generic titles, unlike the *Strange and Wonderful News for Chipping-Norton*, which does exist.

Teniers: David Teniers II (1610–90), a Flemish painter of interiors.

38 *the old mad Florentine, Benvenuto Cellini*: (1500–71), Florentine sculptor and goldsmith.

our ancestors drunk sack: a reference to Shakespeare's hard-drinking character of Falstaff in *1* and *2 Henry IV* and *The Merry Wives of Windsor.*

39 *epigraph*: from 'The Gaberlunzie Man';. David Herd (ed.) *Ancient and Modern Scots Songs* (1769), 84.

writings and evidents: here, title deeds.

Statistical Account: *The Statistical Account of Scotland*, ed. John Sinclair, 21 vols. (1791–9), a survey by parish.

40 *Ardoch . . . Burnswark*: two Roman camps, the first in Perthshire, the second in Dumfriesshire—both 'stative' or permanent camps.

41 *in conspectu classis*: (Latin) in sight of the fleet.

Sir Robert Sibbald: (1641–1722) physician, antiquarian, and naturalist, author of *Historical Inquiries, Concerning the Roman Monuments and Antiquities in the North Part of Britain called Scotland* (1707), *Commentarius in Julii Agricolae Expeditiones* (1711), and *Portus, Coloniae and Castella Romana . . . ; or, Conjectures Concerning the Roman Ports, Colonies, and Forts in the Firths* (1711).

41 *Saunders Gordon*: see note to page 18.

General Roy: William Roy (1726–90), cartographer, surveyor, and author of *The Military Antiquities of the Romans in Britain* (1793).

Dr Stukeley: William Stukeley (1687–1765), antiquarian and founder of the Society of Antiquaries, author of *Itinerarium curiosum; or, an Account of the Antiquitys and Remarkable Curiositys in Nature or Art, Observ'd in Travels thro' Great Brittan* (1724).

old Johnson . . . Marathon: Samuel Johnson, *A Journey to the Western Islands of Scotland* (1775), ed. Mary Lascelles (New Haven, 1971), 148. Marathon was a Greek victory against the Persians in 490 BC.

to have the sculpture taken off with plaster of Paris: to have a cast made of it.

Agricola Dicavit Libens Lubens: (Latin) dedicated willingly and heartily by Agricola.

Caius Caligula Pharum Fecit: (Latin) Caius Caligula built this lighthouse.

42 *Ille . . . pruinis*: (Latin) he who pitched his camp among the Caledonian frosts. Claudian (d. *c.* AD 404), 'De quarto consulatu Honorii Augustii'.

Theodosius . . . year 367: the Emperor Valentinian sent Theodosius to recapture Britain from the Saxons, Picts, and Scots.

Decuman gate . . . Prætorian gate . . . porta sinistra . . . porta dextra . . . prætorium: respectively, the gate opposite the Praetorian gate; the gate nearest the Praetorium, the camp headquarters; (Latin) the left gate; (Latin) the right gate.

your Bond-street four-in-hand men: dandies who drove four-horse phaetons down London's smart Bond Street.

43 *See, then, Lovel . . . see Rome no more!*: adapted from Francis Beaumont and John Fletcher, *Bonduca* 3.5.94–8.

44 *Aiken Drum*: the Scottish protagonist of the nursery rhyme.

the story of Keip on this syde: a reference to a probably apocryphal tale of how the Society of Antiquaries was asked to decipher the inscription 'KEE PONT/HI SSIDE'; all their learning proved inadequate to read it correctly as 'KEEP ON THIS SIDE'. See *Town and Country Magazine* for 1771, p. 595.

old Tully: Marcus Tullius Cicero (106–43 BC) orator and politician, who defended the claims of the poet Archias to citizenship in his speech 'Pro Archia Poeta'.

Quis nostrum . . . ut: (Latin) which of us was so rude and barbarous as to.

the great Roscius: Quintus Roscius Gallus (d. 62 BC), the great Roman actor.

46 *poor's-rates and a work-house*: poor-rates were a levy to support the poor, workhouses were institutions which housed the poor.

as intimate as one of the beasts familiar to man which signify love: crab-lice.

Joe Miller: (1684–1738), comedian.

48 *epigraph*: *Merchant of Venice*, 2.1.45.

in defiance of taxes and times: hair powder was taxed in 1786, which contributed, along with the French Revolutionary fashions for the natural, to the demise of the wig.

49 *the volunteer cohort, which had been lately embodied*: the outbreak of war in 1793 had led to the raising of such volunteer companies across the country; Scott himself was a volunteer.

the club of Royal True Blues: Tory supporters of monarchy and the status quo.

Friends of the People: a radical society in sympathy with French revolutionary ('democrat') ideas of constitutional reform; the Scottish Friends of the People was formed 1792–3.

substitute: a sheriff's appointee who dealt with routine investigation and court business.

50 *the 17th curt. stilo novo*: (Latin) 'the 17th of the current month in the new style' i.e. on the Gregorian calendar introduced in Britain in 1752.

at four o'clock: this would be for dinner, the main meal of the day, eaten at this time in the mid-afternoon.

awful rule and right supremacy: *Taming of the Shrew*, 5.2.114.

giddy-paced times: *Twelfth Night*, 2.4.6.

signatum atque sigillatum: (Latin) signed and sealed.

51 *He hobbled . . . he could*: Charles Churchill, *The Ghost* (1763), iii. 1207–8.

squeezed the orange: a Jacobite coded gesture, implying contempt for William of Orange, who succeeded after the forced abdication of James II in 1689.

a dangerous health: amongst Jacobites it was common to evade laws against treason by drinking 'to the king' while passing the wine-glass over a water glass, signifying 'to the king over the water', i.e. the exiled Stuart.

Charles Stewart: (1720–88), grandson of James II, claimant to the British throne, and leader of the Jacobite rising of 1745.

52 *non-juring chaplain*: the chaplain is an Episcopalian who has refused to swear the oaths of Allegiance and Abjuration (i.e. to support the Hanoverian monarchy and renounce the Stuarts), and consequently lost his post as minister.

52 *oaths of abjuration and allegiance*: see above note. To vote, electors had to take these oaths.

house of Stewart . . . been extinct: Charles Stuart died in 1788; although his brother only died in 1807, he had never made any claim to the throne.

deputy-lieutenant and trustee upon turnpike acts: i.e. deputy to the Lord Lieutenant of the county, and responsible for building, maintaining, and levying tolls upon turnpike roads.

53 *Boethius . . . Buchanan*: Hector Boece or Boethius (1465?–1536) wrote a history of Scotland, *Scotorum Historiae* (1526), which lists a number of imaginary Scottish kings; George Buchanan (1506–82), tutor to James VI (later James I of England), followed Boethius in his *Rerum Scoticarum Historia* (1582).

portraits . . . Holyrood: Charles II (reigned 1649–85) commissioned a set of portraits of Boethius' imaginary monarchs to be hung in Edinburgh's royal palace.

divine hereditary right: the belief that the throne passed to the eldest son on divine authority.

the posterity of Fergus: Fergus was the legendary founder of the Scottish monarchy in 330 BC.

descendants of Banquo . . . Hecate: *Macbeth* 4.1.129–37.

the good fame of Queen Mary: Mary, Queen of Scots (1542–87; reigned 1560–7) had implicated herself in the murder of her husband Lord Darnley, and in adultery with the Earl of Bothwell, subsequently her husband, in the notorious 'casket letters'. Jacobite scholars conducted a lively debate over the authenticity of these letters in an effort to clear her reputation and to maintain her as a national heroine.

ruling elder of the kirk: a senior member of the Presbyterian Church.

revolution principles and Protestant succession: i.e. the principles by which, at the Glorious Revolution of 1688, much of the monarchy's power was curtailed; the English Act of Settlement (1701) and the Scottish Act of Security (1704) barred Catholic claimants from the throne.

sought the base fellowship of paltry burghers: Joanna Baillie, *Orra*, in *A Series of Plays: in which it is attempted to delineate the stronger passions of the Mind*, 3 vols. (1812), 3.6.

54 *King William*: William of Orange.

per contra: (Latin) on the contrary.

55 *Bellenden's rare translation of Hector Boece*: John Bellenden (*c.*1500–*c.*1548), put out a translation of Boethius' Latin history of Scotland in 1536.

56 *sum an account of interest*: work out interest due on a debt.

57 *epigraph*: William Cartwright, *The Ordinary*, 3.1.49–53. The character Moth, who speaks these lines, is an antiquary.

Clogdogdo's . . . malæ bestiæ: from Ben Jonson's *Epicene*, 4.2.65–7. The hen-pecked Captain Otter makes up the word 'clogdogdo', and *malae bestiae* is Latin for 'bad beasts'.

Tilley-valley . . . tittivillitium . . . talley-ho: 'tilley-valley' means 'nonsense!'; 'tittivillitium' is Latin for 'a trifle'; and 'talley-ho' is a fox-hunting cry.

Griselda . . . Grizzel: a reference to the story of patient Griselda in Chaucer's 'The Clerk's Tale', *The Canterbury Tales* (*c*.1387); the beautiful Griselda is of humble origins but marries into the nobility; her jealous and tyrannical husband tests her love of him through a series of trials and humiliations, including imprisonment, the theft of her children, and a disgraced return to her father's house, all of which she bears with exemplary patience, to be reinstated eventually in his affections.

ladies' memorandum-book: *The Ladies Own Memorandum Book; or Daily Pocket Journal for the year 1771* (London and Newcastle, 1770), a page-a-day diary put out for the year 1771.

58 *Vesta*: the Roman hearth-goddess, served by the vestal virgins.

Sebastian and Viola . . . Twelfth Night: the twins who are taken for each other in *Twelfth Night* until they coincide on stage.

Mahound or Termagant: Muhammad, the prophet (570?–632), and Termagant, a Muslim deity.

When folks . . . capon: adapted from William Cartwright, *The Ordinary*, 4.5.56–8.

scarlet-fever . . . civil complexion: the scarlet-fever epidemic is a reference to the red-coats of the British army; Lovel is wearing civilian clothes.

59 *Davie Lindsay*: (1486–1555), Scots poet and playwright.

Dibdin: Charles Dibdin (1745–1814), actor, playwright, songwriter, and producer.

Aroint thee, witch!: *Macbeth*, 1.3.5.

Flanders: British troops fought the French in Flanders (roughly, modern Belgium) in 1793 and 1794.

Lycurgus: the traditional founder of the Spartan constitution.

Mahommed: Muhammad (570?–632), principal prophet of Islam.

60 *Dulcineas*: a reference to Don Quixote's lady-love.

Guebres: ancient Persian fire-worshippers.

Solan goose: gannet.

61 *King Alphonso . . . old wine to drink*: proverbial.

how wags the world: *As You Like It*, 2.7.23.

Auld Reekie: nickname for Edinburgh, so called because it was often overhung by a cloud of 'reek' or smoke.

61 *dipping in the sea . . . hellebore*: treatments for madness.

standing armies and German oppression: the German Hanoverians were maintained in power by standing armies.

cum toto corpore regni: (Latin) here, with the whole power of the nation.

Kilmarnock cowl: conical woollen cap worn by the artisan class.

62 *quarter-session . . . general assembly . . . convocation*: quarterly court of appeal; supreme court of the Church of Scotland; a meeting of bishops and clergy convened by the archbishop.

Boadicea . . . Amazon . . . Zenobia: all warlike women, respectively: the queen of the Iceni who fought the Romans in AD 61 and sacked London; a woman warrior of Greek myth; and the queen of Palmyra who also fought the Romans.

the history of Sister Margaret: Adam Ferguson, *The History of the Proceedings in the case of Margaret . . . only lawful Sister of John Bull Esq.* (1761), a political satire in support of the Scottish militia bill.

He came . . . not to heal!: probably by Scott.

detest a drum like a quaker: the sect of Quakers is pacifist.

63 *the privilege of croaking . . . the grand chorus of the marsh*: compare Aesop's Fable of the Stork and the Frogs.

Ni quito Rey, ni pongo Rey . . . as Sancho says: I mar not the king, I make not the king. Cervantes, *Don Quixote*, Part 2, ch. 60.

scot and lot: a tax, consisting of a basic rate (the 'scot') plus a personal rate (the 'lot').

64 *Pinkerton*: John Pinkerton (1758–1826), antiquary and historian, author of *An Inquiry into the History of Scotland Preceding the reign of Malcolm III* (1789).

Chalmers: George Chalmers (1742–1825), antiquary and historian, author of *Caledonia*, an account of Scottish antiquities (3 vols. 1807, 1810, 1824).

Gordon: see note to p. 18 above.

Sibbald: see note to p. 41 above.

Innes: Thomas Innes (1662–1744) antiquary, historian, and author of *A Critical Essay on the Ancient Inhabitants of the Northern Parts of Britain or Scotland. Containing an Account of the Romans, of the Britains betwixt the Walls, of the Caledonians or Picts, and especially of the Scots . . .* (1729).

Ritson: Joseph Ritson (1752–1803), antiquary and editor specializing in the detection of forgeries. He took issue with Pinkerton in his posthumously published *Annals of the Caledonians, Picts, and Scots* (1828).

65 *Castrum Puellarum*: (Latin) Castle of the Girls.

quasi lucus a non lucendo: (Latin) 'as though the word for grove [lucus] was derived from the grove not shining' a tag used to mock suspect etymologies.

Mac, id est filius: (Latin) Mac, which means son of.

66 *Henry Maule*: author of *The History of the Picts* (1706).

Chronicles of Loch-leven and Saint Andrews: probably the *Liber Cartarum prioratus Sancti Andree in Scotia*, and the lost *registrum* of St Andrews.

Chronicle of Nuremburg: the vernacular version of *Liber Chronicarum* (1493).

Miles: here, knight.

Ragman-roll: the list of those who swore loyalty to the conquering Edward I of England in 1296.

67 *Round Table*: a reference to the chivalric ideals of King Arthur and the Knights of the Round Table.

Qui ambulat . . . quo vadit: (Latin) he who walks in darkness does not know where he is going.

Bruce and Wallace: Scottish patriots. William Wallace (*c*.1270–1305) was the leader of an uprising against Edward I, which led eventually to his execution in London; Robert the Bruce (1274–1329) joined Wallace's rising, becoming king in 1306, and subsequently driving out the English. Bruce himself had signed the Ragman-roll.

68 *the black dog*: a fit of the sulks.

Seged, Emperor of Ethiopia . . . Rambler: Samuel Johnson, *The Rambler*, nos. 204 and 205. In Johnson's moral tale, which Oldbuck may be supposed to have in front of him, Seged endeavours to escape 'the fatigues of war and the cares of government' and to assure himself ten days of unadulterated happiness by shutting himself away in the palace of Dambea; despite all his efforts, the experiment is a dismal failure, and cultimates in the death of his beloved daughter.

70 *epigraph*: George Crabbe, *The Borough* (1810), Letter 9, ll. 210–15.

72 *the line of beauty*: as theorized by William Hogarth, amongst others, the line of beauty was serpentine and essential to producing the picturesque effect in a landscape.

73 *the Fall of Fyers*: waterfall on Loch Ness, 165 ft high.

75 *as high as the mast of a first-rate man-of-war*: a first-rate was the most powerful class of navy ship; its mast would rise some 200 ft above the deck.

77 *Dunbuy of Slaines*: rock near Cruden Bay in Aberdeenshire.

79 *epigraph*: *King Lear* (Folio text), 4.2.66–70.

80 *bouse up the kegs o' gin and brandy lang syne*: a reference to smuggling, widespread until the reforms of the 1780s.

81 *Patmos*: island in the Aegean, to which St John was banished, and where, legend has it, he saw the visions of the apocalypse.

82 *a naughty night to swim in*: *King Lear* (Folio text), 3.4.104–5.

   respice finem, respice funem: (Latin) remember your end, remember the rope's end.

   base proverb: i.e. he that is born to be hanged shall never be drowned.

   sus. per funem . . . sus. per coll.: (Latin) hung by a rope . . . hung by the neck.

   old Mocker: *Love's Labour's Lost*, 5.2.542–3.

83 *rara avis*: (Latin) rare bird.

84 *dumosa pendere procul de rupe*: (Latin) to hang far out over the bushy cliff's edge.

   suave mari magno: (Latin) it is pleasant on the open sea.

85 *meo arbitrio*: (Latin) in my judgement.

86 *epigraph*: John Gay, *A True Story of an Apparition*, 71–8.

87 *O, first they eated . . .* : 'Get up and Bar the Door', David Herd (ed.), *Ancient and Modern Scots Songs* (1769), 330–1.

89 *anno domini*: (Latin) here, probably of this year's brewing.

   Wassia Quassia: a coinage suggested by the near rhyme between 'wassail' and 'quassia', a South American shrub from which a bitter medicinal infusion was made.

   risk of being made a ghost: *Hamlet*, 1.4.62.

90 *walk with Sir Priest . . .* : *Twelfth Night* 3.4.263–5.

91 *Aubrey . . . page*: John Aubrey (1626–97), antiquarian and memoirist. *Miscellanies* (1696), 67. Though the Antiquary gets the page number wrong, the passage is indeed in the middle of the page.

   exempli gratia: (Latin) for example.

   dead palsy: stroke leading to paralysis.

92 *Tenues secessit in auras . . . mansit odor*: vanished into thin air . . . the smell remained. Ovid, quoted by Aubrey, *Miscellanies* 97.

   Lordship of Regality: an estate by royal grant.

   twelve–thirteen: until 1752, the English new year began on 25 March, while Scotland and the rest of Europe dated it from 1 January; hence in England the practice of giving both years for the period 1 Jan. to 24 Mar.

93 *Saint Augustine*: St Augustine of Hippo in North Africa (AD 354–430). The story is retailed in Aubrey's *Miscellanies*, 55–6.

   Lord Bacon: Francis Bacon (1561–1626), courtier, scientist, and writer.

   Reginald Elstracke: Renold Elstracke (*c.*1590–1630), one of the earliest engravers working in Britain.

   Augsberg Confession: devised by Luther and Melancthon in 1530, published 1531; became the articles of faith of the Lutheran Church.

quantum sufficit: (Latin) a sufficient quantity.

Mesmer, Shropfer, Cagliostro: Friedrich Anton Mesmer (1733–1815), Austrian physician who popularized hypnotism; J. G. Shröpfer, notorious eighteenth-century exorcist; Conte Alessandro di Cagliostro (1743–95), a charlatan who sold the secret of eternal youth to the credulous.

Scotch collops: larded veal escalopes and meat balls served in a rich sauce of anchovies, oysters, and claret.

95 *epigraph*: W. R. Spencer, 'The Visionary', *Poems by the Late Hon. William R. Spencer* (1811), 1–8.

the philosopher, who appealed . . . sobriety: the reference here is to the widely known story of Philip of Macedon and the woman who petitions him for justice; refused her request, she replies that she will lodge an appeal from the judgement of Philip drunk to that of Philip sober.

a poem . . . repeated: Scott's note: 'The Fountain' was only written in 1799.

96 *My eyes . . . behind*: Wordsworth, 'The Fountain', *Lyrical Ballads*, 2nd edn. (1800), ll. 29–36.

97 *Lo! here be oakis grete . . . green*: *The Floure and the Leafe*, 29–35. Now thought to be by a fifteenth-century lady, but reprinted as Chaucer by Speght in 1598 and not discredited till after Scott's time.

And many an hart . . . ate: Chaucer, *The Book of the Duchess*, 427–32.

Ah! cruel maid . . . unkind: R. B. Sheridan, 'Ah! cruel maid', in John Aikin, *Essays on Song-Writing; with a Collection of English Songs* (London, 1810), 279.

98 *like dewdrops from the lion's mane*: *Troilus and Cressida*, 3.3.217.

99 *baseless and confused visions*: *The Tempest*, 4.1.151.

syren: fabulous sea-nymphs who with their singing beguiled sailors onto the rocks.

triton: a sea-deity, son of Poseidon, half-man, half-dolphin.

Ephialtes: a Greek demon of nightmares.

100 *Rembrandt*: Rembrandt Harmenzoon Van Rijn (1607–69), Dutch painter.

102 *Why sit'st thou . . . for ever*: by Scott.

103 *a Scotch pint*: about three imperial pints.

104 *epigraph*: Abraham Cowley, 'Davideis', 2.90–3.

more majorum: (Latin) after ancestral custom.

mum . . . fat ale: strong beer.

105 *Gideon . . . Midian*: Gideon defeated the Midian hordes, Judges 7: 20–3.

vervain . . . dill . . . Hypericon: magic and medicinal plants.

106 *Jamblichus*: Iamblichus of Chaleis (d. *c*. AD 325).

with vervain . . . will: proverbial saying also quoted by John Aubrey, *Miscellanies* (1696), 111.

106 *it does allay . . . malefactor: Antony and Cleopatra*, 2.5.50–3.

Peter Wilkins . . . Glum and Gawrie: Robert Paltock, *The Life and Adventures of Peter Wilkins* (1751). Shipwrecked in the Antarctic, Wilkins meets a winged race of 'glums' and 'gawries'.

107 *When courtiers . . . no cold*: probably by Scott.

mid impediment: an event intervening between two others, depriving the first of the legal consequence it would otherwise have had.

Ossian's poems . . . the acute Orcadian: the controversy was over the authenticity of *Fragments of Ancient Poetry Collected in the Highlands of Scotland* (1760), *Fingal* (1761), and *Temora* (1763) claimed by their 'editor', James MacPherson, to be translations from the third-century Gaelic bard. Malcolm Laing (1762–1818), born in Orkney, was one of the sceptics.

old Scaliger: Julius Caesar Scaliger (1484–1558), physician, polemicist, scientist, and philosopher, who was involved in a particularly bitter polemic against Erasmus.

l'embarras des richesses: (French) embarrassment of riches. Harlequin appears in a play of the same title (1725).

108 *Pr'ythee, undo this button: King Lear* (Folio), 5.3.285.

Melancthon: Philip Melancthon (1497–1560), philosopher, theologian of the Reformation, and principal author of the Augsberg Confession (1531).

the Elector of Saxony: Frederick III (1463–1525), ruler of Saxony.

powerful and victorious emperor: Charles V (1500–58), Holy Roman Emperor (1519–56), and King of Spain, Naples, and the Spanish Netherlands. He convened the Diet of Worms which condemned Luther and his works.

Philip II: Philip II (1527–98), King of Spain, the Netherlands, Naples, and Portugal, and husband to Mary I of England. He invented the Inquisition in Spain, instigated the persecution of Protestants in England from 1554, and waged war against Calvinism in the Low Countries.

Horace: Horace, *Odes*, 3.3.1.

109 *Sed semel insanivimus omnes*: (Latin) but we all have been mad once.

old Fust: Johann Fust (d. 1466), German pioneer of printing and eventual owner, with his son-in-law Peter Schöffer of the Gutenberg press, here conflated with Johann Faust (*c.*1488–1541), German wandering conjuror, the subject of Marlowe's and Goethe's plays in which he sells his soul to the devil in exchange for forbidden knowledge and sexual adventure.

sixteen armorial quarters: a coat-of-arms betokening a long aristocratic genealogy, since the shield is divided into sixteen to accommodate all the intermarried houses.

Luther . . . Erasmus: notable leaders of the Reformation.

110 *arranged the types . . . revise*: the compositor sets the type (backwards and upside-down), and imposes it by transferring it to the printing press itself. A proof is followed by a revise—a triple revise is therefore a fourth proof.

fronde super viridi: (Latin) upon the green sward: Virgil, *Eclogues*, 1.80.

Sing hey-ho . . . folly: *As You Like It*, 2.7.181–2.

hobby . . . run it a tilt: Oldbuck puns hobby as hobby-horse (imagined as in a tournament) with hobby as leisure pursuit.

111 *world and worldlings base*: 2 *Henry IV*, 5.3.100.

Earl Marshall: Thomas Percy (ed.), *Reliques of Ancient English Poetry*, 'Queen Eleanor's Confession'.

Heir lyeth . . . wyvis: Scott's own faked-up middle English.

112 *Naiad*: in classical mythology, a water-nymph.

the Bell-Rock: 12 miles south-east of Arbroath.

113 *the distilleries is no working*: the failure of grain-harvests in 1794–5 led to the prohibition of distillation in 1795.

114 *epigraph*: adapted from Richard Brome, *A Jovial Crew*, 2.1.2–6.

115 *old philosopher of the Cynic school*: founded by the Athenian Antisthenes, pupil of Socrates in the fifth-century BC, the Cynics equally despised learning and luxury in favour of an independence from needs.

120 *epigraph*: *As You Like It*, 3.5.93–8.

good down pillow . . . churlish: *Henry V*, 4.1.14–15.

121 *swart spirit of the mine*: adapted from John Milton, *Comus*, 435.

123 *terra firma*: (Latin) firm ground.

terra incognita: (Latin) unknown territory.

Dr H——n: Scott's note: James Hutton (1726–97), geologist.

Kircher: Athanasius Kircher (1601–80), physiologist, mathematician, vulcanologist, and natural philosopher.

Artem . . . ire: (Latin) they have art without art, a part without a part, their medium is to lie, their life is to go a-begging.

125 *bend of bastardy*: diagonal lines running from top left hand to the bottom right hand of a shield, denoting illegitimacy.

Milcolumbus Nothus: (Latin) Malcolm the Bastard.

126 *cito peritura*: (Latin) soon it will perish.

teres atque rotundus: Horace, *Satires*, 2.7.86. Smooth and well-rounded [man].

127 *Illuminé*: a term associated with the German Illuminaten, a secret society founded in 1776 which, on account of its republican and deistic

principles, commonly came in for part of the blame for the French Revolution.

128 *magisterium . . . revived in our own*: the 'magisterium' is the philosopher's stone; 'sympathies and antipathies', attractions and repulsions said to account for natural forces; 'cabala', here, a secret system of esoteric doctrine; 'Rosycrucians', a secret society supposedly founded in 1484, which claimed secret and magical knowledge of alchemy, the elixir of life, natural magic, etc., and were frequently associated in the popular mind with conspiracy theories of the French Revolution.

Abon Hassan: character from 'the Story of the Sleeper Awakened' in *The Arabian Nights*.

scourge . . . rods of scorpions: 1 Kings 12: 11.

strictly entailed: an entail specified the heir and prevented the selling-off of the estate.

like John Bunyan: see John Bunyan, *The Pilgrim's Progress* (1678), end part 1.

130 *epigraph*: *Romeo and Juliet*, 5.1.1–5.

Marcus Tullius . . . intelligo: Marcus Tullius Cicero, *De Divinatione* (44 BC), 2.59. If we do not put faith in the visions of madmen, I cannot understand why we should credit the visions of sleepers, which are even more disordered.

131 *Cicero . . . events*: also from *De Divinatione*, 2.59.

a Daniel: Daniel ch. 2.

132 *What make you from Wittenberg? . . . truant disposition*: *Hamlet*, 1.2.163–7.

133 *multifarious idolaters . . . Golden Calf—the Mammon of unrighteousness*: Egypt is represented as the home of luxury and vice from which the Israelites must escape; the Golden Calf and Mammon represent materialism. Exodus ch. 32; Luke 16: 9.

pressing to death, whipping, and hanging: *Measure, for Measure* 5.1.521–2.

134 *Parnassus . . . the base of the hill*: a summit in Greece consecrated to Apollo and the muses. Oldbuck is referring to the generally accepted hierarchy amongst literary genres whereby epic outranked lyric.

the Antiquarian Repository: London periodical, 1775–86, and revived from 1807 to 1809.

Hearne's edition of Robert of Gloucester: Thomas Hearne (1678–1735), antiquary and editor of *Robert of Gloucester's Chronicle Transcrib'd* (1724).

the Gentleman's Magazine: London periodical founded 1731.

the inscription of Œlia Lelia . . . Œdipus: a reference to the famous riddling inscription in Bologna: 'Ælia Laelia Crispis | Nec vir, nec mulier, nec androgyna | Nec puella, nec juvenis, nec anus | Nec meretrix, nec pudica; | Sed omnia': neither man, nor woman nor hermaphrodite | neither girl, nor boy, nor old woman | Neither whore nor virgin; | But all of them. Oedipus, king of Thebes, solved the riddle of the Sphinx— hence Oldbuck's adoption of the pseudonym.

free of the corporation: i.e. privileged as a member of a town guild.

135 *No more of that, an thou lovest me*: *I Henry IV*, 2.5.286.

Palladio or Vitruvius: Andrea Palladio (1518–80) and Marcus Pollio Vitruvius (fl. 40 BC), respectively, celebrated neoclassical and classical architects and writers on architecture.

after what flourish your nature will: *Hamlet*, 5.2.140–1.

a second Teucer: the greatest Greek archer besieging Troy; he shot from behind the shield of his half-brother, Ajax.

136 *cestus ... awen ... divinus afflatus*: (Latin, Welsh, and Latin) divine inspiration.

Abdiel: the faithful seraph who withstood Satan's incitement to revolt. John Milton, *Paradise Lost*, 5. 896–907.

Galgacus: 1st century AD, Caledonian chieftain defeated by the invading Agricola AD 84.

to publish by subscription: to collect money ahead of publication from subscribers, whose names would appear listed, usually at the front of the book.

137 *ultra crepidam*: (Latin) beyond the sandal. Here, implies that Oldbuck has gone beyond his remit.

care killed a cat: proverbial i.e. even a cat, blessed with nine lives, can be killed by anxiety.

gaudé-day: gaudy-day or feast day, latterly especially a grand entertain- ment held in an Oxbridge college

analecta ... collectanea: (Latin) an erudite joke. Literally, the crumbs picked up by the slave; but in early nineteenth-century usage, literary extracts.

138 *epigraph*: possibly fabricated by Scott.

protested bills: bills which the bank has refused to honour.

139 *the weird sisters ... pilot's thumb*: *Macbeth*, 1.3.26–7.

John Thomson's wallet: see the folk-song, 'John Tamson's wallet' in Wil- liam Motherwell, *Minstrelsy: Ancient and Modern* (1827), Appendix, x. 'John Tamson's wallet frae end to end ... | And what was in't ye fain wad ken, | Whigmaleeries for women and men.'

140 *pole at his door*: a reference to the red and white striped pole that still occasionally designates a barber's shop.

wafers ... wax: a simpler and cheaper way of sealing letters than with sealing wax, a wafer was a disc of flour and gum which when moistened would both act as a seal and take the impression of a seal.

140 *a double letter*: i.e. consisting of two sheets, and therefore costing twice as much.

a frank: a signature from a member of parliament on the letter which sent it post-free.

141 *Falkirk tryst*: a cattle market.

nick-sticks: Scott's note quotes Matthew Prior, *Alma: or, the Progress of the Mind*, 2.214–17.

N. B.: North Britain.

142 *too, too solid wax . . . dissolve itself*: *Hamlet*, 1.2.129–30.

143 *dooms sweer to the road*: very reluctant to go the journey.

like the sybils after consulting their leaves: prophetesses of the ancient world who consulted collections of prophecies written on leaves before making their own.

144 *an insurrection . . . La Vendée*: La Vendée was the regional stronghold of the French royalists who rose against the revolutionaries in March 1793.

pudder over his head: *King Lear* (Folio), 3.2.50.

146 *staying no longer question*: *2 Henry IV*, 1.1.48.

148 *epigraph*: *1 Henry IV*, 2.2.18–20, (not the Second Part, as Scott suggests).

Friar's chicken: chicken broth thickened with eggs.

149 *the Sun*: Tory London newspaper.

the great attempt: i.e. the French invasion.

150 *O crimini!*: (Latin) O what a crime.

151 *a widow's close-drawn pinners*: a widow commonly wore a close-fitting cap with two long flaps falling on either side of the face.

the Master o' Morphie: according to the Dryburgh edition, a member of the family of Morphie, noted for their extravagance and love of good horses.

153 *crede experto*: (Latin) believe the experienced.

Mars armipotent: the Roman god of war.

vale of Bacha: the vale of Tears, Psalms 84: 6.

154 *Hæc data pœna diu viventibus*: this punishment is allotted to those who live long. Juvenal, *Satires*, 10.243.

cram these words . . . your sense: *The Tempest*, 2.1.112–13.

vacare musis: (Latin) have time for the muses.

the Hotspur of the North: see *1 Henry IV* where this name is used of the reckless young Harry Percy.

Almanzor: knight in Dryden's *The Conquest of Granada* (1670).

Chamont: irritable soldier in Thomas Otway's *The Orphan* (1680).

155 *set up your staff*: literally, set up your tent-pole; i.e. take up residence.

   substitute heirs of entail: the first heir to the estate was the 'institute', subsequent heirs the 'substitutes'.

156 *turnpike-gate*: point at which tolls were paid on the toll-road.

   Bucephalus: the favourite charger of Alexander the Great (366–323 BC).

   eighteenpence a side: Oldbuck is suggesting hiring a horse by the stage.

157 *epigraph*: adapted from George Crabbe, *The Borough*, Letter IV, 134–43.

   buzz wig . . . ramilies . . . bob-wig: respectively, a large bushy wig, a wig with a long plait behind finished with a bow at top and bottom, a wig with its bottom locks turned up into short curls.

158 *by way of bodkin*: to ride bodkin was to ride between two others, the accommodation being only for two.

   hedge inn: an inferior public house.

160 *I know each lane . . . side*: John Milton, *Comus*, 310–12.

   hors de propos: (French) inappropriate.

   So sinks the day-star . . . forehead: John Milton, *Lycidas*, 168–71.

161 *its parent lake*: a poetic commonplace.

   Montrose's wars: James Graham, first marquis of Montrose (1612–50) fought on Charles I's side in 1644–5.

162 *the learned Leland*: John Leland (*c*.1503–52), the earliest of modern English antiquaries, whose researches in monastic and collegiate libraries are recorded in a mass of notes edited by Thomas Hearne as *The Itinerary of John Leland the Antiquary* (1710–12). Leland went insane in 1550 (see later in Scott's text).

   Rachael weeping for her children: Jeremiah 31: 15; Matthew 2: 18.

   Heytesburg's sophisms, Porphyry's universals, Aristotle's logic, and Dunse's divinity: William Heytesburg (14th century), Oxford logician and author of *Sophismata*; Porphyry (AD 232/3–*c*.305), philosopher, Neoplatonist, and scholar of religions; Aristotle (384–322 BC) the author of *On Logic*; Duns Scotus (*c*.1266–1308), a Scottish Franciscan who specialized in ingenious metaphysical distinctions.

   the accommodation of grocers . . . and other worldly occupiers: Oldbuck is referring to the practice of using old books as wrapping paper.

   John Knox: (*c*.1513–72), leader of the Reformation in Scotland, and so popularly held responsible for the destruction of churches, monasteries, and manuscripts.

   woodcock caught in his own springe: proverbial; and *Hamlet*, 1.3.115; 5.2.259–60.

163 *magia naturalis*: (Latin) natural magic, a term which covered much medieval science.

164 *the great overshadowing tree of iniquity . . . abomination*: the Holy Roman Church, here described in a pastiche of Presbyterian rhetoric.

165 *knights of the Rosy Cross*: i.e. Rosicrucians, associated with revolutionary opinions.

Queen Mab: the fairy midwife to dreams; *Romeo and Juliet*, 1.3.54–96.

166 *Inquisition . . . Auto-da-fe*: the Roman Catholic tribunal set up to suppress heresy and heretics; Auto-da-Fé is Portuguese for 'act-of-faith', which came to refer to the burning of heretics.

167 *cat and nine tails*: a nine-thonged lash employed in the army and navy as a punishment.

168 *fronde super viridi*: see note to p. 110.

169 *epigraph*: John Milton, *Paradise Lost*, 2.943–7.

Goethe or Wieland: Johann Wolfgang von Goethe (1749–1832), novelist and poet, and Cristoph Martin Wieland (1733–1813), writer of romances with a medieval flavour.

171 *Baalpeor, Ashtaroth, and Beelzebub*: respectively two heathen deities (Numbers 25: 3; Judges 2: 13), and 'the prince of the devils' (Matthew 12: 24).

Tophet: situated to the south of Jerusalem, used first by the Israelites as a place for human sacrifice to heathen gods, and subsequently as a rubbish heap and bonfire site, thus becoming a symbol of hell. 2 Kings 13: 10; Jeremiah 14: 4.

172 *the Electorate*: i.e. the Elector of Hanover.

176 *the wedding of Hermes with the Black Dragon*: god of magic and alchemy, and Satan.

177 *as Deep calls unto Deep*: Psalm 42: 7.

179 *a lapsed fief*: a grant of lands which reverts to the granter upon the lapse of the recipient's claim.

180 *epigraph*: Thomas Middleton and William Rowley, *A Fair Quarrel*, 1.1.155–9.

I bear . . . to start: adapted from Thomas J. Mathias, *The Pursuits of Literature* (1798), Dialogue 4, 73–4.

Hector, son of Priam: the most valiant of all the Trojans, eldest son of King Priam of Troy.

181 *cavaliér servénte*: (Italian) man devoted entirely and professedly to a lady out of love, but not usually a present or future husband!

182 *the schools of Oxford*: now the Bodleian library quadrangle, which boasts a Jacobean gatehouse as described.

patience on the heat of his distemperature: *Hamlet*, 3.4.114–15.

183 *savoir faire*: (French) social know-how.

starting like a war-horse at the trumpet sound: Job 39: 24–5.

a train which takes fire: a slow fuse.

a grant of lands, cum decimis . . . separatis: (Latin) lands on which the duties included all church-tithes because they had not formerly been assessed separately.

Teind Court: the Court of Session also sat as the Teind Court to deal with ministers' stipends, tithes, church property, etc.

localling his last augmentation of stipend: apportioning an increase in a minister's salary among different landholders of the parish.

gules with a sable fess: red with a thick horizontal black band.

battle of Vernoil: battle of Verneuil (1424), an English victory over the French.

184 *Decreet of certification . . . mere evasion*: Scots law. Blattergowl is describing the progress of settling liability to tithes to fund the increase in the minister's salary between a number of landholders.

186 *I am schooled . . . speed!*: *1 Henry IV*, 3.1.186

upon the tapis: come under discussion. From the French, 'tablecloth'.

187 *Have we got Hiren here?*: *2 Henry IV*, 2.4.172 where Pistol refers to his sword as Hiren, borrowing the name of the heroine of George Peele's *The Turkish Mahomet and Hiren the Fair Greek* (1594).

188 *his coral and bells*: it was customary amongst the well-to-do to combine a piece of coral as a teether with bells for a rattle.

æquam servare mentem: (Latin) to keep a quiet mind. Horace, *Odes*, 2.3.1–2.

190 *to throw [the glove] down*: to issue a challenge to a duel.

191 *epigraph*: Thomas Middleton and William Rowley, *A Fair Quarrel*, 3.1.20–6.

193 *Cain, with the blood of his brother on his head*: Cain killed his brother Abel, becoming the first murderer. Genesis 4: 3–15.

194 *before the mast*: the crew and non-commissioned officers were berthed in the forecastle of a ship of war, i.e. Taffril has risen to a commission from ordinary seaman.

195 *caulking a shot-hole*: literally, plugging and tarring a hole in the ship's side; here, dressing a shot-wound.

196 *father Adam*: traditional mode of address to an old man, Adam being the first and therefore the eldest of men.

weigh anchor: literally, to pull up the anchor; here, leave.

197 *a fugie warrant for debt*: a warrant imprisoning a debtor who otherwise might abscond.

in terrorem: (Latin) in order to terrify.

201 *epigraph*: Thomas Dekker, *The Wonder of a Kingdome*, 1.4.71–6.

206 *St Michael and the dragon*: the Archangel Michael cast Satan (or the dragon) out of heaven.

206 *mirth ... frankincent*: myrrh and frankincense. Myrrh, an aromatic resin, was used in embalming, frankincense was burnt as part of the act of worship. They comprised two of the three symbolic gifts given to the infant Christ. Matthew 2: 11.

208 *Pymander*: Hermes Trismegistus, *The Divine Pymander of Hermes Mercurius Trismegistus* (1650), i.e. his book of occult magic.

little plate of silver ... house of ascendency: garbled astrological terminology spiced up with magic numbers and occult signs and conjurations.

209 *planetary hours*: the hour associated with the moon.

a pentagon within a circle ... sword: the magician's circle to protect him from the spirits he raises. The sword doubles as a crucifix and thus offers further protection. Scott's source for this and the vision that follows is Reginald Scot's *Discovery of Witchcraft*.

Fischer with his oboi: Johann Fischer (1733–1800), famous German oboist.

210 *Alle guten Geistern, loben den Herrn*: (German) all good spirits praise the Lord.

213 *Blind Harry*: Henry the Minstrel (fl. 1470–92), author of a major poem on the life of Wallace (*c*.1477).

Davie Lindsay: David Lindsay (1490–1555) Scottish poet, dramatist, and courtier.

217 *epigraph*: Joseph Hall, *Virgidemiarum* (1597–8), 4.3.34–9.

218 *feræ naturæ*: (Latin) wild animals.

Juno ... Pantheon kind of a name: Roman goddess, sister and wife of Jupiter. A pantheon was a temple dedicated generally to the gods.

219 *aureum quidem opus*: (Latin) certainly a work of great value.

Fingal ... Fin-Mac-Coul ... spirit of Loda: see note to p. 107 on Macpherson's *The Poems of Ossian* (1762–3).

221 *Macbeth ... Duncan*: Macbeth, 2.3.42–63.

222 *personal bond*: an acknowledgement of debt with a promise to pay before a certain date or incur set penalties.

notes of hand: written promises to pay specified sums at specified dates.

223 *rari—et rariores—etiam rarissimi*: (Latin) rare—even rarer—very rare.

bonnet-piece of James V ... Dauphin's: all antique gold and silver coins.

224 *Sapiens dominabitur astris*: (Latin) a wise man will rule the stars.

225 *Nicolaus Remigius ... Petrus Thyracus*: Remigius on demonology, *Daemonolatreiae* (1595); and Thyracus on ghosts and possession, *De Apparitionibus* (1605) and *De Obsessis* (1598).

Pinkerton's catalogue: John Pinkerton, *An Essay on Medals* (1784).

Mair: John Mair or Major (*c*.1470–1550), Scottish theologian and historian, author of *Historia Majoris Britanniae* (1521).

Jachin and Boaz: the two pillars set up by Solomon as the porch to his Temple. 1 Kings 7: 21.

226 *Money . . . pay*: Samuel Butler, *Hudibras*, Part 3, 3.624–6.

228 *epigraph*: Ben Jonson, *The Alchemist*, 4.6.40–5.

229 *his genius stood rebuked*: *Macbeth*, 3.1.57.

great Oldenburgh horn . . . de wood: according to tradition, Count Otto of Oldenburg was in 967 offered drink in a silver-gilt horn by a 'wild woman' at the Osenberg—suspicious, he threw the drink away, but retained the horn, which is now in the collection of the King of Denmark.

metaphorical horn: the cuckold's horns.

230 *the commission of the peace*: i.e. magistrates.

Thyself shalt see the act: *The Merchant of Venice*, 4.1.312.

232 *Aha, old true-penny*: *Hamlet*, 1.5.152.

the last call: the last trump on the Day of Judgement.

triangular vial of May-dew: dew gathered in May supposed to have medicinal and cosmetic powers.

divining-rod of witches-hazel: forked stick for discovering water etc.

233 *Bartholinus*: Thomas Bartholin (1659–90), Danish antiquarian.

a green Yule makes a fat kirk-yard: (proverbial) in a warm winter, fatal diseases flourish.

236 *Your toad . . . to name*: Ben Jonson, *The Alchemist*, 2.3.189–91, 193, 198.

237 *epigraph*: John Fletcher and Philip Massinger, *The Beggar's Bush*, 3.2.112, 114–15.

graduated and calculated sigil: the plate of silver formerly alluded to, engraved with lines to assist astrological calculation.

238 *Exchequer . . . claim*: the Court of Exchequer dealt with the Crown's claims to treasure trove. The Crown would normally lay claim to treasure which had been evidently hidden, but in practice it would frequently be made over to the owner of the ground and/or the finder.

the Barons: i.e. the Barons of the Exchequer.

239 *Mine heiligkeit . . . sapperment . . . mein himmel!*: (German) respectively, my holiness, sacrament, my heaven.

three times tried in the fire: compare Zachariah 13: 9.

Dutch burgomaster . . . the Stadthaus: it was customary for a burgomaster to take his turn at funding a banquet at the equivalent of the Town Hall—the Dutch were proverbially great eaters.

241 *wheel*: the wheel of fortune.

242 *of that Ilk*: of that territory. Here, a designation, so, the Knockwinnocks of Knockwinnock.

243   *the wrang side o' the blanket*: i.e. illegitimate.

244   *a dark lantern*: a lantern that could be fully shuttered.

246   *epigraph*: *King John*, 3.3.7–10, 3.3.12–13.

248   *Alle guter Geister*: (German) all good spirits. The prayer would normally finish 'defend us' or 'praise the lord'.

251   *voie de fait*: (French) legal term for assault.

252   *nixies . . . blue spirits and grey*: nixies are female water-fairies; oak-kings are the spirits of oaks; werewolves are men capable of changing themselves into wolves; hobgoblins are mischievous domestic sprites such as Puck; for black, white, blue, and grey spirits see *Macbeth*, 3.6.44–5 and this passage's source, Thomas Middleton's *The Witch*, 1.2.1–7, 5.3.60–1.

254   *rites . . . rarely practised in Protestant countries, and almost never in Scotland*: public Catholic rites were illegal in Scotland.

255   *ignis fatuus*: (Latin) marsh-light.

256   *epigraph*: traditional.

257   *her distaff in her bosom, and her spindle in her hand . . . the more regulated spinning-wheel*: Elspeth is spinning with distaff (a stick on which the raw flax was wound) and spindle which was made to spin the fibres round as they were twirled into thread. This system was superseded by the spinning wheel.

        the fated Princess of the fairy tale: Sleeping Beauty.

258   *ilka land has its ain lauch*: (proverbial) every country has its own law.

259   *the auld harlot*: an allusion to the Whore of Babylon (Revelation 17), a common way of referring to the Roman Catholic Church amongst Presbyterians of the time.

260   *Harlaw*: battle of 1411 in which Donald of the Isles was defeated by the Earl of Mar.

        eating fish: Friday was a Catholic fast-day on which it was customary to eat fish rather than meat.

262   *Prestonpans*: Jacobite victory in the 1745 rebellion; Ochiltree was fighting on the government side.

265   *epigraph*: Fletcher and Massinger, *The Beggar's Bush*, 1.3.165–7.

268   *Excluded from politics by the incapacities attached to those of his religion*: Catholics were excluded from, amongst other areas of public life, all corporate, municipal and parliamentary office until the Catholic Emancipation Act of 1829.

269   *Inigo Jones*: (1573–1652), architect who introduced the Palladian Renaissance style.

        occasional conformist: Protestant nonconformists, prevented from holding public office by the Corporation and Test Acts of 1661 and 1673, developed the practice of 'occasional conformity' i.e. occasionally taking Church of England communion, to get around the laws. The issue was especially inflamed at the beginning of Queen Anne's reign (1702–14).

270 *Fontenoy*: battle of 1745 in the War of Austrian Succession.

272 *Carrick's company*: John Campbell of Carrick, captain of the 42nd, killed at Fontenoy.

cappechin freer . . . palmer: a capuchin friar returned from pilgrimage to the Holy Land, in token of which he would carry a palm leaf.

273 *the union of the crowns*: 1603, when James V of Scotland also became James I of England.

Vandyke: Anthony Van Dyke (1599–1641), court painter and portraitist to Charles I in 1632.

Domenichino: Domenico Zampieri (1581–1641), Italian religious painter.

Velasquez: Diego de Silva y Velazquez (1599–1660), Spanish portraitist.

Murillo: Bartolomé Esteban Murillo (1618–82), Spanish painter specializing in religious works and scenes from low life.

275 *epigraph*: Thomas Southerne, *The Fatal Marriage*, 4.3.6–10.

Spagnoletto: Jusepe de Ribera called Lo Spagnoletto (1591–1652), artist specializing in gory martyrdoms.

St Stephen: the first Christian martyr, stoned to death. Acts 6 and 7.

280 *epigraph*: George Crabbe, *The Village*, 1.333–6.

281 *I was in America*: the 42nd served in America during the Seven Years War (1756–63).

the deil gaed o'er Jock Wabster: (proverbial) there was a devil of a fuss.

heresies of the country: i.e. Protestantism.

she was sib to him nearer than our Church's rule admits of: in Canon law marriage was not permitted within three degrees of relationship—i.e. the number of steps to a common ancestor. Eveline Neville was brought up as the daughter of a first cousin to the Earl's father, so she and the Earl would therefore have had the same great-grandparents.

282 *pride goeth before destruction*: Proverbs 16: 18.

283 *a new Speaker called to the chair*: the allusion is to the Speaker of the House of Commons, who chairs the debate. When a new Speaker is elected he or she traditionally demonstrates reluctance, historically because under Charles I the Speaker was liable to be executed to punish the defiance of Parliament as a whole.

284 *peace-officer . . . baton*: constable and his sign of authority.

285 *highland bail*: to free Ochiltree by violence rather than by putting down money as surety.

government victualler: supply ship for the navy.

286 *epigraph*: probably by Scott.

286 *kittle cast*: a tricky calling.

crops and the powder-tax: the late eighteenth-century fashions for men moved away from long powdered wigs to 'crops', short hair worn naturally. The change was accelerated by the introduction of a powder-tax in 1796.

Quid mihi cum fæmina?: (Latin) What have I to do with woman?

287 *Spartan . . . Helot*: Helots were a class of serf in ancient Sparta.

kolb kerl: Middle German for 'club-bearer'.

ascriptus glebæ: (Latin) tied [to service] on the land.

the Catholic priests in thae times gat something for ganging about to burials: it was customary to present an animal or an equivalent to the Church on a death.

288 *The daughter . . . Corecca slow*: Edmund Spenser, *The Faerie Queene*, 1.3.18, 3–4.

Ira furor brevis: (Latin) anger is a brief passion. Horace, *Epistles*, 1.2.62.

Hector . . . officer of mine: *Othello*, 2.3.241–2.

289 *camp train*: the supplies, wives, and other followers who accompanied armies.

expeditus, or relictis impedimentis: (Latin) unencumbered, or with luggage left behind.

claustrum fregit: (Latin) breaking the door, an aggravation of theft.

290 *remora*: a sucking fish, supposed by the ancient world to stop any ship it attached itself to.

291 *Weave the warp . . . pence*: parodic adaptation of Thomas Gray, *The Bard*, 2.1.49–50 with two wholly spurious lines appended.

the Fatal Sisters: the title of Gray's translation of a Latin version of an Old Norse poem.

292 *officina gentium*: (Latin) the workshop of peoples.

Stern to inflict . . . in death: 'To A.S. Cottle, from Robert Southey', in *Icelandic Poetry*, trans. A. S. Cottle (1797), 34.62–5.

Cressy and Agincourt: famous English victories over the French in 1346 and 1415.

Edward and Henry: i.e. Edward the Black Prince (1330–76) and Henry V (1387–1422), who led the victorious English armies at Cressy and Agincourt respectively.

293 *Harolds, Harfagers, and Hacos*: old Norse kings and heroes.

Mancipia and Serfs: Roman slaves and medieval peasants tied to service on particular lands.

294 *Hector and Achilles, and Agamemnon*: Hector was a Trojan hero, Achilles and Agamemnon Greek warriors in Homer's *Iliad*.

Patrick, the tutelar Saint of Ireland: St Patrick, patron saint of Ireland, was said to be Ossian's son-in-law.

the most admirable fooling: *Twelfth Night*, 2.3.77.

295 *drone and small pipes*: bass and soprano parts of the bagpipes.

Fenians: ancient name for the old Irish.

Proteus: god of the sea.

296 *Sancho . . . sheep*: Miguel Cervantes Saavedra, *Don Quixote La Mancha* (1605, 1615), Part 1, ch. 18.

spolia opima: (Latin) spoils taken by a Roman general from the enemy's general in single combat.

297 *I would not have given it for an ocean of seals*: adapted from *Merchant of Venice*, 3.1.114.

298 *epigraph*: probably by Scott.

our Wilkie: Sir David Wilkie (1785–1841), Scottish painter of scenes of village life.

301 *General Assembly . . . moderator*: The General Assembly, the supreme court of the Church of England, elects a Moderator as chair every year.

chair of rhetoric or belles lettres: professorial chair for the study of modern literature.

306 *epigraph*: Horace Walpole, *The Mysterious Mother* (1768), 1.3.12–13, 29–31.

307 *this vale of sorrow and darkness*: Psalm 23: 4.

311 *the tempter of auld*: Satan.

313 *epigraph*: probably by Scott.

cousin-german: first cousin.

314 *Sheriffmuir*: battle of 1715.

322 *epigraph*: probably by Scott.

procurator for the church: lawyer acting on behalf of the Church of Scotland.

323 *the Stoic philosophy*: ancient Greek school of philosophy which taught indifference and endurance in the face of misfortune; popularly also associated with suppression of feeling.

324 *more sinned against than sinning*: *King Lear* (Folio), 3.2.59.

327 *blotted out of the book of the living*: Psalm 69: 28.

332 *epigraph*: probably by Scott.

the titular's condescendence in the process of valuation and sale: the titular held the title to tithes, which could be sold. Their value would be specified in the 'condescendences' prior to the Teind Court's process of valuation and sale.

Erskine's Institutes: the reference is to John Erskine's *An Institute of the Law of Scotland* (1773).

Coke upon Littleton: Edward Coke's *Institutes of the Laws of England*

(1628–44), a critical commentary on Thomas Littleton's *Tenures* (1422–81), was indispensable because it reformulated English property law.

334 *diet . . . of a heathen Pythagorean, or Indian Bramin*: Pythagoras (b. *c.*580 BC) founded a school of philosophy and mathematics whose members followed a form of vegetarianism. A Brahmin is a member of the priest-caste amongst Hindus, who are also vegetarian.

the first Constituent Assembly: the French Assemblée Nationale renamed itself the Constituent Assembly on 23 June 1789, and proceeded to formulate a new constitution ratified in February 1791. As Oldbuck's remarks suggest, many British Whigs hailed this reform as in the spirit of their own constitutional democracy, and as the excesses of the revolutionaries mounted, typically offered the defence that follows.

335 *Dumourier*: General Charles François Dumouriez (1729–1823), who led the French campaign in Belgium in 1793.

336 *a quid pro quo*: (Latin) something in exchange for another.

a Rowland for his Oliver: (proverbial) Roland and Oliver were two equally matched knights of Charlemagne (see next note), neither of whom could best each other in single combat.

Paladins of Charlemagne: the twelve warrior princes of the court of Charlemagne (747–814), king of the Franks and Christian Emperor of the west.

Suum cuique tribuito: (Latin) to each his own.

337 *a lying-in hospital*: a maternity hospital.

338 *Eheu Evelina!*: (Latin) alas, Evelina.

339 *a discovery which may turn out so much to his own prejudice*: it seems here that by old Neville's will, the Glenallan estate went to the eldest son, and the Neville estate to the younger. The Neville estate would be entailed upon the younger son and his descendants. However, should the younger son not produce an heir, the property reverts back to the elder son's son. It was only in the absence of a son to Glenallan, that Edward Neville had 'free disposal' of the Neville estate. Hence the belated discovery of a son by Glenallan would dispossess the current heir.

the Saxon horn that is preserved in the Minster: an ivory horn given to York Minster before 1042, of debated provenance.

Dr Dryasdust: one of Scott's recurring characters; he reappears, for example, in the Dedication to *Ivanhoe* and the epilogue to *Redgauntlet*.

340 *as an emigrant*: London was flooded in the early 1790s by emigrant clergy and others fleeing France.

341 *Linnæus*: Carl Linné (1707–78), Swedish botanist and plant-classifier.

elisa H: eliding the H.

343 *epigraph*: *The Passionate Pilgrim*, 12.1–4. Current scholarship takes the

view that this collection (attributed to Shakespeare) contains some material by Shakespeare, but that much other material is not by his hand. Shakespeare's authorship of 'Crabbed age and youth', however, has not yet been disproved.

344 *democraws* . . . *the Friends o' the People*: 'democrats' was a term used of sympathizers with French Revolutionary ideas, and especially of those who espoused Thomas Paine's ideas on reform set out in *The Rights of Man* (1791, 1792); the Friends of the People were a reform-minded political organization founded in Scotland 1792–3, widely regarded as seditious.

the new collector: i.e. of land-tax.

the Blue and a' Blue Club: supporters of the monarchy and current constitution.

the peace: in June 1793, Charles James Fox (1749–1806) proposed a Commons petition to the King in favour of making peace.

meal mob: i.e. food riot.

345 *I live not in their report*: *Measure for Measure*, 4.3.155.

346 *Alexander II*: 1214–49.

347 *Quadriga* . . . *scholium* . . . *vox signata*: (Latin) respectively, a chariot drawn by a team of four horses, annotation, particular name.

off this grass: this season.

348 *Sunt* . . . *juvat*: there are those who rejoice in having stirred up the Olympic dust in their chariot. Horace, *Odes*, 1.1.3–4.

352 *epigraph*: probably by Scott.

353 *Bailie Littlejohn*: a Bailie was both councillor and magistrate.

354 *nae liberty-boy* . . . *the riots in Dublin*: a liberty-boy was one who lived in the 'liberties' on the outskirts of Dublin. In 1765, during riots against troops stationed in the city, the prison was broken open and the prisoners released. By transference, 'liberty-boy' took on the meaning of 'standing for liberty'. Ochiltree will have been amongst the troops trying to control the rioting.

ate the king's bread: i.e. been a soldier.

355 *the Lords at the Circuit*: the High Court of Justiciary, Scotland's highest criminal court, travels on circuit round the country.

the res-publica: (Latin) the commonweal.

gouty chair . . . *padagra*: Littlejohn is suffering from gout and so is using a gout-stool to support his leg.

the manual: the manual prescribing drill, amongst other matters.

the present: i.e. 'present arms'.

the Hecaté of the ancients: the goddess who presided over such diverse activities as law, war, athletics, horsemanship, fishing, and cattle-breeding.

355 *quid non pro patria*: (Latin) what will you not do for your country.

356 *in the commission*: i.e. a member of the Commission of the Peace.

precognition: statements collected to put before a magistrate.

Nec lex justitior ulla: (Latin) (loosely) there could be no better justice.

357 *Causa scientiæ patet*: (Latin) the reason is sufficiently obvious.

prima facie: (Latin) (loosely) at first sight, on the face of it.

nebulo nebulonem: (Latin) a scoundrel of scoundrels.

358 *an Egyptian, whose wealth it is lawful to spoil*: Exodus 3: 22 and 12: 36.

the other side of the water: i.e. France.

360 *epigraph*: probably by Scott.

361 *ferry*: i.e. Queensferry.

fragilem mecum solvem phaselum: (Latin) (loosely) to embark with me in a fragile boat.

Rumour . . . with her trumpet about her neck: a commonplace representation of rumour.

362 *Lar Familiaris in Plautus*: domestic spirit who speaks the Prologue in *Aulularia*, or, 'The Pot of Gold', a comedy by Plautus (*c*.254–184 BC). The protagonist, Euclio, finds a pot of gold buried in his house, but pretends continued poverty, a ruse which necessitates the ill-treatment of his housekeeper, Staphyla.

Brownie: a fairy of domestic turn, who would come and do the servants' housework in the night.

Euclio . . . Staphyla . . . Aulularia: see note above to p. 362.

Michael Scott's man: Michael Scott (*c*.1175–*c*.1235) by profession astrologer, and by reputation a wizard.

363 *saw me asunder, as they did the children of Ammon*: 2 Samuel 12: 31 and 1 Chronicles 20: 3.

Œdipus: King of Thebes who solved the riddle of the Sphinx.

butter in the black dog's hause: (proverbial) i.e. [disappeared as thoroughly] as butter down the black dog's throat.

Aulam auri plenam quadrilibrem: a four-pound pot full of gold. Plautus, *Aulularia*, 821.

golden eggs . . . story-buick: the story of the goose that laid golden eggs appears first in the Greek fable of the greedy owner who was unwise enough to kill the bird, thinking to keep all the wealth to himself, rewritten many times over the course of the eighteenth century for children. Ochiltree is also playing with two other proverbial phrases—the term 'goose' as a synonym for fool, and 'a wild-goose chase'.

364 *the labours of Mars . . . of Themis*: Mars was the god of war, Themis presided over justice.

the first of June: presumably 1 June 1794, when the British navy beat the French off Brest.

the Gazette: the *London Gazette* announced victories, defeats, casualties, promotions, and commendations.

365 *the twelfth*: i.e. 12 August, the day when the grouse-shooting season begins.

Omne cum Proteus. . . montes: (Latin) when Proteus drove all his flock to view the high mountains. Proteus herds seals. See Horace, *Odes*, 1. 2. 7–8.

Nimrods: hunters.

We'll hang a seal-skin . . . limbs: adapted from *King John*, 3.1.125.

366 *the alien act*: The Aliens Act (1793) was designed to control the influx of refugees, and introduced powers to detain and expel supposed French agents.

tanquam suspect: the Bailie here misquotes *tanquam suspectus* (Latin) as a suspect.

act of 1701 regulating bail-bonds: fixing maximum rates of bail according to the station of the accused.

meo periculo: (Latin) at my own risk.

368 *epigraph*: *As You Like It*, 2.7.156.

Joe Manton: Joseph Manton, maker of fine guns.

Coemptos . . . Iberis: to trade noble books, collected from many places, for Iberian armour; Horace, *Odes*, 1.129.13.

Cordery: a Latin grammar.

Captain . . . as Milton has it: Milton, Sonnet 8, line 1.

Gens humida pontii the dripping people of the sea; Virgil, *Georgics*, 4.430.

Sternunt . . . phocae: Virgil, *Georgics*, 4.432.

369 *et se . . . in altum*: and threw himself into the deep sea; Virgil, *Georgics*, 4.528.

West Indies: the other main locus of war.

monitoribus asper: hostile to teachers; Horace, *Ars Poetica*, 163.

tanquam suspectus . . . suspicione major: (Latin) suspect, above suspicion.

370 *Petrie . . . Good-breeding*: Adam Petrie, *Rules of Good Deportment, or of Good Breeding, for the Use of Youth* (Edinburgh, 1720).

led captains: hangers-on.

arca auri: box of gold.

371 *rerum cognoscere causas*: (Latin) to know the causes of things.

haud alienum a Scævolæ studiis: (Latin) not foreign to the interests of Scaevola, i.e. to one interested in the law.

letters of four forms: a sequence of letters demanding repayment of debt.

process of diligence: enforcement.

372 *fugie-warrants . . . Border-warrants*: warrant preventing a debtor from decamping, warrant for the arrest of debtors on the English side of the Border.

374 *half-merk marriage*: clandestine marriage.

375 *epigraph*: probably by Scott.

The herring . . . gentle kind: adapted from a popular ballad.

Now haud your tongue . . . Harlaw: based on a Child ballad, but rewritten by Scott to fit the plot of *The Antiquary*.

376 *Percy*: Thomas Percy (1729–1811), editor of *Reliques of Ancient English Poetry* (1765).

Ritson: Joseph Ritson (1752–1803), another editor of ballads, e.g. *A Select Collection of English Songs* (1783).

377 *Ossian's songs of Selma*: James Macpherson, 'The Songs of Selma' in *The Poems of Ossian*.

Hunter's song of the Owl . . . torpid: Scott's note: Anne Grant, *Essay on the Superstitions of the Highlands of Scotland* (1811), 2.260.

378 *Do manus*: (Latin) I submit.

379 *Omni . . . .eduxit*: 'worse than being crippled is loss of memory, no longer knowing the names of servants, or the face of the friend dined with the night before, or the children he got and raised.' Juvenal, *Satires*, 10.232–6.

380 *He turn'd him right and round again . . . anither*: Loosely derived from stanza 7 of 'The Douglas Tragedy' in Scott's *Minstrelsy of the Scottish Border* (1803), 3.6.

381 *a fair-strae death*: literally, death in clean-straw—death in bed.

382 *Brand*: John Brand (1744–1806), author of *Observations on Popular Antiquities* (1777) from which Oldbuck's remarks are derived.

383 *Quintus Curtius*: Roman historian of Alexander the Great.

Nobilis . . . potest: a thoroughbred is ruled by only the shadow of a whip; a hack cannot be livened up even with spurs, Curtius, *Alexander*, 7.4.18.

With that . . . Staying no longer question: 2 *Henry IV*, 1.1.43–8.

Beneficia . . . redditur: good deeds are welcome so long as it seems that they can be returned; when they stretch beyond that point, hatred, not gratitude, results; Tacitus, *Annals*, 4.18.

385 *epigraph*: probably by Scott, a spoof of Erasmus Darwin's *The Loves of the Plants* (1789).

Windsor: Windsor Castle, a royal residence.

A fico . . . golden joys!: 2 *Henry IV*, 5.3.100–1.

386 *Harpagon*: miser in Molière's play *L'Avare* (1668).

387 *Panchresta . . . Basilius*: *panchresta*, universal panacea; *polychresta*, nonsense word; *Pelaso de Taranta*, Valescus de Taranta, a doctor of the

fourteenth/fifteenth century; *Basilius*, Basilius Valentinus, purportedly an alchemist of the fifteenth century.

389 *a writer's office*: a lawyer's office.

second table: the best company dined at the first table.

390 *writer to the signet*: top-class solicitor.

charge of horning: the process by which the court required a debtor to pay his debts and prescribed imprisonment if they were not paid.

in hypothec: the right of a creditor to hold the effects of a debtor as security for a claim without taking possession of them.

the next money term: Martinmas, 11 November.

peremptorie and sine mora: (Latin) forthwith and without delay.

to agé as accords: act as may be necessary.

394 *Royal Charlotte*: mailcoach.

396 *epigraph*: probably by Scott.

warrant of distress, or poinding: list of moveable goods to be sold by court-order to pay off debt.

397 *taxed cart*: (also 'tax-cart') two-wheeled open cart drawn by one horse, taxed as a luxury.

398 *process of battery and deforcement . . . declare myself deforced*: i.e. they would take him to court for assaulting a public official after he had displayed his baton as badge of office. The penalty was, respectively, imprisonment and the forfeit of all moveable property.

He that will to Cupar maun to Cupar: a proverb used of the wilful—Cupar is a town.

phoca barbata . . . phoca vitulina: (Latin) bearded seal or common seal.

capite quarto, versu quinto: (Latin) fourth heading, fifth section.

399 *despectus Domini Regis*: (Latin) contempt of the king.

tanquam participes criminis rebellionis: (Latin) of the nature of those who participate in the crime of rebellion.

per Legem Juliam: (Latin) under Julian law (to do with treason).

400 *Sed pereunti mille figuræ*: (Latin) but there are a thousand modes of dying.

desipere in loco: be silly at the appropriate moment; Horace, *Odes*, 4.12.28.

401 *where the slaughter is . . . together*: Matthew 24: 28.

take the wings of the morning: Psalm 139: 9

Jonah: name commonly given to a man who brought bad luck to a ship—Jonah's ship was overwhelmed in a storm sent by God's displeasure and the crew saved themselves by throwing him overboard.

in nomine regis: (Latin) in the name of the king.

403　*Indian Banians*: Indian traders.

404　*hanging, drawing, or quartering*: the punishment for treason.

405　*epigraph*: probably by Scott.

406　*favete linguis*: be silent; Horace, *Odes*, 3.1.2.

　　　secede paulisper: (Latin) retire for a short while.

　　　supersedere of diligence: delay in legal action.

　　　bear-garden: violent disorder, as in bear-baiting.

　　　bills: bills of exchange, i.e. effectively cheques.

407　*sist on a bill o' suspension*: postponement as a result of Letters of
　　　Suspension, granted to a debtor asking for a review of the situation.

　　　ultimate diligence: here, imprisonment.

408　*evacuate Flanders*: the British retreated from Flanders in January 1794.

　　　Dutch baby-house: a miniature house designed to predict the weather.

409　*old Truepenny*: *Hamlet*, 1.5.152.

　　　olive branch: as the dove returned to Noah's ark with a message of hope.

410　*a soft answer turneth away wrath*: Proverbs 15: 1.

　　　Odi accipetrem qui semper vivit in armis: I hate the hawk who always lives
　　　in arms. Ovid, *Ars Amatoria*, 2.147.

　　　par nobile fratrum: (Latin) a noble pair of brothers.

411　*may you be besieged . . . the chapel of Saint Winnox*: Oldbuck is here
　　　making a rather leaden joke about courtship and marriage. Saint Winnox
　　　is an imaginary saint whose name puns on Knockwinnock

413　*epigraph*: probably by Scott.

414　*hoc erat in votis*: that was what was prayed for; Horace, *Satires*, 2.6.1.

　　　The cry is still, They come: *Macbeth*, 5.5.2.

416　*sting and ling*: by force.

417　*simmered it and wintered it*: discussed it at length.

418　*ashes glow their wonted fires*: Thomas Gray, 'Elegy Written in a Country
　　　Churchyard', 92.

421　*epigraph*: James Hogg, 'Lord Derwent' in *The Mountain Bard* (1807),
　　　134.

　　　Birnam . . . Dunsinane: *Macbeth*, 5.5.27–36.

　　　with fear of change perplexing nations: adapted from John Milton,
　　　Paradise Lost, 1.594–9.

422　*Andrea Ferrara*: late sixteenth-century Italian swordmaker.

　　　the sea fencibles, and the land fencibles: members of the armed services
　　　responsible for home defence.

424　*like Diogenes at Sinope*: a cynic philosopher of the fourth century BC, said
　　　to have lived in a tub.

425　*assessors of the lieutenancy*: advisers to the Lord Lieutenant and deputies.

426   *Caesar and Polybius, and the Stratagemata Polyœni*: Caesar's commentaries on the Gallic Wars, Polybius, historian of Rome, and a manual of military strategy authored by Polyaenus (second century AD).

427   *Raro antecedentum . . . deseruit pœna*: rarely does punishment fail to catch up with a wicked person who has fled ahead. Horace, *Odes*, 3.2.31–2.

430   *En attendant*: (French) while waiting.

GLOSSARY

The glossary lists words in Scots (leaving out those that can be inferred from the context), unfamiliar or archaic words in English, and those legal and foreign-language terms not dealt with in the Editor's Notes. It is derived from the glossary to the Magnum Opus edition, supplemented by material from the Dryburgh Edition (1893), the Edinburgh Edition (1993–), and the *OED*. My thanks are due to Jennifer Michael for her extensive work on compiling it.

abune above

acmé perfection

adept one that has attained to proficiency in anything

aestus (Latin) fire

agger (Latin) rampart

ahint behind

aiblins perhaps

aik-tree oak tree

airn iron

aits oats; **ait-meal, ait-strae** oat-meal, oat-straw

aliunde (Latin) from some other authority, quarter

amaist almost

analecta (Latin) excerpts, scraps, selections

anchoret hermit, recluse

ane one

aneath beneath

anent about

anes, ance once

anglicè (French) in English

anither another

anker a measure of wine and spirits, 8½ imperial gallons

antic antique; or, grotesque

arcanum secret or mystery

armipotent mighty in arms

aroint begone

arquebuss firearm

assoilzie, azzoilzie absolve

atweel certainly

auld old

auld-farrant sagacious

awa away

aweel well

awmous alms

aye yes, always

ayont beyond

baarenhauter a nickname for a German mercenary soldier

backsey sirloin

bail-bond written promise of bail

bailie (in Scotland) the chief magistrate of a barony or part of a county

bairn child

ban curse, swear

band-string string for fastening a collar or ruff

bane bone

bannock loaf of homemade, usually unleavened bread, round or oval in shape, baked on a griddle

bannock fluke halibut

barm yeast

barns-breaking frolic

barouche carriage with seating for two couples

basse-cour (French) poultry-yard

baudrons a cat

bauld bold

bawbee old halfpenny

bead-roll a long string of names; originally, list of persons to be prayed for

bean, bein comfortable, snug

beaver fur hat
bedral beadle
belay to coil a running rope around a pin or cleat
belive, belyve immediately
ben in, within; as a noun, the inner apartment of a house
beyont beyond
bicker a wooden bowl or beaker
biddin waited
bide endure, remain, reside
bield hut, shelter of any kind
big to build; **bigging** building
biga (Latin) two-horse chariot
bink kitchen dresser
birse bristles, temper
bit (adj.) used as a diminutive
black-nebs the disaffected
blatter to speak rapidly and incoherently
blink glance, glimmer, wink
blonde silk lace
blude blood
bode asking-price
bodkin squeezed in between two others
bodle a copper coin of the value of the third part of an English old penny
bogle hobgoblin, ghost
bole small window
boll measure of grain containing, in Scotland, 6 imperial bushels
bolt's head flask used in distillation
bonnet-laird small landowning farmer
bonny-dies trinkets
bountith the bounty given in addition to servants' wages
bourd a jeer, a joke
bourock a mound
bouse, bowse to haul with tackle
bowk bulky
braid broad
branched embroidered, ornamented
brank prance
braw, brawly brave, fine, splendid

braws finery
bridewell jail, prison
brig ship
brock badger
brunt burnt
busk dress hooks for fly-fishing
cadger-powny carrier-pony
callant stripling
caller fresh
calthrop spiked iron ball designed to discomfit cavalry
Candlemass 2 February
cankered ill-tempered
cannle candles
canny safe; trustworthy, fortunate
canton a division of a shield in heraldry
cantrap trick
capper copper
caption warrant for arrest for debt
Capuchin a friar of the order of St Francis
car-cake small cake
carle a man
carlin, carline witch, old woman
carvy-seed caraway-seed
cast lot, fate, chance
castra (Latin) military camp
castrametation art of laying out a military camp
cauld cold
caulking plugging (the seams of a wooden ship)
certie, my certie indeed? (exclamation)
chancy lucky
change-house small inn
chasse (French) hunt
chevaux de frize (French) military defence works
chiel fellow
chip-box a small box made of thin wood
chop-fallen dejected, dispirited

cicerone a guide who shows and explains the antiquities or curiosities of a place to strangers

cinctured belted

claes clothes

clashes, clatter idle gossip

claymore the two-edged broadsword of the ancient Scottish Highlanders

cleed to clothe

clipping-time nick of time

clod throw with violence

clouted repaired

coble fishing-boat

cock-padle the lump-fish

coenobitium monastic refuge

collectanea passages, remarks, etc., collected from various sources

comfits sweetmeats

commons common people

concurrent (n.) an assistant to a sheriff's officer

convenience a conveyance

corbie crow

coronach see **cronach**

coupit overturn

couples leashes for hounds; roof-supporting rafters

cove cave

covinarii (Latin) chariot-borne soldiers

cracks chat

craig rock; also, throat

craigsman one who is dexterous at climbing amongst cliffs

crappit-heads a dish composed of haddocks and oatmeal

creel lobster-pot, basket carried on the back

creesh grease

crimini exclamation of astonishment

croft a piece of enclosed ground, used for tillage or pasture

cronach, coronach the Highland lament for the dead

crousely with confidence, boldly

crown o' the causeway the top or middle of the road

cruppin, cruppen crept

cummer comrade

curfuffle, carfuffle excitement, commotion

curricle light, two-wheeled carriage

curriculum (Latin) light, two-horse carriage

cutikins leggings, gaiters

daft silly

dander, daunder saunter, roam

dee die; also, to do

Deil the devil; **Deil a bit** not a bit, no way

delation accusation, denouncement, informing against

deukes ducks

devel, devvel very hard blow

dial-plate clock-face

diligence stage-coach, legal process

ding force, beat, overcome

dirge funeral-chant, or, more rarely, a funeral drink

dirk highland dagger

discussed (of supper) consumed

div do

dog-horse horse fit only for dog-meat

doited stupid, doating

donnard stupid

dooms, dooms certain absolutely certain

doting, doating foolish, senile

douce quiet, sober, steady

douceur (French) a gratuity

douk duck, plunge into water

doup candles' end

dour, dure hard, impenetrable, stubborn

dow to be able to

dow-cot dove-cot

downa cannot

dram a small draught of cordial, stimulant, or spirits

drap drop

dree endure, suffer

dreep drip
durstna would not have dared
dwam swoon
eard to bury in earth
easel-ward eastward
ee eye (pl. een)
eilding fuel
eithly easily
eneugh enough
epopea the epic species of poetry
equipage equipment for war, travel, domestic establishment, or personal use
eremite hermit, recluse
escritoir writing desk
espièglerie (French) archness
ewking itching
exceptious disposed to make objections
exies hysterics
fae (Aberdeenshire) who
fan, fanever (Aberdeenshire) when, whenever
fash trouble
fashious troublesome
fat (Aberdeenshire) what
fathom a measure of length, usually 6 feet
faulded folded
faur'd favoured; **weel-faur'd, ill-faur'd** well- and ill-favoured
feal-dyke, feal-dike low stone-wall, covered with turf at the top
feck quantity, part; **maist feck** greater part
feckless powerless, of little strength
feel, feel-body (Aberdeenshire) fool
fending provisions
fere well, healthy
feuar landholder paying ground-rent to a superior
fickle puzzle
fico fig
fire-flaught flash of lightning
firlot quarter of a boll
fissel, fissil rustle

fit foot
fite (Aberdeenshire) white
flambeau a torch; a fire-signal or beacon
flaughtering light shining fitfully
flaw squall
flee fly
flightering quivering, fluttering
fliskmahoy a flighty woman
flit depart
flude flood
fly stage-coach
flyting scolding, arguing
forbye besides
fore-end beginning
forenoon morning
forfairn wholly exhausted by decay, or fatigue
fossa (Latin) ditch
founder stun
fowling-gun light gun for hunting wild birds
freestone sandstone
friseur, frizeur (French) hairdresser
fuff puff
fugie warrant warrant to prevent flight
fund found
furze an evergreen prickly shrub
fusht, fusht (Aberdeenshire) tush, tush
fussil rustle
gaberlunzie an itinerant beggar
gae go; **gaed on** went on; **gane** gone
gae-down drinking-bout
gaefa' guffaw
gar compel, make
gate way; as, **his ain gate** his own way
gathering-coal a large piece of coal, laid on the fire to keep it burning during the night
gauger an exciseman
gay, gey very
gear goods; head-gear, head-dress
geck jeer

gelt (German) money

gentle person of high birth

gewgaw a gaudy trifle, plaything, or ornament

ghaist ghost

gie give

gig light one-horse carriage

gill a measure for liquids, one-quarter of a pint

gill-stoup drinking-vessel

gimcrack useless apparatus

glaive a lance or spear

glamour magical delusion

glass-breaker a drinker

gleg active, vigilant

gliff a fright

gloaming twilight

glunch gloomy

gossips woman-friends

goustie, gousty dreary, dismal

gowd gold

gowk silly fool

grane groan

grape (v.) grope

great-coat overcoat

greet cry, weep

greybeard stoneware liquor-jug

ground-officer one who has charge of the grounds and lands of an estate

grund ground, land

gudeman husband

gudemither mother-in-law

gudesire grandfather

gudewife wife, mistress of the house

gull a credulous person; a dupe; a fool

gully large clasp-knife

gyre-carline female supernatural being

gyte beside oneself, delirious

ha' hall

hack-chaise, hackney-coach carriage kept for hire

haddie haddock

haill whole, sound

half-mutchkin a mutchkin equals three quarters of an imperial pint

hallan an inner partition in a house

hallenshaker tramp, beggar

hame home

hand o' writ handwriting

hand-werker (German) skilled manual worker

hang-choice the position of one who has to choose between two evils

hantle great many, or great deal

harns brains

harry to plunder

har'st harvest

hause throat

haver talk nonsense

hegh an exclamation expressing sorrow

hellicate light-headed, boisterous, improper girl

herd man in charge of the cattle or sheep

heritor property-owner liable for certain parish taxes

hersell herself

heugh a crag

heugh-head head of the cliff or precipice

Himmel (German) heaven

hinny, hinney honey, an affectionate form of address

hirple to walk, limping

hoast cough

hollin, holyn holly

hone to grumble, whine, moan

hoodie-craw hooded crow

hooly softly, slowly

hospitium, hospitale, hospitamentum hospice; place of rest for travellers

hotch-potch mutton and vegetable broth

houdie midwife

howk, houk dig

howlit owl

huz us

hypericon St John's wort

ilka every; **ilk ane** every one

illustrissimus (Latin) most illustrious person

indagator (Latin) someone who investigates

indurate hardened or obstinate

ingle fire, fireplace

in-ower and out-ower violently, despotically, against all opposition

ither other

ivy-tod ivy bush

japanned varnished, lacquered

jeeding (Aberdeenshire) judging

jimp scarcely

jink dodge

jocolate chocolate

Joe sweetheart

jolter-headed clumsy-headed

jowing rocking

just-living living fairly, honourably

kaim camp, hillock

kale-blade cabbage-leaf

kale-supper a term applied to Fifeshire people, famed for their consumption of kale or broth

kale-yard a cabbage-garden, kitchen-garden, commonly attached to a small cottage

kame comb

keelyvine pen black-lead pencil

keip keep, stay

kelp seaweed

kemp to fight

ken know

kilt tuck up

kimmer neighbour or gossip

kippage excitement or anger

kirk church, specifically the Church of Scotland

kist chest

kittle doubtful

knevel beat violently

knowe knoll

lachrymatory Roman glass or stoneware vessel found in tombs

laigh low

laith loath

land-louper a vagabond

lapper-milk sour curdled milk

lappet a flap or fold of clothing

larboard left-hand side of a ship, looking towards the bows

lauch laugh

lave remainder

lees lies

leg-bail; to give leg-bail to run off

leze-majesty treason

liege lord, ruler

lift sky

likewake the watching of a dead body previous to burial

limmer (derogatory) woman

list the selvage of a piece of woollen cloth

lists space where tournaments are held

little-ease narrow place of confinement

loan-head head of the lane

loaning lane to a house

loom implement, utensil

lound tranquil, calm

lounder heavy blow

loup leap

lour frown, scowl

luckie applied to an old woman

lug ear

lungie guillemot

magisterium philosopher's stone

mailing a tenant-farm

mane mourn

manty-maker dressmaker

massymore dungeon

maun must

maunder to talk incoherently, ramble

maze amaze, bewilder

meat food in general

merk Scots money worth just under an English sixpence old money

middenstead the place where a dunghill is formed

miff a fit of pettish temper

minnie mother

mirk dark

misca' to abuse verbally

misdoubt suspect, be afraid

monomachia (Latin) a duel

morning-gown dressing-gown

morpeon crab-louse

mote speck of dust

mouls earth; generally applied to the earth that covers a coffin

muckle much, large

naig nag; small riding horse or pony

nain own

napery table linen

near stingy

neb nose

neckercher neckerchief

neist next

neuk nook

nevoy nephew

nick-stick reckoning stick

niffer narter

night-cowl night-cap

oakum loose fibre used to caulk ships' seams

obtestation swearing by a sacred name

oe grandson

oneirocritical relating to the interpretation of dreams

or before

ordinary eating-house or tavern

original (n.) a singular, odd, or eccentric person

orra occasional, odd, unoccupied

outby out at sea

out-rider rider escorting a carriage

out-taken excepting

overlay a cravat, necktie

ower-head precipitately

owerta'en overcome, deranged

owzel blackbird

paddock frog or toad

paiks, his paiks a beating

palmer a pilgrim

palmering tottering, infirm

paraffle ostentatious display

parritch porridge

partan crab

pateræ shallow saucer-like vessels used by Romans for libations

pawky crafty

pease-strae straw from the pea plant

peer poor

peery child's top

peruquier (French) wig-maker

pet a fit of ill humour

petto (Latin) the breast; **in petto** in one's own private intention

phoca (Latin) seal

pibroch music for the bagpipe

pickle a very little, small quantity, few

pictarnie the great tern, or sea-swallow

pike-staff a walking-stick with a metal point at the lower end

pinnace small, light vessel

pinners two long flaps falling down either side of the face and attached to a cap

pirn the reel on which yarn is wound

placebo make-peace

plainstanes pavement

pliskie a mischievous trick

pluff powder-puff

pock see **poke**

pockmanky travelling bag

poinder an official who seizes and sells the goods of a debtor under warrant

poke, pock bag, sack

poppling purling, rippling

pose a secret hoard of money

posie (often rhyming) motto

post-chaise carriage with horses hired by the stage

post-horse horse hired by the stage

postilion rider of a post-horse in the absence of a coachman

pouthered powdered

pouting shooting at young partridges

pow head; or, pull

powsowdie broth

prent print, printed
primer school book
propine present, gift
punaise bed-bug
pursy fat, short-winded.
put-on make for
quadriga (Latin) four-horse carriage
quarters lodgings
quean young woman
quiz to tease
quodammado (Latin) in some degree
quondam (Latin) former
rampauging raging and storming
randy a rude, drunken woman
rapparee a wild Irish plunderer, so called from his being armed with a rapaire or half-pike
rappee coarse snuff
rath quick, early
rattlin thin line or rope, used in rigging to make steps
ready-money cash, or immediate payment in coin
rebeck stringed instrument played like a violin
reck to care, heed
reist to refuse to go forward
remora (Latin) delay
rencontre (French) meeting, duel
repeater a pocket-watch that chimes the hour
reversion the remainder
rickle a heap
rive rob, plunder
road-stead a place where ships may conveniently or safely lie at anchor near the shore
roturier (French) a commoner
roughies torch
routh plenty
rudas cantankerous
rugging take forcibly
rund the selvage of broad cloth
sackbut obsolete wind-instrument
sackless blameless

sain bless
saltire-ways in the form of a St Andrew's cross (or an X)
sapperment corruption of 'sacrament'
sark shirt
saugh willow
saul soul, mettle
saulie a hired mourner for a funeral
saut-backet a wooden box in the shape of a house, with a round hole in the exposed end, for holding salt
sax six
scauding scalding
scaur precipice
sconner, scunner a shudder of disgust
scour run
scull fish-basket
scutcheon heraldic shield
sea-maw common seagull
seere (Aberdeenshire) sure
seerpreese (Aberdeenshire) surprise
semple of low birth, opposed to gentle birth
shagreen untanned leather
shank walk
shathmont distance from the knuckle of the little finger in the clenched fist to the tip of the extended thumb
shaw wood
sheugh ditch, furrow
ship-letter letter carried by private vessel rather than the mail-boat
shirra sheriff
shool, shule shovel
shoon shoes
shouther shoulder
shriegh, skreigh shriek
shrift confession
sibb related by blood
sic, siccan such
side and wide long and wide
siller silver, money in general
sinker one who sinks mine-shafts
sinning cinnamon

sipple to drink slowly, by small sips
skart cormorant
skeel skill, cunning; **skeelfu** skilful
skirl scream
slaistering eating in an awkward and dirty way
slap-bason slop-basin
sleuth-hound slow-hound, blood-hound
slink dishonest
sneck lock
snecked bolted, locked
sneeshin snuff
sneeshing-mull snuff-box
snell sarcastic
snood binding up the hair
soi-disant (French) self-styled
sonsy handsome
sothefast truthful
sort to arrange, manage
sough a feeling, the sighing sound of the wind, to breathe or sigh
souple to soften or mollify
souter shoemaker
souther, sowder solder, repair
sownder, sounder a boar of two years old
spearings information, news
speel climb
spontoon half-pike
spunk spark
stang staff, long pole
starboard the right-hand side of a ship, facing the bows
steek shut
steer, stir disturb
steery commotion
steeve fixed, stable
stick to stab
stickit stuck
stiver small coin of low value from the Low Countries
stouth health
straik stroke
strake struck
strait tight, narrow

striek, streek stretch, lay out for burial
studden stood
sufflamina (Latin) pause a little
swarvit swooned
swear, sweer reluctant, difficult
swither doubt, hesitation, quandary
syne since, ago
tackets nails for boots
tae the one, or, toe
tale-pyet tell-tale
Tammie Norie puffin
tapis (French) tablecloth
target a light round shield
Tartarean infernal, hellish
tawpie awkward, slovenly girl
teinds tithes
tent care
tenter-hook a metal hook
tête (French) head
thack thatch
thrapple throat
three-nookit three-cornered
threep argue, insist
through-stone, through-stane tombstone
thrum tell, prose over
tie-wig a wig with the hair tied together behind with ribbon
till to
tilley-valley exclamation of impatience
tinkler tinker
tintamarre an uproar, confused noise
tippence twopence
tirl cut through, rattle
tirlie-wirlie intricate
tocher dowry; **weel-tochered** having a large dowry, well provided for
toilet, toilet-table articles and furnishings required for dressing
tolbooth prison
toom empty
touzled out ransacked
tow a rope

towmond twelvemonth; a year
toy cap worn by elderly women
travail labour, childbirth
trencher a wooden plate used to serve food
trig neat
trim reprove
troth faithfulness, honesty
trow believe, think
tup-headed ram-headed, i.e. obstinate as a male sheep
turn household chore
twal, twall twelve
turnpike toll-road
tyro novice
ugsome disgusting
ulyie oil
unbrizzed unbruised
uncanny careless, unlucky, inauspicious
unco' very, strange, odd
uphaud support
upsides even with
vallum (Latin) rampart
vide (Latin) see
villain serf
vivers food
vole the winning of all the tricks in a card-game
wad, wadna' would, wouldn't
wale toast
wame belly
wampish toss frantically
wan-chancy unlucky
wanle active, strong, healthy

ware spend
warp four oysters
water-gruel thin soup
wauk wake
waur defeat, worse
wean child
weel well; **weel-favoured** attractive, handsome; **weel-kenned** well-known
weird destiny
weize to manoeuvre, ease gradually
whar where
whase whose
wheen few
whilk which
whisht hush
whomled, whombled capsized
wife-carle a man who occupies himself with a woman's or housewife's work
wile to beguile, deceive
wilyard wild, strange, unaccountable
winsome pretty, cheerful-looking
worriecows, worricows goblins
wool-gathering day-dreaming
writer a Scottish attorney or solicitor
wuss wish
yald, yauld supple, active; or, old
yard wooden or steel spar slung from a mast
yaw to deviate temporarily from the set course
yerl earl
yestreen last night
yule Christmas
yung-fraw (German) young lady

ANTHONY TROLLOPE

An Autobiography

Ayala's Angel

Barchester Towers

The Belton Estate

The Bertrams

Can You Forgive Her?

The Claverings

Cousin Henry

Doctor Thorne

Doctor Wortle's School

The Duke's Children

Early Short Stories

The Eustace Diamonds

An Eye for an Eye

Framley Parsonage

He Knew He Was Right

Lady Anna

The Last Chronicle of Barset

Later Short Stories

Miss Mackenzie

Mr Scarborough's Family

Orley Farm

Phineas Finn

Phineas Redux

The Prime Minister

Rachel Ray

The Small House at Allington

La Vendée

The Warden

The Way We Live Now

THE OXFORD SHERLOCK HOLMES

Arthur Conan Doyle
The Adventures of Sherlock Holmes
The Case-Book of Sherlock Holmes
His Last Bow
The Hound of the Baskervilles
The Memoirs of Sherlock Holmes
The Return of Sherlock Holmes
The Valley of Fear
Sherlock Holmes Stories
The Sign of the Four
A Study in Scarlet

The Oxford World's Classics Website

www.worldsclassics.co.uk

- Information about new titles
- Explore the full range of Oxford World's Classics
- Links to other literary sites and the main OUP webpage
- Imaginative competitions, with bookish prizes
- Peruse *Compass*, the Oxford World's Classics magazine
- Articles by editors
- Extracts from Introductions
- A forum for discussion and feedback on the series
- Special information for teachers and lecturers

www.worldsclassics.co.uk

American Literature

British and Irish Literature

Children's Literature

Classics and Ancient Literature

Colonial Literature

Eastern Literature

European Literature

History

Medieval Literature

Oxford English Drama

Poetry

Philosophy

Politics

Religion

The Oxford Shakespeare

A complete list of Oxford Paperbacks, including Oxford World's Classics, OPUS, Past Masters, Oxford Authors, Oxford Shakespeare, Oxford Drama, and Oxford Paperback Reference, is available in the UK from the Academic Division Publicity Department, Oxford University Press, Great Clarendon Street, Oxford OX2 6DP.

In the USA, complete lists are available from the Paperbacks Marketing Manager, Oxford University Press, 198 Madison Avenue, New York, NY 10016.

Oxford Paperbacks are available from all good bookshops. In case of difficulty, customers in the UK can order direct from Oxford University Press Bookshop, Freepost, 116 High Street, Oxford OX1 4BR, enclosing full payment. Please add 10 per cent of published price for postage and packing.